Series

Paranormal Stories

War on Darkness

Darkness Defined (MM)

Order of Light (MM)

Knights of Nyx (MM)

Moons of Mystery

Sara's Moon (MF)

Charline's Solstice (MF)

Diana's Eclipse (MF)

Kisin Novels

Courting Death (MM)
Death, Love, & Tacos (MM)

Fated Mates
Truth in Exile (MM)

Contemporary Romances

Ulwich Preparatory Academy

Our Last Fall (MM)

Our Secret Winter (MM)

Our Epic Spring (MM)

Oak Haven Romance

One Brave Thing (Enby/M)

All the Hype (MM)
Any Which Way (MM)
A Thin Line (MM)

Ulwich Preparatory Academy

New Adult Romance

Our Last Fall
Our Secret Winter
Our Epic Spring

S Bolanos

1st edition 2024

Disclosures & Content Warnings

These books are intended for mature audiences. It contains adult themes, language, and content, including on-page sex, violence, and homophobic language. Themes of sexual assault are present in references to previous events as well as the sexual assault (off-page) of a major secondary character.

While brutal, its inclusion is intended to show that while the world has grown in how it treats the queer community, it still has a long way to go and there are places that remain rooted in bigotry and violence.

At the time this series was written, the University of Chicago did not have a Men's Lacrosse Athletic Program. However, their Social Sciences program does sound stellar.

Ulwich
reparatory
Academy

Our Last Fall

Contents

Chapter 1

Four Years Ago

Andy

The room filled with a mild glow as I pulled back the curtains. It was still beyond gloomy, but the moonlight would have to suffice; turning on so much as a lamp would be too risky. My hands closed around the cardboard box. It immediately began jerking as I picked it up off the floor and placed it on the desk.

Out of habit, I looked towards the other bed in the room. It was just as empty as it had been yesterday. *Talk about a stroke of luck.* Of course, I doubted Lucien felt lucky since he was the one with chicken pox. We hadn't even had time to get properly acquainted after being moved into the upper level student wing together before he'd had to leave.

I placed a large textbook on top of the box to make sure the lid didn't pop open and send the box's contents spewing across the room. Now that the container was secure, I picked up the piece of paper that had been hidden beneath it. Even in the almost nonexistent light, I could make out scratch marks crisscrossing the page.

Trying to write a letter was stupid.

I crumpled the scarred page, then shoved it deep in the wastebasket beneath countless other similar scraps.

He deserves to hear it from me, anyway.

I glanced at the clock. He'd be here soon. I needlessly adjusted the box, which hopped in response.

Deep breath. He's your best friend. He'll understand. Okay, maybe he won't understand exactly, but he'll still appreciate the honesty. Yeah, the honesty. I can do this.

I shook my hands in a vain attempt to dispel my nervous energy.

"What are you doing?"

I jumped in place and spun around at the whisper. "Mitch. You scared the crap out of me," I whispered back.

He shrugged as he carefully closed the door. "Did you get them?" he asked as he crossed the room to set his own supplies on the bed. The large container of chalk dust shone in the light. "This is going to be our best prank yet. Were you able to get the frogs?" he repeated.

I stood there like a statue, my mini pep-talk already a distant memory.

I can't do this.

"Hello. Earth to Andy. Did you get them or not?"

Mitch is staring at me. I should tell him they're in the box under our Social Studies text.

He lifted his eyebrows and held out his hands, impatience clear on his face.

"I'm gay." My eyes widened in horror. *Fuck.*

"Okay, but did you get the frogs?" Mitch insisted.

"Did you hear what I said?"

"Yeah. Now, are you gonna answer the question?"

"But—don't you have anything to say?" I asked, confused.

The light of the moon flashed against the whites of his eyes as he rolled them. "Does you being gay change who you are? Does it make you a different person than the one who helped me plan this?"

"Well, no."

"Then were you able to get the frogs or not? Because this is going to be a super shitty prank without them."

"They're in the box on the desk," I replied, still in a mild state of shock.

His trademark mischief quickly replaced his exasperated expression. He tossed me the container full of white dust and walked over to admire our prize.

"I got twelve," I added to make up for my earlier lack of response.

"Perfect." He removed the book and carefully picked up the box, which gave a characteristic jolt. "We better get going or we'll miss our window."

Present Day

Andy

I stared up at the vaulted ceiling of the cafeteria. The deep red brick and exposed beams lent the large space a grandeur far exceeding the room's use, but I'd stopped being impressed years ago. Despite Ulwich Preparatory Academy's mission of excellence and only accepting young men from the most prestigious families, it was still a school like any other.

"You gonna be studying with Connor again this year?"

I shifted my focus to my friend as he put his tray away and dusted his hands of the nonexistent crumbs. Calvin Bridges was meticulous to a fault and not one to make a mess—ever. Even his dark curly hair, while cut into a long shag that definitely violated school policy, was precisely styled to give the impression of nonchalance. His navy school blazer hung over a perfectly pressed cream button down and intentionally crooked tie striped with the Academy's colors.

As literally one of a dozen students of color in the entire school, his choices undoubtedly made a statement, loud and clear and one no one dared to call him on. Despite his rebellious appearance, or perhaps because of it, he was also the school's unofficial keeper of secrets.

I emptied the remains of my breakfast into the trash before responding. "Let him take care of his own homework for a while."

Calvin snickered. "Bet he didn't like that."

"Don't say it like that. It was as much his idea as it was mine." Connor and I had had a good thing going for a while, but as one year turned to two, our easy relationship had become strained.

"Sure it was, Andy," he responded with an over-the-top eye roll. We turned to exit the cafeteria together to steal a few minutes outdoors before the second bell and the day's classes.

I glanced back towards a group of guys sitting on a table by the windows. The light illuminated the rowdy crowd as they laughed and carried on. The one at the heart ran his hand through light brown hair and smiled. Mitchum Hudson: Ulwich Academy's star lacrosse player. Athletic perfection and so far out of reach, he might as well have been on another planet.

Pain stabbed through my chest like it did anytime I saw him.

Why did I have to tell him? If I had just kept my stupid mouth shut. If I hadn't...

Calvin gripped my shoulder, dragging me back to the reality that I was standing in the doorway and blatantly staring across the cafeteria.

"I'm coming," I grumbled.

"It's been four years," Calvin whispered.

"I know. And not a single word in between." I pushed open the door to the courtyard with a tad too much force. It rebounded off the outside wall, then nearly crashed into a too-slow Calvin.

"You guys were already drifting apart. You said so yourself."

I cast Calvin a sour look.

"Don't get mad at me for telling it like it is," he said as we settled into our usual spot on the green beside a low stone wall that I was sure served a purpose at some point. "He's a typical jock, just like the rest of them. All muscle, no brain."

I raised an eyebrow. "Unlike us?"

"Unlike you. I'll be lucky if I can pass Algebra II with a low C. You're the brainiac." He stood up on the low wall and struck a classic Shakespearean pose. "I'm doomed to be a starving artist. Forever suffering for my creations, sacrificing my very soul, with no hope of recognition." He paused and glanced down at me to make sure I was paying attention. "Or more importantly, compensation."

The dramatic declaration had the desired effect—I laughed. "Get down from there before you break something."

He snorted. "I think the wall can take it."

I laughed again. "Not the wall, more like your neck."

He waved away my concern, then mimicked walking a tightrope complete with balancing arm swings. I shook my head. Calvin may not have been the same kind of friend Mitch had been, but he was still a good one. Not to mention he understood things Mitch never would.

The Mitch you knew is gone, I reminded myself.

"Look what the cat coughed up." The taunting comment snatched me out of my musings.

I raised my head from the notebook I was scanning to find the school bully headed our way. "It's too early for this shit," I mumbled. Meanwhile, Calvin was already turning to confront him. I sighed inwardly.

Just once couldn't they leave well enough alone?

“If it isn’t Benjamin Price himself, come to wish us good morning. Look Andy, he brought the welcome wagon and everything,” Calvin said with far too much cheer.

Benny’s face immediately twisted at the abundance of enthusiasm; Calvin wasn’t *supposed* to be excited to see him. “They should ship your queer ass back to where it came from,” Benny sneered.

“Are you offering to pay the postage? You could even wrap me up yourself,” Calvin responded with a wicked smile.

Benny’s expression clouded with anger. “As if I would go anywhere near a cocksucker like you.”

Calvin feigned a wound to the chest, then bold as brass declared, “If I’m not mistaken, most of the guys here would do just about anything to have their cocks sucked. Present company not excluded.”

Benny’s cheek twitched and his lackeys looked at each other askance. Calvin had hit a little too close to the truth for their comfort. Going to an all-boys boarding school did leave certain things wanting. Finally, Benny recovered and fired back, “You think you’re special, because your senator mom got you into this school, but we all know the truth—she’s nothing more than a mail-order-bride that used daddy’s money to make a name for herself.”

Calvin vaulted off the low wall to land practically on top of Benny. “My mother got what she was owed and even an idiot like you should know you have to be a citizen to be a senator.”

“Who’d she have to fuck to get those papers? No wonder you’re such a queer.”

“*My mom*?" Calvin's voice pitched high with incredulity. "What kind of shit did your dad make *your* mommy agree to in that prenup? Tell me, was she pregnant before or after signing away her life?”

“Fuck you, you fucking fudge-packer,” Benny snarled.

Point Calvin.

“You kiss your mother with that mouth?" Calvin crossed his arms and popped a hip. "Or have you even seen her since daddy got his heir?”

“One of these days, I’m going to put you in your place, you fucking hapa faggot.”

“Just be sure to shower first,” Calvin said, cool as a stone.

I checked my reaction and watched Benny struggle to contain his. Behind him, Neil and Todd looked confused at their leader’s sudden lack of comeback.

"Motherfucking fairy," Benny mumbled before signaling to his companions.

"Which is it Benny? Am I a motherfucker or a faggot?" Calvin called after them. Benny kept walking, not deigning to respond. Calvin continued to hold his ground until the trio was out of sight.

"You shouldn't goad him. One of these days, he really will do something," I cautioned as I adjusted the notebook on my knee.

Calvin scoffed before joining me on the ground. "Benjamin Price hates himself more than he hates me."

Mitch

I watched the door to the mess hall close behind Anderson Gallagher, obscuring his bright copper hair.

He's friends with Calvin now. He won't ever be mine, not after what I did.

Boisterous laughter erupted around me, directly contradicting my depressing thoughts. I withdrew deeper into myself to escape the offensive sound that had taken complete possession of my life over the last four years. At first it hadn't been so bad. These people were my friends. They cared about me and wanted me to succeed. But as time went by and their expectations chipped at my soul, I realized how horribly wrong I'd been to believe they were friends, because they weren't, not really, not the way Andy had been.

I miss the way things used to be.

A sharp smack landed on my arm and jolted me out of the downward spiral. I returned my attention to the table full of familiar faces, not a one of which knew a damn thing about the real me. "What?" I asked, having lost all track of whatever ridiculous conversation we were having this morning.

"Trixie, man," Brian repeated. An image of a girl with bottled-red hair came to mind. It hung about her sun-deprived face in a pixie cut that wasn't doing her any favors.

My brow furrowed. I hadn't talked to or even thought about her since school dismissed for summer. "What about her?"

"Bro, are you even listening?" Kyle asked, his peach face a mask of exasperation.

"You two still hooking up or what?" Brian repeated. He crossed brown arms made that much darker from a summer spent outdoors over his chest and leaned back with a raised eyebrow. I scanned the eager expressions surrounding me and my stomach turned. Dating Trixie had been an awful decision that I never would have made in the first place if it hadn't been for these relentless assholes.

I shrugged as if she was the furthest thing from my mind, not the least of which because she was. "No, not really," I replied honestly, Beatrix Roberts held zero interest for me and always had. Her stick figure topped with disproportionately large breasts made her look like a cartoon with the personality to match. She'd started with blonde hair that had miraculously turned an awful shade of red when I'd made the mistake of saying I preferred redheads in one of many attempts to break up with her.

"See, I told you," Nate said with all the righteousness of someone proving a point that doesn't need proving.

"Whatever." Aaron rolled blue eyes that had snagged their fair share of the student body at the Mary Barnes School for Distinguished Young Women. "Still doesn't mean you can try."

"Why not?" Nate asked. I couldn't help but be surprised that he of all people had an interest in pursuing Trixie. As my roommate, he'd gotten more exposure to her than the rest and should know she wasn't worth the drama. Then I remembered Nate was a self-professed "boob-guy".

John snagged the toast from my forgotten tray. "It's the bro-code."

I stared down at where the rest of my morning meal remained untouched. If I didn't start eating more, I wouldn't make weight and wouldn't be allowed to start come season in the spring. I pushed at the disconcerting yellow mass of eggs with my fork, but couldn't bring myself to take a bite.

"Not to mention, you don't stand a chance," Brian added, uncrossing his arms and leaning forward to smirk at Nate.

Would it be so bad if I couldn't play anymore?

I looked around at my teammates. They were loud, crude, completely obsessed with the neighboring girl's school, and totally oblivious.

This school is doing a terrible job of turning us into gentlemen.

Nate turned to me and dragged me away from my thoughts yet again. "So, what do you say, Mitch?"

"About what?" I responded, looking once again at the several faces all eagerly awaiting a response and reminded myself for the millionth time to try harder not to sit in the middle.

"Do you think Nate has a right to go after Trixie if you two aren't dating anymore?" John asked.

I shrugged again. "I don't care what you do. Go after her if you want," I replied, genuinely not caring. Nate pumped his fist in the air, much to John's annoyance. "But I'll warn you, she has zero sense of humor."

Nate made a rude noise. "I'm not interested in her sense of humor." The table erupted into guffaws and I glanced back at the door where Andy had disappeared.

Chapter 2

Four Years Ago

Andy

Everything had gone perfectly. More than perfectly. When Mr. Hanover opened his desk drawer tomorrow morning the whole school would hear about it.

"The room is going to be a total disaster," I said, closing the door softly behind me.

"Hanover is going to freak. It'll take weeks to get chalk off of everything," Mitch added emphatically, his eyes sparkling in the glow still coming from the open window. He plopped down on my bed and I walked over to join him. I was too wound up to sit though, so I remained standing.

"You were right," I said. "This is definitely our best prank yet."

"I still can't believe no one has figured out it's us."

"Why would they? We're awesome," I stated, then quickly had to suppress a bout of laughter. It really was unbelievable that no one had guessed it was us after two whole years. I may have been doing pranks at Ulwich since before Mitch transferred in, but they were small time compared to the mischief we got up to together.

Tonight is going so well. The prank went perfect. I told Mitch the truth—most of it anyway. And we're still cool.

"It was a brilliant plan," I said, taking another step closer.

Mitch shook his head, laughing quietly to himself. "I may have come up with the frogs, but you're the reason we never get caught," Mitch countered.

"Pft, I almost got caught plenty of times before you got here."

"Yeah, but you didn't."

"Fair point." I smiled at Mitch who smiled in return. I loved it when he did that, it brightened his whole face and made my insides flutter.

Mitch leaned forward, his eyes shining with merriment. "Can you just see Hanover's face?"

"It's gonna be epic," I said, mirroring his lean in my enthusiasm. One beat passed, then another, as we stared at each other so close we were sharing the same air, grinning from ear to ear. My heart flipped as something between us seemed to thicken.

I blinked and suddenly our lips were pressed together. I hadn't planned for it to happen, it just had. Time seemed to slow as my brain processed the fact that I was actually kissing him, something that I'd barely been brave enough to dream about, and…and it was *perfect.*

Mitch pulled away and time rushed to catch up. "What the fuck," he hissed. His gaze fell on everything but me.

What have I done?

"I've known you're gay for all of two hours." The angry words hit me like a slap in the face.

"I…I…Mitch, I'm sorry. I didn't mean…" I stepped further back with each word.

What have I done?

Mitch's hand shot out lightning fast to stop me. His grip on my wrist tightened to the point of pain and panic seized my heart at the wild look shining from my best friend's eyes. Likely former best friend now.

I swallowed hard. "Mitch, please. I'm sorry. I won't tell anyone. I won't do it again. It was stupid. Please, you have to believe me. I swear." I pulled in vain against his hold as his eyes bored into me. Mitch had always been bigger than me and thanks to lacrosse tryouts, he was now definitely stronger.

He still hadn't said a word. Just that intense gaze that felt like it was skinning me where I stood.

Tears welled in my eyes at the betrayal I'd committed. "Mitch, I'm sorry. Maybe I didn't tell you everything like I should have. But I *swear* I won't breathe a word," I pleaded.

Present Day

Mitch

"Are you coming?" Brian asked as he walked backwards out of the school into the sunlight. John, Nate, and Kyle all glanced over their shoulders in anticipation of my response. I hiked my bag higher up my shoulder and willed myself to keep walking. But I didn't. I remained rooted inside the threshold shrouded in shadow, just out of reach of the afternoon sun.

Nate stopped walking and turned to face me fully, his features twisted into a frown. "Something up?"

Doubt flooded through me at the concern in his voice. Maybe I wasn't doing such a good job of hiding my depression from my roommate as I thought. To my horror, the others pulled to a stop as well, apparently incapable of going anywhere without me in tow, least of all to the informal practice that Coach S had all but ordered our first day back.

"What gives man?" John asked, the painfully bright light shining off his overly greased, dark hair.

I swallowed hard and scrambled for words that wouldn't come. My gaze darted between the four of them all staring at me, waiting for an answer. My grip tightened around the strap of my bag while my heart hammered in my chest. The harder I tried to speak, the more strained my breathing became until I stood there panting quick breaths that only made my pulse spike more. Just the thought of stepping onto the practice field again, of listening to the coach yell and shout and demand, made me want to throw up all of the nothing I'd eaten for breakfast and lunch. Not even the hope of getting benched brought a reprieve, because I *wouldn't* get benched. Coach would force me to eat, just like he'd made Carter lose fourteen pounds in a week in order to make the semifinals last year.

Brian's eyes narrowed and he took a step back toward the school. "What's the deal?"

Panic surged through me and finally brought my voice. "I'll be there in a bit, I just remembered I have to stop by Nolan's office." I took a step back and hoped none of them would dig deeper into the lie.

"Nolan's a prick. Just don't take too long or Coach'll freak." Brian waved for the others to keep moving and I bit back a sigh of relief.

"Yeah," I said, then quickly turned and retreated into the school before one of them decided to join me.

My bag slipped as I rounded a corner so fast my shoes squeaked on the hardwood floors. I fumbled to keep it from flying and ended up with my back pressed against the wall, clutching the bag to my chest and gulping for air. A few precious seconds ticked by and my breaths came a little easier, but they stopped altogether when the sound of approaching footsteps filled the hallway.

I slung the bag over my body this time and took off down the hall once more. I needed to go somewhere I could cool down, somewhere no one would find me. My destination swam into view and I took the steps two at a time, ascending the Tower as fast as my feet would carry me. At last I stood in the center of the circular room facing the massive opening that hadn't held glass for as long as I'd been here. I gasped out a sob that the draft immediately stole and dropped the nearly empty sack to the ground with trembling hands. Tears stung my eyes as I gazed out the would-be window at the green beyond. Already the tiny dots of my teammates scurried about in coordinated patterns.

"I can't do it anymore. I can't live like this." The tears I'd been fighting for what felt like four fucking years finally slipped free as I stepped toward the ledge. The dizzying thirty-foot drop to the ground below swam before my eyes.

Another sob tore free as I stumbled back away from the ledge. I fisted my hands in my hair, desperate for an escape, but too afraid to take the one right in front of me. I sank to the floor in a defeated heap and buried my head in my arms.

Andy

I finished shoving the assortment of textbooks and paperbacks into my bag, then slung the worn strap over my shoulder. The first day back was always grueling. Between getting books organized, establishing a schedule with my college mentor, having to hear about everyone's summer excursions... seeing Mitch... I needed some space.

"I thought you said you weren't studying with Connor anymore," Calvin called out when I was almost to the stairs.

I turned back to face him. "And I'm not. I'm allowed to want to be on my own, you know."

"That's not why you're going up there." The flat statement just missed being a rebuke. Rather than dignify the accusation with a response, I turned back to the stairs.

My foot hovered over the first step as I glanced up the passage. *The Tower*. That's what everyone called it, mostly due to the steps that curved up and to the right until they disappeared; not to mention the huge window at the top. Despite the allure of the name and stunning view, hardly anyone ventured up there. No one wanted to climb all of the damn stairs, which made it the perfect place to go if you wanted to be alone. That was how it had become Mitch and my hangout all those years ago. It was the birthplace of some of our wildest schemes.

I wet my lips.

Will going up there make seeing him this morning hurt any less? I should go with Calvin to the library, or the courtyard, or literally anywhere else.

Despite the logic, I lowered my foot and began the climb. Fifty steps later, I rounded the final corner and started. To my surprise, another student was already there. My shoulders slumped.

So much for being alone.

It was hard to tell who it might be with their back to me. Their focus was centered on the vast window and it didn't seem like they'd noticed my arrival. It looked like they might have been there a while already as they were seated on the floor with their legs stretched out, their school blazer tossed casually beside them. Curious, I took a step closer. It wasn't until my bag hit the floor and he raised his head that I realized I recognized him.

"Mitch? What are you doing here?"

His arm lifted and moved as if wiping something from his face.

Is he crying?

"I could ask you the same thing," he said over his shoulder.

"I come up here sometimes. To think. You know?"

"Yeah," he replied softly without answering my initial question and returned to gazing back out the opening.

I should go.

My fingers wrapped around the canvas strap of my messenger bag fully prepared to do just that. I looked from it to Mitch.

I definitely should go.

Still I hesitated.

But something is clearly wrong.

The strap slid through my fingers back to the ground and I walked towards him. After another moment of indecision, I sat down. We hadn't spoken in years, but that didn't eliminate the reflex to comfort my best friend, even if I didn't have a right to call him that anymore. "Is everything alright?"

He shrugged and continued to stare out at the green landscape below.

To the north, I could just make out the lacrosse fields filled with scurrying bodies. From this distance, they looked like ants. "Aren't you supposed to be at practice?"

"Yeah," he said evenly, still not looking at me.

"Won't you get in trouble for missing it?"

"Probably."

I pulled my knees up and rested my arms on them, not sure how to proceed.

I really should leave. He's not my Mitch anymore. It's not like I know anything about his problems.

I glanced at him out of the corner of my eye.

Then again, he hasn't left yet either.

I took a deep breath and let it out slowly. "Do you wanna talk about it?"

He turned to look at me. His hazel eyes were rimmed with red, reaffirming my belief that he'd been crying. He stared at me for a long minute before turning away.

Way to fucking go, Andy. What am I thinking? We haven't even been in the same vicinity for this long in four years. Not since that night.

Heat burned across my face at the memory.

"I can't stand it." His sudden speech startled me right out of my creeping blush. "There's no pleasing any of them. They all want more from me, but none of them actually want *me*—not the real me. I'm not sure I even remember who that is anymore," he added in a whisper.

"I didn't realize you were so unhappy." He'd certainly never looked that way, always laughing, surrounded by his brainless friends.

"No one does. No one cares."

My hands fidgeted in my lap. "I care," I said quietly.

Why did I say that?

"Sometimes I wish I'd never gone out for the team."

I thought back to all those years ago when he'd first told me he was going to try out. He'd been so excited to be doing something his father had done when *he'd* attended Ulwich. I'd been happy for him, even as I recognized it was signaling the end. "You always wanted to be on the team," I responded.

Mitch shook his head. "I didn't know what it would mean. The things I would lose." That last was so soft, I barely even heard him.

"What do you mean?"

He looked at me and I had to grip my fingers to keep them from fidgeting again as he searched my face.

I let out the breath I was holding when he finally shifted his intense focus to the window.

"It never ends. All I do is practice, play, and work out. I'm barely even passing my classes. I can't afford to fail, but when am I supposed to study with the whole damn team constantly on my back? Not that it would matter if I *did* fail," he added bitterly. "The grades would just get doctored. Can't lose our lead attackman, can we?" He stood abruptly.

Unsure of what to do, I remained seated.

"Mitch, you need to push harder. Mitch, you need to lead the team. Mitch, you have to win," he said as he paced the small room. "And that's just the coach. My fucking teammates are worse." He gestured emphatically as he continued to rant. "Their humor is gross and they're obsessed with getting laid. Not that any of them ever do, but it doesn't stop them from expecting me to sleep with every girl within twenty miles."

I glanced towards the stairwell. His voice had been getting louder with each grievance. Just because no one came up here didn't mean someone at the bottom couldn't hear the echoed conversation. "Mitch..."

"I can't take it. I just wanna go back to the way things used to be, when I was allowed to be a person. Not just some piece of meat to be ground down until there's nothing left. Fucking assholes don't give a shit about anyone but themselves."

"Mitch..." I tried again already moving to retrieve my abandoned satchel.

He's going to get himself in trouble if he keeps on like this. Even if someone from the team doesn't hear, word 'll get back.

"I mean, fuck them. Their idea of a good time is going on a panty-raid at the neighboring girl's school or fucking tea-bagging each other. It's disgusting. Do you remember how much fun we used to have? We didn't do any of that stupid shit. We—"

"Mitch.".

He spun on me. "What?"

I slung the strap across my body.

His eyes darted between the bursting satchel back to me. "Where are you going?"

"Somewhere else."

His face fell like he couldn't believe I'd have the audacity to walk out on him.

I rolled my eyes and gestured to the stairs. "Are you coming?"

At this hour, hardly anyone was in the corridors and we passed through them relatively unobserved. I walked at a good clip, turning down first one hallway, then another and another, until at last I reached my destination. A quick glance showed the passageway was empty.

I walked right up to an over-sized portrait of Walter Ulwich, the founder of the academy, and pulled it away from the wall. Mitch strode purposefully through the opening and I followed behind, letting the giant painting swing shut behind me.

Mitch flicked an equally hidden switch, and the room filled with a soft, yellow glow. "I think I'm going to quit the team."

I set my bag down and let out a sigh. "Why would you do that?"

"Because I hate it. I hate *them*."

"You don't hate them. I know they can be jerks, but they depend on you."

"I don't see why that has to be my responsibility," he said angrily, glaring at the floor.

I stepped deeper into the secret room and placed a hand on his slumped shoulders. "That aside, you're really good. You can't deny that."

"I don't even like lacrosse. How can I be good at something I don't even like?"

"Natural skill?" I offered.

"I miss the way things used to be." His gaze lifted to meet mine. Although his eyes were still red, there was a hardness to them. "Before I—" He shook his head.

I gave his shoulder a reassuring squeeze. "You've been playing for a long time."

"Pretending," he corrected. "I've been pretending for a long time. I never had to pretend with you." His gaze softened as he looked back at me.

I searched his sad eyes, at a loss for how to make this better. We hadn't been close in years, since the last time we'd been in this exact room, but I hated to see him hurting like this. My thumb stroked the tiny patch of exposed skin it rested on. He was warm—probably from working himself up—and he felt good. He'd felt good then, too.

I didn't realize the distance between us had been shrinking until Mitch's mouth was on mine. My hand reflexively left his shoulder to curl around the back of his neck while his arm slid around my waist and pulled me closer even as he kissed harder. I sighed into it and he took advantage of the opening to slip his tongue past my lips.

The shock of it finally gave my brain a chance to catch up. I pulled away and put both of my hands between us. The distance, however, was minimal as his hand stayed firmly planted on my waist. "W-What are you doing?" I stuttered.

His face clouded with confusion. "What do you mean? *You* brought *me* here, Andy."

I pushed against his chest, and he finally let go. "Yeah, so you could vent without anyone overhearing." I took a small step back, still struggling to pull it together.

He licked his lips, and I tried not to think about why they were so pink. "But..."

I can't do this, not again. I don't even know why I brought him here.

"I was just trying to make you feel better," I reiterated, not sure which of us I was trying to convince.

His eyes searched my obviously panicked face.

I nervously wet my lips. They still tasted like him.

He took a full step towards me, forcing my arm to bend and effectively invading my personal space.

I stiffened.

His eyes bored into me, and mine widened in fear.

"What if this *is* what I need to feel better?" He said the words softly, but there was an edge to them, a hardness I was afraid to entertain. Mitch was my best friend—four years couldn't change that—but he was also trouble.

Can I play this game with him?

When I failed to respond, he moved my hand out of the way and captured my mouth again. For reasons that eluded me, I kissed back. The almost soft kiss became more exploratory. My eyelids fluttered as my heart beat erratically. Kissing Mitch felt even better than I remembered. He'd gotten better at it. We both had.

What am I doing? This is a mistake. I know better. This can only end one way.

The knowledge didn't change the fact that I'd wanted this for years, still wanted it.

I can't lose him again because of my selfishness. I have to tell him no.

I pulled away again, but he was less than inclined to relinquish his hold on me a second time. His hazel eyes were super intense as I stared into them.

Say no, Andy. Tell. Him. No.

"Fine." The traitorous word was out of my mouth before I could call it back.

His eyes lidded and he leaned forward.

I quickly sandwiched a hand between us, and he stopped short. "But no sex." At least one lesson I could remember, even if I was barely holding onto it with a white-knuckled grip.

"Okay," Mitch said, leaning forward.

"I mean it, Mitch. Absolutely no sex."

If it doesn't go that far, if I don't repeat the same mistake, then it can't end the same way.

He searched my face for a moment, and my anxiety ratcheted up several notches. It was already too late. That was what he wanted from me. A quick escape, a way to ease his troubles for an afternoon before returning to his reality. I just got him back and now I was losing him all over again for the same damn reason.

"No sex," he finally responded, then promptly recaptured my mouth. There was nothing tentative about the kiss. It was harsh and needy, and I gave it to him. His arm tightened around me once more. I wriggled my hand free and wrapped it around his head, urging him deeper.

This is a very bad idea.

His grip on my waist shifted, and he pushed me against the wall. I let out a gasp at the sharp contact. Before I could say anything, his mouth closed back over mine and his body pressed firmly against me. There was no hiding my groan *or* my growing erection. His teeth pulled at my bottom lip as he freed my top two buttons in quick succession.

"Mitch." Despite how breathless I was, the warning tone was evident.

"I fucking heard you, Andy. No sex." His fingers slipped beneath my collar to caress the now exposed part of my neck.

Feeling his touch on the sensitive skin made me want to feel it everywhere. I desperately tried to rein in my rampant hormones before I did something I would regret even more.

He abandoned my mouth, and I gave a soft moan as his wet lips replaced his hand.

Oh fuck.

His fingers dug into my hips and I realized I wasn't the only one struggling. His lips found mine again, and I was lost, so totally freaking lost.

Oh God Mitch.

Despite my adamant assertion not to let this go too far, I was already a heartbeat away from letting him have whatever he wanted. If he wanted head, he could have it. If he wanted to bend me over something, he could fucking do that too. My fear of consequences was systematically being seared away with each heated second. I clung to him, desperately wanting to hang on to something I'd thought I'd lost forever.

Gradually the kiss faded from outright demanding to light presses until at last he gave them up altogether and rested his forehead against mine. His heavy breathing mirrored my own and, for once in my life, I had literally no words. I could barely even hear myself think over my pounding heart.

"You should go first," he whispered. He was still so close, the air itself felt like a kiss.

"What?" I asked, still trapped in a fog.

He leaned away and looked me in the eye. "You should leave first."

"Oh. Right." I cleared my throat and stepped aside, since he was crowding me. He silently watched me redo the buttons he'd popped, his gaze staying on me as I stooped to retrieve my bag. I did a quick inventory of myself to make sure I was back in order before walking to the secret entrance. I opened the door just enough to peer into the outside hallway. When I was sure the way was clear, I opened it further.

"I'll see you around, Andy."

My heart skipped at Mitch's words. I wanted to look back, but didn't trust myself to actually leave if I did.

What the fuck have I gotten myself into?

Chapter 3

Four Years Ago

Andy

"Come with me." Mitch's words sounded like a death knell in the quiet room.

He's going to kill me.

Icy terror washed through me at the realization. Then Mitch tugged me toward the door and I immediately began clawing at his hand.

"Please. I'm sorry. It won't ever happen again. I swear." My desperate pleas fell on deaf ears. I dug my feet into the area rug. It wrinkled, but didn't offer any resistance. Mitch continued to pull, relentlessly dragging us to the only escape. I tripped over the bump I'd made in the rug and stumbled out the door. I glanced back at my room receding behind us and renewed my frantic attempts to get free.

"Mitch. Stop. I promise I won't say anything. No one will ever know. It'll just be between us. Please," I cried.

Mitch lurched to a stop and used his grip on my arm to pull me closer. "Do you wanna get caught?" he hissed.

I quickly ran through the possibilities. If I made enough noise and attracted a teacher or prefect, then I might be spared. However, then they would want to know what we were doing out of bed after lights out. That could potentially be way worse, especially if they checked the classrooms. I swallowed and quickly shook my head.

"Good. Now be quiet or we'll both be on the chopping block." I barely registered his concern for getting caught before he tugged on my arm again. Once more, I was being towed by Mitch to what was surely my end.

Present Day

Mitch

I hadn't meant to kiss Andy, I really *really* hadn't, but clearly, I was just as incapable of making good decisions now as I had been four years ago. My tongue darted out to taste my lips. I could still feel him there, buzzing beneath the surface. When he'd shown up in the tower, I hadn't known what to make of it. When was the last time we'd exchanged more than a passing glance, let alone spoke? Then he'd... stayed. That had thrown me even more.

My finger tipped the corner of the photograph taken a lifetime ago as I sat on my bed with my legs stretched out—mercifully alone. Within its faded edges, two thirteen-year-old boys laughed with a joy that only ever seemed to come with summer. It was also the first summer I hadn't felt so horribly alone since my dad died. When he'd died in combat two years before, I thought I'd never be happy again. Then came Andy. I'd been at Ulwich all of a year and we'd been inseparable since the moment we'd met on my first day. We'd had the time of our lives getting into all sorts of trouble with never a thought that our fast friendship might come to a sudden terrible end. My smile at the memory slipped, and I chewed on my bottom lip as I continued to stare at the frozen memory.

Andy's eyes sparkled with joy as he leaned across the frame to shove me. Their bright green had been darker in the secret room. Whatever he said, I recognized lust when I saw it. I shifted on my bed, increasingly uncomfortable in my school khakis as I remembered how he'd reacted. The press of his full lips against mine. The molding of his hard yet remarkably soft body. The whisper of a moan as I'd sucked on his neck.

A groan spilled out as I recalled how fucking aroused he'd been, his hard length digging into my thigh while a flush stained his pale skin and darkened his freckles. I palmed my straining dick and focused on his eyes, only they weren't the bright green shining back at me, but ones darkened with want.

His dragging me into the secret room should have been a second chance, an opportunity to get it right this time, but of course I'd fucked it up...again. All I had to do was *not* kiss him. It shouldn't have been that hard. Who was I fucking kidding? Andy pressed buttons on me no prior hookup had ever found. And fuck me if I hadn't done my damnedest to find someone who could. But no one could replace Andy with his snark and being too smart for his own good. That fiery hair that defiantly proclaimed his Irish roots. And those eyes. *Fuck*, those eyes.

I couldn't take it anymore. The hand not holding the picture fumbled with my pants. I needed a release like I needed air to breathe. My fingers wrapped around my pulsing shaft and my head fell back with a groan that came straight from my balls. Absently, I considered digging out some lotion or *something* to make the slide smoother, but I didn't have the patience for it. I stroked once and squeezed the base, nearly choking on another groan. My head popped back up, and I zeroed back in on those insane eyes, memories driving my hand faster. The slight burn of the dry friction only made me more desperate. My breaths came in short pants as fantasy overlaid the memory.

Back in the secret room, Andy wasn't clothed this time, but gloriously naked, all of his smooth skin on display and free for the touching. He curled his fingers in my hair as he pressed his ass back against me. I sucked bruises into his delicate skin until he turned to look at me over his shoulder, eyes darkened with lust, lips parted in invitation. The ache in my balls turned painful as I dug fingers into his sides and yanked him back to claim that mouth.

Pain turned to tingles as I kept fueling the fire, still unable to look away from the photo clutched in my hand. My toes curled in anticipation of the release I so badly needed. It burned beneath my skin, threatening to turn me to ash if I didn't do something soon. I stroked faster and faster, each pass of my fist bringing me closer. A few more seconds, that's all I needed. Just a few more seconds, then I could finally explode.

My balls tightened, and I braced myself for what promised to be an epic finish. Then the door opened. In a blind panic, I shoved the picture out of sight and fell on my side, struggling to put myself away as fast as humanly possible, the oversight of lube now a blessing.

"Jesus fucking Christ, Nate! Knock much?" I finished zipping my pants and glanced up to find my roommate not even remotely apologetic about having walked in on me rubbing one out.

"Don't you fucking start with me," he snapped right back, the slight pink in his round cheeks the only sign that he might be embarrassed. "You don't want to be disturbed? Put a fucking sock on the door like a normal person." He slammed said door shut and stalked over to his own bed and desk. His book satchel landed in the chair with an angry squeak that matched his bad attitude perfectly.

"Excuse the fuck out of me. Last I knew, you were supposed to be somewhere else." My heart pounded as I bickered with him about dorm etiquette. Had he seen what I'd been holding? Had I ruined the picture when I shoved it under the comforter? Nate couldn't know, no one could fucking know. I grabbed at my hair and continued to silently freak out while Nate bitched about his shit day. If he'd seen, if he even suspected, forget not wanting to play anymore, the entire team would fucking crucify me. And if they found out I'd been getting off on a picture of Andy…they'd kill him.

"Hey, you okay?"

The sudden expression of concern ripped me out of my spiral. "What?"

"I asked, are you okay? Look, I get that it's embarrassing as shit to get caught, but it's not that big a deal. Really." He shrugged as he tossed his school blazer over the chair. "Could be worse. Ever been caught by your grandma? Now that shit is fucked up." He laughed, and I knew I was supposed to too, but I couldn't.

"I'm gonna go for a walk. Cool off." I slid off the bed and toed my shoes back on.

Nate's face fell, and he pushed his brown hair back. "Yeah. Okay."

I didn't give him any more information, just walked out of the room without a backward glance. For once, the usually bustling hall was empty. I briefly contemplated going back up to the Tower, but dismissed it when I remembered why I'd gone the last time. With a huff, I turned down an adjoining corridor, walking fast enough to look like I had a purpose, except I had no idea where I was going. My thoughts strayed to the picture that lay hidden beneath my sheets, possibly ruined, for anyone to find. Why had I taken it out? I was always so careful with the damn thing. I doubt even Andy knew I had it, since my mom was the one who'd taken the picture.

After long enough that my legs were actually getting tired, I slowed and sagged against a wall. I wasn't even surprised to find myself facing the East dormitories where Andy's own room was. My fingers dragged across my face and I let out a heavy breath. I'd spent four years trying to let him go and was obviously failing miserably. I glanced down the deserted hall, now shrouded in shadow. Lights out had come and gone while I'd wandered aimlessly through the school in search of an answer I already knew.

"What the fuck do you think you're doing, Hudson?"

Great, just what I needed right now. "Cool your tits, Price."

"What the fuck did you say to me?" Benny asked, bowing up. With his broad shoulders, he made an excellent Midfielder and could probably beat me to a pulp if he wanted to get his hands dirty. Oh, I'd put up a good fight and get my licks in too, but Benny would win hands down.

I sighed and straightened up. Being a hot mess didn't give me license to be stupid. "I said, I'm going to bed."

Benny stepped aside so I could do just that. "You think you're untouchable because you're coach's shiny star."

I couldn't help but glance over at him. Benny fought hard for his position on the team. Benny fought hard for everything. But he'd never have the talent I did. "Aren't I?"

A muscle in his cheek twitched as I passed, but he didn't stop me or say anything else. My own words played in my mind as I made my way to bed. *Aren't I?*

I slipped into the room and let out a relieved breath when the sound of Nate's snoring filled my ears. I shut the door softly behind me with barely even a click, then tiptoed over to the side of my bed and flicked on the lamp. A quick glance showed the light hadn't disturbed him. Reassured, I fished out the photo. Crinkles marred the delicate paper, and I carefully smoothed them out. All in all, it could have been worse. At least I could still see Andy's face clearly. Plus, if I was lucky, my mom had made duplicates and I could get another.

I stole another glance at Nate, then made my way to the closet. Propped at the back was my dad's old army duffel. Mostly by feel and memory, I replaced the damning photo in between the lining and put the bag back exactly how it was with hardly a speck of dust out of place.

In silence, I stripped down to my boxers and undershirt, then slipped between the covers, my mind still circling what I didn't want to admit. I'd tried to let Andy go once. I couldn't do it again.

Andy

I sat my lunch tray on the table and swung my leg over the bench. I eyed the selection before me skeptically. It wasn't a gourmet meal by any stretch of the imagination, but there was one thing it never failed to be—nutritious.

Just once couldn't we have pizza or something?

I stabbed the seared chicken and set about turning it into manageable pieces. My fork was halfway to my mouth when the sight of another tray and its adjoining student manifested in front of me. The useless utensil clattered down, sending wrinkled green beans flying.

"This seat taken?" Mitch asked as he sat without waiting for a response. I glanced over at his usual table to see if everyone had miraculously vanished. Per usual, it was overflowing with rowdy guys pushing each other and laughing. My gaze swiveled back to Mitch.

"What are you doing here?" I hissed.

"Eating lunch with my friend. Is that alright with you?"

"Um, yes?"

Why is he really here? Any minute, the whole fucking team is going to descend on us. He'll be fine, but what will they do to me?

I shuddered at the possibilities.

"You cold?"

"What? No." I retrieved my fork, which had somehow held on to its piece of meat.

"So where's Bridges?" he asked, starting to eat as well.

"Uh, he's getting a lecture or something from the art professor."

Mitch nodded and took another bite.

We're really having lunch together. This is happening right now.

"He's pretty good from what I've seen." I was about to tell him I agreed when he asked, "So are you two…?"

It took me half a second longer than it should have for me to realize what he was blatantly asking in the middle of the cafeteria. I snorted a laugh. "Um, no. Calvin's a friend, that's all."

A smile spread across Mitch's face as he continued to demolish his lunch.

"What about you and—oh, what's her name?—Trixie, that's it."

He groaned. "Heard about that, did you?"

I laughed at the theatrics.

"Nothing there," he answered.

"Oh? What happened?" I prodded. That sounded suspiciously like a story.

He leaned back and scooted vegetables around his plate. "First off, she's absolutely insane."

I laughed again.

"I'm serious. Stay away from all the girls at that damn school. The lot of them are certifiable," he added with a short laugh.

"I think I can manage that just fine."

"You know, I was thinking with it being a new year and all, it might be nice to apply myself a little more," he said, shifting in his seat, his lunch forgotten.

"What did you have in mind?" I asked, leaning forward despite myself.

"I could really use some help with my history paper."

I let out a sigh and started gathering my trash. "If you're fishing to get me to write it for you, then you should know I don't do that sort of thing." I stood up, fully prepared to make a hasty exit and diligently working to hide my disappointment. Why did it have to hurt so much?

Mitch bumped his tray as he got up. "What? No. That's not what I meant at all."

I seriously doubted his request for a study partner had anything to do with the other option. I gave a huff, and against my better judgment, turned back to him.

"Andy, I already wrote the damn thing. I was just hoping you could look at it. I'm sure it's absolute trash, and it's not like the professor really expects anything from me, but just once, it'd be nice to turn in something halfway decent."

"Oh." *Well, I'm an ass.* "Yeah, I could do that."

Mitch looked visibly relieved. He mirrored me and gathered his tray, though it still held most of his meal. "Awesome. Meet in the courtyard tomorrow after practice?" he suggested as he walked with me to the bin.

I mentally ran through any potential conflicts. "That should be fine. You know where the low wall is on the east side?"

His eyes twinkled with mischief as he smiled. "How could I forget?"

It took me a second to realize what he was referring to. When I did, I chuckled. We'd once set off a firework there. It was supposed to be for a prank, but it didn't work as we expected and we'd nearly lost a few fingers. "You know, there's still a blast mark," I said.

"No way."

I nodded. "God, I still don't know how we didn't get caught."

"Probably has something to do with the fact that we booked it out of there like we were on fire."

I laughed again, remembering some of our closer calls.

"So, I'll see you tomorrow then?"

I looked into his hazel eyes, the eyes of my best friend, the same one who had come up with so many of our wild schemes, and the one who had thought it was a good idea to test the firework first. "Yeah, I'll see you tomorrow."

"Cool." He promptly dumped what remained of his lunch and hopped back to join his goon buddies.

I stood there a moment, just appreciating the brilliant grin he'd given me before he left.

Maybe my Mitch isn't as gone as I thought he was.

I shook my head and turned to exit, immediately running into Calvin. "Oh, hey. You're done sooner than expected," I said, continuing my path out of the cafeteria.

He fell in step and the doors swung shut behind us. "Eh, doesn't mean it was any more pleasant to bear. I'm more interested in how *your* lunch went. Do my eyes deceive me, or was that the esteemed Mitch Hudson I just saw you with?"

I rolled my eyes.

"What did *he* want?" Calvin didn't even try to hide his over-the-top inquiry.

"He asked to study together."

Calvin guffawed loud enough to earn us a reproachful look from some passing teachers.

I waved an apology and turned down the nearest hallway. "It's not like that."

He continued to snicker.

"I'm serious. Cut it out." I considered telling him about what had happened the other day, but decided that wasn't liable to help my current situation.

"I'm sorry, it's just too good. First Connor, now Mitch. Keep going like this, and you'll be able to collect the whole set."

"Well, if it does turn into a recurring theme, it'll have to be ar incomplete one. I'm not going anywhere near Benny."

"Good. Because *that one* is mine." He gave me a devilish grin before sauntering down another passageway toward his next class.

Chapter 4

Four Years Ago

Mitch

I shoved Andy into the secret room and closed the door. He stayed quiet for all of three seconds before words started spilling out of him.

"It won't happen again. I don't know what I was thinking. Not a word, I swear. Please don't kill me."

"Kill you? I'm not going to kill you," I snapped at him, more than a little upset that he would ever think that. Rather than be comforted, he blanched.

"W-what are you going to do? Please, I can make this right. Just give me a chance."

I shook my head. "Stop talking. I need a minute." I grasped my head, but it didn't do shit to stop my mind from spinning. Everything had happened so fast. I needed to wrap my head around it and I couldn't do that in his room while he was very loudly freaking out.

Andy's gay. How did I miss that? We spend practically every waking second together. How could I not know?

"You don't have to do this. I'm sorry. Mitch, please," Andy blubbered.

I dropped my hands and looked at him. My gut gave a sickening twist at seeing his wide eyes and pale face.

He's terrified.

I walked over to him, and he flinched. I grasped his arms before he could try to retreat again. As it was, he looked like he was trying to figure out how to make a play for the entrance. We both knew there was no way he'd get to it before me.

"It was an accident," he insisted, water welling in his eyes. That much I knew was true. It had been a total accident, one that couldn't be taken back.

"Stop talking," I said again and shook him, causing a tear to slide free.

"You don't have to talk to me anymore. I understand. Just please, don't hurt me," he pleaded. There it was again, this insane belief that he could ever do or say *anything* that would make me want to hurt my best friend.

"I'm not going to hurt you," I growled.

He pulled against my grip, his eyes still wide with fear and apologies spewing from his mouth. "I promise. I won't do it again. No one will ever know. Please—"

"For the love of God. For once in your life, Andy, stop talking." His mouth opened as if to keep going anyway. I jerked him toward me and mashed my mouth against his. He immediately went stock still. I kissed him harder, forcing my tongue past his salty lips.

He gave a small squeak, but didn't fight me. I released his upper arms to cradle his head and pull his face closer. Kissing Andy wasn't at all like I'd expected. I knew his lips were full, but I'd never imagined they'd be so soft, so pliable. Even trembling, they fit against mine in a way I hadn't experienced before.

His hand left my arm and rose shakily into the air. I braced myself for him to push me away. Instead, his fingers wrapped in my hair and forced my mouth harder against his. Then his lips finally moved. In a single heartbeat, everything shifted. My hands fell to his waist to pull his body tight against mine. Andy let out a gasp and arched into it. The kiss got wilder, and I groaned.

"Mitch," he whispered against my mouth. Whatever doubts I had vanished.

I silenced the rest of his words with a harsh kiss even as I frantically worked to remove his night clothes. I needed to feel his skin against mine, and I needed it now. The stupid fabric bunched and got stuck. I gave a growl of frustration, unwilling to stop kissing him long enough to get the damn thing off of him properly.

A sudden pressure on my shoulders forced me to take a step back. I met Andy's heated gaze as he reached back and pulled off his tangled shirt. It fell by the wayside, quickly followed by his pants. My mouth went dry.

I'd seen Andy naked before, but not like this. Not flush and definitely not aroused. I swallowed past the unexpected lump in my throat and brought my gaze back up.

Andy's chest rose and fell with breathing heavy, not unlike my own, but he didn't look away. He'd meant what he'd said. Andy wasn't fucking with me. He really was gay.

Present Day

Mitch

I rubbed a hand along the back of my neck as I made my way down the hall. The last-minute change to meet inside had been necessary because of a surprise rain shower. For probably the hundredth time, I patted the bag at my side to reassure myself it was still there. Like I could somehow misplace the damn thing while it was strapped across my body. But it wasn't the bag that I was worried about so much as the paper within. What if Andy took one look at it and decided I was a hopeless cause? What if I really wasn't any better than mediocre? What if sports was really all I was good at? And the scariest thought of all—what if no matter what I did, I'd never be able to undo the sins of the past?

That last one smarted, and I rubbed at the familiar ache in my chest, my constant companion these last four years anytime I made the mistake of thinking of the friendship I'd lost, the one I'd ruined.

Get a grip. He's reading your paper. Probably going to give a few grammar tips and send you on your way.

Reality aside, it didn't stop my heart from lurching into my throat the moment I opened the classroom door. The locale had been my suggestion, but it wasn't helping my anxiety like I thought it would. If anything, knowing I would be alone in a room with Andy was actually making it worse.

He glanced up at my arrival and I nearly called it quits right there. I still didn't know what had possessed me to kiss him after all this time, let alone try to inhale him like the last air on Earth resided in his lungs. All I knew was that I'd been thinking about him, about us and what we'd been, and then he'd been there. He'd sat down, talked to me, and for a shining moment, I'd gotten a glimpse of the past before I'd wrecked it. Then he'd taken me to the secret room, and it was like history was doomed to repeat itself. There I was, making all the same mistakes. But it had been different this time. He'd put his foot down—mostly—set rules. It had been a stark reminder that in the four years we'd been apart, Andy had grown up. He wasn't the wide-eyed youth anymore. He was top of our class, knew his own mind, and had boundaries. Hell, even according to the state he wasn't a kid anymore, not since August ninth.

"You planning on standing there 'til the next bell?"

I took a deep breath and a fateful step forward. "No."

He crossed his arms over his chest and leaned back at my grumbled response. The move put him directly in the path of a ray of sunlight streaming through the window. The tension in my chest loosened. Andy had changed, but his eyes were just as green, his hair just as red.

Maybe redder.

A smile tugged at my lips as his eyebrows climbed up his forehead. Finally, he asked, "What's so funny?"

"Nothing." I ducked my head to hide the renegade grin and took a seat next to him. "Let's get this over with." I fished in my bag and pulled out my travesty of a report. The sad part was that I really had tried, and it was still awful. "Go easy on me."

He snagged the papers from my hand, barely missing giving me a paper cut. My eyes went wide as I spied the red pen already uncapped in his hand. "When have you ever known me to go easy on anyone?"

"Look, I know it's probably the worst thing ever, but you could at least sugarcoat it for me."

"No can do. If you want sugar, Mr. Isaac still keeps skittles in his bottom left drawer."

For a second I forgot all about the paper, about my anxiety being here, about how all of this could blow up in my face...again. "Really?" I asked, glancing at the large desk in the front of the room, then back at Andy.

His eyes glinted wickedly, and he flashed a hand that sported a skittle between each finger tip.

"Hell, yes." I vacated my seat in favor of the treat and left Andy to what was likely to be a massacre. Sure enough, the lock was still busted and nestled within the bottom drawer was Mr. Isaac's guilty pleasure.

I swiped a handful, but instead of returning to my seat, I leaned back against the board and watched Andy read my attempt at scholastics. A red skittle found its way into my mouth, followed quickly by a yellow and a green. Back at the table, Andy stared thoughtfully at the pages and painted the damn things red. Between each bout of scribbles, he chewed on the end of the pen.

So that's still the same too.

His hair, his eyes, his habits…his mouth. Even as I had the dangerous thought, I couldn't stop myself. His mouth was definitely still the plush thing that plagued my dreams. Perhaps that was why I'd kissed him, to see if any of it was real, a test as it were. A test I'd failed miserably the second his body reacted to mine. In my defense, at eighteen, a warm anything could get my blood pumping, but nothing could have prepared me for the confident way he'd wrapped his arms around my neck and forced me to kiss him deeper. There was only one word for it—hungry. That was a feeling I was intimately familiar with.

"There."

My head snapped up from where I'd been studying the sugar melting in my hand. I popped the last few skittles and licked the sticky off as I made my way back to the table. The metal legs of the chair squeaked against the ground as I fell into it. "Alright, coach, how bad is it?"

Andy shook his head and laughed under his breath. "I'm 'coach' now, huh?"

I shrugged. "Would you rather I call you something else?"

"The technical term is tutor. Learn it, live it, love it," he said as he brandished the recapped pen at me. "And Andy will do just fine."

"Okay, Andy."

He stared at me for a long second without blinking, then adjusted his attention to the page.

I mirrored his gaze and almost choked at the sea of red. "Jesus Christ, Andy, what happened to taking it easy on me?"

"First off, pretty sure I said I wouldn't. Second, I thought the whole point of this was that you were tired of people going easy on you." He turned those green eyes on me and I swallowed. Andy had that kind of intense stare that dared you to contradict him. It dared you to do a lot of things.

"Yeah, okay. You're right."

The emerald challenge softened into a playful smirk. "I know."

"You know everything." The moment the words left my mouth, my heart stopped. I couldn't help it. They'd just…slipped free.

Andy only hesitated half a beat. "You make that sound like it's a bad thing. Also, you're going to want to wash your hands."

I frowned at him, but before I could do more, he reached out and snagged my wrist. I quickly added "not breathing" to the list of things I wasn't doing.

"Unless, of course, you wanna get busted for raiding the snack drawer."

I forced my gaze away from his sharp eyes and looked down at the captive hand. Sure enough, the melted skittles had left stains on my hand like a rainbow of freckles. My gaze slipped to Andy's firm grip, and the dusting of real freckles on his own hand.

As quickly as he'd snared it, he released my hand and started putting away his pen. "Don't be discouraged. The paper has promise." He gestured at the pages I didn't remember picking up. "Most of that is notes and suggestions for resource materials. Paper's due in a week. Should be plenty of time to clean it up."

"Yeah," I croaked out, because, again, had neglected to breathe.

"I, uh, could look at it again before you submit it." His gaze skittered over the table, but never actually met mine, which was probably for the best since I was pretty sure my face looked like the time I'd gotten beamed with a lacrosse stick.

Andy wants to see me again.

I rolled up the pages and stuffed them into my bag without really looking. "That would be great. I'd really like that," I said, my voice gaining strength.

Andy's roving gaze finally flicked up to meet mine and the small smile he'd given earlier grew to the one I remembered from our childhood, the one he'd given me when he'd declared we'd be best friends moments after meeting me. All too soon it was gone, lost as he shouldered his bag. And fuck, now I was going to bust my ass to make this the best paper I'd ever written, because I wanted to see it again.

Chapter 5

Four Years Ago

Andy

Euphoria coursed through my veins like a drug. Not that I'd ever done those. And euphoria was totally the right word. Right? Normally, I was better with words. Except for right now. Right now, all of my limbs sagged like overcooked noodles and my brain was a delirious pile of mush. I would have laughed if I'd had the energy. Which I didn't. And, fuck, wasn't that great? Euphoria was definitely the right word. That's all I was, a gooey mess of pure euphoria.

My ass twinged, and I winced against the unwelcome intrusion. Okay, maybe a little achy too, if I was being honest. Next time should probably use actual lube. A giggle bubbled in my chest. *Next time*. How could I already be thinking about a next time? My ass still burned, and I was one hundred percent positive I'd be sitting funny for days. Not to mention it had been way messier than I'd expected. But fuck if I cared. I *wanted* a next time. I wanted all the times. Until he did it, I didn't know how much I needed to be completely owned.

Mitch.

I just had sex with Mitch Hudson.

The bubbles of laughter threatened to boil right over into the world. I wanted to roll around like a lunatic, giggling my triumph. I, Anderson Gallagher, had had sex with Mitch Hudson, my best friend and the guy I'd been in love with who knew how long. And it had been incredible. I sighed through the laughter and pressed back into the warm body curled around me.

"Andy?" Mitch whispered into my hair, and hell if that didn't set off a fresh wave of goosebumps. "You awake?"

"Yeah," I squeaked out, then immediately bit my lip to prevent the laughter rioting inside me from spilling over. He snaked an arm around my waist and pulled me tight against him. Laying on the cold floor instead of a cushy bed sucked, but nothing could diminish my happiness at being snug in Mitch's embrace. The tiny part of me that had dared to believe Mitch could ever feel the same way burned a little brighter.

"Do you think I'll make the team?" Hearing the doubt and insecurity in his voice tore at my heart. Even though my back was to him, I knew he had a line between his brows like he got anytime he was worried, and I knew that smile I loved would be pointing the wrong direction. If I could have rolled over and kissed it back right ways, I would have, but his hold on me was too strong and not something I was willing to relinquish just yet.

"I know so," I said with all the confidence he couldn't seem to find.

He chuckled into my neck, the hot puffs of his breath warming the already flushed skin. "You know everything."

"You say that like it's a bad thing," I fired back. It was a familiar tease, and just one of the many things I loved about us. His thumb, already building calluses from hours of practice to try-out for said team, brushed across my lower abdomen and short-circuited my thoughts. The giddy high returned as my words abandoned me once more and I savored the caress.

Yeah, euphoria is definitely the right word.

Present Day

Andy

I stretched my legs out on grass warmed by the late afternoon sun. The light breeze kept the day pleasant and the clouds scuttling overhead offered intermittent shade. I let out a sigh and sank into the ground, letting it steal my tension as I looked down the steep hill to the field below where most of the lacrosse team was also enjoying the perfect day.

"Interesting choice of locale." Calvin's bag fell unceremoniously to the ground and sagged to the side, spilling an assorted collection of paint brushes and sketch pencils, not a pen or textbook to be seen. "Motherfucker," Calvin hissed, flopping to the earth and stuffing the rogue materials back in the bag.

I chuckled and reached into my satchel. "You know, there are these fancy things called cases you could use to keep your shit from trying to escape."

"Order is the ultimate enemy of a true artist. Chaos is my medium." Bag once again reassembled, he shoved it to the side where it threatened to have another episode. "You ignored my comment."

"Don't know what you're talking about."

"Uh-huh. How many times have I tried to get you to come up here with me?" The arched brow was over the top and pure Calvin. The sun highlighted his dark taupe skin, making him seem at once darker and brighter. He let out a dramatic breath and threw himself back, only to pop right back up again. "I see how it is. You help Mitch with one measly paper and suddenly it's okay to enjoy the view." He made a sweeping gesture to the flurry of activity below.

"It's a nice day," I countered, refusing to take the obvious bait. What may have started as one paper had quickly turned into three, including the English Lit one I was currently helping him with.

"I'm not begrudging you, the view—I mean day—is *very* nice," Calvin said as he returned to openly appreciating the players below.

"Do you have to leer like that?"

"If they didn't want to be looked at, then they shouldn't be running around half dressed, coated in delicious sparkling drops."

"It's hot."

He turned his lascivious grin on me and winked. "Yeah it is."

"Shut up, or I'm not giving you your pudding." I held out the stolen goods like they were the Holy Grail.

Calvin's eyes widened, and he made grabby hands. "Gimme gimme." He all but snatched the cup and fished out his own pilfered spoon from his rebellious satchel, humming with delight as he peeled back the lid. "I don't think I'll ever be able to reconcile the fact that *you* are a bit of a klepto."

I rolled my eyes and scooped a spoonful of chocolaty goodness. Filching treats had certainly been something I'd always been capable of, but it hadn't been until I learned Mitch loved the silly puddings that I'd started pilfering them from the cafeteria's secret stash. My gaze traveled across the players enjoying their friendly game. Mitch drew my attention like a magnet. Even from this distance, I could spot him no trouble. His smile threatened to split his face in two as he chased the ball only to steal it. Sweat dripped down his bare back, sliding past the defined dimples into his shorts. He'd changed over the last four years, from an awkwardly tall youth to this pinnacle of athletic perfection.

I adjusted my attention to my neglected pudding, but it couldn't stop my mind from wandering to places it shouldn't. Mitch didn't just look great, he felt it too. His hard body pressing me into the wall while his mouth conquered me with impunity, had been every dark desire I had come to life. The heat of him had threatened to burn me up, steal my senses...

It's just a game.

"Well, yeah. But wouldn't it be better if they played all their games like this?"

My head snapped up at Calvin's response.

"What? Look, you can say what you will, but we are *not* the only people who appreciate a good show around here," he added, waving his spoon at me.

I cleared my throat and banished all thoughts of what Mitch's body felt like against mine. "You think everyone is repressed."

"Aren't they? Just look at your boy." He gestured once more to the players below.

My gaze zeroed in on Mitch, his chest heaving from exertion and practically glowing with happiness. *So much for hating the team.*

"We at least know the shit he gets into and I doubt he's the only one, though maybe the only one with the balls to go for it. How are his balls these days, by the way? Still blue?"

My pudding went down the wrong way and I turned to disabuse Calvin of his belief that anything more than writing was happening between me and Mitch. Before I got the words out, though, he finished his thought.

"You still sticking to your not studying together?"

"Connor," I said as the reality of who he was talking about finally registered.

"Uh, yeah, *Connor*. Who the fuck else would I be talking about?" All the hoping in the world couldn't have stopped the light bulb from going off over his head. "Holy fucking mother of Christ, you boned Mitch."

"No, I didn't, and shut your trap before someone hears you," I snapped and tossed my half-eaten pudding aside.

Calvin's face scrunched with concern as he turned to face me. "Okay, fine, you're not boning him, but... Andy, are you sure it's a good idea to be spending so much time with him?"

I bristled at the implication. "We can be friends."

He searched my face a long minute before asking softly, "Can you?"

My gaze settled on Mitch once more, laughing, having fun, being someone else.

Calvin scooted closer until our shoulders were touching and leaned enough into me to offer comfort. "What do you think he would do if he saw us up here?"

"Probably come over." The words were out of my mouth before I could consider them.

"Yeah?"

I leaned back on my arms without taking my gaze off the figures below. "Yeah. I'm not sure why, but he seems to be trying to renew our friendship. And I... I kind of want to let him try." I glanced over at Calvin where he too stared riveted at the scene below. "Is that stupid?"

He shook his head and his gaze went distant. Calvin had his own demons to slay. One day I hoped more than anything that he'd get the knight in shining armor he deserved, someone to make all the pain bearable, but he'd have to let go of the past first. "It's not stupid, Andy. Just...be careful, okay?" he said, turning his suddenly dark gaze on me.

We looked at each other, then returned our focus to the players. I'd spent four years wrapping my heart in so many walls, it'd be a miracle if they ever crumbled. Connor hadn't even managed to peek over in the year and a half we'd been together. I didn't even know if *I* could break them at this point. But staring down at the first boy I'd ever fallen in love with, I knew, if anyone had the power to break me again, it was Mitchum Hudson.

"Well, today just got a lot fucking better."

The cheery comment startled me out of the dire thoughts, and I searched the area for its cause. Three more players had just joined the impromptu game, Benjamin Wallace Price IV at their helm. His shirt fell to the ground, and Calvin rubbed his hands with malicious glee.

"Do I need to leave?" I teased. Calvin made a grand show of rearranging himself in his pants and I laughed.

"I'm not saying you have to, but it might be in your best interest. Would hate to ruin those delicate sensibilities of yours."

I snorted. "And what do you think *he* would do if he saw us up here?"

"Stomp up here and throttle the living shit out of us. No question." Calvin winked and sat forward to watch the game with far more intensity than he'd started. I shook my head and followed suit. Calvin's obsession never ceased to amaze me. And of the two of us, he was actually the only one who knew how the damn game was played.

Chapter 6

Four Years Ago

Mitch

I just had sex with Andy. Like actual came-so-hard-I-saw-spots sex. With my best friend. Who was gay. On the floor. What. The. Fuck.

"Hey, Mitch?"

I swallowed past a sudden lump in my throat. "Yeah?"

"I'm glad it was you."

I blinked and stared at the back of his head, his red hair a darker Auburn in the dim lighting of the secret room. "What?"

"My first time, I'm glad it was with you."

I pulled back the arm that had been wrapped around him like he was actually made of fire like his hair suggested. "What?" I repeated, as if it would somehow change what he'd said.

He rolled onto his back and propped up on his elbows to look at me. His face twisted in confused concern that almost hid the wince that had passed over it when he'd shifted to a seated position. Probably because his ass hurt. His virgin ass. Because Andy had never had sex before.

"Did you actually not hear me, or are you really going to make me say it again?"

"You've never done that before?" I wondered if it was possible to have an out-of-body experience while you were awake, because I sure as fuck didn't feel connected to mine at the moment.

Andy is a virgin… Well, not anymore. And I'd just… I hadn't even…

Andy cocked his head to the side, his green eyes darker than normal in the low light. “Uh, no. Hence the ‘first time’ comment. It’s cool. I know you’ve been with…people.” Girls. I’d been with girls. The slight pink that rarely stained Andy’s cheeks made it clear that his thoughts mirrored mine. “I know my experience is basically nil compared to yours.”

“But… You haven’t been with anyone, like at all?” *Why am I struggling so hard with this? That’s literally what he just said.* And yet, I couldn’t let it go. I couldn’t be Andy’s first. I just couldn’t. “Touching, kissing, anything?” I asked, my desperation growing.

He snorted, a rude sound that Andy seemed to have perfected for the sole goal of ratcheting up my rapidly increasing anxiety. “When would I have done that? We spend like every waking minute together. Pretty sure if I’d been sneaking around to hook up with guys you would’ve noticed.” He shrugged. “Then again, if I had, then I wouldn’t have needed to tell you I was gay.” His teasing smile danced in his eyes like this was some kind of grand joke, one of the many we’d shared over the last two years. Except this shit wasn’t funny, it wasn’t funny at all. Andy had told me he was gay and instead of being a supportive best friend, I’d dragged him off and…*used* him. Sweet, *innocent* Andy, pure in his love of mischief and books… And I’d stolen it.

Shame boiled rancid hot in my belly like someone had shoved a white-hot poker into me.

Present Day

Mitch

“You’re getting much better,” Andy said, twirling his red pen between his fingers that thankfully had kissed the page far fewer times this go around. “Aside from a few grammatical errors, I’d say you have a solid B on your hands, maybe even an A.”

I bit my lip and waited as he scribbled a quick note in the margin of the last page and highlighted a few more of the grammatical errors. “You really think so?” I couldn’t even remember the last time I’d gotten an "A" without some bogus extra credit assignment that never actually happened.

"We've been through this. I know everything, remember?" The lid of his pen clicked in place. He slid the papers over to me, but didn't release them.

I glanced up at his serious face, so close I could see flecks of amber in his eyes.

"All joking aside, your grasp of the material is really good and your writing improvements are commendable." He blinked, his red lashes fanning briefly over his freckled cheeks. "I'm impressed, Mitch. You've worked really hard. You should be proud of yourself."

My heart swelled at the generous compliment. I didn't realize how much I missed someone building me up, helping me to be better for myself and no one else.

Maybe he can forgive me, maybe I can have my friend back.

The distance between us shrank as if gravity itself was pulling us together. Deep-seated longing slowly worked its way out until it filled every cell. I missed my best friend, my companion and partner in crime. I missed Andy, missed his laugh and wit, missed his spark and mischief. His warm breath fell from parted lips and his eyelids fluttered. Guilt at how I'd treated him back then threaded beneath the ache of longing.

Whatever it takes, I'll get him back.

His breath hitched, and the tip of his tongue traveled over his lips. My gaze followed its path while my mind went to the one place it shouldn't. I remembered every microsecond of kissing Andy. The way his lips had molded against mine, the way his tongue had danced and played, the hunger that seemed to radiate off of him. I wasn't supposed to like it, wasn't supposed to want it. But I did. I wanted it so fucking much it hurt.

I wasn't even sure I was breathing anymore as the space between us dwindled to millimeters. Suddenly, Andy jolted back as if he'd been electrocuted and the fog wrapped around my brain fell. I sat back, putting more distance between us, my heart pounding furiously against my ribs. My gaze darted over to the door and I swallowed. What was I thinking? What if someone had walked in? That'd be a fine way to earn Andy's forgiveness. My fingers clawed into the paper and I dragged it closer.

Beside me, I felt as much as saw Andy's walls go up. He put away his pen with stiff hands and refused to look back over at me. "Like I was saying, keep up the good work."

Bile crawled up my throat at the familiar, flat encouragement. How many times had the coach said the same thing, only to demand more from me? There was no such thing as enough, not when there was more to give. And there always was.

I pushed my chair back and reached for my bag so I could put the paper away. “Thanks again for all the help.” I looked down at his red hair and struggled to find the words that could make this better, some way to restore the fleeting moment of real friendship.

He stiffened as if he could feel my gaze on him and his hand hovered inside his bag. He slowly withdrew it and a thin book. “This should help.” He stared at the book, then stood. Head down, he offered me what turned out to be a thesaurus.

My fingers closed around the worn binding, and his gaze finally rose to meet mine.

“I circled a few words that you over use. This should offer some alternatives. If…” He paused and licked his lips like he had earlier, “if you have any questions…let me know?” The hint of question snagged my attention.

I searched his face, not sure if I understood what was happening. Had Andy just given me…a peace offering? Even after I’d literally just royally screwed up? “Yeah, I’ll do that.” My voice came out unexpectedly thick, but I couldn’t have cared less as the corners of his mouth ticked up in a smile and he released the book.

“You’ll tell me how it goes?” he asked, stuffing his hands into his pockets.

I nodded, not trusting any actual words in the wake of the hope that surged through me like a tidal wave. Andy was actually going to give me a chance to make things right. All I had to do was not fuck it up. Again.

Andy

The bookstore door shut behind me with a tinkling of bells. I stroked the soft leather of my bag, now near to bursting with my latest acquisitions. The books brought with them their own sense of joy, yet despite the hours I’d devoted to getting lost among the shelves filled with other realities, my own continued to haunt me. More specifically, the reality in which I was talking to Mitch again. I didn’t expect this sudden renewal of friendship to last, but a rebellious part of me dared to dream, and no matter how deep I shoved the blind hope, it just kept coming back, relentless, undeniable, determined…

We're studying, that's all, nothing more. Fall training will start in earnest and this sudden desire to improve his grades will be pushed aside.

I shook my head and focused on the ground moving beneath my feet. Three steps away from the only decent bookstore in the sad little town of Hylestad, someone yanked me off the street. Being short didn't bother me most days, but being manhandled was another story altogether.

My feet skidded over the gritty pavement, incapable of finding purchase. Rays of sunshine cut sharp swaths of light in the dim alley. My bag thudded heavily against the brick wall now pressing into my back. A shout filled my lungs but never found voice as a mouth closed over mine. Instant recognition poured through me, washing the fight away. Half a heartbeat is all it took to decide. I slipped into the easy familiarity of the demanding mouth, tasting and teasing with a playfulness perfected with practice.

His lips pulled on mine as he dragged out a languid kiss that we could never enjoy freely in the open. "Mm, seems like someone misses me."

"In your dreams, Connor," I quipped, my gaze flicking to his storm blue eyes.

He snickered a low laugh and pressed me more firmly into the wall. "And what do you know of my dreams?"

Rather than answer, I kissed him again, indulging in the simplicity of the moment and doing my damnedest to let go of the stress from moments before. Our tongues tangled together as I took ownership of the kiss and dragged a needy moan out of him. Connor's buttons had always been easy to push. They were right on the surface. He angled forward and my fingers scraped over his hard-won abs. Calvin wasn't the only one with a type. I splayed my hand over the defined muscles and felt Connor's stomach flex in anticipation.

What is it about athletes? These long, lean bodies. Muscles for days…

My hand itched to explore, but before it could go anywhere, thoughts of another athlete intruded on my appreciation of Connor's eager body. Mitch's muscles weren't all that different, except he was taller, and well, better. I still burned at the memory of him pressing me into the wall, using his whole body to hold me there while he completely owned me, like only he could, like he always had…

Like he always will.

I sucked in a breath and pulled away from the bad decision already in full swing.

"What's the matter?" Connor asked as he endeavored to tempt me with another kiss. "Change your mind again already?"

"Nothing to change. We're not getting back together," I said with all the monotone I could muster. I may not understand why Mitch was suddenly so eager to spend time together, but I did know it wasn't right to take out my frustrations on Connor. No one deserved to be used like that.

He made a rude sound in his throat. "Come on, Gallagher. Doesn't mean we can't still have a little fun now and then. Right?" His hands slid provocatively around my waist, and for a tiny moment, I was genuinely tempted. "That *is* how this whole thing started, remember?" He tipped my nose with his own, his breathing as husky as his words, while his hard-on pressed into my stomach.

I quirked a smile at him. "I remember. Which is exactly why this stops here." I flattened my hand on his chest and pushed. His crestfallen look might have been comical if it also hadn't been so childishly affected, like someone had stolen his candy.

Mitch would never look at me like that.

He huffed and spun to lean against the same wall as me. "Suit yourself, but don't pretend you don't miss me."

"Missing you and *missing* you aren't quite the same. Or are you fishing?" I teased. As remarkable as it was, some days, Connor's insecurities seemed to run deeper than mine.

"Shut your face. I had a rough day. So sue me for wanting a pick me up."

I sighed and didn't say what I'd said a million times before—that right there was why we didn't work. I didn't want to be somebody's pick me up to use only when they were feeling blue. We may go to school with a clusterfuck of bigots, but I deserved to be happy, to be appreciated for who I was, to have a companion, a friend and a lover.

Someone like Mitch.

I growled to myself and adjusted the strap threatening to slip off my shoulders. Mitch wanting help with classes wasn't the same and it never would be.

"Don't get your panties in a twist," Connor griped. "Fuck, you're so serious all the time. Learn to live a little."

"Like you?"

He flashed an obnoxious grin. "Yeah, like me. What do you have in there today?" he asked, poking into my satchel like the nosy ass he was.

"Books."

"Surprise, surprise." He rolled his eyes and withdrew his questing hand.

"About murder."

"Frankly, I don't give a damn if that was a threat or a genre. I keep telling you, they keep the juicy stuff in the back."

"And I keep telling you, I have no interest in reading smut." Especially since the store hadn't gotten any new stuff in ages. Of course, Connor didn't need to know that I'd found the horde of erotica sequestered in the back behind a velvet current three years ago, then promptly devoured every page.

"Your loss. Anyway..." He danced his fingers along my thigh, bringing them perilously closer to my groin. "You sure I can't persuade you?"

I gently, but firmly, grabbed his hand and repositioned it over his own crotch. "Sorry, but you'll have to continue with...self-study."

He unsurprisingly groped himself and leered back. "We'll see. You'll come around eventually. And when you do—"

"I will have clearly lost my mind and should be committed."

He barked out a laugh and pushed his long frame off the wall, abandoning his lewd show. "See you around, Gallagher." He took another step closer to the mouth of the alley, winked, then was gone.

I stayed in the shadows awhile longer and continued to fight with myself. Renewing a friendship with Mitch was likely an even greater act of insanity than renewing a relationship with Connor. And yet, here I was, bound and determined to see if it would work. Except, all my efforts to protect myself from getting hurt again were already suffering heavy losses. The near-kiss the other day was proof of that. I'd just have to make my walls thicker, build them higher, whatever it to took to protect my heart from the one person guaranteed to break it. I wouldn't survive a second time.

My groan bounced back at me in the narrow space and I rested my head against the wall as I grappled with the insurmountable task of not falling for Mitchum Hudson...again.

Chapter 7

Four Years Ago

Mitch

It didn't take long for Andy to fall asleep. My sleep, however, remained elusive, not that I could have closed my eyes if I wanted to. As it was, it took everything I had not to ralph on the floor. Still might have, if I hadn't been so worried about the sound of my dry heaves waking him up. I devoted all my energy to keeping my stomach under control until I was positive he was solidly out.

Once I was confident he wouldn't wake if I moved, I shifted to do just that. Before I could though, he grabbed my arm and wrapped it around his torso, then preceded to use me like a human blanket. Acid boiled in my stomach while pain stung sharply behind my eyes. He was so small, so fragile. I was his best friend. I was supposed to protect him, not…what I'd done.

Eventually, his hold on me relaxed enough that I could remove my arm. I stared at it for a long minute as if it somehow held the secret to go back in time and undo this horrible mess I'd made. It didn't. Nothing could undo what I'd done. I shook it out and got dressed as quietly as I could. Every cell in my body screamed at me to just go, don't look back, walk away while I still could, while there was still a chance of fixing this, or better yet, wake him up, make sure we were on the same page or at least in the same book. I did neither. Instead, I leaned against the wall and slid down to the floor, my gaze riveted on the image of shattered innocence before me. I'd stay just a minute to gather my thoughts and then I'd go.

Except I didn't.

I sat and watched Andy sleep on that hard floor in a cold room that almost no one knew existed. I remained perfectly still as goosebumps roved across his flesh, crawling over him like a thousand tiny insects. Didn't blink when he curled in tighter on himself to ward off the chill. I just sat there and watched, while a hollowness spread throughout my chest. With each second that ticked by, it found and devoured every bright spot of light inside me. All the joy I'd had at the beginning of the night died a slow and painful death.

By the time I got up, I was positive there wasn't an ounce of feeling left in me. I pushed the giant portrait away from the wall and stared into a hallway as bleak as my soul. Did monsters even have souls? Because that's what I was now, a monster. Only a monster could betray their best friend in this entire world's trust like I had. My stomach heaved, and I choked on bile. I sprinted as fast as my feet would carry me to the nearest bathroom.

The stall door bounced on its hinges, its hollow echo as it smacked its neighbor ringing through the room. Pain radiated through my knees as I crashed to the ground and threw up the last two years. Every extra pudding we'd ever stolen, every filched sweet from a teacher's desk, every moment of laughter over a shared summer memory. All of it, gone, and I only had myself to blame.

Present day

Mitch

I swallowed my anxiety as Professor Garza pulled out a manila envelope. He considered me a moment, his brown eyes sharp and scrutinizing, before stepping around the desk that separated us. I willed myself not to assume the worst, but considering everyone else had gotten their grades the normal way, I wasn't doing well. He held out the folder, and I took it with a miraculously steady hand. I immediately flipped it over, only to find the adhesive gluing it shut.

"Um... Can I ask why it's sealed?"

He perched on the edge of his desk, his fingers curling over the top, and smiled. "Figured you might like to share the results with Anderson."

My face went cold as all the blood immediately vacated it. "Why would I want to do that?" I asked, aiming for calm and missing it by a mile.

"I'd recognize his handiwork anywhere."

The desk scraped loudly against the floor as I lurched out of it. "He didn't write it. I swear he didn't. He would never do that. Andy-"

"Is tutoring you," Garza interrupted. "I'm glad. I wish I could convince him to tutor more of my students."

"You...you don't think he wrote it for me?" I floundered, put off by his response.

Garza's mouth twisted into a frown. "Forget the fact that Anderson would never do such a thing, I'm devout in my belief that your own morals wouldn't allow it even if he had offered. You put in the work and the results show that. I'm simply suggesting that Anderson might appreciate sharing in your victory is all."

"Oh, um, okay," I stammered and clutched the folder to my chest. "So, it wasn't bad?"

"Not in the least. One of the best in your class, actually."

A smile tugged at my mouth as I glanced down at the golden envelope. *One of the best?*

"Go on, get out of here." Garza glanced up at the clock. "He should be getting out of Nolan's class pretty soon. He'll probably welcome a good diversion after that," he added with a half-smile.

I did a double take. Had Garza really just knocked one of the other professors? Sure, Nolan was a total tool, but weren't they all supposed to be unified or some shit?

In answer to my unasked question, Garza said, "Being part of the faculty doesn't automatically make us all friends. He is a bit of a fresa."

I frowned at the unusual term while Garza walked back around his desk. In the hall, boys were already pouring out of their last classes and filling the air with excited chatter.

Garza settled back in his chair and resumed grading another class's assignments. After a moment, he glanced back up. "What are you still doing here? If you don't hurry, you'll miss him." He smiled ruefully as I carefully slipped the envelope in my bag and rushed into the crowd outside. I only made it as far as the next junction when a familiar voice called me up short.

"Hud-son." Even dropped to a low bass, the voice and the exaggerated extension of my name carried easily in the vaulted hall. I squeezed my eyes shut and sent up a silent prayer that he was on his own as I turned to address its owner.

"Hey Brian," I said with practiced calm. Despite my hope, he was flanked by Nate and John, his dark brown skin contrasting with their lighter tan.

"Where are you off to in such a hurry?" he asked as he and the others formed a half circle around me.

I nodded to Nate and fist-bumped Brian and John. "Nowhere special."

"Good, then you can come with us. We were gonna head into town."

Just then, I spied a familiar satchel over-burdened with books. "Actually...uh..." I took a step back, breaking their circle. "There was something I wanted to do." My fingers tightened around the strap of my bag while anxiety threatened to turn me into a stammering idiot.

Nate elbowed Brian and smiled crookedly. "Something or some*one*."

"Maybe a certain redhead?" John added.

I groaned inwardly, but was half a second away from letting them assume whatever they wanted, as long as it got me out of this before Andy vanished altogether. Then Brian's gaze shifted behind me.

"Oh shit, it's Nolan. Scatter." Just like that, I was free to pursue the object of my quest as all four of us dispersed without another word.

By sheer dumb luck, I caught up to Andy just as he reached the south exit. His eyebrows raised in surprise at my sudden appearance, and he glanced behind me. He seemed to do that a lot when other people were around. For once, I was with him. I didn't want to share this with anyone else.

"Do you have a minute?"

"What for?" His gaze slid past me to triple check the hallway.

"I got my results for the lit paper."

His green eyes snapped back to me, fever bright. "And?"

I bit my lip. "I haven't looked at it yet, but Garza said it was good." I ran a hand over my bag and thought of the sealed envelope within. "He thought you might like to find out with me since you helped me with it."

Andy made a low, strangled sound deep in his throat. "Well, come on." He grabbed my wrist and started off down the nearest hallway. A hallway that would conveniently lead us to the portrait of Ulwich.

Andy

The lights were still struggling to brighten when I reached for Mitch's bag. I got as far as flipping it open before he danced back with a laugh.

"Eager much?"

"Don't pretend like you're not. Quit with the stalling." I made a come-on gesture with my hand and he laughed again.

"Yeah, you're right. I thought the worst when he asked me to come back after my last class to pick it up." He reached into the bag and pulled out a manila envelope, its seal unbroken.

"You really haven't seen yet?" I asked in wonder.

"Nope. I have to say, when Garza said you'd be just as eager to know, I didn't really believe him." He slipped a finger between the fold and tossed me a smirk. "Guess I was wrong."

"You planning to open it at all?" I deadpanned.

He dropped his gaze back to the folio. "Yeah. Okay. Yeah, I am," he said, but rather than continue peeling the adhesive apart, he hesitated, his teeth sinking into his bottom lip. Then it hit me. He was nervous.

I stepped up to him and placed a hand on his forearm. "Hey, there's nothing to be worried about. You did really well. Garza even said so."

He nodded and licked his lips, then finally opened the envelope. I waited with bated breath as he withdrew the pristine white pages stapled together. The moment the pages were free, Mitch sucked in a breath. Impatience tore at me. From my angle, all I could make out was the red circle around the grade. Finally, his gaze lifted from the page and latched onto mine.

"I did it," he whispered with awe. "You were right. I actually did it." His fingers tightened around the pages. I didn't even need to see the grade anymore, the insanely bright smile on his face was reward enough. "Fuck, Andy, I did it." He barked a laugh and released the paper to flutter to the ground and surged forward, his hands coming to rest on my face.

I went stock still as his lips pressed against mine. My entire brain short-circuited, and I forgot how to move or even blink. My body thrummed like a tuning fork and the air froze in my lungs.

As suddenly as he'd caught me, Mitch pulled away. "Shit. I'm sorry. I just...got caught up. I didn't... I mean..." he stammered along while he rubbed the back of his neck and valiantly failed at looking like anything other than an awkward goose.

I forced my eyes to close and reopen, the shock of what had just happened still playing through me. Without my brain to interfere, all sorts of forbidden thoughts were lighting up with abandon. "It's…fine," I said awkwardly, the words thick in my mouth as I reminded my tongue how to speak.

He gave me a sheepish look, then did what Mitch did best—he ignored what had just happened. "An 'A', Andy. An honest to goodness 'A'. Thank you."

I blinked more naturally this time and fought to refortify the walls he'd casually traipsed past. "You're welcome, but you really did most of the work."

"You're being generous, but thanks anyway." He scooped up the neglected pages and dusted them off, before reverently replacing them in the envelope. Then he bit his lip again and flicked his gaze back at where I was still standing like a shell-shocked lump. His hazel eyes caught the yellow glow of the ancient lights overhead. "We should celebrate."

A familiar wariness snaked through my veins. "What did you have in mind?"

"Something for old time's sake? A prank?" he suggested tentatively. Like the kiss, the idea hit me out of nowhere. But maybe…maybe the answer to all of this wasn't guarding against everything. Just because Mitch could never feel about me the way I'd once felt about him didn't mean we couldn't have a little fun, as Connor put it.

Why shouldn't I enjoy this?

"A prank…could be fun," I conceded. His latest smile completely trumped the previous one and my own begged to be set free. "Who did you have in mind?"

"What would you say to Nolan?"

My smile finally broke free and the corners of my lips curled up in a wicked grin. "I'd say I have an idea."

Chapter 8

Andy

I walked down the hall and did my best not to look like I was up to no good. Luckily, filching art supplies was way less suspect than acquiring a dozen *live* frogs. By the time I reached the art room, I'd only passed two staff members and a handful of students, none of which had spared me a second glance.

After a quick survey of the otherwise empty hall, I slipped inside, careful to make sure the door shut quietly. Calvin's instructions had been remarkably succinct, and I spotted my destination almost immediately. I crossed the vacant room to the tall black cabinet on the far side and let out a sigh of relief to find it unlocked. Calvin had said it would be, just like he'd said the class would be outside working on blending techniques today, but I'd brought supplies just in case he'd been mistaken. Not that I was confident in my lock picking abilities. It had been a long while. Besides, picking locks had always been Mitch's forte.

Giddiness bubbled inside of me. We were doing a prank together. That he'd followed along with my schemes since that first day I'd nearly bowled over him six years ago without so much as lifting an eyebrow had been one of my absolute favorite things about our friendship. About him. Understandably, once I had a partner in crime, the pranks only got more elaborate, hence the epic Dust Frog Caper. Who knows how we would have topped that one if we hadn't broken up.

I paused. "Broken up" made it sound like we'd been dating. Much as my heart at the time would have loved that, I understood now that had never been in the cards nor would it ever be. Mitch might be curious, but he was most definitely straight. All it took was one look at him and his girlfriend, Trixie, with her garish red hair trying to eat each other's faces to confirm the belief. Not that I would ever tell Mitch that I'd stumbled across them in town last term or that I'd stood frozen and watched them until his teammates called him away.

I shook my head clear of the awful memory, then checked the clock to make sure I still had plenty of time. Again, Calvin had said they'd be out most of the period, but there was no sense in dawdling. I undid the straps on my satchel, then removed the books sitting on top to reveal the empty box beneath. It had been significantly harder than I'd expected to find a container big enough to hold the art supplies, but small enough to fit in my bag without being conspicuous.

Smirking at my genius, I set the books down and opened the cabinet wide. Toward the back, tucked away in a dust filled corner, were the promised tubes of paint. I plucked one out to inspect, leaving a perfect ring of dust in its wake. *Lamp Black Acrylic*. Calvin was positive no one would miss it as his mentor and the head art professor, Jankowski, abhorred what was apparently a *very* bad batch. I debated taking all of them, but given the size of the containers, I opted to only take three. Besides, I figured a few missing tubes were easier to explain than all of them vanishing.

I wiped my hands free of the dust on some nearby painter's cloth, then replaced the books and closed the cabinet. Satisfied with my handiwork, I sauntered out of the room, unable to keep my grin to myself.

"Well, well, well. What do we have here?"

I froze mid-step on my way back to chemistry. The paint hidden in my bag felt like it might as well have been a beacon broadcasting my guilt to the entire school. I swallowed down the burst of nerves and turned to face my accuser, then promptly relaxed. "Connor. Aren't you supposed to be in class?"

His sandy blond eyebrows lifted. "Aren't you?" I reflexively clutched the strap of my satchel and his gaze darted to the open straps—because, of course, I'd forgotten to synch them. "What's in the bag, Gallagher?"

"None of your business." I could have bitten my tongue clean off. Why hadn't I just said books?

"Uh-huh." He crossed his arms, accentuating his wide shoulders and muscular biceps that I definitely wasn't noticing...or comparing to Mitch's. Connor tilted his head toward the art room, where the door hadn't closed completely.

I could have hissed with annoyance. Since when did I make such rookie mistakes? Was I really *that* out of practice?

"What were you doing in the art room?"

"Since when do you care about what I do?" I snapped.

Connor nodded to himself and stuffed one of his hands in his pocket as he walked up to me. "That's fair."

I tightened my hold on the bag as he lifted his free hand, fully prepared to defend it. Except he didn't reach for the satchel. He lightly held my chin, lifting it slightly while his thumb rubbed beneath my mouth. I swallowed thickly. "W-what are you doing?"

His gaze lifted from my parted lips. "I'm talking to you, Andy. I'm paying attention. Wasn't that one of the reasons you said we didn't work?"

I licked my lips and glanced behind him, relieved to see we were still alone. But that wouldn't last. "This isn't really the place for this."

"I know," he said with a sigh, releasing his tentative hold. "Shame really. You don't deserve to be anyone's secret."

My breath caught and my eyes began to sting. I dropped my focus to the floor, unable to continue meeting his soft gaze. What was all this about? Did he know about Mitch?

"I'm sorry. I didn't mean to upset you." He fisted the hand that had been holding my face, then shoved it in his other pocket. "This place, it sucks the decency out of you, turns you into someone you never wanted to be. I know we had our issues, but it wasn't all bad, right?"

I lifted my head sharply. "Of course not."

Connor stepped closer and dropped his voice to a whisper. "I still believe we could be good together. Give us another chance. I'll show you."

To my shame, I considered the proposal. He wasn't wrong. We *could* be really good together. We got along well enough. Had enough differences to keep things interesting. But... But we'd both be sacrificing part of ourselves to make it work. I knew that, even if Connor didn't. Agreeing would only hurt us both in the long run.

I took a step back, determined to be strong. "No, Connor." Guilt stabbed my heart at the hurt that flashed in his eyes. "I appreciate what you're saying, I really do, and... And you're not wrong. But it was more than the not talking. You know that."

"We could at least try. I miss you."

His plea tore at my heart. I'd never been wrapped up in Connor the way I'd been with Mitch, but I did care for him. Which was why I had to remain firm. Cutting ties now was the right thing to do—for both of us. I may not deserve to be anyone's secret, but neither did he. One day, Connor would find someone who complimented him and embraced *all* the things that made him an incredible person. And if I was being honest with myself, it broke my heart a little to admit that would never be me.

Mitch

I wiped my hands on my khakis and stepped into the locker room. Thankfully, the rest of the team wasn't here...yet. They'd be along eventually, but Coach Santinelli had asked to speak with me privately. I didn't have to be Andy-level smart to know that wasn't a good thing.

The empty rows of lockers and benches seemed to pass silent judgment on me as I crossed the room, as if they knew all my dirty secrets. For all of its emptiness, it was full to the brim with memories...most unpleasant. There was the bench I'd been standing by when I'd gotten pantsed on my first official day as part of the team. Laughter had echoed off the walls until it seemed like it would break right through the concrete. That was the locker we'd shoved a naked angry Teri into. He'd quit the team a week later. My steps faltered when I passed the spot where'd I'd officially learned what tea-bagging was. For a school full of elitist homophobes, they had some questionable ideas about "fun".

I dried my sweaty palms again before reaching up to knock on the coach's office door. The glass panel was frosted, so I couldn't tell much besides that at least one person was inside. The knock felt overly loud without the loud buzz of the team to fill the silence.

"Come in!"

I slowly opened the door, doing my best to hide my silent hope that the purpose of this meeting was to kick me from the team. "You wanted to see me, Coach?"

Coach Santinelli glanced up from what looked like a new playbook. His sandy complexion had weathered with time and too much sun into something more like leather than skin. He still had a full head of dark hair that he kept short, but if you looked closely, you could make out the rebellious silver strands. The pictures he kept on his desk showed that he'd once been young and attractive. But it was hard to reconcile the youthful smile of the man in the photos with the stern hard ass before me. "Hudson. Come in. Have a seat."

Coach had always been more on the...blunt side, and didn't like repeating himself. I quickly moved to occupy the seat across from him. Despite the plush cushion, I didn't dare get comfortable.

He set his pen down and rested his forearms on the desk while he stared at me intently. "Do you know why I've asked you here today?"

I had a pretty good idea, but past interactions with Coach had taught me the hard way to never supply an answer first. My leg started to bounce and I willed it still. After the silence dragged on for an uncomfortable amount of time, he leaned back and laced his fingers over his stomach.

"Your performance these last few weeks has left a lot to be desired. Care to explain yourself?" Despite the obvious question, I knew better than to mistake it for one.

"I—" My voice hitched. I cleared my throat and sat up straighter. "I've been working on building my grades up." While it had technically only been the one, I wanted to be clear that I cared about all of them.

Coach snorted and pushed out of his chair. "The grades will be taken care of." He waved a dismissive hand as he walked toward the most prominent picture on the wall—Class of '87 Lacrosse Team.

I bristled. Thankfully, his back was to me, otherwise I'd likely still be doing laps when the rest of the team showed up later in the afternoon. Before I could come up with a response, Coach was talking again.

"You have promise, Hudson, like your father."

My gaze cut toward the picture that I'd memorized by heart. I didn't have to see it clearly to make out my dad in his uniform, only a few people down from Santinelli himself. When I'd learned they'd not only gone to school together, but played together as well, I'd been excited, eager to hear the stories. How naïve I'd been.

Coach spun around, his hands clasped behind his back. "I'd hate to see you waste yours the way he did." Coach's lip curled up in a sneer like it did anytime he talked about my dad, which thankfully had turned out to be hardly ever. To say they'd been rivals would have been putting it nicely. Given how much Coach Santinelli clearly hated my dad, it was a wonder I'd ever made the team in the first place. Most days, I wished I hadn't.

I thought about Andy and how we were plotting a fresh prank for the first time in years. That shot of joy buoyed me enough to moderate my response. "I won't, sir. I know the team is counting on me."

"You're damn right they're counting on you." He smacked the flat of his palm on the desk so hard I gave an involuntary jump. "The culmination of the team's efforts will be this spring. And your future isn't the only one riding on getting a sport's scholarship."

I swallowed and dropped my gaze to the floor. This was it. He was going to order me not to study anymore. He'd have my grades adjusted enough to pass, but not enough to raise suspicions with any school interested in taking me on. The prank with Andy could very well be the last time we'd get to hang out, maybe ever. If I'd known four years ago that lacrosse would consume every aspect of my life, whether I wanted it to or not, I never would have tried out for the team.

"Well, what do you have to say for yourself? Can we count on you to carry your weight?" Santinelli demanded to know.

Anger spiked through me and I balled fists in my lap. It wasn't just *my* weight he wanted me to carry; it was the whole fucking team's. We had some damn good players, but they weren't me. Without me, they didn't have a prayer of winning the championship in the spring, let alone qualifying. They knew it. Coach knew. And most importantly, *I* knew it.

I launched out of my seat, practically vibrating with years of pent up anger. This was too much pressure, it always had been, and I was fucking done. If Santinelli kicked me off the team and I no longer had a sports scholarship to fall back on, then so be it.

"What do you think you're doing?" Coach snapped, his glower as fierce as ever. And I... Didn't. Give. A fuck.

"If it's all the same to you, Coach, I think I'll keep studying. There won't be a need to...'take care of' my grades. I'll take care of them myself." I caught his gaze, his deep brown eyes all but blazing with fury at my outburst, and I refused to backdown. "Was there anything else?" I waited a beat before adding, "Coach."

His nostrils flared while his face darkened to the purple side of crimson. "You've just won yourself laps."

"How many?" I asked, crossing my arms over my chest.

"Until I tell you to stop. Now get the hell out of my office, Hudson!"

"Gladly, sir." I turned on my heel and marched out the way I'd come, letting the metal door slam shut behind me.

"Make that double time!" Coach Santelli yelled after me.

I ripped open my locker, which, coincidentally, had also been my dad's. His initials scored into the back seemed to mock me as I traded out my school uniform for practice gear. I snarled at them before slamming the door shut again. It was probably a good thing he wasn't around anymore to see me fuck up my life. After that little display, Coach would likely be making my days a living hell until I left this school once and for all. Which meant I needed to make the most out of this prank with Andy. I might never get another shot.

Chapter 9

Mitch

The light of the half-moon shone through the nearby window, completely washing Andy out. Even his outrageously auburn hair was muted in the dim light. He shook his hands like they were wet and paced in a five-foot area. I laughed to myself. How many times had I seen him do that? Too many to count.

"Nervous?" I asked, walking the rest of the way to him.

"Mitch!" he hissed and promptly smacked me in the chest.

"Ow."

"Why do you always have to sneak up on me?" Despite the accusing question, his face erupted in a grin that made his eyes dance. "Mitch." The way he said it made it sound like it wasn't his first attempt to get my attention.

"Yeah?"

"You ready?"

"Depends. Were you able to get some?"

An evil grin spread across his face as he held up three tubes of black paint.

I smiled in return. I was probably one of two people in the entire school who knew how devious Andy could be.

"Come on, let's go." His urgent whisper had excitement fizzing inside of me like a shaken soda, and if the way his grin kept popping out was any judge, he felt the same.

We sprinted silently through the empty halls like a pair of shadows. At last, our destination loomed before us. As I knelt down level with the doorknob, a sudden bout of giggles hit Andy. I shook my head. Some things never changed.

I took out a bobby pin I'd acquired from my time with Trixie and set to work on the lock. Andy gave a quiet snort, and I glanced up at him. He had his eyebrows raised in silent judgment, knowing damn well where the pin had come from. I gave him a look and returned to my task while he tried to quell his amusement. The door made a soft click. We glanced down each passageway, then slipped inside.

"Okay. Where do we start first?" Andy asked in a hushed whisper as I carefully closed the door.

"Everything Nolan touches all the time, for sure."

"Definitely the eraser then. I'd say the marker too, but there's no way to coat it without it getting on everything else and ruining the surprise," he added as he liberally applied a layer of paint to the dark handle of the board eraser, careful not to get any on himself.

I caught the tube he lobbed at me. "And of course, it can only be black things."

"Hey, you agreed on the color."

"I'm just poking at you," I whispered in his ear as I walked past him. He made a face at me and stuck out his tongue. I chuckled to myself and set about finding several items to doctor as well. Out of the corner of my eye, I saw Andy shift to the wall full of windows, silently coating pretty much every dark item he could find. "You sure it won't dry?" I asked for probably the tenth time.

He scowled at me. "Calvin said this shit takes days to stop being tacky."

I laughed quietly and stepped back to admire our handiwork. You totally couldn't tell. "Can you think of anything else?" I asked aloud.

He stood a moment, holding the nearly empty third bottle up as he considered the room. I watched him mentally tick off all the likely items we'd already covered, as well as the less likely. He chewed on his lip, still musing when inspiration suddenly lit his face. "I've got it!" he shout-whispered. He stepped back and bumped Nolan's notoriously over-stuffed bookcase. Andy froze as the giant structure teetered behind him.

Faster than what I would have thought possible, I reached out and snatched him out of harm's way. I clutched him to my chest as several large books tumbled to the ground right where he'd been standing. The first book made a loud smack as it landed on the floor, while those that collided after were more muffled. If one of those had hit him…

Time seemed to stretch around us as we waited for the noise to be investigated. Andy was so close I could feel his heart beating against my chest. I looked down at him and had to resist the urge to crook a finger under his chin and tilt his head up. In my mind's eye, I did it anyway.

My heart slowed as I looked into eyes the color of summer framed by golden red lashes. I forgot how to breathe as my gaze rested on his mouth. Andy had the softest lips I'd ever tasted. They parted slightly, an invitation I gladly took. He wrapped his arms around my neck and I sighed into him, longing for more. It was moments like this, with him completely cocooned in my embrace, that I remembered how much shorter than me he was. The half a foot difference didn't mean much as I tightened my grip around his waist, fully prepared to lift him so he could wrap his legs around me.

"I don't think anyone is coming, do you?" His question effectively broke the spell, and I crashed back to reality, where the only heart beating furiously was mine.

"I think you're right," I said, releasing him. He stepped over to the fallen books and held up a large tomb that could have easily snapped his neck.

"You okay?" I asked, struggling to keep my sudden anxiety at bay. None of our pranks had ever risked actually hurting one of us.

"Only thanks to you," he responded with a smirk, then promptly smacked me with the book.

We made quick work of righting the room. By the time we were done, there wasn't a trace we'd ever been there. Unless, of course, you touched something black.

"I think that's it," I declared, pleased as punch with what we'd accomplished *and* that no one had investigated the ruckus.

"Wait," he said, pulling me up short.

"What?"

"One more thing." He took back out the remaining paint.

"We've gotten everything. What else is left?"

"I wanna get the chair." His eyes glittered maliciously in the moon's light spilling through the wall of windows.

This is why we're best friends. Imp.

"Okay, but don't paint the whole seat. I have an idea."

I laughed as I fell to the floor in the secret room, too wired to even try to go to bed. Mercifully, Andy was of the same mind. He was an even worse giddy mess than when the evening had started. I tried not to think about how close it had come to being a terrible night instead of the incredible fun it had been.

“I thought for sure our goose was cooked when you bumped that shelf.”

Andy laughed as he joined me on the floor. “I forgot you use all those antiquated phrases,” he said, stretching out and chuckling to himself.

“What’s wrong with my phrases?”

“Come on. ‘Our goose was cooked’? What era are you from?” he teased, then promptly disintegrated into giggles. “Oh god,” he gasped between fits, “I can’t remember the last time I pulled off a successful prank.” He let out a huge sigh and relaxed into the floor. I could.

I angled my body so I was on my side, facing him. He looked at me from his back, his eyes still bright, with a smile playing at the corners of his mouth. I loved him like this: carefree and relaxed, remembering there was more to life than studying and good grades.

He ran his hands over his face and flopped them to the ground. "I feel high. Don’t you feel high?" It was quite the statement, since I knew for a fact that Anderson Gallagher had never once been high.

I chuckled at his animation. “A little,” I said. His eyes danced at the admission. Before I could wuss out, I reached out and caressed the side of his face. When he didn’t immediately pull away, I placed my lips against his. He let out a soft moan as I slipped my tongue past the slight part.

I wasn’t sure what I'd been expecting, but it certainly wasn’t the distinct response I got. He moved his mouth firmly against mine, deepening the kiss. I'd never believed the ridiculous superstition that red-heads stole souls, but in that moment, it certainly felt like Andy was trying to steal mine.

He really must be high if he’s not only letting me kiss him, but kissing me back.

I slid closer, desperately wanting more. Naturally, since he’d said sex was off the table, it was the only thing I could think about.

It’s now or never.

I’d thought a lot about what I was about to do. I owed him this at the very least. It wouldn’t make up for what I’d done—not by a long shot—but it was a start. More than that, though, I wanted to. And even though I had no idea what I was doing, I wasn’t nervous; that’s what Andy was for. Andy knew everything.

Our teeth clicked as I deepened the kiss even more to ensure he was properly distracted.

Here goes nothing.

I released his face to slide my hand down his body. Andy was lean in all the right ways and it took an active force of will to stay focused. My hand hit his waistband and immediately slipped into his pants.

He gasped when my fingers wrapped around his erection, effectively breaking the fevered kiss. "Mitch."

I gave a light squeeze, and his eyelids fluttered. He could pretend all he wanted, but his reactions were showing him for the liar he was. He wanted me, even if he refused to admit it.

A firmer squeeze as I dragged up his shaft.

"What are you doing? We talked about this," he said, pushing up to his elbows even as I maneuvered his cock free. Like the rest of him, it was perfect: long, narrow, and stunningly smooth. I gave it another experimental stroke and his breath hitched. "Mitch, I'm serious."

I finally caught his gaze. "I know the rules. Now stop complaining and just tell me how you like it."

"Like wha—?" A strangled moan swallowed the question as I took his shaft in my mouth. I didn't want him to have any reason to deny this, so I took him as deep as I could manage the first time. "Fuck," he hissed.

I took the word as encouragement. I dragged all the way up, pausing at the cap, and did it again. His hand fluttered over my shoulder, then fisted tightly in my hair when I sucked hard on the head. He gave a deeper moan and finally lay back down. I was beyond shocked that he wasn't going to fight me on this. Thrilled at my victory, I pulled him back inside the cavern of my mouth.

"Easy on the teeth," he hissed. I quickly sheathed them with my lips and tried again. His only response this time was to moan. I did it a couple more times, and he added, "Use your hand." I shifted to do as he instructed. "That's it," he sighed as I found a rhythm between my hand and my mouth. "Now swirl your tongue around the tip."

I did and tasted pre-cum. His body shuddered. I added the move to the rest of the formula.

"Just like that," he moaned. "Mmm." His short nails dug into my shoulder. "Yes," he groaned, returning his grip to my hair. As he spoke, his hips rolled up. "Now—"

I didn't let him finish. I took him as deep as I could.

He gave another strangled groan. "Fuck!" Whatever control he'd been exercising vanished. His hips thrust frantically up from the floor as he held my head steady. I let him drive into my mouth, taking what he needed from me, and fought my gag reflex.

He tasted so sweet and I loved that he was clearly enjoying this, but it wasn't enough. I wanted more. I wanted to make him come. My rhythm returned with renewed vigor as I took back control, adjusting the pattern. Andy moaned deep in his throat as his back arched off the floor. I increased the pressure of my tongue, taking it from base to tip, and swallowed to pull him deeper. He made a high-pitched whine, and I did it again.

"I'm gonna come," he gasped.

Now that I'd found my perfect combo, I wasn't about to relent.

"Seriously. Oh *God*," he groaned. His hand tightened in my hair to the point of pain.

I kept going.

"Mitch—Mitch. You ha-have to stop," he stuttered.

The tip of his cock was practically weeping now. I could taste his imminent orgasm with each stroke. *So close*.

"Stop," he ordered, pulling my hair and forcing me back. His cock made a pop as it came free, and he rolled to the side just in time to ejaculate on the floor.

"Why did you do that?" I asked, not bothering to check my anger.

He didn't answer right away, taking a minute to put himself back together. Finally, he sat up, completely composed, and looked me in the eye. He seemed to choose his words in the face of my obvious irritation. After a moment of studying my expression, he let out a sigh. "Having someone come in you like that is…" He searched for the word. "Different."

I didn't give a shit if it was "different"; that was my choice, and he'd taken it from me. My thoughts must have shown because he gave me a small smile and reached out to hold the side of my face.

"Hey, don't be upset," he said softly. Then he surprised me by leaning forward and placing his lips against mine. The gentle kiss was sweet and tame, lingering. I debated going ahead and deepening it like I wanted to—like I was sure *he* wanted to—then he leaned back. "You're not ready for that yet."

Excitement rushed through me to replace my disappointment—he'd said "yet". The implication alone had me wanting to pull his mouth back.

Before I could, he flopped back, making a noise, and careful to avoid the mess on the floor. "If it's any consolation, that was fucking incredible." He looked delirious as he rolled his head to face me.

I think he might still be a little high.

I tried to focus on the wins I had and resumed my previous position beside him, but stayed propped on my elbow so I could see his expressions better. "Yeah?"

"Yeah," he sighed, turning his gaze back to the ceiling. "I've never walked anyone through it like that," he mused aloud. "You're a quick study." The passive compliment washed over me, lending hope to my crusade. All I'd done was give him head, but the victory felt more substantial.

"I have a good tutor," I responded, settling back down.

He snorted, then yet another laugh attack overtook him. Oh yeah, he was definitely still high. As he sobered back up, he let out a sigh. Tempting this unprecedented easiness between us, I wrapped an arm around his waist. He reflexively turned into it, making the contact more natural.

"What's your favorite part of sex, Andy?" I asked, hoping to keep my streak of wins going.

"Well, the obvious answer is getting off," he replied snidely.

"No shit," I said, jostling him. He laughed like I hoped he would. "Seriously, favorite thing. Before, after, during. Whatever."

"How should I know?" he grumped, sliding closer.

"How should you know? How should you know?" I teased, continuing to jostle him. He released a chorus of laughter. Each new laugh added to the sea of fireflies already filling me.

"Alright. Alright," he said, scooting closer once more, so that if I shook him, I'd shake myself. "Talking afterward is nice."

I scoffed. "Pillow talk is *not* your favorite thing, Andy."

"Oh yeah? What makes you so sure?" he asked over his shoulder.

I tightened my arm around his middle and eliminated the last of the distance between us. For a second, I was transported in time, and it was that night again. Andy felt so innocent curled in the hollow of my body, so right.

Except I'd ruined everything. He wasn't that same innocent boy, but he was still Andy and he was here with me. I nuzzled the back of his neck, inhaling the strange herbal scent he had. "Because I already know what your real favorite thing is," I whispered, giving him a gentle squeeze. A tense minute passed, and I feared I'd just fucked it up all over again.

"How do you know that?" he asked softly. If there had been any other sound in the room, I would never have heard him. Rather than answer, I buried my face in the back of his hair, letting his smell envelop me, and prayed he wouldn't pull away. We both knew how I knew.

Chapter 10

Four Years Ago

Andy

I shivered as I woke, my body aching in both familiar and foreign ways. The night before rushed in to fill me like the best hot cocoa in the world, finding all the tiniest parts of me and suffusing them with warmth. I hummed contentedly and reached out for my best friend. When my hand landed on the cold floor instead, I sat up. I squinted into the dimly lit room as if that would somehow make an extra body magically materialize.

"Mitch?" I whispered, then immediately shook my head. "Way to go, dummy." Another glance around showed his clothes were gone, and obviously he wasn't hiding in one of the nonexistent shadows. There was also no note or any other sign of where he might have gone. I chewed on my bottom lip as I sought my pajamas.

Maybe he didn't leave a note because he's coming right back.

I nearly fell over as I maneuvered my pants on, because damn, that smarted. Truthfully, my body ached more from sleeping on the unforgiving floor than losing my virginity, *that* pain I was more than okay with no matter how difficult it was making getting dressed. One of the giggles I'd fought so valiantly to keep to myself the night before slipped free. I'd never felt so light in my entire life. Yeah, my body hurt like hell, but every sore muscle was absolutely worth it.

"Maybe I don't have to tell him. Maybe he already knows." The hope that had begun as a small ember burned like the sun in my chest. Fear of losing my best friend had made sure I kept my feelings to myself, but now that there was a real chance Mitch might feel the same way about me… Giggles burst free and I immediately clamped a hand over my mouth, my gaze darting to the secret entrance. Which was stupid, really. Hadn't Mitch told me no one could hear us here?

I can't wait to tell him.

I approached the peculiar door and cautiously pushed it away from the wall a crack. In the tiny sliver of the outside world, sunlight filled an arched hallway.

Shit. What time is it?

The door fell back into place as I reassessed the situation. Mitch had probably left already so we wouldn't get caught together and had let me sleep in, because, well, that's just the sort of friend he was.

He's so much smarter than he gives himself credit.

And his heart, fuck, I loved his heart. And his warmth, and his laugh, and now probably his dick. My smile from earlier made a reappearance, and I ventured back to the door.

Now to get from here back to my room without anyone noticing. I smiled wider. *Piece of cake.*

Present Day

Andy

The portrait that hid the secret entrance swung shut and Mitch crowded me against the wall. His hazel eyes flashed in the low lighting and shone with a wildness that instantly had my heart hammering. Strong fingers curled into my hips as our mouths came together like a super magnet. I moaned into him and tangled my fingers in his hair, urging him deeper. He deftly popped my top two buttons and moved to suck a bruise out on my neck. I arched into him and tugged his head back to claim his mouth once more. Mitch didn't argue. He didn't say anything. He never did in my dreams. But knowing it wasn't real didn't change the want coursing through my veins or the need crawling up my spine now, or like it had then. No amount of knowing better could change how badly I wanted him.

His nimble fingers found my fly, and I moaned in anticipation. I knew exactly what it felt like to have Mitch inside of me, owning me like I needed, like only he could, like he always had. Outside, in the real world, I recognized the danger of indulging in the fantasy, but in here, it was safe to want, safe to need. His lips pressed hotly into the side of my neck and I gave over wholly to the sensation. By the time his mouth found mine again, I was panting with desperation and on the verge of begging. The eager kiss gentled, and I sighed into the softness of it. When he pulled back, his eyes held the promise I'd once hung all my hopes and dreams on. I opened my mouth to tell him the truth I should have told him years ago, but before the words could form, something soft smacked forcefully into my head.

My body rocketed back to awareness just in time to catch the next attack. "What the fuck, Lucien?" I snapped as I ripped the pillow away from him. He promptly yanked it back and glared at me.

"You were making gross noises in your sleep. I don't wanna hear that shit." The glower on his face paired well with his tousled, dark hair and sour disposition. I blanched at the implication that my illicit dreams had infringed upon a reality that could and would crucify me.

"Anything else?" I asked, more than a little trite.

He shoved his pillow under his arm and spared me one last menacing glare before stomping back to his bed. While he flopped back down with an irritated huff, I sat up and rubbed at my face. Mercifully, the shock of the rude awakening had done its part to kill my arousal, but sadly, it did nothing for the anxiety now pumping through my veins. More agitated with myself than with Lucien, I flipped the covers back and got dressed. I'd have to be up soon anyway for my meeting with Garza about my application for Chicago's advanced literary program, and this way I could sneak into the breakfast hall early before anyone could find me.

As I slipped out of the room, my mind summoned images better left forgotten. I shoved the memories violently away and hurried to the cafeteria. Unfortunately, the eggs and toast turned to ash in my mouth. I stubbornly drank the entire glass of orange juice so I could at least pretend I'd acquired sustenance and stalked back out of the slowly filling room. A flash of light filled the hallway, and I altered my course to look out one of the many windows that graced this hall. Rain came down in heavy sheets that obscured the grounds and darkened the sky. A fitting display given my current mood. The day promised to be every bit as dismal as my morning, and I wasn't in the mood for any of it.

My hand tightened on the strap of my satchel as if it could actually ward off the depression clawing at my heart. The dreams weren't new, but they were escalating. Something would need to be done and soon, except I didn't know what. What could I possibly do to alleviate the pain of spending time with Mitch, of indulging in his sudden curiosity? Clearly, allowing him to be blow me had been a mistake of epic proportions and now my reason was off its axis.

I spun away from the window and stalked down the hall, not really sure where I was going until I found myself in the tower. Exhausted, I dropped my bag and slumped to the ground, intending to read until I could face the day. But I didn't take out my latest mystery novel or even the epic fantasy I couldn't seem to finish. Instead, I sat with my back against the wall and watched the rainfall through the large window.

Mitch

I took the stairs two at a time, my heart frantically beating against my ribs. *Please be here*. If he wasn't, I didn't know where else to look. I'd already checked the secret room, his dormitory, and most of the classrooms. I'd even asked people, but no one had seen him beyond Lucien that morning, though he'd looked like he'd swallowed razors at the telling.

Thunder shook the Tower as I launched onto the landing with enough momentum to clear half the small space before coming to a stop. I peered around the room, made darker by the storm raging outside that all but guaranteed no one had ventured beyond the safety of the school. On the verge of despair, a flash of light illuminated the rotunda, and I spotted him against the wall I'd surged past.

"Andy." I breathed a sigh of relief that faltered when he didn't respond. Concern once again took hold as a faint whimper reached my ears. His shadowy form twitched, and the sound came again. I stalked over, but it wasn't until I crouched in front of him I realized he was asleep. "Andy," I tried again with the same result. I reached out, intending to grab his shoulder and shake him awake, but that's not where it ended. I cupped the side of his face and stroked his cheek. "Andy."

"Mitch." He said it so softly, I feared I'd misheard.

I scooted closer until I could feel his deep breathing on my face. "I'm right here." He sighed, and I leaned forward, worried I'd missed another whispered word that could help me understand what was wrong. I was completely unprepared for his lips to brush against mine in a tentative kiss. Taken aback, but unwilling to leave, I softly pressed back. His lips parted with a decidedly different whimper. Then he latched onto me.

He swallowed down my muffled sound of shock and licked inside my mouth. Instinct took over, and I tangled my tongue with his, giving and taking as much as he did. My surprise at the sensual response took a back seat as he continued to kiss me like it was the only thing in the world that mattered. His lips molded to mine like they were made for me and they washed away every thought I had about not fucking this up with the rain falling relentlessly, not ten feet away.

"Andy," I finally managed, my voice ragged with need. The kissing wasn't enough, giving him head wasn't enough. I needed more, needed to make this right.

Suddenly, he jerked back and pressed firmly into the wall. "What the fuck are you doing?" He reached a shadowed hand for his bag. "Seriously, what the hell, Mitch?"

I didn't need to see him to know his eyes were borderline feral or hear his breath coming in short, panicked puffs. My brow furrowed. "What are you talking about? *You* kissed *me*."

"I... I did?" The hint of question only threw me for further of a loop.

"Andy, what's going on?"

"I'm sorry. I... I shouldn't have done that." He scrambled to stand in the narrow space that existed between me and the wall. I rocked back on my heels and rose as he shouldered his bag.

"I don't understand. Is something wrong?" Had I somehow fucked everything up anyway? That would be just my luck, to ruin all of my efforts to get him to forgive me, let me back in, and not even know.

"Why are you here?"

"You skipped all of your classes. That's not like you. I was worried."

"As you can see, I'm fine." He shouldered past me and made for the stairs.

"Andy, wait." He hitched his bag higher and walked faster. "Andy," I called again, but he didn't stop.

Andy

I took the treacherous stairs fast enough to risk falling down them if I mis-stepped, Mitch's voice chasing me the whole way. An entire day of classes missed and for what? To end up having the same nightmare I'd been running away from for four years? Except it hadn't been the same, not really. Unlike the predictable chain of events where I wandered down corridor after corridor, calling for him to come back, begging him to let me try again, this one had been different. This time when I woke in the secret room and called out for him, he'd been there. He'd stepped out of the darkness and held my face tenderly while he laughed about my being a spaz.

I swiped away the sting of tears that remembering the dream brought. He'd kissed my nose and told me he'd never leave me, not ever, that he was here. Then he'd kissed me and every childish dream nurtured in the dark had come true. I kissed him back with everything I had, everything I couldn't put words to, surrendered to the love I so desperately wanted to have. But then he said my name, impossible when his mouth was still firmly glued to mine and I realized the lie for what it was—a dream. Only when I woke up, Mitch was really there, and my lips still tingled from the passionate kiss.

I missed the last step and stumbled to the ground floor. The jarring impact set my teeth on edge, but I pushed on. I needed to get as far away as possible to deal with this wretched fucking day before he could stop me. My frenzied pace slowed, and I sagged against the wall.

What the fuck is wrong with me? I should be past all this.

But clearly, I wasn't if today was anything to go by. I needed to pull it together, and fast. The logical thing to do would be to stop seeing Mitch all together, his curiosity and determination to be friends again be damned. Except I wouldn't and therein lie the problem. I was being tortured all right, but I was the one doing the torturing.

There has to be a way to regain control of this before it spirals anymore out of control. Think.

I rounded the corner and ran into someone hard enough for us both to stumble back. My overstuffed satchel shifted, nearly taking me down with it. I floundered to regain control of my body, as well as my masochistic heart.

"There you are. Where the fuck have you been all day?"

I glanced up from my struggle, surprised to see Calvin. "H-hey."

His eyebrows pulled down, and his mouth pressed into a thin line. "Is everything alright? Where have you been?"

"I..uh…fell asleep in the tower," I forced out as I danced from foot to foot. The V between his eyes deepened.

"What's going on? Who cares if you blew off a few classes? I've blown off plenty."

I shook my head. I'd also missed my meeting with Garza, but that was beside the point. "Mitch found me."

"I'm not surprised," he scoffed. "Especially considering he practically turned this place upside down looking for you."

The comment momentarily distracted me, then I remembered why I couldn't be standing here talking to Calvin. "You don't understand. I was dreaming about…" I glanced behind me to be sure no one was around and leaned closer, "*that* night."

Calvin's eyebrows shot up while his mouth formed an O. "I mean, okay, but so what?"

I leveled a glare at him. "I think I was talking in my sleep. I… I don't know what he may have heard."

"You could always ask him," he suggested, ever the pragmatist.

"No, I can't," I countered without elaborating.

"O-kay, well, you better pull your shit together quick, because he's coming this way." He glanced behind me, lending credence to his words, and I cursed under my breath. "What are you going to do?"

I scrambled for a solution without success. "Cover for me."

"Andy," Calvin said flatly, repositioning his gaze back to me.

"Please."

He bit his lip, then said the last thing I ever expected. "Tell him the truth."

My hackles rose. "No."

"All I'm saying is—"

"I don't give a shit what you're saying," I hissed. "Just be my fucking friend." Shock exploded across his face, but I didn't stick around to see what would come out of his mouth. Mitch had longer legs than me and it wouldn't take him nearly as long to catch up.

I all but raced away, heavy satchel thumping painfully against my leg. There had to be somewhere else I could go, somewhere Mitch wouldn't find me. My usual place was out of the question, though, judging by the torrential rain I could still see falling through the windows. The sound of speedy steps filled the hall, and I glanced back to see if either Calvin or Mitch had followed me. Still looking over my shoulder, I rounded a corner and, for the second time that day, ran into someone.

"Watch where the fuck you're going." At the sound of Benny's voice, my head snapped back forward.

Fuck, like today wasn't bad enough.

I ducked my head and pretended I was invisible as I tried to skirt past him.

"Did you hear me, homo?"

I gritted my teeth and diligently ignored the offensive slur. "Sorry," I said, aiming for meek and growling it instead. His lip curled, and he moved to block my path. "What do you want?" I snapped, beyond exasperated.

"I want you to stop fucking with Mitch." Cold dread slid down my spine. Benny knew. "This is our last season and I don't want this weird ass friendship you two have dicking the team over." My momentary scare dissolved into rage. It was because of people like Benny I'd lost Mitch in the first place.

"Fuck you," I snarled.

"What did you say to me, you ginger freak?" Benny asked, his voice dangerously low as he invaded my space, highlighting the height difference between us.

"You heard me. Fuck. You," I repeated, standing my ground.

His face warped with anger, and his eyes burned with barely contained fury. "You fucking piss-ant, I'm going to—"

I cocked my head to the side, unphased by the looming threat. "Tell me, Benny, had any eventful showers lately?"

"What did you say to me?"

Now it was my turn to get in his face. We all had secrets we'd rather keep in the dark, even Benny. I dropped my voice, but held eye contact so he would know I wasn't kidding. "He still goes to those same showers. Three a.m. like clockwork. Just. In. Case." I let that hang a moment and enjoyed watching the blood drain from his face. "I suggest you take a hard look at yourself before you start passing out names."

Face officially devoid of color, Benjamin Wallace Price IV, school bully extraordinaire, staggered back without a word. I shouldered past him like

I had Calvin and continued down the vacant hall. My threat had given me an idea of where to go.

Chapter 11

Mitch

I blew out a breath and flipped the paper over. Nothing about the grade came as a surprise. I'd never excelled at science, and trig-based physics was thoroughly kicking my ass. But not even the deplorable grade could distract from what truly occupied my thoughts and brought me down. I hadn't seen Andy in days, eight to be exact. Sure, we didn't have any classes together, but the school wasn't *that* big. I usually at least saw him around even before we were intentionally spending time together. There wasn't another way to look at it—Andy was avoiding me and had been since whatever had happened in the Tower.

Did I do something wrong?

I wracked my brain, but the only answer forthcoming was that I'd kissed him, or more appropriately, he'd kissed me. *Thoroughly*. Maybe it was because he'd been asleep? He'd certainly seemed awake. How was I supposed to know he hadn't actually woken up when he was—

"You coming?"

I glanced up from my bubble of misery and the hurricane of thoughts clouding it to find Brian's expectant face. Brian was a nice guy, one hell of a defender, and a good friend, but right now there was only one friend on my mind. And he was avoiding me.

I don't understand. We were doing so well, making progress. Or maybe…we weren't? Maybe it's all been in my head and there's really no way Andy will ever forgive me for—

"Did you hear me?" Brian asked as he waved a hand in front of my face. "Where'd you go? You spaced hard there for a minute." Concern tightened his eyes and his mouth turned down. I wasn't stupid. I knew the team was freaking about me being distracted lately, but I also knew I'd stay distracted until I figured this thing with Andy out.

As I stood, I slung my bag over my shoulder, then grabbed the test. "Sorry, man. A lot on my mind. Right now, though, I need to talk with Cohen about some extra credit." Brian winced. Extra credit from Cohen wasn't something anyone ever wanted to need. Lessons were bad enough. They were worse when you had to endure them twice, and that was assuming he was willing to offer any credit in the first place.

"That bad?"

"That bad," I echoed. He gave me a sympathetic shake of his head, then left me to my groveling.

Cohen glanced up as I approached his desk, not an ounce of surprise on his lightly tan face. "Mr. Hudson."

"Hey Mr. C, about my grade—"

"You know I don't subscribe to Coach Santinelli's assertion that anyone on the team gets a pass. There are no handouts here."

"I know," I mumbled, absolutely mortified. "That's not what I want."

Surprise finally registered on his face as raised eyebrows, though the rest of his expression remained unsettlingly neutral. "What did you have in mind?"

"I was hoping you could assign me some real extra credit?"

His features softened with sympathy, and he leaned forward to rest his forearms on the desk. "I don't mean to be cruel, Mitch, but all the extra credit in the world won't help if you don't understand the material."

"Yeah," I sighed, looking down at my feet and scooting a rogue button with my shoe. *Fuck, even the teacher thinks I'm hopeless.*

"Gallagher was tutoring you, was he not? Have you considered asking him for help on this subject as well?"

My heart landed with an unpleasant squelch in my stomach. Oh, I'd thought about it alright, along with about a million other things I was positive would never happen. "I think he might be done helping me."

Professor Cohen considered me a long minute, then leaned back and pulled open a drawer. He took out a thick packet and held it out. "He'll help, I'll make sure of it. You two can start with this workbook. It covers all the material that was on the last exam and some of what will be on the next."

My fingers wrapped around the unexpected offering.

"Anderson is familiar with the material, and it shouldn't take him long to get into it. Complete that entire book, showing your work," he gestured to the test clutched in my other hand, "and we'll see about raising that a letter grade or two. It should also give you a good foundation for the midterm. Ace that, and you'll be well on your way to graduating with a B minus."

I pulled the book closer, stuck between happy shock and crushing disbelief. All of this was pointless if Andy wouldn't be in the same room as me. "How are you going to get him to help?"

"I have my ways." Cohen winked, then pulled out his phone, tapped out a quick message, and returned it to the drawer.

"Uh..." I trailed off, suddenly anxious that my desire to pass the damn subject had inadvertently gotten Andy into trouble. That certainly wouldn't help my case.

"Don't worry, nothing untoward. Promise. A little birdie told me Anderson is hoping Garza will write him a recommendation letter for his application to Chicago U's advanced program. Rest assured, Garza will ensure that he's enthusiastic about the assistance."

"Oh. You sure?" I asked, still not convinced that Andy wouldn't resent me for jeopardizing his chances.

"Positive. I'm also pleased to see you finally taking a genuine interest in your grades. Any particular reason?"

"I don't want to take an athletic scholarship," I whispered, knowing full well that if word got back to coach, he'd have a stroke. Cohen's eyebrows rose once more and his mouth fell open. I didn't blame him. As far as he knew, as far as everyone knew, I lived, slept, and breathed lacrosse. Everyone but Andy. He recovered from his shock, snapping his mouth shut, and busied himself reorganizing his already pristine desk.

"In that case, we'll have to see what we can do about that grade. Won't we?"

Andy

I stomped down the abandoned hallway, still bristling from the meeting with my mentor. I couldn't believe Garza was holding my letter of recommendation hostage in order to get me to tutor someone. And not even in literature. Ridiculous didn't cover it. Ludicrous was more like it. Or maybe even outrageous. But without that letter, I'd never get into the advanced writing program. Still grumbling to myself and mentally running through a thesaurus of vitriol, I pushed open the door to professor Cohen's classroom and stopped dead.

The hopeful smile melted off of Mitch's face and I could only imagine what my own looked like. "They didn't tell you," he said. Not a question, a statement of fact. He shook his head and averted his gaze. After a few moments of tense silence in which I remained frozen in the door, he scooped his books off the table into his bag. "It's okay. I'll… I'll figure something else out."

My heart sank at seeing his obvious disappointment and hearing the hint of despair that colored his words. Was I really going to punish him—punish his grades—because I couldn't keep the past and present separate? When he'd needed a friend the most, he'd turned to me. That had to count for something, right? He stood, and I stepped deeper into the room, letting the door swing silently shut behind me.

"Wait."

"It's fine, Andy. I… understand if you don't want to be around me."

My heart twisted painfully. That wasn't the case at all, it would never be the case. Of course, I wanted to be around him—I'd be glued to him if I could. And that right there was the root of the problem. Even after everything that had happened over the last four years, I still wanted to be his best friend.

"That's not—" My voice cracked, and I regathered myself. After a deep breath, I pushed through the fear that I wouldn't survive this. "That's not true. I'll help." I walked into the room beneath his wary gaze and took a seat in the chair beside where he remained standing. "Garza said you'd have a workbook. Can I see it?" He didn't so much as twitch or blink. "Please," I added.

He stared down at me, uncertainty darkening his hazel eyes. "You don't have to do this. I'll tell Cohen I changed my mind and not to let Garza take it out on you."

"I know I don't have to. I want to," I said without an iota of hesitation.

"Really?" He sank back into his seat, disbelief still evident on his face.

"Really. Now, how about that workbook?" I smiled softly in the hope it would lend credence to my assertion. Because, damn it all, I did want to help, and I *hated* physics, which Garza damn well knew.

Mitch blinked and twisted to retrieve the requested item from his bag. "Did you wanna see the test? I won't lie, it's pretty bad."

"No."

His head whipped around, the hand holding the promised workbook following much slower with the rest of his torso. "Why not?"

I shrugged. "Because it doesn't matter."

"But—"

"But nothing." I placed a hand over his where it had settled on the table, still clutching the thick packet like it was a life raft. "It's in the past and we're going to change it." I winked at him and tugged the workbook free of his grasp so I could flip through and scan the pages. "Plus, it sounds like you've beat yourself up about it plenty. All that's left is to move forward and do better now, wouldn't you say?" I glanced over at him, because he'd yet to utter a syllable.

"Do you really believe that?" The question came out thick, laced with an emotion that I couldn't quite put my finger on and that, admittedly, surprised me.

"If I didn't, I wouldn't be here." Forget the fact that Garza had blackmailed me here under false pretenses. The second I realized it was Mitch, I could have left. I'd figure my shit out and find a way to make this work, enjoy whatever weird game Mitch was playing, because at the end of the day, any time I could steal with him would be worth the inevitable heartache. I cleared my throat and let out a laugh that I prayed he wouldn't recognize as nervous. "Please tell me you brought a calculator."

His lips quirked up in a hesitant smile that grew with confidence until it popped a dimple in his cheek. "Nope."

Chapter 12

Andy

I rubbed my hands down my face as I tried to convince myself for probably the thousandth time that I could do this. But this wasn't editing a paper and giving it back. This would be shoulder to shoulder, constant proximity studying. With Mitch. And I was already doing a shit-tastic job of keeping my emotions in check. I dropped my head back to stare at the ceiling of my dorm room and let out a groan.

"What's got you so blue?" Lucien asked as he stepped into the room with a few books tucked under his arm. At first glance, they all seemed to be textbooks, but further inspection revealed a worn paperback tucked between the school books.

I straightened up and rolled my shoulders to loosen the tension build up. Unsurprisingly, it had zero success.

Lucien set his books down and considered me for a moment. "You had your meeting with your mentor the other day, right? Did it not go well?"

"It certainly could have gone better," I grumbled, stalking over to my bed and sitting with a huff.

My roommate's eyebrows lifted. "Really? I thought everything was on track for your application to Chicago."

I waved a dismissive hand. "It's not the application, per se."

"Then what?" Lucien swiveled his desk chair around and plopped into it, propping his elbows on his knees as he leaned forward.

"Garza is *encouraging* me to tutor another student. Insists that it will look good on my application." Why I didn't come right out and tell him who I was tutoring was beyond me. Probably because I was having a difficult time wrapping *my* head around agreeing in the first place.

Lucien leaned back and frowned. "Is it one of the younger kids? I get how that can be a pain, but surely it won't be all that bad. Not that I think you need *anything* else padding your application," he added with a smirk.

I almost returned it, but the reality of the truth kept my lips in a firm line. "I wish. No, it's another senior in our year. But get this, it's not even in literature."

He held up a hand and shook his head. "Okay, you've officially lost me. What the hell does Garza have you tutoring if it's *not* literature?"

"Physics," I deadpanned and watched Lucien's expression go from mild curiosity to full-blown confusion.

"What the hell?"

"Oh, it gets better. I'm tutoring Mitch." Maybe if I shared, had someone to help keep me accountable, remind me in a roundabout way that *wanting* to be around Mitch was not a good thing, I'd actually survive this somehow. Also, wouldn't hurt to have the explanation for why we'd suddenly be spending so much time together.

Lucien barked a laugh, but when I didn't join him, he speared me with a disbelieving stare. "Wait. You're serious? Like Mitch—Mitch Hudson—Mitch? The school's star lacrosse player and grade-A asshat. That Mitch?"

Well, now I knew exactly how Lucien felt about my would-be pupil. "The one and only."

"Okay, maybe it's not *all* bad. You two used to be good friends, right?"

I leaned back on my elbows and hoped Lucien hadn't seen the flash of pain that statement always brought me. "Emphasis on the 'used to'."

"Shit, man, that sucks. Couldn't you tell Garza no? I mean, sure, it could look good on your app, but it's not Lit and you don't really need it."

"I do, however, need Garza's letter of recommendation if I want to secure a spot in the advanced writing program, which he's currently holding hostage. Without his Alumnus endorsement, I might as well not even bother applying to Chicago." Maybe should have checked my bitterness... While I didn't agree with what Garza was doing, it wasn't really him I was mad at, or Mitch, for that matter. I was mad at myself, because apparently getting ghosted and ignored for four years wasn't enough for me to get over my first crush...first love.

"That's fucked."

I pointed at Lucien. "You said it." I shifted back to a properly seated position and indicated the worn paperback on his desk. "Now you going to tell me about what you're reading or what?" I asked, seeking more familiar territory for us. Lucien and I got along fairly well for two guys that had randomly been assigned as roommates—we both despised sports, were top of our classes, and we loved to read. What we didn't do was make a habit of talking heavy shit. Sure, we'd covered our fair share of family drama, but it was few and far between. And while Lucien might not know it, Mitch was heavy shit. So books.

"Dude," Lucien said with a wide grin as he reached for the book. "This thing has got dragons, like all kinds, and witches, and fae, and what have you." He leaned forward again, checked the door, and despite it being closed, dropped his voice. "It also has sex. Like *a lot* of sex." His eyes widened comically, and I couldn't help but chuckle.

"And who gave you this hella racy book?"

Lucien shrugged. "It's on loan from my sister."

"Your sister?" I echoed. "Isn't that a little...weird?"

"Maybe, but when I saw her a couple of weeks back, she accused me of always reading the same things. Said I needed to 'broaden my horizons' and threw it at me. I told her I could read anything she did, and here we are."

I chuckled again. "Sibling rivalry gets you every time." And wouldn't I know it, being the youngest—and shortest—of three.

"No shit," Lucien said with a huff.

"But you *like* dragons? And I doubt you've never read a book without some kind of sex in it. How is this any different?"

Lucien's face went from its usual tawny chestnut to full on burnt red. He cleared his throat, then before continuing in the same low whisper as before, checked the closed door...again. "It's not *just* a lot of sex, it's a lot of different *kinds* of sex."

Now it was my turn to be shocked. I couldn't help but follow the book as Lucien flipped it around in his hands. Was it possible the book had gay dragon sex? I'd never read a book with gay sex at all. They weren't exactly plentiful at the bookstore in town and I couldn't buy them when I was home for breaks, as my family had no clue I was gay. What I really wanted to do was ask Lucien if I could read it next. But that would be weird, right? Then again, we shared books all the time. Surely this wouldn't be any different just because he'd admitted to it having adventurous sex.

I was about to go for it when Lucien cleared his throat again and ducked his head. He shoved the book into his side table drawer so fast he probably bent the cover. "Anyway, the—story is solid and no way am I gonna let Amari get one up on me for this. She'll now if I chickened out and DNF-ed."

"Can't have that," I said, more than a little disappointed that he hadn't even offered.

"Also, she...um, wants it back the next time I visit." Lucien looked abashed, his cheeks still pink from his confession. "So I'm kind of on a time limit, what with fall break coming up. Sorry." He gave me a weak smile.

Technically, fall break was still *several* weeks away and more than enough time for both of us to read the book, but Lucien had made his position clear. He wasn't comfortable sharing something like that, which was a real bummer, because now curiosity was clawing away inside of me.

Wonder if I could sneak a few peeks at it without him knowing.

"So Mitch..."

I blinked and dragged my attention away from the denied book. "What about him?" I asked dubiously.

"He really as good a player as everyone says?"

"Wouldn't know. Never been to a single match and don't know a damn thing about the game."

Lucien grimaced. "Sounds like your tutoring lessons are going to be a special kind of torture."

I let out a heavy sigh, picturing Mitch's shirt plastered to his toned body. I may not have been to any games, but thanks to Calvin, I'd seen my fair share of practices. "You have no idea."

"You know what? We're both done with classes for the day. Let's go into town and hang out for a bit. What do you think?" Lucien waited patiently for my answer.

Finally, I nodded. "Yeah, that would...that would be nice." I pushed off the bed and we both switched out of our uniforms for casual wear, then set off for town. Luckily, the weather had cooled, and it wasn't oppressively hot as we made the twenty-minute trek into town. We even lucked out with a pleasant breeze. By the time we'd sauntered onto Main Street in Hylestead, I'd all but forgotten about the stressful situation with Mitch, but not so much about the racy paperback still sequestered in Lucien's side table.

He pointed at the bookstore. "Wanna go in?"

"Since when do we *not*?" I snorted and opened the door so he could go in first. We both waved to the clerk on duty, then gravitated toward the shelves, Lucien toward the fantasy section and me toward the murder mysteries. After about half an hour of independent perusing, we regrouped.

"What did you find?" Lucien asked as he rearranged his own stack of finds.

I pulled out a used copy of *Murder, She Wrote*. "Thought it might be fun to check out some classics."

He shook his head and laughed. "You know, if I didn't know you so well, I'd be worried."

"What's that supposed to mean?" I asked, clutching the book and several others in the series to my chest.

"It's just murder, murder, murder all the time with you."

I scowled at him. "Is not."

Lucien's dark eyebrows lifted. "Oh yeah? When's the last time you read something that *wasn't* about people getting axed?"

"They don't all get axed... Sometimes they get shot, or poisoned, or runover. But that's beside the point. I read other things."

He put down the rest of his stack and crossed his arms. "Yeah. Like what?"

"You're not the only one who occasionally dips their toe into romance," I replied with a smirk, unable to resist the dig.

His face fell into a hard scowl. "Okay, smartass. Try this one out." He plucked a book free of a nearby shelf. "It's the first book in a duology. It's got magic, mayhem, and, yes, plenty of death for your morbid soul."

I took the proffered book and wrinkled my nose, not exactly enthusiastic about reading a book about daughters, first or otherwise.

"Don't let the title fool you. It's a great story." Lucien levelled a look at me as he picked up his collection. "At least give it a shot. If you decide you hate it, I'll buy it from you."

"Deal." We made our way to the checkout, laughing as we purchased the latest design of the store's canvas bag to hold our acquisitions, then ventured back into the town.

Lucien smacked me in the arm, nearly throwing me and the bag. "Let's hit up that pizza place."

"Ugh, yes! My kingdom for a slice of pepperoni."

"You're such a dork," he said with a laugh that I echoed.

"And you're not?"

"Pft. Not as much as *you*," he fired back as we turned onto the street with the pizza place.

I lurched to a stop, and laughter stuck in my throat. Leaving the pizza parlor was a rowdy group of guys, laughing and cutting up. And at their heart was Mitch. His radiant smile simultaneously lifted my heart and ruthlessly stabbed it. Would he ever laugh like that with me again?

Lucien stopped a pace later and glanced between me and the group. "Andy?"

I struggled to respond, but couldn't tear my gaze from Mitch as the entire group continued to approach. I'd always been so careful never to run into him in town, confident that my reaction would give me away...kind of like it was now. The group got right up beside us and I held my breath.

Mitch turned his smile on me. And while it was probably a trick of the imagination, it seemed to become even brighter. "Hey, Andy. See you Thursday?"

I tried unsuccessfully to swallow and nodded. "Yeah. Thursday."

Mitch's eyes crinkled with his grin, and my stupid heart skipped a beat. Then he turned to one of his companions and they kept going. I couldn't help but stare after them while I fought with my longing to be the one beside him instead of the one left behind.

"Maybe studying with Mitch won't be so torturous after all," Lucien said, snapping me out of my stupor.

I gave myself a good internal shake and moved to catch up to him. "Oh trust me, it'll be torture."

Chapter 13

Mitch

The book made an ominous thud as Andy dropped it to the table. His laugh at my expression almost wiped away my doubt that I'd ever grasp this material. We'd already had a handful of tutoring sessions, much to the dismay of my teammates, as they regularly coincided with informal practices.

"Don't look so discouraged," Andy said, smacking my arm and returning his attention to the heavy text. "I promise, this will make it easier."

"For you maybe. You're a freaking genius."

"Aw, thanks." Despite the teasing response, he noticeably brightened at the praise.

"I'm serious, Andy. I can't even grasp trigonometry. How am I supposed to understand calculus?"

"And I'm serious, *Mitch*. This will help. They're two different types of math. Trust me when I say I think you'll have an easier go with calculus."

I grumbled to myself, then leaned back, tilting my chair on its back two legs, and crossed my arms. "You could just tell me there's no hope instead of trying to teach me a whole other subject in four weeks."

He let out a huff that sounded like a volume of frustration, then turned to me. "You're a stubborn ass. Quit with the doom and gloom or I'm making you write lines."

The threat provoked a snicker out of me. "Pretty sure you don't have that authority."

He raised a red brow, his green eyes sparking a challenge. "Try me."

I leaned forward, sending the chair crashing back to the Earth. Our faces hovered inches apart as we stared each other down in silence. His green eyes bored into mine without mercy or a single blink, perfectly resolute and convinced of his ultimate victory.

Bet if I captured his mouth and pinned him onto the table, he'd blink.

The rogue thought popped up out of nowhere, nearly disrupting my own efforts not to blink. I pushed it away, refusing to entertain letting the mindless need that lived inside of me anywhere near Andy…again. He shifted, but still didn't bat an eye. Something red popped up in my periphery and I did a double take.

"Ha!" Andy crowed in victory. "I win. Calculus it is and you don't get to bellyache about it."

I blinked again and reached for the object of my distraction—a cup of chocolate pudding.

He snatched it away before my fingers could close around it, and I shifted my shock to him. His eyes glinted with mischief and barely contained mirth. "You can have it… *After* you hear me out."

"Are you…bribing me?" My gaze shifted to the hostage snack. "With pudding?"

"You accomplish more with the carrot than the stick."

I barked out a laugh, then doubled over as they kept coming. "And you say *I* use outdated phrases. What did you do, look that up?"

He shifted in his seat and set the pudding on his other side. Not far enough that I couldn't reach it, though. All it would take was getting practically on top of him to snag it with my longer arms. Which I wouldn't do, because then I'd be pressed against him and there was no telling what I would do.

A smile tweaked the corners of his mouth as he focused on the text. "Maybe," he admitted.

I stopped thinking about what it would take to get the pudding and how I was likely to forget all about the treat if I got that close to him and gave Andy my undivided attention. "Let's hear it. How the hell is calculus going to help?"

"Did you know calculus was invented to explain physics?"

"You can invent math?"

He laughed and scooted closer, bringing the book along with him. The smell of his herbal soap drifted beneath my nose. I breathed out heavily to clear it so I could think straight. "I want you to look at this." He pointed to a section of the page with a picture of light being refracted through a bubble into a miniature rainbow.

"Pretty."

He glanced up at me, his mouth twisted into a frown. "Does any of this look familiar?"

I dragged my attention away from the shapes his mouth was making to read the page. It took three passes, all of which Andy sat perfectly quiet through, until it clicked. Without a word, I yanked out the physics text that rivaled his calculus book and plopped it on the table. A few flips later, I landed on a page with an almost identical image.

"What the fuck?" I glanced back and forth between the long, complicated formula on my page and the short, straightforward one on his. "What the fuck?" I said again.

He laughed and slid over the pudding along with a magically produced spoon. "Willing to listen now?"

I snatched the snack, peeled back the lid, and shoved a spoonful in my mouth. Beside me, Andy watched me with an unreadable expression. I took a slightly less aggressive bite and looked over at him. "Did you want some?"

He shook his head quietly, then seemed to register he was staring. He shook himself and pointed back to the similar pages. "The bad news is that you still have to learn the trig way." I nearly choked on my latest spoonful. He glanced at me out of the corner of his eye, then continued, "But the good news is that you can use this to check your work."

"I don't see how that helps my current problem, seeing as how trig *is* the problem."

"It's not perfect, but I think if you knew you were on the right track, what the reward would be," he pointed at the now empty cup in my hand, "then you wouldn't be so quick to believe you can't do it." His fierce gaze softened. "You're smarter than you give yourself credit for, always have been."

In that moment, I wanted more than anything to kiss Andy, to grab his face and own his mouth, to thank him for believing in me, for being my friend, for giving me a second chance. I pushed past the overwhelming desire, not the least of which because the last time I'd gotten too excited and done just that, he'd freaked. "Okay," I said, discarding the empty cup and scooting my chair closer so that we were huddled together over the texts, "how do we do this?"

Andy

I paced the small room for what was likely the thousandth time, filled with just as much anxious energy as I usually had before I'd pull off a prank. Except this was so much more than a prank. This was Mitch's future. He needed to blow that midterm out of the water if he had any hope of redeeming his grade for this class, not to mention his overall GPA. Of course, if he took an athletic scholarship, no one would care what his grades were as long as he hadn't outright failed.

But if I'd deduced nothing over the last five weeks, it was that Mitch didn't want to be defined by a sport anymore. That, and I had zero sense of self preservation. Hours spent shoulder to shoulder, thigh to thigh, had only fueled more dreams that wouldn't be ignored. Admitting to myself that I enjoyed spending time with Mitch was a hell of a lot harder than it should have been. But I couldn't help it. Every minute we spent together seemed to bring him closer to *my* Mitch, the Mitch I'd lost all those years ago.

A swath of afternoon light cut across the floor and I looked up right as the secret door swung shut. "Took you fucking long enough."

"You try sneaking in here in the middle of last bell," he fired back.

Right, last bell, I'd nearly forgotten. I'd been so eager to learn the results that I'd begged off my last class of the day and headed straight here. Rather than admit how anxious I was, I waved a dismissive hand. "Do you have the results or not?"

He gave me a crooked smile and flashed that damned dimple as he pulled out a manila envelope, sealed just like the one Garza had given him. I surged forward, already reaching for it, only to be stopped by Mitch's hand on my chest. "Curse you and your long arms," I grumbled as I pushed against the immovable barrier, my fingers curling in the air well short of their goal.

"Someone's impatient," he laughed while continuing to hold me at bay.

I let out a huff and dropped my arms. "You're not the only one who worked hard for that."

"Suppose you have a point." He let his hand fall and walked to the center of the small space. There, he lowered his school bag to the ground, where it slumped over on its side while he fingered the seal. I joined him and took a steadying breath that did absolutely nothing to quell my tide of nerves.

Please don't let me have failed him.

"Here." He shoved the envelope in my hands.

"What?"

"You open it."

I made to pass it back. "Mitch, I can't..."

He pushed it back toward me. "Please?"

I took a moment to register his own state of nerves—the pinched line of his mouth, the wariness in his eyes, the tightness pulling his shoulders together—and nodded. I used my thumb to peel back the tacky flap, then glanced at him again before pulling out the results. To my surprise, Cohen hadn't given him the usual single-page report. He'd given him the entire hefty exam.

Probably so we can review any errors.

"Well? How bad is it? I know you don't sugarcoat, but maybe make an exception this time?" Mitch licked his lips, and I followed his gaze back to the pages in my hand and the circled grade. At seeing the red number, my chest swelled with pride and it took every ounce of willpower not to crow with delight.

"No need."

"Fuck." He dropped his head back and squeezed his fists against his eyes. "I knew it was too much to hope for. So much for thinking I did well."

Some of my excitement bubbled over and I laughed. "No, Mitch, there's no need to sugarcoat, because you did fine, better than fine. You aced it."

He straightened and snatched the exam from me. "I did?"

"You totally did." Pride radiated from my chest to glow in each nerve ending.

Mitch glanced back up at me with my grin threatening to split my face in two. "Is that... That says ninety-eight. Does that say ninety-eight?"

"Yeah, yeah it does."

He ran a hand through his hair and stared down at the page in disbelief mixed with wonder. "Holy fuck. We did it."

"*You* did it," I corrected. The pride coursing through my veins turned to raw energy that had me vibrating in place. Taking a page out of his playbook, I surged forward and slammed him with a bruising kiss. Unlike when he'd done it to me, he only had a moment of shock before responding in kind.

The exam fell heavily to the floor as he opened up and kissed me back just as hard. The energy inside me turned white hot and blindingly bright.

Nice as the kiss was, it wasn't enough. I needed more of an outlet before I was burned from the inside out. I continued to snatch at his lips while my fingers found his buckle. Once it was free, I tackled the button. Mitch pulled back with a gasp and released his hold on my head, though fuck if I knew when it had gotten there.

"Andy, what are you doing?" he asked as I slipped a hand past his waistband.

I hummed with delight at finding him already hard and stole another kiss before falling to my knees. "Should think it's pretty obvious." I tugged his briefs down to reveal my prize. His erection bounced free, the head already swollen red, and my mouth watered.

"You don't have to do this."

I grabbed hold of him and heat pulsed through my hand to fill the rest of me. "Would have thought you'd caught on by now that I don't do anything I don't want to." I brushed my thumb over his slit and leaned forward.

"Andy." I glanced up at the insistence in his voice. His chest heaved with rapid breaths and the flush of arousal stained his cheeks while his fingers dug sharply into my shoulder to keep me at bay.

"Trust me," I said softly, and bypassed my original destination to place a gentle kiss on the side of his cock. He shuddered and the hand gripping my shoulder relaxed ever so slightly. I lay a trail of delicate kisses down his shaft until I could bury my nose in his groin. The intense musk of him swallowed me whole, and I barely suppressed a groan of need. Mitch had no such reservations, as his own groan sounded like it was ripped from a strangled throat.

I rocked back on my heels and licked my lips in anticipation. This time, when I leaned forward, he didn't stop me. I took my time pulling him in, savoring the feel of velvet over steel. When his length edged the back of my throat, I hummed in contentment. Why the hell had I waited so long to taste him? I took him a fraction deeper before wrapping my tongue around him and working my way back to the tip. His haggard moan was the perfect encouragement. I seriously doubted this was the first time Mitch Hudson had ever gotten head, but I'd be damned if it wouldn't be the best.

Mitch

I threaded my fingers through Andy's thick, red hair, shining copper in the light, and focused on not letting my knees buckle. Fuck, was this really happening? My mind couldn't wrap around it at all. One minute I'd been staring at the highest grade I've ever gotten in science, the next, Andy was on his knees with my dick in his mouth.

The barest hint of teeth brushed over my increasingly sensitive dick. I hissed and tightened my hold on his hair. I felt as much as heard him snicker as he swallowed around me. Fuck, that felt good. My grip relaxed as he found a steady rhythm, his tongue routinely wrapping around my shaft like he'd found the best damn lollipop in the world. I slid my fingers through his hair and refused to give into the urge to ram down his throat until I came or collapsed.

He pulled back with a slurping pop. I looked down as he continued to stroke me, but he wasn't looking at me. Without warning, he lapped at my sac, then promptly sucked a ball into the heat of his mouth.

"Mother of God!" I cried out. My relaxed hold on his hair turned white-knuckle as I rode out the sensation. He released it only to lavish attention on the other and my hold on him became the only thing keeping me upright. Fuck, why hadn't I thought to do this for him? No sooner did I adjust to the latest tide of stimulation than he swallowed my dick back down. I let out a strangled moan that he echoed. "Shit, sorry," I said and forced my hand to stop pulling sharply on his hair.

He hummed like he had earlier, and the vibrations rippled through my cock to wrap around the base of my spine. Fuck, I wasn't going to last much longer. Already my fingers tingled with the promise of imminent release. *Warn…need to warn him.* The thoughts came sluggishly as they forced themselves through the haze of mind-blowing sensation.

"A-Andy." His name came out raw and barely audible. I swallowed the zero moisture in my mouth. "And-dy, I'm… I'm gonna…" He swallowed me deeper than he had before and I lost the words. I lost everything as I shot down his throat. My fingers tightened in his hair once more and he moaned, but there wasn't a damn thing I could do about loosening the hold as my orgasm tore through me like a freight train. He finished licking me clean and I finally relinquished my death grip on his hair only to fist a hand in his shirt and drag him to his feet.

"Mi—"

I slammed my mouth on his, not caring that I could taste myself on his tongue. In fact, I sought out every trace of seed I could find until all that was left was Andy, pure, perfect Andy. At last, I pulled away, solely by virtue of the fact that I was out of breath. "Holy fucking shit, Andy. That was..." *Unexpected. Incredible. Insane.*

"An A-plus." He smirked, obviously satisfied with reducing me to an incoherent mess that couldn't finish a sentence.

"Fuck you." I laughed and yanked him in close, wrapping my arms around him, pinning his own between us, and rested my head on his. "Fuck," I repeated as I panted in his hair. By some miracle I hadn't actually pulled any of it out, though not for lack of trying. When my breathing finally got back under control, I whispered, "You didn't have to do that."

"I know," he said into my chest.

I counted it a special kind of victory that he hadn't pulled away yet and tightened my hold around him. While my body relaxed, my mind whirled in a million directions, most of which centered around how incredible the last ten minutes of my life had been.

Damn, Andy is good at that. Like really, really good.

I wasn't so naïve to think it would be the best blowjob I'd ever have, but it certainly held the record to date. My sigh of utter relaxation was halfway out when the realization of how Andy would have gotten so good at giving head finally sank in. The breath lodged in my throat and I lurched back. Andy on his knees for a bunch of faceless guys was not something I wanted to envision, but too late. The damage was done.

Andy tilted his head to the side and frowned as I put myself away, then leaned down to snatch the test off the floor. He followed my jerky movements, the concern on his face deepening. "Mitch?" I moved to grab my bag, and he placed a hand on my arm, halting me in my tracks. "Are you okay? Are...*we* okay?"

The uncertainty in his voice made me want to die. "Yeah," I croaked, not even the least bit believably.

"What is it?"

I grabbed at the first thing that came to mind. "You swallowed."

His eyes widened with surprise. "I knew what I was doing."

The image of Andy kneeling for some faceless stranger flashed again. I forced the image back with a rage that unnerved me, then proceeded to pummel the ever-loving shit out of it.

Something must have shown on my face, because he immediately added, "Shit. I didn't mean to upset you." The unexpected worry snapped me out of my downward spiral.

"What? No. I'm not…upset." A lie, but not the one he'd think. "I feel…" I floundered once more for something to fill the blank, anything to explain my weird ass reaction to getting blown by my best friend, literally the best of my life thus far. "Guilty." The word left my lips and dropped like a stone that grew until it filled the entire room.

Why the fuck did I say that?

Andy grabbed my bag from the ground while I remained frozen and incapable of breathing. A small smile turned up the corners of his mouth as he draped the strap over me, then placed his hands on my chest. Warmth pooled where his fingertips rested. I couldn't help but wonder if he could feel my heart racing beneath his palm or could tell that my lungs seemed to have forgotten how to work.

"You have nothing to feel guilty about." He rose on his toes and brushed his lips lightly over mine before lowering back down. "I'm really proud of you, Mitch." I stared into his green eyes framed with copper and took a shaky breath. He blinked as I let it out slowly and drew another. His freckles bunched as his smile grew. "What do you say we go acquire ourselves some well-earned pudding from the kitchen?"

"That sounds like a good idea."

"I agree," he said as he took the test from my limp fingers, slipped it back into the forgotten envelope, then secured it safely back in my bag. He turned away to grab his own things, then led the way to the secret door. He peered out into the hall, glanced over his shoulder at me, and eased out of the opening. I followed mutely after him, knowing now what I'd known all those years ago—Anderson Gallagher had the power to destroy me. The question was, would he still be there to pick up the pieces when he did?

Chapter 14

Mitch

Every muscle burned as I made a break for the goal. Dalton, our primary goalie, took a defensive stance in the crease, prepared to stop the play Brian and I were running. Brian skid short of the crease, but when the ball left his net, it didn't hurtle into the goal.

I swiveled on my heel, sweat streaming down my bare back, to catch the rubber ball flying toward me. As I turned, a flash of copper on the hillside snagged my attention. Andy. I did a double take. And Calvin. For a split second, I forgot about the ball racing toward me and fully capable of giving me a concussion. Was Andy here for me? Or was he here because Calvin was here? Calvin almost always watched our practices. The entire team knew; it wasn't like he was sly about it. But it was also an unspoken agreement, similar to the one I'd made about Andy, that Calvin was Benny's problem. If Benny wasn't doing anything about it, then none of us were going to bother either.

"Hudson!" Santinelli shouted from the sideline.

I shook off the distraction and held up my stick in time to get body-checked. Blue sky filled my vision as I hit the ground hard enough to crack my back and knock all the air from my lungs. I blinked in a daze as clouds lazily drifted across the sky far above and transported me back to a different time.

Andy and I were laying in the grass on a hot summer day. He'd come to visit me for a couple weeks and I'd just told him about how my father had died before I'd come to UPA. Unsurprisingly, he'd been supportive and empathetic, asking me questions about my dad, but never pushing. He even understood that I was still kind of angry at him.

At one point, while we were calling out shapes in the clouds, we'd gone into a companionable silence. Then he'd said that while he wasn't really religious, he believed my dad was still out there. Stating that energy could neither be created nor destroyed and at their core, wasn't that what souls were anyway? Pure energy. So, really, how cool was it that my dad was out there? He could be anything. A star, part of a new planet, maybe even a comet or black hole. But wherever he was, he was part of the fabric of the universe—just like I was.

He'd looked at me with those bright green eyes of his, a soft smile curling his lips. I knew then what I'd known the first time I'd met him, I—

"Mitch? Mitch. Can you hear me?"

I blinked a few times, but instead of Andy's warm eyes, Nate's dark blue ones greeted me. The happy memory continued to slip away like mist dissipating with the dawn. I groaned and rolled to my side.

"Shit, man. That was brutal. You alright?" Nate took a step back as I sat up and braced my stick across my knees, my breathing still pretty labored.

"Yeah. I'll be good."

"Hudson!" Coach shouted again as he stalked closer. "This is no time for chasing butterflies. Get your head in the game. You're no good to me if you're not on your feet." He jerked his thumb violently toward the locker rooms. "Hit the showers. Hawthorne, you go with him. Next time I see you out here, Hudson, your head better not be up your ass." With that, Santinelli stormed off, already barking orders at the rest of the team to get their shit together.

I fought the urge to hurl my stick at Santinelli's fat head. Fucking asshole.

"Come on, we better get going before he comes back." Nate extended a hand that I gratefully took. Without his help, I probably would have fallen back on my ass. "You good?" he asked again as he helped steady me.

I took a deep breath that felt like fire in my lungs and let it out slowly. "I'll live." We trudged in silence toward the lockers and I glanced over at him, noting the pinched line between his brows and the way his lips were pressed into a thin line. "I'm sorry."

"What for? It's not like you asked John to freaking demolish you."

I shook my head, though I couldn't say I was surprised. Despite hanging with the same crowd for years, I wasn't entirely convinced John actually liked me. "It's not fair that you got kicked from practice too. You didn't do anything." The rest of the team—hell, maybe not even coach—might not realize how hard Nate had been busting his ass to rise in the ranks, but I did.

"Eh, it's not like it really matters." He shrugged like it was nothing, but the defeat in his eyes betrayed him.

I threw an arm around his shoulders. "Fuck that noise. What do you say we get cleaned up and grab some ice cream from town?"

Nate looked at me like I'd lost my fucking mind, which, given my head-space over the last several weeks, wasn't entirely out of the question.

"What? You're rank, man," I said with a straight face.

He barked out a laugh, but thankfully didn't push me off. I definitely would have fallen on my ass. "You're on, but the first round is on you."

"First round? How much ice cream you planning to eat?" I teased.

Rather than answer, he held open the metal door for me. I slid free of his shoulders and made my way inside. It took me a shameful amount of time to get my bruised as fuck body cleaned and dried. But Nate didn't complain or rush me. He could be kind of a nuisance, but he was a real stand-up guy, always had been.

By the time we made it to town, the ache in my chest and back had mostly subsided. The bell over the door to the creamery dinged as we stepped in from the warm afternoon.

"Hello, boys. What'll it be?" the pretty young woman staffing the counter asked. I gestured for Nate to go first, and he didn't hesitate to step forward.

"I'll take a three scoop Neopolitan in a waffle cone, on his tab," he added with a smirk, pointing his thumb back at me.

I frowned as I joined him at the counter. "Really, man? Three scoops? How are you gonna eat all that before it melts?"

He flashed me a self-satisfied grin before walking off with zero shame to grab a drink at the water fountain while his obscene order was being put together.

"Lose a bet?" the young woman asked.

"Something like that. Can I get two scoops of mint chocolate chip in a waffle cone?"

She flashed a pleased smile and her cheeks turned rosy when I returned it. We were probably about the same age. This was likely her afternoon job, which made it unlikely that she attended the all girl's school.

I paid, leaving a hefty tip, and joined Nate at the table he'd claimed with both cones in hand. "Here's your monstrosity."

"It's not a monstrosity, it's a work of art."

I snorted and took a seat. "Whatever happened to committing to a flavor?"

"Neopolitan *is* a flavor," he countered as he tasted the top scoop.

"Maybe, but I don't really think independent scoops of chocolate, vanilla, and strawberry are the same thing."

"That's because you have a limited imagination."

I snorted. My imagination was plenty healthy, hence why the coach had accused me of chasing butterflies at practice...again. If I couldn't stop getting distracted by thoughts of Andy while there was a live ball, then I'd really get hurt instead of just getting my bell rung like earlier.

Nate leaned forward 'til his cone was practically dripping on the table and nodded toward the young woman that had fixed our ice creams. "What do you think of Deborah?"

Was that her name? I hadn't even looked. "She's cute," I said with a shrug. "Why do you ask?"

"I think she recently graduated from the public high school. Seen her around town a bit. She's super nice." Nate stared wistfully at the brunette currently greeting a small family.

"Oh yeah? You like her?" I crunched into a bite of chocolate. Nate and I had talked about girls throughout the years. Though, now that I thought about it, it had been a while. That was probably on me.

He ducked his head and hiked a shoulder. "Maybe. What about you? Now that you're single and all."

I winced inwardly and glanced at the young woman again. She really was cute and clearly every bit as sweet as the ice cream she served. Her brown hair was pulled back in a short bouncy ponytail and her apron hugged her curves in a way that was eye-catching without being lewd or inappropriate. From a purely subjective point of view, she was very attractive, classic girl-next-door, and...not my type in the least. I realized Nate was still waiting for a response and shifted my gaze back to him. "Nah, not really my jam."

Nate smirked. "That's right, she's not a redhead."

I nearly dropped my cone on the floor. "W-what?"

His cheeks tinged a light pink. "Word might have gotten around that the reason Trixie dyed her hair that awful burgundy color was because you said you were into redheads." He tilted his head to the side and considered me. "You were never really into her, were you?"

"Is it that obvious?" I asked with a grimace.

"Not to the rest of the crew, but we've been roommates for four years. You never seemed…excited to meet up with her."

I blanched and tried to hide it behind a giant chomp of ice cream that instantly made my teeth numb. If Nate had noticed that, what else had he noticed?

"Yo, don't worry. If you don't like her like that, then you don't. What I don't get is why you kept dating for so long if you weren't into it, not to mention telling her you prefer redheads."

I sighed and slouched in my chair, abandoning what was left of my ice cream. I had no idea how Nate had managed to go through so much of his. My stomach was churning from all the sugar. "Would you believe me if I said I tried *multiple* times to let her down easy? Everything from saying I didn't have time to date to outright telling her we should be friends. The hair thing was kind of a last ditch effort to get her to get the hint."

"Damn." Nate let out a low whistle. "Wish you'd have said something. I could have helped."

My lips twisted into a dubious frown. "How? By taking her off my hands?"

"Shit, man. No. I'm not an asshole like that," Nate said my forcefully than I expected. "I know I've joked about things in the past, but that was really for the rest of the guys. I wouldn't do that to you. But we could have figured *something* out. You shouldn't have to date someone you don't like just because everyone expects you to."

I swallowed and stared down at the linoleum tabletop. Maybe I should have given Nate more credit over the years, let him in a little more, instead of suffering in silence. "You're a great guy, Nate."

He rolled his eyes. "I know and nice guys always finish last." He scowled at the remnants of his cone before popping it in his mouth.

We stood, and I clasped him on the shoulder. "Not always. Don't do shit to appease the rest of the asshats. You're a good-looking guy and hella nice. Anyone would be lucky to have you. The way you *are*." I glanced over my shoulder to see what the adorable Deborah was doing—wiping down the counter and refilling the toppings. "I'm gonna pop outside and thaw a bit, maybe take a little walk. You go talk to Deborah."

Nate's mouth fell open and his gaze darted uncertainly to the young woman he was clearly crushing hard on. "I don't know if you've noticed, but I'm shit at talking to women."

"Take your time and be yourself. You've got this." I squeezed his shoulder and gave him a wink before making my way back into the sun.

Chapter 15

Andy

I glanced out the window at the stunning afternoon beyond, not paying nearly enough attention to the day's lesson. My gaze wandered over my peers, looking equally bored with Professor Isaac's monotone presentation about the awfulness that was the Twenties. I debated sneaking out one of my own books to read instead. It wouldn't be the first time I feigned absorption in the class text to hide a better book. But alas, Isaac had yet to direct us to a particular page or even to take out the massive history tomb. I slumped in my chair and continued to let my gaze wander, however when I caught sight of a familiar face in the small window of the door, I immediately straightened.

My eyes widened in alarm as Mitch smiled and offered a small wave, then pointed down. I frowned and shook my head slightly. His gaze darted to the professor, whose back was still to the class as he scratched out relevant events on the board and back to me. I did a quick survey of my peers to see if anyone else had noticed our audience, but everyone seemed thoroughly absorbed in their own misery. I brought my gaze back to Mitch and shook my head again. Was he crazy? What was he thinking popping up like that?

His hazel eyes rolled in obvious agitation, and he gestured more forcefully for me to look down. With a frown, I did so to see my expectantly bare desk. I looked back up at him and shrugged in confusion. He threw his hands up, and for a second, I thought he might have a fit right there in the hallway. Then he mimed a lifting motion.

I frowned harder and returned my attention to the desk. It didn't lift to reveal a storage cubby like the ones in the younger classes did. On a whim, I reached under the desk and felt around, praying I didn't encounter something gross. When my fingers found folded paper taped to the underside, my eyes widened in surprise and I glanced over at Mitch, still popping in and out of the window like a loon. He gave me two thumbs up and disappeared again.

I chewed on my bottom lip as I carefully extracted the paper and unfolded it in my lap. With a last look around to make sure no one was paying me any attention, I glanced down at the scribbled note.

Play hooky with me

I stared at the note, reading it several more times, but the four words didn't change. A quick glance at the door showed Mitch hadn't reappeared either. I quickly ran through all the reasons this was a horrible idea. I never skipped class. Except for recent events, I'd barely had a sick day. I couldn't simply walk out in the middle of a lesson. I just…couldn't.

I crumpled the paper and shoved it into my blazer pocket, then my arm went straight into the air. "Professor Isaac?"

The professor turned around and looked at me over his glasses. "Yes, Mr. Gallagher? Did you have a question?"

"No sir. I'm actually not feeling well and was wondering if I could be excused." Anxiety tightened around my chest at the bald-faced lie.

"I hope it's nothing too serious."

"I don't think so. Maybe just low blood sugar," I offered, already starting to wuss out.

To my amazement, Isaac nodded and gestured toward the door. "See that you take better care of yourself in the future, young man. Growing bodies need nourishment. As a matter of fact," he began as he turned back toward the board to resume the lesson.

I quickly scooped up my satchel and zipped out of the room before he could change his mind. Out in the hall, I shook my head and settled the bag more securely around me. "I can't believe that worked."

"What excuse did you use?"

I nearly leapt out of my skin. "Why do you always have to sneak up on me?"

He scoffed. "It's hardly sneaking if you already knew I was out here. It's not my fault you can't see what's in front of your own nose." I stuck my tongue out at him and he chuckled quietly. "Come on, let's drop your bag off and get you changed."

"What? Why?" I asked, suddenly realizing that Mitch wasn't in his school uniform, but in light denim and a faded green tee. My gaze rebelliously latched onto where the thin fabric stretched across his chest and my fingers buzzed with desire to reach out and smooth the wrinkled fabric. I jerked back to awareness as he divested me of my satchel.

"First, dropping off this monstrosity," he said as he slung the heavy bag over his own shoulder, "means you don't have to lug it around. Second, having it in your room will make it more believable that you've only stepped out for a minute. As for changing, it'd be pretty fucking conspicuous for us to be wandering around town in uniforms when we're supposed to be in class."

"We're going to town?"

"You have a better idea?" Mitch countered as he started walking toward the east dormitories. I faltered, momentarily surprised that he knew where my room was. Then I remembered he'd been there before. By the time I finally got my feet moving, he'd made it nearly all the way to the adjoining hall, walking like he didn't have a care in the world. I raced to catch up with him and he glanced over at me, humor dancing in his eyes right beside the mischief.

"Shut up. You know I don't skip."

"Didn't say anything," he said with a teasing smile that belied his words.

"You were thinking it."

"I'll have to keep better tabs on my thoughts if you've become a mind reader." He tossed me a crooked grin and turned the corner. I followed beside him and couldn't help but wonder what thoughts Mitch could possibly be worried about me reading.

Mitch

I couldn't say why I was shocked to discover Andy owned jeans, but I most definitely was, and skinny jeans to boot. They clung to his legs, outlining muscles with every step he took. He surged a couple paces ahead of me as my own steps slowed to appreciate how his equally fitted dark teal shirt shaped his back and stopped shy of his tight ass.

Stop thinking about Andy's tight ass.

Despite the order, my gaze lingered on the captured globes. Fuck, Andy looked good in jeans. Everyone knew that the school uniform wasn't doing anyone any favors, but this was a fucking crime. Suddenly, the ass I was not supposed to be staring at like some depraved lecher stopped moving. I quickly jerked my attention to somewhere safer, which happened to be a chalkboard sign on the sidewalk.

"You alright? What are you thinking about?"

Peeling you out of those tight pants and spanking that perfect ass until it burns red.

I blinked in alarm at the unexpected conclusion of the wicked thought. What was it about Andy that brought out the animal in me? Was it the air of innocence he still possessed even now, though I knew he was far from it? Was it that he was almost a year younger? Or was it me? Maybe I really was just a base animal that couldn't control himself.

"Hello. Earth to Mitch. Do you read me?" I blinked again to find Andy standing right in front of me, his auburn hair shining like the purest copper in the sunlight and his expressive emeralds flashing with humor.

"What? Yeah. I was just…" My gaze darted past him to the sign. "Reading." His eyes squinted as he frowned and I gestured behind him. "Isn't that the bookstore you used to sneak off to all the time?"

He twisted around to look and then turned back, his face morphing into shock. "You remember?"

There were a lot of things that I remembered, especially where Andy was concerned. I remembered how he hated carrots with a fiery passion of a thousand suns and how he believed that smoked Gouda was superior among cheese while Havarti could rot. I remembered how animated he got when plotting a prank or talking about his family. I remembered how his lips tasted and how his body seemed to fit my hands perfectly. I remembered how he always made me feel like a person, like I was enough.

I didn't say any of that, though. Instead, I smirked and said, "Of course." A smile that could light even the darkest room stretched across his face. "Also, it's literally the only bookstore in town."

His smile flipped into a scowl, and he popped me in the arm. "Just for that, we're going in."

Laughter bubbled out of me as he grabbed my arm and dragged me into the small shop crowded with every kind of book imaginable. "Okay, we're in," I said when he finally released me between two leaning towers of paperbacks.

"Oh, no you don't. We're not leaving until *you* get a book."

I shook my head. "I'm not a great reader like you, Andy. What good would a book do me?"

"Why do you do that?"

"Do what?" I asked as I plucked at a worn cover nearby.

"Belittle yourself."

"I do not," I scoffed, moving my attention to another frayed edge. His hand covered the fingers worrying the binding, and I met his steady gaze.

"Yes, you do. You're not dumb, Mitch. I keep telling you that. Maybe one day you'll believe it. As for what a book could do for you, books are an escape, a way to be someone else, even if it's only for a little while."

I curled my fingers inward, but his hand stayed over mine, his thumb absently stroking my wrist. My pulse pounded faster at the minute contact. Was it possible Andy really could read minds? That he already knew all the things I was too scared to say out loud?

He gave my hand a light squeeze and raised his eyebrows. "Still like sci-fi?"

I nodded without thinking as I leaned forward. This moment certainly felt like fiction and I'd do just about anything to keep it going. Andy's full lips quirked up in a soft smile and quickly became the only thing I could see. The thousands of books around us vanished, the musky scent of old paper and dust gone to be replaced entirely by Andy's herbal scent and the sensuous curve of his mouth.

"Come on." He squeezed my hand again, and I blinked to find the world once more as it should be.

I let out a sigh as the fantasy slipped through my fingers.

Andy nudged me in the ribs, his smile still bright and completely oblivious to my inner turmoil. Guess he couldn't read minds after all. If he could, maybe this wouldn't feel so fucking impossible. "Don't be like that. This place may not have the largest selection of literature, but I'm sure we'll find you something you'll enjoy." I smiled back at him—though I doubted it reached my eyes—and let him lead me deeper into the cavern of words.

An hour later, he did indeed find a book I found interesting enough to read about space pirates…because, well, fucking space pirates. We stepped up to the counter and he placed down not one, but five books.

"Really, Andy," I said as he added a tote with an image of a dragon curled around a hoard of books.

"What? I can't come to a bookstore and not very well buy a book. And we need something to carry them in since *someone* made me leave my satchel at the school."

"Well, *someone* carries too many things in said satchel. There wouldn't have been room anyway."

He snorted and thanked the cashier before shoving the receipt into the bag. Then he slung it over his shoulder, looking quite pleased with himself. "There's always room for books." He took a step toward the exit and I suddenly realized I had no idea where *my* book had gone.

"Shit."

"What's the matter?" he asked, his hand already on the door.

"I don't know where I put my book. Damn it, I actually really wanted to read that."

A smile brightened his whole face, and he patted his new bag. "I've got it."

"But… You didn't have to do that."

He shrugged and finished pushing the door open. "I wanted to. Besides, that's what friends are for, right?"

I floated in a haze of wonder as I trailed after him back into the lazy afternoon. Andy had actually called us friends, something I'd never thought to hear him say again after the horrible mess I'd made of our friendship. I was definitely reading that fucking book now.

Chapter 16

Mitch

I made my way down the hall scattered with the occasional student. Most of the school had taken advantage of the half-day to venture into town or catch up on assignments, leaving the walkways mostly abandoned. That suited me just fine. Pretending that I cared about the same things most of them did was getting harder every day. So what if Trixie was dating Ronald Harrington? Who cared that the lacrosse schedule had been rearranged or that the school board of trustees had their quarterly meeting coming up? Not me.

The hall turned and opened up to a larger passage. My pace quickened. I didn't want to be late for my study session with Andy, and I'd stupidly left my bag in my room. I may have done well on my midterms, but seasons weren't won by giving up on practice after winning one key game. Not to mention, I enjoyed my time with Andy. It was the rare occasion that I could actually be myself, that I didn't have to pretend. He didn't expect me to be perfect and didn't judge me when I struggled. The routine we'd fallen into mostly wasn't awkward as long as I didn't think about certain things and kept my hands to myself.

The adjoining hall that led to the dormitories came into view, and my stride lengthened. To my horror, Brian stepped out of the wing flanked by John, Kyle, and, of course, Nate. I cursed inwardly and nearly tripped. Brian's gaze roved the almost vacant hallway until it rested on me. His eyes narrowed, and he stalked forward, not at all his usual, easygoing self.

"Hey guys, what's up?" I asked as I forced my feet to keep moving forward instead of turning around and sprinting as fast as possible in the opposite direction, notes be damned. The group walked up the middle of the hall, blocking my original path. I veered to the side to go around. As one, the group shifted to cut me off once more.

"I'll tell you what's up. Where the fuck have you been?" Brian asked, his finger jabbing at me in the air.

I swallowed and took an involuntary step closer to the wall. "What do you mean? I've been here."

"You've been blowing off practice," Kyle said, his enormous arms crossed menacingly over his chest. As the school's starting goalie, Kyle really wasn't someone you wanted to be on the wrong side of.

"They aren't formal practices," I argued.

John scoffed. "You know as well as we do that doesn't mean shit as far as Coach is concerned. Practice is mandatory, formal or not."

"Excuse the fuck out of me for giving a shit about my grades," I snapped. Nate opened his mouth to—I hoped—back me up, but Brian held up a hand to cut him off before he got so much as a sound out.

"Since when is studying a priority? You've never shown any interest in it before. Why now?"

"Things are different." The truth about not wanting to play anymore sat on the tip of my tongue. But much as it burned in me to confess everything, I couldn't do it. Too much was at stake to take the risk.

"Different like how?" John asked, a scowl etched into his sunburned face.

"If you're worried about having grades good enough to get accepted to college, the scouts don't care. The school will take care of it," Nate offered in a way that I imagined he found helpful.

"Maybe I'm tired of the school taking care of everything. Is it so wrong to want to earn it on my own?"

"Yeah, it fucking is." Brian stepped forward and pushed me. I stumbled back into the wall and stared at him in shock. Brian and I were close, or as close as anyone on the team really was.

"What the fuck?" I moved to sidestep the lot of them, only to have Kyle cut off my escape with his imposing frame.

"You're not the only one on the team, Hudson. Don't dick this up for the rest of us," Kyle rumbled.

I let out an aggravated huff and directed my response to Brian, who was clearly in charge of this little intervention. "Look, I'll be at practice today, okay? Satisfied? Now, move, I have somewhere to be."

Brian placed a hand on my chest and forced me back against the wall. A growl slipped free before I could rein it in. He dropped his arm, but not the glower. “Not good enough. You need to fucking show up. None of this half-assed playing bullshit. You’re our lead Attackman. Act like it.”

“Fine, whatever.”

“You’re not hearing me. Either you get your shit together or we’ll be having this chat with your faggot tutor.”

My jaw. “Don’t talk about Andy like that. You know he’s off limits.”

“Not anymore," Kyle said, taking up a position beside Brian. "Consider your standing blanket of protection for that pillow-biter stripped. The fag is fair game.”

White-hot rage burned through me, getting hotter with each word. “You don’t fucking touch him.”

“What are you going to do about?” Brian glanced at the others, who all mirrored his sneer. “How do you think that pansy-ass, fucking queer—”

My fist hit Brian’s jaw mid-slur.

He stumbled back and looked up at me, clutching the side of his face. “You son of a motherfucking bitch!” He launched himself at me. Unfortunately, I didn’t get my hands up in time to prevent his own fist from slamming into my face. Stars exploded in my vision and all reasonable thought went up in smoke.

I pushed off the wall and caught Brian in the middle hard enough to send us both crashing to the ground. We scrabbled for the upper hand, pushing, pulling, and hitting whatever we could reach. Hands ripped at my shirt and arms until a hit from Brian sent me flying. I raced to get back on my feet, only to have John and Kyle crash into me while Brian regained his own footing.

Brian wiped at his mouth and looked at the blood on his fingers before stepping up to rejoin the others. “You’ll pay for that. Thought we were friends.” John moved aside and Brian’s fist landed squarely in my gut.

I clutched my middle and met him glare for glare. "Go fuck yourself."

Nate stepped forward and inserted himself between us. “Stop. This has gone too far. We’re going to get expelled and then no one plays.”

Brian fingered his jaw again. “No, we won’t.” He shoved Nate out of the way and pulled back his arm again.

Andy

I followed the noise until I turned a corner and found the source. Nathaniel stumbled back as Brian pushed him out of the way to get to Mitch. Both of their faces twisted into snarls as they slammed into each other with enough force to make me flinch. John and Kyle leapt in to join the fray, clearly eager to get their licks in. Without a second thought, I dropped my bag and sprinted toward them. My feet skidded across the floor with a horrible screech as I came to an abrupt halt and slammed into John. He flew back, and I spun to face Kyle just in time to get socked in the mouth.

I tasted the metallic tang of what was undoubtedly a split lip and clocked Kyle right back. The shock on his face before he fell was well worth any reprisal I might endure. A glance over at John revealed he was well on his way to regaining his bearings. Meanwhile, Brian and Mitch were in a free for all of swinging fists, rolling on the ground. Nathaniel spun to confront me. Instead of waiting to find out what he would do, I barreled into him with my full weight. While not much compared to his, it was sufficient. Not expecting the hit, he fell hard into Brian, who'd just come out on top. The two crashed to the ground in a heap of angry limbs, shoving at each other and spitting curses.

Mitch scrambled to his feet then immediately began advancing on Brian, unadulterated rage sparking in his eyes. I caught his arm, and he looked down at me. He blinked, and the fury clouding his vision gave way to surprise. "Andy? What are you doing here?"

"Saving your dumb ass. Come on, let's go." I tugged on his arm.

He stumbled a couple of steps, then pulled back as he looked around at the others. "But—"

"But, nothing. We need to get out of here before any of the faculty shows up." I yanked harder on his arm and he fell into a lurching run. We sprinted through the dormitories, which were mercifully empty, until we skidded up to a side exit.

"Where are you going? They'll just find us again." Mitch panted beside me, hands on his knees, casting furtive glances down the twist of hallways we'd navigated.

"Trust me. I know a place." My fingers brushed the hidden key at the top of the doorjamb as I winked at him. I quickly used it to open the exit. Sunlight poured through the opening, momentarily blinding me. I stashed the key back where I'd found it and dragged Mitch through the opening. He hesitated, and I rolled my eyes. "It automatically locks. Now, come on."

Not a soul watched us slip out of the dorms or skirt along the outer buildings or even bolt across the quarter mile of open terrain. Few had any reason to venture this far north of the campus. Well, few without illicit intents. I smiled as I spied our destination lurking on the edge of the woods. The forgotten shack held a plethora of discarded junk from the school, everything from canoes and nets for a lake commandeered by the township a decade ago to outdated sports equipment from the seventies.

"How did you find this place?" Mitch asked, turning in a circle as he gawked at all the stuff.

I moved over to one of the grime covered windows and shifted a moth-eaten sheet to allow a ray of dim light into the otherwise dreary room. "You're not the only one who finds neat places." Truthfully, Connor had found it, then shared it with me while we'd been dating. It was the perfect spot to get lost for a few hours without worrying about someone showing up unexpectedly.

Mitch glanced over at me like he wanted to ask another question, but returned his attention to the room at large instead. "This place is freaking ancient."

"Been here at least forty years." I squatted down and swiped a finger along the dusty floor. "Better news, no one has been here for a while. They won't think to look for us here. I doubt they even know it exists."

"That's a relief." There was a brief pause, and then, "Fuck."

I looked up at the expletive and found Mitch plucking at his ripped shirt. My gaze traveled up his long torso to his mouth twisted into a frown and the rest of the damage that had been done to him. Brushing my hands off, I stood and walked over. "You gonna tell me what all that was about?"

Mitch's shoulders stiffened and his gaze darted off to the side. It seemed like that would be the only answer I'd get when he broke the silence. "The team isn't happy about how much practice I've been missing."

I frowned. "Okay, but it's not like you're skipping for the hell of it. You're studying."

"They don't see it that way." His shoulders sagged. The heavy air of defeat around him hurt my heart.

"I don't get it. If they're so fucking awful, why do you stay? Just quit the team. No one deserves to be treated like that."

He let out a cynical laugh and lifted his gaze to meet mine. "If only it were that easy."

I wanted to argue that it was. All he had to do was walk away. He wouldn't be alone. He'd have me. But the sheer level of sadness swimming in his eyes held my tongue. "You're gonna have one hell of a shiner," I said instead, indicating Mitch's face. A little closer and I could actually touch him. I fought back the impulse to do exactly that and dropped my hand even as he raised his, and took a step back.

He flinched as he touched the quickly purpling bruise on his cheek, dangerously close to his eye. Even in the gloom, it was easy to tell the bruise would be massive. "You didn't get off so unscathed yourself," he commented in return.

"What do you mean?" I asked, stopping my retreat.

He took a step closer, shrinking the distance I'd opened between us, and reached out. His thumb brushed lightly along my bottom lip. A jolt of electric pain shot through me at the contact. He took another half step closer, all but eliminating the meager distance remaining. His brow furrowed, as if he was inspecting the damage. "Looks like it hurts," he whispered.

My mouth parted slightly as his thumb traced the path again. I wanted to tell him it didn't hurt, but wasn't sure I trusted myself to speak. Not when he was so close and all I could think about was how good his hands felt. Then his lips closed on mine, harsh and needy. His insistence swallowed the resulting sharp lance of pain as the force re-split my lip. I didn't care. Any pain was worth enduring if it meant I could have Mitch like this. Desperately, or maybe stupidly, I kissed him back every bit as feverishly. The heady mix of pain and pleasure making me higher than I already was.

Suddenly, he pulled away, our lips sticking together until the last possible second. My heart raced even as my breaths got shallower. Every cell in my body zeroed in on him, inexplicably and perfectly in tune with his every movement.

His eyes widened, and he dropped his hand as if finally realizing what he'd done. "I'm sorry, I..." he stuttered.

"Take it off," I ordered.

"Take what off?"

"All of it," I said, and eliminated the distance. My mouth closed over his like I planned to suck the very essence of him out while my fingers set to work eliminating his ruined shirt.

He shrugged his shoulders back as I forced the material off of him. The shirt fell to the floor with a muffled thump. I expected him to argue like he had when I'd gotten to my knees, but he didn't. He separated from my mouth long enough to pull his undershirt over his head and kick off his shoes while I tackled his pants.

My fingers touched bare skin and my mind went utterly blank. All that existed was the warmth suffusing my hand as I ran it up his torso. I was touching Mitch. Finally, after all this time. Logic struggled back to the forefront and brought with it caution. Already I was losing myself in him. I mentally shook myself out of the fog that had swallowed me.

Control. I can do this if I stay in control.

Chapter 17

Mitch

Andy grabbed my arm for the fifth time that afternoon and dragged me around a pile of junk. On the other side, the space was remarkably clear and dominated by a makeshift cot. Andy fluffed the sheet and a cloud of dust went up. I fanned the motes out of my face and was rewarded with the vision of Andy finally stripping his own clothes off. I suppressed a groan and hated how hard I was just at the promise of touching his bare skin.

He kicked away his pants, then stepped close to yank me down for another searing kiss. My hands automatically went around his waist, but he stepped back again before I could crush him against me.

"Where the fuck did I put it?" he mumbled to himself as he searched along some cluttered shelves. "Ah-ha." He pulled out a small bottle, then promptly flipped it over to read something on the bottom. Then he checked a string a square foils. How he could read anything in this gloom was beyond me, but it didn't stop him from concluding, "Still good. Perfect." He set it back down within easy reach of the odd pallet. I pushed away all thoughts about why this cot, a bottle of lube, and condoms would be here—or how Andy would know about them—and focused on the only thing that mattered right then. This was actually happening.

I stepped back in close and caught his face so I could steal another kiss. Even after all this time, Andy still had the softest lips I'd ever tasted. I hungrily snatched at them, mindless of what that could say about me. My hand ran down his side while I shifted my focus to his neck. He let out a soft moan and shuddered. My hand continued to rove until it rounded over his ass. I pressed him against me and a groan rose from my throat, deep and almost feral.

He yanked back, the sound of our combined harsh breathing filling the otherwise silent space. His eyes practically burned as he took in every inch of me from head to toe. "Hands and knees."

I took a whole step forward before I faltered. Had I heard that right? He caught the hesitation, but didn't move.

"You can say no, and this is as far as this goes."

I blinked, still struggling to process the unexpected development, and searched his face while my mind ran a veritable gauntlet. Could I do this? Could I really bottom for Andy?

His face softened. "You don't have to do anything you don't want to. All you have to do is say the word."

Consent. He was asking for consent. Exactly what I should have done four years ago. I swallowed hard and stepped closer, my mind already made up. "Okay." I leaned forward and swiped my mouth against his, the sharp tang of metal from the split in his lip grounding me.

I can do this.

Without another word, I did exactly as he'd instructed and got on my hands and knees. Embarrassment warred with doubt as I felt him move behind me. I told them both to shut the fuck up and tried to relax.

He placed a hand on my hip, and I flinched. "I promise I won't hurt you. You can stop this anytime. No questions. No guilt. We walk away like it never happened."

I seriously doubted that last was evenly remotely possible given how far things had already gone, but even if it was true, I had no intention of backing out now. I glanced over my shoulder at him. He knelt behind me every bit as naked as I, his red hair blazing in the thin ray of light he'd let in earlier. A tightness in my chest loosened. That was enough. "I trust you."

He leaned forward to snag a quick kiss, his body pressing against mine as he laid across my back to reach my mouth. All too soon, though, the skin to skin I ached for was gone.

I dropped my head between my shoulders and worked on not freaking the fuck out about what was about to happen. It couldn't be all bad, right? I wasn't dumb. Plenty of guys bottomed. It was normal; it was balance; it was… A slick finger slid delicately over my hole and I yelped in surprise.

"Sorry, should have warned you it'd be a little cold." He chuckled, but didn't remove his hand. Truth was, the temperature had little to do with it, and it didn't hurt, it felt…nice? "Remember, all you have to do is say the word."

I nodded, and it turned out that was my warning as he slowly worked his slim finger inside.

My entire body rebelled at the intrusion, even my shoulders clenched and my fingers white-knuckled in the sheet. I focused on my breathing and worked through convincing each muscle to relax. It didn't hurt exactly; it was just weird, and I felt exposed, like I was on display. My cheeks burned and suddenly I was grateful Andy couldn't see my face.

"There you go," Andy whispered as he deliberately moved his finger in and out, ratcheting up the weirdness to a million.

When he added another, I almost called it quits, promise to myself or not. Then he pressed all the way in and curled his fingers as if looking for something. I was about to ask him what the fuck he expected to find when pleasure hummed through me like someone had hit a bell. A moan nearly choked me, and Andy chuckled again.

"*That* is called your prostate." He stroked it again just as gently, and my cock twitched back to life. "You're welcome."

"Are you planning to give me anatomy lessons the whole time?" I panted as he continued to methodically work me open, ensuring to show attention to the treasure he'd found.

"Would it help?" The laughter on the edge of his voice spread a warmth through me I hadn't expected.

Fuck me, yeah, it probably would.

I was about to tell him as much when he removed his fingers. Never in a million years would I have thought I'd actually miss them. Then something decidedly not an index finger pressed against my hole and I shot straight back to panic. He worked his way in with slow, shallow thrusts like he had with his fingers, and I worked on the same process of forcing myself to calm the fuck down. Behind me, Andy's ragged breathing mirrored my own and guilt surged through me. Had he been this freaked when I…

He slid deeper suddenly, and I nearly choked at the incredible fullness of having all of him. "We can stop," he said softly as he held perfectly still.

My thoughts whirled in a million directions until they all circled one. *I can do this.* "No," I finally croaked, then immediately panicked again when I realized how that might sound. "Keep going."

His hands stroked lightly up my sides as far as his reach would allow and flowed their way back down, tracing every minute outline of muscle I had as if following a map. The anxiety coiled in my chest eased again and I let out a breath. That. I needed Andy to touch me, ground me, remind me it was him.

"Curiosity killed the cat," Andy whispered.

I took another deep breath. "Satisfaction brought it back."

His thumbs stroked over the dimples in my back. "Tell me when you're ready." The thoughtful check-in only served to further highlight the differences between this and all of my other experiences. Andy may not like it, but he cared. He was still my best friend, and that was all I needed.

"Okay. I'm good."

His rhythm started slow and purposeful. Thankfully, I didn't tense up again and the foreign sensation settled into an interesting buildup of pressure. An odd sort of good I hadn't expected. He sank all the way in and on the backstroke, adjusted his hips. I gasped as his ensuing thrusts stroked over my prostate again and again. Andy's pants filled my ears, joining my own as well as a moan. Because fuck, that felt good.

"Give me your hand."

I didn't even think, just adjusted my balance and did as he said. He took it and guided it to my outrageously hard dick where his fingers wrapped around mine. The groan that fell out of me wasn't even human as I tightened my hold, and fuck, if Andy guiding my hand didn't instantly become the single most erotic moment of my life. My entire body stiffened as my orgasm hit me with the same surprise everything else had.

"Shit. Fuck," Andy hissed. Then he was gone and my ass was left clenching nothing. I moaned at the awful ache of emptiness while Andy's heavy breathing increased until he grunted and his own release splattered across my back. I dropped my hand to the ground before I could fall over from the head rush.

Andy

I stayed fixed to the ground for a solid minute, as if roots had sprouted from my knees and sunk through the layers of flooring and earth. Gradually, my breathing returned to normal, and I blinked away the last of my post-orgasm fog. The splatters of cum across Mitch's back stood out in stark contrast to his tan skin, and my stomach twisted.

Check on him. I need to check on him.

Despite knowing what I needed to do, those weren't the words that came out of my mouth as I stood on shaking legs and kicked the used condom out of sight. "Give me a second to find a towel or something. Don't move."

"Fuck that," he grumbled, and promptly rolled away from his own mess to lie on his back. He let out a sigh and closed his eyes without glancing over at me. The insecurity I thought long since buried reared its head as if its grave had been a shallow one instead of the deepest pit I could dig. My gaze kept sliding over the rumpled sheets to the evidence of Mitch's release.

Why did I think this was a good idea? Why didn't he call my bluff?

"That was…different."

My gaze flicked back to Mitch's face. He blinked at the ceiling, then turned his head to look at me. I braced myself for the worst. When I wanted to break something, I really went all fucking out. "Bad different?"

His mouth didn't curve into a smile, but it seemed to shine in his eyes. "No. Just…different."

I shakily released the death grip on my anxiety and extended a hand to help him up. "We should probably get going before it gets too late." His strong fingers wrapped around my forearm and my heart thudded hard at the feel of his hands on me.

"Yeah. And I have a practice I have to get to."

"You can't be serious." He snorted in response and I fought the urge to shake my head in disbelief, or better, argue. How could he possibly want to go to that stupid practice after what his teammates had done? After what we'd done? Sure, the fight had been about his missing practice, but surely his black eye was reason enough to skip, not to mention how uncomfortable he'd be.

He straightened up, and though he tried to hide it, I caught the twinge of discomfort. I'd prepped him as much as possible, but all the prepping in the world couldn't account for the sheer newness, that ache of emptiness after being so full.

I miss that.

I ruthlessly crushed the rogue yearning. I didn't bottom, not anymore, not for a long time. Of course, losing control like I had today also wasn't something I ever did either. Mitch released my arm, and I bent to grab my clothes from the floor. Doubt continued to ricochet inside me as he walked around the barrier meant to obscure the cot from anyone that might happen by to retrieve his ruined uniform. I focused on setting myself to rights before joining him. At the vision of Mitch's sculpted back, though, my fingers faltered on the last few of my shirt buttons as they remembered what he'd felt like beneath them. *Warm, hard yet pliable…mine*. I shook off the thoughts and forced my fingers back to their task, then found my shoes.

"Probably a good thing they'll bench you after what happened," I said to distract myself.

"They won't."

I glanced up at his deadpan response, but he still had his back to me. A surge of worry snuffed out my rampant anxiety. I finished tying my shoe and stood. "Then I suggest you find some way to sit out."

Mitch turned and gave me one of the saddest looks I'd ever seen mar his beautiful face. "You know I can't do that, *especially* after the fight."

All of my doubts about what we'd done officially took a backseat to my concern for his wellbeing. He'd said before that he didn't want to play anymore, had dropped countless clues over the last several weeks, but only now was I finally getting the full picture of what these last four years had done to him. The tightness around his eyes spoke of an exhaustion that had nothing to do with the physical. The slump of his shoulders stood testament to a wariness that came from being beaten down constantly. Was it possible that I was the only person in Mitch's life that actually saw any of this? That cared?

"Mitch."

He sighed and stepped closer. I was so busy searching his face, the sudden press of his lips against mine took me by surprise. Where the kiss before had been borderline manic in its fervor, this one was slow and purposeful. It wrapped gently around my heart and called to the deepest parts of me that seemed to exist solely for him. When Mitch pulled away, he took a part of me with him. I licked my lips, tasting him there, along with a longing I didn't dare entertain.

"You could always pretend to be sick. I've got an excellent trick for that."

He laughed quietly and touched his forehead briefly against mine before leaning back. "Thank you for caring."

My heart twisted in my chest at the unwitting confirmation of my suspicion that no one was looking out for Mitch. "That's what friends do."

"You're right." His hazel eyes glowed with the same small smile that tugged at his lips. "You're right."

"I'm usually right."

He laughed softly again as he trailed the backs of his fingers along my cheek, then dropped his hand. "Okay, smarty pants, know a way out of here that doesn't land us in hot water?"

I offered him a crooked smile and stepped past him to the back wall. "Is that a real question, or are you actually doubting me?" I asked with raised eyebrows as I pushed open the nearly invisible back door. Beyond, the dense foliage of a forest unwilling to give up its evergreen crowded up to the shack.

"You sly bastard," he said in awe as he approached the open doorway and the late afternoon light.

I gestured to our left at a narrow path that hugged the building and disappeared into the tree line. "If you head that way, you'll end up at the Green in about half a mile. I'll go the opposite way and circle back to the dorm. Or…" I trailed off, not sure how willing I was to tempt this unusual easiness we'd stumbled upon.

Mitch stepped in close while I floundered, invading my personal bubble once again. I fought the urge to swallow and betray the nerves his presence caused me while my heart struggled to find its normal rhythm. "Or," he prompted.

"Or we could walk straight ahead together and…" *And never look back.* "And then part in three-quarters of a mile. That would put you at the practice field sooner."

Mitch looked back at me with those startling perceptive eyes, his lips hovering centimeters away from mine. "And where will that leave you?"

As much a fool for you as I've always been.

I swallowed down the honesty, giving way to my anxiety at last. "I'm not worried about me."

We stared at each other for a moment that stretched into eternity, then Mitch took a step back and looked away. "I don't want to risk it."

The words were like ice water being dumped over my head. Of course not. The whole point was to not get caught together. Taking the alternative path just to steal a few extra minutes together was stupid, reckless. I nodded and took a step toward the winding path that extended in the opposite direction of Mitch's destination.

"Andy."

My traitorous heart hammered against my ribs as I looked back at him over my shoulder.

"I..." He hesitated, then seemed to change his mind. "Be careful. I'll see you tomorrow at lunch," he finished, then turned and settled into a slow jog. I watched him go until the sweep of branches completely obscured him.

Chapter 18

Mitch

Andy was right. I should have skipped practice, and it had absolutely nothing to do with the sting in my ass. *That* I could work with. What I couldn't was the way the team watched every move I made as I stepped into the locker room. Brian especially gave me such a withering expression that my skin should have blistered. Much like mine, parts of his face were swollen, and Kyle and John didn't look any better, though I couldn't recall ever hitting Kyle. Maybe I had. The whole fight was a blur.

I glanced toward the far end of the locker room where, mercifully, fewer people were staring at me like I was an ant under a microscope. As promised, the walk here had been relatively short, but it had been long enough for all the aches and pains to truly set in. I wanted a shower something fierce—for hot water to pummel relaxation into my sore muscles. Considering how much my ribs hurt, I was a little surprised Andy hadn't remarked on any other obvious bruises. But a shower would be weird. No matter that I still had dried blood on my cheekbone.

I took a deep breath that my ribs instantly protested and made my way to my locker. A few of the guys went back to getting ready for practice as I peeled off my ripped shirt with care. I was focusing on not falling over when Kyle's voice boomed loud next to my ear.

"Where's your twink-ass little friend?"

I glanced at him in confusion. First off, Andy wasn't a twink and Kyle calling him one told me he'd never actually *seen* a real twink. Second, why the fuck would Andy be in the lacrosse locker rooms? Before I could find any words, though, Brian cut in.

"You've got some balls, Hudson." Not an uncommon phrase for this group, but normally it was followed by rowdy cheers and ribbing. Brian's face had yet to lose the scowl and his voice had a definite note of challenge.

I reached into the locker, ignoring the pain that lanced across my side, and grabbed the armless tank. Brian's face continued to darken as I pulled it over my head, then reached for my shorts. "Would have thought you'd be pleased. After all, my *balls* are here."

Brian's lip curled while John tried to hide a snort of laughter behind a cough. "You're damn right they are. And you'll keep them here or—"

I finished adjusting the drawstring on my shorts and cut a look at Brian. "Or what? You gonna find a new attackman that can score like I can? You gonna convince coach to let Hendricks start? Tell me, what the fuck are you gonna do, Brian?"

He narrowed his eyes at me and dropped his voice. "You can't watch him twenty-four-seven, Mitch. You so much as show up late for one practice and our next...*conversation* will be with Gallagher."

My throat stuck as I fought the urge to swallow hard. When had my friends gotten so violent? Had they always been this way, and I'd just been too out of it to notice?

"But, Daniels, I wanted to get some payback on that fire crotch," Kyle griped as he rubbed his jaw. I did a double take. *Andy* had done that to Kyle's face? Shit, I needed to give him a high five...and probably make sure he hadn't split his knuckles.

Brian continued to glare at me as he answered our whiny companion, "And you'll have it." Kyle was on his way to a full-out celebration when Brian held up a hand and cut his gaze to him. "The second Hudson stops being a team player. Understood?" he finished, making sure I realized the question was for me as well.

"Ugh." Kyle groaned like it was the worst news he'd received all year. "Yeah, yeah, I get it. Little shit gets to keep his face the way it is...for now." Still grumbling to himself, Kyle walked off, leaving me with Brian and John, who still hadn't moved or spoken since he'd propped a shoulder on the locker beside me.

Brian's hard stare bored into me until I nodded. Then the grim line of his lips flipped into a grin and he clapped me on the shoulder. I nearly dropped from the sheer shock of the one-eighty. "You've got a hell of a right hook on you, Hudson. Let's see if we can't put it to better use on the field." He squeezed my shoulder a hair tighter than normal, then gestured for John to follow him. "See you out there."

I waited until most of the team had filtered out of the locker rooms before sagging against my locker. The cool metal on my back didn't do shit for the sting behind my eyes or the tightness in my chest. Not a one of my teammates had batted an eye as Brian and Kyle blatantly threatened bodily harm to Andy. Not a one had moved to interfere or stop them from cornering me. I don't know what I'd been expecting, but clearly my belief that we had each others' backs was a delusion. This wasn't a team, this was a cult. I bent down to slip on my sneakers, painfully aware of how tight my body had become. I'd been so close to escaping, to finding happiness, but if I put even a toe out of line, it wouldn't be my ass they came for.

I straightened and shook out the tension threatening to pull me under. Andy's worried face from the shack filled my vision and determination burned in my veins. "I can do this. I can be the person they want *and* fix our friendship. I won't be forced to choose, not again."

"Hudson, who are you talking to? And what the hell happened to your face?" Coach Santinelli asked as he exited his office.

"No one. Nothing, sir," I replied quickly.

He squinted at me a moment. "Good, then get your ass out there and start running suicides. And while you're at it, have Hendricks and Bellwether join you."

I kept my groan to myself and gave him a sharp nod. "Yes, sir." Then I turned on my heel and jogged out of the locker rooms to give the others the bad news.

Andy

The public library was more populated than I'd expected, but the constant sound of people searching for books and whispering was oddly comforting. I made a mental note to come by more often. While Ulwich's library might be more grand, the town library had a significantly better selection of fiction and horror, not to mention fewer people who wanted to make my life a living hell.

I glanced at the stack of books I'd checked out about half an hour before in complete disregard of the TBR pile waiting for me at the dorm. The plan had been to read at the little table I'd secured by one of the tempered glass windows while I waited for Calvin to finish at the church, but I hadn't so much as cracked a single book. Instead, I kept replaying the events of the last couple of weeks.

I still couldn't get over how...*normal* lunch with Mitch had been. He'd let me top him and the next time we'd seen each other it hadn't been weird or strained, or tense, though I was dying to know how he'd got through practice. If I'd been braver, I might have found a secluded spot to watch the practice for myself, but I'd gone straight back to my room where I'd worried myself sick. And yet, lunch had been normal, our study sessions continued to *be* normal. But I couldn't wrap my head around how. What was I missing? There had to be something. Something staring me in the face. But what?

"Fancy meeting you here," Calvin said as he dropped into an empty chair across from me. He unwound a fancy blue scarf from around his neck. I'd never gotten into fashion or fabrics, but knowing Calvin, it was probably cashmere. He set it beside him, but left his light jacket on. Fall had turned crisp without much warning, unless you took into account that it did that every year around the end of October. Finally, after all the production, he pushed his curls out of his face and leaned forward to rest on his forearms. "Been here long?"

I gave him a wry expression. "Don't pretend like you aren't hoping that I'm ready to go."

He placed all ten fingertips against his chest. "Moi?"

"You can save the act. I'm all set," I said as I reached for the bag holding my latest acquisitions.

"Oh, thank God, I'm starved."

I chuckled as he wrapped the scarf he'd literally just taken off back around his neck in a double loop. "Work up an appetite with all that confessing?" I teased.

"You have *no* idea." Where I'd expected his usual theatric flare, he actually sounded sincere.

I hesitated with the strap over my shoulder, but the weight of the bag still resting on the mahogany table. "Is everything okay? I know I've been..." I rolled my shoulders, not ready to admit to the quagmire of Mitch-drama I'd landed myself in, not even to Calvin. "But you can always talk to me. I'm still here."

Calvin stopped fiddling with placing his scarf just so and gave me a considering look. After a few seconds, a soft smile lightened his expression. "Thank you, that... It means a lot to hear you say that."

Despite the nice way he said it, I felt sucker-punched. What the fuck had I missed? How shitty of a friend did I have to be not to know something was clearly going on with him? I shifted the full weight of the bag to my shoulder and walked with him out of the library. Once outside, I cleared my throat and glanced at him out of the corner of my eye. "So, um, *is* there something you wanted to talk about?"

He turned slightly to look at me and lifted a dark brow as we set off in search of sustenance. "Is there something *you'd* like to talk about?"

I nearly swallowed my tongue. It never ceased to amaze me just how *good* Calvin was at reading people. You'd think after four years of friendship I'd be able to remember these things. But I'd also been a major suck of a friend lately. The least I could do was give him honesty. "Short answer? No. Long answer...yes."

He threw his head back with a hearty laugh. "Those are both short answers, Gallagher."

I chuckled and rubbed the side of my nose. "Suppose they are."

"Maybe. But I think I know what you mean, and I'm right there with you."

I paused on the sidewalk. The savory scents of authentic Italian wafting around us from one of our favorite places. "Really?"

"Yeah." He nodded a few times. "Yeah," he repeated, then gestured to the entrance of Capri. "How about here?"

"Smells good to me."

He laughed and pushed open the door, simultaneously signaling the host for two while holding the door for me. "Seriously, Andy, don't you have enough books?"

"That would be like me asking if you have enough art supplies," I countered as I let the heavy bag drop to the floor and took a seat at the table they had directed us to. Thankfully, we seemed to have beat the dinner crowd and hadn't needed to wait.

"Which you've totally done," he said in an appropriately scandalized voice. Unlike at the library, Calvin removed both his scarf and jacket, which he draped with care over the empty chair beside him before settling in.

I waved him off and kept my sweater decidedly on. It was always too cold in this place. "Know what you're having?" I asked as I peered at the menu.

"Still thinking. You?"

"Leaning toward my usual."

"Of course you are," he mumbled as he continued to peruse his own menu with intense focus, as if we hadn't been here dozens of times.

The server approached the table, effectively heading off my rebuttal. "Good afternoon. My name is Patrick. What can I get you?"

"Two waters to start, and I believe I'm ready to order." I glanced at Calvin, who gave me a quick nod, then passed my menu to Patrick. "I'll have the chicken and shrimp carbonara."

Calvin snapped his menu shut and passed it to the server as well. "And I'll have the day's special."

Patrick tucked the menus beneath an arm. "How would you like your steak?"

"Medium, unless the chef would recommend it another way. Thank you."

Patrick nodded. "Will there be anything else?"

"Fried mozzarella," we said the same time. "And a side of sour cream," I added.

"I'll have your waters right out," Patrick said before leaving to put our order in.

I leaned back in my chair and looked at Calvin. "You had no idea the special today featured steak, did you?"

"*No*," he groaned. "And now I *really* want a bottle of Hamacher Pinot Noir." He gave an exaggerated pout. Besides the fact that I seriously doubted they had that exact bottle here, no way were they serving us alcohol without our IDs showing twenty-one.

"Woe is you," I said with a laugh.

"For real." He glanced off in the direction our server had gone. "Maybe Patrick will be my consolation dessert," he said wistfully.

"Calvin!" I shout whispered and tried not to let my laughter get out of control.

He shrugged. "What? He's cute."

I rolled my eyes and shook my head. "Okay, yeah, he is kind of cute."

Calvin did a prim shoulder shrug as if to say "See?" then he unrolled his cutlery with a flourish, placing the napkin across his lap. "Now I want to hear all about how your application to Chicago is going."

Our waters arrived—mercifully, after we'd both admitted to how cute the server was—and I lifted my glass. "Only if you do the same."

He smiled and mirrored me, clinking our glasses together. "Done." We never really talked about how we might end up at the same university, but I had to confess, the possibility held a certain amount of appeal.

Chapter 19

Mitch

I smiled at Brian's antics as the team filed out of the lockers, a little because I should and a little because I wanted to. We may not see eye to eye on a lot of things, but I couldn't begrudge his dedication to the team or his rightful title of captain. Also, there was the small fact that he was supposed to be my best friend…on the team anyway. The fight in the hall had already become old news, swept under the rug and out of sight exactly like I'd expected it would. Of course, just because no one was talking about it didn't mean I wasn't still paying the consequences.

The team split apart into predetermined groups for drills, and I fell in step beside Hendricks and Smith to run laps around the practice field. The three of us settled into an easy jog to warm up that would undoubtedly turn into grueling sprints the second coach realized his shitlist wasn't giving it their all. I glanced over at Oliver Smith and wondered what he'd done to land himself here. Hendricks, I knew. Guy tried way too hard to stand out. And while he had talent, he played angry, like he had something to prove, and too often let his mouth run away with him. For that alone, he'd probably never make it to a starting a position.

Head down, focus ahead, do as you're told. That's the only way any of us make it out of here.

I followed my advice and hunkered down, pulling ahead of the others. At least today, my ass didn't hurt like it had been when the coach had originally ordered me to run laps before practice. I shook my head and pushed the memory away. Practice would never be a safe place to think about Andy. Not the way he hadn't hesitated to tell me exactly what to do or the way he'd taken care of me, and definitely not the way he'd seemed to genuinely care. I growled to myself and poured on more speed until my lungs and legs burned in unison.

Browning grass raced beneath my feet and in my periphery, I caught sight of the other two gaining ground. We made another complete circuit and Coach glanced our way, but didn't give us the nod to stop. I growled my frustration at being forced to continue instead of training properly like the others. My gaze flicked over at a low laugh beside me, where Connor's long legs easily kept pace with my strides.

"Welcome to the B-team. How many weeks is this now?"

"Fuck off, Hendricks."

He did a bit of fancy footwork that undoubtedly had gotten him on the team in the first place and started running backwards, now doing double time to keep up. "Hey, does this mean you'll be riding the pine this spring and someone else will get to play for change?" He smirked, and I debated telling him it was his smart mouth keeping him from starting.

"We're supposed to be running, not talking." I pushed my straining limbs harder to outstrip him, but the fucker switched to running normal again.

"Yeah, but talking is more fun. Besides, you're not *winded,* are you? Maybe you should volunteer to take a back seat and let someone else shine."

"Chill out, Connor," Oliver wheezed behind us, struggling to keep up with our increasing speed. "Are you trying to dig us in deeper?"

Connor made a dismissive noise. "Relax. It's not like *we're* the ones who've been blowing off practice and showing up late or being half-assed."

I let the digs wash over me. Connor could say whatever he liked; it wouldn't change anything. No matter how much I might wish otherwise, I would keep starting short of a major injury and he would stay second string.

"Hudson!" My head snapped around at Coach S's shout. "Get your ass over here and show Walters and Monroe how to do a proper BTB."

"Yes, Coach," I replied instantly, and peeled away to join the group of demoralized, frustrated faces, even though a stitch already burned along my side and my feet ached from the relentless running. A water break would have been great, but as Coach's hawk eyes tracked me across the field, I thought better of it. I'd take my licks and keep going. I knew what I was getting into the second I'd decided to try to win Andy back, and I refused to have any regrets.

Andy

I closed the paperback and basked in the fleeting euphoria of having finished a good book. The fantastical escapades of a prince from another dimension stealing across the vale to abduct not one, but two brides in order to keep the magic in his kingdom alive had been an unexpected delight, with far more romance than I'd predicted. That hadn't diminished my overall enjoyment of the book though and I eagerly anticipated the sequel due to release next spring. Honestly, the only thing that could have possibly made the story better would have been if the unwitting king had found a groom instead of a bride.

A sigh escaped me as I rested my head against the wall and wondered if Mitch had finished his space pirate book yet. I didn't expect that he had, but I did hope that he'd at least started it.

"Something bothering you?" Lucien asked as I reached for another book inside the dragon tote.

"Just the usual dysphoria of finishing a good book."

Lucien nodded in understanding and returned to emptying his satchel of the notes from his study group. "Series?" he asked over his shoulder.

"Next year."

His face twisted in mock pain. "Harsh."

"Yeah. Interested?" I held up the nearly discarded paperback.

He straightened and held out a hand. "I'll take a look." I tossed it over without a second thought. "Genre?" he asked as he snagged it out of the air.

"Fantasy with a touch of realism."

"Cool." He flipped it over and began perusing the back jacket. A couple of minutes later, he nodded to himself and tucked the book beside his desk lamp. "Is it okay if I get it back to you after the holiday weekend? Normally I'd get it to you sooner, but I'm actually bouncing early."

"No problem at all. Early, huh? Must be nice."

He shrugged and pulled his button down over his head. "Eh, it might not be so bad if they didn't expect me to participate in all the religious shit."

"Family still ignoring you're atheist?"

"Yep." He tugged on a plain tee and switched out his khakis for more comfortable lounge pants, then flopped on the bed in a giant puff of expelled air.

"At least you'll have something good to read to distract yourself."

"Hell fucking yes." He leaned forward to snatch his current book from the desk and settled down.

I chuckled to myself and settled in with my fresh story. Twenty minutes later, I realized I'd yet to move from page three, but couldn't tell if it was the story itself I couldn't seem to get into or that my focus had gone up in smoke. My mind kept straying to an alternative story line for the book I'd just finished, one in which the dashing prince who had no desire to be king fell for a cute lab assistant with red hair and an inquisitive mind. I pushed the fantasy away, but it kept coming back, and each time the prince looked more and more like Mitch.

Damn it, I never should have had sex with him.

A groan drifted out of me, and Lucien shifted on his bed. I refrained from glancing over to see if he was looking at me and doubled down on my efforts to engage with the words perched on my lap. The harder I tried, though, the more the words blurred until I gave up and switched it for a different book from the bag. When I reached down, I caught Lucien gazing over at me curiously. I studiously ignored the look and opened the new book without even glancing at the back jacket or title.

Not even a paragraph in, I'd already slid into a revision of one of the hottest scenes of the reluctant king story. One in which the stubborn prince pressed the unwitting extra bride against the wall in the lab, except it wasn't the sassy maiden, but me whose shoulders pressed into unforgiving iron and wood as Mitch conquered my mouth and wedged his leg between my thighs. The scene didn't even take that much imagination as Mitch had done much the same in the secret room at the start of term. His hot mouth searing kisses into my skin while his fingers dug mercilessly into my sides and forced all my want to the surface.

I jerked violently at the sudden rush of longing that flooded through me and pinched the bridge of my nose to ground myself. The move did shit for all to relieve the stress behind my eyes or quell my rising erection.

"You okay over there?"

I fumbled the book in my hands, nearly tossing the damn thing across the room, and ended with it clutched against my chest like the meager pages would attempt to break free and fly away of their own accord. Upside, my chub was definitely gone now. "Uh, yeah..."

Lucien stared at me for a solid second without blinking, then turned his attention back to his own book. I let out a sigh and tried to do the same.

"You, uh, wanna talk about it?" he asked awkwardly.

I chewed on my lip and debated the wisdom of trying to talk to Lucien about my issues, not in the least bit tricky because I couldn't actually say anything about Mitch and I wasn't about to tell him I was gay. "Um… I have this…report," I floundered.

"Okay. What about it?"

"It's…not going the way I expected?"

"Are you asking or saying? What's the report about? A class we share or one on your own?"

I instantly regretted the attempt to seek an unbiased opinion about my predicament at the rapid-fire questions. "That's not important," I said.

Lucien's face scrunched up in a confused scowl and his book tipped back, momentarily forgotten.

"I mean, the issue isn't the report itself so much as I think I'm on the wrong track. If you'd asked me four y-weeks ago," I quickly amended, "I could have told you exactly how I would have finished it, but now… Now I seem to have gone off on a weird tangent and I don't think my original…thesis holds." I risked another glance at Lucien to see what he was making of my awkward as fuck attempts to relate the situation I now found myself in with Mitch.

His mouth twisted to the side as it usually did whenever he was thinking hard. Finally, he said, "If the new thesis isn't working, drop it. Sounds to me like you already know what the report needs. You're just too scared to go for it."

I turned to face forward as Lucien's words sank in. Weird as it sounded, he might be onto something. Except…except pursuing the original thesis meant going back on every promise I'd ever made to myself. Fuck, now I was using this ridiculous metaphor with myself.

"Hey, Anderson?"

I glanced up, but Lucien still had his gaze focused on the book in his lap. "Yeah?"

"If you wanted advice about dating, you could have just said so." His lips quirked up in a half smile and he looked at me out of the corner of his eye.

So much for being cunning.

"Right. Yeah. I'll remember that…next time," I said to fill the void. He gave a small nod and returned his full attention to the book he was pages from completing. I, on the other hand, suffered in silence, running over all the ways the situation with Mitch could blow up in my face at any second, and never made it past the first page.

Chapter 20

Four Years Ago

Andy

Showered and dressed to face the day, I ventured out in search of my best friend. It took an active effort to keep my face from splitting into a grin as I walked the halls. I exited the West Hall and made my way to the Green and the muted hum of cheerful voices. I quickened my pace, practically racing the last several yards, eager anticipation fueling me until at last I vaulted over the low wall that still bore marks of our misguided firework prank.

The smile I'd fought so hard to keep at bay broke free as my gaze fell instantly on Mitch. He stood laughing with some of the other team hopefuls, including his new roommate, Nate. The smart thing to do would be to wait until later to tell him the rest of what I should have told him the night before, but my excitement trumped my patience. I took a few steps closer and raised a hand to catch his attention. When that didn't work, I called out.

"Mitch!"

His gaze swept in my direction, but didn't settle, although no one else was nearby. Then he turned back to Nate and laughed again. My smile dissolved.

He looked right at me. No. He looked right through me, like I wasn't even here, like last night hadn't happened, like…like… He acted like he doesn't even know me.

My breath hitched, and I stumbled backwards. How delusional could I be? There wasn't a snowball's chance in hell Mitch could ever feel the same way about me, no matter what had happened last night. We'd all heard stories about some of the more interesting things that the boys of Ulwich Prep had been caught doing. It didn't mean anything. But it did to me and my best friend would know that, except…except he wasn't looking at me.

I ached to call to him again, demand that he see me, acknowledge what had happened between us, but I couldn't pull in enough air to convince sound to come out of my mouth. Tears pricked my eyes and I shook my head.

This has to be a dream. A really, really bad dream. Mitch couldn't…wouldn't abandon me like this. Not my *Mitch.*

Yet there he went, across the Green without so much as a half-hearted wave or blink in my direction. As far as he was concerned, I didn't exist. It wasn't until my back bumped into the low stone retaining wall, I realized I hadn't stopped retreating.

"Hey, Gallagher."

I glanced up from my imploding world at the greeting. "Hi, Bridges," I offered and immediately returned my attention to Mitch's receding form, which was currently being swallowed by the rest of the lacrosse team. Why wouldn't he look at me?

"Does he know you're in love with him?" The whispered question right next to my ear practically sent me shooting out of my skin. I spun around to confront Calvin. His characteristically unkempt curls hung in his face as he leaned against the low wall. He swept them out of the way, revealing dark brown eyes set in a lighter brown face dominated with open curiosity.

"What? No. Why would you say that?" I glanced off to the side, illogically terrified that he could have somehow heard something I'd never been brave enough to voice aloud.

Calvin glanced toward the players where they were starting an impromptu match. Then his features clouded with confusion and he shifted his attention back to me, his dark brows scrunched together. "He at least knows you're gay, right?" he asked clearly, though not loud enough to be heard by anyone not right next to us.

My eyes widened at this fresh horror. There wasn't a doubt in my mind that fear was plastered clear as day across my face as I looked back to where Mitch was being congratulated by his new teammates.

New friends.

I brought my gaze back to Calvin, swallowing past the hard lump threatening to cut off all my air. "So, it's true. You really are…" I trailed off, not bold enough to say it aloud as he clearly was. More than a few rumors centered around Calvin's sexuality.

He shrugged and held his hands out. "I am who I am. I'm proud of it and don't see any reason to change just because it makes some people uncomfortable."

I stared, amazed at his level of confidence and a little envious. It had taken me almost fourteen years and an insane attraction to my best friend for me to come to this realization, but he acted as if he'd always known.

He rested his elbows on the wall and stared right back. "I also notice you didn't deny it."

My jaw dropped. However, trepidation quickly overrode the astonishment. How did he know? Did everyone know? Were there rumors about me too? Was that why Mitch didn't want to be seen with me?

Calvin picked up on the shift and held out his hands again, this time in a placating gesture. "Don't worry, your secret is safe with me. If you don't want anyone to know, no one will. Though, full warning, being seen with me might make you guilty by association," he added with a crooked smile.

I let out the breath I was holding and cast one last look at the spot where Mitch had completely ignored my existence. "He knows," I whispered. Calvin's face fell at my tone, as did his hands. My own fisted by my side as a tide of self-loathing rolled through me. "I told him what I am. I… I don't think we're friends anymore."

"Who."

I glanced up sharply. "What?"

"Who," he repeated. "You told him *who* you are. You're not a 'what' Andy, you're still human, just like he is."

I shook my head, unable to accept what he was saying. It certainly didn't feel that way. The rejection stabbing through my heart threatening to rip it in two was testament to that.

"How did it go when you told him?" Calvin asked cautiously, inching a little closer.

I thought back to our unbelievable night, what he'd said, what we'd done. My traitorous heart, still freshly bleeding, fluttered at the memory. "Not at all like I expected." Calvin raised an eyebrow at the unusual response. "It's complicated," I added without elaboration.

His curious expression morphed into an amiable smile. "I like complicated."

Present Day

Andy

I stared down at the book in my hand, already having forgotten why I picked it up. The week had been a special kind of mind fuck and clearly my retreat to the library and the crassness that was Calvin were not proving to be the diversion I desperately needed. I still couldn't believe I'd had sex with Mitch. It was one rule. One. Nevermind that we'd both gone on like nothing had happened, nothing had changed. The only mercy was the fact that Mitch hadn't pointed out that I'd been the one to break it.

"I'm telling you, one of these days he'll realize the error of his ways," Calvin said as he replaced one book only to remove another. I looked up from my tumultuous thoughts and wracked my brain to figure out what we were talking about now. Calvin was notorious for skipping around in a conversation.

I glanced around for some sort of clue. Shelves rose around us, cluttered with books and creating a haven of reclusion from the rest of the library. It wasn't perfect, but it offered a modicum of privacy for some of our more…interesting conversations. At last, my mind caught up with what he'd said and I rolled my eyes.

"I still don't get it. I mean, Benny. Of all the people to have a crush on…" I glanced over at Calvin, curious if he'd deny it. When he didn't even acknowledge it, I shook my head. "Seriously though, he's such an ass."

"But, you see, that *is* why." He held out his hands for emphasis and stared between them like he really could see Benny's ass. "Mm, you don't even know. Boy's got an ass you could bounce a quarter off of." Despite my own pervasive funk, I couldn't help but laugh at the lascivious look he gave the imaginary ass. Calvin was hands down the lewdest person I'd ever known and while we may not agree on a lot of things, I wouldn't give up his friendship for the world.

The muffled sound of books falling to the carpeted ground snatched the humor from my lungs. I immediately shoved my nose back in my book which turned out to be one of my acquisitions from the book store. The topic of murder seemed appropriate as the source of the disruption sauntered into our cultivated bubble.

"Look at what we have here. It's Club Faggot." The usual three culprits followed the insult. Benny's lackeys laughed at the tired insult while their fearless leader rested a shoulder on the nearest stack and glared at us. He gave no hint that he recalled the threat I'd given him in the hall that day, nor had he ever sought me out.

"Fuck off," I said, doing my best to ignore the vulgar charades Neil and Todd were performing behind him. "We're not bothering anyone."

Benny's face twisted into a sneer. "You're bothering me." The palpable shift in mood made the alcove shrink from small to minuscule. The hair on my arms stood on end and I could practically feel Calvin gearing up for a verbal fencing match.

"Then leave," I suggested in an attempt to prevent things from escalating.

"What if I don't want to? What are you going to do about it?" Benny pushed off of his perch, inspecting his fingernails as he ventured deeper into our sanctuary, then knocked over the stack of books Calvin had been creating. His goons snickered in the background while Calvin made a sound that was a cross between an indignant squawk and an angry growl.

"I'm gonna start by getting Professor Jackson," I said quickly, aiming for nonchalance as I glanced up from my book. "I don't think he'd appreciate learning how you're treating the materials."

"Oh yeah? And how do you think he'd appreciate finding out about you two fucking up here?" Benny snarled back.

Calvin gasped and struck an exaggerated pose of insulted horror. "We are in a sacred space of learning. And, *ew*." He looked at me for emphasis, mouth agape at the preposterous notion.

I rolled my eyes and went back to my reading, determined not to let any of their prodding get to me. I had enough problems to contend with without adding someone else's homophobia to the mix.

Benny sucked on his teeth and took a step back. Bully he may be, but he wasn't stupid. He couldn't prove we'd been doing anything suspect, and forcing the issue would only draw attention to his own involvement.

"Whatever, homos." He made one last hideously vulgar gesture and stalked off, closely followed by Todd and Neil.

"One of these days," Calvin commented wistfully as he watched Benny leave.

I glanced after the trio. "I'm not one to judge—really, I'm not—but seriously? How can you still say that? He's a jerk and he'll always *be* a jerk." Calvin's only response was to hold his hands back up and wriggle his eyebrows suggestively. I threw my hands up in defeat. "To each his own."

"Speaking of which, you still carrying that flame for Mitch?" he asked without even glancing over his shoulder.

Some days, I really regretted telling Calvin what had happened four years ago. Not the whole thing, but enough. I groaned. So much for not thinking about it.

"You're friends again, right? You've been spending a lot of time together at the very least," he added, switching books once more from the now rebuilt stack.

"You could say that. And for the record, I'm trying to keep that *particular* light extinguished." *Not that it's working.* I shook my head. "But he makes it really hard. I don't think he has any idea how hard he makes it."

"I *bet* he doesn't." I met Calvin's snide response with a book to the shoulder. "Ow," he said, rubbing the point of impact. "Have you told him?"

"I'm trying to make things better, not worse." I hadn't told him the whole truth four years ago, and I had no intention of doing so now.

"Just saying. Maybe if you slept with him..." I shot Calvin an angry look in lieu of another book. He held up his hands defensively. "It was just a suggestion."

"The whole thing is a mess." I hung my head and massaged my aching temples. There was absolutely no way I was going to tell him I'd tried that, and it hadn't done shit. If anything, I was more confused than ever.

Calvin abandoned his books and sat beside me. "If you would tell me more about what happened that night, maybe I could help better."

I glanced at him from the refuge of my folded arms. "I've been dreaming about it again."

Calvin's face fell. "Judging by the way you say that, it's not the good bits."

I shook my head and buried my face back in the protection of my arms. "It's always the same. I wake up cold and alone. I search the room, but there's no clue to where he went. He's just...gone."

We sat in silence for a minute while I relived the nightmare. The aching cold that had settled into my bones without a warm body beside me to stave off the chill. The naïve joy swallowed by despair when I realized he was never coming back, not to the secret room, not to me, not ever. I stared unseeing over my arms at the sculpture of books Calvin had created. The colors blurred together indiscriminately, and the architecture became a shapeless blob.

"I remember thinking at the time how smart he was to already have gone, that he was protecting us. So we wouldn't get caught together." My chest constricted as I fought back a sob. Four years didn't make the truth of it hurt any less. If anything, recent events made it hurt more.

Calvin's warm hand steadily rubbed along my back, a reassurance that only pushed me closer to falling apart.

"He's going to do it again. He's going to ghost me. I can feel it," I croaked. It wasn't until the words left my mouth that I realized that was the root of my distraction, the unshakable fear that Mitch would get close only to abandon me again.

"Maybe you should do it first."

"We both know I can't do that anymore than you can let go of what happened with Benny."

The back rub suddenly turned into a gripping side hug. "Benny," Calvin said wistfully. He glanced over at me with his characteristic exuberance. "Did I ever tell you about that shower?"

I laughed despite myself and used the palm of my hand to rub away the evidence of my near meltdown. The fear was still there, bubbling beneath the surface, but I welcomed the distraction. "Only like a hundred times."

"There I am, innocently walking into the showers, minding my own business," he went on undeterred. "And who do I find?"

"Benny," I supplied.

"Benny," he echoed. "Jacking off in the shower."

I laughed again at his animated retelling of a story I'd heard enough times to tell myself and had used to bluff Benny into backing down.

"Being the gentleman I am—"

I snorted. Calvin was about as far away as Benny was from being a gentleman.

"Excuse you," Calvin reprimanded me. "Like I was saying. Being the gentleman I am, I coughed to *discreetly* let him know he had an audience."

I couldn't help but wonder how long he'd had the audience before the "discreet cough".

Calvin ignored my snicker and continued his elaborate tale. "In true Benny fashion, he turns to me and says, 'You just gonna stand there, or are you gonna help?'" His mimic of Benny's gruff voice sounded more like a bad noir crime film than a real person.

"What did you do?" I prompted on cue.

"What was I supposed to do? He *literally* invited me. Now, in my defense," he held up a finger for emphasis, "I was only planning on giving him head. How was *I* supposed to know how he was going to want to finish?" His eyes opened wide as if he himself still couldn't believe the unexpected turn of events.

I chuckled. Against all my efforts to remain sullen, Calvin had cheered me up. He had a gift for that, and one I'd cherished since we'd first become friends.

"I still dream about that ass," he sighed, staring off into the distance dreamily.

"You're ridiculous," I said and shoved him in the shoulder. He swatted me away, but thankfully returned to Earth. "One of these days, Benny is going to end you."

Calvin scoffed at the threat as he jumped back up. "Bet you Benny still dreams about it too," he said with a wink.

Mitch

My lunch tray slid across the table, its contents virtually untouched. "But get this," Andy continued his tale, his arms waving animatedly and his eyes sparkling with humor. "Carver then has the audacity to ask if the 1940 version was that different from the 2005."

I leaned across the table, my lunch completely forgotten. "He did not."

"He totally did," Andy said, trying to get his laughter under control enough to continue the story.

"Everyone knows the 1995 mini-series is the best. I mean, Mr. Darcy."

Andy's eyes widened, and he smacked the table. "Right!" We laughed at the same time and he struggled to sober up.

"What did Garza have to say?" I prompted.

“So, I shit you not. Garza looks him dead in the eye and says, '1813'. No one in the room is even breathing at this point. Carver is fucking oblivious and is now insisting that there was no such version and he can’t be penalized for something he couldn’t find. Garza narrows his eyes—I swear Mitch, I’ve never seen anyone look so insulted in my life. Anyway, he straight up deadpans, 'The book, not the movie.'”

I smothered a laugh. “Please tell me Carver stopped talking.”

Andy leaned back, the light sparking in his green eyes. “God, no. Dumbass then goes on to say, ‘Wait, there’s a book too?’”

“He didn’t,” I groaned.

“I thought Garza was going to kill him right there.”

“With, what? Laser beam eyes?”

Andy waved a finger at me. “You laugh, but if looks could kill, Carver would be walking around with two holes burned right through his skull.”

“How did he even get into your class?”

He shrugged and scooted his tray back in front of him. “Probably used Spark Notes.”

I bit my lip to keep from laughing and placed a hand next to his tray. “Wait.”

Andy glanced up, his water bottle already to his lips.

“You mean I could have been using those this whole time?”

He snorted water up his nose and spluttered it out all over his neglected tray.

“What? I’m serious.”

He reached across the table and shoved me. “Fuck you.”

“It was too easy. Also, you know I would never. Lit may not be my forte like it's yours, but I at least respect books enough to read them.”

His lips quirked into a smile despite that he was still avidly cursing me. “Fucker, you owe me a new lunch. No, more than lunch, two puddings at the very least.”

“You want me to filch you puddings from the kitchen?”

“You heard me.”

“You realize I could probably ask for a dozen and they’d hand them over no questions asked?”

His green eyes sparked with mischief. “What’s the matter, Mitch? Afraid you’ve lost your touch? Besides, everyone knows they taste better when they’re stolen.”

My grin stretched from ear to ear. “And will I have a partner in crime for this little escapade?”

“Do you need one?” he asked, the challenge clear.

“Need is a strong word.”

He smirked. “Admitting defeat already?”

“I said, *need* is a strong word… But what if I *want* one?” I clarified, leaning forward once more to rest my arms on the table. “What do you say?”

His eyes darted between mine as he pondered the proposal. I held perfectly still and waited in silence. At last, he stopped chewing on his lip and smiled. “Okay, but we go now.”

“Now? Andy, are you nuts? It’s the middle of lunch period.”

He lowered his voice to a conspiratorial whisper. “What’s the matter? Chicken?”

“Never. Bring it. What’s the plan?” I asked just as quietly, intending to call him on his bluff. I should have known better. Andy didn’t bluff.

He glanced around to make sure no professors or snitches were nearby before hunkering close enough that our foreheads almost touched. My mind flashed to his red lashes fanning across his freckled cheeks as he blinked and looked up at me, eyes filled with doubt, lips parted… Then the memory was gone. “You’ll get up first.” He pointed subtly, his hand hidden between us, back toward the kitchens. “Carla still has a sweet spot for you, says you look just like her grandson.”

“And how do you know that?”

He rolled his eyes. “Because she says it literally every time you go down the line.” I couldn’t help but smirk at learning that Andy knew that. “Shut up, you’re getting off track. Anyway, return your tray straight to her and ask about her grandson. You don’t have to get too involved, just enough to keep her distracted while I slip around the line.”

“Okay, and how am I supposed to steal the outrageous number of puddings I owe you?”

“Easy. I’m going to create a diversion. Also, two is not exorbitant, and in case you hadn’t already guessed, one of them is for you.”

“You’re so generous,” I teased. “Then what?”

“Then we meet back up with our spoils of war.”

“The usual spot?” I asked, fully expecting him to know where I was talking about.

He snorted. “Naturally. Ready?”

"Ready." I leaned back, grabbed my tray, and stood like it wasn't weird I was relocating in the middle of lunch.

No one stopped or questioned me as I made my way across the room. I dutifully dumped my trash in the receptacle nearest the line where the lunch custodian Carla was, in fact, conveniently standing. Excitement surged through me as I engaged her in conversation about her grandson Liam, who turned out to also be into lacrosse, while Andy slipped behind her like a flame-haired ghost.

I was just starting to wonder what the distraction was supposed to be and how long I would have to have this pretend conversation when a tower of trays slid free of their perch to clatter loudly on the tiled ground. Carla spun around with a gasp of alarm and ventured into the kitchen to investigate. I followed close on her heels to…help.

She was re-stacking the last of the trays when I slipped away to the massive pantry, still propped open to resupply the line. Andy's determination to go through with the heist made more sense now as I recalled the door had typically been locked when we'd come like thieves in the night to raid its contents. I secured the two puddings as well as some spoons on my way out, then headed straight for the low wall we'd often met at when pranks had been our life.

Andy glanced up when I hopped over the wall and settled down beside him. "What took you so long? I thought you got caught," he said as I tossed him his pudding.

"Me? Never." I held out a spoon for him.

"Please, you totally stayed and helped clean up."

"You say that like you wouldn't have." I bumped his shoulder and his bite of pudding smeared across his cheek.

He let out an indignant yowl and popped my spoon so it splattered chocolate on my nose. "Brown noser," he accused with a laugh, then wiped his face clean.

"Ha ha, you're such a comedian." I searched my bag for a napkin, but had to settle for trying to get it all off with my fingers.

He laughed again and set his pudding aside. "Oh my God, you're hopeless. Come here, before your face turns into Revenge of the Pudding." He fished out a spare napkin from his bag, wet it with some water from his water bottle, then grabbed my face and turned it towards him. The cool cloth made short work of the mess, but all I could think about was how strong yet gentle his grip was on my jaw. The more I thought about his fingers, the more my face heated, until I was positive I looked like I'd been left to bake for days in a summer sun.

I cleared my throat and pulled away when he finally declared me once again decent for polite society and released me. All of my focus centered on my half-full cup of pudding, but the burn remained. "Any plans for the long weekend coming up?"

"Nah," Andy said, reacquiring his pudding. "Will probably end up staying here and reading since the holidays are coming up. No sense in making the trip back home only to come right back. You?"

"Same. When you say reading, please tell me it's not school books."

He laughed like I hoped he would. "No. I have a new stack I'm working through. Should be able to make some good progress too since Lucien is leaving a few days early."

"No shit."

"Yep." He pulled his last spoonful free and smiled over at me, his green eyes sparkling while the sun set his hair ablaze. "I'll have the whole place to myself starting next Wednesday."

Chapter 21

Andy

I pulled open the door, the scribbled note clutched in my hand. Light pushed into the dusty space of the forgotten classroom from curtainless windows. It had only taken a decade to solidify the nondescript room's reputation as being haunted or, better yet, cursed. When the school had dared reopen it for Professor Marco's exclusive lecture hall five years ago and he'd promptly had a nervous breakdown after a scant three weeks, speculation had burned through every grade like wildfire. Now only the bravest ventured up here and only then on a dare.

"Connor," I whispered as loudly. When no response was forthcoming, I shut the door, mindful of creating any noise that might attract unwanted attention. It clicked shut in almost perfect silence and I turned back to the neglected space. I took a hesitant step forward, my gaze dancing over the desks pushed to the sides, the haphazard cluster of bookshelves shoved together, and the shadows lurking in their depths for any sign of life.

This room isn't really haunted. Pull yourself together.

"Connor?" I called again, louder this time, and immediately felt like an idiot. "That's it, I'm leaving. I don't know why I came up here." I crumbled the familiar scribble, turned to beat a hasty retreat, and came face to face with, well, a face.

"Looking for someone?"

Every hair on my body stood on end and my stomach lurched as my muscles tried to do the same. A jolt of adrenaline sent blood rushing through my ears and made recognition slow in coming. When it did, I could have sprouted claws. "Jesus fucking Christ, Connor. What the hell is wrong with you?"

His uninhibited laughter filled the room, made slightly less creepy now that it held another living being. Though how much longer Connor would remain alive after scaring the living daylights out of me was anyone's guess. He glided his long, lithe frame across the room with the grace of a dancer, completely unperturbed by the fright he'd given me.

"Did you want that alphabetically or by severity?" he asked, his tone light and teasing as he leaned against the monolith of a teacher's desk, his legs stretched out, ankles crossed as he braced on his arms. A broad grin stretched his cheeks and lent a hint of whimsy to his wit. Connor had a special gift to make a joke out of literally anything. Appropriateness need not apply.

I rolled my eyes, my smile threatening to steal across my face. "If you conned me into coming up here just so you could pretend to be a ghost, I'm leaving." *Never should have come up here in the first place. My issues with Mitch are leading me to make even more questionable life choices than usual.* The cruel thoughts wiped away the smidgen of joy Connor's antics had wrung out of me.

In the blink of an eye, Connor vacated his perch and gave up all pretense of his casual repose. "Wait. That's not why." I eyed him skeptically, but didn't venture toward the door. Excitement danced in his eyes as he side-stepped toward the shelves, arms still out to halt my movement. "Besides, if you leave now, you'll miss the best part."

"Best part, huh? And what would that be?" I asked, my repressed smile twitching at the corner of my mouth.

Curiosity killed the cat.

Satisfaction brought it back.

The unwelcome conclusion to the rhyme sounded eerily like Mitch, and it instantly transported my thoughts to when he'd said it to me. With crumbling willpower, I forced the memory away. If I relived it any more, I'd run screaming down the hall. I brought my focus to where Connor had finally made it to the cluster of bookshelves. Guilt coiled like a viper in my stomach as I took in his enthusiastic grin. Connor deserved better. I just couldn't get him to see that.

"Wait right there," he emphasized, before ducking between the shelves. A moment later, his head popped back out, his hair noticeably mussed. "Promise you won't leave."

I rolled my eyes again, making sure he saw the exaggeration. "I promise I won't leave until I see whatever inane surprise you've concocted this time." He flashed another broad grin that nearly split his face in two and vanished again. I moved over to assume his vacated position on the desk. Connor loved surprises...and fun. That's what drew me to him originally. He knew how to have unapologetic fun and I...desperately needed that.

But even good things have their problems.

I stared solemnly down at my feet, lost in my dreary thoughts. Connor wasn't entirely to blame for why we'd broken up. He wasn't even mostly to blame—though I'd let him believe he was. It wasn't my proudest moment, and that guilt was unquestionably what had brought me up here at the whim of a note slipped into my bag, even though I knew this to be a mistake.

The pure note of a trumpet jerked my head up. The instrument was swiftly joined by what had to be a trombone and the more identifiable melody of a piano and bass. A long leg, bare but for a navy sock, emerged from behind the shelves, curling in time with the music. A laugh stuck in my throat as an elaborate arm toss joined the appendage. Connor's long limbs were definitely one of his greatest assets, and he knew exactly what to do with them. He peeked a head out, still not giving away the main event. I shook my head and gave up on restraining my laugh when he waggled his eyebrows at me.

Oh god, please let him be wearing clothes.

The music dipped, and all three revealed pieces retreated. When the brass blared in triumph, he slid out from the curtain right on cue, his socked feet carrying him an extra yard before he came to a complete stop. A loud burst of laughter erupted out of me and I clamped a hand over my mouth, darting an anxious glance over at the door. Connor sashayed his way closer, twirling a monstrous pink boa in time with the salacious music and taking his time crossing the room.

Each swell of music brought a new provocative move. He spun around and glanced over his shoulder at me before shaking his ass like there was no chance of someone happening upon this outrageous show. I sunk my teeth into my bottom lip to hold the laughter at bay. It was for naught. A loud burst of laughter erupted out of me as he trailed the stretch of feather up his body and tossed his head back like it was the most sensuous sensation he'd ever experienced. When he was close enough, he looped the boa over my head and used it to pull himself closer. I struggled once again to muffle my humor. He fake pouted and tossed his head like he was tossing a mane.

"Darlin' you have got to learn to loosen up. Live a little, sweetheart," he drawled despite not being the least bit southern.

I blew a feather out of my face and couldn't help but smile. Getting me to loosen up had become a mission of sorts for Connor. Shame it hadn't taken. "You really are too much sometimes, you know that?" I hooked a finger in his boxers and popped the elastic. The striped light blue cotton and his white undershirt were the only things left of his uniform. Where the hell he'd found the black suspenders, I wasn't sure I wanted to know.

He flipped the boa back around and draped it around himself like a classic lounge singer. "I happen to think I'm just the right amount."

"Perhaps you are," I conceded, now officially grinning.

"There ya go, sugar." He dropped the feathered death trap to hang loosely around his hips and stepped back in close. Habit had my eyes already half-lidded in anticipation. His mouth swiped against mine in a teasing invitation I couldn't help but accept. He draped his long arms around my neck and preceded to explore my mouth with eager abandon. "Missed you," he whispered playfully, angling his hips to show me just how much he'd missed me. If there was one word in the entire English language to describe Connor Hendricks, it would be forward.

I laughed and sought out his defined hip bones beneath the ostentatious feathers. "Connor."

"Connie," he corrected, his voice thick with lust, then recaptured my mouth. His hand glided up my thigh toward my crotch and I lurched back. Suddenly, the saxophone harmonizing with a piano in the background became a discordant jumble of noise instead of the seductive lure it was meant to be.

"No," I said as firmly as I could, considering my tongue had just been in his mouth.

He recoiled at my vehemence. "Is it the name thing? Fuck, Andy, it's not like I even like it all the time." Despite the angry statement, I could still detect the hurt laced underneath.

"Connor—Connie… Fuck." I scrubbed my hands over my face, at a loss for the right thing to say while he continued to put distance between us. How did I let myself keep getting sucked into these situations? Getting back together, even fooling around, would be an epic mistake. "No, that's not it. You *know* that. How many times do I have to tell you?"

His eyes flashed angrily. "Then what?"

"I can't give you what you need. I wish I could." I held my hands out by my sides in a hopeless gesture of surrender.

"Do you?" The sharp words cut me to the quick and guilt welled up.

"I'm sorry." Connor identifying as genderfluid had been an…interesting development in our relationship. I cherished the trust he'd placed in me when he confided how he felt. Given how deeply I cared for him, accepting and supporting him unequivocally had been a foregone conclusion. But that had never been enough to dispel his insecurity. No amount of reassurance would ever convince him that his identity wasn't why we'd broken up. That I wasn't rejecting who he was.

He crossed his arms and tossed his head. "Whatever."

"Don't be like that," I said as I watched the pure vibrancy that was Connor's truest-self disappear beneath a veneer of propriety, projecting what the world expected. His colors dimmed and darkness wrapped around him tighter than the boa. It killed me. "You deserve to be happy."

"So do you, but you won't take your head out of your ass long enough to see that other people are there."

"What is that supposed to mean?"

He tossed aside the boa like it was trash and refused to look at me. In a few steps, he was close enough to the shelves to snag his hidden pants.

"Connie," I said with more force as he began tugging them on.

"Connor," he snapped harsh enough to make me flinch. "I'm weird and queer, Andy, not stupid. Whoever broke your heart did one hell of a job."

I recoiled at the astute accusation. A defense sat unsaid on my tongue. Four years ago, I'd promised I wouldn't tell anyone what had transpired between me and Mitch, and I wasn't about to break that now. Literally the only person who knew had guessed, and I'd been too raw to deny it properly.

Connor let out a heavy sigh and dragged a hand through his unkempt hair. A second of tense silence passed, and he looked back at me, his trousers hanging open at his waist, undershirt half-tucked. "You should go."

"Connor," I said softly and stepped toward him.

He averted his gaze. "Just fucking go, Andy."

I swallowed past the hard lump of guilt lodged in my throat. Without another word, I made my way to the door and slipped silently back into the hall.

Mitch

I shrugged into my jacket and followed the guys out of the West Dormitories. Walking to town to spend an evening staring at half-dressed chicks from the girl's school wasn't exactly my idea of a great time, but showing up didn't just mean for practice. There was a whole song and dance that went with being on the team. You either learned to hum along or suffered the consequences.

Nate nudged my shoulder, his hands already wrist deep in his letterman, and tilted his chin at me. "You sure you're cool with coming along? No one would blame you if you wanted to sit out seeing Ronald and Trixie pawing at each other all night."

Despite his reassurance, I knew no excuse would get me out of this. "Nah, it's fine. Like I said before, I'm cool. She's free to date whoever she wants." So long as it wasn't me.

Brian glanced back at us and slowed his steps until he was close enough to sling an arm around my shoulders. I forced my own to remain relaxed and kept walking like his determination to keep me in check wasn't in any way out of the normal. "Sup, bro?"

"Nothing. Tired from all those damn laps."

"Coach will let up eventually, you'll see," Nate said in support.

Brian squeezed my shoulders, and I bit back a snarl. He was taking this team captain business way too seriously for my liking. "Give him time. Old fucker will forget he's mad." Unlikely, especially when he had so many spies on the team keeping tabs on me. But if I had to run an extra lap for every hour I spent in Andy's company, I'd run a million and never begrudge them.

"Sure," I responded by rote.

"That's the spirit. So you cruzin' for a new honey now that Ronald stole your girl?" Brian teased.

I bit my tongue from reminding him that Trixie wasn't my girl and hadn't been for a while. "Think I'm gonna fly it solo next term." Several pairs of eyes swiveled to stare at me in disbelief. "Keep my head in the game, you know?" I added quickly.

"What about the Finals ritual?" John asked, looking like I'd just told him his grandma had died. Even Nate side-eyed me, and there was nothing pleasant about the look Brian was sending my way. The guys took the whole getting laid before a big game to a new level. It had actually been how I'd lost my virginity… I did not have pleasant memories about the experience. Being tossed into a room by a bunch of rowdy upper classmen and expected to perform with some girl I'd never even met before had been a weight of pressure that made it damn near impossible to do so.

I couldn't help but wonder if my father had been subjected to such ruthless demands or had perpetuated them. I shivered and hoped that wasn't the case. When I'd wanted to join the lacrosse team four years ago, it had been to feel a kind of kinship with a man I could never spend time with again. Sadly, that wasn't what had happened.

"It'll be fine. Don't want to risk getting distracted, especially with all the scouts Coach is planning on bringing." I checked my relieved breath as Brian nodded in acceptance of my answer and released me to stumble along with the others. In his absence, Nate sidled up next to me. I glanced over at him and the telltale line of concern between his brows. "What?"

"You're seriously not going to do it?" he whispered, his gaze darting to the others.

"It's not a big deal, Nate."

"Maybe, but…"

"Look, I have bigger shit on my plate right now than worrying about getting my dick wet in some laxtitute," I snapped.

He held his hands up defensively. "Shit man. I didn't mean any offense. Just wondering is all."

"Leave him be," Brian called from the front of the group. "There's still plenty of time for a pretty little thing to change our boy's mind. Isn't that right, guys?"

I groaned to myself as the heckles of the others circled around me. Just fucking great. Now every last one of them was gonna try to hook me up just so they could keep to their ridiculous superstition of getting laid the night before a major game in order to secure victory.

Chapter 22

Mitch

I padded down the hallway, quiet but confident, no more than another fleeting shadow. Beyond the windows, darkness reigned, punctuated only by a half moon hanging low in the sky. I paused at the junction of passages and checked to make sure the way was clear before venturing into the East Dormitory. It may have been years since I'd taken this journey, but the way was branded into my memory and, at its end, a flame of red that shone like a beacon in my mind's eye.

My foot scuffed on the ground and a sharp squeak rang out into the muffled darkness, gone almost as soon as it emerged. I slunk closer to the wall and looked around. Price was doing the rounds tonight and he could be an absolute ass about violating lights out. Not that I was overly concerned about getting caught. I could sneak out of the entire school and back in with none the wiser...and had. No, it wasn't me I worried about. Then again, it rarely was.

I let out a sigh of relief as my destination came into sight. Once more, I checked to make sure the hall was void of witnesses before crossing it and twisting the doorknob. Pride at my success, however, evaporated when I softly shut the door and found the room completely empty.

Fuck. Where is he?

Lucien, I expected to be gone, but Andy wasn't one for sneaking about unless he had a reason. My stomach soured at what reason my best friend might have to be out of his room at night. The same one that had kept me out of mine perhaps? I ventured over to the desk by his bed and found his latest book lying open to a page, face down, a bookmark beside it. Without thinking, I picked it up and placed the ribbon between the folds of paper and set it back down. Andy hated having bends in the spines of his books.

He wouldn't have left it like that if he didn't intend to return soon.

My gaze caught on the flashlight poking out from behind some of his larger school books, and I smiled. Still a rebellious imp. Andy never could walk away from a good book, usually to the detriment of all else. Which begged the question, what had taken him away now? The obvious answer to all of it was that he'd ducked off to the restroom, Benjamin Price be damned. Reassured in my conclusion, I shifted to a perch where I could easily watch the door without being seen by anyone that might pass in the hallway and resigned myself to wait.

Within a few brief minutes, the knob twisted once more, and the door opened and shut with the barest of clicks. Even with his back to me and the room shrouded in shadow, I'd recognize Andy anywhere. He stood a moment, his hand pressed to the door, then let out a sigh that slumped his shoulders and turned around. The second his gaze landed on me leaning on his roommate's desk, he jumped.

"What are you doing here?"

I frowned and straightened up. "What do you mean? You said—"

My heart fell as Andy's face lit with understanding. Somehow, watching him put together the pieces of my own misguided conclusion was infinitely worse than his surprise.

I'm such a total idiot. I shouldn't have come.

"You're here because I said Lucien went home for the holiday," he stated evenly, then paused and glanced at the floor as if he was searching for something.

Probably a way out of this mess. What was I thinking?

"I can go if you don't want me here," I said, already stepping towards the door. It had been a mistake to come, to believe he wanted me.

Andy's head shot back up and he snared me with those bright green eyes. "What? No. I mean, I suppose I did sort of invite you. Why else would I have told you Lucien had left early?" Hearing the logic out loud didn't make me feel any better. It had obviously been a mistake, and he'd never had any intention of me sneaking in here.

"It's fine," I said, trying to hide my epic disappointment.

"You don't have to go," Andy whispered into the gloom. Saying I didn't have to go was not the same thing as wanting me to stay, and in the darkness, it was nearly impossible to tell which way he was leaning.

With a frustrated sigh aimed more at myself than him, I spun to the window and grabbed the curtain.

"Mitch, wait."

I looked down to see his hand on my arm. Andy appeared equally surprised to find it there, but didn't remove it. I brought my gaze back up to his as the curtains whisked softly behind me. The ambient light pouring through was more than enough to see the slight panic on his face. My hand fell back to my side as I released the thick fabric. "It's okay, Andy."

His hand tightened on my arm and tugged at my pulse. "You can stay."

I searched his face and found no more clarity in the low light than I had in the darkness. "I'll only stay if you want me to." *I won't make the same mistakes again.* When he failed to respond, I had my answer. Some mistakes just couldn't be undone. Wherever the last few months had brought us, we weren't there and probably never would be. "I'll go."

His Adam's apple bobbed in the moonlight and he flicked an anxious glance at the empty bed of his roommate. When his gaze met mine again, he was sporting a small smile that looked a tad forced. "And waste such an incredible opportunity? Besides, you're already here." The hand on my arm relaxed, as did his smile into something more natural, something more Andy.

He still hadn't been exactly clear about *wanting* me to stay, but he was also making it increasingly difficult to leave. Saying no to Andy was never something I'd quite mastered and wasn't sure I really wanted to. I took a step towards him and slid my hand along his cheek to cup his face, then brought my lips to his. He let out a sigh as he melted into the touch, the reaction equally less and more than what he'd given me the last time we'd been truly alone. It was just going to have to do. I used the caress to pull him closer and deepen the kiss. His hand glided along my arm, but didn't go further. I hated how I never felt like I understood the rules with him. They always seemed to be changing, and I always seemed to be losing.

I was about to break free and just call it a night when suddenly, his demeanor shifted. His grip on my arm tightened once more, and the kiss became more aggressive, his tongue sweeping boldly inside my mouth to tangle with mine. The heat of it blindsided me and I reached out with my free hand to grab his waist and steady myself.

As abruptly as he'd deepened the kiss, he released it altogether and stepped back and out of my reach. My hands fells away as he put first one foot, then four between us. An ache I was becoming very familiar with pulsed out to encompass my chest with each pained beat of my heart. I watched in silence as Andy stepped back to the desk by his bed and opened a drawer.

"Plus, the things here are better than what's in a forgotten shack in the middle of the woods," he said, removing a bottle and placing it on top of the book he'd clearly forgotten all about.

The wicked look in his eye and the crooked smile did the rest. I took two long strides towards him and crushed his body against mine. This time, when I kissed him, his hesitation was gone.

Andy

Every fiber of my being ached for Mitch to keep touching me, kissing me, wanting me, and no amount of logic could dispel it. I fisted a hand in the front of his shirt, needing him closer, but still terrified of the cusp I hovered over. This wouldn't be like last time or even the time before that. We weren't fourteen anymore.

It's not too late. I can still stop this.

Our lips danced a hair's breadth apart. However, he didn't take control of the non-kiss. But I wanted him to, I wanted him to take me because I was his, always had been, always would be. Still, he waited in silence for permission.

Always such a gentleman.

I tightened my fingers in the thin fabric of his nightshirt and yanked him closer. Our mouths collided with all the force of years of pent-up frustration, at least for me anyway. While our tongues tangled, his fingers slipped beneath the hem of my shirt where their tips burned molten pools on my side. He kissed me harder and stroked his large hands over my ribs. I moaned into him and the part of my brain responsible for rational thought short-circuited. I needed Mitch with a fierceness I'd never admit to in broad daylight, but here in this bubble of sub-reality, here, I could want.

Maybe…maybe if he has me again, then I can finally move on, let him go.

The wrongness of the whole thing still troubled me. It wasn't right that I suddenly wanted to bottom again, and for Mitch no less, especially since I hadn't been able to give Connor the same. The one and only time we'd tried to switch things up, I'd had an acute panic attack, complete with hyperventilating and body wracking sobs. It had taken Connor hours to calm me down and we hadn't tried again. Undoubtedly, that had contributed to our inevitable breakup along with so many other things. But I didn't want to think about how horribly I'd wronged Connor or how this was probably a terrible mistake. I just wanted to be Mitch's one more time.

All I have to do is stay in control. Remember what this is.

Plan in hand, I relinquished his shirt in order to yank mine off. He quickly followed suit, and I sucked in a breath at seeing his chest laid bare. The light in the shack was inadequate at best, nowhere near enough to appreciate the fine coat of hair dusting his pecks, or the cut of his abs, or the defined V disappearing into his lounge pants. It wasn't until he took a half-step closer that I realized I'd reached out or that I was shaking.

Fuck, pull it together. Stay in control.

And yet, my breath still hitched as my fingers contacted with his chest and splayed out so that my entire palm was pressing against him. Pure want burned through me like wildfire and in the ashes all that was left was need. My gaze flicked up to his. While I couldn't make out the hazel of his eyes, it didn't change the fact that he was watching me in silence. I dragged in a ragged breath as I suddenly realized that I'd stopped breathing the moment I'd touched him.

Control. Stay. In. Control.

I coasted my hand up to cup the side of his neck and pulled him down for another kiss. He leaned into it, owning my mouth while his larger frame crowded me against the bed. I moaned and tangled my fingers in his short hair. Need pulsed in time with my already aching cock. It wasn't enough, it would never be enough.

Fuck it.

I ripped my mouth away from where I was basically trying to eat him and turned around before he could see the flash of desperation on my face. His hands slipped along my waist as he nibbled along the back of my neck, his nose tickling my hair, his moist breath sending shivers down my spine. I pressed back against him and had to smother a whimper at the feel of his cock pressing into my ass. At this rate, he wouldn't even get inside before I came like some pubescent twit first discovering his dick. I flailed blindly around on the desk until my fingers found the bottle of lube.

"Here." The word came out husky and raw, giving voice to all the desires threatening to strip me bare.

He pulled away slightly and took the bottle from me. Anxiety threaded through my delirious need as I moved to remove the rest of my pajamas.

His hand closed over my wrist, halting me, and my heart lurched into my throat. “What are you doing?”

“Should think it’s obvious.” The comment came out snappier than necessary as I fought not to let my fear get the best of me.

He used his hold on me to spin me around. “You sure?” The quiet question ghosted out to stroke my cheek, then slithered its way down to settle in my heart. He was going to make me say it. In that moment, I loved and hated him. I didn’t want to admit how much I wanted this, how I burned for him, had never stopped burning. But he didn’t deserve to know that. He’d forfeited that right when he’d abandoned me to navigate all of this on my own.

I hovered between indecision and the absolute certainty that I’d already decided about what would happen tonight the second I’d mentioned Lucien leaving early for the holidays. “I’m sure.”

Mitch’s mouth closed back over mine, gentle and firm, and solidly on the wrong side of all the walls I’d erected around my heart. I wrapped my arms around his neck and arched into him, urging him deeper. He slid a hand down my backside and hooked it under my leg, then with hardly any effort at all, he hoisted me onto the bed. The mattress sank beneath me, much more inviting than an unforgiving floor. I reached greedily for him while at the same time trying to tug my pants off once more.

He joined me on the bed, miraculously free of his own garments, and pressed me into the pillow with another kiss that stole my breath and made my toes curl. I gave up trying to get my pants off and once more wrapped my arms around him, my trimmed nails digging into his back. He shifted to lay a trail of hot kisses along my neck while his hands divested me of my pajamas. I bowed off the bed as his slick fingers wrapped around my dick and stroked. The moan that fell out of me bounced around the room and only made me harder. I struggled to regain control of the situation, but I couldn’t see straight, let alone think straight. His fingers danced over my sensitive shaft, then turned their attention to my balls. I writhed beneath the gentle torture.

“For fuck’s sake,” I hissed, at the end of my rope and hanging on by a thumbnail. “You need to…need to…”

Before I could get the words out, his fingers ventured lower and tapped at my entrance. I gasped as electricity blasted through my system. My entire body tightened, refusing admittance even though this was something I desperately wanted. He leaned forward once more and tangled our tongues in a slow dance that both grounded me and sent me soaring while he continued to rub circles around the sensitive muscle. When his finger slid inside with almost no resistance, I moaned into him. Within a matter of minutes, those moans turned to heavy pants and even louder groans. Then he massaged my prostate and stars danced behind my eyes. Mitch may not have been the smartest kid in school, but he was a fucking incredible student.

I gripped the base of my cock, not ready to let go, and on the verge of begging. Like the astute observer he was, Mitch removed his fingers and replaced them with the head of his swollen cock. He added more lube, then worked his way inside. Every inch, every centimeter threatened to unravel me, until at last he was all the way in, filling me up and making me his. His forehead pressed to mine as we both adjusted to the overwhelming sensation. Then he stole a sweet kiss that made my heart flutter. My fingers dug into his back once more as I fought off the tide of emotion determined to pull me under. Thankfully, he took the response as encouragement and moved, first slowly, then with stronger thrusts until the bed creaked and the sound of our harsh breathing filled the room, punctuated by the occasional moan.

My orgasm danced closer and closer. I drew a shuddering breath and a distant sound tickled my senses. More than lost in the moment, I pushed it away until I realized it was getting louder. My eyes flew open. "Oh, shit."

Mitch paused, concern clear on his face in the moonlight streaming through the window. "What?"

I strained to hear the one sound that could ruin everything. Footfalls. Approaching fast. "Benny. He's coming."

"Fuck. What do—" Mitch didn't have a chance to finish as I pushed him off the bed. He fell with a loud thump and I winced, but there wasn't time for apologies as the doorknob turned.

I quickly lay back down and wrapped a hand around my flagging cock. The ensuing moans were purely theatrical and the best I could do given the circumstance. I didn't dare look down to see if Mitch had scooped his clothes under the bed with him. My hand continued to stroke my cock with a fervor that sparked a bit of life. The door opened and I willed myself to keep going.

"What the fuck is going on in here?" Benny asked, his gaze sweeping the room for something—or someone—that shouldn't have been there.

When his gaze landed on me, his face twisted in revulsion. “Fucking hell, Gallagher.”

Not an exhibitionist by any stretch, it took everything I had to keep moving. “Ever heard of knocking?”

“Jesus, you fucking fag. Stop.”

“Since when is it a crime to get off?”

“I’m right here,” he snapped, a scowl stamped across his face.

I raised an eyebrow and deliberately stroked up slowly, adding a moan for good measure. “Are you just going to stand there, or are you going to help?” The look of furious outrage that exploded across his face was almost worth nearly getting caught with Mitch in my bed.

“Fucking queer, keep that shit to yourself.”

“That a no?”

“Go fuck yourself.”

“Trying,” I fired back without mercy. “So help or get out. What’ll it be?”

Rage sprinted across his face, and his cheek twitched. “Keep it down,” he ordered, and slammed the door shut. I counted to five and listened for his receding steps before letting out a sigh of relief.

“That was really fucking close,” Mitch said as he rose from his hiding place.

“Yeah, it was,” I responded and grabbed his arm to tug him back onto the bed. Already my body was perking back up at his proximity.

“Maybe I should go.”

I faltered. “You’re not done, are you?” I glanced from him to his still erect cock. He ducked his head and I couldn’t help but wonder if he was blushing.

“Did you finish? Sounded like it got pretty close.”

Ooh, Mitch liked to listen. That was interesting. I shook my head and reached for him again. My fingers scratched along his scalp as our lips came together once more.

“Are you sure?” Mitch asked. I nodded and got as far as my tongue in his mouth before he threw the brakes again. “Aren’t you worried he’ll come back?”

I let out a frustrated huff and refused to give up my hold on him, not now that I finally had him in my grasp. “Trust me, Benny won’t come back here tonight for anything short of an explosion. Now are you good? Because I’m gonna need you to finish what you started.” Without waiting for a response, I slammed our mouths back together.

Mitch's capable fingers ventured once more to my ass and I let out a deep groan as he sought out my prostate. Between heart beats, his hard length replaced his fingers. Every nerve sparked back to life as I clung to him and continued to conquer his mouth as he conquered my body. Kissing became more difficult as each thrust stole more of my breath. He cradled my back with one hand and moved his other to cup my ass. The firm hold pulled me further open, and he slid a fraction deeper.

"Mitch," I gasped, his name falling like a whispered prayer from my lips as I fell back.

He followed after, sucking fervent kisses on my neck and anywhere else he could reach before at last wrapping a hand around my aching cock and stroking in time with his increasingly rapid thrusts. I wrapped my legs around him, altering the angle just enough so that the next few thrusts stroked my prostate just right. My breath caught, and I clawed at his shoulders, needing to hang onto something as he systematically took me apart.

"Come for me." His growl went through me like an arrow.

I grunted as the pain of it shattered me into a million pieces. The shock of my climax was still rolling through me when he jerked above me. His release spilled inside, filling me with a warmth that would have made me come if I hadn't already.

He leaned down to swipe my lips with a kiss once more before collapsing to the side. "Fuck."

Yep. That about summed it up. The instant the post bliss haze cleared, logic rushed in to fill me with cold. *What have I done? What part of that was staying in control? Fuck fuck fuck.*

I slipped off of the bed and thanked my lucky stars my knees didn't buckle; they were certainly shaky enough, not to mention the characteristic sting in my ass all but guaranteed that I wouldn't be doing anything comfortably for the next day or so. Oddly enough, I didn't give a shit.

Worth it.

I pushed the echo of the thought from four years ago away and pulled out a mostly clean shirt from the hamper. It wasn't perfect, but it would do. I cleaned up the best I could and glanced out of the corner of my eye to see Mitch doing the same. Deafening silence filled the room and while I ached to fill it, I couldn't find the words that wouldn't ruin what we'd just done. I bent to grab my pajamas from the floor and did a double take at seeing Mitch climbing back into the bed. The plaid fell from my suddenly numb fingers.

"What are you doing?"

"I'm gonna need a minute," he said as he flopped back and made himself comfortable.

The urge to argue the impracticality of him lingering even a second longer than necessary rose and promptly died. After all, hadn't I been the one to say that Benny wouldn't bother us for anything short of nuclear fallout? And it wasn't exactly like I was eager for Mitch to go.

So much for self-preservation and controlling the situation.

I grumbled to myself about my total inability to deny him and crawled in beside him on the narrow bed. "Fine," I conceded, spearing him with a glare, "but only for a minute. And don't you dare fall asleep."

"Yeah, yeah. No sleeping, got it. Now scoot over."

"Me? You're the one taking up all the room, you damn giant. Why don't you go lay on Lucien's bed, then you'd have plenty of room," I huffed and turned on my side, facing the window and putting my back to him.

"That requires movement. Besides, I'm already here. Now seriously, you're hogging the pillow."

"Ugh." I sat up and punched the pillow back to give him more of it. "It's not my fault you're too big."

"I wasn't too big a minute ago."

My jaw mentally dropped. Looking down at him in the low light, it was nearly impossible to tell if he'd meant for that to be a dick joke. Rather than call him out, I dismissed it and rolled once more to face out as far as the tiny bed would allow. "You're incorrigible," I grumbled.

"You know I don't know what that means."

"Liar."

He chuckled behind me and shifted to commandeer what was apparently his part of the pillow. "Fine, I do."

I barely suppressed a shiver as the warm words caressed the back of my neck. His moving around had brought him substantially closer than I expected, though why this closeness affected me so much when he'd been closer earlier boggled the mind. Suddenly, his long arm draped over my side and his hand felt around the edge of the bed.

"What are you doing now?" I whispered.

"Just making sure you're not gonna fall off."

“I’m fine.” Despite my reassurance, his arm stayed draped across me. I hated how much I liked having it there, knowing that although I’d literally thrown him to the floor earlier, he didn’t want the same to happen to me. “I mean it, Mitch, don’t fall asleep. I don't know how you sneaked in here to begin with, but it will be damn near impossible to sneak out come morning.” Silence filled the room like a living thing. I waited a moment, but no response was forthcoming. “Did you hear me?” I pressed.

“I heard you,” he whispered. Another tense moment passed and all the anxiety I’d kept at bay snuck out from the depths to plague me once more.

I must be out of my mind. Why did I think this was a good idea? It was one rule…

“Andy?” Mitch’s sudden whisper startled me. At my tiny jump, his arm curled around me, pulling me closer.

I swallowed before answering. “Yeah?”

“Why did you let Benny talk to you like that?”

“What do you mean?”

“The gay slurs. Why didn’t you stick up for yourself?”

I shrugged, which had the added consequence of Mitch’s arm tightening even more. My back pressed firmly against his chest and my heart stuttered. I snuffed the ember that stubbornly refused to stay dead and focused on the unusual query. “There’s no point in it. That’s just who he is. Benny is harmless. Besides, arguing wouldn't have been conducive to getting him to leave.” I expected that to be the end of it, when I felt Mitch’s nose brush my hair as he buried his face in the back of my neck. My breath caught and I willed my stupid heart to find a steady rhythm.

“No one is harmless,” he whispered, his breath tickling the sensitive hairs. His arm tightened briefly in conjunction with the morose words, at once protective and possessive. I swallowed past the sudden lump lodged in my throat and found no words.

Chapter 23

Four Years Ago

Mitch

A shout came from the opposite end of the makeshift field. I knew I needed to pay attention or risk getting hit by either the ball or a body, but my mind was still stuck on the image of Andy standing on the hill waving emphatically to get my attention. His red hair shone copper in the morning sun and even from this distance, I could see the green of his eyes. My gaze passed right over him and he staggered back as if physically struck. I winced at the echo of the blow that landed in my gut.

What have I done?

Someone tugged on my arm, pulling me back into the game. Sweat trickled down my back as I moved forward to cut toward the goal. I dodged Benny before he could body check me for my trouble and passed the ball to Brian. He was less fortunate evading the Middies. The friendly match continued, but my movements were mechanical, my body moving by rote rather than desire to win.

Eventually, the game came to a stopping point when the existing lacrosse team spilled out onto the Green. Shouts went up as the coach started listing the names of those that had made the cut. I knew I made the team long before my name was called. I knew because Andy had told me so. Against my better judgment, I glanced over to where I'd spotted him earlier. The low stone wall stood immovable at his back, a witness to countless schemes and animated conversations. It was a place I treasured and one that had always brought me comfort. Andy stood staring down at the chaos on the field, except he wasn't alone.

The Senior Captain slapped me on the back and congratulated me again on making the team. His voice joined the rest of the enthusiastic commendations and celebratory cheers. But it was all white noise. All I could see was Andy talking to Calvin Bridges. And Calvin was smiling.

I turned away from the sight twisting my stomach into knots and melded into the crowd. Andy didn't need me. He'd moved on.

It's for the best.

The thought brought me little comfort as the tiny spark of hope that I could somehow be redeemed went out.

Present Day

Mitch

The tension in Andy's body slowly relaxed as his breathing deepened into the steady rise and fall of slumber. I tightened my arm around his waist and pulled him closer into the cocoon of my body, though he was in no danger of falling off. He shifted in his sleep and I feared I'd inadvertently woken him up. But rather than turn and berate me for still being there, he snuggled back against me. I let out a relieved breath and burrowed my face once more against his neck.

He had a point. Sneaking out of a secret room was one thing, sneaking out of a dorm room that wasn't yours was substantially more conspicuous. Despite the logic and the risks, though, I wouldn't leave. Even if he woke right now and demanded I go, I'd stay. I wasn't about to make the same mistake twice.

Not for the first time, more like the millionth, I wondered what would have happened if I had stayed that fateful night. Would Andy have forgiven me? Would he have understood? What if I hadn't turned my back on him the next day or all the days after that? I thought back to the one and only time we'd run into each other before he'd found me on the verge of committing another grave mistake in the Tower at the start of term.

It hadn't even been a year since we'd spoken. He'd come tearing down the hall like hell itself was after him. Too preoccupied with looking over his shoulder, he hadn't seen me crossing from an adjoining hallway. We'd collided. While I kept my footing, he'd gone sprawling. Books tumbled out of his bag, equal parts worn paperbacks and massive texts. He immediately started gathering them and only when the last one was secure did he look up .

The look of abject horror as the blood drained from his face when he realized who he'd run into would haunt me until the day I died. At the steady beat of feet hitting the ground, we both looked back the way he'd come. He turned back to me, the tiniest spark of hope in his eyes when I didn't call attention to where he was. The footsteps got louder and my gaze flicked up to make sure no one had emerged at the end of the hall yet. When I glanced back down at him, he didn't even seem to breathe as he awaited judgment.

"Go." One word. It was all I could manage, and it nearly killed me. He scurried to loop his bag over his head and got to his feet. He took two steps, then hesitated, glancing over his shoulder at me. I wanted to scream at him to run, but more than that, I wanted to run with him, away from this awful place and all the horrible mistakes I'd made. Instead, I turned to face the oncoming threat. I sensed him leave, taking that herbal scent that was wholly his with him.

John, Todd, and Aaron skidded to a halt before me, their gazes searching the otherwise empty hallway. "Oy, did you see where that ginger freak went?"

My jaw tightened, and I forced it to relax. "What's it to you?"

Three pairs of eyes snapped to me. "That queer has it coming," John said, joined by a host of cruel laughter.

It had taken everything in me to keep my shoulders from tightening up. I shoved my hands in my pockets and met his gaze without blinking. "How do you know he's queer?"

"He just is."

I shrugged. "But how do you know?" John frowned and looked to the others, who were no more helpful in coming up with a reasonable response. I stepped forward with a confidence I didn't possess. "You know what I think? I think you should leave Gallagher alone."

"Why are you protecting him?" Aaron asked at the same time recognition lit in Todd's eyes.

"You two used to be friends." I winced inwardly at Todd's assessment. He narrowed his eyes at me and I braced myself for the inevitable conclusion. If they believed Andy was queer, it wouldn't take much of a leap to think I was too. "But you're not anymore."

John crossed his arms. "So, why protect him now?"

"Consider it for old time's sake. He backed me when I needed it. I'm just returning the favor."

"And what'll you do if we go after him anyway?" John asked.

I speared him with a glare. "You really want to find out?" I couldn't believe it as the lot of them shuffled their feet and averted their gazes. Feeling braver than I had a right, I decided to push my luck. "So, it's settled. No one touches Andy. Ever." I'd waited for nods of acceptance and prayed this wouldn't come back to bite me in the ass. Even if it did, I wouldn't take it back. Andy would always be my best friend, even if I didn't deserve him.

Back in the present, curled up tightly with the man in question, I inhaled the scent of him and hoped that having Andy close would help keep the sins of the past and the nightmares they brought at bay for at least one night.

Andy

I shifted in my sleep and met the resistance of an arm draped across my waist. The hand attached to it coasted along my side to reposition itself higher up. I let out a contented sigh and snuggled back into the steady warmth behind me. My fingers interlaced with the hand's and pulled it closer to my chest. I was hard pressed to come up with a time I'd been more comfortable, more at peace.

The only way this could get any better is if it was actually Mitch curled around me.

My sleepy mind was more than okay with this and happily indulged in the wonderful fantasy that he would hold me so close. The responsible part of my brain that recognized it as morning and that I needed to wake up, had its own reality check: It *was* Mitch and he *wasn't* supposed to be here.

My eyes flew open, and I tossed aside the arm like it had burned me. "Mitch," I hissed in the early morning light streaming mercilessly through the window. It had to be at least seven by now, which meant the first bell for breakfast had already rung.

The rejected arm made a stubborn return and tightened around me like a constrictor. “Go back to sleep, Andy,” Mitch mumbled sleepily, nuzzling into my back.

The part of me that desperately wanted to believe the fantasy skipped with joy. The rest of logic, however, would not be denied. “You weren’t supposed to fall asleep,” I admonished, scooting to the edge and slipping out from under his arm and under the covers. Mitch blinked back at me, not looking nearly as sleepy as he should, though his bed head was rather impressive. I brought my hand up to my own hair, which no doubt looked like I’d had epic sex the night before, which I had, but that was beside the point.

“I think it was warranted.” His casual response only got my ruff up further.

“You’re not supposed to be here,” I argued. “How the hell do you expect to get out of here without drawing any attention?”

“I won’t.”

I straightened up, my irritation momentarily forgotten in surprise. He slung his legs over the side of the bed and my rebellious eyes couldn’t help but drink in every inch of him. He looked damn good in the dark. He looked positively edible in the daylight. I tore my lingering gaze away from his chest and met his unabashed face. “What?”

“Please, Andy, give me a little credit.” He walked over to the closet, but not mine, Lucien’s. In a matter of seconds, he had an entire uniform laid out, but it wasn’t until he slipped on the jacket that I realized the two were nearly the same height. He rolled the sleeves up and tugged the pants as low as they would sit on his hips without falling off. “Not perfect, but it'll do. And since he won’t be back until next week, I have plenty of time to return it.” He straightened from tying his stolen shoes and looked over at me. “You planning to get dressed?”

My mouth opened and closed again without any words coming out. Mitch's gaze slipped from my face and traveled south. I quickly spun away and started yanking out my own clothes before he could see the reaction his looking at me had. My cheeks burned as long forgotten memories of getting dressed in front of Mitch like it was no big deal resurfaced. We could pretend all we liked, but this was different. We were different.

Deep breath. You can do this. Just stop over-thinking everything. Easier said than done, of course.

I finished doing the last button and pulled on my vest, then spun to face Mitch. "There, how do I look?"

He gave a low chuckle and stepped forward, abandoning his perch on Lucien's desk. His fingers slid beneath my folded collar and he used it to pull my mouth to his. We came together with a suction of air that threatened to dissolve my resolve to remain calm and impassive. He deepened the kiss, his tongue slipping past my parted lips to claim what it wanted with abandon, and I could feel myself sliding deeper into the fantasy.

Sex with Mitch was one thing, but this was something else. I wanted to grab him and crush his mouth to mine, to tangle my hands in his hair and hold him as close as possible, to never let him go. I stubbornly kept my rebellious extremities by my side rather than wrap my fingers around his forearms in a caress that would only encourage him. My denied heart twisted painfully in my chest while I continued to kiss him back, unable to stop myself.

I can't do this. I can't be Mitch's friend with benefits. It's killing me. I'm falling in love with him all over again.

I was actually beginning to wonder if I'd ever fallen out of love with him in the first place.

This is just another game for him. What will happen to me when he tires of playing—again?

"Mitch," I said with all the force I could muster.

I have to tell him. I have to stop this.

He pulled back slightly without acknowledging my tone. "You're gonna want to wear your collar up today," he said with a wicked gleam in his eye as he flipped it up.

"What? Why?" I asked, caught off guard by the unusual suggestion.

He leaned forward to whisper in my ear, his lips trailing along my cheek, and my heart skipped. "Because you have a hickey." When he pulled back, his trademark look of mischief danced across his features like Puck himself was looking back at me.

"What?" I raced over to the window to check my reflection and pulled back the now popped collar. Sure enough, a mouth-sized bruise marred the side of my neck. "What the literal hell, Mitch!" Even the collar up barely hid the mark. "Motherfucker."

He laughed while I frantically inspected the hazy image. His response only solidified my earlier assessment that this was all just a game to him.

Does he even understand the ramifications of what he did? What it means?

He'd marked me, like a possession. I was literally branded…as his. My stomach fluttered. I ruthlessly murdered all the butterflies and refused to acknowledge that being marked by Mitch was in any way something I wanted.

"Are you trying to get me in trouble?" I asked, still inspecting the mark.

"Keep," he corrected.

I spun around to face him, stunned for the fourth time that morning and yet again at a loss for words.

"Keep you in trouble," he added with a devious smile.

"I'm gonna murder you." After all, I'd already massacred a rabble of butterflies. What was my best friend?

"Yeah?" Mischief sparkled in his eyes that showed zero signs of remorse for what he'd done as he inched his way toward the door.

I mirrored his movement. "Yeah."

His laughter rang out as he spun and raced for the door. It flew open, and he tore out of the room. I sprinted after him, grabbing my scarf on the way out and resigned to return for my satchel after I murdered him. We sped down the corridor toward the dining hall. With his long legs, he should have had more of a lead, but I gained ground even as I wrapped the scarf around my neck to hide the evidence of our night together. A giddy joy I hadn't experienced in years filled my chest and fueled my limbs.

Abruptly, Mitch skidded to a halt. Confused, I looked ahead to see what could have caused such a reaction and barely saw the teacher in time to do the same. Professor Stein quirked an eyebrow at us as we walked sedately past him side by side. I did what I could to school my ridiculous grin, but could do nothing about the excitement running rampant inside me.

"Gentleman," he said flatly.

"Professor Stein," we echoed in unison.

The hallway was abnormally quiet as we continued to walk. Mitch glanced over his shoulder several times before finally catching my eye. My grin finally broke free, and we sprinted in tandem all the way to breakfast.

Chapter 24

Mitch

I leaned against the wall with my arms crossed and hoped I didn't look too conspicuous. A few students wandered the halls, some I recognized from my classes, others I didn't. While Ulwich was a legacy school, not everyone could stay. Some moved, some got transferred. Whatever the reason they left, they rarely came back. Part of me envied them, another part recognized that if my Uncle Teri hadn't gotten me in at Ulwich, I never would have met Andy.

A door further down the hall opened as another class let out for the day. Luckily, it was a group of lower classmen and none of my teammates. The memory of the last time I'd run into them like this made me wince and I shifted my gaze back to the door of Garza's classroom.

Finally, it opened. Andy filled the doorway, and I stood straighter, a smile already tugging at my lips, though he hadn't seen me yet. He was glancing over his shoulder, still talking to Garza. I bit my lip to stop myself from shouting at him to hurry already and prevent the grin in danger of cracking my face. While he continued talking, I let my gaze travel down his body, appreciating the way his buttoned blazer accentuated his slim shoulders and highlighted his waist. Not everyone could pull off the academy uniform, but Andy wore it well.

The navy blazer made his copper hair that much brighter and paired well with his ivory freckled skin. Of course, I'd rather be peeling him *out* of the uniform, but that was beside the point. It didn't hurt that Andy *always* looked good either. Even the way the unremarkable khakis hugged his trim waist and ended in a perfect cuff just before his polished Oxford loafers set my pulse racing. Or maybe that had more to do with his legs.

They may not be as long as mine, but they'd been able to wrap around me just fine. And *that* was a feeling I wouldn't soon forget.

"Sure thing, professor, I'll get right on that," Andy said as he stepped through the door. The heavy wood swung shut, and Andy lifted his gaze. When it landed on me, a smile instantly blossomed on his face and glowed in his eyes. "Hey, what are you doing here?"

I fought the urge to close the distance separating us and snare him with a kiss. Instead, I shrugged. "Thought it was a nice enough afternoon and wondered if you'd be interested in going for a walk. We could head toward town or stick to the woods. Whatever." I had to bite my tongue to stop babbling. That wasn't a problem I normally had, but considering how well everything had been going since we'd slept together, I was worried about messing things up. I still couldn't get over how easy it had been between us. I'd expected full on awkward or for Andy to withdraw, but he hadn't. He'd continued to tutor me in physics and even helped with my recent Lit paper. It was likely we'd turned a corner, and as much as I wanted more from Andy, I also didn't want to do anything to jeopardize the progress we *had* made.

"It is a nice day, isn't it? I suppose I could go for a walk." He gave me a quick once over, no doubt taking in the fact that I was already in jeans, a knitted sweater, and a jacket. "I'll change real quick. Meet you at the wall?"

"Sure thing."

A whopping ten minutes later, Andy walked up to our usual spot, and I had to remind myself to breathe. He looked positively edible in a forest green cable-knit sweater that was definitely heavier than mine and skin-tight jeans so dark blue they might as well be black. If I'd wanted to greet him with a kiss before, I wanted to drag him into the woods and devour him now.

"That was fast," I said, grateful my voice didn't pitch like my stomach did as he stepped close enough to smell his herbal scent.

He gave me a cheeky grin. "Well, my mentor meeting with Garza went longer than expected and the sun sets earlier now. Hope you weren't waiting too long."

"Nope," I lied as we fell in step and angled for the edge of the woods. I glanced at him again and worked diligently to keep my dirty thoughts of rucking up his sweater and leaving hickeys all over his torso to myself. "You gonna be warm enough?"

"I was literally sweating as I left the school. Far as I'm concerned, this feels great."

I shook my head. The winter chill had set in with a vengeance, and we'd already had snow twice. But I also didn't want to point out that I remembered how easily he got cold...or the fact that he'd just shivered. "I kind of feel like an ass for not asking sooner, but how's the mentorship going?"

Andy darted me a quick look, surprise dominating his small smile. "It's going really well. My grades are all up—"

I rolled my eyes. "No surprise there."

"Shut up," he said with a chuckle that only fed the light filling me. "Like I was saying, grades are good. I'm on my way to being valedictorian, though it seems I have a little competition there."

I frowned, my eyebrows pinching together. The idea of *anyone* out-smarting Andy was ludicrous. "Really? Who?"

"Price, if you can believe it."

"No fucking way."

Andy nodded, though he didn't look like he believed it himself. "Way. But I'm not really worried. It's not like I *need* to be valedictorian." He shot me a glare as I guffawed. "What's so funny?"

"Can I get that in writing? Tell me with a straight face that you won't do everything short of cheating to make sure that title goes to you." I lifted my eyebrows as I waited.

He rolled his shoulders, and his beautiful mouth twisted into a scowl. "Fine. I will. But only because it will look great on my final transcript."

"Oh yeah, *that's* the reason," I teased. He bumped me with his shoulder and I was tempted to wrap an arm around him to keep him close. It would also help to stave off the shivering he would adamantly refuse to admit he was doing. Except with the school not that far off and students wandering around in search of early evening plans, here wasn't as safe or free as I would like. "So, um, you know which university you're going to?"

"Yes!" Andy quickly glanced around as several startled birds took flight. "I mean, yes," he repeated in a softer tone, that did nothing to diminish his enthusiasm. "I've already submitted to Chicago University. Garza is making me apply to some backups, so I'll be doing that over winter break. But, honestly, it's Chicago or bust for me. Now all I'm waiting on is for Garza to finalize his letter of recommendation and hopefully my acceptance letter, though he says they like to drag their feet to make applicants sweat."

"I have every belief you'll get in. How could they not want you?"

Andy gave me a sheepish smile, and my heart did a silly flip. "You really think so?"

"Do you really have to ask?" I responded softly.

He let out a self-deprecating laugh. "No, I suppose not." He glanced at me again, this time a light of curiosity in his eyes. "I know it's a sensitive topic, but what about you? I know that Santinelli is almost everyone on the team's mentor, but do *you* have any colleges you'd like to go to?"

My steps slowed as I turned his words over in my head. I really hadn't given it much thought and even with my grades being better, my chances of getting accepted somewhere weren't great. Plus, without a scholarship, no way could my mom afford it, and there wasn't a chance I was letting my uncle foot the bill for that too, not after covering Ulwich's steep tuition. I came to a full stop and considered Andy, an idea forming. Chicago had a lacrosse team. They weren't a big name in the sport by any means and I doubted coach would have encouraged any of their scouts to visit, but that didn't mean one couldn't.

Andy stood watching me, having stopped when I did. He wrapped his arms tightly around his torso and gave a full body shudder.

"That's it, enough of this."

"Enough of what?" he asked, his teeth chattering on the "t".

I slipped off my jacket and held it out for him. "You're obviously cold, Andy, and I'm not gonna stand by while you stubbornly pretend you're not. Now turn around."

"But—"

"No buts." I shook the jacket for emphasis. He pouted and grumbled under his breath something about me being obstinate, but turned and let me help him into the still warm sleeves. I hiked it over his shoulders and he spun back to face me, still scowling. "There. Now, isn't that better?" The jacket fit me perfectly, but it nearly swallowed Andy whole. I chuckled to myself at how freaking adorable he looked in the oversized outerwear and pulled the lapels tighter.

Andy gazed up at me, his green eyes bright beneath his copper lashes, his cheeks pink from the cold, and his lips parted as if he'd planned to say something.

My heart hammered as I smoothed the front of the jacket over his chest and stared back at him. Forget dragging him into the woods to make out. I wanted to kiss him here, right now, witnesses be damned. How had I gone so long without his lips on mine? When I'd given into the impulse four years ago, it had been more than enough to make me want them all the time. But I'd been scared. And I'd wasted so much time.

"Mitch?"

Hearing Andy whisper my name helped me reach the conclusion I should have reached all those years ago. He deserved the truth. "Andy, I... I need to tell you something—I should have told you a long time ago—about us. Me, really." I hesitated, my gaze fixed on where my thumb rubbed along the zipper, still anxious despite knowing this was the right thing. "I owe you the truth. I—"

"It's okay, Mitch. I know."

I flicked my gaze up to meet his, my breath catching even as my heart threatened to explode out of my chest. "You do?"

"Yeah." He gave me a soft smile and took a small step back, causing my hands to fall free of him. "I get it. You're curious. This isn't really you, and I'm... I'm okay with that. Really."

I was pretty sure my brain was leaking out of my ears, because I had no idea what he was talking about. With a shake of my head, I stepped closer. "Please, let me finish. You deserve an apology."

Andy

How naïve could I be? Sleeping together didn't magically erase who Mitch was... Who I was. This was always doomed. We would never work. Mitch would never be *mine*. And yet, I'd childishly let myself indulge in the fantasy and hoped we had more time before we had to confront this conversation.

I took a deep breath and tried not to let my hurt show as I put on a front of acceptance. "Seriously, Mitch, there's nothing to apologize for. Like I've said before, I knew what I was doing. There's no need to let me down easy." Despite my valiant effort to maintain eye contact, I couldn't do it *and* suppress the stinging building behind my eyes. I dropped my gaze to look past his shoulder, where I wouldn't have to see his confused expression. I didn't have it in me to break this down for him. He was experimenting, I got it. There was no need to make this more painful than it already was. He was straight. I was not. Nothing was ever going to change that.

"Andy, please, just listen to me. I should have been upfront with you years ago, but I'm not brave like you are. You trusted me with your truth, and I should have trusted you with mine. I'm—"

I wasn't really listening; it was too painful. Why couldn't we have continued pretending? Why did it have to come to this?

Movement behind him caught my attention. I squinted and instinctively leaned forward to make it out. The indistinct shadows solidified into the outline of several people. "Oh shit," I hissed, then promptly dove into the trees. No way was I letting Mitch get caught by his homophobic teammates on what probably looked like an intimate walk with me.

"What the fuck?" he asked, stepping closer to the shrub I'd ducked behind. "What are you doing?" He leaned down like he was going to come after me despite my waving for him to go. Then a braying laugh, like a hyena with the flu, cut through the otherwise peaceful landscape, and Mitch straightened to look back the way we'd come. The noise came again and Mitch cursed under his breath. For as long as I lived, I doubt I'd ever be able to forget John's God awful laugh.

"Yo, Hudson! What are you doing out here all on your lonesome?" a voice I was pretty sure belonged to Kyle asked. Given that the only thing I could see from my vantage was Mitch's back, all I had was guesswork.

Mitch's gaze flicked to my hiding spot, and I held my breath. Then he moved closer to the voices. Fortunately, his response masked my sigh of relief. "Figured I'd take my happy ass for a walk, take in the fresh air. It was nice until you bozos showed up." He laughed, but there was no joy in it.

"Well, you look like a loser, wandering around by yourself." Judging by the wheezy laugh that followed, that had to be John.

"A cold loser," maybe Aaron added.

Mitch shrugged. "Don't know what you mean. Feels great out here to me." My hands reflexively curled around the opening of Mitch's jacket around me. He'd been dead-on about me being cold, but I should have been more adamant about refusing. Except it had felt good to have someone take care of me, to have *Mitch* take care of me.

"We're headed to town to hang at the arcade. Join us." *That* was definitely Brian Daniels, and it wasn't a request. Even from my limited perspective, I could see Mitch's shoulders stiffen.

Several beats filled the silence until I wanted to burst from the woods like some kind of jack-in-the-box, just to cut the tension. At last Mitch said cooler than I would have been able to, "Sure. Sounds like a good time." Then he stepped aside and held up an arm. "Lead the way."

The sound of footsteps grew louder until I caught glimpses of the group. Per my suspicions, Brian, Kyle, John, Aaron, and to my surprise, Nathaniel, Mitch's roommate, were all there. Mitch let most of them past and only turned to fall in line when he was even with Nathaniel. He glanced in my direction again, a strange mix of emotion on his face, and shrugged one shoulder, offering me a half smile that didn't touch his eyes, as if to say, "What can I do?"

I remained perfectly still as I waited for them all to leave. Once they were too far to make out clearly, I stood and started making my way back to the school, careful to stay in the trees and out of sight. I clutched Mitch's jacket tighter around me, both to stave off the cold and to inhale what lingered of his warmth. Even as his tangy scent soothed my nerves, my heart cracked.

How could I have been so foolish as to let Mitch back in? Being friends again was one thing, but fooling around was not only dangerous to my heart but our physical wellbeing. Tears that I told myself I would never cry again spilled free to chill on my cheeks. Would I even be able to push Mitch back to arm's length now that he was back in my life? Whether or not I could was beside the point—I had to. And I had all winter break to figure out how.

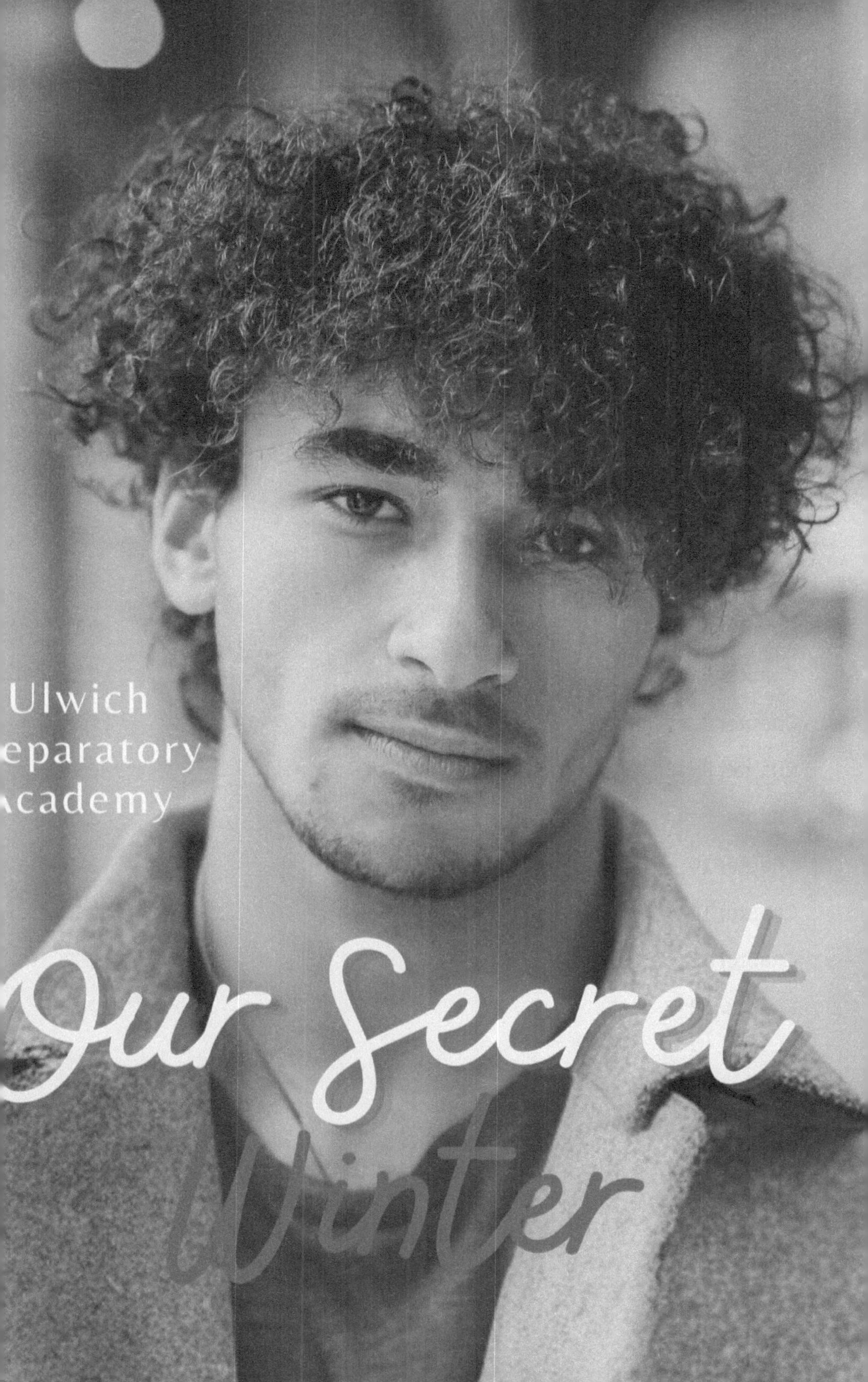
Ulwich
eparatory
Academy
Our Secret
Winter

Contents

Chapter 1

Calvin

The empty pudding cup sat beside me on the grass, forgotten as I leaned forward to give the impromptu lacrosse match below my full attention. With the arrival of the school's key Midfielder and two Defenders, the friendly game had evolved into a full-on practice match. No pads or helmets meant the body checks stayed fairly tame, but you wouldn't find me complaining. The sweaty bodies below glistened in the afternoon sun, a veritable feast for my eyes. It never ceased to amaze me how a school consumed with homophobia didn't see how shoving a bunch of developing boys in proximity to each other wouldn't foster at least a little exploration.

Andy, my companion and only real friend in this hellhole of repression, had long since abandoned me. Lacrosse held no interest for him, surprising considering the star player, Mitchum Hudson, had once been his best friend and seemed determined to be so again. I winced as a Middie and an Attackman came together hard enough to be heard even from this distance. Benjamin Price stared down at his latest victim, who remained on the ground in what was likely a state of shock. With his broad shoulders, thick torso, and muscular legs, Benny was a beast on and off the field. A veritable Laocoön or Farnese Heracles. My fingers tingled as I ran through the list of Grecian sculptures and imagined running them over the living model currently dominating the game.

What I wouldn't give to get my hands on that.

...Again.

A smile curved my mouth as I scooped the fallen art supplies back into my bag along with the cleaned pudding cup and spoon. I straightened up and cast a glance back down at the field below. The poor Attackman had found his feet, and the match had resumed, though it was clearly winding down. They'd be heading to the showers at the locker room next. If I meandered my way along, I'd arrive just in time for my appointment, and if I was lucky, a peek at all that exquisite flesh.

I yanked my loose tie off and stuffed it in my bag, where it hung out like a mustard-striped navy tongue. Next, I undid several buttons and yanked on the stifling collar. The uniform they forced us to endure was just another symbol of oppression and one I openly rebelled against. I rolled the cuffs of the navy jacket, exposing the white satin underlining, and pushed back the hair that had fallen in my face. The tight curls—a stunning Mars Brown with Burnt Sienna highlights—hung substantially longer than code dictated and were a constant nuisance. But it was either tie them back or cut them off, both of which were tantamount to admitting defeat. Unsurprisingly, the damn things tumbled back in my face and stuck to the sweat dampening my forehead. Not that I was out of shape, far from it, but the way was long and the afternoon exceedingly warm.

At last, my destination came into view. Rather than venture into the locker room proper and enjoy the view and the AC, I sought a bit of shade off to the side and waited for my quarry to emerge. The coolness of the painted cement offered a welcome reprieve from the heat and a convenient lean-to. I fished out a sketchbook and pencil, and made sure the rest of what I would need was within easy reach.

The pale cream of the fresh rag paper held all the promise of creation and none of the inspiration. I blew out a breath and stared at the soft white canvas. If I could not round out my portfolio, then I might as well kiss my chance at the Art Institute of Chicago goodbye. Of course, there was always Yale, but Chicago held my heart. I glared resentfully at the stubbornly blank page and graphite poised above it.

You'd think drawing people would be easy for me, considering how many I see all the time.

But not the way Jankowksi wants them, layered with nuances of vulnerability and authenticity.

Therein lie the rub, while I could see those things in others, translating it to canvas meant exposing a part of myself I'd locked away since I was nine.

And some doors should never be opened.

With a disparaging grunt, I fell back on tried and true. By the time my appointment arrived, my rendition of a Quaking Aspen was in full form on the once pristine page. I glanced up out of the corner of my eye without raising my head. My perch in the shade lay far enough from the main entrance to be inconspicuous and mostly hidden from view—unless, of course, you were looking for me.

Brian went rigid as he spied me lurking in the shadows. After a beat, he made his way over, movements jerky like an automaton in sore need of oil. His stunningly dark skin, an intriguing mix of Vandyke Brown with Medium Hansa Yellow undertones, at once absorbed and reflected the afternoon sun. As the only other student of color in our grade, it was a true shame he hadn't been able to look past my orientation to foster any kind of friendship or camaraderie.

"Bridges," he grumbled under his breath as he stopped close enough to be heard, but far enough to deny association. I smirked as I took my time putting away my sketchpad with exaggerated care. The longer I took, the more growly he became. It was no secret Brian didn't like me, of course, he'd liked me even less since I'd caught him and another boy giving each other hand jobs.

At last, I procured the pack of smokes from my bag. His eyes lit up, then immediately darted around to make sure no prying ones were nearby. He reached out, and I pulled the open carton back out of reach. "Payment first."

His face twisted, and his hand fell back to his side. "I don't have it."

Cute how they always think I don't know.

"Don't be coy, darling." He winced at the endearment, and my lips tweaked up in a wicked half smile. "Post came yesterday and *someone* got a delivery." I held out a hand and waited patiently. He ground his teeth and grumbled incoherent insults as he liberated a small wrapped package from his bag. He plopped it rudely in my hand and glared daggers at me.

"Happy, you damn fairy?"

"Immensely." I curled my fingers around the vacuum sealed box and held out the carton of cigarettes with a few greener companions nestled inside. He snatched them from me and didn't bother to check the contents before shoving the poor, abused packaging into his bag. "Pleasure doing business with you."

"Fuck off," he sneered.

"Is that an invitation?" I bat my lashes as I pocketed the high-end cosmetics. It wasn't my fault he had connections to the esteemed company through his sister. Now, whether he stole, bought, or somehow coerced her into gifting the expensive items, I had no idea, nor did I care. It clearly was worth the price, since this was by no means our first such deal.

He rolled his eyes without deigning to answer, then turned to stomp sullenly off with his contraband.

"Oh, tell Tanner I said hello," I called out before he could get too far.

Brian stiffened once more, confirming my suspicion that the two hadn't ceased their extracurriculars despite being caught. Of course, I'd never out either of them on principle, but Brian didn't know that nor would he likely believe me if I told him as much. Plus, it was nice to remind him he was not as untouchable as he acted. He stole a few moments to pull himself together, then resumed storming off.

I chuckled to myself, pleased with a good day's work and content with the knowledge that my client base was well and truly in line. Secrets were a dime a dozen in this place if you paid attention, and it paid to do so. A deeper shadow fell across me, briefly dimming my merriment. Curious if it was another client in need of another trade or a new petitioner, I glanced up once more.

Ah, the latter.

"Benjamin." Nothing could be done to school the wicked grin that stretched my cheeks. Sadly, I didn't seem to have anything he couldn't acquire on his own, not to mention the only secret I had on him fell squarely in the sacred column. I straightened up from slouched repose to be of an even height with him, but didn't abandon my casual stance. "Fancy seeing you here. What can I do for you? Any particular *needs* I could help you with?"

The slight tightening around his eyes was the only indication he'd caught the targeted emphasis. "What are you doing here? You know your queer ass isn't allowed anywhere near the locker rooms."

I pushed off the wall to invade the fringe of his personal bubble, undeterred by the hostility and a touch emboldened by the fact that he'd sought me out. "There's no such rule against it."

"There is, if I say there is, you fucking fagot."

"Ooh…" I shook my head from side to side. "Tsk tsk. You sure you wanna do this, Benny? Here," I purred. "All alone, without your boys to back you up? Last time I checked, you liked to have… a hand." Shuttered fear danced behind his eyes as he no doubt remembered something he tried hard to forget. Meanwhile, the same memory was emblazoned in gold and given a position of prominence in a hall of fucking glory in my mind. "That's what I thought. Now, if you'll excuse me, I have other business to attend to."

Unable to resist riling him up more, I lazily dragged my gaze down his body. Once more, the fantasy of molding that incredible physique in smooth, wet, pliable clay filled my thoughts and made my fingers itch to reach out and test the firm muscle before me if only to make sure I got the consistency right. By the time my gaze found his face once more, his ears burned a fantastic Alizarin Red with steam practically billowing out of them while he fought not to swallow his tongue.

I winked and blew him a kiss, which he didn't catch. "See you around, Benny." I walked past him close enough to feel the tension and anger radiating off his statue-like form. No more slurs followed me as I made my way back to the school proper to inform my client that their shipment had arrived.

White silk hung in elaborate folds from King Kelani's sleeves as he met with the latest supplicant. The trade agreements settled without quarter or malice, but with a firm stoicism that bespoke of a wisdom beyond the young ruler's age. Many had made the mistake in the past of believing the ostentatious prince would become a weak and malleable king. However, Kelani had assumed his role with a dignity and form unbeknownst to his predecessors. After all, what need had he for an army when he held sole control of all the supplies essential to his hostile neighbors?

Chapter 2

Benny

My efforts at keeping my expression neutral went wholly unappreciated as the headmaster himself shot me a pointed look. I diligently didn't roll my eyes and returned my focus to the cluster of fresh faces currently filling the atrium. Ulwich Preparatory Academy's latest batch of would-be gentleman looked about with wide eyes filled intermittently with wonder and uncertainty.

New class, more like lambs fresh for the slaughter.

Anxious eyes darted toward me and I tried harder to remove the scowl from my face, to no avail. I recalled my own amazement and expectation upon enrolling. A legacy whose place was solidified by money and prestige, a fact my father never let me forget for a moment. The Price name was precious, inscrutable, and powerful, and I dare not do anything that might tarnish it. All lies, of course, puffed up circumstance and money lining the right pockets.

I rolled my shoulders, and one of the underlings shrank back into the herd. He wouldn't last long. This school had a nasty habit of taking anything it saw as weakness and crushing it beneath an iron heel. You either grew thicker skin or learned how to put on armor. Trouble was, no one bothered to warn you how much the armor would come to chafe.

"In conclusion, we look forward to having you all join our esteemed ranks next fall." Headmaster Torsney straightened and flattened his formal robes. The navy velvet hung heavily to the floor and swished lightly on the ancient wooden floors.

Fucker has got to be burning up in that shit.

"Mr. Price—that's Benjamin Wallace Price the Fourth—will now lead you on your tour of the grounds." Torsney gestured over to me and I plastered my fakest sincere smile on my face. The parents erupted into a muted tizzy over the news of who their personal guide would be, while most of the youths looked at me with the level of fear I expected from the lower grades.

With a resigned sigh I mostly kept to myself, I stepped away from the wall. "If you'll follow me, we will begin by visiting the dormitories. The youngest grades are situated closer to the teachers' wing in the event of an emergency, but as boys age out, they are transferred to one of three other halls." I turned down the wide expanse of walkway.

This particular route granted an impressive view of some of the school's trademark architecture, including the vaulted ceilings and elaborate stone archways. Never mind that the students themselves would have no occasion to venture this way, but then again, this wasn't for them, was it? This whole charade was so families could feel better about shipping their sons off to live without them. Some of these boys wouldn't see their parents and loved ones for months at a time, others for years.

Sometimes the years are preferable.

I shook off the melancholy thought and concentrated on the task at hand. Spinning on my heel, I began walking backwards. "Traditionally, Ulwich aims to keep bunk mates with the same assignment for the duration of their education. A built-in friend, if you will." I smiled, and the parents tittered happily again. Meanwhile, several of the boys eyed each other skeptically. They had the right idea. Forced bunkmates rarely made for friends. Becoming a prefect certainly had its draws, namely that I had to do these ridiculous tours, but it did have the fantastic perk of coming with my own room. I barely even remembered my original bunkmate.

The tour dragged on for another two hours until I was satisfied that the parents and children were too tired to ask any more inane questions or complain. I left them back in the atrium for a pretentious lunch with the faculty and excused myself to my own diversions. Sadly, though, no reprieve was found in my room. Shortly after arriving, a knock came at the door.

"What?" I snapped, already knowing who would be on the other side. The door had scarcely opened when Neil and Todd came tumbling inside.

"Where have you been all morning?" Todd asked as he flung himself into my chair.

"Yeah, you missed class," Neil added, thumbing through my school books.

I scowled at the pair of them, completely oblivious to me not wanting to be bothered. "I had that stupid fucking tour this morning. You know how Torsney likes to parade me about."

The two shared a look, one of the few examples of successful bunkmates. I wasn't sure how they'd stayed friends or why they bothered to stick around me, likely for the same reason everyone else did. At least they didn't simper.

"Torsney is an ass hat with a prick so small not even a blue pill could save it," Neil declared with conviction.

I snorted a laugh, because it probably wasn't far from the truth. In a sudden spark of energy, I surged up from my seat on the bed. "Let's get the fuck out of here."

"Where did you have in mind?" Todd asked, promptly vacating his stolen seat.

"Somewhere fucking else. Town or something."

Neil rubbed his hands together. "And how long will we be somewhere else? Will we be back in time for, say... afternoon classes?"

I smirked and grabbed my discarded jacket. "We'll see. I've had enough responsibility for one day."

Calvin

Professor Jankowski looked back at the sketch, his brows coming together with an intensity that matched the puckering of his mouth. He didn't need to say it, I already knew, and it was written plain as day across his face.

"Calvin."

"I know," I cut him off, not wanting to hear the words I knew would follow.

"This is not what I meant."

"I know." With another huff, I launched out of my seat to stalk across the room. I stopped to survey the cluster of canvases left to dry. The skill employed wasn't remarkable, but what room did I have to talk? At least they'd *done* the assignment.

He let out a frustrated sigh, and I heard the unmistakable sound of paper whispering to the desk. "We've been through this." I braced myself for the lecture coming; cutting him off would only delay the inevitable for so long. "Art is pain."

"I'm aware."

"Then why won't you let yourself feel?"

"I feel just fine," I snapped back, spinning to face him. He grabbed the flat sketch of my priest from the table and waved it at me.

"*This* is feeling? Come on, Calvin, you're better than this, or at least I thought you were. I've seen your landscapes, the joy you suffuse in a sunrise, the sorrow of an empty hillside bathed in moonlight. Where is *that*? Because it's not here. I have first years that can't manage proportions putting more emotion into their sketches."

I glowered and turned away. The pointed insult needled my pride, but I couldn't do what he asked. Letting feeling out meant letting feeling in, and that wasn't something I could afford to do. I swept the dark curls out of my face and retrieved my bag from the floor. "Fine. I'll try again."

"I know it's hard, Calvin," Jankowski said as I reached for the pathetic attempt at a portrait. "People are complicated, and capturing those nuances is a momentous task. But I wouldn't ask it of you if I didn't know you could rise to the challenge." My fingers clenched into a fist, then I snagged the limp page from him and made my way out. "I'll give you a month's extension, but the deadline for applicants is dwindling. Make it count."

I nearly crumpled the evidence of my failure into an indistinguishable ball. Instead, I carefully slipped it between pages of my sketchbook where it could remain safe and whole. The only way to get better was to learn from mistakes, but fuck if I knew what this one could offer me. I left the art room and only paused twice on the way to my dorm to check key alcoves for customer requests. At finding none, my mood darkened further.

My roommate Greg glanced up at my storm cloud entrance, unsurprisingly without a word. Our entire first year bunked together I'd assumed he was mute given that he never said a word, then I'd overhead him talking with some of his classmates and realized it was me.

"What?" I snapped as I flung my bag on the bed, sending art supplies tumbling free.

In lieu of a verbal response, his dark gaze flicked to my desk equally strewn with pencils and charcoals and a sole envelope. I snatched the small missive up and sat back on my pillows. Greg rolled his eyes and returned to whatever mindless task he used to occupy his time. My fingers deftly fished out the folded square, and I flicked it open, a smile tugging the corners of my mouth.

1. I've done as you said. 2. Hauntings are always worst at midnight.

~L

Instantly, my spirits lifted. Granted, Leonel's code could use some work, but even if Greg had read the note, I doubt he would have been able to infer its true meaning. Considering today had been absolute shit, this wasn't so bad as far as consolation prizes went. After all, in a scant two nights, I'd be getting laid. To celebrate, I yanked out my sketchbook and turned to a clean page.

The portrait remained neglected while I drew the pencil in a broad arc over the page. Bold strokes tapered into delicate scratches that filled the room and went largely uncommented until a perfect rendition of the main atrium of the school dominated the page. I flipped my pencil around and used my pinky to smudge some shading, grounding the image solidly in the late afternoon.

The room depicted held no life, but the shadows of memories filled the emptiness. I'd been frightened to be surrounded by so many strangers, had fought my mother on coming to this place I was sure held nothing but horrors for a boy who couldn't pass even if he wanted to. I sighed and my pencil hung from limp fingers as I let the tide of the past wash over me. The horrors had come, but that day I'd gotten a different surprise. I'd caught another of the boys looking at me. The weight of the world seemed to rest on his shoulders, the burden heavy as if he was Atlas himself, but when he'd looked at me, his demeanor had softened.

At first, I'd believed the look to be one of curiosity. I looked like none of the other boys, with my dark mop of curls and skin like smoky quartz to his delicate fawn. But as the orientation went on, I realized he wasn't looking at my differences, he was looking at *me*. When I'd finally offered a tentative smile, his eyes had widened like I'd caught him doing something wrong. He stopped looking and melded into the crowd to be replaced by a different boy that seemed to wear darkness like a cloak. *He* had smiled at me, a feral thing that made me want to seek out the nervous boy and cling to him for both our sakes.

My pencil scratched violently across the page, digging deep enough to rip the resilient material and mar the once beautiful image. I took a steadying breath and decided to take advantage of my sudden rush of emotion. The portrait slipped free of the pages and I spent the next three hours trying to add any of the compassion or put-upon patience Father Miles had any time we spoke.

Chapter 3

Benny

I slumped in my desk, not even remotely paying attention to the proofs Stein was scribbling on the board. Of course, I wasn't the only one whose attention had found other venues of distraction. The angled calculus text before Gallagher undoubtedly gave Stein the impression that his pupil was fastidiously following the lesson. It also hid the paperback nestled in the bend of the sizable textbook. I wasn't surprised that he didn't feel the need to pay rapt attention, though I wondered if he had any idea that we were neck and neck for the coveted title of valedictorian.

Probably not. That assumes anyone realizes I'm more than just some jock.

Truth be told, the team kept me plenty busy and would keep me busier if I actually landed team captain. How Coach justified drawing out the announcement like this, I had no idea, but much longer and it would be more than students he'd have to answer to.

I was on the verge of excusing myself to literally anywhere else when the classroom door flew open to reveal a flushed student. He was younger than the class he'd burst in on by at least three years, though I recognized his pockmarked face from some of the lacrosse practices. His gaze swept the room until it landed on me.

"Excuse me, young man," Stein said, "you are interrupting my class."

The boy's gaze snapped to the irate professor. "Yes. Sorry, sir. Professor Nolan needs Benny, I mean Mr. Price, at once." His focus swiveled back to me. I hesitated only long enough to receive an approving nod from Stein before standing and making my way out of the room.

That's one way to get out of class.

The nameless youth scurried down the hall at a clip just shy of a run. We made our way down the hall to a room on the far side. He opened the door much like he had the one to my class and rushed in. "I've got him, sir."

Professor Nolan turned to face me, and I choked on a laugh. Black paint smeared across his forehead and jaw, which was currently clenched tight enough to crack rocks, a stark contrast to his exceptionally pale complexion.

"Benjamin Price, you will get to the bottom of this." He gestured to his desk, and I realized his entire hand was coated with black as well. I bit the inside of my cheek to keep from laughing aloud and addressed my attention to the three items that lay on his desk that I suspected to be the culprits of his appearance. Each one consisted of a dark material that had no doubt helped to hide the paint from detection.

I cleared my throat. "Of course, sir."

"Excellent. I want the miscreants apprehended and punished severely."

"Naturally."

He nodded his approval, then tsked loudly when he made the mistake of painting the arms of his chair when he leveraged them to stand. Bitterly muttering beneath his breath, he turned to the board and the entire class erupted in laughter.

Motherfucking Christ.

Nolan spun in place, simultaneously trying to bring the class under control and find the source of the outburst. While I could have helped, I wasn't suicidal enough to point out the cheeky smiley face now painted on his ass and staining his khakis. Thankfully, he didn't need the assistance after all, as he finally noted the pointing and looked down. Fury splotched his face purple, and he spun to hide his violated rump against the wall.

"Benjamin!"

"I'm on it, sir." I stepped forward to carefully retrieve a thoroughly painted book from the desk, leveraging an empty bag from the trash so I didn't end up looking like Nolan. Considering all the items, including Nolan's chair, were all originally either black or equally dark, I had a sneaking suspicion this wasn't everything. "May I advise not touching anything else dark in the room?"

Nolan was borderline apoplectic as he looked back at me. "They will pay for this."

"Yes, sir," I said again, taking my evidence and stepping back out into the hall. The door swung shut behind me and Nolan was already yelling at the students all sorts of vitriol for this outrageous stunt.

"Maybe, if you weren't such an unbearable prick, shit like this wouldn't happen to you," I said to the empty hall.

This certainly wasn't the first time Nolan had been the victim of a prank and I seriously doubted it would be the last. Though the last one to cause such a ruckus had been over four years ago. The Dust Frog Caper, as the student body referred to it. The chalk drawing of a frog bearing Nolan's trademark mustache waiting for him on the other side of the pull down had been hilarious enough to solidify the prankster's place of infamy. But it paled compared to the sheer chaos that had erupted when a furious Nolan had then opened his desk only to have a dozen frogs spring free to spread chalk dust on everyone and everything. No prank had ever come close to that scale before or since… until now.

I reached out a finger to touch the exposed spine of the otherwise safely wrapped book. At first impression, nothing seemed amiss, then I pulled my finger back and revealed the tacky paint hiding in plain sight, paint that was now staining my finger. "Son of a bitch." I more securely wrapped the book, confident that the substance would stubbornly remain intact, and retrieved a napkin from my pocket. Unfortunately, it didn't do shit. In fact, it made it worse.

Now officially pissed, I stormed down the hall toward the art rooms. My temper and frustration grew in equal parts as I discovered the rooms were void of any occupants. I slammed the book down on a nearby desk. "Motherfucker."

"Sorry, no one here by that name."

I spun around at the cheeky comment and spied none other than Calvin Bridges perched upon a chaise, no doubt intended for posing models. He had the audacity to wiggle his fingers at me in a wave that set my teeth on edge.

"Where are the others?"

"Out." He didn't even blink as he delivered the flat response. Frustration bubbled beneath my skin. Asking Calvin anything was one hundred percent at the bottom of my list, but in lieu of someone more qualified to talk to, he'd have to do. I snatched the book back up and crossed the room.

"Explain this," I demanded, thrusting it at him. When he didn't take it, I dropped it with a loud thud on the table sitting beside the chair.

His outrageously long lashes fanned darkly over his cheeks as he looked down at the item in question. He inspected it a moment, then leaned back on the couch. I ground my teeth at his nonchalance, but refused to be goaded into asking a second time.

"That would be Lamp black acrylic paint," he declared. "Terrible stuff. Prefer oils myself."

I took a deep breath in through my nose to foster patience I absolutely did not have. "How do you know what it is?" He shifted his head slightly, causing the rampant curls to fall in his face as he quirked an eyebrow at the accusing undercurrent.

"You shouldn't have tried to wipe it away. You need paint thinner for that shit."

"Where is the paint kept?" I asked, determined to focus on the reason I was here and not on his attitude or the way his dark hair curled around his brown eyes. He gestured over his sketchbook with his pencil at a closed cabinet. "Care to be more specific?" I growled, already regretting this entire endeavor.

He rolled his eyes and made a grand show of setting his work aside. His long limbs stretched out like a snake uncoiling as he extricated himself from the plush chaise. I took a step back as he stood so we wouldn't be standing on top of each other. The only thing more remarkable about Calvin's lithe height matching my six-one was the confidence with which he carried himself, like he owned the damn school instead of it being the other way around. This wretched place owned all of us.

"Take your time, why don't you," I snapped irritably as he meandered at a snail's pace over to the indicated furniture.

He glanced over his shoulder, the navy broadcloth of his uniform jacket bunching. "I intend to," he purred, the words thick with insinuated promise while his dark brown eyes shamelessly took me in. My chest puffed up out of reflex while my ears burned. I hated when he looked at me like that, something he never failed to do when there was no one else around. Before I could say anything, he unlocked the cabinet and threw open both doors, then let out a gasp.

I surged up beside him, heedless of the proximity. "What? What is it?"

He held a hand to his mouth in mock coyness. "It seems someone has liberated that detestable paint."

"Are you fucking serious? I swear, you limp-wristed flamer, if you had anything to do with what happened in Nolan's class—"

"Ooh... What happened to Nolan?" he asked, his eyes sparkling with intrigue.

"Nothing."

"Doubtful if it has your knickers in such a twist."

I ignored the prod and looked deeper into the cabinet. To my relief, a few bottles lurked in the back labeled Lamp Black Acrylic. I snagged two bottles and noted the circles of dust highlighting another missing three. Given how difficult the shit was to get off, it was unlikely the culprit had gotten away unmarked. "Who else has access to this?"

"Besides me?"

I rounded on him and resolved not to show how much having him this close was affecting me. "Is that a confession?"

His eyes narrowed as a sinister smile pulled at his full mouth. "I'm very good at confessions, Benjamin. Have any you'd like to share?" Unable to stand his proximity anymore, I jerked back and used closing the cabinet to hide the reaction. "What's the matter, Benny? Are there some deep dark secrets you need to unburden? I'm all..." his gaze flicked down and back up again almost too fast to catch, "ears."

I curled my lip at him and squeezed the tubes of paint so hard I feared they'd burst. "Listen, flit-"

"Working our way down the alphabet today?" he interrupted, his Cheshire grin growing. "Wouldn't it be more fun to work your way down something else?"

Fucking Calvin Bridges and his fucking insinuations.

I pivoted on my heel, nearly forgetting the wrapped book in my eagerness to get the fuck away from him. His laughter chased me out of the room and continued to ring in my ears as I made my way to the headmaster's office to report.

Kel's laugh filled the atrium and abraded Einar's ears. The king's bejeweled robes swept in an elaborate arc as he turned away from the young prince. Prince Einar saw no humor in these proceedings, however, and resented the implication that he'd come, like so many others before him, to court the self-assured ruler. He tightened his hold on his sheathed sword and followed after to the throne room with its ornate adornments that lauded the king's power. King Kelani assumed his seat with all the regal bearing befitting his station and considered the prince, the supplicant, as one might consider a fish before gutting it for dinner.

Chapter 4

Calvin

Leonel glanced up at me, nervous anxiety written in every line of his body from the dark rose flush staining his cheeks to the tightness of his shoulders. "You're not going to tell anyone, right?" It was hard to miss the edge of defensiveness… or hint of threat.

I diligently refrained from giving face to my surprise. Not that the implied threat was new, but normally they asked that question *before* we had sex. I let out a slow breath and offered him a reassuring smile as I moved to squat down beside him. To his credit, he only flinched a little at the proximity. For some reason, having me near him without clothes was perfectly acceptable, with, however, apparently bore different implications. "No."

His gaze shuttled away to look opposite me. Anger and a fierce need to comfort him in this time of doubt warred within me. Against my better judgment, I reached out to comb his brown hair behind an ear. He stiffened at the touch and the anger inched a little closer to winning.

"No one you don't want to will ever know what happened here," I said softly and dropped my hand.

His gaze danced back toward me, fear to believe swimming in their mahogany rings.

"Do you remember what I told you to do next?" He nodded mutely. "Good." I caught his gaze to make sure my next words took. "However you feel about what happened here is your business, but aftercare is important."

"I got it," he snapped. His gaze fell once again, but at least didn't wander too far this time. "Thanks," he finally added, with the tiniest hint of humility.

I smiled and straightened up, then offered him a hand, that to my surprise, he actually took. "You say that like I got nothing out of this."

His cheek twitched, and I won my first genuine smile of the night. Teasing the men I slept with was always a bit of a gamble that paid off about as often as it blew up in my face. He glanced around, taking in the thin mattress and twisted sheets that still bore the evidence of what we'd done minus the condom. I'd disposed of that while Leonel had been pulling himself together. I'd learned the hard way that actually seeing it triggered the skittish ones more often than not. "Do you want any help cleaning up?"

Once again, I worked to school my face, but as generous as I found the offer, it was also abundantly clear that Leonel was ready to run as far and fast as his legs could carry him. "No, I'll take care of this. You go on and sneak in a shower before your roommate wonders where you've gone off to."

He offered another weak smile and gingerly gathered up the last of his things. Unexpectedly, he paused and glanced over at me, the shy nervousness back in full force, along with a heavy dose of fear that pinched his brows and clouded his eyes. "Does this mean... I mean, does this make me..." The floundering and inability to come right out and ask it would have been laughable if it wasn't so damn heartbreaking. Fuck this school and what it did to generations of confused adolescents. Leonel was technically older than me, though not by much, and *this* was how he had to explore his sexuality.

"No, Leo, you're not gay. Curious, maybe, but not gay."

Hope lit his eyes and soured my stomach. "Do you know?" he asked like I possessed some magic eight ball about what people's sexual preferences were.

"Not always, but sometimes," I admitted, an image of a young boy looking across a crowded room and truly seeing me flashing through my mind.

Fucking motherfucking damn. I never should have drawn that Christ forsaken atrium.

I pushed away the tide of resentment threatening to further dim the evening and nodded towards the door. Some days I wondered if I was taking this whole sexually liberating the repressed too far. "You should get going. Be careful of the prefect doing the rounds." Leonel offered one more nod and left without a backward glance, just like they all left. There had only ever been one that had stayed, had wanted to be held and comforted, who hadn't had shame in their eyes.

I swallowed against the sudden tightness in my throat and glanced around the empty room. Once a bustling classroom like all the others, rumors and superstition had led it to be abandoned, closely followed by several neighboring rooms as well, which made it the ideal place for illicit interludes. Encouraging those rumors had been a no-brainer the second I recognized the potential of such a space.

I scooped up the sheets and tried not to think about the boy with the penetrating gaze who felt so much as I balled them up. They joined a collection of odds and ends that would also find their way back into the school proper, be it the laundry or the trash.

An hour later, not a speck of evidence remained. The mattress rested between the multitude of shelves squished together and the lube rejoined the remaining condoms in a hidey-hole hidden behind loose backing. Satisfied the place once again looked every bit as derelict and haunted as it was supposed to be, I gathered my own things and made my way to the less used showers on this floor, confident they'd be empty.

Worry scratched at my nerves as I made my way back to the dining hall in the hopes my friend would be there. I rounded a corner and the solid form of someone moving much too fast slammed into me. My breath came out in a grunt and I looked down to see copper red hair no bottle could ever reproduce. Relief instantly flooded through me.

"There you are. Where the fuck have you been all day?"

Andy glanced up from his efforts to restore his bulging satchel, surprise clear on his face. "H-hey."

The worry I'd just lost came back in a rush. "Is everything alright? Where have you been?" I asked again.

"I... uh... fell asleep in the tower," he said, evading the real question as he hopped from foot to foot as if our conversation were an inconvenience. My frown deepened. Andy only went to the Tower when he was thinking about Mitch, though he'd never admit it. "Missed all my classes," he added, though we both knew that wasn't the root of the problem.

"No one gives a shit if you blew off a couple of classes. I've blown off plenty. What's really going on?"

He stubbornly shook his head. "You don't get it." True, I didn't get a lot of things. Like why people thought being gay was a big deal or why anyone believed acrylics were better than oil or how a single stroke could decide if a painting was a masterpiece or absolute rubbish. His green eyes flicked up, the tiny ring of amber encircling his iris holding all the pain of old wounds. "Mitch found me." *There* it was.

"I'm not surprised. He practically turned this place upside down looking for you." The strange part being that Mitch and Andy didn't really share any classes, so how had he known Andy wasn't in his?

Andy startled at the comment and the fidgeting returned with a vengeance. "You don't understand. I was dreaming about..." He glanced around and lowered his voice, "*that* night."

Well, fuck.

"What of it?" I asked. Andy had only told me the barest details of *that* night, but it didn't take a genius to figure out that something besides making out had happened, something that had destroyed one of the most beautiful friendships I'd ever seen.

Andy's gaze cut to sharp shards of uranium glass. "I think I was talking in my sleep. I... I don't know what he may have heard."

"You could always ask him," I suggested. *Maybe then we could finally get to the bottom of this ridiculous intrigue.*

"I can't," he countered, stubborn as ever.

Movement in the background caught my attention, and I glanced behind Andy to find the root of his troubles glancing frantically over the heads of the thickening dinner crowd. If I hadn't already suspected that more was going on, the panic shining in Mitch's autumn eyes confirmed it. I brought my attention back to Andy at odds with warning him and holding him hostage a little longer to give Mitch a fighting chance to fix whatever he'd broken. Suddenly, Mitch caught sight of us and immediately began pushing through bodies with determination. I mentally sighed in exasperation. Much as I wanted to help Andy by letting Mitch catch him, Andy wouldn't see it that way, and Andy was my friend, not Mitch.

"You better pull your shit together." Andy's face clouded in confusion, and I darted my gaze behind him. "He's coming this way." Andy glanced over his shoulder and hissed a curse. "What are you going to do?"

"Cover for me."

"Andy." His name came out flat and full of rebuke. I understood my role in Andy's life and how our friendship had come to be, but this was getting ridiculous.

"Please?" he asked, desperation emanating off of him.

The battle to do what I knew would help and what Andy thought would, raged once more. My teeth sank into my bottom lip as I searched his face and settled on something in the middle. "Tell him the truth."

The worry in his eyes vanished in a flash of anger. "No."

"All I'm saying is-"

"I don't give a shit what you're saying," he cut me off. "Just be my fucking friend." I took a physical step back at the force of his words and he pushed past me to leave me to deal with his mess. I barely got my shock under control by the time Mitch approached, his eyes feverish.

"Hello, Mitch," I said, absently leaning against the wall and blocking his path to buy Andy his precious seconds.

"Where is he?"

"Who?" I raised my eyebrows and projected an innocence that no one in their right mind would ever buy.

"You know damn well who." Anger tightened his shoulders and clenched his jaw. Then, as suddenly as it had taken him over, it was gone. Those same shoulders sagged in defeat and he ran a hand through his hair. "Please, Calvin, where did he go? I need to... I need to talk to him."

"I'm not sure where he went," I admitted. "He seemed to be in a hurry. You two have been spending a lot of time together lately. Maybe he needs space."

Mitch's eyes darkened, not with anger this time, but with doubt. "What did he say?"

Not seeing the harm in it, I related as much of our conversation as I dared. "All in all, I gather he's embarrassed." I angled away from the wall and wrapped a hand around the strap of my bag. "Give him time," I suggested gently.

His shoulders drooped even more as the defeat took root. He nodded quietly, causing his light brown hair to fall in his face. Rather than push it clear, he seemed to shrink behind the wall it offered. Then, without another word, he turned and made his way into the dining hall. Almost immediately, his teammates swarmed him. His responding smile was as broad as any of theirs as they launched into animated chatter about the

Senior Captain finally being named, but I couldn't help but wonder if any of them could see the sadness that lingered in his eyes.

Unwilling to subject myself to anymore drama for one evening, I adjusted my course for the library. There was a windowsill there with my name on it. And with everyone else preoccupied with dinner, there would be no one to stop me from climbing up to the coveted perch.

The ambassador spun away in a whirl of green robes and stalked off. Kel remained resolute, standing beside the parapet, and watched in silence as his greatest councilor left to fulfill other obligations. The kingdom itself would keep so long as the king betrayed no signs of weakness. Much as it pained King Kelani to send his reluctant ambassador on such a perilous mission, there were treaties to be made and alliances to seal. Would that his own marriage could bring such fortuitous tidings, but the king as yet remained unaffected by his many suitors.

Chapter 5

Benny

I stomped down the hall toward the cafeteria, my stomach bubbling more with acid than hunger. Today was about as shit as a day could get. First, Coach had finally made an announcement about who would be Senior Captain—Brian, not me. Then, I'd fallen half a letter grade in chemistry thanks to a couple of ambiguous questions on an over-weighted exam. Then, I'd been called to report to the headmaster's office about the motherfucking prank on Nolan, of which I had nothing. We'd spent literal fucking hours turning that classroom upside down for any clue as to the culprit and only gotten painted hands for our trouble as we found the two-dozen other booby-trapped items. And as if all that wasn't bad enough, Anderson fucking Gallagher had just threatened me. Maybe not in so many words, but the intention was clear—he knew what I'd done... and with who.

And what did I do about it?

Did I feign ignorance about "eventful" showers?

No. I stood there like a goddamned idiot.

My fist collided with the stone wall of the atrium, and pain radiated from the point of impact. I snatched it back with a grunt and inspected the torn skin around the knuckles. Bright pink shone through raw skin and pricks of red grew in tiny puddles that burned. I flexed my fingers and shook out the shock waves of hurt. The move only made it feel like my pulse was throbbing in my hand.

"Fuck!" The curse rebounded off the distant walls and was flung back at me. Having lost my appetite, I turned around and headed back into the heart of the school where hopefully I wouldn't run into anyone that I'd be more willing to hit.

Thunder boomed through the encroaching night, shaking the walls and matching my mood perfectly. I'd almost made it to the library when the phone I wasn't supposed to have vibrated in my pocket. A quick glance around didn't reveal any peers or professors; with luck, they'd all still be in the dining hall for at least another hour. I slipped into the library and found a shadowed alcove. Only then did I remove the contraband.

I squinted against the bright light of the screen and the missed call notification. As if possessed, the device began vibrating once more. My stomach rolled as I stared in unsurprised, muted horror at the caller id. I swallowed down the bile creeping its way up my throat and accepted the call.

"Hello, sir."

"Benjamin, what is the meaning of this?" I winced at the fury-laced question and wished the alcove were deeper.

"Father-"

"I have to hear from O'Connell that the Daniels boy has been named Senior Captain."

"We only found out this morning," I argued, but the words went unheard.

"And what's this nonsense I hear about you being unable to apprehend petty vandals? Children, Benjamin, fucking children," he said in his usual gritty manner right over me.

I ground my teeth and forced myself to keep quiet. Pointing out that the prank had been far too sophisticated and well-planned to be committed by first years would be pointless. I'd yet to meet an entitled brat capable of picking locks, which they would have had to have done in order to access Nolan's room, not to mention the paint they stole.

"Are there any other failures you'd like to regale me with?"

The question dripped with scorn and disappointment that slithered into my belly. "No, sir."

"With conviction, boy. You're a fucking Price, for God's sake."

My shoulders tightened as steel ran up my spine. "Yes, sir," I replied.

"Get your act together. I didn't send you to that school so you could make a mockery of our name."

"Yes, sir. I wo—" The line cut out before I could finish. I looked at the phone in my hand and seriously debated breaking the piece of shit in two and flinging the pieces as far as I could into the stacks. I'd never wanted to come to this school, had begged to attend a regular school, one that would…

The soft shuffling of shoes whispering on carpet as someone entered the library intruded on my thoughts. I quickly pocketed the device and ventured deeper into the quiet. Still seeking sanctuary, I wandered to one of the few places in the library that actually managed to be isolated. By the time I emerged in the sheltered hollow of shelves, my anger had faded, leaving me empty. Truth was, it didn't matter what I did—I could be Captain, Prefect, Valedictorian, Prodigy—it still wouldn't be enough for Benjamin Wallace Price III. Nothing ever would be.

Calvin

At the sound of a muffled voice in the library, my pencil paused over the page. Not that I was worried. Short of someone thinking to look up, no one would ever find me stretched out on the wide ledge of the stained-glass window that dominated and looked out over the library. Balanced an impressive ten feet above the ground, it would take a flash of lightning backlighting me and broadcasting my shadow to betray my presence.

I studied the image that filled the over-sized sketchpad with its eleven by fourteen page. Stacks of shelves wove and twisted in intricate patterns, revealing the unseen labyrinth of books we called a library. From this vantage, I could see a lot that no one else thought to consider. The toy covered in dust, spirited away to the tallest shelf, where it had remained hidden for who knew how long awaiting its owner's return. The arched alcoves that provided a refuge for friends and lovers to whisper in corners. And of course, my own retreat, nestled just below me, a veritable island of isolation surrounded by literature. There, I didn't have to put on a show, be the loud and proud gay man they all needed me to be. There, I could be myself. Andy and I had spent many an afternoon sequestered in the oasis, quietly appreciating the luxury of peace.

I flipped to a fresh page and debated what to draw next. The altercation with Andy came to mind, but I really didn't want to think about how he'd basically shoved our friendship in my face. I'd kept his secrets and made sure they didn't spread, no matter how much the rumors wanted to sprout like weeds. For four years, I'd ensured that only three people in the entire school knew that Andy was gay, despite our friendship and the speculation it inevitably created. My pencil scratched an oval on the fibrous material, Andy's anger clear in my mind.

At the whisper of fabric, though, I paused and looked out at the refuge below. I recognized the student slinking into the space immediately. He walked to the center of the bedroom-sized space and paused. I watched in silence as he raked his hands along his short hair that I imagined felt like crushed velvet. Then he intertwined his fingers behind his head. The move stretched the muscles across his chest and strained the cotton button down to its limits. A heavy sigh drifted up, perfectly matching the obvious distress that had hold of him.

He squeezed his eyes shut, clearly fighting some unvoiced emotion. When he finally dropped his hands, it was to brace against the bookshelf before him. Tension defined every taut muscle starting at his neck and working its way through his shoulders and back on down through his legs. The shirt clung to his form, an insubstantial armor against the demons that plagued him. Where his jacket had wandered off, I had no clue, but without it, the purity of pain lay exposed. Each line of definition stood in high relief thanks to the ivory fabric clinging to his torso, a testament to the immense well of feeling before me.

My pencil whisked softly of its own volition along the page, having found its muse. His fingers dug into the shelves, sliding books free of their path, as if seeking a purchase from the insurmountable weight determined to crush him. He remained miraculously still, while the graphite continued to glide with a life of its own, filling in every speck of white space with the agony of a boy who felt too much and had no way to express it, standing not seven feet away.

The longer he stood there, the more life the likeness gained. It captured the tightness of a jaw working hard to keep from giving voice to the sorrow permanently etching itself into broad, sculpted shoulders. Each pass plucked out details of pain. Eyes scrunched against the agony. White-knuckled fingers, torn and marred with a raw pink. A mouth pressed to a thin line. My fingers grew weary and smudges stained each finger as I worked tirelessly to have the 2D image echo reality. Layers upon layers of shading added light and dark to a tortured soul. A boy with all the weight of the world sitting on his shoulders and no idea how to put it down.

Chapter 6

Benny

"You wanna hit up the game store?" Todd asked as we left Malcom's Sporting Goods empty handed. Neil glanced over. No doubt curious what my response would be. I'd been an outright cantankerous son of a bitch since news had dropped about the captain's assignment. Of course, they didn't know the full extent of my anger and frustration, and I preferred it that way.

"Nah. Don't really feel like it." Truth be told, I didn't much feel like anything. Their faces fell and I only just didn't roll my eyes in open exasperation. "You two go on. I'm gonna..." I searched for an acceptable single pursuit that didn't require them fucking dogging my every step. "Walk around."

They shared a look, surprise clearly written on their faces. In all fairness, it was rare that I ventured off on my own. "You sure, boss?" Neil asked.

"Would I have fucking said it if I wasn't?"

Neil held up his hands. "No offense, just checking." He shared another look with Todd. If either had an actual pair between them, they would have called me out for acting like a bitch. Unsurprisingly, they didn't. "We'll see you around," Neil said at last.

"Whatever." This time I did roll my eyes before stomping off without another word, not giving a shit what they did as long as they left me alone. I thrust my hands in my pockets and wandered down the semi-populated sidewalk, the greatest mercy being that it wasn't stifling hot.

Thank fuck this fall is almost over.

The unremarkable town of Hylestead passed by me in an indistinguishable blur of colors and shapes. Nothing held my amusement and if I was being honest, I didn't have a damn clue where I thought I was going. On a whim, I turned toward the cafe that occasionally had decent pastries, not that I was supposed to be eating those. I could practically hear my father's voice gruff with scorn in my ear as he reminded me for the millionth time that an athlete's body was sacred, that a powerful mind required proper nourishment, that sweets were for the weak. Never mind the man himself had no such qualms indulging in most decadences.

That's all I need, my father bitching because I've put on weight. What the fuck does it matter as long as it doesn't affect my performance on the field?

With that, I stepped into the quaint cafe. Pristine little white tables filled the intimate space while thin blue curtains gave it a welcoming glow. The tension that had been riding my shoulders for days relaxed slightly as I spied the glass display and its impressive assortment of forbidden treats. Mental calculations of how much exercise I'd have to do to burn off the excess calories ran through my mind as I inventoried the options and stepped up to the counter.

"Pastries, Benjamin? You know better." The reproach crashed through my determined indulgence. Guilt surged up inside of me, quickly followed by overwhelming anger.

I spun around to give the insolent voice a piece of my mind. However, when my gaze fell on the Amazonian blonde, long hair cascading over her shoulder, hip popped out and hands placed upon them with a button down on the verge of losing its battle with the barely contained cleavage, I couldn't help but smile. Her lips quirked into a wry smirk and her blue eyes flashed as she stepped up to the counter and feigned looking at the display. She bent at the waist, purposefully putting on her own display of all her best assets. She glanced over her shoulder at me and I half expected her to wiggle her ass, which the short plaid skirt did next to nothing to keep hidden.

"If you must indulge, though, I'd say get creamed." Her eyes glinted wickedly, and my smile broadened. "I mean, the Boston Cremes," she amended as she straightened up, her ample breasts bouncing almost out of her shirt.

"Savannah." Her smirk widened to a grin, and she held open her arms. I gladly stepped into the embrace, the press of breasts against my chest further distracting me from my otherwise dreary day. "What brings you here?" I asked as she stepped back, taking the modicum of comfort with her.

She rolled her baby blues and gave a dismissive wave of a hand decorated with sparkling rings and bracelets that clinked together. "Needed a break from those bitches."

I snorted and the attendant that had been standing in the background trying not to swallow his tongue at Savannah's provocative display leveled her with a scorn-filled glare. Sensing censure, Savannah twisted and arched an eyebrow of challenge at him, then turned back to me.

"We should do lunch," she suggested in a perfect imitation of her high society mother. "It's been too long since we caught up."

My eager smile twitched a hair wider. "Okay. When were you thinking?"

She deflated with an exasperated sigh, her hand falling to hang listlessly by her side. "Uh, how 'bout now, dipshit?"

I laughed outright, a full sound that burst out of me and prompted the judgmental assistant to shift his glare. "You really don't want me to have any sweets."

"Fuck that. We're getting the sweets and a sandwich. Your treat." She winked.

I laughed quieter and stepped up the rest of the way to the counter and the thoroughly scandalized attendant. "You heard the lady. That'll be two Boston Cremes and two turkey clubs."

"Two, Benny? You flirt. You'll have to fuck me extra hard to work that off," Savannah said, smooth as silk when she accepted the food. The attendant fell into a coughing fit and dropped my card twice before ringing us up.

"You just couldn't help yourself, could you?" I commented as we took a seat at one of the painted white ironwork tables on the private patio.

She shrugged. "Not my fault he's a prude. People fuck and not all girls are dainty flowers."

"No, some of them are captain of the State Championship Girls' Volleyball team, could give sailors a run for their money, and just happen to have perky tits and a nice ass."

"Damn straight." She took a massive bite, shoving renegade bacon back in her mouth and I shook my head. Savannah Strickland was a picturesque debutante at all social events and gatherings, smiling sweetly and saying all the right things to all the right people. She could work a room with the best of them and had. But beneath the fine veneer polished to a mirror shine, she was every bit as crass as Calvin, maybe more.

"The highlights look good," I said, indicating the honey streaks combed through her impressively straight curtain of hair, hair that also happened to be hugging her full breasts.

She gave me a wry smile and slid the hair back over her shoulder, offering me an unobstructed view. "You always have been good at noticing things like that."

I smiled back at her not fooled in the least. She continued to study me and I shrugged since there was no sense in denying either the spoken or the unspoken accusation. I knew what I liked, always had. Finally, she blinked and cocked her head to the side.

"Really is a shame we don't work." Her gaze slid over me appreciatively much like her hands once had and I felt myself hardening beneath the unabashed scrutiny. Tempting as it was to forget my distractions in her inviting body, we really were better friends.

"Please. You broke up with me the same day—at the same time, I might add."

She laughed and shook out her hair, causing the honeyed locks to glow golden as they hit the light. "Okay. Fine. I did. Doesn't mean I can't be sad about it. You've got a nice dick. The rest of you isn't so bad either," she added belatedly.

"Oh, I see," I said as I polished off the last of my sandwich. "It was purely physical."

She let out an exaggerated gasp that put her already strained buttons to the test and reached out to place a hand over mine. "Benny. Did you catch…feelings?"

We both let out a hearty laugh that raised my spirits even more. Savannah really was a good friend, even if we were a terrible match romantically. Though for a time, it hadn't really been up to us. The Stricklands and the Prices aligned would have been a power couple to shake the status quo. Or it would have been if our grandfathers hadn't gotten into a snit about someone cheating at cards—or maybe it was a bet? Either way, no one remembered who did the cheating or what had started it all, only that whatever machinations that had existed in regards to creating permanent family ties were to cease and be forgotten immediately.

We sobered up and tackled the remaining sweets. She glanced up at me as she licked her fingers clean of the white filling and my mind instantly sank into the gutter again, no doubt her goal. "So, have you talked to the big man lately?"

The gutter dried up and cracked, rents ripping through the foundation to expose bedrock. "I take it, you've heard."

"News travels fast."

"No shit."

She reached out a hand again, this time all elements of playfulness gone. "I'm sorry, Benny."

I gave her hand a light squeeze and pulled back. She left her hand on the table another moment, then pulled it into her lap without pursuing the conversation, a gesture I was more grateful for than the original outreach. Savannah was one of the few people from my family's social circle that I could speak with honestly. She understood the unbelievable pressure I was under, because she experienced it too. The fact that she'd found a way to both conform and rebel was one of the many reasons I genuinely liked her. But for as much as we had in common, we saw the world in very different ways.

While I adored her and she was strikingly beautiful, she believed in pedigree and materialism. Those stunning highlights probably cost at least a couple hundred dollars and would undoubtedly get replaced in a month or so when she grew bored of them. Each ring on her finger bore a genuine stone in a solid gold setting. Even the bangles were a far cry from costume jewelry and likely worth a fortune on their own. The cheapest thing on her was the mandated school uniform and even that cost a shiny penny if my own was a mark to go by.

Where she basked in the world wealth and status brought her, I resented it. Then again, that resentment hadn't stopped me from taking advantage of the doors that opened for me at the mere mention of a name, which I suppose made me a pampered hypocrite. I glowered at the remnants of our shared meal, now even deeper in the darkness than I'd started.

"I know you say you don't gossip, but you're a blue-balled liar. Tell me all the latest dirt that's been happening at that warped cock fest of a school," Savannah artfully navigated the waning conversation. I gave her a look and she leaned forward to prop her amble bosom on the table. "I'll tell you mine if you tell me yours."

We spent another hour trading nonsense about our respective schools. When we finally parted ways, I simultaneously felt lighter and heavier. I enjoyed spending time with Savannah, but she was also a painful reminder of the world that awaited me when I left the refuge I'd carved out here.

Calvin

Holy Trinity rose up before me, no less grand for its small size. Like the rest of the town, it boasted a mix of aged brick and granite as well as stained glass that rivaled the school's. A sense of peace settled over me as I stepped through the banded, double doors into its hallowed halls.

Ornate pillars rose up to support the vaulted roof decorated with exposed beams and more stained glass, inviting pockets of multi-colored heaven into the space of worship. To the far left, a smattering of prayer candles offered their own flickering glow, while soft organ music kept the handful of parishioners company.

I double-checked the time and made my way over to the confessional booth. This time of day many were still at work and I slipped inside the sound-padded room without delay. The interior thick velvet curtain settled into place to add another layer of crimson silence. The firm seat beneath me held no comfort despite the thin cushion, no doubt to discourage confessors from devolving into scruples.

I clasped my hands together in my lap and not for the first time longed for the rosary my grandmother had gifted me with before she'd passed. The traditional olive wood beads weren't the least bit ornate, but nonetheless beautiful in their simplicity. A shadow passed behind the lattice to my right as a figure settled on the other side.

"Good day, my son." The warmth of Father Miles' voice brought a smile to my lips as did the subtle admission that he'd seen me arrive. It had been an unexpected gift to find a sympathetic priest when everyone else seemed determined to condemn me.

I drew the cross over myself. "Forgive me, Father, for I have sinned. I'm still gay."

The partition snapped back to reveal Father Miles in full-on grumpy bear mode. "Calvin, if you cannot take this seriously…"

I smothered the rest of my laughter. "Sorry, Father. It's just too easy."

He narrowed his Azo Brown eyes at me and his mouth drew into a thin line in his pale face. "You know where his Holiness stands. You can either confess real sins or make way for those in need of genuine contrition." He waited for me to nod before settling back with a harrumph and snapping the divider closed.

I took a deep breath, let it out slowly, and crossed myself again. "In the name of the Father, and of the Son, and of the Holy Spirit. Amen. Bless me, Father, for I have sinned. It has been..." I faltered a moment then pushed forward. "Three weeks since my last confession. I am an artist in my final year of primary school and pursuing a scholarship for secondary." My words filled the hushed space, then were swallowed by silence.

"What sins would you like to confess, my child?" Father Miles gently encouraged once more back to his easy, affable self.

"Last week I... I helped a boy at my school."

The shadowy figure shifted, and I did the same in my own uncomfortable seat. "This does not sound like a sin."

"I fear the Lord would disapprove of my methods. We engaged in sex outside the bounds of matrimony." My fingers tightened around my imaginary rosary. "I'm not sorry for the act itself, but... I know I should be."

"We've been through this. Forgiveness requires contrition."

"I am sorry, just not for me. I know who I am. I'll never apologize for being myself, but others are not as blessed."

"You cannot confess the sins of others." The gentle reprimand wasn't anything I hadn't heard before, but it still smarted.

"I know, Father, but they have no one." I let out a heavy sigh and leaned back against the unforgiving wall. "They have questions, doubts, and only me to answer them."

"The Lord works in mysterious ways."

I snorted at the implication that fucking my way through the senior class could in any way be part of God's greater plan. "There are some that fear too much to come forward. My heart breaks for them." I squeezed my eyes shut and fought the image determined to surface, the same one that had led me to confession early.

"Anything else?"

I pushed the image away and focused on smaller sins. "I was disrespectful to my mentor. He provided guidance, and I lashed out. He is a good man and does not deserve to be punished for my failures. You see, I've been avoiding an assignment for weeks—one that seems particularly difficult for me." The image I'd been fighting for days pushed forward and refused to be denied a minute longer. "And... one more thing. I saw a boy suffering. But I did not offer aid. I... I drew him."

"Was this suffering physical?" Father Miles asked, an edge of rebuke to the question.

"No, Father," I hastily clarified. "As far as I could tell, it was only suffering of the heart." Not just the heart, though, a deep soul hurt that had come to life on my page, captured for eternity in graphite and pulp. Guilt tore at my insides. "But I feel terrible. I should have extended comfort or at least warned him he wasn't alone as he believed." I stared down at my hands and pictured what Benny's reaction would have been if I'd been insane enough to do either. Fury without question.

"Why did you refrain?"

I curled my fingers until the knuckles turned white. My mind's eye filled with the tightness lining his shoulders, the subtle twitches of hard-won muscles fighting an unseen force. The wealth of sorrow and heartache that had filled the intimate space while Benny quietly fell apart and tried to keep it all together. Finally, I gave the only excuse that made sense. "Because he deserved to hurt in peace."

Father Miles' silhouette nodded beyond the lattice. "Your heart is good, though your… methods could stand improvement. As penance, you may not use the ill-gotten image for your assignment. You must obtain an honest rendition."

"But, Father," I argued, turning toward the division.

"Contrition, Calvin."

I crossed my arms and grumbled beneath my breath, though not quietly enough.

"This is your penance. You would not have confessed this sin if it did not weigh so on your heart. Thus, your atonement must start there."

I sighed in defeat and slumped against the wood at my back. "I really hate it when you're right. Okay. Fine. I won't use the portrait for the assignment." Even though it's the best fucking thing I've produced in months.

"Or…"

I stiffened and clenched my jaw. "Or the Admissions Portfolio."

"Better." I let out an aggrieved sigh at the unfairness of it all. How the fuck was I supposed to get an "honest" rendering of Benny without him beating the shit out of me? "Calvin. Is there something you'd like to say?"

"No, Father." The silhouette nodded once more, and I straightened.

"God, the Father of Mercies, through the death and resurrection of his Son, has reconciled the world to himself and sent the Holy Spirit among us for the forgiveness of sins in the name of the Father, and of the Son, and of the Holy Spirit, Amen."

As he finished, I crossed myself once more and echoed, "Amen."

"God has freed you from your sins. Go in peace."

"Thanks be to God." I took a moment to gather myself, then exited the confessional, the weight of my guilt lifted to be replaced by the pressure of figuring out how to fulfill my penance and the assignment.

Back out in the nave, I pulled my rebellious curls back and held them at the back of my head for a minute. My gaze flitted around the church, taking in the statues and crosses while I debated lingering a while longer rather than returning to the school right away. Eventually, I dropped my hair to fall loosely around my face and headed for the door. At some point, someone had pulled the massive doors shut, likely to keep the unusually warm fall out.

I pushed open the smaller door and stepped into the fading afternoon. Shadows stretched in long swatches across the sidewalk like a bright paintbrush dragging charcoal. I tucked a renegade curl behind my ear, still struggling with how to fulfill my penance, then looked up. And froze. At the end of the breezeway stood none other than Benjamin Price.

He stared at me in silence, then his gaze slid past me to take in the elegant facade of Holy Trinity and the placard boldly proclaiming it as a Catholic church. I swallowed and braced myself for the inevitable ridicule to follow as his gaze once more settled on me. Ten years I'd kept my faith quiet, avoiding the derision bound to accompany the observance of an openly gay man having religion. All of it gone, in one chance meeting.

Benny remained quiet and my anxiety rose, all the peace I'd found in absolution diminishing with each passing second. Then he blinked and continued on his way without uttering so much as a syllable. I remained frozen for another few seconds before rushing to the end of the sidewalk and looking after him in wonder. Maybe there really was such a thing as holy ground.

Kel straightened to his full height and braced for the battle to come. Not a king in this moment, but a man burdened by the expectations of an ungrateful kingdom. Though even without his majestic robes he was no less a king in control of every moment and still the strongest ruler Prince Einar had ever had dealings. The young prince debated seizing advantage of the king's precarious position and leveraging this perceived weakness to aid in his own trade negotiations. Expectation filled the silence as decisions waited to be made until, at last, Prince Einar bowed his head and let the proud Kelani pass unhindered. Even a king deserved to set his mantle down once in a while.

Chapter 7

Calvin

I placed the book on its precarious perch and inspected my work. Designing an alarm system out of books, while inspired, wasn't easy. I frowned and switched out one paperback for a heftier hardback. The collection of color improved, but the structure wobbled. With a frustrated huff, I removed the entire top layer and set about reconfiguring the base.

A glance to the side showed Andy every bit as lost in thought as he had been all the other times we'd hung out. I'd wanted to talk to him about what had happened in town with Benny, but he clearly had other things on his mind. He lifted his head to look in my direction without truly seeing.

Maybe what Andy needs is a distraction from his thoughts.

"So… I ran into Benny in town the other day." I paused, a fresh book in my hand. "Well, not actually ran into, but you get the idea. He saw me after my visit with Father Miles." I gently leaned the heavier book against a red-backed monstrosity. Encyclopedias always made the best noise when they fell. "Can you believe it? He didn't say so much as a word. Not one. Hell, he barely even blinked at me." I sat back on my haunches, pleased with how this latest book-trap was developing.

Andy turned a page of his own book, though I doubted he'd read so much as a word. I rolled my eyes and returned my attention to the masterpiece before me. It didn't take a genius to know Andy's preoccupation centered on his increased time with Mitch, but I'd learned the hard way not to bring up the Attackman out of the blue.

"It was weird," I continued with my recounting. "I don't think I've ever had an interaction with the guy that didn't also include a slur and profanity." Except one, I could think of one. The memory flitted through with its fuzzy feels and I sighed.

Why couldn't we have stayed like that?

We didn't have to be lovers, but would friendship really have been so far-fetched?

Of course, the very thing that would make us tolerable friends was also the number one thing stopping us. Benny saw my truth…and I saw his. "I'm telling you, one of these days he'll realize the error of his ways."

Andy glanced up again and this time his gaze actually focused. "I still don't get it. I mean, Benny… Of all the people to have a crush on."

My hand twitched at the accusation and nearly sent the whole sculpture crashing down. What I had with Benny wasn't a crush, more like morbid curiosity, bordering on obsession. Explaining that to Andy, though, would only solidify his belief, so I said nothing.

"Seriously though, he's such an ass."

The fuzzy memory came back, and a wicked grin spread across my face as I turned to Andy. "But you see, that *is* why." I held out my hands, miming Benny's spectacular ass, which had most definitely made it into my spank bank, though I only pulled it out on the rare occasion when nothing else would do. "Mm, you don't even know. Boy's got an ass you could bounce a quarter off of." I squeezed the imaginary butt and could almost feel the firm flesh giving way. Blood rushed through my veins and my cock twitched.

Fuck me. Looks like I'll be jacking off to that later.

Andy's laugh—which had become rare these days—filled the intimate nest of shelving and books and brought a different smile to my face. At the muffled sound of books falling though, our momentary happiness fled, and we each returned to our previous occupations, me to my structure and Andy to his book. As expected, the crash was followed by the emergence of Benny and his friends, if they could be called that.

"Look what we have here. It's Club Fagot." Neil and Todd mimed fucking each other in the background while Benny leaned a shoulder on the nearest shelving. I rolled my eyes at the lewdness and paid them no mind.

Amazing how it is perfectly okay for them to pretend to bend each other over, but when I do it for real, it's suddenly a crime.

"Bugger off," Andy said without raising his head. "We're not bothering anyone." I mentally frowned at the sharp dismissal and realized how tight his shoulders were.

So, that's what it is. Should have known he'd be sensitive about sex after breaking up with Connor and spending so much time with Mitch.

"You're bothering me," Benny spat, his face twisting into a sneer that marred his features. Andy's wince was barely perceptible beyond the tightening of his fingers on his book.

Oh, fuck that.

I dusted my hands and prepared to take the focus away. Benny I could handle, the others would follow him. Before I could intervene, Andy spoke up again.

"Then leave."

Benny stepped deeper into our sanctuary of literature. "What if I don't want to? What are you going to do about it?" In a flash of movement, he flipped a precariously balanced book and sent all my efforts crashing to the ground. I choked on my outrage and lurched up from the ground to deal with the brute head on.

"I'm gonna start by getting Professor Jackson. I don't think he'd appreciate learning how you're treating the materials." Once more, Andy's calm intervention stopped me.

What's gotten into him? Since when does he go at it with Benny?

Unsurprisingly, Benny bowed up at the blatant threat. "Oh yeah? And how do you think he'd appreciate finding out about you two fucking up here?"

Shock hit me in the chest, and I let out a gasp. "We are in a sacred space of learning. And… ew." I glanced over at Andy and hoped he'd understand that it was nothing personal. Andy was cute, but not remotely my type, nor was I his. And while I'd absolutely fooled around up here with others, I also wasn't dumb enough to get caught.

Andy rolled his eyes and turned back to his book, like that was the end of it. Benny's glare, on the other hand, couldn't seem to decide which of the two of us was most deserving. Determined to get to play at least a little, I gave him my best come-hither smile.

"If *you're* volunteering, though, I could be persuaded to violate the sanctity of knowledge." I could be persuaded to do a lot of things if it meant getting to taste Benny again.

His lip curled as if the suggestion was hands-down the most revolting thing he'd ever heard. Of course, we both knew better. "Whatever, homos." He flipped me off, and I clutched my chest as if restraining my beating heart. His face soured further, then he and the others stalked off.

"One of these days," I sighed as I watched Benny's tight ass walk away.

"I'm not one to judge—really, I'm not—but seriously? How can you still say that? He's a jerk and he'll always *be* a jerk."

I shook my head, because there was no way I could ever make Andy understand. Instead, I held up my hands once more in the shape of Benny's perfect ass and wiggled my eyebrows.

Andy threw up his hands in response. "To each his own."

"Speaking of which, you still carrying that flame for Mitch?" I asked, seizing the opportunity to dig into what the hell was going on with him, more concerned than ever after that little showdown with Benny. I glanced over my shoulder to find him staring down at his pages, his face twisted like he was going to puke all over it.

Shit.

"You're friends again, right? You've been spending a lot of time together at the very least," I commented, trying a different tactic.

"You could say that. And for the record, I'm trying to keep that particular light extinguished."

I diligently didn't snort. Andy not liking Mitch was like watercolors not running.

He shook his head and added, "But he makes it really hard. I don't think he has any idea how hard he makes it."

"I *bet* he doesn't," I snickered, less successful at keeping my opinion to myself a second time. Out of nowhere, a book smacked into my arm and nearly destroyed the tower of books I was working to rebuild. "Ow-wa." I glared at him as I rubbed the shallow injury. If that was what he was playing at, then kid gloves were coming off. "Have you told him?"

He instantly looked like he'd swallowed something tart. "I'm trying to make things better, not worse." We'd been through this—many times. He'd balked at all of my "methods" and refused to budge beyond the current nothing he'd held onto for four years.

"Just saying. Maybe if you slept with him…" I ventured again. His green eyes lit with anger and I thought for sure a hardback would be flying my way shortly. I held up my hands to prepare for the onslaught. "It was just a suggestion."

"The whole thing is a mess." The defeat in his voice as he hung his head hurt my heart. What good was I as a friend if I couldn't help him with this? Never mind I'd been trying to do just that for the last four years with no success.

I gave up my tower and sank down beside him. "If you would tell me more about what happened that night, maybe I could help better." He untucked his head enough to peek at me over his arms.

"I've been dreaming about that night again."

Fuck.

"Judging by the way you say that, it's not the good bits," I said, hoping that I was wrong. Andy had only shared the smallest amount of what had happened, but it had left an impression.

He shook his head and buried his face so that only his vibrant, burnished copper hair remained in sight. "It's always the same. I wake up cold and alone. I search the room, but there's no clue to where he went. He's just... gone." My heart ached for Andy. Whether or not he chose to admit it, he'd been in love with Mitch, and if his current miserable state was anything to go by, still was.

Thank God I've been spared this agony.

"I remember thinking at the time how smart he was to already have gone, that he was protecting us, so that we wouldn't be caught together," he said after a while, the edge of his voice raw with emotion. I placed a hand on his back and offered what comfort I could. His breath hitched, and he shuddered at the touch. "He's going to do it again. He's going to ghost me. I can feel it," he croaked.

"Maybe you should do it first," I whispered, still rubbing his back.

"We both know I can't do that anymore than you can let go of what happened with Benny." Like I needed the fucking reminder. Unlike some, I didn't lend more weight than the interaction deserved. It had been a dalliance, nothing more. Granted an unexpected, fucking amazing dalliance, but that was all, and it was time to remind Andy that.

I gave up my attempt at comfort, which was obviously doing nothing, and wrapped an arm around Andy's slumped shoulders. He let out a wheeze as I squeezed tightly and sighed. "Benny. Did I ever tell you about that shower?"

Andy laughed despite himself and glanced over at me. "Only like a hundred times."

Seeing his smile again gave me hope. I may not be able to fix whatever was going between him and Mitch, but I could offer a distraction from his troubles. So, I recounted the one and only sexual encounter I'd ever shared with Andy like I had every other one of the hundred times. I hadn't told him everything, but enough to arm him in the event he ever needed it, not that he should considering the “no-touch” order Mitch had issued to the lacrosse team shortly after they’d had their falling out, but I was positive Andy wasn’t aware such an order existed. Normally, I didn’t condone leveraging someone’s sexual history for blackmail, but if Andy ever had occasion to need a secret that could save him from harm, I wanted him to have one. Besides, this wasn’t just Benny’s secret, it was mine.

Chapter 8

Benny

Going up to the library oasis had been a mistake, not the least of which because I'd gotten my foot crushed by a fucking encyclopedia of all things on my way up there. I'd taken one look at Calvin and immediately been transported back to the sidewalk in front of the church. He'd been so shocked to see me, which was fair, considering the only reason I'd been anywhere near the place had been because of my lunch with Savannah. The insults practically wrote themselves. *Calvin*. Lewd, crass, unashamedly gay, running a black-market trading scheme, not to mention all the other shit he got up to that no one would ever admit to knowing about, Calvin...was Catholic? Not possible.

But then his shoulders had tightened defensively, and the briefest flicker of fear had flashed in his eyes. I was many things, but I wasn't so much of an asshole to mock a man for having the audacity to believe in something. That fear hadn't been in his eyes at the library, but challenge had. Calvin had everything he needed to bring me to my knees and turn me into a laughingstock for the entire school. It wouldn't even take an hour before my father would be calling and demanding retribution.

I pushed away the idle thoughts and focused on the task at hand. The hallways opened before me, shrouded in darkness and devoid of life, with only the occasional lamp to light the way. I'd gotten a much later start than usual for the evening rounds due to being called to the headmaster's office—again—to explain that the culprit of what was now being heralded as the greatest prank in school history could not be found. That had gone over like a ton of bricks and I'd dragged my feet going about the rest of my school appointed duties.

The telltale squeak of a shoe scuffing on the floor rang through the hallway. I immediately altered my course and turned down the West Dormitory. A shadow darted across the hall and I quickened my pace. It hovered by the wall, oblivious to my silent approach, and peered down the dimly lit corridor.

"Looking for someone?" I asked loud enough to be heard.

The kid jumped practically out of his skin and whirled to face me. This time, the shrill squeak didn't come from his shoes. "B-Benny."

"What are you doing out of bed, third year?"

He swallowed and the little blood remaining in his face drained away. "I-I was j-just g-going to the b-b-bathroom."

"Are you finished?" I asked, knowing full well that if he hadn't already been, he'd likely pissed himself when I showed up. He nodded vigorously. "Back to your room. Lights out is lights out. No exceptions. Keep a fucking bottle in there if you have to or, better yet, don't drink before bed. Grow some fucking senses."

"Y-yes sir."

I crossed my arms and glowered at him. "Well? What are you standing around for? Get." The preteen fell over his feet in his eagerness to comply. I waited for him to vanish into what better have been his fucking room, then resumed the nightly ritual.

The North dormitory and the dining hall were both quiet. I glanced down the main hall for the East Dormitory that was still consisted entirely of older boys. Seeing nothing amiss, I made to keep going. That's when another squeak reached my ears. Unlike the scuff of a shoe, this noise had a higher pitch to it, like hinges in need of oil, or... the sound came again.

Or a bed rocking.

Anger surged through me as I stomped down the hallway, tracking the intermittent sound. With the addition of a faint moan, indignant outrage replaced my anger. Over my dead, fucking body was someone going to have the balls to sneak someone in their room on a night I was doing rounds. The sound mocked me all the way to the door itself. As I reached for the door, a thump reverberated through the floor and another moan came. I immediately twisted the knob, my gaze already sweeping the room in search of anyone that had no right to be there.

"What the fuck is going on in here?"

Moonlight poured through the drawn curtains, illuminating an immaculate room and one perfectly made bed at the far side. I scoured the space until my gaze landed at last on the room's supposed sole occupant. Too late, I realized the error of barging in. Anderson Gallagher sat buck ass naked on his bed, unabashedly stroking his cock despite the fact that someone had just walked in.

"Fucking hell, Gallagher," I snapped and lurched my gaze to his face.

"Ever heard of knocking?" he asked without stilling his hand. I thanked the darkness that he couldn't tell my face was burning.

"Jesus, you fucking fag. Stop."

"Since when is it a crime to get off?" he fired back.

"I'm right here," I snapped in a desperate attempt to get him to at least acknowledge he had an audience.

He raised an eyebrow, then without so much as a goddamn blink, he deliberately stroked himself, adding a loud moan for good measure. As his fist tightened around himself, his eyelids fluttered, but didn't close. "Are you just going to stand there, or are you going to help?" He might as well have gotten up and slapped me for all the effect his words had. I fought to control my temper and the horrifying realization that Andy didn't just know that "something" had happened in those showers, he *knew*.

"Fucking queer, keep that shit to yourself." As far as rebukes went, it was limp-wristed. Not that Andy seemed to be having a problem with that at the moment.

Fuck. Stop thinking about cock. Andy's or anyone else's, for that matter.

"That a no?" the persistent fucker asked, still working himself and adding the odd moan.

"Go fuck yourself."

"Trying. So help or get out. What'll it be?" he threw down.

Help or get out. Almost verbatim what I'd said to Calvin two years ago. Seemed Andy's threat in the hall that day wasn't idle. He *knew*.

Heat surged up my neck, and I had to clench my jaw tight enough to keep from screaming. Finally, I managed, "Keep it down," then slammed the door shut and got the fuck out of there.

Calvin

I glanced over at Greg's bed, where his silent, judgy-self had been asleep for at least a couple of hours now. With the stealth of practiced ease, I slipped from the sheets and quietly gathered my things. The shower caddy already held shampoo and body wash. I added the conditioner worth its weight in gold and slipped on the house shoes I'd purchased for the sole reason that they never squeaked. The towel I'd procured earlier got tucked under my arm and I was set. I chewed on my lip for a moment, then caved and returned to my desk. The sketchpad lying there still held the image I wasn't allowed to use, but that was neither here nor there. I'd figure something out. I pulled open the drawer and added the lube I found there to the caddy. I'd earned some me-time.

And who knows? Maybe I'll get lucky.

Doubtful, but a guy could dream. All else failed, my hand was more than sufficient to get the job done. Still smirking to myself, I ghosted out of the room and began the journey to the rarely used second floor showers. During the day, the bathrooms themselves were frequented enough, but at this hour they were blessedly empty—which was the whole reason I was here now.

I made it there without event, avoiding the elevators, as the damn things would alert anyone within a hundred feet that they were in use. I'd learned that lesson the hard way. But for all the years I'd been sneaking around the school—be it for my client exchanges or hookups—I'd only had a few close calls. I was nothing if not a master of stealth. Not even the awful squeal of the rusted hinges of the restroom door gave me pause as I reached my destination, though, perhaps it was time to add a bit more oil.

Inside, the mint green tile shone almost clear beneath the fluorescent lighting, and a wave of serenity washed over me. Though outdated by a couple of decades, the tiles never failed to remind me of a spa I'd once gone to with my mother. Sadly, the school did not boast seaweed wraps, but the water was hot and the pressure steady. I made my way past the sinks and walked around the wall separating the showers from the rest of the bathroom. Six shower heads lined the tiled walls, including a handicap accessible setup at the far end.

I took my time removing my night clothes, folding them, and placing them on a bamboo bench that rested against the dividing wall. Then I walked over to the shower in the middle of the nearest wall and turned on the spray. While the water heated, I removed everything from my caddy and placed it within easy reach. By the time I returned from securing the caddy with my clothes, the water was sufficiently hot. I stepped beneath the spray and released a sigh that bordered on a moan as the scalding water pounded my muscles. After a few indulgent minutes, I reached for the shampoo. The bottle of lube caught my eye, and I winked at it.

“It’s you and me tonight.” I laughed, then moaned again as my fingers massaged the lather into my scalp. Best part of showering at this unholy hour? I could make all the noise I wanted and no one would say a damn thing.

Chapter 9

Benny

There is no way Andy was telling the truth. It's been two years since that happened.

I swallowed. Sometimes it didn't feel quite that long ago, others longer. I shook my head as I turned down the latest abandoned hallway.

This really is a useless practice. No one is ever out of bed after curfew. Well, except for that one dumbass.

I continued down the vacant corridor, my mind wandering back to its original track, the same one it had been on since I had made the mistake of confronting Andy about Mitch virtually abandoning the team. I'd done a fair job of pushing the interaction to the far reaches of my mind and pretending it had never happened, but tonight had brought it roaring back to the forefront to torture me during this waste-of-time round.

Everyone knew Andy and Mitch had been friends before, but that had all changed when Mitch had become the school's star lacrosse player. Now, apparently, it was changing back. When I'd bumped into Andy that day, it'd seemed like an ideal time to confront at least one of them about it. Mitch may not have exactly been a friend, but he was vital to the team, and the team was suffering due to his lack of focus. Andy had never stood up to me before. I hadn't expected our chat to be any different.

Wrong.

I blew out a sharp puff of air. When he'd first voiced the low-key threat, I hadn't wanted to believe it. How could he have gone so long without saying anything? I'd certainly given him and Calvin plenty of reason to use the information against me. I ground my teeth together. Truthfully, it was a goddamn miracle the entire school didn't know.

Calvin's a damn gossip queen.

Even as I thought it, I knew it wasn't true. Calvin didn't share secrets. He collected them. For what horrid purpose was anyone's guess.

Probably blackmail. Definitely for his illicit trading scheme. Which I'm sure he doesn't think I know anything about.

I hooked a right and suddenly found myself in front of the second-floor showers. The same showers that he'd found me in two years ago. I glanced around the barren hallway.

It couldn't hurt to look, if only to confirm that Andy was just having a go at me. All threats aside, there's no way he was actually serious.

Confident in my assumption, I boldly strode to the door. I cringed as the rusty hinges squealed and glanced back down the barren hall, positive that the ruckus would have alerted the entire fucking school to what I was doing. When the obscene sound faded, there was still a steady noise filling the room: running water.

Someone's taking a shower.

The ridiculous thought floated by unattached. My legs moved with a life all their own, powered by I didn't even know what.

No fucking way. It has to be someone else. There's no way that he's continued to take showers here at three-fucking-am for two years. Just. In. Case.

I rounded the privacy wall and stopped dead. Sure enough, Calvin Fucking Bridges was standing by a stream of water covered in soap—naked. *Very naked.* My gaze followed the path of suds as they slid their way down his slick back. They swirled in the dip above his ass, then streamed down his long legs with their light layer of dark hair. The bubbles I'd been tracking finally left his body, and I dragged my gaze back up. Muscles in his back rippled as he went through the motions of cleaning. He didn't look the same as before; he looked better. Though how that was even fucking possible was beyond me. My heart pounded. I'd have given almost anything if I could just look away, or at least fucking blink, but my eyes stayed glued to his light brown skin with its warm peach undertones.

He still hasn't seen me.

No sooner did I think it, then he turned around.

Fuck me. When did he start working out?

Calvin did not look like the kind of guy to possess a six-pack—perpetually skinny, maybe—but not toned. Even with suds still obscuring half of him, I could clearly see the definition, the outline of firm pectorals, the perfect ridges of his abdominals, the pronounced V that invited a wandering gaze to keep exploring. Heat rushed through me as I continued to take in every sculpted inch of him. The same heat that had sprung to life as I'd stood outside and stared at the door just thinking of the possibility that he might be within.

"Benny."

At the sound of my name, I dragged my gaze up to his face, where his brown eyes were wide in surprise.

He's still not afraid of me.

The thought came unbidden. Then the reality of the situation hit home, and that this was an almost perfect role reversal of what had happened two years ago.

I need to leave. Turn around and go. I have my answer. Turn and GO.

The urgent logic asserted itself and yet, my rebellious gaze fell to the tiled floor and landed on a bottle by the soap.

That's not shampoo.

Calvin watched in silence as I stripped off first my shirt, then my pants, quickly followed by my boxers. I threw them to some dry corner and stalked up to him. I snatched the bottle of lube from the floor and tossed it at him. "Expecting someone?" I wasn't sure why I asked or why it even mattered. I just knew that it did.

"Never hurts to be prepared," he responded, a cheeky smile teasing his lips. His eyes blatantly traveled down and back up my body, inspiring another wave of heat. I stared back at him and tried not to think about what I was doing. "Same as before?" he inquired with a raised eyebrow.

God, yes. I still had fucking dreams about his mouth on my cock and what it had felt like to have him inside of me. I was getting hard just thinking about it now. Correction, harder. Blood had rushed to my cock the moment I'd laid eyes on him.

"Not quite," I responded, then before he could say anything else, I placed a hand on his surprisingly defined chest and pushed him back under the water.

He stared at me unblinking, still not an ounce of fear in those dark eyes. The last of the soap washed off of him and I wrapped my hand around his cock. He stiffened beneath my fingers and my pulse spiked. I tightened my grip and stroked up his length, rubbed my thumb across the tip, then slid back down again. His eyes lidded and he gave a low moan.

"Tell me when you're getting close," I ordered. I waited for the commentary, the judgment, anything. All he did was nod.

I looked down at where I had hold of him. His cock, like the rest of him, was several shades darker than me. I gave the spongy cap an experimental squeeze. It was different touching someone else like this, yet there was still an echoing stir in my cock. Not to mention, there was something intoxicating about hearing him groan as I worked him, but that wasn't what I really wanted.

I knelt down and studied him for a moment. Still no quippy remark. I wanted to know what he tasted like, had thought about it far more than I cared to admit. Slowly I took the head into my mouth and was instantly surprised at the difference in feel from my fingers. I swirled my tongue around the tip, and he rewarded me with a throaty groan. My cock twitched in response. My lips slid further down his shaft as I took more of him in. I ran my hands up the front of his muscled thighs and stroked his Adonis belt with my thumbs while I admired the neatly trimmed nest of dark curls surrounding my captive prize.

His hips threatened to buck as I added the flat of my tongue and established a rhythm. The sound of the water spraying around us mostly hid the noises I was making, but did little to cover his increasingly husky breathing. It was fucking hot. To know that I was doing that, I was making the self-confident Calvin Bridges lose his cool. He let out a heavy moan as I methodically worked my tongue up and darted it across his slit. Finally, I had my answer to what he tasted like.

He's salty, almost sweet.

I took all of him back in again and his breath hitched. "I'm gonna come," he groaned. I quickly released him, a little sad to have to stop. His groan this time was decidedly more disappointed.

I stood up, and he watched me in perfect silence like he'd done everything else, like he'd done two years ago when I'd been unwilling to turn him away. I snaked an arm around his waist and tugged him away from the wall. Our cocks brushed together, and a thrill surged through mine. For a moment, we stood chest to chest, face to face, his golden-brown eyes seeing everything inside of me I worked so hard to keep from the world. My gaze flicked down to where his lips hovered on level with mine.

I wonder what the rest of him tastes like.

I ignored the thought and took his place by the wall, facing it instead of leaning on it as he had been. Whatever insanity had brought me here tonight, I was done waiting. It was time to see how good my memory really was. The lid of the lube made a snap as it opened and trepidation shot through me.

What am I doing? This is wrong. This is insane. This is—a seriously lubed finger circled my hole, then slipped inside—*fucking incredible*. I groaned and pushed back. My memory didn't do it justice.

"Easy." The soft word was like a caress, matching the way his other hand was massaging my ass cheek. He added another finger, and I got harder.

Fuck. Why does that feel so good?

Then he moved, slow and shallow at first, then deeper until he stroked that spot inside me I'd been too afraid to touch myself. I redefined my definition of good. He took his time working me open, gradually increasing his pace, then slowed again when I started pressing back in time with his thrusting fingers.

God damn it, Cal.

I wanted to shout at him to stop fucking with me and just take me already, but I was struggling with coherency too much to try to form a proper sentence. Another finger. My whole body simultaneously reveled and rebelled at the invasion. Another delicate brush of my prostate.

God, I'm not gonna make it.

No sooner did I adjust to the feel, than all three fingers were gone. I sagged against the wall, resting most of my weight on my forearms.

I don't know if I should be relieved or upset.

His fingers kneaded my cheeks, and my moan turned desperate. Then he pulled them back apart. My breath caught when I felt his swollen head at my entrance.

About fucking time.

Impatient, I made to push back, only to have his hands turn to iron and prevent me from moving. No comment or anything, just a silent command to hold still. A shudder ran through me, but I didn't force the issue.

If he goes any slower, I'm going to pass out from anticipation.

He slid past the first ring and I let out a whine.

Fuck fuck fuck. Oh god, was he this big last time? I don't remember this at all.

My hand fisted against the slick tile, and I forced it back flat.

"Breathe, Benny," he whispered.

I wasn't aware I had stopped. I dragged in a shaky lung full of air. As I let it out, he drove the rest of the way home and stopped moving. His lithe fingers started massaging the small of my back while he stayed deeply rooted, his impressive cock stretching me. I focused on the touch instead of the burn. I knew Calvin was an artist, but this was different. He confidently traced patterns in my skin, as if he could see something no one else could.

Maybe he can.

I drew in another deep breath in time with the swirls he was creating. When I exhaled, the last of my tension went with it. I relaxed, and he slid a fraction deeper, his cock expertly angled to rub across my prostate. A groan from somewhere deep inside of me emerged as I hung my head.

That, that is what I remember.

Pleasure spiraled as the memory I'd clung to and this new reality merged. Then he moved. He pulled out halfway, and I whined again. *What the fuck is wrong with me?* He pushed back in all the way to the hilt. *Fuck me, that's good.* Gradually, he established a rhythm of long, deep strokes. His painter's hands digging into my sides started to feel like the only things holding me up. I let out another moan and reached for my cock. *How is it possible for anyone to be this hard?*

"Fuck you're tight." The low hiss nearly sent me careening over the edge. Already, I could feel it building to a breaking point.

I don't want to come so soon, but if he keeps talking like that, I won't have a choice.

His grip loosened, and he pulled nearly all the way out. I could have cried with frustration. Before he could stop me, I rammed back and took all of him at once.

"Fuck!"

I echoed his exclamation as I came hard enough that the light green tile turned white.

Our ragged breathing surrounded me as we came down from our respective climaxes. His hair brushed the middle of my back as he folded to rest his forehead on me. He finally slipped out and an overwhelming emptiness took its place. The ache of absence warred with the satisfaction of fulfillment. Suddenly, I realized the water was still falling all around us.

Neither of us said a word as we stepped far enough apart to clean up. He passed me the soap in perfect silence and we took turns in the spray that miraculously still held warmth. We rinsed off and got dressed, the haze of release still firmly wrapped around my mind and keeping my body a relaxed collection of muscles. It was a motherfucking miracle I didn't collapse as I put my pants on. I still felt like I should be lying in a heap on the floor, though it wouldn't have helped the ache in my ass, an ache that wasn't entirely bad.

That hadn't been at all like I remembered it. It had been a hundred times better.

I looked over at Calvin gathering his things where we'd just…

What the fuck did I just do?

I walked over to him and he raised an eyebrow in that infuriating way he had. "Not a fucking word of this to anyone." A smile played at the edge of his lips. He mimed zipping his mouth shut, locking it, then throwing away the key.

Real fucking cute.

"This doesn't make me gay," I said emphatically.

He snorted a laugh, and I glared at him. He held his hands up defensively, but kept to the silence.

I glared at him again for good measure and had to resist the urge to give him another once over.

You'd never know…

I dragged my thoughts away from what he really looked like beneath the plain cotton tee and loose lounge pants. Without another word, I exited the showers and made a beeline for my room. I was already deep under the covers by the time it occurred to me I hadn't ever actually finished the round.

Well, fuck.

I sat up, and something pulled at my side. My hand quested beneath the covers for the source, but came up empty. I flicked on the lamp and investigated more thoroughly, my hand patting along the under sheet.

Nothing in the bed. Maybe it's on me.

At last, I found the cause of my inexplicable discomfort. Three perfect scratches, easily an inch long, graced my hip with a matching set on the other side. I snickered to myself.

Perfect composure, my ass.

I wasn't even thinking as I pulled out the notebook I kept under the bed. Pages filled with scribbled words flipped past until at last I found a blank one and continued the story I'd been working on for the last two years.

The indomitable Kel had met his match…

Chapter 10

Calvin

The filing cabinet squeaked and groaned in protest at the sudden force of me plopping atop it. Almost instantly, the sound of my great aunt's voice scolding me for sitting on the furniture filled my mind. I smiled as my over-sized sketchpad landed with a hard smack on the desk before me. Great Aunt Winnie hadn't been able to break me of the habit and I didn't expect Ulwich Prep to have much success either. I leaned back on my arms, my legs kicking aimlessly, while I awaited Professor Jankowski to return and give me my passing grade. Unsurprisingly, my mind wandered back to the same merry-go-round it had been circling for the better part of three days.

Benny gave me head. Benjamin Fucking Price actually got down on his knees and put my dick in his mouth. Willingly.

Giddiness bubbled through me like Dom Perignon. I still wasn't sure what surprised me more, that it had been *the* Benjamin Price or that he'd been so goddamn enthusiastic. Probably had as much to do with all my thoughts being centered on my dick, but I could have sworn he'd sighed—in disappointment, no less—when I'd warned him I was on the edge. To be fair, I'd been pretty fucking disappointed myself, so it was possible I'd actually heard my own sigh. Hard to tell with the water crashing around us, but I was inclined to believe it was Benny. Of course, getting to slide into that tight hole, his intense heat wrapping around me…yeah, that might have made up for it.

Benjamin Fucking Price.

A smile tripped over my lips. Bringing the lube had been a stroke of genius. Shame I hadn't thought to keep a spare condom in the shower caddy. Even as I considered starting to do so now, I dismissed the reckless idea. Getting caught with it wasn't worth the risk. So what if we'd gone bare? Benny was officially one of two guys in my entire life I'd ever done that with and I took my health seriously. I trusted he did as well.

With a body like that, he'd have to.

"I see you've done it."

The comment merged so perfectly with my latest mental victory lap, it took me a second to process the intended meaning behind the words. I blinked the fantasy away and realized that at some point Jankowski had arrived. Though how I'd missed it when he was standing right fucking in front of me… I shook my head at my distraction and focused on what had captured his attention—the sketch of Benny in the library.

"This is incredible," Jankowski said, like I'd expected he would when I'd completed the damn thing in the first place.

Shit.

"Wait. Not that one." He glanced over, his mouth pressing briefly into a thin line as I hopped off the cabinet and stepped forward. I took the pad from him, careful not to crumple the exposed page and opened the book to the more recent, honestly obtained portrait. "This one," I said as I passed it back.

Surely Benny knowing I was there this time counts as honest. Right?

Jankowski gently took the pad back and glanced down at the fresh image. The moment his gaze landed on the page, though, he jerked away. "Calvin, how many times do I have to tell you? You cannot give me pictures like this."

"Oh please, art is art. And he's not even a minor. Even I have some moral standards." I gestured at the image, because *obviously* that wasn't some kid. His scowl deepened as he stared at me. "What?"

"But it is still a student. Correct?"

"Irrelevant," I countered.

"Calvin, I do not want to see my pupils this way. It's unethical."

"It's *art*. At least look at the damn thing before you decide I'm too morally depraved."

"I didn't say…" He let out a heavy sigh and pinched the bridge of his nose as he often did when we debated subject matter. With obvious reluctance, he finally looked down. He gave another put-upon sigh like I was torturing him instead of offering some of my best work, maybe ever. "It's exceptional. Your attention to detail is as astute as ever. But the eyes… those are incredible. You've captured a world of emotion and you can only see half his face."

I knew exactly what he was talking about. Lines arched gracefully up the page to form the sculpted landscape of Benny's back. Shading had brought the two-dimensional sketch into a world all its own where I could reach in and touch the quivering skin, flush from heat and arousal. You could just make out his hands in the background, bracing him against the wall while he turned to look over his shoulder at me, his lips parted slightly, still spit-slick. Everything about his face was incredible, the openness, the raw vulnerability, the way his eyes shone with lust and sheer desperate *need*. I'd jacked off to it no less than three times. First time I'd ever jacked off to one of my works, so I guess, point Benny. Fine, two points Benny. The first for taking me by surprise and making me finish before I'd intended.

"Why not the other?" Jankowski asked, bringing my thoughts back to the present.

I crossed my arms and leaned against the cabinet. "This one's better."

"I'd say they both admirably display your talent. But the first... might be better received."

My spine stiffened. Why couldn't the male form be beautiful? It was okay to depict women like this, but heaven forbid a man be portrayed as vulnerable, as wanting. Being those things didn't make him weak, they made him strong. Not to mention, I'd intentionally left out anything that might be conceived as explicit, stopping well above the spectacular curve of his ass. No Dimples of Venus, no exquisitely muscled thighs, not so much as a goddamn nipple. I'd even left out the water, for fuck's sake.

"I'm not using the other. You can judge me for this one or not at all."

"But why?" he asked, his gaze flicking up at my serious tone.

"Personal reasons." I shrugged and left it at that.

He simply shook his head and returned his focus to the piece. Suddenly, he jerked and ripped back to the previous portrait with as much care as anyone can frantically flip between two pages. "Is this...Please tell me this isn't..." His voice dropped to a whisper as he turned eyes wide with horror on me. "For the love of God, Calvin, please tell me this isn't Benjamin Price."

An evil grin spread across my face. Though admittedly, I was impressed he'd gathered that from half a profile. "Well, they are the same person, if that's what you're asking."

He snapped the book shut and dropped it to the table like a living, breathing Benny might actually emerge from the layers of graphite. "I understand you pride yourself on the outrageous, but have you no sense of self-preservation? At all?"

"I survive just fine." I plucked the discarded sketchpad up and tucked it securely back in my bag.

"And what do you think Mr. Price will do if he finds out about those?"

"Beat the living shit out of me, I imagine."

"Jesus," he hissed. "I can't display this. If Benjamin isn't even in my class and *I* can figure it out, others will as well." He glanced at me out of the corner of his eye. "Are you two… No. Don't answer that, I don't want to know." He straightened up. "I will accept this as your assignment—you clearly have the skills—but it will not be included in the fall exhibit." I made to argue, and he held up a hand. "It's not up for debate, but it is time we cultivate this skill set. For your next assignment, no more of this side view nonsense. I want a full frontal."

"You sure about that?" I asked with a smirk.

He nearly swallowed his tongue as his words caught up with him. "Clothes *on*." My smirk broadened to a grin. Clothes on could be just as salacious with the right details. Jankowski finally found his voice and his glower. "In addition, I want a self-portrait."

"Now wait a minute. I'm not creating some pretentious piece of—"

"I'm fully aware of your opinion on the style, however, this too is also not up for debate. I've been far too lax in accepting your excuses and *that*," he gestured at my satchel and the sketchpad within, "proves it. Your portfolio is nowhere near complete. You have your grade, but if you want to keep it, you'll create the pieces."

My jaw tightened along with my death grip on the strap of my bag. This was blackmail, pure and simple. I should know. I leveraged this tactic all the time with my clients.

Jankowski softened the tiniest bit. "Remember, artists—even great ones—rarely get to choose their own subjects."

I huffed and pushed my way past him to make my way down the hall. He might as well have added that great artists were also usually dead by the time they were recognized as great. Begrudging acceptance gradually tempered my anger. There was no way Jankowski would ever understand my abhorrence of self-portraits. Most really were of pretentious ass wipes puffed up with their own self-importance, but there were the odd few that stood out as genuinely remarkable. Those told a story and I didn't want my story to be told.

Too late, I heard the telltale catcall. I lurched to a stop, my hand going instinctively to protect my satchel and its precious contents. I'd die if something happened to those sketches. Before they could gain more on me than surprise, I squared my shoulders and locked eyes with Benny. My fingers curled over the flap, my thoughts instantly going to the condemning pictures within, and I smiled.

Benny

I'd run into Calvin over the years a hundred times, no, make that a thousand, and it had never affected me before. But today, it did. I swallowed hard at the lascivious grin pulling at his lips and, for probably the first time in my life, was grateful that he always looked at me like that. Nate and Todd would never be able to know something was different, even if I did. There was no distinguishable difference. He always leered like a lech because he knew it got under my skin. The more I squirmed, the more he did it. It was an awful game and one we couldn't seem to stop playing. And now, now all I could think as he looked at me like that and caressed his bag was how fucking envious I was of the damn bag.

Fuck. Double fuck.

It had taken over a day for my ass to stop smarting and half that for me to start aching to have him fill me again. All my years of avoiding this part of myself were gone in an instant. Blood roared in my ears and he arched one dark eyebrow, that knowing smile still painted on his face. With growing desperation, I slammed down all my walls, barbs and everything, then fell back on the familiar.

"What the fuck are you looking at, queer?"

His eyes glinted with a malevolence that immediately froze my heart and stilled the air in my lungs. What if he told? I had nothing to stop him, no argument, no leverage, only this unbearable want crawling up my spine bolder than ever. He removed his hand from the satchel and inspected his nails like he had all the time in the world. Only Calvin Bridges could calmly face off with three grown athletes without an ounce of backup and remain cool as crystal.

"That really the best you can do, Benny?" He tsked his teeth and shook his head slowly from side to side. "If you're going to insult me, Price, the least you can do is get creative." He glanced up at the ceiling as if pondering the ultimate insult. Then he dropped it again, eyes wide with inspiration, long fingers of both hands spread out in the air. "I know! You could tell me I have a small dick."

Todd and Neil snickered behind me at Calvin's self-imposed insult. I couldn't bring myself to even do that, no matter how smart it would have been. We both knew that Calvin didn't have a small dick by any stretch of the imagination. Fuck, even thinking about it made my ass clench greedily. If he kept making cracks about his dick like that, I'd end up sprouting wood. I needed to get control of this now. I took a step toward him and his open grin settled back into a smirk.

"What'll it be Benny?"

"Telling you that you have a small dick assumes you even have one."

"Ooh." Calvin placed the fingers of one hand against his chest in mock injury. "Benjamin, do we need to play doctor?"

I rolled my eyes. "When's the last time you even saw a doctor?"

His eyes sharpened, betraying that I'd struck a nerve. He didn't have many, and they were damn near impossible to find, but he did have them. "Three months ago, you fuck twat. Clean bill of health. What about you, Benny? Up to date on your rabies shots?"

"Like I would put my teeth anywhere near you." A traitorous image of his cock gagging me while my nose pressed into his pubes and he moaned above me flashed through my mind. I fisted my hands and pushed the image away, determined not to let him get the best of me. "Speaking of people willing to be near you, where's your little sidekick?" I leveled my hand at my waist.

"Yeah," Neil snickered, "Where's fire crotch?"

Calvin's gaze flickered to him at the pedantic insult. "How the fuck should I know? We're not attached at the hip."

"Really?" I crossed my arms. "You two seemed pretty... *tight* once upon a time. Let me guess, he gave up when he figured out you didn't have a dick to find."

The muscles in Calvin's jaw worked furiously while his eyes burned with anger. As soon as the emotion surfaced though, it was gone, no more than a pan flash. "Andy has absolutely zero interest in my dick. I can be gay and have friends without wanting to fuck them, asshole."

"You sure about that? Last I checked, you only had the one friend, and he's nowhere to be seen." I held out my arms to encompass the hallway that currently only held the four of us.

"Hasn't been for a while," Todd chimed in. I glanced back at him and he tipped his chin at me. I barely didn't roll my eyes at the unnecessary assist and returned my attention to where Calvin was working harder than usual to remain neutral.

"How much has to be wrong with you that not even other queers want to be around you?" I asked.

"Go fuck yourself."

"Seems to me like he's moved on... or is it moved back? Now that Mitch is back in the picture, he doesn't need or want you. Face it, you were never anything more than a placeholder to him." With each word, Calvin's shoulders tightened more and more until the tension practically rolled off of him and he had a death grip on his satchel.

"You don't know what you're talking about." His glance slid behind me. "At least my friends aren't a bunch of boot-licking sycophants. Did you get a say or did daddy buy them outright for you?"

"Watch your fucking mouth," Neil growled while Todd bowed up.

I held up a hand to forestall them before it escalated to actual violence and continued to worry the open wound I'd uncovered. "Bought or not, at least I know they have my back. Tell me, does Andy have yours when it matters, or only when it suits him?"

Dumb and Dumber fist bumped behind me. "That's right, ride or die you pansy bitch," Neil added like the idiot he was. I barely checked my eye roll and took another bold step toward Calvin, who glared absolute death at me.

A part of me instantly missed the lascivious look that seemed a permanent part of him, capable of stripping you bare and fucking you where you stood. The other part recognized that I wasn't supposed to want that, wasn't supposed to want *him*. He remained rooted to the spot as I leaned forward and dropped my voice so it wouldn't carry. His sharp gaze cut to me and I almost checked to see if the look had drawn blood.

"Does anyone at this school actually know who you are? Do they care? You talk a lot of smack, but admit it, at the end of the day, you're an island, always have been."

"Haus," Todd called. "We throwing down or what?"

I stepped back and looked down my nose at Calvin, not easy considering we were the same height. “What’s that? Nothing to say, Bridges?”

The rage simmering in his eyes crystallized into ice. “Oh, I have plenty to say.”

A spike of fear shot through my chest. Despite my gnawing uncertainty, I didn’t back down. Calvin could’ve destroyed me years ago. He hadn’t then, and I didn’t expect he would now. “Let’s hear it.” The challenge fell from my lips and every muscle braced for the worst.

His icy gaze studied me, then his lips twisted into an almost smile. Releasing his white-knuckled grip on his bag, he flipped his hair back. “No, I don’t think I will.” The air of nonchalance was pure grade-A bullshit as he made a grand show of stepping around me to continue on his original journey.

Todd and Neil moved with the same coordination they did on the field to stop him. I waved them both off and they looked at me askance.

“Let him go. He’s not worth our time. He’s not worth anyone’s time.”

Calvin’s shoulders tensed as he passed between them, the only sign I’d struck a nerve. No one moved as he walked unhurriedly down the hall. When he finally disappeared around a corner, the tightness in my chest eased and Neil and Todd rushed me.

“Damn, boss, that was cold,” Neil said, clapping me on the back.

“I don’t remember that last I saw him actually shook. How’d you know the dig about Andy would get to him?”

I blinked away the last sight of him. “Good guess. Figured if Mitch flaking to hang with his old buddy fucked with the team, then Andy was probably doing the same.” It was more than that, of course. Being unique brought with it a level of isolation whether you wanted it or not, and Calvin was nothing if not unique.

King Kelani’s rage could have burnt down the entire palace if it hadn’t been so cold. The aloof king had fielded countless attempts to undermine his rule over the years. In fact, such attempts had only reinforced his reign, made him bolder. Prince Einar had longed to be the one who brought the emboldened king to heel, who reminded Kel that he was not the only significant player in this game of crowns. But now that Einar had at long last accomplished his impossible task, he could not maintain the King's level glare. He had not anticipated his victory to taste so bitter.

Chapter 11

Benny

I stood in front of the door to the second-floor showers and hesitated. More than anything, I wanted to go inside, to be claimed by him again, to just *be*, but I faltered, unsure of the reception I'd receive after what had happened in the hall. Calvin and I'd had several run-ins throughout the week, but that one haunted me. The ghost of hurt in his eyes had been real and I'd put it there. And why? Because I was afraid he'd reveal what we'd done to Todd and Neil? That was part of it, but not the part that mattered. Calvin could have exposed me for the liar I was years ago. Hell, I kind of hoped he would. Then I could finally stop pretending. No, after nights of tossing and turning, I could finally admit the truth. To myself, if not to Calvin. I'd violated our unspoken rules of engagement. Made him hurt because I could, because it was expected of me. I'd gone for the one thing I knew would bring him to his knees in some misguided attempt to prove he didn't have power over me. Except he did. He always had.

My fingers wrapped around the handle. Would he send me away? Demand retribution?

Is he even here?

I pushed the door open. The damnable hinges squealed with a horrible cacophony of metal against metal, alerting the whole fucking world of my weakness. It swung shut with a decided thump and the sound of running water filled the room. The tension wrapped around my chest relaxed slightly, but didn't dissipate altogether. The need to know quickened my steps until at last I rounded the wall dividing the showers from the rest of the bathroom.

My breath caught and my stomach lurched into my throat as my gaze fell on Calvin's light brown body leaning against the pale green tile. Water cascaded over him, caressing every exposed inch of his gloriously naked body before running off to vanish down the embedded drain. He raked back damp curls from his face while his other hand stroked up his length with a firm grip. His fingers slid all the way up his cock with practiced ease until they encapsulated his swollen head, then purposefully slid back down.

By the time I dragged my riveted gaze away from the mouthwatering sight, my pants were uncomfortably tight and Calvin's eyes were boring into me. Apologies for the awful things I'd said bubbled up, closely followed by the overwhelming desire to beg for his forgiveness, offer him whatever he wanted so long as he'd touch me again. I swallowed down all of it and it swirled unpleasantly in my stomach.

We stared at each other with nothing but the sound of spray hitting tile filling the air. The whole time he continued lazily stroking himself like he didn't have an audience. He squeezed the base of his shaft and arched against the wall, his heading falling back at the pleasure of it. I didn't even bother to check my groan as sheer fucking want turned to liquid fire pulsing in my veins. Calvin raised his head and looked at me once more, his eyebrow characteristically raised.

"You just going to stand there and cream your pants or are you gonna come over here so I can fuck it out of you?"

One minute I was across the room, the next Calvin was shoving me under the spray, his hand like a vice around my aching cock, making me gasp. I didn't remember taking my clothes off or what I had done with them. I didn't remember when I'd decided to come here. I didn't remember anything for the next hour.

Calvin

My thoughts were a muddled mess, like paint splatter on a white wall, the color running together and no discernable image in sight. I absently checked the enclave that held a statue of some forgotten scholar who'd undoubtedly paid a shit ton of money for the ugly piece. But not even the three folded slips of paper could pull me out of the quagmire. Benny had come back, the unmistakable glint of fear and desperate want shining in his eyes. Part of me hadn't expected him to show. Hadn't wanted him to.

His taunts about Andy had cut deep and still stung. I hated him for taking our typical banter that far. Despite forgiveness being a tenant of my faith, I'd never been very good at it. It galled a bit that I'd not only been pleased that he *had* shown, but that all my plans to punish him by turning him away had gone down the drain the second I'd laid eyes on him.

I slipped into the art room and let out a relieved breath to find that no one else had arrived yet. My usual desk toward the back of the room squeaked as I sat, reminding me of the door to the showers. Hate fucking wasn't something I really ascribed to. I made a point to always be tender with the men I slept with, recognizing it was likely their first time and no one should have to endure a first like I had. But ascribed to or not, that's exactly what I'd done with Benny. He hadn't protested the rough handling or punishing pace. He'd taken it like a champ, almost like he thought he deserved it.

... And that's where my brain dissolved, like a water-based blue paint reaching across soaked paper until it was translucent. I wasn't that person. As mad as I was at Benny, I didn't use partners that way. Not even Benjamin Price *deserved* to be treated like that.

"Penny for your thoughts?"

I blinked and glanced at the desk beside me where Keagan sat waiting for my response. At some point, the rest of the class had come in and somehow I'd missed it. I returned my focus to him, noting that he'd copied the way I'd done my tie, or more accurately, hadn't, as well as untucked half his button-down. Though I doubted he realized it was actually a French Tuck and intentional style choice on my part rather than a means of rebellion. They said imitation was the highest form of flattery. I found it fucking annoying.

"Have you decided what you'll be submitting to the art show in the spring?" Keagan asked when I neglected to answer his first question.

The sketch of Benny looking over his shoulder while water cascaded around him flashed through my mind. I ground my teeth, more than a little perturbed with myself that I couldn't seem to keep my thoughts away from Price. "No," I responded flatly, then turned to remove a less damning sketchbook and the art text.

"Huh, normally you have like ten things already lined up and the rest of us are trying to squeeze in anything." He gave a humorless laugh, reminding me that despite being in a room full of shared interests, I had no friends here. Whether it was because I was gay, better than them, or both was anyone's guess. "Maybe this will be my year to take the showpiece."

I barely contained a snort. Snow stood a better chance in hell than of Keagan being awarded the coveted showpiece slot. "What are you planning to submit?" I asked, feigning interest. Anything was better than thinking about my last encounter with Benny.

"Like I'd tell you. Last thing I need is you pulling another stunt like you did our sophomore year."

"The assignment was landscapes. It's not my fault Hunter, and I chose the same one to paint." It didn't matter how many times I said it was an accident, pure coincidence. No one believed I hadn't done it on purpose to show him up. The debacle had solidified my reputation among the school's art community as an egotistical upstart. It certainly didn't help that the piece had captured the aforementioned showpiece.

"Yeah, yeah. You start your self-portrait yet?"

I stiffened. "Not yet."

Keagan gave me a quizzical look. "For real? It's due in like two weeks. No way you'll finish in time."

"Yeah, well, I guess I'll be asking for an extension then, now won't I?"

His blue eyes turned cruel. It was a subtle shift, but one I'd learned to pick up on early in life. "Thought for sure you of all people would've had that done in no time."

My grip on my sketching pencil tightened until it snapped, compounding my irritation. That was my last 6H graphite. I'd have to order more and they definitely wouldn't arrive anytime soon, thanks to the brand I preferred. I chunked the broken pieces into my bag and pulled out a 2B. If I was lucky, I could salvage the other and eek out a few more sketches before it was unusable. I didn't bother responding to Keagan's less than subtle dig at my "over-inflated pride", instead sliding down in my seat to review the pieces of paper I'd retrieved on the way to class.

I unfolded the first, mindful of prying eyes. It was from Connor, thanking me for the boa and letting me know he had more pot whenever I needed it. The next was more crumpled paper than folded note. The shaky handwriting betrayed their nerves as they asked for flavored lube for their girlfriend. Despite the nom de plum they'd used, there wasn't a doubt in my mind it was a request from Tanner, and it definitely wasn't for a "girlfriend". The note joined the first, and I reached for the last. My eyebrows rose in surprise at the request. It wasn't every day a student at Ulwich had the balls to ask for anal beads. Hell, I didn't even have any. Then again, I'd never had a partner interested in exploring anything beyond my dick in their ass.

Shaking my head, I stood and walked over to the art supply cabinet. There were still a few minutes before class officially started. More than enough time to take care of this. I fished out a paper mixing cup and poured undiluted acetone into it, then dropped the scraps in one at a time. The paper may not have completely dissolved, but they were a far cry from legible. Best way to keep secrets was to make sure there was no evidence. I was nearly done cleaning up when I spied my pouch of backup art supplies shoved into a corner of the cabinet from when I used to sneak into the classroom to draw in solitude. That was before I'd been tall enough to get onto the ledge in the library.

Back in my seat, with scant seconds to spare, I unzipped the uncharacteristically demure pencil bag and let out a whoop.

"Mr. Bridges, was there something you wanted to share with the class?" Jankowski asked from the front of the room with an exasperated expression that could rival Father Miles'.

"Found another 6H, but I don't plan on sharing," I replied with a cocky grin.

Jankowski stopped just shy of rolling his eyes and turned to the board to start class. "For today's lecture we'll be covering…" His voiced drifted out of focus as I twirled my unexpected prize and flipped to a fresh page.

Chapter 12

Calvin

The door squealing open barely even registered as I entered the showers. *Will he be here?* Part of me was genuinely curious; then again, he'd either already been here or shown up shortly after me the last four times.

I don't hear anything. Maybe he won't show.

I tempered my disappointment. I always knew what this had been. Having fun with Benny was bound to have a short shelf life, even if it was nice to learn someone's body, all the tiny things that drove them wild with pleasure. That wasn't something I'd had before. Twice was my previous all-time high, and that had been as much desperation as good timing.

Oh well, it was fun while it lasted.

I folded my clothes and rounded the division, where a grin immediately split my face. I quickly reined it in. It would never do for Benny to know how much I was enjoying our random hookups. So maybe the enjoyment wasn't strictly getting to know *any* person's body, but Benny's specifically. Stripping away his reservations to reveal the unbridled lust lurking beneath the surface was a special kind of high. I'd debated what I would do if he showed up again after that day in the hall. All sorts of scenarios had come to mind, but in the end, seeing the aching want in his eyes had decided me. Whatever else I could do, it wouldn't ever have near the satisfaction of bringing Benjamin Price to his knees.

He's so fucking proud.

And already naked, I was pleased to note. My grin threatened to make a reappearance as I shamelessly appreciated the view. Muscles wrapped around him like they'd been sculpted and rippled as he moved, every motion intentional and confident.

An athlete's body without question. And those squats are definitely helping. He has a fantastic ass. Like a perfect bubble. Tight and round.

My cock twitched at the thought of what I was going to do to that ass and I slowly worked my gaze back up his spectacular body. Either Benny hadn't heard the damnable door or he was ignoring me. He walked over to the same shower we'd used the last couple of times.

"Not that one," I called out. He spun around, clearly startled, and I smirked.

Little distracted, Mr. Price?

He glanced back at the shower. "What?"

I walked across the light green tile to a larger station on the far side of the room. "This one tonight." There was no missing the reproachful look he gave the handicap set up. Truthfully, the bench was too small to be of any actual use, but that wasn't why I chose it.

As if reading my thoughts, he asked, "Why?"

The knob twisted in my hand, sending out a wave of steam as the cascade of scalding water hit the floor. I looked at him through the curtain. "Because you're gonna wanna hold on to something." He swallowed as anxiety and what could only be excitement flashed across his face. I quickly yanked him under the waterfall before he could find some witty retort. "I'm going to fuck you until you can't stand, Benjamin Price. Now hold on tight." I spun him around so he'd be able to hang onto the support bars and sat on the absurdly small seat in front of him.

He made a dramatic show of placing his hands on the metal, but otherwise didn't comment. I ignored his condescending look and eyed his erect cock before me, already beaded with a perfect opaque drop.

I haven't even touched him yet.

I could barely hear his light moan over the water as I took him in hand. I squeezed the base and pulled up.

"Tall order," he finally quipped in response to my bold promise. I was impressed he managed to say the goading statement as flatly as he did, especially since it was immediately followed by a deeper moan.

So so proud Benny Price. I licked up the length of him and he shuddered.

"Do you have a book of tricks or something?" The breathy question lacked the sting it was undoubtedly supposed to have.

Or something.

"It's called imagination." I placed my lips around his swollen head and gave a light suck, earning me another moan.

I slowly took in more of him, hollowing my cheeks out and adding pressure with my tongue to the underside of his shaft. His moan became more pronounced. I settled into a pattern of lick, stroke, suck. Above me, his breathing became more ragged with each second. A quick look showed that he was finally taking the support bars seriously. I smiled inwardly and, without losing my pace, reached out for the lube I'd sat beside me.

"It's about being comfortable with your body and knowing what it wants," I said between mouthfuls.

"And you think you know what *my* body wa—" His snarky comeback died as I slid a finger past his entrance. His head fell back and his mouth opened in a silent moan as he gave himself over wholly to the sensation. I brushed across his prostate with a featherlight touch. His entire body shook and his cock twitched against my lips. I curled my tongue around his pulsing shaft and he dropped his head back between his arms where another moan fell out of him.

My mouth stayed on his cock as I began to work his ass. The water drowned out most of his fantastic responses, but I could still feel his heavy breathing on my wet hair, each moan a caress urging me on. When I was confident he was ready for it, I added a second digit. He let out a guttural groan from deep in his throat and squeezed around the pair.

He makes the best fucking sounds. What I wouldn't give for three hands.

My cock was twitching eagerly and aching. Finally, I slid in a third finger. He let out a tiny whine, and I tasted more pre-cum. I immediately abandoned my rhythm, but kept moving my fingers, wanting him nice and prepped for the pounding I had in store. His body tensed at the intrusion and relaxed in record time, without any coaxing or guidance.

He's getting better at this.

No sooner did I have the thought, then he gasped. I glanced up to see him white-knuckling the bars. "I'm gonna..." he groaned, fighting back his own need for release. "I don't... I don't want..."

Not so proud now.

His cock made a wonderful pop as I released the head, only to recapture it.

"What do you want?" I asked, alternating between stroking and sucking, careful not to overstimulate that glorious bundle of nerves inside of him.

He can't possibly hold on much longer.

The moan he let out was nothing short of primal. The sound wrapped around my neglected cock and squeezed without mercy. I choked on my own groan of need, but refused to relent.

Hell, I'm not gonna make it much longer.

"Tell me."

He groaned and shook his head, eyes squeezed shut. I threatened to remove my fingers, and he gasped out, "Your cock! I want your cock." The words rang with desperation and defeat.

Not good enough.

I slowly licked him from base to tip. "And where do you want my cock? In your mouth? In your ass?" It definitely had not eluded my attention how much Benny enjoyed having my dick in his mouth. Hell, with his enthusiasm, he'd be graduating from novice to fucking pro in no time.

"God damn it, Cal. You know where I want it," he said through gritted teeth.

"I do. But I want you to say it." I gently brushed that small globe of pure pleasure, determined to make him beg. He sucked in air and his whole body stiffened, squeezing my fingers so tightly that I simultaneously feared for circulation and despaired for my cock.

Shit. I've pushed him too far.

Benny took a deep, shaky breath that expanded his flushed chest and stretched his pecs. He held it for a few seconds, then released it in stuttering bursts only to do it all over again. I watched, fascinated as he fought back his climax.

He really doesn't want to come any other way.

"My ass. I wanna feel your cock in my ass," he said when he exhaled for the third time.

Better.

"Ask nicely."

He whimpered as I withdrew my fingers. "Please. Oh god, please, Cal." He tried to look at me, but could barely keep his eyes open enough to focus.

That'll do.

I slid my fingers across his slick skin, tracing the contours of his body, and repositioned myself behind him. He moaned as I drew light patterns on his quivering flesh, buying time for him to come down from the edge. I stroked myself and considered how to proceed. I'd never brought him so close before taking him, nor had I ever neglected myself for so long while doing it.

This should be interesting.

I pressed my body against his, tight enough for him to feel my insanely hard cock digging into his back. True to form, he groaned in anticipation, and his grip slackened. "You're going to want to hang on," I whispered in his ear. I cupped his ass and gave it a slight squeeze, stealing a minute to appreciate just how wonderfully round the damn thing was. When his fingers encircled the bars once more, I took him in one long drive, the heat of him swallowing me deep. His gasp echoed back on the tile. I held him tight against me once more and waited. He took a couple shaky breaths before I asked quietly, "You okay?" His only response was to moan and hang his head. "Good." I stepped a fraction back, pulling out until the head of my cock was barely inside him. His sound of frustration was maddening, but I refused to move.

You want it? Come get it.

I placed my hands on his ass and gave it the barest tug towards me. He got the message. I stared transfixed as he settled into his own driving rhythm, pushing back against me in order to claim the dick he so desperately wanted.

"You have no idea how fucking hot it is watching you fuck yourself on my cock." He pushed harder, and I struggled to maintain my footing without holding onto him.

"Stop… talking," he gasped, even as he rolled his hips.

"Why would I, when you so clearly like it?"

He made a small noise that might have been another whimper.

"You like hearing how fucking tight your ass is. About how good it feels to have my cock so deep inside you."

He groaned, and his pace quickened.

"Harder," I ordered.

He obliged and moaned again.

Oh fuck.

I wanted to slap his ass, but wasn't sure if he wouldn't turn and slap me back or just outright come. Neither was ideal, so I ignored the impulse. He slowed, and I realized he was starting to shake.

"Cal… I… I can't…" he panted.

Oh good, my turn.

I closed the distance again so that my body was touching as much of his as possible, sliding my cock back in deep. His panting was edged by a moan he couldn't hold back. I barely didn't shudder at the delicious feel of him squeezing me.

Why do I insist on playing these games with him? Even with all of his impatience, sex with him is like fucking endurance training.

I licked the salt from his back before pressing my lips against his shoulder blade. "Don't let go," I whispered. He had all of half a second to comply, then I took him hard and fast. I held onto his body for support as I drove in and out of him like it was a race to the finish line. And it felt like it. God, it felt like it. Each driving stroke sent crackles of energy radiating through my nerves, pushing me closer and closer to the pinnacle. I kept to the brutal pace until my rhythm abandoned me, then gave one last pound and finally gave out.

"Mother of fucking Christ," I hissed as Benny let out his own cry. The sharp sound somewhere between ultimate pleasure and pain ricocheted around the room and pulled every ounce of cum I had out of me. It took longer than usual to blink the world back into focus, and I noticed that his hands were practically ghost white from how hard he was gripping the bars.

Good call on those. Though I think I might have over-delivered. Not sure how well my *legs will hold up after that.*

My breathing gradually returned to something akin to normal, and I stepped away, albeit shakily. Benny's hands slipped from the bars and fell to his side like they were made of lead. He finished rinsing and started about getting dressed. I followed suit and finished in time to watch him try not to fall over putting his pants back on.

He doesn't look steady at all.

"Aren't you a smug fagot." The snide remark caught me off guard.

Oh, hell no. He could talk to me like that in the daylight, but not here, and certainly not after begging me to put my cock in his ass not twenty minutes ago.

"This still doesn't make me gay."

I raised a disbelieving eyebrow at the adamant declaration. Funny part was, I didn't believe Benny *was* gay, something in between for sure, but that was a moot distinction at this point.

Someone is definitely overdue for their reality check.

I stepped towards him and grabbed his buckle. His eyes went wide as I used it to pull him towards me and completely invade his personal space. "You're right, Benny, having my cock in your mouth and in your ass doesn't make you gay. Nor does having it there several times a week. But do you know what does?" He swallowed as I stared into his eyes. "Thinking about it every single day in between."

I released him and he staggered back, having to catch the nearby metal bar for support or risk falling over. His eyes flashed to it and back towards me, but I was already walking towards the door. Despite my outburst, there wasn't a doubt in mind that he'd be back.

I've got your number, Benjamin Price.

Whispers of war filled the hall. King Kelani studied the room with a practiced air of indifference, though the set of his mouth betrayed his concern. Things had not unfolded the way he'd expected, nor the way he'd been promised. Before long, an alliance would be necessary, but no suitor could tempt the young king's frozen heart. To love was to show weakness. To care, to invite snakes into his bed. But much as the young king would have it differently, the kingdom could not survive on the shoulders of one man. An alliance would have to be made.

Chapter 13

Calvin

I sat back against the stonewall and officially gave up my attempts to math. Far as I was concerned, the only tolerable math was geometry, since it was the closest to art, and Algebra II could go stuff itself. As a solidly average student, I neither possessed the drive nor the skill to dominate every exam the way others did. Now dominating a class of would-be artists with a stellar interpretation of the Starry Night—*that* I could do.

My fingers hovered over my bag while I debated filling the rest of the time with a fresh sketch. It was a beautiful day and the clouds scuttling overhead begged to be drawn in all their fluffy wonder. But I didn't reach inside and grab a pencil or mentally review which colors would best capture the opaque wonders. Instead, I sank my teeth into my bottom lip and glanced over at Andy, still completely immersed in his Lit II textbook.

Benny's words from the hall came back to me and soured my stomach, all the more cruel for their truthfulness. I curled my fingers inward and withdrew my hand to nestle it awkwardly in my lap. It wasn't like I could begrudge Andy our somewhat stilted friendship. I knew what I'd signed up for just like he recognized the inherent risks to his reputation in associating with me.

But still…

"Hey Andy."

He lifted his head, his bright red hair catching the light like burnished copper. It took him a few blinks before his focus centered on me. "What's up? Give up already?" he asked cheekily, a small grin tugging at his mouth.

"Ha ha." I made a production of setting aside the textbook and turned back to him. "*Actually*, I wanted to check in on you. You seem… better," I hazarded.

His shoulders stiffened slightly, and the vague smile fell from his face. A breath later, his entire body seemed to sag against the wall at his back. "I suppose I am. Mostly anyway." I glanced around, then scooted closer.

"Still worried Mitch is going to ghost you?"

"No?"

"Well, that sounded super convincing."

He let out a heavy sigh and let his Lit book tilt over his lap. "It's… complicated."

"I believe we've established my affinity for complicated," I teased. His cheek twitched, but no smile emerged. I debated letting him in on the unexpected intrigue I found myself in with Benny. Maybe if Andy knew how much I *understood* complicated, he'd be more willing to open up about whatever was going on with Mitch. Much as I wanted to be there for him, I also didn't want to betray Benny's trust… again. I'd had my reasons before, but Andy didn't need my protection anymore, hadn't for a long time.

Before I could decide what to do, Andy glanced over at me, his Phthalo Emerald eyes holding a hint of anxiety. "Calvin?"

"Yes, Anderson," I replied with all seriousness. Like I hoped, a tentative grin tweaked the corner of his lips.

"I… I wanted to apologize."

My brows immediately scrunched together. "What for?"

He scratched a nail along the seam of his trousers, where all of his focus was now centered. "I've been a pretty shit friend lately."

"Andy-"

He held up a hand. "Don't. Don't do that thing you do where you say it's no big deal. It's a big deal to me. You've been the most supportive, quirkiest, understanding friend I've ever had—I honestly don't know what I would have done if you hadn't come along—and I've been so wrapped up in my own issues that I haven't really held up my end. So, yeah, I'm sorry."

Warmth pulsed out from the center of my chest, spreading like ripples on a pond to fill every part of me. Even my toes tingled. A sudden lump formed in my throat and I blinked back an uncomfortable stinging in my eyes. "Is it weird that I kind of want to hug you?"

He rolled his eyes, abandoning his miserable demeanor, and gave me a wry smirk. "Go on already."

I eagerly reached out to claim the generous hug he was offering. While I side-hugged Andy all the time, our physical interactions were very limited, both out of necessity to maintain some kind of decorum and because he generally didn't like to be touched, though I suspected that would be different if Mitch were the one doing the touching.

I sank into the embrace, resting my chin on his shoulder. To my surprise, he actually squeezed back. The feeling of warmth intensified, and I blinked away the stubborn mist clouding my eyes. When it cleared, I saw Benny standing several yards away, staring at me, his expression unreadable. I cleared my throat and pulled away from my friend and the unexpected gift he'd given me.

"Thanks. So… things are going well with you two, then?" I asked in an awkward attempt to get things back on track while at the same time glancing over Andy's shoulder. Benny looked to be putting down roots, his gaze unblinking on a face of neutrality. I tucked a rebellious curl behind my ear, inexplicably self-conscious.

Surely one hug won't call into question whether or not Andy and I are an item…

Still, I couldn't shake the fear that Benny might be thinking I'd lied about it. But I hadn't. Andy and I just weren't interested in each other that way. Sure, it would've been convenient as fuck if we were, but that wasn't the case. He had his type, and I had mine… which was currently staring me down like I had a sign over my head blinking *Liar Liar* in bright neon.

Benny finally blinked and glanced back the way he'd come. I sagged with relief, then immediately tensed back up when I realized Todd and Neil were joining him. If ever there was a time for them to go after us, this was it. We'd let our guards down, we were exposed; we were sitting too close, we'd just hugged for fuck's sake, and Benny had witnessed it all.

His buddies caught up and, without so much as a backward glance, he led them away before the two could spot us. Mild disappointment wiggled in my chest, pushing aside my relief at not being harried.

Is he really not going to come over here?

"Hell-O." A hand waved in front of my face and I dropped my gaze from Benny's receding form back to Andy.

"What?"

"I said, things are going about as well as they can be," he responded to the question I'd entirely forgotten asking.

"Oh. That's good," I replied absently, my gaze sliding over his shoulder once more.

Is he avoiding me? Did I push him too far? What the fuck? That fucker better not be avoiding me. How does he expect to keep doing this if he's gonna be weird about it?

Maybe he doesn't want to keep doing this...

I dumped a mental gallon of paint thinner on the murky thought. It didn't matter what I said; I had Benny's number, no question. In fact, I had half a mind to go after them and provoke an altercation myself just to prove I couldn't be ignored. Forget the fact that I'd been relieved not ten seconds before that he wasn't going to say anything about the hug. Calvin Bridges was *not* someone so easily pushed aside.

"So..."

I let out an exasperated huff and returned my attention to Andy. Couldn't he tell I was having a minute? "So, what?"

His flame-colored brows rose at the sharpness of the response at the same time a smile flitted across his lips. "So, you going to tell me what's been going on with you?"

Oh. Maybe he could tell.

Fuck.

That's worse.

"You know you can tell me anything, right?" He placed a reassuring hand on my knee. "Judgment free zone. Always." My gaze flicked to the last place I'd seen the trio and back to Andy's face, open and waiting for an answer. "Well?" he prompted.

I've been fucking around with Benny for weeks and it's been freaking amazing, but I think I might have fucked it all up by calling him out on his homophobic bullshit and normally I wouldn't care, except I'm not ready to give it up.

... Yeah, I can't say that.

"Um... I don't think I'm ready to talk about it." Andy nodded in quiet acceptance, and I immediately felt like an ass. Here he was actively trying to be a better friend. And how did I react? By spinning the tables and pulling the same crap he'd been doing. I mentally smacked myself in the face and tried for compromise. "But... I promise to tell you about it when I am."

His face relaxed into an amiable smile. "That's fair. Same here. Deal?" He held out a hand, and I took it.

"Deal."

Benny

I couldn't take it anymore. Day by day, it chipped away at my sanity. Every time I closed my eyes, held my breath for too long, or dared to stop moving, Calvin's lips pressed into my shoulder, hot, velvet soft, firm. I'd almost come on the spot at the intimate touch and I hadn't stopped burning since. I wanted—no, needed—more with a desperation that terrified me. One absent kiss was all it had taken to turn me into a walking torch. Except there was only one thing I could think of to tame the inferno and that was to level the field.

It wasn't the first time I'd thought about kissing Calvin, or even the fourth or fifth. Fuck, it wasn't even the fiftieth, but it was the first time it had dominated all of my thoughts, nearly to the exclusion of all else. I couldn't function like this. Something had to be done… and soon.

"Heads up!"

I got my stick up just in time to catch the rogue toss and send it back out.

Fuck. I need to get it together.

I jogged after the others as we wrapped up the last of the drills. The season was still several weeks away, but Ulwich was determined to bring home that trophy and we were the team that was supposed to make it happen. Plus, now that Mitch was back to attending the informal practices with more regularity, everyone was getting their heads in the game.

Everyone but me.

We made it through a few more plays, followed by yet more dexterity drills. Donovan got tagged for suicides, Neil ended up running laps with his stick over his head for failing to keep his arms up, and Connor almost beamed the coach with the ball when he called him a pansy and was now doing pushups until the snow fell. How I escaped unscathed when my playing reflected my split attention was beyond me, but I wasn't about to look a gift horse in the mouth. I trudged off with the others toward the lockers, feeling frayed at the edges and eager to wash off the sweat and grime already drying on my skin.

A spun towel darted in front of me to land with a sharp crack on McNeil's ass. He let out a yelp and reached for his own towel to return the favor. I quickly vacated their area before I could become collateral. All around me the team stood in various stages of undress, nearly all of them bitching about the brutal practice. Occasionally, the conversations drifted to what people were doing over the weekend or whether we really stood a chance at taking the title this year. We'd come painfully close in the past, but we were all done with second place and for most of the starters, this would be our last chance. For many, the scouts coming would be their only ticket into a decent university. Heaven knew they didn't have the grades.

I glanced over at Mitch horsing around with Brian and Nate while Kyle hovered imposingly on the periphery. John stepped up and said something that had all four of them laughing. The whole scene should have been shocking, considering the lot had been in a full-on brawl in the hall only a few weeks ago, but that was how this place worked. On the surface, it looked like they'd all made amends, but I knew better. There was a tightness around Mitch's eyes that betrayed the strain of the front he was putting on, not to mention that fight had started over Andy. Mitch wouldn't forgive that so easily, but the only way his standing protection of his friend would hold was if he kept playing his part—which was exactly what the team wanted.

I shook my head and moseyed over to my locker, where I peeled off my clinging tee. It fell in a sweaty heap and I massaged the back of my neck. Sadly, my fingers did absolutely nothing to alleviate the built-up stress. Mitch wasn't the only one struggling to keep up appearances. My own game performance needed some serious work or coach was going to notice and a higher authority would have something to say. Last thing I needed was my father breathing down my neck about me being a failure at this too. Forget the fact that I wouldn't be allowed to take a sports scholarship even if I was offered one, I'd either be going to the University of Chicago as a legacy or Yale for the prestige. While one actually had a lacrosse team, the closest I'd get to it was watching from the sidelines. Even if I made the team, my father would never allow it. I tossed the rest of my clothes into the bottom of the locker hard enough to make it shake.

Maybe if someone else's fingers do the massaging, it would work. I wonder if Savannah is available.

Except I didn't want Savannah to work out the kinks tightening my shoulders and making my neck stiff. I wanted the long fingers of an artist to knead out the stress, to whisper filthy promises as he traced patterns I couldn't understand on my needy flesh. I wanted his moist breath to send a cascade of goosebumps down my back before he pressed those mouth-watering lips into my fevered skin.

"He lives!" Todd shouted.

I jerked at the sudden burst of sound right beside me and pushed away the fantasy. The last thing I needed was to chub up in the locker room. I'd gone this long without incident and I planned to keep it that way. If my father had found out about me losing the position of captain as fast as he did, I didn't want to think about how quickly rumors of his son getting a boner in the shower surrounded by his naked teammates would reach his ears. Not that some of them weren't worth getting a boner for, but that was a headache I didn't need.

I glanced in the direction Todd was looking and found Neil rolling up like he'd been run over by a fucking truck. "You look like shit," I said as he dropped onto the bench. His lip twitched in a half-hearted snarl as he worked on unlacing his shoes.

"Coach is really out for blood these days," Todd commented as he reached into his locker for a fresh towel.

"Probably has something to do with you-know-who," Neil grumbled.

As one, we all glanced over to the school's lead Attackman, acting like he didn't have a care in the world. On cue, Hendricks walked into the locker as well and glared absolute death at Mitch. While his absence had undoubtedly brought Coach down harder on the rest of us, it struck me as unfair that one man was expected to lead the school to victory. This was a team sport, after all, and that kind of pressure had a tendency to break people rather than help them rise to the challenge. My shoulders gave a sympathetic twinge to the weight he was carrying. I got it, I did, but I had my own burdens to bear. I couldn't carry his too. Mitch Hudson would have to figure it out on his own.

I was mid wrapping a towel around my waist when my gaze snagged on something shining coppery bright on Mitch's jacket hanging in his locker. While Mitch had dated almost with perfect singularity strictly redheads, there was only one person I knew of at either school with hair that color… and that short. Suddenly, I knew without a doubt that Andy had not been alone that night I'd busted in. And I knew who he'd been with.

"Motherfucker," I growled.

Todd straightened up from his lean on the lockers. "What's up?"

"Yeah, something wrong?" Neil echoed.

“What? No, I smacked a blood blister is all.” Their faces twisted in sympathetic winces. “Forget it. Let’s get this stink off and get out of here.” I snatched my soap out and stomped over to the already half-occupied showers the sound of Mitch’s forced laughter raking down my spine.

Chapter 14

Calvin

Excitement simmered beneath my skin, giving my step an extra spring as I all but sprinted through the dimly lit hallways. Moonlight poured through large windows to create large pools of Radiant White that rippled at my passing. Funnily enough, the very reason I could walk about so boldly after hours was the exact reason I was practically vibrating with anticipation.

Perhaps a little more caution wouldn't be a bad idea. If it gets out what we're doing, the fallout will be epic. Also, pretty sure Benny will beat the shit out of me.

Thinking of Benny sent another thrill through me, and my pace quickened. Finally, my destination solidified before me and my heart skipped and started only to race some more. I bit my bottom lip and willed the damn thing to slow down before it exploded and approached the door with none of my usual caution. It swung open in perfect silence and glanced up to find the hinges shiny with grease.

Benny.

A smile stretched across my face at the image of Benny doctoring the hinges to literally keep this quiet. Without the typical squeal echoing on the tile, the room held an uncanny absence of sound. My grip tightened on my towel as I stepped deeper into the vacant space.

Maybe I beat him here.

I shrugged to myself. Getting here first wasn't unusual, though it begged the question of when Benny had found the opportunity to oil the hinges.

Guess I'll just get started without him.

I walked past the stalls and rounded the corner that separated the sinks from the showers proper. My smile instantly slipped and my heart stilled with a sickening thud. I struggled to get my disappointment under control and took another step like my entire evening hadn't been completely derailed.

"You're still dressed," I said, taking in Benny from head to toe. Dressed was an understatement. He still wore his complete uniform though the tie had been loosened, his shirt was partially untucked, and his blazer was noticeably rumpled.

He pushed off the wall where he'd been leaning with his hands stuffed in his pockets. "I wanted to do something different."

"Different," I echoed as I continued to approach.

Different could be promising. Even as I thought it though, trepidation shot through me. Different could also be trouble.

"Yeah," he said softly as pulled his hands free and used his body to herd me until my back was pressed against the wall he'd just vacated. My heart sprinted at an alarming pace and my breath caught in a telling gasp as the cold tile leeched its chill past my thin shirt to suffuse me with dread. This was why I never let my guard down. Now it was too late. I was cornered and alone. No one would hear me scream.

I crushed the increasing anxiety before it could take anymore root than it had.

Benny has never physically hurt me.

The reassurance did nothing to temper the inexplicable panic now racing through my veins.

Get a grip Calvin. You're still in control.

"I'll make you a deal," I said, catching his eye. "Tell me a secret—something I don't know—and you can do whatever you want." He stopped a foot away, not technically crowding me, but close enough to be uncomfortable without knowing what he was about.

Benny's eyes narrowed with obvious skepticism. "Whatever I want?" Unwilling to let on how much the situation was unnerving me, I played along.

"Depends on the quality of the secret. But sure, why not?" I shrugged and gave him a smug grin. It was a tall order. There wasn't much that happened in this school that I didn't know about.

Benny shifted and looked me dead in the eye, as if weighing his options.

What secrets do you have, Benjamin Price?

"Alright. Connor and Andy were sleeping together."

I snorted a laugh. "I already knew that. You're going to have to do better." Admittedly, I was a little impressed that he not only knew that they had been, but that they weren't now.

"You know about that fight a few weeks back? The one in the hall by the East Dormitories?"

"I mean, I didn't see it, but yeah. A bunch of guys from the team got into it. What about it?"

"Did you know Mitch threw the first punch?"

"What? Why would he do that?" I asked, frowning. Mitch wasn't known to be violent or even to be in fights at all. Sure, he'd had a couple, but nothing to suggest he would ever *start* one.

"Probably because they were digging into Gallagher."

Okay, that part is news. But something still isn't adding up. Mitch knows Andy is gay. He's known for years. Even if they were laying into Andy, that's nothing new. Why would it bother him now?

"That's not the interesting part."

I threw my hands up. "Jesus Christ, get on with it already."

"Andy was in the fight too," Benny said, leaning forward. "He dragged Mitch out of there at the first chance. No one knows where they vanished to, but when Mitch made it to practice later that day with a black eye, he came from the woods on the east side of the field."

What the literal hell? Andy was in a fight and didn't tell me?

I put a hand on Benny's chest to prevent him from getting any closer. He stopped at the touch, but didn't back off.

The East Woods. What's in the East Woods? The only thing there is that godforsaken derelict shack. Why would they be there? Unless, of course…

My jaw fell in shock at what felt like the likeliest answer, the only thing that would explain both of their unusual behavior of late.

Holy shit. Mitch is sleeping with Andy.

Motherfucker.

"I'm going to assume by your reaction that was something you didn't know." Benny's words startled me back to the present where he was standing very, *very* close to me.

"What? No. I mean, not in the way you're thinking." Truthfully, I had no idea what Benny was thinking, only that I suspected he might be a hidden treasure trove of secrets. He knew about Andy and Connor. He clearly had suspicions about Andy and Mitch. What else could he know?

"Does it qualify?" Benny asked, one sandy eyebrow raised.

"I suppose it does." I eyed Benny nervously. I hadn't actually anticipated having to deliver on my end.

This is what I get for being an over-cocky ass.

"What do you want?" I asked, a little afraid of the answer.

"Your mouth."

I barked a short laugh. "Sure, I mean, that's kind of normally how this goes, but if that's what you want to waste your secret on."

What a relief.

"I don't want you to give me head, Calvin."

If his expression hadn't been so deadly serious, I might not have believed him.

Who turns down head?

My eyebrows shot up in surprise as an alternative came to mind. "Rimming?" I hadn't ever actually done that before, but there was a first time for everything.

I'm sure I can manage.

"No," he scoffed, leaning even closer. He was practically laid out against my entire body by this point, despite my hand still on his chest. Before I could guess again, his lips brushed mine.

My surprise turned to full-blown shock. I pulled back as far as the wall would allow. "Benny."

"You said whatever I want," he whispered, closing the distance to hover a hair's breadth away. Short of physically removing myself from the situation, I was out of options.

"I did. But..." I faltered.

What the hell is happening right now? How does this fit into our arrangement? Does it fit? Kissing is... kissing is... Well, kissing is kissing.

His hand slid along my jaw to hold my face. He seemed to be waiting for the rest of my argument... except I didn't have one. I searched his face and reined in my sudden panic. I swallowed.

"Okay."

Benny's mouth closed over mine without any of the hesitation I felt and it was like someone dumped high gloss varnish over a lusterless painting. My world exploded into vibrant hues as his lips moved with defined purpose against mine. I fisted my hand in the fabric of his shirt while I struggled to think of the last time someone had actually kissed me. His tongue slid in and I gave a muffled sound of surprise.

He's on a goddamn mission.

I tangled mine with his and let go of my reservations, sinking into the exploration and letting the colors sweep me away. I got so lost in it that for a moment I completely forgot that we both were still dressed.

"Whoa," I whispered when he finally pulled away. "You're really good at that," I added.

Perhaps he's more experienced—in some areas at least—than I gave him credit.

"I can't be bad at everything," he said as his hand slipped from my face. My cheek tingled where his fingers had trailed. I was tempted to tell him I thought he was actually quite good at a lot of things, but was more interested in getting back to the kissing.

I nearly forgot how much I like this.

I relinquished my death grip on his shirt and dropped the towel I was somehow still holding in order to capture his face with both hands. He didn't stop me when I mashed our mouths back together, hungry for more.

Fuck me, that feels good.

I let out a moan as he deepened the kiss once again and arched off the now warm tile into his even warmer body. The heat of his hand burned through my tee and into my lower back as he pressed me harder against him. My breath caught at the overwhelming intensity of it, and I nipped at his lip before getting sucked back in. By the time he pulled away again, we were both struggling for air and every cell in my body felt saturated with the purest color. I couldn't have said what day of the week it was, let alone how long we'd been at it, nor did I care.

"You should get back to your room," Benny said quietly and far steadier than I could have.

"I still haven't showered," I snickered, sliding my hands from his lightly stubbled cheeks to cup his neck.

This is going to be a great fucking night.

He didn't so much as blink when he countered with, "I have to finish the rounds." My enthusiasm, along with the riot of color inside of me, dimmed.

Is he serious? No, he can't go, not after that.

"Or you could stay." I gave him a wicked smile, determined not to give up so easily, and rubbed against him suggestively. Even that small move sent tendrils of aching pleasure through me. He leaned forward and gave me a smaller kiss, barely more than a mild pressure, but didn't respond.

"Stay," I whispered, my eyes already half-lidded with the hope of another mind-altering kiss.

"Your room, Calvin," he responded sternly.

Fuck. He's serious.

"Fine," I huffed and dropped my hold on him.

Back to being the prefect already. So much for my great night.

He put distance between us, and I waited. "What?" he asked, sounding a bit irritated.

"Aren't you going to say it?" I asked.

"Say what?"

He's playing stupid, he has to be.

"Say what?" I mimicked in my poor imitation of his gruff voice. "You say it every time."

"I don't know what you're talking about." He turned to leave.

I caught his arm, and he looked back at me. "Yes, you do. You always say 'This doesn't make me gay.' Well, let's hear it." Benny gave me a level look and didn't respond. "You're really not going to say it." I searched his face, but found nothing even remotely enlightening.

I don't believe this.

"Go to your room. It's past curfew." He straightened his shirt, though it did nothing to smooth the fist of wrinkles I'd put in it and walked out of the bathroom, leaving me standing there like an idiot.

What the fuck just happened?

I twisted my hands with impatience as I waited for my turn to speak with Father Miles. It would be my luck that every Catholic in town and their brother would come to confessional today. I stifled an aggravated groan as yet another person made their way over. With a forced smile that I hoped at least looked genuine, I gestured for them to go before me and kept my position at the end of the line. They nodded in thanks and I reminded myself yet again that this was a house of God and throttling petitioners for taking too long would be frowned upon.

Finally, the last person left the booth. I danced from foot to foot and offered a weak smile as they took their sweet ass time getting the fuck out of the way. When they moved far enough off that I wouldn't have to push past them, I surged into the booth, snapping the door shut and whipping the curtain closed. I did the fastest cross of my life and rushed out, "Forgive me Father, for I have sinned," before Father Miles could utter so much as a syllable.

He cleared his throat. "What sins would you like to confess, my child?"

"I kissed a boy, and I liked it." The words burst out of me in a giant whoosh, taking all of my air.

Father Miles sighed on the other side of the latticed partition. "Calvin, how many times-"

I yanked back the divide and Father Miles' gray-laced, bushy eyebrows shot up in surprise. "Sorry, Father. I don't mean to be flippant and it's not really a confession. But I did. I kissed a boy, and it was amazing." I flopped back into the hard seat and ran both hands over my face. "Like really, really amazing and I hadn't been expecting it at all and I'm not entirely sure what it means, but I *really* want to do it again." *And again, and again and again.* I glanced over at the open divide as my exuberance trailed off. "Sorry, I just really needed to tell someone."

Father Miles held up a finger and leaned forward to open the door of his side of the confessional. He poked his head out a moment, then ducked back in. "What do you say we move this conversation to somewhere with more comfortable seating?"

I smiled and eagerly launched out of the booth to follow him through the nave, past the prayer candles, and into his personal office. He removed his ceremonial robe, hung it up, then turned back to me. His Raw Umber eyes crinkled at the corners as he opened his arms. I stepped into the hug not so different from the others he'd given me over the years, though I was substantially taller than I'd been at nine. He gave my back a firm pat and released me to take one of the seats in front of his heavy desk.

"I'm so happy for you, Calvin."

Light filled my chest as I took the chair opposite him, which was in fact way more cushioned than the one in the confessional. "Yeah?"

He pushed back up from his seat and walked over to the cabinet that traditionally held the communion wine. "Yes," he said as he pulled out a bottle and two plastic cups. "This calls for a celebration."

I laughed as I took the proffered cup filled with crimson liquid, bubbles floating across that taught surface. "You sure, Father?"

"I won't tell if you won't." He winked and took a sip. I mirrored the motion and had to laugh again.

"Grape juice."

"What else would it be?" he replied with a smirk. I shook my head and took another sip, leaning forward to rest my forearms on my knees. "Tell me about this boy."

I let out a sigh and stared into the sugary depths of my drink. "Where to even start?"

"The beginning perhaps?" Father Miles suggested as he settled back in his seat.

"That might take more time than we have and I… I kind of want to protect his identity. If that's okay? Not that I think you would tell anyone, but I feel like I owe it to him, if that makes any sense."

Father Miles held up his glass in a salute. "I will respect your wishes. You need only say whatever you feel comfortable sharing."

I nodded, appreciating the understanding and the inherent support. I'd come to Father Miles many times over the years for both spiritual and secular guidance. That he had remained such a resolute advocate for me over the years meant more to me than words would ever express, especially since my bio-father hadn't really ever been part of my life. I took a steadying breath to calm my nerves and took another drink.

"For starters, it's the same boy from the drawing I'm not allowed to use."

"That so?"

"Yeah." I rolled the plastic cup in my hands. "It's also the same boy from my first day at Ulwich, the one that I connected with. I don't think I mentioned that before."

"You did not. Go on."

I chewed on my bottom lip and tried hard to fight the smile threatening to dominate my face yet again. "I still can't believe it actually happened. I mean… it was kind of a bummer that it was *all* that happened, but…"

"Calvin," Father Miles admonished, a frown pulling his mouth down at the corners.

"I know, I know. He's not like the others, though, Father. He doesn't need my help." *Not anymore.*

I couldn't help but think back to the first time I'd been intimate with Benny. But it wasn't the sex I thought about or the way I'd coaxed him gently through it, reminding him to breathe and helping him to relax. It was the moments after that. The way he'd slid down the wall, his legs too weak to hold him, and I rushed to break his fall. The way he'd curled against me and rested his head on my shoulder. He'd let me hold him until the water ran cold, my fingers gliding through his short hair and trailing down his arm. When we did finally part ways he hadn't been embarrassed or ashamed of what we'd done, he hadn't raced off without a backward glance, he'd looked at me with sadness in his eyes like he really didn't want to leave. The same sadness that had been in his eyes the other night when he'd told me to go back to my room.

The plastic crunched in my hand as I tightened my hold on the flimsy cup. I quickly downed the contents before they could spill all over Father Miles' elegant rug and placed the cup on his desk with a shaking hand.

"Is everything alright, my son?"

"I…" The words lodged in my throat.

Father Miles' features gentled, and he reached out to place a hand on my knee. "What is it?"

"I'm scared," I admitted, unable to hold his gaze.

He squeezed gently. "What do you fear?"

"This… changes things. I don't know what the rules are anymore… or if there ever were any."

He patted my knee and sat back, his warm smile shining in his eyes once more. "Perhaps a little faith would be warranted?"

"Should have known you'd say that," I said, rolling my eyes, though I knew he hadn't meant it as an empty platitude.

"Trust that the Lord will lead you where you need to go." He spread out his hands. "Now, what you do when you get there is up to you."

And that was the rub, wasn't it? What was I going to do?

Chapter 15

Benny

I tugged on the striped, cotton pants, opting to change straight into my pajamas rather than stay up and study or immediately tackle my nightly obligations. Still, my gaze drifted to the closed door and the undoubtedly barren hall beyond.

It won't hurt anything to miss one night. No one will know.

The bed let out a puff of air as I landed unceremoniously on it and stared up at the ceiling.

The responsible thing would be to do the round.

But I couldn't. I knew what would happen. I would do the round—or only half—then end up in the showers… again, just like I always did lately.

Where I'll find Calvin.

Or I won't.

I wasn't really sure which was worse. The bedsprings squealed into the deepening night as I rolled over. I shut my eyes tight and wished for the escape of mindless slumber, but sleep was proving more than elusive. With a huff that hit the wall and bounced back at me, I rolled to my other side in the vain hope that it would prove more conducive to passing the fuck out.

I can't do this anymore. I'm not even sure what this *is. Why did I have to mess everything up? Why couldn't I just leave well enough alone? Things were fine the way they were, still confusing as fuck, but at least I understood the rules.*

I squeezed my eyes tighter, like it could block out the persistent thoughts. If anything, it made them louder.

Why did I have to kiss him? Why?

Even wondering was dangerous, as it immediately provoked memories of Calvin's warm body pressing against me while his hot mouth devoured mine and his delicate fingers held my face. After denying the urge to kiss him for borderline a decade, I'd feared that finally kissing him wouldn't live up to the impossible standard I'd concocted over the years. But it had, it had been absolutely everything it needed to be, raw, surprising… perfect.

I let out a sigh and turned over again.

This is fucking miserable. What time is it?

I sought the clock, barely visible in the gloom. Three a.m.

Of course it fucking is.

I raked my hands over my face and flopped them back to the bed, a chant of "Don't do it," playing on a loop in my head.

I have to tell him.

The determined thought came in direct contradiction with every ounce of self-preservation I had. But I couldn't lie here for another second and wish it all away. I stood up and shook myself, doing what I could to steel my resolve.

That's it. I'm gonna tell him. I can't see him anymore.

I didn't even notice if the hallways were empty, but it was unlikely there was anyone about to see me stomp through them. It was well past lights out and no one was brazen enough to be out of bed on the nights I was scheduled for rounds.

No one except Calvin, of course.

My pace quickened until at last I was standing in front of the door to the showers. My nerves returned with a vengeance along with the chant that had implored me to stay safely sequestered in my room.

I should have stayed in bed. What if he's not there?

What if he is?

I swallowed my anxiety and pushed the door open. The bathroom's sole occupant didn't hear it close behind me.

Why does he have to be attractive?

Every line of Calvin seemed so intentional, from his perfectly straight nose and angular jaw, to the way his leg was propped on his other knee where he lay on the bench by the sinks. Even his button down had a precision to it.

Wait a minute.

"You're still dressed," I said, officially announcing my presence.

Calvin's head swiveled towards me. He then immediately scrambled up off the bench. His long fingers fidgeted with the shirt, straightening the barely creased fabric, then moved on to tuck his hair behind his ear. The dark, silky strand immediately slipped free. Its length was just past code, but no one ever said anything to him about it. I suspected no one ever had. Calvin had beautiful hair.

"Hey, I…" He stopped and cleared his throat, then tucked the rebellious strand again. It didn't cooperate any better the second time. He rubbed his arm, scrunching the fabric of his navy jacket, and his gaze flicked towards me, then down again.

What the hell is going on? I've known Calvin for years and never seen him act like this. Even when I'm saying horrible things to him, he's still the picture of self-confidence and always has a witty retort ready to go.

What's wrong with him?

My eyes narrowed. I reconsidered the fact that he was still completely dressed.

Is he trying to tell me he doesn't want to see me anymore?

The thought brought with it a small rush of anger. He took a deep breath and tried again. I braced myself, fighting back my contradictory emotions. After all, wasn't that the exact reason I'd come here?

"I wasn't sure what you would want to do." Finally, his gaze met mine. In contrast to his behavior, their honey brown was steady, sure.

Calvin is still in his school uniform—the uniform he hates—because I was in mine last time.

All of my nerves and anxiety fell away. I knew exactly what I wanted to do. My single-minded determination of why I'd come here evaporated, leaving the real reason I'd gotten out of bed at three a.m., the same reason I was always here. I searched Calvin's face with its unusual mix of uncertainty and confidence.

How can he be so open? Never any judgment, just acceptance…

And he's still in his fucking uniform.

As I walked towards him, I knew what I had known at the beginning of the night when I'd refused to leave my room—I couldn't stop seeing him. I would keep coming here in the small hours of the morning until he stopped being here. Hell, I might even go off and find him if he wasn't. No matter how much I might wish otherwise, I couldn't quit Calvin Bridges.

He didn't say a word when I grabbed his arm and dragged him around the privacy wall. Nor did he argue when my mouth closed over his and forced him flush against the tile. My fingers slid along his face and into his stupid, soft hair as I kissed him deeper. He kissed me back, and I felt the featherlight touch of his hand on my wrist. I trailed my fingers across his neck to his collar. One button was quickly followed by another.

He let out a sigh edged with a moan as I tasted first his throat, then his clavicle, pushing the blue and cream fabric out of the way as I quested for more. His head turned as I worked my way back up his neck, tasting him the way I'd wanted to for years.

"Tell me a secret," I whispered.

"What do I get if I do?" The husky question made me light-headed.

"One in return," I said, then promptly recaptured his mouth. I'd known kissing him would be a mistake, not because he would use it against me or anything else so gauche, but because I wouldn't be able to stop. My want of Calvin had started when I was scarcely more than a boy and had only grown over the years. When I released him, I wasn't sure whose breathing was more ragged. I returned to his neck. This time, his sigh was definitely more of a groan.

"I wasn't sure you'd come," he immediately offered, albeit a little breathless.

And yet here he was.

"Now you," he prompted.

"I almost didn't."

"Why did you?"

"Uh-uh. One secret, that was the deal," I countered, unwilling to admit the truth.

Uncertainty flashed in his eyes. It disappeared to be replaced by acceptance. He grabbed my face and pulled it towards him like he had the other night. I let out a groan as his teeth pulled on my lip and pressed him harder into the wall. I wanted to make him feel good, but not just good, really good, needed him to know how far gone I was.

I mindlessly conquered buttons until I reached his buckle. He arched back as my mouth followed the same path as my questing hands. He sucked in air in a small gasp when my teeth closed on a nipple at the same time my hand wrapped around his cock.

God, everything about him…

I couldn't decide what of him I wanted next. I wanted all of him, had wanted it for so long. My fingers tightened around his shaft and I dragged up until it popped free. His resulting groan decided me. I kissed down his torso, stalling at his navel, tasting every part of him on my journey even as my hands ventured to explore his newly freed chest.

He didn't stop me as my lips closed around him. I didn't expect him to. He never had before. I sucked on his wonderfully swollen head, taking my time and enjoying the soft sounds of pleasure he was making that were gradually increasing in volume. His hips bucked when I took the rest of him inside and added my tongue. His fingers scratched along my scalp. They tightened and released as he rode the rising wave.

"I'm gonna come," he groaned.

I knew it was true, could taste it in the beads leaking out of him. I hollowed my cheeks and pulled harder. His whole body seized, and he gasped as he gave out. His release shot down the back of my throat. I swallowed and didn't let go until it was clear he was done. I slowly pulled away, sucking him clean as his cock fell free. Then my fingers deftly righted his trousers while my mouth resumed its languid trail up his quivering torso.

Damn, his skin is smooth.

My hands glided beneath the open shirt to his sides, then I used his body to pull me up. By the time I made it fully upright, his mouth was waiting for me. I pressed him tighter against my aching body and devoured his lips with the same need I'd swallowed his cock.

"You made me finish," he said, his voice deep and frayed at the edges.

"I did," I responded as his lips molded perfectly against mine, adding to the high that had hold of me, a high I'd gladly chase for as long as possible.

"What about you?" he asked, teasing another kiss.

"Next time," I said, stealing it from him.

"Next time?" I could feel the hint of his smile against my mouth, and it made my heart skip. My hands drifted along his abdomen and chest, mapping the contours of his body with my fingers.

Calvin is a fucking hairless wonder.

"I like that you don't wear an undershirt," I said, leaning down to place a kiss on his chest.

He gave a low chuckle while his fingers danced featherlight over the back of my neck. "Pure laziness, I assure you."

"You know," I began as my hands continued to rove. "No one would ever guess you look like this underneath." His eyes glittered with mischief.

"*That* is purely selfish," he said, arching into the touch so I could more easily explore his back. "Call it my secret."

"Your secret, huh?" My lips ghosted along his angled neck while my eager fingers traced the definition of his back. "I suspect there's few people who know it."

"A few," he said with an arched brow and a wicked gleam in his eyes. "Perhaps a couple more than who know what a gifted kisser you are."

"That many?" I teased. He gave me a crooked smile.

"I suspect your numbers have been grossly exaggerated."

"You seem awfully confident about that." I hovered a breath away from his lips.

"I know you, Benny," he said, punctuating the remark with a kiss that only made me ache more.

He was right. Calvin knew me better than my own friends and family. What's more, he understood and accepted me exactly the way I was. He'd never asked for more and didn't expect perfection. With him, I had the luxury of being enough. I slid deeper into the kiss.

"Tell me a secret," he whispered.

"I masturbate to you," I said without hesitation.

He groaned and fisted his hands in my shirt as he conquered my mouth. "I really wish you hadn't finished me," he said as he drifted a hand down and squeezed my ass, pressing me tightly against him. "I could still..." he offered when I moaned.

"Next time." The shaky assertion seriously lacked conviction, but he took it anyway.

He nodded. "I'll make it worth the wait."

"You always do," I responded before tasting his lips again. While I explored his mouth, my hands reluctantly gave up their adventuring and set about redoing his buttons.

"Really, Benny?" he asked when I was nearly done.

"We've already been here too long," I said as I did the last button.

"We have, haven't we? Much longer and people will show up to take *real* showers."

I gave a small chuckle at the cheeky joke.

He smiled back at me. "I like it when you laugh."

"I laugh."

"Not like that, you don't." Before I could ask what he meant, he followed up with his own question. "When is your next round?"

"Thursday."

"I'll be here."

King Kelani held Prince Einar's gaze for a minute that stretched into eternity. The king never conceded, never negotiated. His power had always been absolute. The suitors that had come before had been incapable of enticing him with anything grander than fleeting interest. Now the esteemed Prince Einar had played a hand he had not expected. Perhaps he'd finally found a worthy partner capable of seeing beyond his mantle.

Chapter 16

Calvin

I shoved the door open with far too much force and practically launched myself into the room. *Please still be here.* Even as I had the desperate thought, the sound of running water filled my ears. I quickly rounded the division, stripping as I went.

Benny turned as my shirt crumpled against the wall and fell unceremoniously to the floor. I greedily devoured the sight of him. Water ran down his wonderful body in rivulets that dipped and explored every defined inch of him the way my fingers itched to do.

Fucking hell, he's hot.

He was flushed as well, the pink coloring his barely tanned skin. I wasn't sure if it was because he had already started without me or from the scalding water, sending waves of steam throughout the room. Judging by how hard he was, I suspected it was the former.

"Sorry I'm late." I pulled off first one shoe and then another. "I ran into Stein and Jackson and had to double back and take a different route. And my stupid bunkmate decided tonight, of all nights, to give a shit about his grades. He spent the last three fucking hours studying and I couldn't get away without raising suspicion." Apologies poured from my mouth. "I got here as soon as I could." I stumbled as I tried to walk and remove my pants at the same time.

Finally, I was free and strode with renewed vigor towards him. He managed one step away from the wall before I reached out to cup the back of his neck and pulled his mouth the rest of the way to mine. The force of my momentum was so great we fell back against the slick wall. My body firmly pressed against all the hard lines of his while I devoured his mouth with a hunger that had grown since he had sucked me off four days ago.

I let out a groan as I remembered how hot his mouth had been and the way his hands had roved across my torso. I physically ached for him to touch me again, to touch me everywhere.

We haven't even done anything and I'm barely keeping it together.

"Did you finish?" I asked huskily, barely dragging in enough breath to form the question.

"What do you think?" He thrust his hips forward so that his very hard cock stabbed in my belly. I let out another groan and conquered his mouth again, prompting him to elicit his own delicious moan.

Fuck. He really does only want to come the one way.

"Why are there so many fucking days between Monday and Thursday?" I growled.

"It's called a week."

"It's too long."

Oh god, the feel of him is going to drive me insane.

I raked my fingers down his back and he made a sound deep in his throat, arching against me. I abandoned his mouth to nibble across his jaw and then down to where his neck met his shoulder. My teeth grazed the increasingly sensitive skin, and he made a sound akin to a whimper. His fingers slid through my damp curls, encouraging me.

"Your hair is amazing." The breathy compliment was unexpected. I smiled against his flush skin, then placed a kiss further up his neck.

"Yours could stand to be a little longer," I whispered as I brushed the palm of my hand across his border-line crew cut.

"Why?" The breathless question hitched when I nipped at his shoulder again.

In lieu of a response, I reached back to where his hand was still tangled in my hair and tightened his grip. He let out a sensual groan as if it was actually his hair we were pulling. I released my hold and tasted his sweet skin again.

I'm going to leave a mark if I don't move to something else. Reluctantly, I pulled away from his neck.

"Don't stop." The husky request almost undid me and I struggled to get control of my spiraling desire.

He shivered as I whispered in his ear, "If I don't, you'll have a hickey."

"Who fucking cares?" He turned his face, questing for my mouth. My teeth sank into his bottom lip and I pulled. He let out a deep moan. This kissing thing was obviously working for both of us.

"You will when you have to figure out how to hide it," I said low.

His breath caught. "Do it." The insistent command sent desire coursing down my spine.

God, does he even know what he's asking?

To prevent myself from giving into the temptation, I kissed him back more aggressively. He bucked his hips forward and I ground against him.

He's so fucking hard.

I released his mouth and placed a kiss on his jaw, his Adam's apple, his peck, tasting and teasing as I went. His soft sounds of enjoyment following in my wake. I shifted to keep going and his hand cupped the back of my neck, halting my progress. He gently pulled me back up level with his lusciously swollen lips.

"That's not where I want your mouth," he said, then captured me hard enough to make me moan.

Fucking-A Benny.

My right hand slipped around to press into the small of his back. He eagerly arched into me. "I still need to make up for being late," I said between kisses.

"You came. That's all that matters."

"I always come." He gave a primal groan and tangled both of his hands in my hair.

Fucking hell.

The pure unadulterated need in Benny was going to have me coming, and I hadn't even touched either of our cocks.

Time to remedy that.

I rolled my hips forward, and our erections rubbed against each other. He made a small noise at the back of his throat.

Sounds like someone enjoys that. Good, I did too.

I dropped my head to place kisses on the sweet spot between his neck and shoulder that I was supposed to be avoiding as my hand drifted down between us. I wrapped long fingers around both of our cocks and gave a light pull. Benny's body reacted better than I could have hoped. He straightened in surprise even as his cock twitched in my hand and he moaned into my ear. I slowly worked both of us together, pulling gasps of pleasure from him with each fist.

"Fuck, that feels good," he groaned.

I slipped a finger between our cocks and dragged again. His hips bucked, and I swallowed his moan. My movements got faster, bordering on frantic.

"I've wanted to do this a while," I confessed.

"Why… why… sooner?" he gasped.

I would have laughed if I'd had the breath to spare. He wasn't the only one riding dangerously close to the edge. "I wasn't sure how you'd take it."

He gave a whimper. "Cal, please."

I knew what he was trying to ask, but I wasn't sure I'd make it at this point.

"We need to get you ready," I whispered against his neck.

"I've waited long enough." He was right, and I felt terrible. My hand drifted down his backside. "I'm good," he added.

I chuckled. "Benny," I started to scold just as my hand slid in between his cheeks and kept sliding.

"Like I said." He pressed back into my hand, the warmth of his ass easily swallowing my finger.

"Fuuuck," I exhaled.

He's more than prepped.

I subconsciously slipped another finger in, loving how he pulled me deeper.

Oh god, I'm going to come. Shit shit shit. This is the last time I wait.

"I swear to god, if you don't put your cock in my ass soon, I'm gonna…" His threat disintegrated into a strangled cry as I squeezed hard at the base and pulled my fist up our shafts.

I was a fucking masochist; I was never going to make it, but I wouldn't deny Benny what he wanted. I removed my hands and spun him around. His ass thrust back against me and my already strained control crumbled a little more. There was no pretending to try to cool down; he couldn't wait and neither could I.

I pressed the head of my cock against his hole and slowly pushed in. I bit down on my lip hard enough that I might have drawn blood. Even the sharp pain did little to distract from how fucking good he felt. His tight ring quivered around me and I could have cried. At this rate, I wasn't even going to get inside before I fucking exploded.

"For the love of god, Cal," Benny whined. "If you go any slower…"

"If I go any faster, I'm gonna come," I barely managed to respond. All of my concentration was focused on going as slow as possible and praying that Benny's impatience wouldn't get the better of both of us. I was shaking by the time I slipped past the last ring of tight muscle and found my entire length buried inside of him.

"I...can't..." Benny didn't finish. His whole body tightened as his release took over.

I cried out as he squeezed me from the inside, forcing the orgasm that I'd been fighting against. I griped his body against mine as I rode out the wave.

I'm not even a one-pump chump.

His channel quivered and then I did something I'd never done before—I immediately got hard again.

"Fuck yes," he moaned, pushing into me.

The things you do to me Benny Price.

I wrapped my arms around to rest my hands on his chest and pressed him more firmly against me, while I trailed kisses from his ear to his neck and across his shoulders. "What do you want?" I asked softly.

"What I want?" he echoed quietly as he turned his head to press his mouth against mine. The angle was awkward, but that didn't stop him from sliding his tongue inside to tangle with mine. I gave into the kiss completely. I was so wrapped up in Benny, it wasn't even fucking funny.

"Whatever you want," I whispered, brushing my lips against his. As I said it, I realized how true it was. I'd give him anything he wanted. All he had to do was ask.

He let out a sigh as he moved his hips backwards and forwards, slowly working himself on me. It was maddening. During the day, he could be a total prick, but here he was shockingly erotic. My fingers dug into his pecs. Another deliberate roll of his hips. He rested his forehead against mine and my eyelids fluttered as he stroked me with his body.

"Slow," he finally whispered, barely audible above the water. "Take me slow, Cal." He caught my eyes and I could have drowned in their light green, a stunning, undiluted Celadon that stole my breath.

Have they always been that color? I wondered as I stole a languid kiss, tasting his lips even as I thrust slowly into him. While the other quested down, I wrapped one hand around his shoulder. I wanted more of him. I wanted all of him. My fingers closed around him and he hardened at the touch. *That's my man*. The possessive thought barely even registered as I continued to drive into him at a deliberate pace while I stroked his cock.

Never in a million years would I have thought such a tedious rhythm could drive me to the edge so quickly. Despite all my efforts to keep the rhythm moderate, my thrusts grew sharper and more insistent as I chased my second, impossible orgasm.

Benny let out a moan so deep I felt it wrap around my cock and squeeze. He reached back and dug his fingers in my ass cheek. The touch almost pushed me over the precipice, as did the inexplicable desire for him to reach further.

I let out a gasp as I imagined what it would feel like to have his fingers inside of me while I drove into him. My thrusts became frantic. I wanted him to do it. Needed him to. And that absolutely fucking terrified me. His fingers dug in enough to bruise, forcing me deeper and harder against him. The feeling only heightened my fantasy. All sense of sanity slipped away as I rode him hard towards completion.

"Benny!"

His cry came a second after mine. He thrust into my hand and came every bit as hard as I did. My heart rate, like my breathing, skipped and started in ragged bursts.

I don't think I've ever come so hard in my life.

After a few seconds, he shifted beneath me so that he could turn and rest his back against the wall. "You okay?" he whispered, stroking my hair back from my face.

Fuck. I was really hoping he wouldn't notice. I was pretty sure my death grip on him was the only thing keeping me upright.

I gave a half-hearted groan. "That's the last fucking time I wait," the unfiltered honesty slipped out. *Fuck.*

"Wait for what?" he asked, placing light kisses along the side of my face while his fingers trailed down my back.

Mother of Mary, that feels good.

"I haven't gotten off since Monday." *Why did I tell him that?*

A small smile appeared on his face right before he caught me in a slow kiss that threatened to finish turning me into a puddle, and I sighed into him. "Me either," he admitted.

Something fluttered low in my belly. I ignored it and focused on the wonderful feel of his hands exploring my exhausted body. "I love the way you touch me," I said softly into his shoulder.

"How's that?" A finger trailed down my spine, and I lost my words for a minute.

"Like I'm special. Like I'm worth touching," I finally answered. He shifted slightly and I looked up.

What's wrong with me? Why am I saying all of this?

His gaze searched mine. "I don't want to be mean to you anymore." His words were so sincere, I felt a little bad for my resulting chuckle.

"We all have our roles to play."

"What do you mean?" he asked, his brow furrowed.

I looked back at him curious if he really didn't know. "You're the school bully, and I'm the flamboyant fag. That's just the way it is." I smiled in an attempt to take the sting out.

His face still clouded over.

"That's not true."

"Yes, it is," I sighed.

His fingers felt like butterflies on my face. "You're more than that. You always have been." He leaned forward and tentatively placed his lips against mine.

We stayed like that a moment until I pressed back. He immediately opened up to me and my tongue slid inside to taste him. His fingers wrapped back into my hair and he deepened the kiss, claiming my mouth in a way no one ever had before. It stole my breath and what remained of my senses. I wanted to stay lost in that kiss until graduation.

A distant sound invaded my perfect bubble of bliss.

"Shit," I hissed, breaking the kiss.

"What?" he asked, trying to recapture me.

"That's first bell."

"Shit."

"Yeah." I made to pull away, hoping my legs would hold, and realized we were stuck together.

When did he turn off the water?

"Ow," he said with a laugh as our dried skin pulled apart. He chuckled, eying the red on his chest and I looked down to see much the same on mine. I took a step and my leg threatened to buckle. Benny's hand shot out to steady me. "You okay?" he asked, concern coloring the words.

"Yeah," I nodded, pulling my hair away from my face. "Definitely not doing that again."

His smile was positively wicked. “I think it worked out,” he said, quirking an eyebrow.

At that moment, I hated we were in a school full of bigots and repressed homophobic assholes. I didn’t want to race away, sneaking down hallways to avoid being caught together. I wanted to stay. I wanted to soothe the red out of his chest and kiss that smile until he stole my breath again.

He blinked, and the spell broke.

Get a grip Calvin. This isn’t you. That isn’t what this is. No matter what happens in here, out there, he’s still Benjamin Price.

Chapter 17

Benny

I absently doodled on my page while Professor Garza droned on in the background. There were a few token notes, but nothing relevant. Not that it mattered, Social Studies was an easy class, and I had already read ahead three chapters. I finished out the latest geometric design as my mind wandered back to the other night.

When he hadn't shown at the usual time, I'd gotten anxious; worried I had really fucked everything up by insisting on kissing him. Then he had burst into the showers, ditching clothes like he was on fire. More miraculously, he had seemed relieved to see I was still there. The kiss he conquered me with had instantly set me alight, as if his fire was catching.

I probably could have come from that alone.

Everything after that had spiraled completely out of hand; not that that was a surprise. But he had been different, wilder. I still wasn't sure which Cal I preferred: the calm, dominating Cal who knew every button to press to get me to the edge and keep me there, or the out-of-control Cal that had given me everything he had to the point he had to hold on or fall over. Truthfully, I appreciated them both, but I suspected I was leaning more towards this newer version.

My pulse quickened as I recalled the way he had kissed me afterward. Still needy, but also lingering. His arms twined around my neck, holding him up—yes—but also keeping us close. I lost myself to the memory that was quickly evolving into a full-blown fantasy.

The heat of his breath on my already flushed skin. His beautifully long fingers tracing patterns across my shoulders. Those honey-colored eyes staring into me. Calvin had never been afraid of me, but there had been something else in that look, something I couldn't quite put my finger on. *And that mouth of his. Astounding how lips that give birth to the filthiest things can also give the sweetest kisses.* My tongue flicked over my own as if I could taste him there.

"Mr. Price."

I jerked in my seat and looked up to see Professor Garza eying me speculatively.

"Are we disturbing you?" Garza asked.

Oh fuck.

I fought back the very different heat trying to creep up my neck. My gaze slid past the obviously perturbed instructor in search of a clue on the blackboard. A random string of off-kilter circles.

Eight circles. In a line. Hawaii. That's what we're covering.

"The US government presence rewrote the constitution, severely restricting King Kalakana's powers. Hawaii eventually became a territory in 1898 and the fiftieth state in 1959. Did I miss anything?" I asked, mentally crossing my fingers.

Garza's eyes narrowed before he finally turned away. I let out a silent sigh of relief.

I have got to get myself under control.

I looked down at my useless notes.

Calvin is part Hawaiian.

"As an interesting side note, there are over one hundred documented waterfalls between the islands," Garza commented, returning to the lesson.

Now there's an image.

I pictured Calvin standing beneath a tropical waterfall surrounded by flowers in every color imaginable. It was a far better sight than the mold-colored tile in the showers. He slicked back his dark hair, allowing water to cascade like a lover's caress down his gloriously naked body.

God Calvin is beautiful. He doesn't need to make art; he is art.

Those seductive eyes caught me, filled with honey and lust. They promised all sorts of wicked pleasures. I let out an involuntary groan. I desperately wanted any carnal sin that man could imagine. He gave me that rogue smile of his as if he knew what I was thinking and crooked a finger, beckoning me to join. The look alone was enough to make heat flood through me again, clouding my thoughts in a haze of desire.

"Yo, you alright?" The question was accompanied by a light touch on my arm.

"What the fuck do you want?" I hissed, just barely remembering to keep my voice down. Anger over took me as the beautiful fantasy I'd created dissolved into dust motes.

"Chill. You just seemed to be working yourself up over there." Todd gave a subtle glance to where I was tenting.

Fuck.

All the anger flowed out of me, doing its part to bring me down.

Get it the fuck together.

I met Todd's concerned look. *At least he stopped me before I made a complete spectacle of myself.*

"I'm sorry, man." I shook my head, though it did little to ease my frustration. His expression immediately went from one of indignant concern to outright shock. "What?" I asked, furrowing my brow. Then it hit me: I'd apologized.

I never apologize. For anything. What kind of asshole friend am I that an apology is noteworthy?

Fucking hell. This is all Calvin's doing.

Imaginary Calvin winked at me from his private waterfall.

Fucking hell. I need air.

I raised my hand.

"Yes, Mr. Price?" Professor Garza asked, sounding exceptionally put upon.

"I need to take a piss." His jaw ticked as snickers rippled through the classroom.

"You're excused." He didn't comment when I slung the messenger bag across my body; class was close to letting out, and I needed something to help hide my persistent hard on.

I slipped out of the room and drifted down the hallways towards the cafeteria.

If I keep checking out like that, I'm gonna be in real trouble. I have to do something.

The problem was I had zero desire to do a damn thing about it. I liked the way things were going, and frankly, could stand for a bit more. Sex with Calvin was phenomenal, but talking was nice too. Hell, just holding him was pretty fucking incredible.

To my surprise, the object of my thoughts appeared across the way, turning into the main hall from an adjoining corridor. He was already smiling, but when his gaze fell on me, he practically shone.

My stupid grin rose in response, even as something fluttered in my chest, throwing off my heart's regular rhythm.

I wanted nothing more than to cup the side of his face and capture that smile with a kiss. Then trail my hand down his arm and intertwine our fingers even as I stole another. He would give a small teasing laugh, implying he thought I was being silly, but wouldn't stop me. Together, we'd walk to the mess hall or courtyard or anywhere we could sit and be together. We'd talk about our day and our classes, all the while staying in perfect contact. I'd have to brush the hair out of his eyes, because the stuff really was too long. He'd smile and give me that look. The one I couldn't quite put my finger on. I'd get lost in his honeyed gaze and…

"Benny." My name being called from somewhere behind me brought me up short.

Now that the trance was broken, I could clearly see Anderson Gallagher walking beside Calvin—*not me*. I blinked and realized I'd already cleared half the distance between us before I had been stopped. The flutter in my chest turned painful as cruel reality asserted itself.

I couldn't just walk up to Cal and kiss him in the hall. I couldn't go anywhere near him; couldn't even touch him. Not here. Not with all of these people around. At some point, classes had let out and the massive hall was quickly filling with bodies, adding physical barriers to the invisible ones that already separated us.

"Hey man." I barely recognized the voice as belonging to Todd. Rage at the unfairness of it all burned away the remnants of pain in my chest. I twitched beneath his restraining hand. "Take it easy. It's cool. You can get him some other time."

I stole one last look at Calvin's receding form next to Andy. The same Andy who had made him smile and was about to have lunch with him like it was no big deal. *They* would sit and talk and laugh. A growl bubbled up, feeding off the anger that already had a hold of me.

"Whoa. I don't know what the fuck Bridges did to set you off, but I swear, I thought you were going to tear him apart right here in the hall," Todd laughed.

"Don't worry, we'll get him next time," Neil added.

Where the fuck did he come from?

I spun around without warning. “No one fucking touches Calvin Bridges but me. Understand?” I hissed through clenched teeth.

My two idiot friends looked at each other, clearly taken aback by the vehemence of my statement.

“Sure thing, man.”

“No one but you.”

“We can mess with him now if you’re really that pissed. They usually head to the courtyard when the sun’s out,” Todd offered unhelpfully.

The thought of seeing him again had the flutters threatening to return. They were quickly tempered by my fear of what I might do to Todd or Neil for treating Cal the way we always had. Or to Andy for having the good fortune of actually being able to spend time with him.

We all have our roles. Calvin’s words came back to me and I wanted to be sick.

“I’m over it. Besides, I wanna get a jump start on drills. My passes have been shit lately.” They exchanged another look before I turned to make my way to the practice field. My passes had never been anything less than perfect.

Calvin

Andy glanced over at me as I stared after Benny. “Um… what the fuck was that about?”

“Huh? What?” I tore my gaze away from the trio’s retreating silhouettes, wondering the same thing. “I… don’t know.” When I finally looked over at Andy, his mouth curled down in a wry scowl. “What?”

“That was hella convincing.”

“I’m serious,” I argued. “Don’t have a clue. Why would I know why Price was stalking over here?” Not with death in his eyes, but with the familiar longing I’d grown to recognize when we were truly alone together.

“Maybe because you know just about everything that happens in this twisted place. What the fuck happened? Did you do something?”

My gut twisted. I had done something alright—I’d done *a lot* of somethings—and it was quite possible those somethings were catching up with me. It would seem Benny and I needed to have a chat about keeping up appearances. I tucked a curl behind my ear and tightened my grip on my bag. “Umm…”

"Calvin." Andy stopped halfway through the door to the cafeteria and looked back at me with an expression that would brook no nonsense. I scrambled for something to fill the void that would make sense *and* account for my awkward response.

"Look, we got into it the other day. Okay?" I exclaimed in a loud huff and pushed past him.

"What happened?" Andy asked as he stepped up beside me and grabbed a tray. I simultaneously wanted to groan at the worry in his voice and kick him in the shins for deciding that *now* was the time to be the perfect friend.

"He... accused me of being the one to do that prank on Nolan." *Sort of.*

Andy paled and his tray caught on a dip in the bars meant to support it. He quickly righted the plastic before food could go everywhere. "Shit. I didn't... I mean... If he's..."

I placed a light hand on Andy's arm. He looked over at me, his Emerald eyes almost Sap Green with fear. "It's okay. I took care of it." He didn't look convinced, so I knocked his shoulder. "I can handle Benny."

He relaxed a hair. "You sure about that? He seemed pretty intense in the hall."

I snorted to hide the fact that I wasn't at all sure about anything. If Benny couldn't keep his shit together and play his part, then this whole thing we had going would blow up in both of our faces. We finished acquiring our food and drifted over to the usual table. I forced myself not to keep obsessively checking the entrance for Benny and his cohort's entrance, but it didn't stop me from noticing that he never showed. Which was probably what led me to suggest we relocate to our spot by the stone wall outside the second we were done eating. There was only one place Benny would be if it wasn't here.

For all the years Prince Einar had kept distance between himself and King Kelani, who could fathom that a day would come he'd long to approach the king. Not for border disputes or threats to sabotage supply lines, but to bask in the king's radiance. Would that there was no need to keep their newly forged alliance secret. But rival nations would not sit idly by upon learning that their greatest obstacle had further fortified his rule.

Chapter 18

Benny

I was completely obsessed with Calvin's mouth. From the moment he'd placed his lips on my back, I hadn't been able to think about anything else; I wanted those damn things everywhere. I couldn't even come anymore without imagining them on my body. Even more than on my flesh, I craved to feel those lips on mine. I'd been nervous about asking for it. Terrified it would ruin everything. What if he freaked out? What if he said no? But he hadn't. And while he was far from confident when he'd agreed, it was absolutely worth the risk.

I smiled to myself, recalling how he had wrapped around me to deepen that first kiss, similar to what he was doing now. Calvin's nails scrapped along my scalp, grounding me in the here and now. I groaned and pressed into him harder.

God, I love how he pulls on my bottom lip like that. I gave a moan and rolled my hips forward, seeking even more contact.

When our cocks rubbed against each other, he gasped, and I grabbed the chance to tangle my tongue with his. He arched into me and I left his delicious mouth to taste other parts of him. He groaned again and dug his fingers into my back as I found the tender spot on his neck.

"Fuck me," he hissed, then promptly caught the bottom of my ear between his teeth.

I made a strangled sound somewhere between a cry and a moan, and immediately ground against him again. He gave another groan before catching my mouth in a kiss savage enough to steal both our breaths.

He pulled away gasping for air even as he arched back. I took the invitation and followed the curve of his neck with my lips. His leg bent as he hooked his knee on my hip pulling me closer still.

I love how he always wants more of me.

I let out a groan as I dug my fingers into his thigh. There was a low whine deep in his throat as he tangled his hand in my hair. The stupid stuff was finally growing, but it still wasn't long enough for him to do much besides run his fingers through it. Still, I imagined it was more and moaned in response.

"God, Benny," he panted.

My hand slid higher up his leg as I tried to grip it tighter. He groaned again and a fresh wave of desire swept through me. I was already so close to losing my senses and we hadn't even played with our cocks yet. My hand quested down. Calvin let out a strangled moan as my fingers wrapped around his length.

"I want you," he gasped, breathless.

Fuck yes.

I released him, and he immediately caught my mouth in a kiss hard enough to bruise. I eagerly returned the tangle, reflexively pulling his leg higher.

"Something different tonight," he said when he finally released me.

I would have been more intrigued if he hadn't sounded so uncertain.

"Oh?" I queried, taking his hand in my free one and bringing it to my mouth. His eyes hazed with lust as I took his middle finger into my mouth and wrapped my tongue around it.

"Not that either," he responded shakily.

"Rimming?" I echoed his guess from eons ago.

His eyes sparkled, and his confidence seemed to return. He moved his stolen hand to wrap around my neck and claimed my mouth, biting my lip again for good measure. He was completely out of breath by the time he released me.

"What do you want, Cal?" I asked, returning to that sweet spot on his collar. I drank the water flowing over him as if I could somehow drink him up, too.

"Inside," he moaned, practically crawling up my body.

I hesitated, not sure if he meant what I thought he meant.

When I didn't respond right away, he added, "I want you inside of me."

"No," I said quietly, regretting the word even before I said it.

I let his leg slip through my hand back to the floor as he shifted his hand to my chest.

He pushed me back slightly, forcing me to look at him.

Much as I didn't want to, I met his gaze. All the playfulness from before was gone, as was the lust; seared away by the anger that now burned in its place.

"What do you mean 'No'?"

Oh yeah, he's pissed.

"Exactly that. No," I repeated.

What is wrong with me?

His eyes sparked, and his jaw tightened. Mounting rage wrinkled his brow and pulled at his mouth. "I have given you everything you have ever asked for. Repeatedly. I ask for one thing, and you have the balls to stand there and calmly tell me no, as if what *I* want doesn't matter?"

My heart sank to plop uncomfortably in my stomach.

How do I make him understand? It's not that simple.

"One fucking thing." He shifted and water fell between the distance he'd created. The cold of the spray was in stark contrast to the fire burning in his eyes. "Why?" he asked. The sinister tone seemed more than the one word could possibly convey.

"Because this is still just sex to you." Of the dozens of explanations to choose from, I had no idea why I went with that one. I had thought he was angry before; I was wrong.

He shoved me and I stumbled back a couple of steps.

"What the fuck is that supposed to mean!" he shouted, moving out from under the chill water. "That's what it's always been, Price."

I flinched at the sharp way he said my name.

Calvin stormed over to where his clothes were stacked. He didn't even bother trying to dry off as he started to get dressed. He got frustrated when they stuck and started shouting again. "One fucking thing, Benny! One. Fucking. Thing. And that's your fucking answer? Un-fucking believable!" He violently pulled his shirt down, nearly ripping it. "This whole fucking thing was a mistake. I don't know what the fuck I was thinking." He stepped towards the exit, then spun back around and got in my face. "Congratulations. You're not gay, you're just an asshole!"

My face burned at the rebuke, and I still had nothing to say for myself.

His gaze searched mine another moment, then he turned on his heel and marched out of the showers, slamming the door behind him.

When the hallway disappeared behind the closed door, air finally rushed into my lungs. I gasped as I fell against the wall and slid to the floor. The freezing water continued to fall all around me, highlighting my isolation. I hung my head in my hands, still searching for the words I should have said to him.

What have I done?

Chapter 19

Benny

"Fuck off already," I snapped at Todd and Neil, who had done nothing more heinous than breathe.

"What crawled up your ass and died?" Neil asked.

On any normal day, I would have verbally torn him apart for having the balls to talk to me like that. Today wasn't a normal day. Yesterday hadn't been either. As it was, it took everything I had not to claw at my scalp and growl out my frustration. What the fuck had I been thinking? Why would I tell Calvin no?

On the surface, I could admit that it petrified me what switching things up would do to our tenuous dynamic, but deep down, I knew it was more than that. I just didn't know what.

What is wrong with me?

I thought about how fast he'd hidden the hurt of rejection behind a mask of anger until the anger overtook everything else. I couldn't even blame him for shouting and storming out while I stood there like a total and complete ass.

I should have chased after him.

But what would I have said?

I glanced up to find Todd and Neil hovering a modest distance away and eying me like I was a ticking bomb ready to explode at any minute. They weren't wrong. I'd managed to go four days, avoiding so much as a glimpse of Calvin. Four. Whole. Days. Which was exactly four days longer than I'd ever gone without seeing him since we'd started at Ulwich ten years ago, bar holidays and summers. Going so long without seeing him before wouldn't have been easy. Doing so now that things were… complicated was significantly harder. Every night I wanted to go to him. He was there. I knew because I checked. Every night. I wanted to explain my reasons for denying him, except I didn't understand them myself.

With a shout, I drove my fist into the nearby support. Thankfully, it was wooden and didn't crack my entire hand wide open, but it still hurt like a motherfucker. Todd and Neil flinched while I embraced the throbbing agony radiating up my arm. Anything to distract from thoughts of Calvin. The pulsing pain encompassed everything like a second heartbeat.

Calvin's heartbeat. Beating in almost perfect time with my own. I could feel it in his lips when they pressed against mine. Feel it when he buried his length inside me. Feel it where he placed his hand over my heart and pulled me tight against him.

I clenched my aching hand into a fist and grunted more at the pain of the memory than at the pain that lanced across my knuckles.

"Um, you okay?" Todd's hesitant question was the final straw. No, I wasn't okay. I wasn't in any way, shape, or fashion, *okay.*

"I've gotta go. I'll catch up with you two later."

Neil stepped forward, but stopped shy at actually blocking my path out of the lockers. The place had been my sole refuge and one of the few places actually safe from Calvin. I could think of a couple others that might do the trick, but couldn't take the risk that he might know about them as well. "You sure you don't wanna go see the nurse?" His gaze flicked down to my massacred hand.

"It's fine," I growled and took another step, but not before Todd latched onto the inspired idea.

"Don't know, boss. Heard that new nurse has a hell of a pair of knockers."

Neil glanced over at his buddy. Sometimes I could swear the two shared a brain. "She may be a little older, but who cares when you've got a full pair pushed in your face?" They snickered as one and fist-bumped. A poor choice of celebration as witnessing the move only made my hand throb harder.

"I don't want some old lady's tits in my face." *But a pair of young ones might do…*

"Aw, she's not that old," Neil argued. "Forties at worst."

I frowned at their pathetic attempts at enticement and pulled out my phone.

"Who you callin'?" Todd asked, peering around to glimpse the screen. Instead of answering, I dialed and waited for the call to pick up. Two rings later, I got my wish.

"Sup?" I tried not to think of the pressure releasing around my chest as relief, but that's what it was.

"Can you meet me at the heart?"

"When you thinking?"

"Now?" I held my breath as I waited for an answer.

"Be there in thirty."

I let out the breath and didn't even care about the curious looks Todd and Neil were giving each other about my unusual behavior. "See you then, Savannah."

Todd threw up his hands. "I see how it is. You blow us off for your own tits on demand."

I had no intention of explaining to either of them that wasn't how this was at all. Instead, I offered a leer and let them believe what they wanted as I sauntered past and made a beeline straight East toward the girl's school.

Thirty minutes later, the telltale crunch of leaves announced another person approaching. I abandoned my perch against the tree carved with a heart and arrow that had most likely been made years ago by some star-crossed lovers between the schools. Savannah and I weren't that by any means, but the spot was easy enough to find when you knew where to look and was dead center between Ulwich and the girl's school.

When Savannah emerged from the trees, it wasn't the risque outfit she'd been sporting in town she wore, but the much more proper presentation of a distinguished young lady of society. Her buttons were done all the way, not a one of them straining. Her shirt was tucked into her plaid skirt, that wasn't even rolled to make it shorter. She even wore her school tie and had on a neat, trim blazer. She looked great and although the image was in stark contrast to the rebellious one she often donned, she still looked every inch herself.

An unfamiliar pain stabbed at my heart, and I launched myself at her. She let out a grunt as I wrapped my arms around her waist and squeezed tight enough to make her wheeze. Rather than pull away or tell me to ease up, she rubbed my back and gave me a light squeeze in return.

"Hey, what's wrong? Did something happen?" Her soft voice washed over me and I fought to rein in the sudden tide of emotion. So many things had happened, I didn't even know where to start.

I gave her a last squeeze and pulled away, only to rake my hands through my over-grown hair for want of something to do with them. "Yes. No. I don't know. I fucked up... maybe. No. Pretty sure I fucked up. And I...I don't know what to do. I don't know how to fix this." I met her blue gaze when I ran out of words. The concern I found there at once hurt and soothed something inside me. Savannah would figure this out. She could fix it.

She has to.

"Come here." She grabbed my wrist and led me over to a stump worn smooth with time. "Sit. And start at the beginning." I did as she asked, but only her hold on my arm kept me from popping right back up again.

"There's this guy at school—"

"Benny, did you hit him?" She pointedly looked at my scraped knuckles. "I know they're all a bunch of putzes, but your father will kill you if you get into a fight at his stupid alma mater."

"Trust me, murder is definitely in my future if he ever finds out about this, but I didn't hit anyone."

"O-kay... so, what's going on?"

I looked at her out of the corner of my eye, her ponytail pulled over her shoulder like a river of gold. "Do you remember Calvin Bridges?"

She snorted and leaned back to rest on her arms. "You mean the guy you've been obsessed with since you started at that fucked up school?" I shot her a look, and she rolled her eyes. "What? We both know it's true."

I huffed and rested my forearms on my knees, my gaze focusing on the forest floor. It didn't do any good to argue with her, especially since she was right. "Yeah, him." I twisted my hands together and wondered why I was stalling. Of all the people in the world I could talk to, I trusted Savannah the most. We'd grown up together, and she knew literally everything about me.

So why am I anxious?

"Well, what about him?" she prompted when I remained quiet.

"I... I mean we..." She raised an eyebrow at my uncharacteristic stammering. "We've been fooling around," I finished in a rush. "A couple of months now," I added, my face heating as I kept my gaze firmly fixed on the ground.

"Aww, Benny, are you blushing? That's so fucking adorable," she cooed.

I shook her off. "Shut up. No, I'm not. Don't be such a fucking twat."

She brushed her hair back over her shoulder and smirked at me, clearly not buying my shit. "The young prince finally decided to pursue the elusive king."

I sat up and met her knowing gaze. "Seriously, Sassy? You're gonna go there? Now?"

She shrugged as if it was of little significance. "I mean, writing those stories was *my* idea to help you deal with your obsession. At least that two-bit quack was useful for something." I envied her ability to be so flippant about therapy. That was certainly a luxury I would never have. Even if I could convince my father to let me see someone, I'd never be able to trust that the sessions would truly be private. "So..."

"So what?"

"Oh my god, Benny. For fuck's sake, tell me all about it." She leaned forward, her eyes alight with eagerness, and I couldn't help but chuckle.

"Well, the sex is fucking incredible. Like damn." She beamed and gestured for me to keep going. "And I... uh, I kissed him."

Her eyes said it all. She knew exactly how long I'd wanted to kiss Calvin Bridges. "And how was it?"

A smile twitched at my lips as I dropped my gaze back to the leaf-riddled ground. "Really good." When she didn't immediately have something to say, I looked back up at her. This time, her eyes were filled with a touch of wonder. "What?"

"Nothing. It's just... you really like this guy."

I opened my mouth to argue, but couldn't make the words come. "Shame I fucked it all up."

Her face fell and all the previous joy disappeared. "What happened?"

"He asked something of me I don't know if I can give him."

"Care to be more vague? You didn't call me out of Debate so you could pussyfoot around the issue."

"Shit, Sassy. You didn't have to ditch Debate." If I'd known, I never would have insisted she meet me so soon. Savannah had fought hard to be on the team and even harder for her position as captain, it was one of the few extracurriculars she'd been able to choose for herself.

She placed a hand on my knee and squeezed. "It's no trouble, I promise. You wouldn't have called if it wasn't urgent. Now, out with it. What did he ask?"

"He asked to switch." Her brows drew together in a deep V that matched the frown tugging at her mouth. "It sounds stupid to say out loud and I'm not even sure why I said no. If it was literally anyone else, I wouldn't think twice about it, but not him."

She considered me for a long minute. "Anything else?"

I knew what she wanted, the underlying reason I wouldn't top Calvin, but some secrets weren't mine to tell. I shook my head. "I don't know how to fix this. He was so angry and I… I don't know…"

"Oh, Benny. I think I have an idea." I looked up at her with unexpected hope and found a knowing look in her baby blues. "Casual has never been enough for you. That's one of the main reasons we didn't work. You always want more and you hate sharing."

"Savannah—"

"No, hear me out. You know I'm right. You need more than casual sex." She tilted her head and seemed to weigh her next words. "I think you two should date."

"Are you out of your damn mind!"

"Face it, Benny, you've been half in love with the guy for years. It only makes sense you want more of a commitment."

"Being obsessed and being in love aren't the same thing."

"No, they're not. But facts are facts. Your world has practically revolved around that guy since day one and when you finally gave in, it only got more pronounced. I don't think I've ever heard you tell a story about that place that didn't somehow come back to Calvin. You can deny it 'til your last breath, but if you had seen the goofy smile on your face just from *thinking* about kissing him, you wouldn't have a leg to stand on."

I thought back to that day in the hall when I'd been beside myself with anger solely because Andy could spend all the time he wanted with Cal and I couldn't. "I really hate you sometimes."

"No, you don't, you love me, and you love that I call you out on your shit. Date him, Benny, it's what you want." I continued to scowl at her, even though I knew she was right. Leave it to Savannah to find the heart of a problem with almost nothing to go on.

I gave up my futile battle and dropped my head in my hands. "It would never work. We'd get caught. I don't even know how we haven't gotten caught already."

"I seriously doubt that no one has ever managed to date at that repressed school." I blinked as I realized that once again, she was right.

People had gotten away with dating right beneath everyone's nose. Even better, I knew them. Except I couldn't very well ask Andy how he'd pulled it off, especially after he'd threatened me not once, but twice. That left Connor.

I could do that.

A tiny spark of hope blossomed in my chest, then promptly went out. "He'll never go for it."

"You don't know until you ask." Unexpectedly, she threw her arms around me and squeezed. "It's so nice to see you happy." I snorted. At the moment, I was a far cry from happy. She pulled away and punched me in the shoulder. "Don't give me that. We were great in our own way, but you never smiled like that when we were together. Now, when do I finally get to meet the infamous King Kelani?"

I threw my head back and laughed. My first answer was when hell freezes over, but then it occurred to me I wanted her to meet him, to get to know how wonderful he was. "One step at a time. He actually has to agree to date first."

"I'm sure you can convince him." She winked and bumped her shoulder into mine. "Then you can introduce us."

I reached for her hand and gently squeezed her fingers. "Thank you, Sassy. You're an amazing friend."

"I know." She gave me a self-satisfied smirk. "Now, what's the deal with the hair? Since when did you stop buzzing it?"

My eyes went wide before I could check my reaction to the laissez-faire question and heat surged up my neck to burn on my cheeks.

Her mouth fell open. "Oh. My. God. *He* asked you to grow it out."

"What? No. That's stupid."

She giggled in vicious delight. "He totally asked, and you did it. Imagine that, Benny Price willing to change his appearance for someone else."

"He didn't ask," I continued to argue while fending her off. She paused, her hand inches from my head, my fingers around her wrist the only things keeping her from her destination, and raised another eyebrow. "He didn't *ask*," I grumbled.

Her attack relaxed as she smiled back at me. "You really are gone for this guy."

"Sassy."

"I'm not teasing. I just... maybe I'm a little jealous."

"Why?" I frowned as I released her, suddenly concerned that maybe our breakup hadn't been as mutual as I thought.

"Because you're willing to fight for what you want. You always have been, and I hope… I hope someday someone can look at me the way you look when you think about him."

"You will," I said as I pulled her in for another hug. She squeezed back. But we both knew the truth. Whoever Savannah ended up with would be purely for social gain. For that matter, so would I.

Chapter 20

Calvin

He has to show. He just has to.

I laced my fingers behind my head as I paced the room again. Three different fucking nights I'd shown, and he hadn't; I'd waited for hours, one night even to the first bell, and still nothing.

He's definitely avoiding me. Why do I have to overreact about everything? Maybe if I'd taken a breath and actually explained why I asked what I did, then maybe he wouldn't have been so quick to say no.

My jaw tightened, and I fought off a fresh wave of anger as I recalled what else he had said.

How could he think that? It hasn't been just about sex. Not for a while.

I liked Benny, like, really liked Benny. And it didn't matter that it was stupid or didn't make sense or that Andy was right. None of it changed how I felt. What had started as a game had evolved into something else. Even mad at him, I had still dreamed of being able to sit and laugh together, to not have to say goodbye at the end of the night. Sometimes in my dreams we talked for what could have been hours, learning about each other in a new way, and others we wouldn't say a word, just lie wrapped in each other's arms. The usual longing sprang up at the thoughts.

I'm a fucking mess. I have to make this right. He'll understand if I tell him. He has to.

But why should he?

The renegade thought slashed through my stubborn optimism. I certainly hadn't given him any reason to believe me or even want to hear me out. That he'd failed to show for over a week stood testament to that. I let out a cry of frustration that echoed back at me from the washed-out green tiles.

But that's why I'm here now. If he won't show at the usual time, then I just have to try an unusual one.

I yanked at my school tie, tearing it loose. I fucking hated the damn thing and everything it stood for, not to mention the constricting button down. Angrily I pulled the shirt loose, taking out my frustration on the only thing handy: my clothes.

I should have at least swung by my room to change and drop my bag. I glanced at the discarded pack, once again toying with the idea of at least pretending to do schoolwork. I shook my head and resumed my pacing.

I couldn't risk going back to the room and getting held up. What if I missed him?

It was a dim hope that he would even bother to check the showers at all. Still, I clung to it.

Please show.

"Yeah, but Neil will always be second string, unless you're planning on getting injured soon."

"As if. All I'm saying is that he can't expect to leave the bench without putting in more effort. You know?"

I spun around at the voices. There in the doorway stood Connor Hendricks and, holding the door open, was Benny.

All of my calm evaporated as I realized what I was looking at: Benny was with Connor. Connor and Benny were in the fucking showers. Together. Suddenly, him not showing at the usual time made a whole lot more sense. He'd moved on.

Benny quietly met my accusatory glare.

"Are you fucking kidding me!" I yelled. My body was shaking, I was so pissed.

Connor gave Benny a questioning look, which he missed, as he was still staring at me. Finally, Benny ducked his head and said to Connor over his shoulder, "I'll handle this."

I puffed up with rage. *Over my dead, flamboyant fucking body is Benjamin Fucking Price going to handle* me.

Connor shot me an anxious look. "You sure?"

"Yeah. Finish the round for me? I'll get him back in his room," Benny finished, his gaze returning to me.

Since when does he do the round with someone else? Is that the excuse they're using?

My thoughts were in serious danger of spilling out in an exceptionally elevated tone. Between the tile and the open door, people clear across the school would be able to hear me.

Connor placed a hand on Benny's shoulder and if I could have breathed fire, I would have. "Yeah. I got it. Just don't do anything stupid," he said, sparing me one last look before vanishing back into the corridor.

I managed to keep it together long enough for the door to close before unleashing. "Connor? Are you fucking serious!"

"It's not what you think," Benny said at nearly the same time. I ignored him.

"Is *that* why you've been avoiding me? Or have you just not known I was here? Did you even bother to check!"

"I knew you were here." The flat statement was like adding kerosene to my already blazing bonfire.

"So, what? You just moved from one fucking fag to the next! Did you choose him because you knew he'd be up for it? Or does it even matter?"

"It's not like that."

"Like hell it's not! You're willing to fuck him, just not me, is that it? What the literal fuck, Benny!"

"If you would stop shouting, I could tell you," Benny said calmer than a stone as he walked deeper into the room.

I trailed after him, unwilling to let him out of my sight now that I had him. I rounded the divider hot on his heels, a fresh rebuke ready. "I can shout all the fuck I like. You don't get to tell me what to do."

"I know that."

"Then what makes you think you can do it now!"

"I'm not. I'm asking you to let me explain. Why do you always have to be so dramatic?" he asked, leaning against the tiled wall, the picture of chill. It was infuriating. *He* was infuriating.

"I am not dramatic!" I shouted, immediately recognizing the irony of such a response. My mouth snapped shut to prevent more outrage from spewing out of me. I counted to three, then managed to say without yelling, "Fine. You want to explain, then explain. What the fuck are you doing here with fucking Connor Hendricks?" The tail end of the question rose in both volume and pitch. At this rate, I was going to leave general shouting and enter the realm of screeching. I fisted my hands in a vain attempt to get myself under control.

"Honestly? I was trying to figure out how he and Andy kept it quiet for so long, but I chickened out and started talking about the team instead."

"Why the hell would you want to know something like that? And why would you ask Connor? He's a fucking idiot! I'm the one who came up with the damn code. You could have asked me!"

"Why am I not surprised?" Benny mumbled to himself.

"What?"

He took a deep breath and caught my eye. "Because I wasn't sure how you would take it."

"Take it? Take what? Why wouldn't I be able to take whatever it is?" I asked, waving my hands around.

Benny gave me a knowing look. "You mean, besides the fact that you tend to overreact?" He neglected to say like how I kind of was right now and added, "You're a little hard to pin down, Cal."

It was the first time he'd said my name in weeks and I hated to hell how it felt like a balm on my burning skin. I didn't want to be side-tracked into feeling better; I wasn't done being mad at him.

"I do not overreact," I said flatly. He stared at me and I wavered. "Okay, maybe I overreact a little," I conceded.

That's the most he's gonna fucking get.

He didn't blink.

I huffed. "Are you going to answer the fucking question or not? Why would you want to talk to Connor about him and Andy?"

"Because I want to date you, Cal. I want more of you than just hot shower sex and making out. I want to get to know you, spend time with you. Out of here." He gestured at the surrounding room.

"Date me? But you've been avoiding me."

"I wanted to give you a chance to cool off."

"What about Connor? You were *here* with Connor." I glanced towards the door where Connor had vanished; where he'd dared to place a hand on Benny—*My* Benny. "You're not fucking Connor?" I asked, still feeling uncertain.

"I'm not fucking Connor," Benny replied with the ghost of a smile.

I stared down at the tile floor and scrambled to get my thoughts back in order. None of this was going the way I'd planned. "But… you said no," I finished finally, lifting my gaze to meet his.

I hate feeling like this, so unsure and anxious. This is what Benny does to me. How can I possibly want more of it?

Benny's small smile melted into his suddenly sad expression.

"Cal, I'm sorry. I—"

"I need to tell you something," I cut him off. Without waiting for any sign of acceptance, I stepped towards him. "You have to let me explain why I asked," I elaborated. My heart beat so hard against my ribs it was a miracle it wasn't echoing back.

Benny searched my face for a moment. "Okay."

I'd never heard such a magical fucking word. I closed the remaining distance between us in two long strides and mashed my mouth against his. My hands went up to his head, where I slipped my fingers in his hair. It was still pretty short, but it was long enough now that I could tighten my fingers and hold his face even closer as I tangled my tongue with his. Benny gave a soft moan, and I ate it up, hungry for more. My chest was heaving and air was just a memory by the time I pulled away. "I'm sorry. Two weeks is a long time to go without kissing you," I said, still trying to get my breathing regular.

His hand slid up my neck to cup my face, and I could have melted. "I know," he said, snaring me.

I lost myself to it as his arms wrapped around me. I barely even noticed when he spun us so I was pressed into the wall. My body reacted all on its own, arching into him, craving as much contact as it could get. I reluctantly broke the kiss and dragged in a lungful of air. His own hot panting warmed my face. Benny could kiss like no one else, but I had to do this; he had to know. "I need you to understand," I said, still a little breathless. "It's… it's not just about sex." I looked at him, getting nervous again. My speech had sounded pretty great when he wasn't actually standing in front of me. Now that he was, I wasn't sure I could go through with it.

Man up, Bridges.

I took a steadying breath. "I mean, I know that's technically what I asked for, but you need to know why that's a big deal. At least, why it's a big deal for me." I waited for him to interject or call me stupid, but he just waited to hear me out. I swallowed and went on. "My first time… doing *that*—my first time doing anything—wasn't exactly great. It was with—"

"Warren Singleton," Benny finished.

I stared at him in horror. "Wha- How do you… How do you know that?" I asked, leaning away as far as the wall would allow. An emotion I couldn't place passed across his face. Sadness? Regret? Shame?

"He might have said something." Benny didn't look pleased to be sharing.

"Said something?" I echoed. If I hadn't been so overwhelmingly stricken, I would have started shouting again.

"It was in the locker room not long before he left."

"How many people know?" I asked, my voice rising.

"Shh," Benny soothed, concern clouding his face as he brushed my hair back. "Not many. There were just a couple of us there. No one really believed him. He was an ass known for telling tall tales. Everyone just chalked it up to that."

I felt like I was going to be sick.

He bragged about it.

No matter what Benny said, I didn't believe it was just a couple.

All these years…

"It's okay, Cal. You don't have to explain anything. I know," Benny whispered, then pulled me into a hug. I clung to him as his words sank in.

There are people out there who know. People who know Warren raped me and they did nothing about it.

I squeezed Benny tighter and buried my face in his shoulder.

"I'm sorry." His soft words brushed against my ear and reminded me why I was here.

I released my death grip on his neck and leaned back. I stole a smaller kiss to steady my nerves before continuing. "Then you know why it was a big deal for me to ask." It wasn't a question, but he answered it anyway.

"Yeah," he said softly. "I didn't want you to think that was something I needed from you, because it's not."

"I know. Just like I know you would never ask it of me. But…" I swallowed. "But it *is* something I want from you." I caught his faded green eyes and fought back my uncertainty. "I can't exactly undo my first-first time, but I would really like my first time bottoming—by choice—to be with you."

There, I said it. The words are out.

We stayed perfectly still, staring at each other for a long minute.

"Okay."

That really was starting to feel like a magical word. I smashed my mouth against his, obliterating the last of my anxiety about having this whole wretched conversation. His hands wrapped around me and I moaned into the touch.

God, how I've missed this.

My arms wrapped back around his neck as I struggled to get as much contact with him as humanly possible. Suddenly, he pulled away.

"What?" I asked, my doubts immediately resurfacing.

"But not here."

"Not here? If not here, then where?" I asked, confused.

"We'll meet in my room," he said, returning to tempt me with another kiss.

"Are you insane? Do you have any idea how risky that is? What if we get caught?" I asked, completely incredulous.

Benny, of all people, should know better.

"You're being dramatic again."

I bit off the rest of my argument.

"Besides, if we meet on one of the nights I do the rounds, then who will catch us?"

That's a fair point.

"Fine. Be stubborn and crazy. You're on a round tonight. Let's go," I said.

He chuckled and brushed his lips across mine. "Not tonight. Tonight, you just go back to your room."

My mouth opened, fully prepared to argue, only to be silenced by a kiss that would not be denied. "I missed you," I sighed when I was finally at liberty to talk again.

"I missed you too."

"So date, huh?" I asked with a crooked grin.

"Yeah, or something like that," he responded, leaving me to grab my satchel.

"I might have a few ideas," I said, shouldering the bag.

"I bet you do."

Kel's smile may have started dubious, but the king quickly regained his usual air of confidence. Einar mirrored the expression and gently took the king's hand to formally seal their courtship. The ambitious prince placed a bold kiss on the king's knuckles and vowed to ensure this courtship to be one for the ages.

Chapter 21

Calvin

I stared off into the distance, still not sure what to make of the whole thing. Date Benny? Did I want that? The answer that continued to shock me was yes. Not just yes, fuck yes. There was just one problem—I'd never dated anyone before.

Can't possibly be that hard. Can it?

I glanced over at Andy. He'd been able to do it for over a year and no matter what he said to the contrary, he might as well be dating Mitch now. Sure, I'd come up with the basis of the code they used, but the actual dating part had been all of them.

"What are you doing this weekend?" Andy asked, looking up at me, no doubt having sensed my irrational stare.

Here it was, my opportunity to come clean and maybe ask for some advice. So in true Calvin style, I looked right at the opportunity...and completely ignored it. "Nothing." I shrugged as if it would make my lackluster answer more believable. Andy blinked those intense Phthalo green eyes at me, but didn't call me on my obvious shit. "You?"

Oh, my fucking God. Did my voice just crack? Jesus fucking Christ. I'm going into town with Benny, not marrying the asshole.

Thankfully, the most Andy did was quirk an eyebrow. "Not much. Finish a book. Study with Mitch."

I wonder if Andy has told Mitch what "studying" really means…

"Sounds...like fun." Andy's expression immediately morphed into a glower. "Don't say it. I remember the deal. I can't give you grief about anything when I'm not sharing either." Except thanks to Benny, I knew exactly what he wasn't sharing and wanted to give him so much fucking grief. But I wouldn't, because then I would have to answer questions about the shit I'd been up to.

... like agreeing to date Benny.

Calm down. It's not a big deal. It's lunch, that's all.

I glanced over at Andy again and almost caved. If anyone could put me at ease about this whole mess, it was probably him. Then again, if this little escapade blew up in my face, the fewer who knew about it, the better.

I cleared my throat and stood up, even more awkward at how abrupt it was. Andy looked up at me, his book perched on a knee. "It's getting late. I should go." His face clouded over and I could have smacked myself. It was only ten o'clock, and I'd literally just said I wasn't doing a damn thing with my weekend. For someone who prided themselves on keeping a low profile when it came to illicit activities, I was doing a shit job of it now. "Right. Uh, see you later."

"See you later," Andy echoed as I spun on my heel and all but fled the library so I could obsess about what to wear for half an hour, then race to town. Where I would meet Benny. For lunch. On a date.

Fuck me.

Benny

My gaze traveled over Calvin's body with reckless abandon. While it wasn't like I'd never seen him out of his school uniform, everything about his ensemble screamed sex... and nerves. He reached up to pull at the collar of his deep purple shirt for the third time since I'd spotted him. The tee bled into dark wash skinny jeans that made my own pants tighten. Fuck, he looked incredible, even with the heather gray peat coat, oddly light against the darker, winter colors. He stopped outside the cafe and looked around, his honeyed gaze not settling for more than an instant as he perused the area.

I chuckled to myself and pushed the door of the cafe open. "You planning to just stand there, or did you want to eat something?" He whirled around and I swear to God he actually jumped.

His gaze raked over the facade of the quiet little building, then took in the street once more. He walked swiftly inside and yanked the door shut before it could close naturally. "I'm here. Now what?"

"Now, we get something to eat." I placed a hand on the small of his back and gently steered him over to the counter with its healthy display of decadent sweets. He glanced from the glass to me. "Whatever you want, my treat. Actual food is on the board." I pointed to the chalkboard declaring the day's specials, along with the regular selection.

He licked his lips and stared at it, but didn't say anything. The grumpy attendant from before took one look at me and scowled. His gaze also traveled to the door, no doubt to see if my inappropriate companion had returned. Little did he know that the anxious man before him could give Savannah a run for her money in terms of impropriety.

"What can I get you?" the attendant asked when it was clear no one else would be joining us.

I glanced over at Calvin. His dark curls were in fine form and just as rebellious as ever. I resisted the urge to curl one of them around my finger and instead asked, "What'll it be?"

His dark brown eyes held a hint of panic as his gaze flicked to me. He opened his mouth, but nothing came out. Not a quip, not a snarky comment, not so much as a syllable.

More than a little shocked, I turned my attention to the board. "How about… a turkey club and a… chicken avocado wrap." Hopefully, one of the two would suit Calvin and I'd simply eat the other. My gaze fell to the sweets, that much like the man beside me, I couldn't seem to resist. Also, much like Calvin, it all looked too good to choose. "And two eclairs."

"Bear claws," Calvin piped up out of nowhere.

I smiled and corrected myself. "Sorry, make that two bear claws."

"Will you two be dining inside or on the patio?" the attendant asked as he accepted my card, thankfully without dropping it this time.

"The patio, if that's alright."

The attendant smiled pleasantly and nodded, though I couldn't help but think how much less pleasant he would be if he knew the two young men before him were on a date or if Calvin was acting more like himself.

"Thank you," I said as I took the receipt and led the way out the back door to the four-season private patio. I took a seat at one of the many empty tables and Calvin did so as well, his gaze shifting around almost frantically as he settled into his chair.

"Are you sure this is a good idea? What if someone sees us?" he asked under his breath while he leaned back to see through the narrow gap between the rail and wall to glimpse the main street beyond.

I couldn't help but chuckle at how hard he was trying to see. "You of all people should know hardly anyone from the school comes to this part of town. After all, the church is only a block or two from here. And even if someone did happen by, the odds of them seeing us are slim to none."

He huffed and straightened up. His fingers plucked aimlessly at his coat, which he'd neglected to take off, while his gaze kept searching the otherwise empty patio. "What do we do now?"

I frowned slightly, a little worried about the fact that he couldn't seem to settle down. "This is it. We sit, eat… relax," I added with emphasis. He shot me a look and immediately returned to scanning the area. "What's the matter?"

His nails dug into his sleeve, and he clenched his jaw. "I haven't done this before."

"Haven't done what?" I scoffed. "Eat at a cafe? Granted, this one is a bit of a hole in the wall, but—"

"Date." His eyes snapped to me, their brown depths holding a familiar challenge. For a second, I let myself get lost in them. I loved that look. He had so much spirit, so much fight. He'd never taken shit from anyone, least of all me. That look alone had kept me in his orbit like a moth drawn to a flame, willing to get burned for a glimpse of the sun. Then what he said sunk in.

"What? You've never…" His eyes narrowed before darting away and I immediately stopped talking. Was it really possible that he'd *never* been on a date before? Now that I finally understood the source of his weird behavior, it was kind of adorable. Calvin Bridges was nervous.

He cleared his throat and tugged at his sleeve some more. Before I could say anything, a server arrived with the food. They set it down and thankfully walked off without lingering to make idle chatter. Calvin glanced over at the two plates and without looking up asked softly, "Which one is yours?"

"The one you don't want."

He reached out and hesitated, then pulled over the chicken and avocado wrap. "Thank you," he mumbled, his head still bent. He took a bite, and I half expected him to make a quip like Savannah had about having to work it off. Instead, he glanced up briefly from the wrap and said, "This is good. How is it I've never come here before?"

"They're a little off the beaten path and don't look like much from the street."

He nodded, and we each took a bite. After another minute, he took a drink of water and asked, "So what exactly does this *dating* thing entail?"

The way he said dating made it sound like a curse, and I had to fight back a smile.

"Nothing too complicated. It's generally a lot easier than people make it out to be. Like I said before, we sit, eat, chat."

"Chat about what?" The question held a hair more of his usual fire.

"About whatever. Though the idea is to get to know each other better. Likes, dislikes, ambitions, fears, that sort of thing."

"What, like friends?" he snapped.

I did my best to hide my wince. We may have known each other for years, but friends were something we'd never been. I took a deep breath and bought time by taking a few bites of my club. "How about we start simple and see where that takes us? I'll ask you questions about yourself and you answer… or you don't." He finally looked at me, lips parted in surprise, doubt flooding his beautiful brown eyes. I reached across the table to still the hand in danger of fraying his sleeve, and he froze as my fingers settled over his. "You don't have to share anything you don't want to." I waited a beat, then settled back in my chair. "Tell me what your favorite thing to paint is."

"Why do you assume I paint?"

I shrugged. "For starters, everyone knows you're one of the best artists at the school. Your work is often displayed in the annual alumni event. And I don't just know you paint. I know you prefer oils… because you told me."

"Oh." He tucked a stray curl behind his ear. Unsurprisingly, it popped free. "I like landscapes, though lately I've been focusing on portraits."

"Why portraits?"

He choked on his latest bite and his response came out raspy. "Jankowski says I need a more rounded portfolio if I want to attend AIC."

I blinked in surprise. "Chicago, huh? Why there?"

He snorted and shrugged out of his coat. It flopped over the back of his chair, and he pushed his sleeves up before retrieving his wrap. "Because they're the best. Second choice is Yale, but that's a last resort." To hear anyone talk about Yale as a last resort was beyond laughable, but coming from Calvin, it not only fit, I didn't doubt for a second that he'd get in no question.

"What do you want to do once you have your art degree?" I pushed.

His mouth twisted to the side. "Ideally, be super famous and have my artwork coveted around the world. But realistically? Anything to do with art. Like seriously anything. I'm not picky."

"How are the portraits coming along?"

His eyes widened. "They're, uh, coming." He cleared his throat and waved a hand in the air, clearly dismissing the topic. "What about you? You gonna be a career-Middie?" he asked as he reached across the table to steal a piece of fallen bacon from my plate. He popped the stolen goods in his mouth and looked back at me, where shock was most likely stamped across my face. "Don't get me wrong, I'm not knocking it. You definitely have what it takes to go pro or at least collegiate. Your transitions are on point and you certainly have the endurance." He winked, and I didn't even have it in me to respond appropriately to the obvious sexual innuendo.

"You know what position I play?"

He frowned. "Of course, I do. What, I can't be gay *and* like sports?"

"No, no, of course not. That's not what I… I'm just surprised."

He waved a piece of lettuce at me. "No, surprising is how you didn't get fucking beamed by the ball when Roger body checked you last week." For a hot minute, I was worried that my jaw had actually fallen off and landed on my plate.

How long has he been watching me play? That happened during a friendly game. It hadn't even been a legit practice.

He smirked and settled back in his chair. "I actually rather like lacrosse, beyond the obvious reasons." His gaze slithered over me and I nearly swallowed my tongue.

"How come you never went out for the team?" I asked before I could rethink the logic of such a question.

Sadness chased away the heat in his lingering gaze. "How do you think that would've gone?"

Absolutely terrible. Forget my own reasons for not wanting him anywhere near the lockers, because I wouldn't be able to control myself if A, he looked at me or B, he looked at someone else, there was the fact that most of the team comprised narrow-minded homophobes. He could have been the best player on the team and they still would've torn him apart.

"Exactly," he said when I didn't respond.

"What position would you have played if you could have?" I didn't ply him with false platitudes about how he should have tried anyway. We both knew what a horrible decision it would have been.

"What's the matter, Benny? Afraid of a little competition?" His eyes sparked with challenge. Of course, he would have been a midfielder. "Now you know I like sports. What about you, any creative bones in that ridiculously sexy body of yours?"

I was too distracted by the compliment to consider my answer before it flew out of my mouth. "I write a little."

His dark brow arched. "That so? And what does the illustrious Benjamin Price write about?"

The reality of my ill-conceived confession hit me and I struggled to make it disappear. "Nothing. They're stupid stories. Trifles." I pushed one of the bear claws over to him and took a sizable bite of my own to stop the words.

"I'd be interested to see some of these… trifles," he said, the words like a seductive purr as he plucked his treat from the table.

No. Hell no. Hell fucking no.

"Tell me more about these portraits you're working on. The subjects anyone I know?"

His cheek twitched. "Well, I've been ordered to do a self-portrait and you know me."

"Why, when you say self-portrait, does it sound like the worst thing ever? Would think that'd be fairly easy."

He let out an exasperated breath and dusted his hands of crumbs. "Because it *is* the worst thing ever. Self-portraits are self-aggrandizing, vapid, indulgences of an over-inflated ego."

"Tell me how you really feel," I chuckled.

He gave me a pointed look with a touch of mirth at the edges. "I am, if you would listen. Now, as I was saying. Pompous artists create self-portraits. They think they're better than other subject matter. Who cares what the artist looks like? It's how they see the world that people want to experience, not their own perception of their self-importance."

"Is that what you aim to reveal in your art? A different perspective?"

A wistful smile played over his lips. "I aim to show people what they can't see for themselves." His passionate response immediately begged the question of what he was so afraid to discover about himself. However, now that I finally had him relaxed, there was no way I was about to throw a wrench into everything by actually asking.

"In that case," I leaned forward on my elbows and laced my fingers together, "I look forward to seeing this year's gallery."

That wicked smile that might as well have been a baited lure designed especially for me appeared once more. "Don't hold your breath."

Once Calvin actually relaxed, the date became everything I'd hoped it'd be. Not to mention, learning about him was substantially easier when he was the one supplying the information. And while he'd surprised me with some of the things he already knew about me, I'd managed a few surprises of my own. Clearly, he didn't believe I'd been paying attention all of these years.

"I'm sorry, I can't see it," he said with a wide smile, his empty plate long forgotten before him. "Hard rock or maybe even classic I could understand, but jazz and blues? Nope. Not possible. You sure you're not secretly a heavy metal buff? That at least would make more sense."

"And your devotion to Streisand is logical?"

He gasped and held a hand to his chest. "You take that back. The illustrious Barbara is beyond reproach."

I bit my bottom lip to hold back an idiotic grin. "Stereotype."

"Hypocrite," he fired back.

I let out a huff and rolled my eyes. "We just can't help ourselves, can we?"

He threw his head back, exposing the column of his throat, and laughed. The rich sound sent low-key want pulsing through me. This is what I wanted, all I had ever wanted, to just *be* with him. The laughter trailed off and he looked back at me, a carefree smile light on his lips. I could get addicted to smiles like that paired with his warm, brown eyes sparkling with happiness.

Who am I kidding? Is there a part of him I'm not already addicted to?

"I don't suppose we can." While the words were in direct response to my observation, they also seemed to hold more, not quite innuendo, but something deeper. "Ten years is a long time to know someone without really knowing them." The tip of his finger drew designs in the ring of condensation created by his glass of water.

"Old habits die hard?"

His gaze lit back up to me, seeing me the way he always had. The want grew to a buzz beneath my skin like I'd had a couple glasses of wine at a social mixer. "No one said they had to die altogether. It's part of who we are now. I don't see any reason to change who I am. Do you?" he asked softly.

"Yes," I said without preamble or fluff.

He tilted his head to the side and his dark curls swayed while he continued to pull at the water on the table. "I don't think you do. Not who you are, anyway. Maybe how you approach the world. But I've never found anything wrong with *who* you are." His steady gaze, without reproach or judgment, filled me with unexpected warmth.

Maybe if more people had looked at me like that in my life, then I wouldn't have come out so damn rotten.

Suddenly, the joy on his face clouded over. He leaned across the table, coming out of his chair slightly in order to reach my face. His hand cupped my jaw while his thumb stroked my cheek. "What's the matter?"

"Nothing," I managed, though the word came out thin.

"That's right, nothing, because there is nothing wrong with you, Benjamin Price. That's not to say a little self-improvement isn't warranted." His gentle smile turned cheeky, and he patted my face before resuming his seat. I struggled to wrap my head around what had just happened and how close I was to selling my soul to get it to happen again. My tongue darted out to wet my lips, and Calvin's gaze immediately dropped to my mouth. Lust radiated off of him, adding to the palpable shift in mood.

"Let's get out of here." I stood up a hair too fast and had to steady the table.

There was literally nothing decent about the lascivious look Calvin gave me as he peeled himself out of his chair and took his sweet time putting his coat back on. By the time the damn thing settled on his shoulders, all I wanted to do was grab his lapels and yank him close so I could mash our mouths together. If I wasn't convinced the attendant would find a way to get me barred from this place if he saw something like that, I would have.

"And where do you plan on taking me, Mr. Price?" Calvin crooned, his voice unabashedly laced with sex and promise as he smoothed his coat along his sides. Normally I hated it when people called me Mr. Price, a fact Calvin was well aware of, but the way he said it had blood rushing south and left me lightheaded.

"A walk," I croaked out by the grace of God alone. "We're going for a walk."

He immediately dropped all pretense of advance. "A walk. Why?"

"To cool down."

His lips twitched, and his eyes glinted with wicked glee. He took a step forward and placed both hands flat on my chest. The heat from his palms might as well have been a brand for how they burned into me. He leaned closer to whisper in my ear. "What's the matter, Mr. Price? Something got you all hot and bothered?" I nearly choked on the groan I was desperately trying to hold back. We absolutely needed to leave before I not only got banned from this tiny haven, but thrown into jail for indecent exposure.

I grabbed his hand and proceeded to drag him out the side gate toward the main street, where hopefully the threat of witnesses could keep my rampant libido in check. His laughter bordered on a giggle as he let me man handle him, but ceased altogether when we reached the thoroughfare. Just like that, his anxiety resurfaced. “It’ll be fine,” I reassured him. “No one from the school comes over here.”

He took a deep breath and nodded, then took a step to come abreast of me. We meandered a few blocks in relative silence that miraculously wasn’t awkward. I could count on one hand the number of people I’d ever had companionable silence with in my life.

Suppose I shouldn’t be surprised Calvin is one of them.

As if knowing I was thinking of him, he cast me a furtive glance and I realized he was chewing on his lip. “Something on your mind?”

“Maybe.”

“After ten years of being bold and in people’s faces, *now* you wanna play coy?” I teased.

“Shut up.” He pushed my shoulder, and I laughed. “I…” He glanced over at me again, uncertainty in his eyes.

“What is it? Did you hate it? You did and you don’t want to do this again.” The different options poured out of me until he held up a hand to stem the tide. I snapped my mouth shut and waited for what he wanted to say. If he didn’t want to date, I’d understand—I’d be disappointed as fuck, but I’d understand and respect his decision.

His mouth drew into a grim line, and my internal list of self-recrimination queued up. Why did I always have to push? Why couldn’t I be satisfied with what we had? Why wasn’t it ever enough? Why did I let Savannah talk me into this? At his words, though, all the thoughts scattered.

“We still have to keep up appearances. I know you don’t like it, but things at school have to stay the same. You know that, don’t you, Benny?”

I did know that. I hated it with every fiber of my being, but I knew that. Unwilling to voice it, I simply nodded.

Calvin let out what sounded suspiciously like a relieved breath. Then, without warning, he grabbed my arm. “Come with me,” he said like I had a choice, given his vice-like grip. He tugged me into a narrow alley between two buildings and kept walking at a good clip, his long legs eating up the distance with confidence, as he turned first one corner, then another and another. Right when I couldn't stand it anymore, he turned a final corner into a sun-filled alley behind some commercial stores I'd never heard of and threw me against the wall.

No sooner did my back collide with the aged brick than his mouth was on mine. My gasp of surprise turned into a moan as he curled the fingers of both hands in my hair and completely dominated me. I slipped my hands beneath his coat to caress his sides. He took that as his cue to press more firmly against me. His tongue tangled and teased while he ground against my already straining erection. My resulting groan bounced loudly in the narrow space, but I didn't give a shit. The whole goddamn town could show up, and I still wouldn't care, as long as Calvin was kissing me like this. In fact, if he didn't stop, I was liable to come in my pants.

"Jesus fucking Christ," he gasped, his voice ragged from lack of air. "Sitting across a table from you for three hours was like fucking torture." He didn't wait for a response before reclaiming my mouth with a determination that made my knees weak. I clung to him, digging my fingers into his shirt, desperate to reach what I knew lay beneath. His mouth traveled across my jaw to catch my earlobe between his teeth.

"Oh God, Cal," I moaned, aching for more even though I knew I couldn't have it.

"Benny." The harsh whisper of my name cradled my ear and sank deep inside, turning my need acute. All I could manage was a half-strangled grunt as I clawed my way back from the precipice. Abruptly, Calvin's hands were gone from my face and undoing my buckle. Reason made a valiant effort to return, then promptly shattered into a million pieces when his skilled hand wrapped around my aching dick, the pleasure of it bordering on pain.

Oh God. Fuck. No no no no no…

I squeezed my eyes shut at the same time his fingers tightened around my shaft. Multicolored stars danced across my lids and I forced them back open just in time to see Calvin drop. His lips wrapped around me and I bucked off the wall. The intense, wet heat of his mouth swallowed me down, taking me deep. This time, the stars danced right across the far brick wall. Logically, I knew I should stop him. This wasn't the place. But I couldn't. I couldn't tell him no again. Whatever Calvin wanted, he could have.

I reached a hand out and tentatively brushed the curls from his face, already so close I didn't know how I was even hanging on. Seeing his lips stretched around me threatened the tenuous hold. His mop of dark curls bounced as he bobbed his head, each pass adding to the sweet, unbearable ecstasy. Then he looked up. His dark gaze latched onto mine and it was like someone gut punched me with a sledgehammer. My breath caught in a groan and my fingers reflexively tightened in his hair as I shot my load down his throat. He didn't move, didn't pull away, didn't even fucking blink, just knelt there holding my gaze captive while he took everything.

At last, I sagged completely depleted against the wall. While I was aware of him touching me, it felt more like an out-of-body experience, like it was happening to someone else far away from my fog of satiated bliss. He leveraged my belt loops to pull himself back up and caught me with a more sedate kiss that still managed to stir the embers of my desire. When he pulled out of the kiss, his lips were wet and the remnants of tears from his eyes watering were drying on his face. Without thinking, I reached up and wiped them away.

"I had a great time today," he whispered, and stole another sweet kiss.

Doubt wrapped around my heart. *Was that why…* I shook my head. "You didn't need to—"

He placed his lips against mine again to silence me. "I know. But I really, really wanted to." Another kiss and he stepped away, magically still as put together as ever, while I felt like I'd been fucking wrecked. He tugged his coat straight, though it didn't need it, and looked back at me with that perfect honey brown gaze, a soft smile curving his mouth. My chest ached for that smile.

Savannah was wrong. I'm not half in love with him.

"See you around." He winked and turned to leave. I stepped away from the wall and he spun back to catch my arm, his touch light but firm. "Oh, and Benny, I would absolutely love to do this again." The smile in his eyes told me he wasn't exclusively talking about the sex.

"Me too."

His smile broadened and seemed to fill him until he rivaled the sunlight falling around us. He gave my arm a gentle squeeze and once more turned away, this time walking down a side alley with the confidence of someone who knew exactly where they were going. I stumbled back into the wall and clutched my chest over my pounding heart. I may not know where I was going in this life, but I knew I would never tire of Calvin Bridges.

Chapter 22

Calvin

The door to the haunted classroom swung open, and I'd never been so relieved to see Andy in the four years we'd been friends. "Thank fuck you're already here," I said as I forced the door back closed.

Andy looked up from his book, a quizzical expression on his face. "I still don't understand why we couldn't meet in the library like usual." He slipped a bookmark between the pages and set the paperback aside.

"Because what I want to talk about, we can't talk about in the library, or outside, or anywhere else someone might overhear us." I wrung my hands and glanced over at the blocked-out window of the door. "If someone did…" I didn't want to think about how epically bad it would be if anyone heard this conversation.

"What did you do? Are you in trouble?"

"No. Yes." I dropped my bag on the dusty desk and let out a frustrated huff. "It's complicated. But it's also not. Honestly, I'm not really sure what to think anymore. This whole thing was supposed to be a laugh, a fun way to pass the time. Except now… And what the fuck does that mean—it's just about sex—anyway? Besides which, I met him in the middle. Dating isn't exactly my forte and honestly, if the sex wasn't so good, I wouldn't have even considered it. Who would have guessed dating Benny would be nice, of all things? But why won't he top me, Andy?" I looked over at Andy every bit as lost as I'd been the last couple of weeks. His mouth hung open and his bright emerald eyes were wide. "Are you listening? Don't just sit there. I need help."

"Back up. Did you say you've been fucking Benny?"

"Yeah, didn't I mention that? Keep up. That's not the point."

"Benny," Andy repeated. "Benjamin Price."

"Yes, moving on."

"How long have you been sleeping with Benny?"

I rolled my eyes. "First, no sleeping is happening. I can promise you that. As for how long, a couple months, but the dating thing is new," I clarified.

"You… you're *dating*… Benjamin Fucking Price!" Andy shouted.

"Would you keep your voice down?" I snapped. "If I'd wanted the whole damn school to know, I wouldn't have asked you up here."

"Fuck the school. How could you not tell me you were fucking Benny?" Andy demanded to know, his face turning blotchy red with indignant outrage.

"Oh, you mean like how you told me you were fucking Mitch?" I countered. All the red drained from his face while his mouth opened and closed without uttering a sound. "And for the record, pretty sure Benny knows too."

Andy swayed in place, and I rushed over to steady him. He blinked at me as I held him, his gaze distant. "How… how did you know?"

I let out a sigh and made sure he wouldn't fall over before stepping back. "Benny actually helped me put it together. He mentioned that you'd been in that fight with Mitch and the others from the team. Which you also didn't tell me." I scowled at him, still pretty pissed about that as well.

His eyes narrowed to glare right back. "That doesn't mean—"

"He also said that after you two disappeared, he saw Mitch coming into practice later that afternoon."

"So what?"

"From the East Woods." The little color Andy had gained paled once more. I gave him a knowing look and leaned against the nearby bookshelf. "Still want to deny something is going on between you two?"

He shook his head and stumbled back on shaky legs until he bumped into an old desk. He sat down heavily and looked up at me. "So… you and Benny… again. What started that?"

I shrugged. "Don't know. Went up for my usual shower one night and he just sort of showed up. He seemed surprised to see me at first, but he stuck around, then he showed up again. I kept waiting for it to stop, but he kept coming back." I crossed my arms and bit the inside of my cheek while I studied the ground.

"Okay, so you two have been fooling around for a while. What's this dating business about? And did I hear you correctly about actually *wanting* him to top you?"

I raised my gaze to Andy once more. He still appeared shaken for sure with his hands clasped before him tight enough to white knuckle, but he clearly was attempting to keep it together. "The dating thing is...interesting."

"Why are you dating at all? Wasn't aware that was your thing."

"It's not, but it's not all bad. Believe it or not, Benny isn't actually a total prick, or at least he isn't outside these walls." I gestured to the room and the school in general. "As for the why..." I trailed off, my face unexpectedly heating. "I guess I look at it as a compromise of sorts. Quid pro quo. He wants to date. I want him to top me."

"You lost me again. Why would you need to trade anything?"

Embarrassment blossomed inside of my chest and made me queasy. "Because when I asked, he said no."

"He knows," Andy deduced, without missing a beat.

"He knows," I echoed. "But the reason he gave at the time was that it was because this was still just sex to me. What the fuck does that even mean? What's wrong with sex?" I asked, my voice gaining strength and a noticeable edge.

"Is it?"

"Is it what?" I lashed out, my embarrassment morphing into frustrated anger.

"Is it just sex?"

All the wind left my sails, a tempest dissipating to leave my metaphorical boat adrift in the vast ocean. "I..." *don't know.* The words were right there on the tip of my tongue, but I couldn't bring myself to say them aloud.

He sat back in his seat and gave me a look that seemed to peel back my layers of bullshit with all the mercy of a palette knife. "Sounds like a hell of a lot more than sex to me."

My hand fisted. "What are you trying to say?"

"Something you clearly don't want to hear. There's only one reason I can think of that you'd be twisted up about anyone. Face it, you're falling for him."

I barked out a humorless laugh. "I am *not* in love with Benjamin Price."

Andy raised an eyebrow at the vehemence of my denial. "I didn't say you were *in* love with him. I said you were well on your way."

I blanched and cut my gaze away to glare out the windows at the outside world.

"The Calvin I know wouldn't date, wouldn't even barter to get what he wants. He'd move on to someone more willing. That tells me something is special about Benny for you. You're not treating him like your other conquests."

"Speaking from experience?"

"That was uncalled for," Andy snapped, giving me a glimpse of that infamous Irish anger he did such a good job of keeping in check. "You know damn well shit is complicated between Mitch and me. Always has been."

"Planning on elaborating?"

"Are you?"

I opened my mouth, fully prepared to give him a piece of my mind concerning his own hypocrisy, then deflated. Wasn't that why I'd asked him up here after all? Because I was feeling out of my depth? "What do you want to know?"

Try as he might, Andy couldn't school his surprise fast enough. "Really?"

"Yeah." I slid down the shelves and slumped to the floor. "And don't worry. If you're not ready to talk about what's going on with you and Mitch, then you don't have to. But I..." I stared at my hands, then curled and uncurled my fingers. "I don't know what I'm doing, and that..."

"Freaks the hell out of you," Andy said as he took a seat beside me.

I stared at him in shock unsure of when he'd gotten up or why he was willing to help at all given how long I'd kept this from him or how I'd thrown my knowledge of what he'd been up to with Mitch in his face.

He smiled and bumped my shoulder. "Let's forget the fact that this is *Benny* we're talking about and start at the beginning. Minus details, please. There are some mental images you can't unsee." He winked and I smiled in return. Thank fuck for Andy.

Benny

"Fancy meeting you here."

I started at the unexpected greeting and spun away from my desk to find none other than Calvin Bridges leaning against the doorjamb of my room, dark curls framing his handsome face and a sinister grin quirking his lips up in a half smile. My grin stretched my lips as the light Calvin seemed to carry with him filled me like a second sun. A split second later, logic asserted itself and I launched out of my chair.

In three long strides, I was by his side, his devious smirk filling my vision. I grabbed his arm and yanked him inside, my gaze searching the miraculously empty hallway beyond before I slammed the door shut. "Are you out of your damn mind? What were you thinking coming here?"

He shrugged as he wandered across the small room, taking in the space. "Funny how I've never actually come over here in all these years." He had a point there, though I suspected his reasons weren't all that different from the ones that had led me to avoiding his as well.

"It's the middle of the fucking day."

"Your point?" he asked as he trailed a finger along a poster of the Chicago skyline.

"Exactly that. Are you insane?"

"Maybe I wanted to practice the route." His brown eyes gave up their perusal of my walls and snapped to me. Instantly, a ball of nerves twisted in my gut. It would seem my efforts at distracting him and hoping he'd simply forget all about wanting me to top hadn't done shit.

Should have known better.

"At any rate, no one saw me coming here and no one will see me leave." He meandered toward the desk and the slew of books open on it. "Such a diligent student," he teased as he reached forward to thumb one of the pages.

My gaze slipped past him to the open journal entry I'd been working on. In a few steps, I inserted myself between him and the desk. "This is a little brazen, even for you," I said as I closed the notebook behind my back and slipped it under a textbook.

"You think so?" he asked, stepping close enough that I could feel his body heat. I bit back a groan of anticipation in an effort not to encourage him. It was all useless though. All Calvin had to do was look at me to know how badly I wanted him.

"What exactly was your plan?"

"What do you think?" Another half-step and my back pressed into the edge of the desk.

My breath faltered and my eyelids fluttered at his nearness and the promise practically radiating off of him. "Cal." What was intended to be a rebuke or note of caution came out a whisper that bordered on a whimper saturated with longing.

"Yes, Benny?" he whispered back. His breath mingled with mine as he closed the distance and captured my mouth before I could come up with anything.

My fingers dug painfully into the wooden desk at my back while he curled his own long fingers around the back of my neck and held me where he wanted me. His tongue delved past my lips to steal the moan I was trying so hard to keep in check. Unadulterated want pulsed through my veins and kept me at his complete mercy. My arms ached with the effort of keeping them behind me and became the only thing holding me up as he conquered my mouth with reckless abandon.

He pulled at my bottom lip before ghosting kisses across my jaw. "What are you thinking about, Benny?" The low whisper directly in my ear sent a shiver down my spine that landed in my already aching dick. I swallowed hard and tried to think about anything but what I wanted right now. He wrapped his tongue around the shell of my ear and my knees threatened to buckle. "Are you imagining me spinning you around and fucking you right here?" His hand slithered between us and squeezed my straining erection through my trousers. I grunted, but couldn't seem to form words. "Are you fantasizing about me sinking into your tight ass? Stretching that tight little hole of yours with my hard cock?"

The filthy whispers caressed my ear, the heat of his breath only adding to the sensory overload. But as much as I wanted all of that and then some, it was broad daylight. "Cal... Cal..." I struggled to find my voice as he continued to palm my dick and my eyes tried to roll back. Much more and I'd come right here with no more than a few words and a light brush, the only mercy of which was I had clothes on hand. He lowered his head to suck lightly on my neck and the groan I'd been fighting so hard against rolled out. Finally, I forced words out. "My door doesn't lock any better than yours. Anyone could walk in here at any given moment."

He gave up the hickey I knew he would never give me, no matter how much I wanted him to and looked at me with lust-filled brown eyes. "You should do something about that, then."

I didn't even think twice. I extricated myself, grabbed my chair and dragged it over to the door where I promptly used it to brace the handle. Fuck if it was weird and would attract all sorts of attention if someone tried to get in and couldn't.

This is a bad idea. A really, really bad idea. It's the middle of the day. What if Neil or Todd decide to drop by? There will be no mistaking the sounds coming out of here.

At least no one will be able to see that it's Calvin. But how will I get him out without anyone knowing he was here to begin with?

I was so lost in my thoughts, I didn't realize until it was too late that Calvin had snagged the poorly concealed journal until I looked up and found him holding it open. Horror rushed through me, evicting any lingering desire. "Wait."

He glanced up, a knowing smile twitching at his lips. "Would this perchance be the writing our dear Benny is too modest to claim?"

"Don't. Give it back." I stepped forward, intending to snatch it before he could read too much, but he spun out of reach.

"King Kelani looked out over the balcony at his vast kingdom below," he read aloud. "His subjects scurried about their daily lives mindless of the compassion of their benevolent ruler. Would that Kel had someone to share his lonely kingdom with, but to rule absolutely was to rule alone." Calvin glanced up, his smile wider. "I don't know what you're so worried about. This is actually pretty good."

"Cal, please." I held out my hand in the vain hope he'd pass it over. No such luck. He flipped a few pages back to another passage.

"White silk hung in elaborate folds from King Kelani's sleeves as he met with the latest supplicant. The trade agreements settled without quarter or malice, but with a firm stoicism that bespoke of a wisdom beyond the young ruler's age. Many had made the mistake in the past of believing the ostentatious prince would become a weak and malleable king. However, Kelani had assumed his role with a dignity and form unbeknownst to his predecessors. After all, what need had he for an army when he held sole control of all the supplies essential to his hostile neighbors?" The laughter dancing at the edge of his words as he read aloud vanished as he blinked at the page in confusion. Without a word, he began flipping back through, pausing only long enough to read a few lines before finding another page.

"Cal."

"What is this? It... it..."

"Cal," I tried again.

He looked up, and I saw he'd already made all the connections. "Cal," he echoed. "Kel... I'm Kel."

“It’s not…” I gave up as soon as I started. It would do no good to deny it. That journal was exactly what he thought it was. We stared at each other for a long minute, then his gaze dropped back to the page.

“Looks like just about everyone is in here. The Councilor is obviously Andy. Hostile neighboring nations are definitely the homophobic assholes like Brian and John.” He set the journal aside and leaned against the desk in a much more casual perch than the one I’d had a scarce few minutes ago. “A king, huh?” he asked with a crooked smile.

“Shut up.”

He snickered and pushed off the desk. Once more, he closed the distance between us and I stood there, too mesmerized to move. “What about you, Benny? You gonna tell me who you are?”

“No. Absolutely fucking not.”

He laughed, and the sound slipped past my mortification to settle warmly in my chest, then just like before, he leaned forward to steal a kiss. This time, I didn’t pretend like I had restraint and wrapped my arms around his waist as I gave into it completely. Sadly, the kiss was much shorter lived, though once again he leaned in to whisper in my ear. “Whatever you say, Prince Einar.”

I jolted with surprise and he used the opportunity to slip free. He paused at the door, where he’d already removed the chair while I regained my senses. His hand wrapped around the knob and a desperate need to keep him here if only for a few seconds longer rose in me. “You free this Saturday?”

The smile he gave me wasn’t the one I wanted, the one I craved. It was small and a little sad. “Actually, already have plans that night.” He glanced back toward the door. “Really should get going. Just wanted to make a point.” He offered a wink, then slipped out without so much as a whisper of fabric to betray his passing.

I sat heavily on the desk. My fingers closed around the damnable journal and chunked it across the room hard enough to dent the drywall on the far side. “Fuck.”

Chapter 23

Calvin

The church filled with the usual hum of voices as we waited for Saturday Mass to begin. My fingers rubbed together absently as if I held a phantom rosary. Father Miles had greeted me along with several other parishioners when we'd arrived an hour before. I'd hoped coming so soon would have given me a chance to speak with Father Miles in private before the sermon, but no such luck.

Not that it would have done much good.

What could he possibly tell me I didn't already know, or that Andy hadn't said himself? I let out a sigh and stared down at my empty hands, still seeking something that wasn't there.

This is why I avoid feelings. They're a complicated mess that drag everyone down.

Things had been so much simpler when it was only sex. Fun, light, no expectations. It would go on as long as it went, and then it would be over. A fun story to look back on. It pained me to admit it, but I was woefully incompetent when it came to navigating my own feelings. Others' weren't so bad, but mine? Easier not to have them.

After Andy's accusation that I could be falling for Benny of all people, I'd gone out of my way to prove that wasn't the case, take back control, reassert the unusual balance between Benny and myself.

That had gone spectacularly horrible.

I'd had this grand plan of freaking him out—which I had—but I never could have anticipated the way he'd look at me. That soft smile he almost never shared, glowing in his eyes as he turned to find me in his doorway bold as brass. His pure joy at seeing me had hit me in the gut full force and it had taken everything I'd had to keep the smirk on my face and casually walk into his room rather than race over to him. Not even getting him riled up had changed things. All I'd really established was that I knew of all the right buttons to push and that Benny made me reckless. For God's sake, I'd nearly given Benny a fucking hickey.

What is wrong with me?

I stared up at the stained glass in the ceiling. The early evening meant the sky beyond was too dark to truly appreciate their beauty, but the colors still managed to be striking with the illumination from within the church.

And that damn journal. What was that about?

Page after page of a fantastical story about a young king ruling with confidence and a wisdom beyond his years.

Alone.

I squeezed my hand and longed for the press of worn olive beads against my fingers and the inherent comfort they brought. The truth of his assessment as me being cold and calculating hurt more than anything. Except I wasn't those things with Benny, not anymore. Even though I'd gone to his room with the explicit purpose of proving I was, it wasn't the same as it was, hadn't been for a while. Coming to terms with that, however, and understanding this evolution was fucking with my head.

Maybe I should have skipped Mass and gone out with him.

The look on his face when I'd said I had other plans had physically hurt my chest. I didn't want him to be sad or disappointed. I wanted him to smile at me like he had when I'd shown up, so fucking happy to see me he couldn't hide it.

That's it, I'm bailing. I'll atone with Father Miles later.

I stood up and turned to exit the pew and ran smack into someone. "Sorry," I mumbled with my head down in shame at getting busted trying to sneak out mere minutes before the sermon was due to start. With a heavy heart, I slumped back down.

"It's okay. Is this seat taken?"

My head snapped up at the familiar voice and my jaw fell. "What are you doing here?" I asked a little too loudly, earning myself several reproachful hushes. Abashed, I ducked my head once more and scooted over to give him more room to sit. He did so without hesitation, taking his time unraveling his thick scarf from around his neck to reveal the faint blemish still marring his warm ivory skin.

"Is this okay?" he asked softly once he was fully settled. I glanced over at Benny, still in shock to see him here. He gave me that smile that glowed in his eyes and made my stomach flip-flop.

"Yes." The word leapt out of my mouth with abandon. His smile widened, and more shushing ensued as Father Miles stepped up to the pulpit. I glanced behind me at the middle-aged woman basically giving me a death glare. When I spun back, Benny was still looking at me. I dropped my voice and asked again, "Why are you here?"

"Because I wanted to see you."

"But you're not religious," I countered.

"You are." That smile again.

"Eh-hem," the woman behind us cleared her throat rather aggressively. I scowled at her, and she glared right back. With a huff, I turned forward once more as Father Miles' steady voice reached out to the congregation and Benny did his best to smother a chuckle. I rolled my eyes and sagged against the bench.

When something warm brushed along my finger, I jolted in my seat and nearly came out of my skin. It wasn't until I looked down that I realized that my hand had found its way beneath the substantial bulk of Benny's scarf. The soft touch came again, and my brain finally connected what was going on.

I licked my lips and looked over at Benny. His light green gaze met mine, filled with calm and patience. I glanced back down at our concealed hands and swallowed thickly. Then, before I could psyche myself out, I hooked my finger with his. A sense of rightness settled in my chest. I let out a shaky breath I prayed he didn't notice. He tugged lightly against my finger, then gently rubbed his thumb along it and my heart fucking soared.

Fuck you, Andy. Fuck you for always being right.

I did my damnedest to focus on the sermon, but my thoughts kept straying to the man beside me and the intimate glide of his thumb along my knuckle. Each pass chipped away at my concentration until my awareness of Benny beside me consumed everything. I blinked in confusion when the tiny spot of warmth that had become my world disappeared. It wasn't until I glanced over at Benny that I realized the congregation was already dispersing.

Fuck me. I missed the whole damn thing. Hopefully, Father Miles doesn't ask about it when I come in for confession next week.

Shaking my head at my distraction, I followed Benny out of the pew, my gaze riveted on the thick hunter green scarf as he wrapped it back around his neck to ward off the chill awaiting outside. The woman who'd been giving us a hard time slipped in between us, which allowed several other people into the aisle, creating even more distance. I choked on my mounting frustration as I lost all sight of Benny amid the press of bodies and bubble of voices.

Determined to ditch the lingering crowd as fast as humanly possible, I ducked off to the side and tugged my peat coat tightly closed before stepping through one of the smaller doors into the frigid winter beyond. My gaze traveled over the lazy river of people vacating the church, but no hint of Benny emerged.

Fuck. Maybe I imagined the whole thing.

I rolled my eyes. *Great. What the fuck does that mean if I'm fantasizing about Benny coming to church with me? Fuck you, Andy. Fuck you so much for putting these thoughts in my head.*

Despite the concern that I might have dreamed up the whole impossible experience, I continued to search the crowd. I rubbed my freezing hands together and brought them to my face to blow on them. My breath misted in a white cloud and did little to add warmth.

Fuck this. I'm crazy for standing here like an idiot.

I was about to tuck my hands into my pits when a voice warmer and more seductive than mulled wine stopped me. "Here, let me help with that." Benny tugged off his gloves, and I vaguely wondered why I hadn't thought to put my own on as he stepped forward and wrapped my hands in the very real warmth of his.

"Hey," I said at last, which wasn't at all the smooth quip I'd intended.

"Hey," he said back with that smile that melted my insides despite the fucking sub-zero weather. He glanced around at the dispersing people and looked back at me. "What do you say we get out of here."

I nodded, unable to muster up actual words.

"You gonna be okay?" he asked, giving my hands a gentle squeeze.

"I have gloves."

He quirked an eyebrow. "And where would these gloves be?"

"In my pocket," I replied like the dunce I apparently was now.

Jesus Fucking Christ, pull yourself together. Just because Andy says a thing doesn't make it true.

Without preamble, Benny liberated my gloves along with my forgotten scarf and all I could do was stare at him in wonder as he first tugged on each fitted finger, then wrapped my scarf around me. With each loop of the insanely long scarf I'd thought was fashionable, I turned to more mush, unable to tear my gaze away from Benny's pure Celadon eyes.

Except he is. Oh fuck, Andy's right. I'm falling for Benny.

Some darker part of my mind cruelly pointed out that I was a lot farther along that path than I wanted to entertain, but I could barely admit this little bit. I couldn't handle what the rest implied.

"There," he said, tugging the scarf, "much better." His gaze finally came to my eyes, and I saw what I so often saw when he looked at me these days, desire, want, things I was too terrified to label, but didn't stop them from fluttering with abandon in my chest. I was already leaning forward, eyes half-lidded for a kiss, when my brain finally caught up and a reminder of where we were stabbed through me.

"We should go."

"I have just the place." He grabbed my hand with his equally gloved one, though fuck if I knew when he'd put them back on, and led me down the nearest side street. Once he was sure I was following, he released me and glanced over. "I still can't believe I didn't know you were Catholic, not to mention a practicing one."

"What? Because I'm gay, I can't also believe in God?" I snapped, still shaken by my own unwanted revelation.

Benny's brow furrowed with genuine concern, and I immediately wanted to take back the harsh rebuke. "That's not what I meant at all. I think it's great you have faith. I was merely stating my surprise that *I* didn't know."

This time, it was my face that screwed up in confusion.

What was that supposed to mean?

Before I could ask, he halted by a door and pulled out a set of keys. I glanced around and didn't recognize the area, impressive and a tad disconcerting given how much I'd wandered the back alleys and small streets of the town over the years. "Where are we?"

He glanced up at the nondescript facade. "No place fancy." Still confused, I followed him into the subtle warmth and immediately felt my nose defrost. Before I could ask again where the fuck we were, he launched up a narrow flight of stairs and only paused to open another door at the top. "Here we are." The lights flicked on to fill what appeared to be a modest studio apartment with soft, yellow light.

I began removing my scarf by rote as my gaze traveled over the room, taking in the perfectly made queen bed, the microscopic kitchenette, intimate table set for two. I did a double take. The plates were very clearly set out for dinner and even had a candle ready to be lit sitting between them. In the background, a bag marked with the logo of the popular Chinese joint in town sat on the counter. I turned my gaze back to Benny. “What is this?”

He shrugged and offered a sheepish smile. “I thought you might be hungry after Mass and didn’t want you to worry about being seen in town.”

My heart squeezed at the thoughtfulness as I continued to shrug out of my coat. “What if I hadn’t wanted to come?”

He shrugged again, his own winter gear already divested and hanging on the coat rack. “Then it would have gotten cold. I could always come back for it later.” He added my things to the rack. “We don’t have to stay if you don’t want to. Like I said earlier, I just wanted to see you.”

Fuck it. Fuck all of it. I couldn’t take it anymore. If I didn’t do something soon, my chest was going to explode. “Benny.”

He turned back to me, clearly braced for a negative response. “Yeah?”

“I hope that microwave works.”

“What?”

I closed the distance and smashed my mouth against his with zero finesse. He let out a muffled sound of surprise that turned to a moan as I slipped my tongue past his lips to tangle with his. My fingers curled through his hair, so much longer than it had been three months ago, and urged him deeper. His fingers gripped into my side and I groaned with barely contained need. “Supplies,” I gasped out at last.

“Side table,” he managed between hungry kisses.

I abandoned his mouth only long enough to get a good heading, then snatched at his pliable lips once again as I dragged him back toward the bed and everything else we needed. My fingers traveled up his soft shirt and set to work, fumbling open the buttons until I found the desired flesh beneath. Benny’s breath caught as I pushed the fabric from his shoulders and he immediately reached to tug my shirt free. Our arms tangled a moment as I sought to liberate him from his undershirt and he struggled to yank off my sweater. I laughed and gave up my pursuit to help.

“Fuck,” he hissed when it fell clear. “Still no undershirt. Are you crazy? It’s like twenty degrees outside.”

“I told you. I don’t like them.” I ran a hand up his now bare chest, my fingers gliding with ease through the light, silky strands of his chest hair, then dropped it to his buckle. "I like undressing you," I said as I flicked the tongue of his belt out and stole another eager kiss.

"Why's that?" he asked, more than a little breathless.

So many reasons.

I teased his lips with another kiss while I mentally ran through the list. It was intimate, not transactional like my previous encounters had been. It let me explore his body the way my fingers longed to. It made all the rest of the world fall away so that it was only us. I tugged on his pants, simultaneously popping the button loose, and leaned in close as I slid my hand inside to cup his plump cock. "What do you think?"

Instead of answering, he groaned and captured my mouth hard enough that we fell back on the bed in a tangle of limbs. His kiss didn't stop there. The fiery brand of his lips pressed into my throat and ventured down my chest. He paused to nip and suck lightly at a nipple and I arched into the lavish attention with a moan he echoed.

While I was distracted, he set about undoing my pants. He abandoned his determined pursuit to torture the rest of my torso, sucking kisses down my abdomen that made my stomach quiver with expectation. His fingers hooked over my briefs and removed them, along with my pants, with practiced ease. He ran his hands up my legs as he settled back on the bed that was substantially more inviting than the meager cot I'd procured for the haunted room.

I looked down at him and groaned at the hunger I found there, not as he looked at the cock I knew he loved, but at me. My head fell back into the pillows, which I promptly tossed aside as he wrapped a hand around me and gave a decisive stroke. He leaned down to place a tender kiss on my inner thigh, then lapped at my balls. Blood pulsed through my aching cock and a drop of pre-cum squeezed out.

I registered the firm muscle of his tongue licking up my shaft to steal the drop right before the intense heat of his mouth swallowed me whole. A strangled moan caught in my throat as I bucked off the mattress, lost to the intensity. He groaned around me, more than capable of taking whatever I could dish out. The vibrations rippled through my sensitive cock to my core and I tangled fingers in his hair, both to cling onto something and eager to encourage him.

He moaned again as my hold tightened and swallowed around me before returning to his rhythm. The ecstasy of release danced within reach, tingling in my spine and tightening my balls. I fought against it as I flailed for the drawer and the promised lube within. Out of the corner of my eye, I noted the drawer was stocked with a hell of a lot more than lube, including a healthy supply of condoms. I ignored the rest and snagged the bottle right as Benny took me deep. The intense pleasure of it threatened the tenuous hold of my pending orgasm.

"Stop," I gasped out, not sure if I could last a second longer.

He immediately pulled off and looked up at me with eyes blown wide with lust and colored with a hint of concern. Before he could voice any doubt, I leaned forward to conquer his spit-slicked lips then used my hold on his hair to roll us. Confusion shone in his light green eyes for a second. I popped the lid free of the lube and leaned down to press my lips against his once more. His doubt melted away as his mouth and body molded against mine. Hoping the lubricant wasn't too cold, I rubbed my thumb gently along his entrance. He moaned into the kiss and I pressed my middle finger in, only encountering the mildest resistance before sliding as deep as I could.

"Oh, god, Cal," he gasped as I added another finger and curled them delicately against his prostate.

"You like that?" He gave a whimpered moan in response and I slowly thrust the fingers in and out, being sure to stroke the bundle of nerves. "You like me stretching you open, don't you? Like me inside of you. Making you mine." His eyes rolled back, and he arched into my hand, squeezing my fingers with his gloriously tight ass while his hands fisted in the sheets. "Fuck, you feel so good. So tight and greedy for me." I dropped my head as he tightened around me again. My gaze caught on the fading bruise staining his neck that I never should have given him and my mouth moved toward it as if pulled by some magnetic force. I licked at the marred flesh and sucked lightly on the mark as I scissored my fingers in and out of Benny's willing body.

"Wait."

The breathless command instantly froze all of my movements. I pulled back from his neck, thoroughly chastened. I knew better. What the fuck was I thinking, deliberately marking him like this?

He angled his head up and pulled a featherlight kiss from my lips. "I didn't mean stop altogether," he whispered, then added with a cheeky grin, "Just warning that I was going to come if you kept that up."

I slowly removed my fingers and saw the loss of them on his face. "We can't have that now, can we?" I snatched at his lips, then rocked back on my heels. My hand closed around one of the discarded pillows and I pulled it close. "Get that tight ass in the air." Benny dutifully lifted his hips, and I placed the pillow beneath them. That done, I wrapped a hand around my length and stroked enough to add a liberal coat of lube to it before guiding it toward his already clenching hole.

I smothered a moan as I pressed slowly in, keeping an eye on Benny's face. I'd never had the pleasure of watching my partner as I sank into them, had never wanted it before, but I very much wanted to see Benny's reactions. I watched as his face tightened from the burn of the initial breach, saw his flushed chest flex, then relax as he remembered to breathe. I sank a little deeper with each shallow thrust and saw each gain register until the cringe on his face dissolved into sheer fucking ecstasy when I bottomed out. My pleasure at being so incredibly deep barely even registered, I was so enraptured in his reactions.

Fuck, Benny. What have you done to me?

I didn't need an answer to the question; I already knew it. I gave a slow, deliberate roll of my hips, gliding out and back in, then did it again and again, taking my time building Benny's pleasure, because as much as he liked it fast and dirty, he also loved it slow and purposeful. He squeezed around me and I gave up my hold of his thighs to fall on my arms over him. My gaze fell once more to the almost-hickey on his neck. This time I didn't hesitate. My mouth closed over the mark and I sucked hard as I thrust into him. Benny gasped out a groan and snaked his arms under my shoulders and dug his fingers into my back.

I moaned and my thrusts got sharper and sharper until the slow pace I'd been maintaining became a frantic pound. My arms ached from holding me, but I couldn't bring myself to move because it would mean Benny would let go. I shifted my angle and swallowed Benny's cry of pleasure with a sloppy, savage kiss he eagerly returned. The need for release saturated every fiber. Electricity surged up my spine. Heat coiled low in my belly. And an unbearable ache I'd do just about anything to hang onto built to blinding heights.

"Cal!" Benny shouted, clamping down tight around me as his orgasm ripped through him to pulse in hot streams onto his chest. I didn't even manage another thrust before I shattered apart with my own cry and collapsed on top of him.

Benny

I let out a contented breath and combed my fingers through Calvin's silken locks, one hundred percent positive I couldn't be more in love with him if I tried. He shifted on my chest and let out a groan that sounded like he'd run an entire game with two overtimes. And, fuck, if that wasn't exactly what he'd done. I still wasn't sure if my legs would hold if I tried to stand or finish disintegrating into jelly.

I glanced over at the setup on the table. All my grand plans to make topping Cal special like he deserved had gone up in smoke faster than sage brush in a draught the second he'd rolled us. Not that I was complaining. Jesus Christ, man could fuck like no one else. I placed a tender kiss on the top of his head and he let out a stuttering sigh. My hand slid from around his waist where it had been keeping him close and I shifted to roll him off of me.

"Where 're you going?" he mumbled into my chest.

I chuckled and tilted his relaxed face up to steal a kiss. "You stay here. I'll be right back." He groaned as he rolled to the side, but didn't protest. I slipped into the bathroom to relieve myself and cleaned up a bit before returning with a warm towel for him. To my surprise, he was no longer laid out on the rumpled bed, but standing. He offered me a smile that suffused my chest with an entirely different heat than the one from earlier and my lips stretched into an echoing grin.

"How you doin', stud?" he asked as he stepped forward to steal a kiss and the towel I'd brought.

"Stud, huh?"

He hiked his shoulder in a half-shrug and finished cleaning up. When he was done, he grabbed his briefs from the pool of his pants and tugged them on. I shamelessly followed the motion, and he snickered before stealing a quick kiss. "About that microwave..."

"It works." I wrapped the loose sheet around my waist and wandered over to heat-up the food. We didn't bother with the candle or even the plates and table, but settled on the floor amid the heap of pillows and plucked at the food straight from the cartons. It came as no surprise to me that Calvin was proficient with chopsticks, though I despaired at his need to put soy sauce on everything.

"Don't judge me," he said, snapping his chopsticks at me before stealing another piece of chicken from my carton.

"Is it judgment if you're wrong?"

He snorted and dunked the already sauced chicken into his veritable bowl of soy. "Maybe I like salty things." His eyes glinted wickedly, and I bit my lip to keep from laughing. He finished chewing and sealed up the cartons nearest him, then leaned back on his arms to take in the room. I mirrored him in closing up the remaining containers. When I was done, he asked, "So you gonna tell me what this place is or not?"

"It's exactly what it looks like. A studio flat above a shop," I said as I stood and took the leftovers back to the kitchenette.

"You know what I mean. Whose is it? How do you know about it? Why are we here?" he asked in one continuous stream as he followed me back to the bed. I replaced my stolen sheet and slipped beneath it. He settled beside me and poked me in the ribs.

"Ow," I laughed and turned on my side to face him. "What was that for?"

"You going to answer the question?"

I rolled my eyes and propped up on my elbow. "What do I get if I do?"

His mouth twisted in a frown. "First off, you should tell me anyway, but fine, I'll see your terms. You answer my question and I'll answer one of yours."

Ooh, I loved this game. "The place belongs to my friend Savannah. She rents it out to students to make extra cash on the side, since her parents are always cutting her off."

"Savannah, huh? Couldn't help but notice the... extra in the side drawer," he added with a smirk.

"If you're not so slyly asking if Savannah and I were involved, the answer is yes, but that was a long time ago. We're much better as friends. Do you need a list of my other partners?" I asked with a raised eye brow at the same time, hoping that didn't count as my question.

"No. Do you need mine?"

I slid a little closer and glided a hand over his firm stomach. "No. I know you would tell me if you thought it was relevant."

"I would," he said softly as his fingers trailed along my side, tracing the patterns only he seemed to know.

"My turn." He smiled, but didn't cease his drawing. "What are you doing?"

"Hm?" he hummed while his fingers continued to play.

"Whenever you touch me, it's almost like your drawing. I'm curious what."

"Oh, that? Nothing in particular, mostly just memorizing."

"Memorizing what?" I asked, leaning into him, completely enthralled.

"You. One of these days I'm going to sculpt you in clay and I want to make sure to get it right."

I frowned down at him. "What, like some Patrick Swayze-Ghost bullshit?"

Calvin's hand stilled as laughter rolled out of him. His eyes danced with humor as he finally sobered up. "For the record, I would make a fantastic Demi Moore, but no, not like that. Think more Pygmalion." As he said it, his hand resumed its sensuous roving.

I searched my knowledge of history for the name and almost laughed when I found it. "That's the Greek guy who had his ivory sculpture brought to life by the gods, right?"

Both of his eyebrows rose in obvious surprise. "It is."

I frowned at him in mock insult. "Are you calling me the perfect woman?"

He laughed again and used his hold on my waist to tug me closer for a kiss. "Obviously."

I got lost in the sweep of tongues and let my hand trail lower until it hit the band of his underwear. I was on the verge of asking if he still wanted me to top when he asked a question of his own.

"When did you know you were bi?"

I didn't think he was asking because having doubts about his own sexuality so much as he was simply curious. "Truthfully?"

"No, lie to me," he quipped with a relaxed smile and no sting.

"I used to think everyone was. It wasn't until right before I came here that I realized that wasn't the case."

"What happened?" His hand glided up my chest, distracting me from my response.

"My father," I said without thinking. Too late to take it back, I elaborated. "He found out my mother was "encouraging" my eccentricities."

Calvin's frown deepened. "I'm not following."

I let out a sigh and rubbed my thumb along his lower abs. "Benjamin Wallace Price the Third is a man with very decided opinions and didn't want any son of his to be, as he put it, a fucking fairy. He offered my mom a choice. She could raise me as she saw fit and fend for herself, or she could take a sizable settlement and disappear." My fingers curled on his stomach as my own rolled with rancid anger. "She took the money."

"Benny." The soft compassion in his voice tightened my chest.

I shook my head, eager to return to the lightness we'd been enjoying. "It was a long time ago." A smile tugged at my lips as I looked into his honey brown eyes, the same eyes that had first captivated me across a crowded room full of strangers, eyes that had seen the real me. "Of course, any doubts I may have had vanished when I got my first crush on a boy."

His eyes sparkled as a smile spread across his lips. "Oh? And who was that?"

I looked down at him, a little surprised, then leaned close to taste his smile. "Do you really not know?"

His eyes widened as my meaning sank in. He delicately wrapped a hand around the back of my neck and pulled me down for a more thorough kiss. I moaned softly into him, my hand drifting lower to palm his thickening cock. He ground up into the touch and slipped his fingers into my hair. "When do we have to leave?" he asked.

I moved to free him from his briefs. "We don't. We can stay as long as you want."

His tongue swept past my lips in a deep kiss that ignited all the parts of me that had belonged to him for as long as I could remember. He drifted his hand back down my chest to my hip and tugged it toward him. I broke from the kiss long enough to reacquire the lube from the stand, then tugged his briefs the rest of the way off. Calvin pulled his legs free, then guided me to straddle him. I leaned back down to get lost in his mouth again as he slipped an already lubed finger in my ass. The teasing touch had me moaning into him and eager for more in a matter of seconds.

"Calvin," I panted, his in so many ways I wasn't brave enough to voice for fear of losing him.

He tugged at my lips one last time, then pulled his fingers free. Without prompting, I straightened up and reached back to guide his thick cock to my entrance. My breath hitched as I slowly lowered myself down, but I couldn't bring myself to look away from Calvin's captivating eyes. Their honey brown both seared my soul and grounded me. I didn't bother to fight the moan or subsequent flush that rose when I finished settling. He thrust up slightly to meet me and I loved how full I felt, loved even more that it was him that made me feel this way.

His hands glided over my thighs as he stared back at me with a reverence that made my heart flutter and heat rise in my cheeks. They continued their journey, caressing my hips and coasting up my chest to hover over my struggling heart, then settled back on my waist. We stared into each other, years of history and understanding passing in the silence.

I fought the overwhelming need to tell him how I felt, how he'd stolen my heart ten years ago with a half-smile and a shy wave. The words pushed at my chest, demanding freedom, but I held them back, determined to hang onto this perfect moment for as long as I fucking could. His fingers tightened on my hips as he searched my face like all the things I couldn't tell him were written there for him to read.

He released my side and lifted a hand to curl around my neck once more. I leaned down to meet him halfway, eyes already half-lidded in anticipation. "You're a masterpiece," he whispered just before our lips connected. I moaned into him as his fingers tightened almost possessively in my hair, then gentled. He laid back down and all I could do was get lost in his eyes as I finally started to move. For at least one night, there wasn't anyone else, no overbearing fathers, no oppressive expectations, nowhere we had to be, just us lost in each other.

Chapter 24

Benny

I glanced down the hall for probably the hundredth time and checked my sigh of disappointment. Empty. Still.

How long does it take to have a year-end meeting with your art teacher for fuck's sake?

I shoved my hands deeper into my pockets and leaned back against the wall, hiding me from view to resume my impatient waiting. Though at this rate, all the people I'd spent the last hour evading would stumble across me before Calvin deigned to emerge. True, I could have given him this surprise anytime, but after going to mass with him and our night at the flat, I wanted him to have this now, though a part of me wondered if he already knew about it.

Finally, the click of a door latch filled the expansive hallway, and I hazarded another peek. Calvin stood outside the art room; large sketchbook tucked under his arm as he bid goodbye to Professor Jankowski.

I wonder if he'll ever show me the art he doesn't share with the rest of the world.

Not that I hadn't seen his work before. His landscapes were so surreal they looked like they belonged in a fantasy world, but it didn't take a genius to know Calvin had plenty of art that never reached the eyes of others. The door latched closed, and he turned to make his way down the hall toward where I'd been waiting. I ducked back out of view and listened to his footfalls as he approached. When he was close enough, I reached out and yanked him down the smaller hallway.

He let out a squawk of indignation and barely caught the sketchpad before it could crash to the ground. I cupped the side of his face and pressed our lips together to prevent the tide of expletives undoubtedly coming my way. There was little doubt in my mind that a goofy grin stretched across my face as I released him to take in his perturbed expression. Fuck if this man didn't tick every box I had.

"Are you fucking insane?" he hissed, hiking his sketchpad higher under his arm while his gaze darted around for witnesses I already knew weren't there. Truthfully, yeah, I was probably a little insane, being crazy about Calvin made me reckless and the more time I spent with him, the less I cared.

"I wanted to show you something."

"And it couldn't wait 'til light's out? What the fuck is so important you need to risk exposing us?" Despite his angry tone, at the mention of 'us' my heart did little flip-flops I'd given up trying to ignore. At the end of the day Calvin wasn't upset about getting caught. He was upset that *if* we got caught, then we'd have to stop… and he clearly wasn't ready to do that. "Why are you smiling like a goddamn idiot?" he snapped.

"I have a surprise for you."

He straightened up as light chased away the darkness that had been clouding his features. "A surprise?" His eyes narrowed again. "I swear to fucking god, Benjamin Price, if you scared the shit out of me so you can show me your dick, I'm going on strike."

I smothered a laugh, because sound carried and *that* would definitely lead someone to where we were standing far too close for people who supposedly hated each other. Damn, Calvin was cute when he was angry. I brushed the curls away from his face, enjoying their silky caress as I tucked the rogue strands behind his ear. "I promise I didn't ambush you to show you my dick."

The spark in his eyes dimmed a little, and I almost laughed anyway at his sullen disappointment. "Then what is it?" he asked, a tad more irritably. Part of me still worried that despite what he said this really was still about sex for him while I'd already jumped in with both feet, but the dates he kept going on and our night in town gave me hope that I'd win him over, eventually.

"Follow me." I did a quick double-check to make sure no one else had walked up while I'd been distracted, then ventured down the side hall, making my way back toward the main atrium and offices there. Behind me Calvin muttered to himself about unnecessary secrecy and a certain someone being obtuse and why should he follow me, anyway. That he continued to bitch to himself as we traversed little used hallways in this part of the school further solidified my belief that he didn't know where I was taking him.

Finally, we pulled up in front of a heavy door with a patch of bleached wall beside it where a plaque had once been mounted. He squinted at the bare spot and the intricate detailing on the otherwise nondescript oak door and frowned. "Where the fuck are we?"

My suspicions confirmed, I produced an old iron key and unlocked the door. "Why don't you come inside and find out?"

He narrowed his eyes at me, then boldly strode past into the long-forgotten room beyond. I'd done my best to clean the place up, but there was only so much I could do without arousing suspicion and it was a far cry from its former glory.

"Benny."

At his gasp, I looked up from gently closing the heavy door. Wonder dominated his face and his lips parted in wordless awe as he took in the small space. His gaze danced from the dusty pews and large cross dominating the table at the far end to the elaborate stained glass set in the far wall. The afternoon sun peered through the painstakingly cleaned surface to create a riot of color that stretched from the floor to halfway up the wall.

"What do you think?" I asked, pushing my hands in my pockets once more, suddenly anxious that he wouldn't like it.

He spun around to face me, his brown eyes wide while his mouth opened and closed without emitting a single syllable. In all the time I'd known Calvin, I'd never thought it possible to actually make him speechless. He ripped his gaze away from me to stare at the room again. "I don't understand. How did I not know this was here? How did *you* know it was?"

I shrugged and leaned against the wall next to the door. "When the school decided to avoid any religious entanglements in the seventies, they removed the placard and shut the chapel up tight. I had to memorize blueprints of the school for those ridiculous tours. That's how I found it."

Calvin gently set his satchel and sketchpad on one of the still very dusty pews and looked back at me. "And the key?"

I smirked. "I'm a Price not a saint. No one will miss it." I held it out and his hand shook as he reached for it.

"Why are you giving it to me?" Confusion swirled in the honeyed depths of his eyes as his fingers wrapped around the iron and he took a step closer.

"I thought you might like a place where you could worship in private without anyone finding you or having to go all the way into town."

He licked his lips and swallowed hard. Fear trickled through my happiness. Had I overstepped? He'd pointed out before that I wasn't religious. Was this a weird thing to do? Suddenly he stepped forward, key still in hand, and mashed his mouth against mine. My hands reflexively went to his sides to keep us both steady and pull him closer.

Calvin

Every ounce of feeling currently overwhelming me poured through me into Benny. His hands wrapped around my waist and I pressed my entire body into him, desperately seeking an outlet for all the emotion bubbling inside. Fuck if anyone outside of my family had ever done anything so sweet or thoughtful for me before. And damn this sensitive asshole for making me feel like this.

My fingers tightened around the relic of a key, grounding me as I panted for breath. It still wasn't enough. Even kissing Benny senseless didn't come close to scratching the surface. I wanted—no, *needed*—to make love to him until neither one of us could move for hours. My fingers tightened even more to the point I feared I might actually snap the ancient iron as the word I'd been avoiding with blind determination finally forced its way to the surface.

Fuck me, I'm in love with Benny.

Damn you Andy and damn you too Benny.

I pushed away from him enough to pocket the key before I could break it or, heaven forbid, lose it. A quick glance at Benny showed him looking at me with those soft green eyes the color of algae on a crystal spring, undiluted and pure. *Fuck*. I licked my lips and debated returning to kissing him within an inch of his life. Come to think of it, that sounded like a splendid plan and an even better way to keep avoiding what I didn't want to admit. Feelings always ruined everything. Life was better, less complicated, when they weren't involved.

"I take it you like it," Benny said with a smirk.

I leaned forward to taste his lips again and steal a kiss he didn't deny me. "You could say that." His hands dipped beneath my shirt to caress the bare skin beneath as I kissed him deeper. I moaned into him and pulled away. "I'm not having sex with you in here. I may be depraved, but even I have limits and sex in a place of worship—even a neglected one—is a hard limit."

Benny's brows scrunched together. "I didn't bring you here so you would have sex with me and I have never once thought of you as depraved."

My heart fluttered alarmingly, and I took a half step back. "Why did you?"

His face relaxed, and he offered me a sad smile. "Like I said, I thought you would appreciate it and could find peace here."

Goddamn it, Benny.

My eyes stung, and I took another step back, officially taking me beyond his reach. He remained leaning against the wall, silently watching me freak the fuck out. What was he thinking? Was he judging me? Did he think I was nuts? Why couldn't I keep my shit together? I took a shaky breath that did absolutely nothing to quiet my pounding heart or steady my nerves. I seriously sucked at emotions. "Fuck."

"What's the matter? I'm sorry if this wasn't okay. I didn't mean to upset you."

I shook my head as the stinging behind my eyes intensified. "Stop."

"Cal." My heart lurched painfully at the concern in his voice.

"Don't call me that." I couldn't take this. My breath came in quick bursts as I fought to get myself back under control.

"I don't understand. If you don't like me calling you that, why didn't you say something sooner? I would have stopped."

I shook my head again, though if it would have been possible to squeeze my heart, that might have helped more, because that wasn't it at all. I loved it when Benny called me Cal, absolutely fucking loved it. It was intimate and made me feel special, treasured. "Stop," I gasped out. "Just stop it."

"Stop what?" Benny asked, sounding more confused by the second. And, oh God, I hated that, I hated making him feel unsure, because fuck it all, I was in love with the fucker.

"Being nice to me. I can't... I can't..." I struggled to keep air in my lungs long enough to finish the thought, but how could I? I couldn't be in love with Benny. I just couldn't. Being in love brought heartache and pain. Happily ever after wasn't real and even if it was, guys like me didn't get them. Not because I was gay, but because I was *me*. And here he was making me believe it was possible, making me want it, stupid hearts and all.

He straightened up against the wall, and a wave of hurt crashed over his face. “Well, fuck.” Those two words might as well have been a dagger being plunged straight into my heart for how much pain they caused.

“No. It’s not… I…” I scrambled to find some way to explain that didn’t involve the truth, but as Benny pushed off the wall and turned toward the door, I ran out of options. “Wait!” He looked back at me and frowned. “Wait,” I repeated calmer, then pinched the bridge of my nose. “Shit. Fuck. I can’t believe I’m going to do this.”

“Do what?” he asked as he resumed his position against the wall.

I dropped my hand and looked toward the ceiling in search of divine inspiration. All I found, though, were cobwebs and the knowledge that I couldn’t avoid this forever and keep Benny too. “Okay. I need to tell you something.”

“So tell me already. What’s with the big fucking production?”

I winced at the anger in his words. “You don’t understand. It’s not that easy.”

“Spit it out already.”

“Okay. Okay,” I repeated, more for myself than him, aiming for more calming breaths that did absolutely fucking nothing.

“Fuck this. Find me when you feel like sharing.” He shifted to leave again, and I surged forward to stop him.

“Okay, I’m sharing. But first you have to promise not to get mad.” He snorted and rolled his eyes. “I mean it, Benny. Promise you won’t get mad, because I need to tell you something, but I’m pretty sure you’re gonna get mad. Like next level pissed.”

“Tell me what it is already.”

“Promise first.”

“Fine, I promise. What’s the big deal?”

“I love you,” I blurted and instantly a weight lifted from my chest, only to have anxiety rush in to fill up the space when he didn’t say anything. “Did you hear me? I said I’m in love with you, asshole.” I pushed hard against his shoulder, but he remained as immovable as ever.

“I heard you.”

“And? Why aren’t you mad? You’re supposed to be mad.”

He raised an eyebrow. “Do you want me to be mad?”

That took the wind out of my sails. “Well… no. But… but why aren’t you? I feel like you should be.”

His eyes softened, and a small smile tugged at his mouth. “Because I love you too, asshole.” Five words. Five words is all it took for Benjamin Price to turn all the bones in my body to jelly. Five, because I wasn’t counting the part where he called me an asshole. Thank God I was already standing so close to him or I’d have landed on the floor when I keeled over instead of latched onto his mouth while his arms wrapped around me.

My fingers scraped across the back of his neck as I urged him deeper, delving my tongue past his lips to steal his breath as much as he was stealing mine. He tightened one arm around my waist while he threaded fingers gently through my hair. When we finally pulled apart, my lips were swollen from the fierce kiss and we were both breathing hard. “Why didn’t you say anything before?” I finally asked.

His lips quirked up in a half smile as he continued to comb through my hair. “Why do you always have to be so dramatic? If I hadn’t thought you’d run for the hills, I’d have told you weeks ago.” I opened my mouth to protest the assumption and closed it again when he raised an eyebrow in challenge.

“Fine,” I huffed. “I’m a little dramatic, but I… I don’t do emotions. Love is complicated and messy. Casual sex is so much easier.”

“Maybe, but it’s not half as rewarding.” His mouth closed back over mine in a sensuous kiss that went all the way to my toes. I melted into him, finally recognizing the way Benny touched me for what it was—love, Cupid’s arrow, little bubble hearts, big ass fucking card, love.

“I’m still not having sex with you in here.”

He chuckled softly and the warmth of it spread through my chest to continue thawing my once carefully frozen heart. “I didn’t tell you I love you, so you’d have sex with me.”

“Why did you?” I asked, tipping his nose with mine and lightly brushing his lips.

“Because I do.”

I arched into him at the admission and tangled our tongues once more. We kept both our hands in semi-respectable positions despite the evidence that both our bodies craved more than the heavy make out session. Even that toed the line of too risque for a chapel, but I figured as long as all clothes stayed on, God wouldn’t find it too grievous an offense.

Chapter 25

Calvin

I opened Benny's door, not surprised to find him pacing the dimly lit room. The curtains hung open, allowing just enough moonlight in to illuminate the obvious anxiety on his face. I sighed inwardly and slipped into the room, gently closing the door behind me. As the latch clicked back into place, Benny spun around and attempted to hide his concern with a forced smile.

"Hey," he said and seemed to rock in place, as if unsure if he should step forward or stay there.

I smirked and decided for him. "Hey yourself." I pressed my body against his, enjoying the way his muscled physique pushed back, and brushed a light kiss against his lips. When that failed to ease the tension bunching his shoulders, I dropped my head to place a kiss on the side of his neck. He shuddered as I sucked on the sensitive skin. Finding all of Benny's erogenous zones had become somewhat of a mission for me, but I refused to let his subtle moan distract me from my true purpose this evening.

"Any trouble getting here?" he asked as I tugged him toward the bed, still kissing the side of his neck.

"What do you think?"

"Right. Yeah. Stupid question."

I chuckled into his throat at how nervous he was acting. Not even the first time we'd been together had he been such an uncertain ball of anxiety, at least not as far as I could tell. Maybe he had been and I simply hadn't known him well enough yet to recognize when he was low key freaking out.

"What's so funny?" He whispered into the shadowy darkness.

I lifted my head to meet his gaze. "You. Relax. It's not like we've never had sex before."

He took a deep breath and let it out in a huff. "But this isn't like that. We haven't..."

"Switched. The word you're looking for is switched. It's still not a big deal. Think of it as simply trying out a new position. If we like it, then we add it the other things we like to do. If we don't—"

"If we don't," he interrupted, worry coloring the words.

"If we don't," I continued, catching his eye, "then we don't add to the list of wonderful sexy things we do to each other." A small laugh escaped him and some of the tension eased away. "Now kiss me already before I change my mind and leave you with your hand."

His laugh was a little stronger this time, and he did as I asked, covering my mouth with his in a slow, deep kiss that had me aching in no time. I slid my hands down his back and into his pajamas to squeeze his ass unable to help myself. Man really did have an ass made for squeezing, and pounding, and gripping. I moaned as the kiss took on new life and my desire to be buried deep inside the man I loved briefly won out. Much as I wanted to do this, there was no denying I was a natural top. It was simply the way I was built, and I doubted one night of switching would suddenly make me verse. Still, stranger things had happened, like actually wanting Benjamin Price of all people to top me in the first place.

"On the bed," I said, following my command. Benny drifted after me, his mouth greedily chasing kisses. I tugged on his bottom lip with my teeth and settled back on my elbows. He made to lean down and keep kissing me and I shook my head. "Uh uh, I want that hot, wet mouth of yours wrapped around my cock." I could feel his hungry gaze on me as it traveled down to my tented pants.

Benny rebelliously stole one more kiss, then hooked his fingers on the waistband of my lounge pants and pulled them down. My cock bobbed free and throbbed when he moaned like a starving man. He settled between my thighs, then leaned down and licked me from base to tip. My head fell back with a groan as he wrapped his lips around my length and took his sweet ass time swallowing me down. His hand joined the mix, stroking while his tongue swirled around the swollen head and darted across the slit.

I hissed and fisted my hands in the sheets. Much as I wanted to watch and give Benny exactly what he desired, if I did that, then this evening would be over far too soon and doubted I'd be able to convince Benny to try again, love or no love. I reached blindly for the lube I'd noticed on the nightstand when I'd come in while Benny took me deep again. My hips curved off the bed, seeking more of that glorious heat, and I used the opportunity to draw my knees up.

"Here," I gasped, all but flailing the bottle at him. My cock came free with a pop and he stared at the bottle as if he didn't know what he was supposed to do with it, even though he'd been the one to leave it out. "You need to prep me." I waved the bottle at him again and he accepted it with jerky movements, glaring at it. The high from his giving me head was quickly wearing off in the face of his scowl. "What are you worried about?" I panted. "We've talked about this."

"I don't want to hurt you."

"You won't. Have I ever hurt you?"

"It's not the same," he grumbled,, and I couldn't help but laugh.

"Please, Benny," I said with a smirk, "it's not like I've never played with my ass. How do you think I got so good at it?" More muttered grumbling, but at least it was accompanied by the cap flicking open this time. "How about this? Think about what you like and just do that?" I was about to give up hope when he finally squeezed some of the liquid out and rubbed it between his fingers. Then he lowered his head back to my flagging erection and expertly brought me back to life. I curled my fingers in his hair that was finally long enough to grip properly and encouraged him to keep going.

His slick fingers gently massaged my balls, and the familiar tingle wrapped around the base of my spine. My grip on his hair tightened in warning and then relaxed as he abandoned them to pursue a different prize. The tip of his finger circled my entrance and slipped inside at the same time he swallowed my cock down as deep as he could. I groaned at the dual sensation and shoved a fist in my mouth to stifle the sound. Benny grunted as I squeezed around his finger then worked the digit in and out of me with agonizing slowness. Between my efforts to stay as relaxed as possible so Benny wouldn't panic and not coming from being blown within an inch of my life, I didn't think I could last much longer. If this is what I did to Benny, point me, all the fucking points me.

I smothered a sharp cry as Benny added another finger and stroked my prostate. "Fuck, yes," I moaned as I arched into his hand. "Oh God. Fuck. Again. Do it again." He obliged, sucking on my head as his fingers massaged deep inside me. "That's it. Just like that. Fuck." My fingers tightened in the sheets and I panted through the ecstasy as my orgasm danced dangerously close. It wasn't getting any better than this. "Fuck me. Shit. Fuck. God." I couldn't even curse straight as Benny continued to fuck me with his fingers and his mouth.

By the miracle of God, he pulled off before I completely combusted. His fingers slipped free, leaving my stretched ass clenching air. I moaned in desperation of my denied release while Benny tore off his pajamas that I'd entirely forgotten about and repositioned himself. My fingers ached to bury in his hair and guide his mouth to mine, but instead I lay there gasping for breath and trying to cool down so I didn't come from an unlikely breeze of air. Maybe I should have anyway, because the second Benny's cock touched my rim, I closed up tighter than a steel drum and no amount of telling myself to breathe could get me to relax.

"Cal?" Benny's warm hands caressed my thighs. I reached out lightning fast to grab his wrists and keep him from moving while all the fear I'd worked so hard to get past warped and twisted inside of me, fear I thought I'd conquered years ago. "Cal," he tried again, even softer.

"Just… just wait," I squeezed out through strangled lungs. Talking proved to be a major mistake as a sob quickly followed.

"Calvin. Talk to me."

I shook my head violently from side to side.

"What can I do to help?"

My chest stuttered as I fought through another sob. "A minute. I need… a minute."

"We don't have to do this. Not now, not ever." Benny's quiet concern did nothing but spread guilt through my rampant anxiety.

"I know," I sobbed. "But…"

"But what, Cal? We don't have to do anything you don't want to. You know I don't need this."

Tears poured freely down my face as blubbered, "But *I* want this. It's *my* body, Benny. I should be in control of it, not the other way around."

"What do you need me to do?"

I took one shuddering breath and then another as I struggled to come up with a way to feel less powerless.

"You're in control here. We only do as much or as little as you're comfortable with," Benny reassured me.

Control, that's what I needed, to be in complete control of what was happening. Suddenly, I had an idea. "Lay on the bed." He quickly got up, and I swiveled around to take his place on my knees at the end of the bed. When he lay down, I straddled his thighs and took another steadying breath, already feeling the tension in my chest ease with the reversal. Benny reached out for me, though, and I recoiled. "Don't. Don't touch me. Hands on the bed frame above your head." Even in the dark I could tell Benny was confused, but he did as I asked without comment and the anxiety eased again.

"This better?"

"Yes. Is that okay?"

"Whatever you need, Calvin, I'm here for you." Damn if that didn't make me love him more. I'd kiss him if I wasn't positive I'd turn into a sobbing disaster too afraid to ever try this again, because clearly my trauma was still as ripe as it had ever been.

I patted the sheets until I found the lube again. My slicked fingers sought out Benny's very dead erection. I gently tugged, but it wasn't until I leaned down to place a kiss where his groin met his hip that his cock twitched with any signs of life. It took a few minutes of dedicated attention until he started plumping back up in my hands. My heart hammered as I considered what I was about to do.

"Fuck," I hissed and leaned across his statue-like form. "I need to see you." The lamp switched on, revealing Benny with both hands curled around the bed frame, the flush of arousal darkening his chest. He watched me as I took him back in hand, his lids fluttering as I tightened my slick grip and stroked hard. "Tell me how much you like it."

The groan that rolled out of him was exactly the encouragement I needed. His knuckles went white and the muscles in his arms flexed as he worked to keep his hands to himself. His head tilted back, exposing the column of his throat, as I continued to work him like I knew he liked. While his gaze was elsewhere, I reached around to see if I needed to be prepped again after my episode. Fortunately, it only took a little more stretching to get me to the point that I could accommodate Benny.

I released his cock and repositioned myself over it. I could feel Benny's eyes on me, but I didn't dare look at him for fear of losing my nerve. Instead, I devoted all of my attention to slowly lowering myself down, every centimeter of distance giving myself the same reassuring guidance as I'd given so many others over the years. Take your time. Don't forget to breathe. Relax. Go as slow as you need to. Deep breath in, now let it out. With that last one, Benny's cock breached my entrance. I repeated the list of instructions over and over until, at last, Benny was all the way inside. My last deep breath came out in a whoosh and I could have laughed for joy. I'd done it. I'd actually done it. And now that the hard part was over, I could work for the more fun bits.

My teeth sank into my bottom lip as I slowly pulled up and slid back down. It took a few unsteady tries before I found the right balance and was able to shift enough that each slide stroked my prostate. I let out a low moan and ventured a squeeze. Pleasure arced like lightning up my spine and my head fell back as I continued to fuck myself on Benny's pulsing cock. Suddenly, I realized he was shaking. I forced my attention back to him and kept rolling my hips.

His features were tight beneath the lamplight, his whole body vibrating with the effort of holding perfectly still. I tightened around him and ground down hard. The muscles in his neck bulged and his hips jerked with the urge to drive up and meet me. I leaned back and gripped his thighs for support as I rode him hard, my cock bouncing with each drive of my hips.

"Oh God," I moaned, hovering closer to a precipice I hadn't expected. "Touch me. For the love of God, Benny, please. I need you to touch me." I gasped as he wrapped one hand around my aching cock and gripped my thigh with the other. It only took a few thrusts into his tight grip for me to crash down on his cock and shatter into a million pieces. I squeezed around him as ribbons of cum spurted out of me to splatter on his chest. Benny let out a grunt, and I collapsed spent beside him.

Benny

I ran fingers lightly up and down Calvin's back as he panted for breath beside me. I'd never had a dry orgasm before and was not in a rush to repeat the experience. Calvin's slow torture of my cock to bring it back to life and then my inability to actively participate as he rode me past the point of reason had the poor thing still throbbing hard.

"Are you okay?" Calvin asked where he lay curled on his side into me.

"I should be asking you that."

He reached out and traced a finger in the cum on my chest. "I honestly didn't think I'd climax."

I gently snagged the hand on my chest and brought his finger to my lips where I sucked off the release, then kissed his palm. He moaned and curled a hand around the side of my face in order to turn me toward him for a different kiss. I rested my forehead against his and rubbed my thumb along the back of his still captive hand. "*Are* you okay?"

He let out a shaky breath and nodded. "I am now. Thank you and… I'm sorry."

"Please don't be sorry. We knew this wouldn't be easy."

He groaned and buried his face in my shoulder. "Maybe you did. You sure you're alright? Did you even come?"

"Yeah, I think so. Sort of anyway."

Calvin snorted and shifted to reach for my very obvious erection. "You think?"

"If you love me at all, please don't touch my dick. I'm so over-stimulated, I think it's more likely to fall off than do anything else."

"I'm sorry."

I pulled him closer. "I already told you not to be. I'm fine. I'll be fine. You're the one I'm worried about. Don't ever freak me out like that again. Jesus fucking Christ, I thought I'd hurt you." He winced and I curled into him in blatant disregard of my abused dick. I grunted at the unsurprising pain that radiated through me. "Hey, look at me." I tilted his chin up to see those honey eyes that had captivated me over ten years ago. "I love you."

His gaze searched mine for a moment before he snuggled closer. "I love you too." He leaned forward and brushed my lips with a tender kiss. Without a second thought, I cupped the side of his face and kissed him back, slow and gentle at first, then with gradually increasing intensity he returned with fervor.

"How long can you stay?" I asked when the kisses slowed to mere presses. I'd only spent one complete night completely wrapped up in him and could already tell I was completely addicted to it.

He smiled knowingly and leaned back to glance at the digital clock on the nightstand. "A little while longer, but not much." Instead of saying exactly how much longer he burrowed back in my embrace, and let out a sigh.

"So, is this something we're going to be adding to the list of things we do?"

He chuckled into my shoulder. “The snuggling for sure. As for the other… no. Not now at least.”

I let out the breath I’d been holding, because I really wasn’t sure if I could go through that again.

“No need to sound so fucking relieved,” he teased, smacking me on the chest and getting his own drying cum all over his hand.

I snickered. “Serves you right for trying to beat me up in my own bed.”

“Don’t know what you’re laughing about. You’re gonna clean it up.” He held his hand up in front of my face and arched a challenging eyebrow.

Per the unspoken challenge, I gently wrapped my fingers around his wrist and proceeded to lick him clean. His stifled moans were reward enough for the daring move, and my rebellious dick threatened to come back to life after finally deflating. I willed the damn thing to stand down and released his now differently wet hand. Calvin leaned forward and stole a kiss that made me hate he had to leave.

A short while later, we were both properly cleaned up and dressed once more in pjs. He stopped a short way from the door and turned to offer a small wave that I returned. I watched him ghost soundlessly down the hall until he disappeared, then closed my door with a sigh, already looking forward to when I’d get to see him again.

Prince Einar watched as King Kelani stood at the balcony and surveyed his vast kingdom beyond. It was unprecedented for the King to remain in the Summer Palace during the Solstice. Yet here he was. With Einar.

With the rest of the court away, Einar didn’t hesitate to step up beside the young king. Their alliance was still tenuous, but he had hope that it would persevere. He placed a hand upon the king’s lower back in a familiar gesture that had gotten countless before him exiled, or worse. But the King had no sharp words for him, only a smile that rivalled the rising sun.

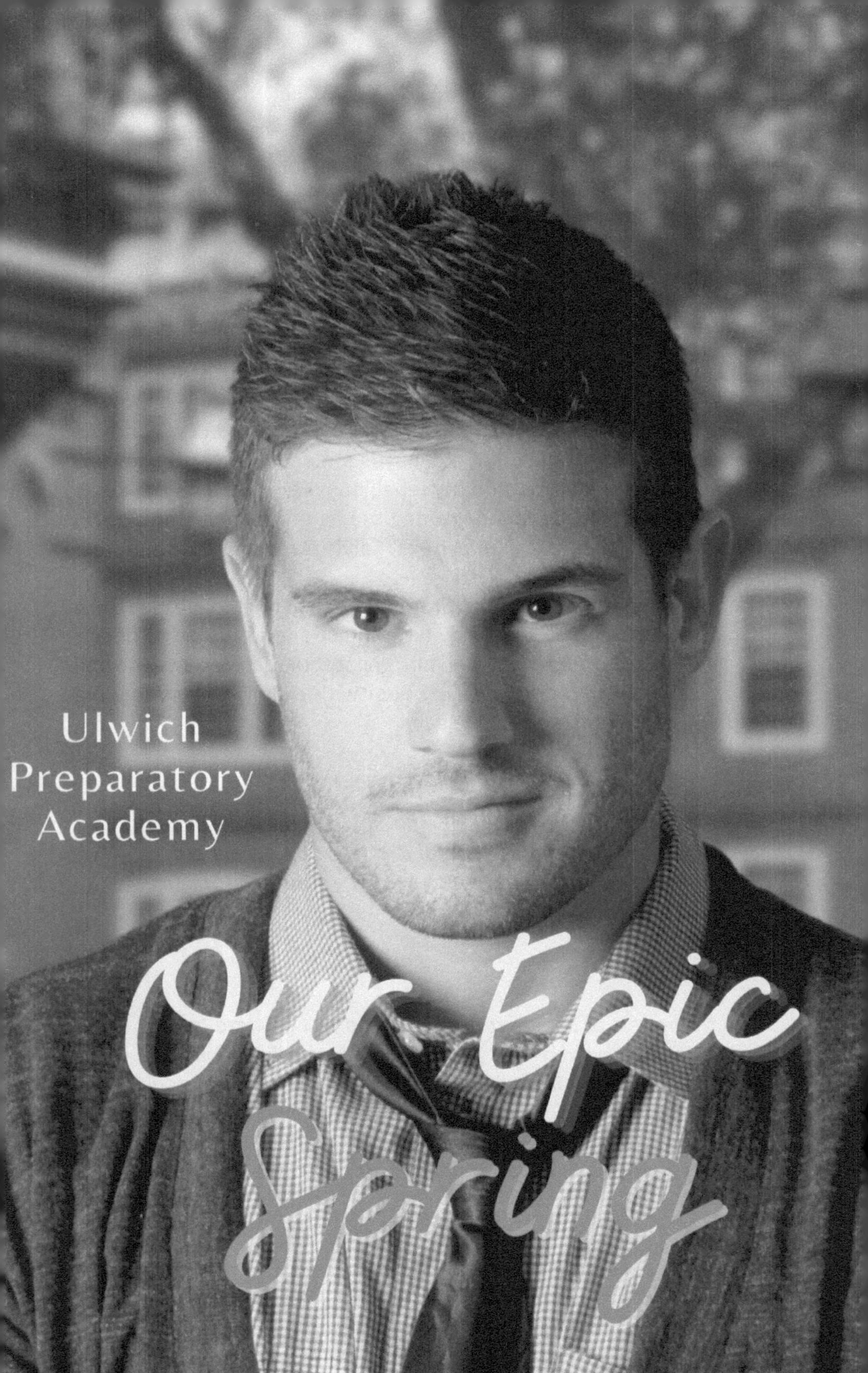
Ulwich
Preparatory
Academy
Our Epic
Spring

Contents

Chapter 1

Andy

I tightened my coat against the cold and pushed into the warmth of the main hall. Behind me, countless students milled around in the courtyard as their drivers unloaded their luggage. The shouts of greeting and laughter disappeared when the great doors shut behind me. My nose tingled as heat suffused the frozen tip. I wiped at the phantom drip that thawing always brought and looked around at the handful of students clustered inside.

No one spared me more than a passing glance before returning to their conversations with friends they hadn't seen in almost three weeks. I didn't pay them any mind. There was only one pair of eyes I was interested in, and they weren't here.

Stop it. Even if Mitch was here, he wouldn't be waiting for you. Get a grip.

Sadly, all my attempts to "get a grip" over winter break hadn't been very successful. I still dreamed about him every night, still looked forward to seeing him any chance I could, to hearing his laugh. I'd even scrolled through some old pictures of the two of us while at home. That was one mercy, at least, of not being able to have a cell phone on campus—I couldn't indulge the nostalgia.

Heat crawled up my neck as I thought about how much... attention I'd devoted to those old photos. I tightened my grip tightened on the handle of my rolling suitcase and launched forward. Once I was safely in my room, I let out a relieved sigh as I unwound my obscenely long scarf—thank you, Calvin—and shrugged out of my coat.

I dusted off the remnants of snow from the gray wool and then from my hair before it could melt. The luggage made a muffled thud as it landed on the bed and I flashed to Mitch hovering over me, holding me close while he—

"There you are, you sneaky little scamp."

The memory blasted apart. I looked up to find Calvin perched in the doorway. "Hey," I said, grateful my voice didn't crack. "Didn't see you at drop off."

He sauntered into the room. "That's because I didn't *get* dropped off."

I paused mid-unpacking to stare at him in disbelief. "You didn't go home for the holidays?"

"Nope." He shoved my suitcase aside and plopped on the bed.

"But... but you always go home for the holidays. You fucking *love* Christmas, not to mention any excuse to leave this hellscape."

He shrugged and feigned a sudden interest in his cuticles.

I gave an exasperated cry, then stomped over to the door and slammed it shut. Unpacking could wait and with any luck, my dorm mate, Lucien, wouldn't return until later. "Alright, spill. What on earth could have possessed you to stay?" I sucked in a breath as a horrible possibility occurred to me. "Did something happen to your mom?" I'd be a little surprised if something had and I hadn't heard about it, given she was the senator of Hawaii.

Calvin clucked his tongue and rolled his eyes. "Always so dire, Gallagher. I *chose* to stay."

"You did not."

"Oh, I definitely did, and it was *so* worth it." He let out a happy sigh and flopped back to lay stretched out on the bed, missing the open suitcase by a fraction of an inch.

"You still haven't told me why."

He rolled his head to face me, the goofiest smile plastered across his light brown face. "Benny."

"Are you fucking serious? You gave up the holidays with your family to fool around with... Benjamin Price?" I asked, remembering to lower my voice at the last second. Shut doors could only muffle so much and those fuckers didn't lock. Benjamin Price IV was money, prestige, and all the arrogance that went with it. Granted, nearly all the students at Ulwich Prep came from a similar background, but Benny was, well, *Benny*. He'd been our personal tormentor, along with his two goons, Todd and Neil, for almost as long as I'd been at Ulwich.

Calvin propped up on his elbows. "Not *just* to fool around, though we did a fair bit of that," he added, his cheerful smile turning wicked. "Turns out, he never goes home for Winter Break if he can help it. Family drama and all that." He waved a dismissive hand, though I suspected there was a lot more to it than that.

I crossed my arms over my chest. "Still waiting for a why."

"Ugh, would you let me tell the story? So impatient." He sat back up and spared me a playful glare. "Like I was saying, Benny didn't go home for the holidays and I didn't want him to have to spend them alone."

"Uh-huh."

In an uncharacteristic moment of visible nerves, Calvin averted his gaze and chewed on his bottom lip.

I straightened up and let my arms fall. "What? What is it?"

That goofy smile he'd been sporting earlier twitched at the corners of his mouth as he looked up at me. "I told him I love him."

I held my breath, not sure how I should react. While I personally didn't agree with Calvin's fascination with Benny, that didn't give me license to be an asshole.

"And he said it back." Calvin barked out a laugh and covered his mouth with his hands as he disintegrated into giggles.

All the air I'd been holding surged out of my lungs like I'd been punched in the gut. Here I was trying desperately to figure out some way to stay Mitch's friend and not lose myself, and Calvin was living my dream. The guy he loved loved him back. Something I would never have, because the guy I loved was straight and I... wasn't.

"Oh my God, you have to see this." Calvin started rummaging through his pockets. I took advantage of his distraction to wipe the devastation from my face. Finally, he pulled out something that looked like a necklace. "We got each other Christmas gifts."

"He got you jewelry?" I asked as I squinted at the smooth wooden beads.

"It's not jewelry, it's a rosary. To replace the one I left at home."

I wasn't sure what was more shocking, that Benny had gotten Calvin a rosary or that Calvin had one to begin with. "And you got him a gift as well," I said slowly, struggling to keep up with what had been going on with my friend while I'd been distracted by my own woes.

"Well, *made* not bought." He shrugged and carefully tucked the rosary away. "But he seemed pretty pleased with it, so I'm not stressing." He leaned back on his arms again, his smile seemingly now a permanent part of him. "What about you? How were holidays with the folks?"

"Um, holidays were... fine." I flashed to the endless dreams of Mitch's hands on my body and quickly shook them off. "Shannon was a total pain in the ass per usual, but as she keeps reminding me, that's a sister's job. Mom and Dad were their usual festive selves. Nothing of note," I bold faced lied. I wasn't ready to come clean to Calvin yet about how he'd been right–I couldn't *just* be friends with Mitch.

Calvin's smile settled into a suspicious frown. "Uh-huh. Did you come out?"

I gritted my teeth. He asked me that after every break and my answer remained the same as it had for the last five years. "No."

"No need to get defensive." He held up his hands in mock surrender. "You're acting cagey is all. What about James? Where was your hot stuff, big brother, during these mind-numbingly boring celebrations?"

I rolled my eyes. While I was most definitely not Calvin's type, my brother, however, was. Course, it didn't hurt that he towered over me by a good seven inches. "Meathead shipped out for a tour in Sudan at the end of November."

"No fucking way. He actually enlisted? I know you said he'd talked about it, but I honestly never thought he'd go through with it. When the fuck did he manage that?"

"Apparently, sometime last year, and never bothered to tell anyone. Fucker's already gone through boot camp and been deployed and everything." I scowled at the frayed corner of the comforter. Once again, I was the last to know anything in my family. Suppose it came from being the youngest, but that didn't make it suck any less.

Mitch

I barreled down the corridor just shy of a full sprint. Thanks to the team congregating at the drop off circle like leopards waiting to pounce, I had to go the long way around and hadn't been able to meet Andy like I'd wanted. I'd harbored a small hope that he'd be waiting for me—would be as eager to see me as I was to see him—but he was smarter than that. Knowing him, he was already unpacking in his room. And since everyone *else* was still camped on the school's front lawn to catch up with friends as they arrived, this was the perfect time for us to connect without prying eyes.

I chewed my lip as I ate up the seemingly endless miles of hallway separating us. Reconciling with Andy dominated every thought, and after the incredible night we'd shared last semester, I finally felt like I had a real shot. The soft way he'd moaned my name had inspired hope and truth be told countless nights of hard-ons.

A smile cracked my cheeks as I finally spied his door. The sandstone-colored plaster actually looked bright for once, instead of its usual oppressive dark. And while I seriously doubted it, even the wooden wainscoting seemed to shine as if freshly polished. I willed my pounding heart to calm the fuck down and did what little I could to school my grin. I wrapped my fingers around the cool bronze of the handle and took a fortifying breath.

This was it. After four and a half years, I was finally going to tell Andy the truth.

I twisted the knob and pushed the door open before I could lose my nerve. And stopped dead. Every happy thought that had propelled me here, every ounce of optimism that I could actually mend what I'd broken, died a horrible death in point-two seconds.

Andy stood beside his bed, snowflakes still clinging to the ends of his auburn hair, though he'd already removed his winter coat. He turned to face me in slow motion, confusion and anxiety stamped plain as day across his freckled face. I shifted my focus from his stricken expression to Calvin Bridges, who lay propped on his elbows. On Andy's bed. Where he was smiling. Well, not anymore. His happy expression had dimmed to one of curiosity when I burst into the room. And he hadn't moved from where he was comfortably sprawled out. On Andy's bed. The bed where we'd... Where Andy had...

This was a mistake.

"Mitch." Andy's voice snapped me out of the trance I'd fallen, and I blinked for what felt like the first time in days. "What are you doing here?"

Fuck my life. All the progress I thought we'd made last semester, gone in an instant. "I... uh..." I floundered, tearing my gaze away from Calvin's knowing smirk. I longed to look at Andy, to have him deny my worst fear, but couldn't bring myself to meet his furrowed gaze. Had he lied to me about him and Calvin? What was it he'd said? *Calvin's a friend*. But I was Andy's friend too, and some of the things we'd done had definitely been more than friendly.

I swallowed down the urge to spew the breakfast I'd been too excited to finish. Acid rolled around in my stomach as Calvin joined the faceless shadows of Andy's prior hookups that haunted my nightmares.

"Mitch, are you okay?" Andy asked, taking a step toward me. I reflexively took a step back to maintain the distance between us and involuntarily looked over at Calvin again.

"Sorry, I should have knocked. I didn't realize you'd have company." I risked a glance at Andy and found his green eyes clouded with confusion. He darted a look at Calvin and I fought the urge to do the same. "I'll... I'll just go. Leave you two to... it."

For the love of God, stop talking and fucking leave already!

Knowing I should leave as fast as humanly possible and actually doing it, however, apparently wasn't going to happen. I continued to stand there, my feet glued to the ground, and my mind blanking out in a desperate attempt to avoid thinking about Andy and Calvin *together* and failing fucking miserably.

"You know what? I actually have some errands to run." Calvin hopped off of Andy's bed like he was fucking popcorn. "You boys catch up. I'm sure you have *a lot* to talk about," he said with a sickeningly sweet smile as he patted Andy's cheek.

The death glare Andy gave him could have burned a hole in the wall, but Calvin sauntered toward the door and coincidentally me, whole and hale. Of course, Andy would be mad. I'd ruined their afternoon by showing up completely unannounced and uninvited. And now the person he actually wanted here was leaving.

Calvin paused in front of me, and I dutifully stepped aside. "Don't have too much fun without me," he crooned and blew Andy a kiss over his shoulder. Andy rolled his eyes and his normally plush lips twisted into a scowl. Calvin offered me a wink and waltzed out of the room, leaving me all alone with an obviously irritated Andy.

"Look, I'm sorry. I shouldn't have come in here like that. Definitely should have at least knocked. I'd hoped to catch you out front, but it's a fucking disaster out there and snowing and—"

"Did you need to talk to me about something?" Andy snapped, cutting through my babbling.

I thought briefly about why I'd come here, about what I'd thought about almost non-stop since Andy had moaned my name. Then I thought about his absolutely stricken expression moments ago when I'd showed up out of the blue.

"Mitch?" The concern in his voice tugged at the part of me that only he seemed able to reach. "Are you alright?" He took a half-step toward me and I danced a full one back.

"Y-yeah. I'm good," I lied, rubbing the back of my neck. A quick look at his narrowed eyes said he wasn't buying it.

"So, what's up? How were your holidays?" Small talk. Andy was doing small talk and I could have fucking died.

"Good. Yours?"

He shrugged and moved to unzip his luggage. "Same old same."

"Suppose that's good," I replied, like I had any idea what that entailed these days. "My mom is good," I offered, unsolicited.

"Mine too," he responded by rote and I sent up a silent prayer for a meteor or *something* so this awkward ass conversation could end. He pulled out a small stack of clothes and I spied the dark jeans he'd worn the day we'd gone to the bookstore in town together.

Fuck, his ass had looked good in those. I shook my head to clear the traitorous thought.

"*Was* there something specific you wanted to talk about?"

I dared to meet his gaze and got snared in his emerald eyes, like I always did. My tongue might as well have been wool for all the good it did me. His copper brows arced gracefully on his forehead while I struggled to get enough moisture back in my mouth to speak. "I... uh... I was hoping we could maybe keep studying together?" I stammered out at last.

He tilted his head to the side and seemed to consider me. "Study?"

"I mean, I know the tough subjects are over and I'll have to deal with like a shit ton of practice and you're probably also really busy, but it's been nice having grades I can be proud of for a change that I actually earned and–" *Shut. The. Fuck. Up.* My mouth snapped closed, and I pressed my lips together to keep it that way.

"Sure..." Andy dragged out, his gaze distant. Abruptly, he refocused on me, and I felt like an ant beneath a magnifying glass. "We can continue studying."

"Really?" I asked, not entirely positive he meant it or if I had some masochistic tendencies I wasn't aware of.

He hiked a slim shoulder. "Yeah, why not? I'm assuming you'd still like to avoid having to take an athletic scholarship, right?"

A tightness in my chest eased. Andy actually wanted to help. That was awesome, though how I was going to deal with this new wrinkle of Calvin and Andy being friends with benefits without turning into an absolute caveman was beyond me.

I'll figure it out. I still have to fix this. Before it's truly too late.

Slightly encouraged, I nodded. "Yeah. Yeah, that would be great. I'll... uh... see you around." I spun on my heel to beat a hasty retreat that fingers crossed wouldn't look like fleeing the scene before my tongue could start wagging again.

"Hey, Mitch," Andy called after me.

I fought to keep my flinch from showing and turned to look at him. "Yeah?"

"Don't mind Calvin. He's just really excited about this guy he's seeing. Apparently, they had a very... *eventful* holiday."

"Oh–okay," I stammered to cover my surprise.

So, Andy and Calvin aren't *seeing each other like that. And we're still friends. He said so himself.*

Andy shrugged like it was no big deal. "Anyway, I'll see you around."

"Yeah," I said, my lips twitching in an almost smile as an ember of hope reignited.

Chapter 2

Mitch

John continued to heckle my roommate, Nate, about his latest crush on the girl that worked at the ice cream parlor in town. While I didn't agree with John's assessment that she was way out of his, John was right about one thing: you missed a hundred percent of the chances you didn't take. If Nate wanted *any* shot with her, he'd actually have to make a move. But despite the Nate's loud bravado, everyone at the table knew he wouldn't do shit.

"Alright, alright," I interjected. "Let the poor man breathe. He might be Lucy's type."

"Short and boring with a micropenis?" John deadpanned.

Nate let out an indignant squawk and lunged across the table to throttle John while the rest of the usual lunch crowd devolved into jeers and snickers.

"I'll show you a micropenis," Nate snarled as he grabbed for John's blazer.

"Oh no! He's threatening me with his tiny dick. Someone please save me!"

I rolled my eyes at John's exaggerated pleas for help. The table continued to get rowdier with each passing second, and I couldn't even say it was new. The lacrosse team was *always* like this. You could put the whole lot of them together and still not get the maturity of an average toddler. I looked down at a sharp jab in my ribs.

"What about you, super star? No way you're still pining over Trixie," Brian taunted, his white smile bright in his dark face.

I checked an eye roll and settled for a scowl. "I broke up with her. Remember? No pinning here."

He waved away my answer and sadly did *not* drop it. "Please, I've seen the way you look at her and Ronald." I tensed at the accusation. Whatever Brian thought he was seeing, I could assure him that wasn't it. "Pretty sure she'd take you back if you showed any interest."

This time, I did roll my eyes. *That* sure as fuck wasn't going to happen. "She seems happy with Ronald," I sidestepped rather than lay into the millions of reasons I had absolutely no interest in renewing a relationship with my ex. And it was true. She really did seem happy. The two were always smiling and laughing when they were together. If anything, I was jealous of that.

"Okay, but there's gotta be someone. At least for the Championship."

It took every ounce of willpower I had not to react. I knew exactly what he was talking about—and it was exactly why I wanted out of this fucked up crowd. All any of them cared about was winning, and that included participating in that ridiculous ritual of getting laid before a big game for luck. Truth be told, that's why I'd hooked up with Trixie in the first place; a decision I immediately regretted.

I chanced a glance at Brian to find him wiggling his black caterpillar eyebrows at me and huffed with frustration. He may have been my best friend on the team, but he didn't give two shits about my actual happiness, only that I didn't fuck up our best chance yet of bringing home that trophy.

"Sure, whatever," I said without feeling. I gazed out at the cafeteria, which was gradually thinning out as other students finished their breakfast and left. When I spied a familiar mess of bright red hair, the anxiety Brian had dumped on me melted away and my shoulders relaxed. We'd been back at school for two whole weeks, and while it seemed I'd lost some—check that, most—of the ground I'd made before Winter Break, at least Andy was talking to me.

Andy threw his head back and let out a rich laugh that filled the room while Calvin continued to gesture wildly beside him. Once upon a time, I'd been the one to make Andy laugh like that, and if I had my way, I would again.

"Dude, are you even paying attention?" Brian shoved me and I nearly fell off the table.

"The fuck, man?" I scowled down at him.

"You got a side chick we don't know about or what?"

Fuck, why does it always have to be like this?

"You're worse than my fucking mother. I don't have some secret chick." I gritted my teeth together to keep the rest of everything brewing inside of me from spewing, and sought out Andy once more. Maybe he'd be up for studying later. I was really liking this whole decent grades I actually fucking earned thing.

I found them both much closer to the main entrance. The ten foot tall, double doors were swung wide to allow the mass of students to flow in and out. He and Calvin chatted animatedly as they wove through the early morning bustle. A small grin tugged at my mouth, an echo of the one brightening Andy's face. He shook his head at something Calvin said, but when he looked up, his smile slipped.

I followed his gaze to find the source of the shift. Sure enough, marching into the cafeteria was none other than Benjamin Wallace Price IV followed by his usual cronies. His gaze zeroed in on the pair now standing stock still, as if waiting for a penalty toss. Benny brushed the hair back from his forehead as a menacing smile twisted his lips. Some of the guys had joked that the reason he'd started growing his hair out was to impress a girl, others believed it was to piss off his dad, a few had even dared to say it made him look nicer and like a Grade A douche. Whatever his reasons were, there was nothing *nice* about Benny.

I vaulted off the table, barely catching Brian's snide remark about "morning entertainment" and moved to intercept their beeline for Andy and Calvin. Unfortunately, I got held up by a flood of second years that didn't know how to get the fuck out of the way. I was still pushing my way through the wave of pimply preteens when the trio reached their goal.

"If it isn't the Queer Brigade," Benny sneered while Todd and Neil snickered behind him. "You two off to braid each other's hair?"

Calvin folded his arms over his chest, clearly unconcerned about the obstacle, while Andy's face morphed into a put upon expression. "Jealous, Price?" Calvin clapped back.

"Of having your filthy faggot fingers near me? As if." Benny's lip curled with disgust and Calvin's perfectly shaped eyebrows climbed up his forehead.

"Damn, Benny, sounds like someone needs to work off some steam. What's the matter, no one touch that pecker for a while?" Calvin cocked a hip and threw a crooked smile that I could only describe as sinister. "I'm sure your *boys* would be more than happy to help you out."

"The fuck you say?" Todd snarled and took a step forward, his hands already balled into fists. Benny threw out an arm. Todd glared from Calvin to Benny, but stopped his advance.

"You think you're cute with your dick jokes and blatant disregard for the rules around here, but you won't always have mommy's title protecting you and we both know the only reason you're in this school at all is because it's the only thing your shitty ass dad wanted from you and you couldn't even do that right."

Calvin bristled, and Andy shot him a worried look. I didn't know much about Calvin, but even I could tell that was way out of line. Dead silence descended on the remaining students as the two faced off. I stole the opportunity to escape the horde of second years. I'd just cleared the last row separating us when Calvin tilted his head to the side, his face creepily calm.

"I don't need protecting. I can handle myself and I can handle *you*. And you're one to talk. Big daddy's money has bought you everything, including your dignity. Tell me, *Price*, will you still be under Daddy's little thumb when you leave this place or will you finally grow a fucking pair and live your own fucking life?"

"Listen here, you fucking flamer, you and your sidekick twink need to remember your fucking place," Benny snapped, his normally tan features turning an angry shade of purple.

"Please. We both know I'll always be on top," Calvin said with a sinister smirk at the same time Andy shouted "I'm not a twink!" his face turning a blotchy red that made his freckles burn.

"That's enough," I said, stepping between them.

Five pairs of eyes swiveled to focus on me. In less time than it took to do a pick and roll Calvin's eyebrows rose in obvious surprise, Todd and Neil looked at each other, Benny's jaw clenched tight enough to make a muscle in his cheek twitch, and Andy stared at me in open confusion.

"You wanna run that by me again, Hudson?" Benny asked, his voice dangerously low.

"They're not bothering anyone. Just leave them alone."

"I think that's our cue," Calvin whispered behind me. He tugged a still frozen Andy around me, darted a quick glance at Benny, then slipped out, probably to their usual spot by the crumbling stone wall in the courtyard.

Benny glanced over his shoulder at Todd and Neil. "I'll catch up with you two bozos later." They shared another look and scurried out the way they'd come, thankfully away from Andy and Calvin. When he turned back to me, his better-than-you attitude was back in full force. "You've got some fucking nerve coming at me, Hudson."

"Fuck you, Price. You know Andy is off limits."

He snorted. "You think I give a shit about that ridiculous edict you made years ago? Which you've done shit all to enforce, by the way." His words hit me square in the chest. I'd stayed away because it was the price I had to pay to keep Andy safe, or that's what I'd told myself for four years. The truth was much darker and riddled with guilt. I clung to the tiny ember of hope that I could make things right with Andy, earn his forgiveness, and squared my shoulders.

"I've done more than you'll ever know. But standing up to you now for your homophobic bullshit is something I've wanted to do for years." I stepped closer, invading his personal bubble, and refused to blink as I stared him down. "So, yeah, Andy is off fucking limits. Unless you wanna see how the rest of this plays out?"

Benny bared his teeth and his eyes looked like they were trying to laser through me. "You think because you're Coach's golden boy, you can do whatever you want. But I've got news for you, Hudson. In here, you may be a legacy, but out there, you're fucking no one. One day your shine will fade and you'll be just another average schmuck like the rest of them."

"And you're any better?"

"You don't have a fucking clue." Benny shook his head and laughed to himself. "If I were you, I'd be more worried about myself. You're so adamant about protecting Gallagher? What do you think will come of making a scene like this? Be careful you don't give the team any more reasons to hate him than they already do." His gaze flicked toward the table where I'd been sitting before and where a good chunk of the team was staring in slack-jawed shock.

My heart sank to dissolve in the bubbling acid of my stomach. I'd been so hellbent on getting Benny to stop harassing Andy that I'd violated the number one rule to keep him safe. I'd just made a public scene... in front of the team. My feet felt like they were in cement shoes as I watched the team pass questioning looks between each other. And in the middle of them all, Brian looking pissed enough to spit nails.

I forced my heavy feet to move back toward the table while I floundered for some way to blow this all off. There had to be some way to get the target I'd painted off Andy's back. Problem was, all the ways I could think of meant giving him up. Again. And I just couldn't do that.

Chapter 3

Andy

The frayed edge of a paperback caught my attention as I stuffed the last of my notes into my satchel. It was the last of the books I'd bought when Mitch had gotten me to play hookie last semester. Everything about that afternoon had been perfect, the way he'd left a note in my desk, his laughter, the way his smile seemed to brighten the afternoon, that fucking shirt that clung to every muscle on his torso...

I shook my head and tried to push all thoughts of what Mitch looked liked in that shirt, or out of it for that matter, from my mind. My jaw tightened as the wayward thought stubbornly brought memories of what said torso had felt like beneath my fingers as I explored every defined inch of him. I fought to keep a growl of frustration to myself. The whole point of letting Mitch top me—again—had been to get him *out* of my system. Instead, it seemed to have exactly the opposite effect. He dominated every waking and definitely every sleeping minute of my day.

"That's it, I'm done waiting. What the hell is going on with you?"

I glanced up at Calvin towering over me with both hands on his hips and an absolutely-no-nonsense scowl on his face. Rather than deal with the blatant attitude, I devoted my focus to convincing the buckle of my satchel to close.

"Don't play that shit with me. I've waited weeks—*weeks*—Gallagher for you to tell me what's going on with you and Mitch. And I am done with that shit, you hear me? Now, what happened last term? And what the actual fuck was that scene in the cafeteria about?"

"I don't know what you're talking about." I swung the strap over my shoulder, but the familiar weight of too many books didn't bring its usual comfort. There was no way Calvin was going to let this go, *especially* after that stunt Mitch had pulled with Benny the other day. Truth be told, I wasn't anymore enlightened about that than Calvin.

"Like hell you don't. Time's up, freckles. I want the dirt."

"There's no dirt." I stepped around him and reached for the door only to have his hand prevent it from opening.

"Nope. You're not going anywhere until I get answers. I've been more patient than a mother fucking priest. As it is, I'm expecting my sainthood any day now. I already know you two are sleeping together, so you can quit playing coy."

I groaned and massaged the bridge of my nose. "We're not sleeping together."

"Like fuck you're not."

"Do we have to do this here? Now?"

"Yes, and yes. Why else do you think I suggested this dusty fucking room for free period?" Calvin asked, crossing his arms over his chest, his lips twisting to the side.

"Because it's raining?" Sleeting more like, but that was beside the point. I should have seen this coming when he chose a place we were all but guaranteed not to be disturbed. His eyebrows rose, and he kicked out a hip as he waited me out. With a sigh of resignation that I swear started in my toes, I let my satchel slip free to slouch with a heavy thud on the ground. "Fine. What do you want to know?"

He made a strangled sound in his throat and his eyes bulged wide as he threw out his arms. "Everything, obviously. When did it start? *How* did it start? Why the fuck have you waited so long to tell me?"

I resisted the urge to roll my eyes and pinch the bridge of my nose. He was one to talk, I'd still be in the dark about him and Benny—which I still couldn't wrap my head around—if he hadn't had a crisis of emotion last term. Instead of being a dick about it, I made my way over to the dust-covered teacher's desk, wiped a small patch clear, and sat on the edge. "First of all, I didn't tell you sooner, because I figured you'd freak out."

"Freak out?" he interrupted. "Who's freaking out?"

I frowned at him and his mouth snapped shut. "Like I was saying, I knew you'd make it into some big deal and it's not. It was a thing that happened. That's all. It doesn't change anything."

Calvin snorted. "*First of all*, you and Mitch boinking *is* a big deal. And second, it changes everything. Thirdly, third? Whatever. How many times did this 'thing' happen?"

"Twice. More depending on how you define 'thing'," I said, my cheeks burning from the memories the admission brought.

"Holy shit. What *have* you been up to, Gallagher?"

"Ugh, do we really have to do this?"

"You bet your skinny ass we do," he said as he plopped down in a desk facing me without bothering to clean it first.

"I don't have a skinny ass," I argued.

"Matter of perspective. Now quit stalling and spill. And don't skimp on the details."

I took a deep breath. Despite his adamant demand, I had zero intention of giving Calvin any additional fodder to torture me with than absolutely necessary to escape this room. "I suppose you could say it started after I started tutoring him. We—"

"Liar," Calvin interrupted. "It started before that." I glared at him. "Don't even. You *never* want to tutor anyone, even though professors and students have been asking for years. The only way you would have agreed to help Mitch is if something happened. Try again."

"I really hate you."

"You really don't. Out with it."

"Fine. I found him in the Tower before then. He was really upset and kept talking about quitting the team and expectations and a whole bunch of other things. Before we could get into trouble, I dragged him off to the secret room and somehow we ended up making out," I blurted in a rush. By the time I finished, my chest was heaving like I'd been forced to run a mile.

Calvin blinked at me and remained silent for all of a second, then snapper out of whatever stupor he'd fallen. "Are you fucking serious?! You've been fooling around that long and I'm just *now* learning about this?"

"Would you lower your voice?" I darted an anxious glance at the closed door of the haunted room. "And we haven't been fooling around the whole time. The next time something happened was when he got a good grade in Lit. He wanted to celebrate, so we did a prank."

"I knew you two were behind that!"

"Shut up."

"Hey, I'll have you know Benny tried to pin that shit on me."

"Considering you're now pinning Benny, I'm not sure what you're complaining about," I countered.

A smug grin stretched across his face, and he settled back in his seat. "Proceed, good sir. You did the prank, then what?"

"We went back to the secret room and..." I trailed off, wishing more than anything I could beam out of this room or teleport or *something* to avoid having to finish this sentence.

"And..."

I groaned and covered my face with my hands. "And Mitch gave me head," I mumbled.

"Sorry, didn't quite catch that. Come again."

"And Mitch gave me head," I repeated, dropping my hands to find him sporting a smirk. "Goddamn you. You just wanted to make me say it again."

He shrugged, unconcerned with the rebuke. "And... how was it?"

"Considering he made me coach him through it? Really fucking great."

Calvin let out a whoop and I darted another frantic look at the door. "So it was *his* idea? Way to go, Gallagher."

"Seriously, would you keep your voice down?"

He waved a dismissive hand. "Then what?"

"Jesus fucking Christ," I hissed. At this rate, I'd end up cursing more than Calvin ever did. "Abbreviated version: when he got an A-plus on his physics midterm, I blew him. After the fight in the hall, I topped him in the old shack. And he topped me over the long weekend in October. There, that's all of it. Satisfied?"

Calvin held up a finger and paused, his mouth opening and closing twice without any sound emerging. "I think... I... Can we back up to the part where *you* topped Mitchum Hudson?"

"It's not a big deal," I said through clenched teeth.

"Okay, yeah, it's not. No judgment. If the man wants to bottom, the man wants to bottom. Where I'm stuck is the *you* topping part. You're a bottom, Andy."

"I didn't bottom with Connor," I argued.

"Doesn't change the fact that you're a bottom. Sure, people can't always tell, but you've got bratty bottom energy leaking out your fucking ears."

"That's not a thing."

Calvin's face turned serious. "Tell me I'm wrong."

"You're..." I trailed off. The words sat on the tip of my tongue, but I couldn't force them past my lips. The brat part was debatable, but he wasn't wrong about the other. "I hate you."

Instead of arguing the legitimacy of my hatred, he slumped back in his seat and brushed his nearly black curls back with both hands. "Shit, Andy. That's... a lot."

Understatement of the fucking year.

"So what's going on with the two of you now?" he asked. "Have you hooked up again?"

"No," I said a little too quickly.

He narrowed his eyes. "But you want to. And if I'm reading Mitch's *interesting* behavior right, he does too."

"What does it matter?"

"Uh, it matters because you're clearly not. If you're both into it, I fail to see the problem. Consenting adults and all that."

"It's not that easy," I said, propping my elbows on my thighs and once again dropping my head into my hands.

"How so?"

"Because this is a game to him. He's straight, Calvin. Nothing I do is going to change that. This whole mess is a recipe for disaster. I mean, look at what's happened already. He stood up to Benny on our behalf, and—"

"Yours," Calvin corrected.

"What?" I said, momentarily abandoning my misery and lifting my head.

"None of that was for my benefit. And that fight last semester was about you."

I shook my head, not buying it. "The team—"

"The team was pissed he was blowing off practice to spend time with you."

"We were studying. He wants to improve his grades so he doesn't have to take an athletic scholarship." I clapped a hand over my mouth the second the words leapt free.

"That's news."

"Shit," I hissed. "I wasn't supposed to say anything. Please don't tell anyone."

Calvin gave me a scandalized look. "Since when have I ever told a secret?"

"Right, of course, sorry. I know that, I just, I'm so twisted up over this whole thing. You're right, I don't want to stop spending time with him and the sex is *really* good, but this isn't sustainable. There's no scenario where any of this works out."

"So what?" He held up his hands defensively when I scowled at his flippant attitude. "Hear me out. So what if this is a game? Games have rules and are supposed to be fun. Have *fun*, Andy. Carpe diem. You only live once, might as well make the most of the ride and at least you'll get some incredible fucking out of it."

"Calvin."

"Sorry, I meant incredible fucking memories." He gave me a wry smile that belied his correction, and my frown deepened. "Don't be like that. You had a pretty relaxed relationship with Connor. This isn't all that different."

"Except it's not a relationship." And it would never *be* a relationship. My heart gave a twinge of pain that I studiously ignored as Calvin continued to make his case.

"Fewer strings then. Have your fun and when you're done, walk away." He shrugged and pushed up from the desk.

I envied how easy he made it sound, like there was anyway I could play with fire and *not* get burned. Was that how it had happened with Benny? They'd just been messing around and it turned into... more? But that wouldn't happen with Mitch; there would be no *more*. He had lacrosse, and I had... books. We didn't make sense. Truth be told, I wasn't even sure how we'd become such close friends to begin with.

"You coming?"

"Huh? Yeah." I shook off my funk, retrieved my satchel, then headed for the door again.

"Hey." Calvin's hand on my arm brought me up short, and I turned to look at him. "At least consider it. You deserve to have fun, Andy. If he's willing and eager, then the only one stopping you is you. Besides," he added with a broad grin as he released me, "what's the worst that could happen?"

Oh, I don't know. I fall completely in love with Mitch all over again only to have my heart and all my dreams shredded into a million pieces when he inevitably walks away?

Instead of telling him the truth about my concerns, I said, "I'll consider it."

He nodded, practically oozing self-satisfaction, and pulled the door open. I trailed behind him into the hall that was mercifully devoid of eavesdroppers and wished yet again that I'd told Calvin the full story five years ago.

Chapter 4

Andy

I glanced around the library with its endless towers of books and massive vaulted ceiling. New terms usually meant a sudden influx of students clogging up the aisles and monopolizing the tables. It would eventually thin out like it always did, but not today, and the steady hum of low voices filled the massive room.

Even though I *knew* everyone was focused on their own assignments, I couldn't shake the feeling that they were all staring at me. Well, not me specifically, more like my six-foot shadow. More than anything, I wanted to escape the curious looks and disappear into the secluded alcove where Calvin and I normally spent our time when we were in the library. But no way was I about to take Mitch anywhere that might be construed as private. Prying eyes or no.

"Come on, the history section is this way," I said, veering left.

"It's not exactly my first time in the library." Mitch snorted and bumped my shoulder, making me bristle with anxiety. Had anyone seen? Did they think something was going on? Fuck me. Was anyone from the lacrosse team in here?

I stuffed my rash of nerves down and focused on why we were here—to help Mitch prepare for his World War II assignment. It wasn't until we were surrounded by rows and rows of books that I finally started to relax.

"You okay?" Mitch asked as I ran my fingers along the spines to further ground myself.

Rather than answer his concern, I dropped my hand. "We should divide and conquer. You take these shelves and I'll check the ones at the other end. We can meet in the middle and compare what we've found."

Mitch grimaced and rubbed the back of his neck. I diligently did not stare at how the move highlighted his defined biceps or tightened his shirt across his chest. “Um, I thought I said, but finding resources is kind of what I’m struggling with.”

“You did say. But you’re not alone.” I forced myself to meet his hazel eyes and the small smile shining in them. As predicted, my traitorous heart gave a happy little flutter. I slapped it back into the cage where it belonged and put on my most professional smile. “Besides, how can I help you get better at finding appropriate resources if I don’t know what I’m working with?”

The hopeful light in his eyes dimmed. “Yeah. I guess.”

Guilt clawed at my insides. It wasn’t Mitch’s fault that I was struggling with boundaries. I squeezed his upper arm. “Just give it your best.”

“Okay. I can do that.” He took a big breath like he was facing down a firing squad and turned to the shelves.

I debated lingering and pointing him in the right direction, but ultimately, my point stood. This was the first time we were preemptively tackling a project together, and I needed to know what I was working with before I could fix it. I left Mitch to his muttering and moved to the opposite end of the row. Ideally, I would have been on a separate row altogether searching for material, but I had a suspicion that if I wasn’t there to keep an eye on him, Mitch would start panicking.

I’d pulled only one book and was reaching for another when someone else pulled it out the other side of the shelf. No sooner did I realize I could see straight through to the next row than a familiar pair of blue eyes blocked it from view.

“Well, well, well. Fancy meeting you hear,” Connor purred.

“It’s the library. A lot of people are here.” It was both a statement and a warning.

He glanced to his side, then returned his focus to me, wearing a smug grin. “So I can see.”

Engaging would be a mistake, but I’d also learned the hard way that ignoring him wouldn’t work either. “What do you want, Connor?” I asked, already exasperated with the whole interaction.

“Seeing as how we’re in a library and all, I figured some studying might be in order. No sense in… studying on our own when we don’t have to.” He smirked at his sad double entendre and wiggled his eyebrows. At least no one who might overhear could possibly know that “studying” was our code for hooking up.

I fought the urge to rub my forehead. "I'm running out of ways to tell you no. What's it going to take for you to get it?"

"You could always try shaking things up and say yes for a change."

I shifted further down the aisle, hoping that he'd let it drop if we were closer to people who might question his persistence. Unfortunately, he simply tracked me on the other side, replacing the book and removing another to keep me in sight.

"Maybe you're running out of ways to say no, because you don't actually *want* to say no," he pressed.

"That's definitely not it," I grumbled under my breath.

He pushed his hand through the stacks, and I nearly jumped out of my skin when he touched my hip. Thankfully, it was on the opposite side of where Mitch was standing. "Just admit it already. You miss us. I know I do."

I nearly bit my tongue off to stop myself from correcting him. He didn't miss *us*. If we were really honest with each other, there'd never really been an "us". We were simply two guys who'd found a way to pass the time in this hellhole. I took a steadying breath and forced my voice to be calm. "You're lonely. It has nothing to do with missing… whatever we were."

Hurt flashed in his normally exuberant eyes. "You're really gonna say that to me? What, do two years mean fucking nothing to you?"

"That's not… I didn't mean… Look, we had something, okay?" I amended guiltily.

Just like that, his smug smile was back in full force. I rankled at the realization that I'd just been played. Yet another reason we didn't work. "See, that wasn't so hard. And we can have something again. You just have to give it a chance. Starting by taking that stick out of your ass. Better yet, I got a stick for you."

I flashed to Mitch, holding me tight as he systematically took me apart one thrust at a time. My resulting flush at the wayward memory burned past my collar. I reflexively ducked my head and angled my body to make sure Mitch couldn't see. Sadly, the same could not be said for Connor.

"Someone likes the sound of that. I know it didn't go so well the first time, but I promise I could make it good for you," he entreated softly. His attempt at topping me hadn't just gone poorly, it had been an unrivaled disaster that resulted in me having an acute panic attack.

I did not need this today. Or any day, for that matter. "For the last time, we're not…" I glanced at where Mitch was steadily working his way closer and dropped my voice. "We're not *studying* together." To my chagrin,

Connor clocked where I'd looked and I could already see the gears turning. "Connor, please. We ran our course, okay?" I added in an attempt to divert him from any hasty conclusions.

Too late. "Have you moved on? Is that what it is?" He pulled his shoulders back, anger radiating off of him, as he stared intensely at me from the other side of the shelf.

"Would you lower your damn voice?" I hissed.

"I'll lower my voice when you stop lying to me. What's the real reason? All I've heard is a lot of empty bullshit."

I slid back down the line of books to put more distance between myself and the ever-encroaching Mitch. "This is really not the place for this. But fine, have it your way. Not that it's any of your fucking business, but I have *not* 'moved on'. Where the fuck would I even move on to? This whole place is filled to the rafters with self-righteous bigots. Most of which can *hear* you," I emphasized.

To my relief, he glanced to his side where the shelves ended and several students had just commandeered a table. But I could still see the tension as he clenched his jaw and his nostrils flared while he tried to control his anger. Finally, he turned his fierce gaze back to me. "This conversation isn't over."

I sagged with relief as he stomped off, not even bothering to replace that latest book he'd removed. Fuck. How was this my life? The breakup had been mutual. Or at least I'd thought it had been. But given how persistent Connor was being about getting back together, maybe I was mistaken.

"What was that about?" Mitch asked right beside me.

I smothered my startled shout, turning it into a weird garbled squeal. "Jesus fucking Christ, Mitch. Why do you *always* have to sneak up on me?" I glared up at him, barely noting the stack of books he'd acquired.

"Wasn't aware I was sneaking, seeing as how we were *supposed* to meet up in the middle." He frowned, probably because I wasn't anywhere near the middle by this point.

I released a heavy sigh and worked to get my attitude closer to something resembling detached professional. "Right, sorry. Let's see what you've found."

He gave me a wary look, but surrendered the books. "So, really, what was that about? If Connor's giving you shit..." I fought the urge to roll my eyes at his blatantly threatening tone.

"He wasn't giving me shit. And even if he was, I can fight my own battles." I scanned the spines of the four books he'd found, then started flipping through them. He actually hadn't done half bad.

"If he wasn't messing with you, what did he want?"

"He wanted to study together." I picked up the lone book I'd secured and compared it to what he'd found. I could feel his eyes on me, but refused to let on that the conversation with Connor had been anything more.

"I thought you said you didn't tutor."

"I don't," I replied absently. Finally, I set aside one of his books and replaced it with the one I had. "You have a really great start here. It might even be all you need for your project." I held up the one I'd discarded. "Only reason I'm not including this one is because you have another that's almost identical and it's better."

Mitch

I really wanted to focus on the positive that I'd actually found passable books for my history assignment, but I couldn't get Andy's comment about Connor out of my head. If Andy hadn't tutored Connor before, then why did Connor make it sound like he had? And why had he gotten so mad when Andy told him to take a hike? It didn't make sense and the whole thing left a sour taste in my mouth.

"Are you listening?"

Apparently not. I shook my head and looked at Andy. "Sorry, what were you saying?"

"I think we should meet up again after you've had a chance to get some notes down."

"But—"

He held up a hand. "You'll be fine. If you get stuck, you know where to find me. In the meantime, I need to meet with Garza."

I frowned. "You didn't say anything earlier about a meeting with your mentor."

"I forgot." Andy might have sounded calm to anyone else, but I could clearly hear his irritation. Was it me? Had I done something to upset him? Maybe I was pushing too hard for him to help. I mean, yeah, I totally needed it, but if he was hating spending time with me... My heart shriveled in on itself.

"Um, yeah. I'll figure it out."

"You've got this." He gave me what I was sure was meant to be a reassuring smile, grabbed the book he'd dismissed, and walked past me. I turned in time to see him replace the book in the spot where I'd found it, then leave without a backward glance.

I clutched the books to my chest as I struggled with a sudden ringing in my ears. This wasn't at all the way I'd seen the afternoon going. We were supposed to sit shoulder to shoulder, laughing while we took notes. And I couldn't get past the suspicion that the meeting with Garza was really an excuse to get away from me.

With heavy steps and a gut full of disappointment, I trudged my way to the nearest table. The cluster of second-years looked up as I sat. They were quiet for a second, then fell into excited whispers. I tuned them out and took out a pen and some paper.

Not even thirty minutes later, I admitted defeat. Maybe the books were useful, maybe they weren't. I wouldn't know because I hadn't been able to read a single damn paragraph. My mind was busy going in circles with what to do about Andy. How was I supposed to fix what I'd broken if he insisted on keeping me at a distance? And something was *definitely* up with fucking Connor. Jesus, wasn't it bad enough that he went out of his way to irritate the shit out of me, now Andy too?

Resigned that I wouldn't be accomplishing shit without Andy there to keep me on track, I packed up my things and took the books to the checkout desk. Once everything was stamped and put in my satchel, I exited the library.

I adjusted the strap on my shoulder for the millionth time as I stepped into the wide hallway. I had no clue how Andy walked around with so many books all the time. This shit was heavy.

"Look at you with all your books," Connor sneered from behind me.

I slowed, but didn't turn around. "Fuck off, Connor." What had he been talking to Andy about? I'd never seen Connor study. Ever.

"Yeah, I don't think I will." He tugged on the strap of my bag, threatening to send the heavy load crashing to the ground. Several students walking by slowed to see what the commotion was about.

Be cool. Connor being a dick is nothing new. Reminder in hand, I turned to confront him. "What do you want?"

"From you?" He barked a cynical laugh. "Nothing."

"Right then, see you on the field." I spun on my heel, but didn't manage to get anywhere before he called out again.

"I am curious about one thing."

"And what would that be?" I asked, facing him again. A smarter man would have kept walking. Except no one had ever accused me of being smart. I was pretty sure Andy was the only one who believed I even *had* brain cells.

"What's up with you and Andy?"

Fear clawed into my husk of a heart. Did he know something? Had he seen something? I'd been careful… except for all the times I wasn't. Sneaking into Andy's room to have sex and almost getting busted by Benny came to mind. "Nothing."

He swiped at his nose with his thumb, his blue eyes icy and cruel. "Didn't look like nothing."

"For fuck's sake, Connor. He's tutoring me. Don't believe me? Ask Garza. Or Cohen. We're studying, that's it."

His eyes widened, and I finally recognized the edge in his eyes for what it really was—rage. "You've been studying together?" he said, his voice going oddly high.

"That's what I said. It's not a big deal. We studied together last term too. He's doing me a solid." I didn't know what Connor's beef was, but he was really starting to freak me out. I shifted my grip on the satchel, ready to drop it if I had to.

"Last term." Unexpectedly, he dropped his head, causing his sandy hair to fall forward and sway as he shook his head with a menacing chuckle. His eyes were almost feverish when he looked back up at me. "Tell me, *Mitch*. Are you enjoying the *perks* of studying with Andy? The late nights, the secret meetings." His gaze flicked over me from head to toe and I fought the urge to recoil from the unbridled hate shining in them. "Bet he really rides that ass. He's got a real knack for it."

"I don't know what the hell you're talking about." We'd never had secret study sessions. Then something about the way he said it struck a nerve, and all the pieces fell into place like some evil puzzle. Suddenly, the faceless guys Andy had been with weren't faceless anymore. I didn't remember dropping my bag or even pulling back. But I'd never forget the look on Connor's face when my fist smashed into it.

He stumbled back, hands going to his bleeding and definitely broken nose. "What the fuck!"

I advanced on him, and he snarled. Fucker had *touched* Andy, and he was going to pay for it. I was almost on him when hands grabbed my arms and pulled me back. "Let me go! Asshole has it coming!"

"Fuck you, Hudson!" Connor shouted past the wall of teammates that had shown up out of nowhere and who were currently dragging me away.

"What's your deal?" John asked, echoed by Niel.

"I don't give a shit what his deal is," Brian snapped. "Get him out of here. And you," he rounded on Connor. "Get your ass to the infirmary before I let him finish it."

"He started it! I didn't do shit!"

"Get, Hendricks! We all know you've got a mouth on you. And not a fucking word about this or you'll learn what it really means to ride the bench."

I glowered at Connor as he clenched his fists. Finally, he flipped us the bird and crawled off to get his face looked at. Fingers crossed his face would stay fucked.

Chapter 5

Mitch

John threw me into the locker room after half the team practically carried me out of the school. "Fuck!" I shouted, slamming my palm on the metal.

"No shit. What the fuck is your problem, Hudson?" Brian asked as he stood in front of me, his brown face twisted into an angry glower.

"You shouldn't have interfered. Asshole had it coming." I pointed an accusatory finger at him. While he hadn't been the one actually holding me back, he was the team captain and the only reason Connor wasn't fucking pulp right now.

Kyle scoffed. "No one is disputing that." John fist bumped him and the two chuckled.

"Enough!" Brian's deep voice cut through the escalating jeers. "What I wanna know is what the hell you were thinking."

I glowered at him, not missing the fact that my so-called teammates were also cutting me off from the only exit. One thing was for certain, I'd die before I told them the real reason why I sucker-punched Connor. An image of Andy on his knees for the jerk flashed unbidden through my mind.

Brian held up his hands. "Actually, I don't wanna fucking know. We all know Hendricks has a chip on his shoulder. If you don't know how to ignore him by now, that's on you, but I'll be damned if I stand around and let you take pot shots at teammates."

"Are you for real? Let's not pretend that he's ever been anything more than an alternate and the only way he's getting my starting position is if I'm dead." Truthfully, I might have wished before that the coach *would* replace me with the second string. But not Connor. Not now.

"I'm getting real sick of your attitude, Hudson. Would have thought you learned your lesson last term," Brian said and murmurs of agreement came from the rest of the team.

"Almost a shame that ginger freak wasn't involved." Kyle rubbed his jaw. "I still owe that shit stain."

I had to fight back the urge to go after Kyle the way I'd gone after Connor. If all these assholes would just leave me be, leave Andy be, then there wouldn't be any problems. But the last thing they needed was more ammunition against Andy, especially Kyle. I wouldn't put it past the meathead not to ambush him out of the blue.

"Stow it," Brian snapped. "Look, I get Hendricks was probably mouthing off like he always does. Maybe he hit a nerve, maybe he talked shit about your mama, *maybe* I don't give a damn. Whatever beef you two have, it ends now. Next time you decide to lose your temper in the middle of the school where every first year and their teddy bear can see you, it's your problem."

I stopped my furious pacing and looked at him. "What are you talking about?"

"Really? I know you're not the brightest crayon in the box, but even you can't be that stupid," Brian sneered. "Outbursts like that have consequences."

"Then just boot me from the team already." The others might have seen it as an empty challenge, but from the considering expression on Brian's face, I almost believed it might actually happen. And wouldn't that be a fucking relief? No more games, no more pretending. I'd finally be free. Well, free-ish.

"This is about more than the team!" Brian's shout filled the locker room and created an odd metallic echo.

I frowned. "What?"

"That's fucking assault, Hudson. You know, the kind of shit you go to jail for? That's criminal record shit. You're not a minor anymore. Grow the fuck up."

I chewed on the inside of my cheek as his words soaked in. There was a chance he really was trying to keep me out of trouble. I mean, we *were* supposed to be friends. But then again, he, Kyle, and John hadn't been so worried about facing time when they were beating the shit out of me in the hall last term. Biggest difference between that and what I'd done, aside from being out-numbered, was that they hadn't had any witnesses.

"Well, what do you have to say for yourself?" Brian pushed. The rest of the team stared intently, waiting for my response.

Finally, I threw up my hands. "Fine. I'll back off of Hendricks. But you need to make sure he stays out of my way or next time he'll have more than a busted face."

"That's more like it." Brian smirked. "Don't worry about Hendricks, we're already taking care of it."

I took an involuntary step back at his ominous undercurrent.

"Jesus, Hudson. I meant someone is going to talk to him. Make sure he knows what's up and doesn't talk about what happened to anyone he shouldn't. Last thing we need is one of the professors who actually 'cares' sticking their nose where it doesn't belong." I didn't really think Brian's air quotes were called for, but then the teachers caring had never been a foundation of this damnable school.

"What about the other students that saw us?" I asked warily.

"Pft, those shit-for-brains aren't going to say nothing," Kyle interjected before Brian could respond.

Brian turned on him. "Seriously, dude. What's with you and shit? Learn some better insults." He shook his head and faced me again. "He has a point, though. Younger or not, everyone knows to keep their mouth shut. And even if someone is dumb enough to say something, so long as neither you nor Hendricks give it any credence, they'll have no choice but to drop it." He stepped toward me and I stubbornly ignored every instinct to back away. He clasped my shoulder, squeezing hard. "Don't worry, your spot on the team is safe."

Dread and despair swirled uncomfortably in my chest. If I'd thought they'd ridden me hard last term, it was going to be a cakewalk compared to the grind they were going to put through now. I swallowed and prayed that Brian wouldn't read the reaction as fear. When he finally released me, there wasn't a doubt in my mind that there were bruises on my shoulder. He glanced around, taking in the portion of the team that had followed us out to the locker rooms.

"Since so many of us are here, we might as well run drills."

There was a collective groan, but no one protested—at least not where Brian could hear.

Andy

That could have gone better. I tossed my satchel onto my desk chair and sat on the bed. Haring out on Mitch probably wasn't the smart move, and with my luck, he'd just track me down. Given what had happened the last time we'd been alone in my room, that sounded like the worst of bad ideas. Solution? I just wouldn't be here for him to find.

It was still pretty early in the evening, but I grabbed my shower caddy, my plaid pajamas, and headed to the showers. Maybe the steam would help clear my head. Thirty minutes later, I felt squeaky clean, if not exactly relaxed. I needed to do something about Mitch. But what?

I was absently drying my hair and tumbling the conundrum over in my head as I made my way back to my room when someone shouted. I pulled up short and looked around, not sure where the call had come from thanks to the way sound carried in the hallways.

"Andy!"

I spun around, surprised to find Calvin running up to me. His dark curls bounced around his light brown face until he came to a panting stop in front of me. "Uh… You okay?" I asked, at a loss.

"Me? What are you doing?"

"Going back to my room. What does it look like I'm doing?"

He shook his head and straightened to his full six feet. "I would have figured you'd be at the infirmary by now."

Cold washed over me. "Wh-what? Why?"

"Because Mitch hauled off and broke Connor's fucking face, that's why."

"He did what?!" My voice carried down the hall, coming back to me again and again in a demented echo. "Why the hell would he do that?" I hissed much quieter.

"Hell if I know. I can't get a peep out of anyone. So either no one actually knows why or they're too scared to talk."

"Shit. Here, can you take this back to my room?" I asked, shoving my things into Calvin's arms without waiting for a reply.

"Sure thing, Andy," he muttered dryly.

"Thanks," I called over my shoulder as I hurried to the infirmary. I stopped to catch my breath just outside and glimpsed someone already talking to Connor, who was lying in one of the two beds. I peered closer.

Whatever was being said, Connor didn't like it, judging by his increasingly sour expression, or what I could see of it beneath the bandage on his face.

Finally, the guy talking to him stepped back, and I realized almost too late that it was one of the lacrosse players. I quickly ducked out of sight and flattened myself against the wall for good measure. It was probably only a few seconds, but it felt like forever until I heard footsteps walking past and the door closing. I snuck a cautious peek to verify the coast was clear before straightening.

Connor was glowering at his lap when I quietly stepped into the room, conscious of the window behind me. The same one I'd seen his teammate through.

"You look like shit," I said, reaching for the blinds.

He looked up, his glower turning into a wide grin, and immediately winced, reaching tentatively for his nose. "Two visitors already. At this rate, I'm going to start thinking people actually like me. Ooh, *and* you're wearing my favorite pajamas." He might not be able to smile without hurting himself, but his leer was doing just fine.

"What was all that about?" I asked as I finished closing the blinds and moved to occupy a free chair beside the bed.

"What was what about?"

I glanced back at the door, just in case the guy from earlier had returned, but no one was there. "Alright, don't tell me. What about your face? Care to tell me what happened there?"

"I ran into a door," he replied without missing a beat.

"Seriously?" I sat back and gave him an incredulous look. "That's how you want to play this?"

He looked away, plucking absently at the blanket over him. "Don't know what you mean."

"For fuck's sake, I know it was Mitch. The whole school probably knows by now. What I don't know is why."

His expression darkened, but he still wouldn't meet my gaze. "You know how boys like to gossip. It's nothing."

"Your face says otherwise." I leaned forward again, resting my forearms on the bed, and softened my tone. "Please tell me. I ran over here as soon as I heard. I could have found out sooner, but I'd gone to the showers."

He finally lifted his gaze and a small smile tilted his lips as he reached to brush my hair back. "Explains why it's wet." Then he shifted his focus to look me in the eye. "Did you really run over here?"

I huffed a laugh. "Yeah, I kinda did. So, you going to tell me or not?"

His face fell again. "You really want to know, talk to Hudson. I didn't exactly do this to myself."

"I just might. But it'd be nice to have a heads up for what I'd be walking into."

He dropped his head back and let out an annoyed sigh. "Damn, Andy, and here I thought you actually gave a shit."

"Don't be like that. I do. I just also have a strong sense of self preservation. Unlike someone else," I added in an attempt to lighten the mood.

He rolled his head to look at me. "I know people call you a lot of nasty shit, and I hate that, I really do, but no one actually knows you're queer. Your secret is safe."

That wasn't exactly what I meant, but it was still good to know. "That mean you're not going to tell me what you said to him?"

"Why do you assume it was me? Golden boy has been on my case for years."

I leveled a stern look at him.

"Fine. I was maybe mad about how you brushed me off earlier and was mouthing off. Nothing new there." I was sorely tempted to press for more details, but given how pink his face was getting, he was embarrassed enough as it was.

I sighed and sat back. "Okay." We sat in silence a few moments before I finally asked what I probably should have started with. "So, how are you doing?"

He snorted, resulting in a pronounced wince. "Well, my face hurts like hell. The doc says they were able to straighten everything out, so there shouldn't be any damage to my looks." He gave me a wink. "He also said I should be healed enough by the time the season starts for real and could play. Assuming I ever get off the bench," he mumbled.

"I'm glad you're okay. And I do hope you get to play."

"Eh, I could be better." He gave me a thorough once over. "I wouldn't say no to a sympathy hand job."

I smiled right back and reached forward. His eager grin slipped when I grabbed his wrist and placed it over his groin. "Then I guess it's a good thing Mitch broke your nose and not your hands."

"That's cold. Fine, I guess I'll just have to seduce the nurse."

"Isn't she like fifty?"

"Forty, actually, but she's got *amazing* tits."

I wrinkled my nose. "Ew."

"Yeah, yeah. Not your jam. More for me." He rubbed his hands together gleefully and I finally gave into the eye roll I'd been holding off.

"You're gross. Try not to do anything *too* strenuous. If you're still in here later, I'll see what I can do about stopping by."

He batted his golden lashes at me as he crooned, "Aww, you do care."

"Try not to let it go to your head."

"Don't I always?" he asked, suggestively grabbing himself through the blanket.

I scoffed, but didn't dignify the provocative question with a reply. I pushed back and headed for the door. "See you later." I caught sight of the nurse coming to check on her patient and dipped back out of view again.

"Hellooo, nurse," Connor catcalled as I slipped into the hallway to track down Mitch.

Chapter 6

Andy

Finding Mitch was proving a hell of a lot harder than I'd anticipated. When I kept coming up empty, I assumed he was out at the practice fields, but when a good chunk of the team returned for dinner and he wasn't with them, I had to reevaluate. He wasn't in the Tower. I was fairly positive he wasn't in his room, and he wasn't in the secret room, either. There was only one place left I could think to check.

I slipped out of the school and ghosted across the lawn toward the storage shack I'd taken him to last term. I cleared the last of the overgrown trees and, sure enough, there was a muted glow pushing against the closed sheets covering the windows. With a resigned sigh, I stepped up to the door. I still wasn't sure exactly what I wanted to say to him, but I also couldn't afford to put this off. That was twice now Mitch had made a scene, and I was as clueless now as I was then as to why.

The old door squeaked as I pushed it open, on alert in case it *wasn't* Mitch inside. My caution proved to be unwarranted when I found him pacing by the dim light of the lantern Connor and I had kept out here.

"Found you," I said, closing the door behind me.

He spun around, his eyes wide with surprise. "Andy. What are you doing here?"

I stepped deeper into the shack, teasing loose the second layer of sheets to help obscure the light better from the outside. "I could ask you the same."

He rubbed the knuckles of his right hand, though he didn't seem aware that he was doing it. "I needed some space. A place to think."

"About why you broke Connor's nose?" I guessed. Judging by how red he went, I'd hit the nail dead on. I shook my head. "I can't leave you alone for five minutes without you getting into some kind of scrape. How the hell did you survive those four years without me?" I let out an ironic laugh, but it did nothing to mitigate the hurt pulsing in my chest anytime I thought about that time.

"I didn't," he replied softly. "Fuck, Andy, I don't know what's wrong with me."

"That makes two of us. What the hell were you thinking? Right in front of the library? In what universe does that seem like a good idea?" I asked, my voice gaining strength and no small amount of anger as I advanced on him.

"You can save the lecture. I already got it bad enough from the team. Stupid of me to think you actually came here as my friend. But then I've never been very bright, have I?" he clapped back with a sneer.

I smacked a nearby shelf, causing dust to fly into the air. "No. You don't get to do that. And I am your friend. Or I'm trying to be. But you don't exactly make it easy."

He scoffed and took a step toward me. "Oh, because you're so easy to get along with? A real open book."

"Fuck you. I'm not the one getting into fights left and right."

"I. Was. Provoked," he snarled.

By now we were in each other's faces, or as much as we could be, given our height difference, and just barely the right side of shouting. "That's no excuse! You can't go around hitting people just because they pissed you off!"

"Easy for you to say. Tell me, Andy, what is a good excuse, huh?"

I was officially beside myself and floundered for a calm response. "There isn't one!" I finally yelled, throwing my hands up.

"I beg to differ," he growled so low I almost didn't hear him. To my astonishment, he caught both my wrists and smashed his mouth down on mine.

My anger turned white hot, and I struggled to free myself from his grip. When that didn't work, I kissed him back violently, sinking my teeth into his bottom lip. He hissed and released my hands. I managed to get them between us before he grabbed my waist and crushed me against him. My fingers clawed into his shirt as he bit me right back. I hated how turned on I was, how even furious with him, I wanted him more than anything else.

Whatever discipline I might have had left went up in smoke when his hands dipped past my waistband and he scratched his nails over my ass. Carpe diem, then. That's what Calvin had said. If I couldn't stay away, then I might as well enjoy myself. And angry sex I could do.

Since I wasn't having any success creating distance between us, I shifted my efforts to getting his shirt off. Most of the buttons gave way without argument, though a few flew off to ping elsewhere in the room. I'd barely gotten his torso free when he shifted his grip to tear off my shirt. Then it became a free-for-all of clothing flying in every direction.

He tossed his pants aside, revealing his already leaking cock. My mouth watered in anticipation, but that wasn't what this was. I shoved his chest, and he dropped to the ground onto the makeshift pallet, already reaching for the lube on a nearby shelf. I borderline tackled him as I joined him on the rumpled sheets, creating a thin barrier between us and the cold, hard ground.

He snared my mouth again as I angled to get him underneath me. But no matter how I tried, he refused to roll over. "No. Like this," he finally growled, digging his fingers into my scalp as he pulled me down for another searing kiss.

I growled right back and gave it up as a lost cause. Fine, he wouldn't bottom, or at least not the way I needed him to, and I sure as fuck wasn't bottoming again. Neither my sanity nor my heart could take it. I yanked the lube away from him and shifted to be on my knees with his legs bracketing me. Then I blindly added lube to my hand and rocked forward so our cocks were lined up.

Mitch dropped his head back with a deep groan as I wrapped as much of my hand as I could manage around us and squeezed. My attempt at measured strokes faltered as his fingers tightened in my hair to the point of pain. He used his vice-like grip to pull my head back and expose my throat, which he sucked on so hard, I gasped.

He wrapped his free hand around mine, which had stalled out mid-stroke. I whined at how much better his large hand felt on my cock and writhed in his grasp. Abruptly, he released my hair and yanked me forward. I reflexively moved my legs to straddle his hips as he hauled me into his lap and buried my hands in his hair while I conquered his mouth. He took over stroking us with firm, sure strokes that sent pleasure zipping down my spine.

Everything became a blur as I ground against him and thrust into his hand. I didn't even register that he'd released my hip with his other hand until his finger tapped my entrance, somehow already slick, though I didn't recall seeing or hearing the lube again. There was absolutely nothing dignified about the sound I made as he circled the sensitive rim, then pressed deep inside.

I arched back, simultaneously releasing my white-knuckle hold of his hair and sinking deeper onto the probing digit. "Fuuuck," I groaned as he added another finger, creating that delicious burn I craved. Then he twisted his fingers both on our cocks and inside me, and all bets were off.

I leaned back, bracing myself on his thighs, and rocked my hips with wanton abandon. The dual sensation of fucking into his fist and onto his fingers bordered on over-stimulation. But I couldn't stop. Didn't want to. Release danced closer, starting as an intense tingling at the base of my spine and increasing until I felt saturated from head to toe with pleasure.

Mitch somehow captured my mouth, though I was too far gone to know how. Our teeth clacked together as he claimed me with another fierce kiss. He nipped at my lips, sinking his teeth in and pulling.

My entire body tightened, and I fell over the edge with a wordless cry, rocking against him to milk every last drop of mind-numbing pleasure. No sooner did I stop twitching from my explosive release, then he removed his fingers to grip my hip with bruising strength, his hand flying faster and torturing my over-sensitive cock.

"Fuck. Fuck!" He grunted as he shot his load to mix with the mess I'd made. For a few moments, the only sound was our harsh breathing as we came down from our respective highs. With each breath, reality set back in with a vengeance.

I lurched away from Mitch, furious at myself, furious at him, furious at the whole goddamn world. His eyes followed me as I snatched an undershirt off the ground to clean the cum off my chest. I didn't even know who it belonged to, and I didn't care.

"Andy?"

I ignored the plea and felt around in the gloom for the rest of my clothes. "We need to go." My fingers found the distinct fabric of trousers. I held them up. When I realized they were too long, I threw them at Mitch. He caught them right before they collided with his chest and the sticky mess there. "Get dressed."

"Andy," he said again, more forcefully.

I clenched my jaw and refused to look at him. If I did, I'd break.

"Talk to me."

My chest tightened at the soft entreaty. I couldn't do this here. I couldn't do this anywhere. What I needed was to get out of here before it was too late. Except it already was, wasn't it?

What is wrong with me? Why can't I stay away from him?

"Are you upset about something?"

The shirt crinkled in my fisted hand. Upset didn't come close. I relaxed my death grip and silently turned it right side out.

"I can't know what's wrong if you don't tell me." He got to his feet and took a step toward me. Conflicting desires threatened to split me in two. Part of me wanted him to wrap me in his arms, protect me, care for me, never let me go. Another part wanted to run away as far and fast as my legs would carry me. I settled for the middle ground.

He took another step, and I threw out a hand. "Don't." He halted, the confusion coming off of him in waves.

"Is this about what happened with Connor? Benny?" he guessed.

It wasn't about either of them, though perhaps it should have been. He had no right to approach Benny on my behalf. I didn't need anyone to fight my battles for me. As for Connor, I earnestly wanted to know what that fight had been about, but delving into why I would give a shit about what happened to Connor Hendricks would open an entirely different Pandora's Box. I wasn't even managing this one.

"No." I slipped on my nightshirt.

"But you *are* mad," he stated, pulling on the rumpled pants. My fingers faltered as the tide of hurt I worked so hard to keep down rose up sharply.

"Yes."

"You planning to tell me what it's about or just keep pushing me away?"

I rounded on him, surprised to find him fully dressed and glaring at me over his crossed arms. "You have some fucking nerve to say that to me." His arms sagged and his face fell, because of course he fucking knew what I was talking about.

"Andy—"

"No. What the hell happened, Mitch? I know we don't talk about it and I act like everything is fine, but it's not. You. Fucking. Left. Without so much as a goodbye or explanation, you walked out of my life." I begged my mouth to snap shut, for the flow of words finally giving voice to the pain I'd kept bottled up all these years to stop, but the dam was broken and no amount of wishing was going to change that. "You left me when I needed you the most. Why?"

He shook his head like he couldn't accept what I was saying. His arms fell to his sides and his mouth opened, but no explanation emerged.

"Answer me, goddamn it!"

He flinched at the shout and looked back at me. "I was scared, okay?! I was scared." Shock rippled through me at the confession, but I didn't let my sudden surge of empathy distract me.

"And I wasn't? I trusted you, Mitch. I trusted you with everything. For Christ's sake, I was in love with you." The words flew out on wings of vitriol before I could realize what they were. I snapped my mouth shut, but it was too late.

His face scrunched in pain like I'd socked him in the gut. "What? Why didn't… You never…"

"Seriously? It was hard enough telling you I was gay. I figured I'd work up to the being in love with you part." I fisted my hands in my hair and willed myself to stop talking. But it was too late. Now that the seal had cracked, everything was tumbling out, everything I should have told him then. "Yeah, I chickened out on telling you the whole truth that night. I had no idea what kind of reception I would get. Let's face it, this school has a dark reputation when it comes to dealing with anyone that doesn't perfectly fit the mold."

"Andy, I—"

"Then when you…" I trailed off and squeezed my eyes shut against the stinging.

Why does it still hurt so much? I'm supposed to be past all of this.

But I wasn't. It hurt just as much now as it did then… and it would hurt even more when he finally left for good. Which would probably be right after this epic disaster of a conversation. If that was the case, then this would likely be my last chance to get it all out. My fists tightened at my sides as I forced myself to finish.

"When you brought us to that secret room… I thought you knew. That you'd always known, and I wouldn't need to say it." I took a deep breath that was more of a gasp. "Then you were gone. Just… gone." I cast my gaze down at the ground as the well of hurt bubbled high enough to drown me. "You know, at first, I was stupid enough to think you were protecting me—protecting us," I added in a whisper. How naïve I'd been. My eyes tightened as the anger and betrayal washed through me and I snapped my gaze back to him. "I figured out the truth pretty quickly."

"It wasn't like that," he argued, taking another step toward me.

Anger burned in my chest. I focused on that to the exclusion of all else in the hope that it would keep me from crashing to the ground in a sobbing heap of hurt. "Then what was it like, Mitch? Enlighten me."

His steps halted, and he looked down at his feet where he used the toe of his shoe to push at some invisible pebble. "When you said you'd never done that before, I… I panicked. I never meant to hurt you, Andy," he said to the floor.

"But you did. You broke my heart, and you didn't even have the decency to do it to my face. What were you afraid of? That you'd lose your spot on the team if they suspected? Or that sleeping with me would turn you? Or maybe you were afraid of being guilty by association."

He finally looked up, my own pain reflected on his face. "What? No. Andy, that's not… No one in the school even knows for certain that you're gay. It's all speculation."

"Then what was it?" I snapped. "Because, newsflash, that's not how it works. That's not how any of it works!"

"I know that!" he fired back, his arms flinging out to the sides as his temper started to get the better of him. Like he had since the day I'd met him, he pulled the rage back in and stuffed it down. The reflex only made me seethe more. Just once I wanted him to be completely honest with me *and* himself.

The silence stretched between us, growing tighter with each passing second. We glared at each other across the short distance separating us, until his face softened. At last, he broke the silence. "I really need to tell you something. I should have told you then. Andy, I—"

A wail of sirens split the air and drowned his words. We both looked toward the source of the sound—the school.

"Fire alarm," I said, grateful for the intervention. "We should go." I made to move toward the door and Mitch stopped me.

"It's probably just another drill. Please, can't we just stay here? No one will miss us."

"They'll do a head count." I stepped around him and double checked to make sure we hadn't forgotten anything too damning, but all that was left was the lingering smell of sex and disappointment.

"Andy, please. Let me say this one thing."

I walked up to the back door and put my hand on the knob. "Same route as last time?" The handle twisted, but before I could open it, Mitch's fingers on my wrist pulled me up short. Against my better judgment, I looked at him.

"Wait." His eyes bored into mine, shining with a million unsaid things. Pain lanced through my chest as I wondered if they'd ever be said or if I'd ever have the strength to demand them.

I reached up with my free hand to cup the side of his face. Even that small contact sent tingles radiating up my arm. Despite our argument or the hurt still roiling inside me, I knew I couldn't give him up. I'd cling to him against all reason for as long as possible. Much as I wanted to, I couldn't hide from it anymore. I still loved Mitch and probably always would, even if he could never feel the same. Lying to myself was one thing, lying to Mitch was infinitely more difficult. So I didn't.

"We're still friends, Mitch. Albeit, really weird, fucked up friends, but still friends." Fucked up was definitely the way to put it. Whatever we were, we'd never be able to go back to being the friends we once were.

His grip loosened, and he opened his mouth, undoubtedly to tell me now that this was all over, that getting involved had been a mistake, and he wanted to take it all back. I braced myself for the worst, not sure if my broken heart would make it back to the dorm or simply lead me off into the woods to get lost in despair. Then the siren cut out.

I glanced toward the front of the shack, where the sound was no longer emanating from the school in the distance. "We better hurry." Before he could come up with some other way to hold me, I slipped outside.

Chapter 7

Mitch

It had been almost an hour and Andy still hadn't shown. While it probably wasn't the first time he'd ever skipped out on studying during free period, it *was* unusual. And the third time this week. Which didn't make a lick of sense given he'd been the one who'd suggested meeting during the allotted "study period". Except it did. I'd exhausted all the other options, including last-minute meetings with his mentor. There was only one reason left—he was avoiding me. Not that I could blame him after he'd dropped that bomb on me last week, but it sure would've been nice to actually finish talking about it. He wasn't the only one who needed to get some stuff off his chest.

I glanced at where Calvin sat a few tables over. He seemed pretty absorbed in whatever he was sketching and not the least bit bothered by having an entire table to himself, despite how packed the rest of the tables were. I stared down at my unopened notes, not entirely sure what to do with myself without Andy's guidance, then returned my gaze to Calvin and the suspiciously empty chair beside him. The one that normally would have held Andy.

Calvin flipped the page of his massive sketch book. I glimpsed two figures before he tucked it under and started scribbling on a fresh page. I was on the verge of giving up altogether when he held the pad up and gave me a hard look. It took me a second to realize he'd written something on the page in giant letters: *Did you need something?*

Okay, yeah, he knew I was staring. Busted, I scooped up my things and awkwardly moved to sit at his table. He raised an eyebrow when I sat across from him, but didn't seem surprised.

"Before you ask, no, I don't know where he is. Yes, he's still alive. And, yes, I know he finally told you the truth," he said, turning his focus to transforming the words he'd written into something else.

I swallowed thickly. None of that should have come as a surprise. Andy needed a confidante and that sure as fuck wasn't me. But it still hurt like hell. "Um, thanks. I guess I did want to know all that," I said awkwardly while I watched his pencil glide across the page.

"And yet, you're still here. At significant risk to your reputation, I might add." He flicked his gaze up briefly.

I couldn't help but glance around the study hall. He wasn't wrong. I caught a number of heads ducking back down when my scan reached them. *Fuck this place. I can't even talk to someone without winding up the gossip mill.*

"Start talking or start walking. You're killing my vibe," Calvin said without raising his head.

I quietly cleared my throat and glanced around again before leaning forward. "Is he okay?" I asked as loudly as I dared.

He snorted. "That's subjective."

"You know what I mean. Is he… is he avoiding me?" I asked in a whisper. Shame lapped at my insides, making me cold.

Calvin sighed heavily and leaned back enough to cause his dark curls to shift, but kept his attention on his sketch. "What do you want me to say, Mitch? He's hurting. He's *been* hurting for four fucking years. Damn, almost five now." He shook his head and I couldn't tell if it was sadness for his friend or irritation at me pinching his light brown face. "At least he finally told you. Been trying to get him to do that forever."

I blinked, taken aback. Was it possible Calvin had been advocating for me? I dismissed the thought. Calvin didn't give two shits about me. If he'd been trying to get Andy to confess, it was for Andy's benefit, not mine. I shrank in on myself, the weight of all my mistakes pushing me deep into the seat. Maybe if my guilt got heavier, the ground would actually swallow me whole.

"Well?"

The sharp question snapped me out of my spiral and I looked up to find him gazing at me intently, his brown eyes so fierce it looked like he might stab me with his pencil. "Well, what?"

"What are you going to do about it?"

"I don't know what you mean. What can I do? He won't even be in the same room as me, let alone talk to me."

He tsked and started gathering his things. "Way I see it, you can either keep throwing yourself a pity party or you can *make* him listen to you. You know as well as I do how obstinate he can be. Don't give him a choice."

"And how the fuck am I supposed to do that?" I snapped a little too loudly.

Calvin slid his gaze to the side, drawing my attention to the eager ears around us. "Normally, I'd say that's your problem to solve, but you're clearly hopeless and apparently, being in love has made me soft."

Wait. Calvin was in love? With who?

"*Jesus fucking Christ.* You can wipe that ridiculous look off your face. It's not Andy." He continued to mumble irritably to himself as he took his sketch pad back out and flipped to the original piece he'd been working on, then swiveled it around so I could see it better.

My jaw dropped as I took in the meticulous detail and familiar faces. "That's… that's…"

"That's exactly who you think it is, and if you'd like to keep all your teeth and any chance of repairing shit with Andy, you'll keep it to yourself."

"Is he…" I floundered. This definitely wasn't the place to be asking about anyone's sexuality, let alone Benjamin Wallace Price IV's.

"Taken? Why yes he is," Calvin filled in with a wicked grin. He knew damn well that wasn't what I was driving at, but also made it pretty clear that it was none of my fucking business. He snapped the pad closed and put it away once more.

I swallowed, heat rising in my cheeks. "That was… unexpected. I'm happy for you. Both of you."

He gave me a thoughtful look, then huffed a small laugh. "You really mean that, don't you? I always assumed that the reason you ghosted Andy was because he and I have so much… in common. But I'm starting to think I was wrong. Very wrong."

"I… I…" Fear curdled my stomach and tangled my tongue.

He held up a hand. "I'm not the one you should be telling any big secrets to. But as I'm feeling particularly magnanimous today, I've decided to help you. A little." My hope must have shown on my face, because Calvin immediately scowled. "I said a little, asshat. I'm not your fairy fucking godmother."

"I'll take whatever I can get at this point. At least before I could see him in passing. This is unbearable."

"Just think how *he* feels." I doubted anything could skewer me more than the pointed look Calvin gave me. "Fuck, it's like kicking a puppy," he muttered to himself, then finished putting away his things and rested his arms on the table. He stared at me with an expression that made me feel like I was being weighed and measured. Finally, he nodded. "Here's what you're going to do. You need to get Andy in a position where he can't just run off every time the conversation gets hard."

I couldn't help but snicker at the way he said it. "Got experience with that, do you?"

He huffed. "You have *no* idea. Typically, I'd be against ambushing him, but..."

"But he's Andy."

He nodded. "Like I was saying, you need to get him on his own. Corner him, if you will. I can make that happen."

"Uh..." He had a point. When he put it like that, it sounded sketchy as fuck, but I was also desperate. "How?"

"The Senior Trip to DC is coming up. You're going."

I snorted before I could think better of it, earning myself a reproachful glare. "That sounds nice, but you're forgetting two things. The trip is already full and there's not a chance in hell Coach will let me go."

"*You're* forgetting two things. One: I don't forget *anything*."

I swallowed anxiously at the undercurrent of threat. Everyone knew Calvin was keyed into every scandalous thing that happened at Ulwich and he was probably the only one who knew what was real and what was rumor. "What's the second thing?"

He smirked. "I'm Calvin Fucking Bridges. You leave your douchebag coach to me. As for the trip being full. Tristan Holt had to drop out of the trip due to a family emergency."

"Fuck. That's awful. Those slots are coveted. Did someone die?"

"No. His father got busted for insider trading and his family is trying to control the fallout by limiting the flow of information."

"How the hell do you know that?" I hissed.

His evil grin returned, and I reminded myself to never get on Calvin's bad side. "I have my ways. Anyway, you're going to go to Professor Cohen and tell him you'd like to take Tristan's spot. If he asks how you know, just say you promised not to tell. The professors know what's going on with the

Holts. If he waffles, tell him you worked out with Stein about some extra credit."

"But I haven't. And why go to Cohen?"

"Because Cohen and Garza supervise the trip every year. They're the ones who initially put it together." How did I not know that? I stifled my surprise and focused on the rest of Calvin's oddly specific instructions. " *After* Cohen agrees, you're going to haul ass to Stein and do whatever it takes to get him to assign an extra credit... something," he finished, waving his hand around to encompass the mysterious assignment.

"Okay... Seems a little backward to me. Wouldn't going to Garza make more sense, seeing as how he's Andy's mentor?"

"Possibly, but there's also a greater chance Andy will find out beforehand. He can't learn about it until it's too late to back out. Now, if you'll excuse me, I apparently have some work to do." He stood, and I mirrored h im.

"Wait. When is it too late for him to do anything about it?"

Calvin gave me a level look. "When he's on the plane."

The blood drained from my face. That really was an ambush. How was I supposed to keep this from him for two weeks? Then again, it shouldn't be that hard, given how good he'd gotten at avoiding me.

Calvin slung his bag over his shoulder and re-situated the items inside before looking back at me. "Oh, and Mitch."

"Yeah?" I asked, suddenly nervous as I met his stoney gaze.

"You break him again and you'll wish you'd never heard of Ulwich Preparatory Academy." He continued to stare at me while the ominous threat sank in, then turned to go. "I wouldn't waste any time if I were you. Cohen will be leaving for his weekly poker game in an hour. You'll want to catch him before that."

Chapter 8

Mitch

Andy was late… again. I wouldn't even be surprised if he didn't bother to show at all. So much for "still being friends, albeit really weird ones". Much as I hated to admit it, him skipping out was ruining whatever progress I'd made with my classes. Though it was a toss up if it was my distraction with him clearly avoiding me or that I was simply a hopeless student that was straight up murdering all my efforts at focused study.

I slumped back in my chair and ran both hands over my face. Out of the corner of my eye, I noticed John glancing in my direction. Maybe it was better that Andy was avoiding me after all. The team had been extra attentive since I'd sucker punched Connor. Brian's reality check still rang in my ears. If it hadn't been for Andy's explosion at the shack, it might have been the *only* thing ringing in my ears.

He said he'd loved me. Emphasis on the past tense.

I knew I'd fucked up back then, that I was a complete monster for the way I'd used him, but now I was also a total and complete asshole. I'd never felt so damn lame as when I'd tried to say I'd left because I was scared. That was horseshit. I wasn't scared. I'd walk over molten glass for Andy. Fear had nothing to do with it. I'd left because I was ashamed, disgusted with myself, and felt like the scum of the earth. All those feelings had compounded in the wake of his confession.

I was an hour into the study block with nothing to show for any of the time I'd wasted. If ever there was a time to throw in the towel, this was it.

"What are you doing? Study period isn't over yet," Andy said, settling in the chair across from me.

I stalled, my book halfway into my bag. "You're here."

"Of course I am," he huffed without meeting my gaze as he continued to unpack his things. "I said I'd help, didn't I?" He finally looked up, and I wasn't sure if I'd ever seen his vibrant green eyes so... vacant. "Show me what you've got on that history assignment."

For a second, fear that he'd found out about Calvin's and my scheme for "extra credit" froze my lungs. Then he gave me an impatient look, and I realized he was referring to the World War II assignment I hadn't made any progress on.

"Well?" he pressed, quirking an eyebrow.

"I, uh, don't really have anything," I admitted.

His gaze sharpened and suddenly I really wanted that unnerving "not-quite-home" look to come back. "You've been here over an hour," he deadpanned.

"And where were you?" I countered.

His jaw clenched. "Contrary to what you might believe, I have other priorities besides making sure you do your homework."

I was pretty sure a slap would have hurt less than his clipped words. "I don't believe that," I mumbled.

"Could have fooled me." He paused unloading and organizing his things. "Look, Mitch, I know I promised to keep helping you with your assignments, but you can't rely on me to make them happen. You need to be self-sufficient."

I bit back sharply pointing out that I *had* been doing all of it on my own, which was why I'd needed his help in the first place.

He dropped his gaze to the wooden table between us that had probably witnessed thousands of conversations like this one. "It's probably for the best that I'm going on the DC trip next week. We could clearly use the space from each other."

I was really glad he was still looking down and couldn't see me cringe. Suddenly Calvin's grand plan didn't seem so genius anymore. If Andy thought we needed space—which I super disagreed with—then he was going to be pissed when he learned I was going on that trip as well. I just really hoped Calvin could deliver on the other part of his scheme, since the way things were going, Andy would still find a way to avoid me.

Finally, he straightened up and released a long-suffering sigh. "Okay, where did you get stuck?" He reached for my history textbook that I'd set back on the table when he'd arrived.

Rather than answer his question, I crossed my arms and extended my legs in the perfect image of the dumb jock he thought I was. “Who says I got stuck?”

He narrowed his eyes, then asked with more sass than should have fit in his body, “If you didn’t get stuck, then why don’t you have anything?”

“Didn’t feel like it.” Two could play this game.

He bristled, reminding me every bit of my cat back home. "So then," Andy continued, like he was putting together pieces of a puzzle, "you've basically sat here acting helpless because you expect me to do it for you. And I'm supposed to, what? Walk you every fucking step of the way? I'm not your mother."

“Jesus Christ, Andy,” I snapped, leaning across the table. “Is that what you really think?”

He deflated slightly, but didn’t back down. “You’re not exactly giving me a reason not to.”

“Does how much I busted my ass last term mean nothing to you? Have I once asked you to do any of my work *for* me?”

He glanced to the side, his normally lush mouth pinched into a grim line. “I’d rather not discuss last semester.”

I scooted closer to the table, my sort-of whisper threatening not to be a whisper at all. “Yeah? Well, I think we should. And while we’re at it, we can cover that bomb you dropped a couple of weeks ago instead of running off.”

His eyes burned a villainous green as he glared at me. “Running off?” he asked, his voice dangerously low. Too late, I realized the horrible mistake I’d made. “At least I’m still fucking here. So I was late for a few study sessions. Excuse the fuck out of me for having other shit on my plate.” He seethed for another minute, practically vibrating with rage while red climbed up his neck.

I scrambled to find some way to walk back my epically poor choice of words.

Abruptly, he snapped the textbook shut and shoved it back toward me so hard I let out a grunt as it collided with my ribs. “You know what? I don’t have to put up with this shit.” He pushed his chair back with a loud screech, causing several people to look our way. Great, now we were a public spectacle. “Fuck you, Mitch. Good luck managing your school work while I’m gone.”

I watched as he shoved the last of his things into his already over-stuffed satchel and stormed out. What the fuck was wrong with me? This wasn't the place *or* the audience—because, yep, John was still there—for any of the conversations we were way overdue for. I fought the impulse to chunk my book after him and buried my head in my hands, stifling a miserable groan. Was it possible for a plan to blow up in your face before it had even happened? Because if so, Calvin was going to skin me alive for fucking up his well-laid scheme.

Andy

Goddamn Mitch. The balls on him. The audacity! Running off. I wasn't the one who ghosted my best friend for four fucking years. Make that *five*. So I needed time to deal with my shit. Sue me.

The bitter thoughts tumbled over each other as I stalked through the hall, the ominous cloud over me scaring off anyone who might think to stop me. As if today wasn't already fucking bad enough. Suddenly, someone grabbed my arm. Expecting it to be Connor—because of course it would be Connor—I spun around to confront him, fully prepared to rip his arm off if that's what it took to get away. Maybe he'd be a little less zealous in trying to get together then.

"Whoa, what crawled up your ass and died?" My red haze instantly cleared at the sound of Calvin's voice. He released my arm to hold up both of his hands in surrender.

"You're lucky I didn't deck you," I snarled.

His eyebrow lifted in obvious skepticism. Right, because there wasn't a chance in hell that I could actually take Calvin in a fight. He was taller, stronger, and, unlike me, actually worked out. Though you'd never know it given the painstaking effort he went through to hide how fucking ripped he was.

"Don't look at me like that." I crossed my arms and glowered off to the side.

His face clouded with concern. "What's going on, Andy? This isn't like you."

"It's been a shitty fucking day, that's what."

"This sounds like a chat better had *not* in the hall where anyone can overhear." He turned on his heel and started walking with the obvious expectation that I would follow.

I was tempted to yell after him that I didn't *want* to have a "chat", but instead, rushed to catch up. We walked in silence until we reached the haunted classroom. Thankfully, there was still some sunlight pushing into the dusty room. I didn't know how he could stomach being in here after dark. I certainly wasn't that crazy.

No sooner did he shut the door behind us than he rounded on me. "Spill. Something's got you all fired up and I want to know what it is. And *don't* even try to leave shit out. It's confession time."

"What happened to letting me tell you things when I'm ready?" I grumbled, dropping my satchel and stomping over to the windows where the feeble light was strongest.

He scoffed. "We tried that, and it still took me cornering you. Now quit stalling. Out with it." He shrugged out of his navy blazer and gave it a good snap before settling it over a mostly clean chair.

"There's nothing to tell. I got into a fight with Mitch, that's all. Not even a fight, really."

"Liar. No way you're such a surly shit after a 'non-fight'," he said with air quotes before recrossing his arms.

I rolled my eyes and leaned against the window, mindless of the grime. "Fine. He accused me of running out on him."

Calvin let out a low whistle and shook his head. "That ballsy fucker. What else?"

"What else? That's not enough for you?" I snapped.

"No, because I know you, and I know there's more. Now what else?"

I rolled my shoulders as I thought about why I was so late to the study session again and the awful fucking news I'd gotten right before. "So I *have* been dodging him. We, uh, fooled around a couple weeks ago and I maybe blurted out the truth about how pissed I've been with what he did four years ago."

"Wait. Wait." He held up his hands and shook his head, obviously struggling to wrap his head around what I'd said. "You told Mitch you're in love with him?"

"I told him I *was* and how much he hurt me. Surprise. He didn't have shit to say about it."

"To be fair, you did kind of blindside him."

I glared at him. “You really want to talk about fairness?”

He winced and dropped his hands. “Actually, no. No, I do not. Okay, so I’ll agree, his nonresponse is super shitty, and it’s even shittier that he called you out for running.” He let that hang for a bit, giving me a knowing look that made it clear where he stood on that. “What else?”

“What else?" I asked in disbelief. "What more do you want?”

“The rest of it,” he countered. “You’ve been managing your issues with Mitch for years and while there’s a lot kicking up right now, there’s no way that’s all of it. I’ve got all night and I’m not letting you out of here until you come clean.” He rested against the oversized desk and stared me down.

Sometimes I really hated how well Calvin could read me. He was a lot like Mitch in that way. I glowered out the window at the setting sun. Calvin might be fine in this abandoned room at night, but he knew damn well I wasn’t. It didn’t take much to realize that daylight was literally slipping through my fingers and that Calvin was *not* bluffing. I wouldn’t put it past him to tie me up if he felt like he had to.

“I found out Connor’s going on the DC trip,” I muttered. My irritation spiked all over again at saying it out loud.

“Goddamn it!” Calvin smacked the wooden desk, and I jumped at his outburst. Before I could ask what all that was about, he noticeably collected himself. “Okay, that’s not ideal, but I can work with that. I get why you’re,” he waved at me and I bristled all over again. “I take it you’re worried he’ll use the trip to push you to get back together?”

“No shit. And with my luck, we’ll end up stuck in the same hotel room.”

“The fuck you will,” Calvin snarled, taking me by surprise.

“What?”

“Andy, I might not be going on this trip, but over my dead body, are you sharing a room with that asshole.” He scooped up his jacket, and I realized he didn’t have his satchel with him.

“Where are you going?” I asked, straightening up.

“To fix this shit,” he said over his shoulder before leaving me alone in the haunted room.

I glanced out at the setting sun and rubbed my forehead. I really needed a fucking vacation from all of this drama.

Chapter 9

Andy

Peace and quiet at last. Well, as quiet as a plane full of boarding passengers could be. The important part was that I wasn't sitting next to Connor. I glanced down at the ticket Garza had handed me only a few minutes ago to confirm my seat number. I let out a small whoop as I reached my row and realized I had the seat by the window. A few people nearby gave me judgy looks, but fuck them. *I* had a window seat.

I mentally went through everything I'd packed for the hundredth time as I stowed my luggage in the overhead bin and shimmied into my seat with my satchel. Not that it would do me any good if I forgot something. I'd just have to hope anything that hadn't made it into the luggage could be easily acquired once we were in DC.

Once I was settled with my current paperback secured in the pouch in front of me and my satchel tucked safely under my seat, I snatched the "In flight Safety Guide" from the same pouch as my book. People continued to board, and with each person who paused by my row, I flicked a glance at the empty seat beside me. As each of them moved on, my excitement grew. Was it possible I'd actually have the row to myself?

Giddy at the possibility, I continued to scan the brochure in anticipation of the preflight instructions that would be happening any minute now. Not that any of the information had changed since I'd last flown a couple months ago, but it never hurt to be prepared. A sudden thump in the seat beside me tempered my hope that I'd had all the space to myself.

I glanced up, but only caught the barest glimpse of whoever would be joining me before another passenger squeezing by hid them from view. I adjusted my focus to the seat and was surprised to find a paperback on it.

To my amazement, it was the same book I'd bought Mitch last term. He'd said he'd started the space pirate book, but I was dubious about what that really meant. Whoever the owner of this book was had already conquered half of it. Maybe sharing the row wouldn't be so bad if it was with another bibliophile. At least it'd be quiet.

A hand came into view, grabbing the book, and I quickly shifted my focus back to the pamphlet, still internally chuckling that of all the books my flight companion could have, it would be that one. Seriously, what were the odds? Then the owner of said book plopped into the seat. I reflexively looked up, and all the blood drained from my face. Turned out the odds were really fucking good.

"Hey, Andy," Mitch said with his bright smile.

I glanced around, not really believing my eyes. Maybe I'd passed out at the airport and this was some weird nightmare. Or maybe someone's luggage had fallen out of the overhead compartment, hit me on the head, and now I was hallucinating. It was the only logical explanation for Mitch to be sitting beside me on the single most exclusive field trip our school had. The one with a fixed number of spots that filled up months and even sometimes a year in advance. The one I was looking forward to, so that I didn't have to see his stupid, handsome face.

"Uh, Andy, could you please blink? You're freaking me out." He lightly touched my arm and reality came crashing down. I wasn't hallucinating. This was real. Mitch was sitting beside me… on a fucking airplane.

I barely retained the wherewithal to lower my voice as I hissed, "What the hell are you doing here?"

"Um, going to DC?" He cocked his head like I was being dense.

I glanced around almost frantically for any sign of Garza or Cohen, but of course the bastards were in first class while the rest of us lowly students had to make do with economy. "Listen, I don't know how the hell you finagled your way onto this plane, but you need to leave. Now. Being on the team may afford you a certain amount of protection with the Academy, but I seriously doubt you can get away with skipping out-of-town like this."

"What are you talking about? I got my ticket from Garza, same as you."

"This isn't funny, Mitch. You could get in real trouble. And you couldn't have gotten your ticket from Garza because you weren't even fucking here when he was giving them out!" I shout-whispered.

He rubbed the back of his neck and at least had the decency to look abashed. "You're sort of right. I had to catch a cab to the airport, because

Coach wouldn't budge on the early morning practice. Garza let it slide, but made it clear that I was responsible for getting my ass here and if I missed the plane, that was on me."

My mouth opened and closed, but I couldn't find any words. Finally, I huffed and turned forward to stare at the back of the chair in front of me. "Un-fucking-believable." I shoved the Safety Guide unceremoniously back into the pouch and took out my book. Unfortunately, not even obstinately focusing on the typed pages could minimize my hyper-awareness of Mitch as he settled into his seat. I tightened my grip on the paperback and refused to give into the urge to look over at him.

I vaguely registered the flight attendants going through the inflight checklist and the emergency exits or the pilot's speech about getting ready for takeoff. I couldn't even recall if I'd turned the page in the last five minutes.

The plane jolted as we were taxied to the runway. Every dip, sway, and lurch set my teeth on edge, and I still refused to look up. How the hell had he managed to get on this trip? It had to be some shady ass shit for me not to know about it.

Out of nowhere, I sensed him getting closer, and I recoiled against the seat. He gave me a curious look as he reached past me to flip up the shade. "Kinda defeats the point of having the window seat if it's closed." He smiled, but I couldn't bring myself to return it. He slumped back against his seat. "Guess that means we won't be chatting during the flight." He released a heavy sigh and opened his book.

I blinked and continued to stare at him for another minute as the plane turned on the tarmac to line up for takeoff. But he didn't look back up. Not even when we started to gain speed. It wasn't until I was turning my attention to glance out at the scenery flying by faster and faster that I realized he'd put a stick of gum on the armrest.

Without thinking, I unwrapped it and popped it in my mouth. Then we were airborne and there was no going back.

Mitch

The flight was, in a word, uncomfortable. In two, excruciatingly painful. Andy refused to look at me the entire flight and the only words he said to me were when he had to pee and needed me to move.

So far, this absolutely was not going to plan. While I was impressed as hell that Calvin had not only pulled this off, but had also gotten me in the seat next to Andy, I maybe should have asked for some advice on what to say. Because Andy was next level pissed. I couldn't even remember the last—if ever—he'd given me the cold shoulder like this. Cornered Andy was one scowly grump. He barely even glanced out the window.

I tried like hell to read, but the tension strangling our row made it impossible to focus. Finally, I gave up and watched the flight tracker, counting down the miles until we reached our destination. When that got old, I started counting how many people had hats, then glasses, and so on.

It wasn't until we touched down and I jolted awake that I realized I'd fallen asleep. I looked around groggily, taking in the antsy movements of passengers eager to disembark. When we docked at last, I lurched out of my seat, taking advantage of my height and size to secure our spot in the awful line to de-board. I popped open the overhead bin and pulled down Andy's luggage. Even if I hadn't seen it dozens of times when we were younger, I still would have known it was his, thanks to the Star Wars luggage tag.

I stepped back as much as I could to give him room to get out and passed him the handle. He mumbled something that might have been a thanks but could have just as easily been a request for me to go to hell. Either way, he pulled the handle up and rolled it in front of him, giving me an unobstructed view of his pert ass in tight jeans while we waited to leave the cylinder of misery.

"Ulwich Prep, over here," Cohen said loud enough to be heard over the buzz of voices. We angled toward him, but when we pulled up to the small circle, I got my second major hit of the day—Connor was here.

I bit back a snarl and slid an inch closer to Andy as Connor stared absolute hate at me. Lucky for him, his nose seemed to have healed fine and either the bruising had truly faded or he'd gotten hold of some makeup to hide it. Wouldn't be the first time a guy on the team had "borrowed" concealer from a sister or a girlfriend. But his luck would run out if he thought he could get between me and Andy again.

"Seven, and… eight. Looks like that's everyone. Glad you could join us, Mr. Hudson," Professor Garza said, prompting the other five students besides Connor and Andy to turn and look at me.

I offered a half-hearted wave and shifted the duffel on my shoulder. Now that I could see everyone, I couldn't help but feel woefully out of my depth. Extra credit or not, these guys were *smart*. Except for Connor. I had no fucking clue what that asshole was doing here. What happened to DC being an exclusive trip?

Cohen and Garza herded us to the pickup zone and then into a waiting taxi bus. On the drive to the hotel, they went over the general rules and expectations for the trip. All of which boiled down to "you're all adults, act like it and we won't have any problems". All in all, I was having a hard time managing my disappointment at how my grand plan had started. And if I was being honest with myself, I didn't expect it to get any better.

We pulled up to the hotel, which was way nicer than I would have expected after being stuffed into the tiny ass seats on the plane. If this was why we'd had to endure that, then I was A-okay with it. Hopefully, the beds would be as cushy as the rest of the place. As we wandered after the professors, I couldn't help but take in the extravagance that surrounded us. Not that any of the others took note—not even Andy. But then, most of them had grown up with anything and everything they could ever want for, with attending Ulwich being another jewel in their crowns.

Not me. My mom did well enough between her job as head nurse at a posh retirement home and the money my dad left after he passed, but it was nothing to get excited about. I was only at Ulwich Prep by the grace of my Uncle Terry. Though some days I questioned if that was a blessing or a curse. I glanced at Andy, who was still stoutly pretending I wasn't there, and reevaluated that sentiment. Anything that brought Andy into my life was definitely a blessing.

"If all of you would please gather around," Cohen said as Garza stepped up beside him. "We have your room assignments and keys. Now before we give them out, I want to reiterate that *any* damage or unauthorized room charges—I'm looking at you Hendricks," he narrowed his gaze at Connor, who responded with an asinine thumbs up, "will not be taken lightly. Your families will be invoiced for the excess and you will be shipped back to the academy—also on your dime—to face disciplinary action. That goes for any trouble as well."

There was no pretending that the last comment wasn't intended for Connor *and* me. Judging by the angry look Connor shot me, he knew it too. Not that I planned on starting anything with him, but I wouldn't idly sit by if he did either.

"Now that we've got that unpleasantness out of the way," Garza said with a sincere smile, "onto the room assignments. You can get your keys from Professor Cohen, as your names are called." He referenced his clipboard. "Elliott, you're with Bricker. Smith and Gardener. Gallagher and…"

I held my breath. Why hadn't I thought about this part? What if Andy ended up rooming with someone else? Or worse, Connor? Fuck, I really needed to start thinking shit through.

"Hudson," Garza finished. "Which means Hendricks, you're with Adams."

Andy stiffened beside me and I refrained from laughing my ass off at the stunned expression on Connor's face. I owed Calvin big time for this. I wondered how he'd feel about a lifetime supply of sketch books.

Chapter 10

Andy

This was a disaster. That was the only word for it. A complete fucking disaster. I stopped just shy of snatching my room key from Garza, though judging by the look he gave me, my irritation was right on the surface. It just wasn't fair. This trip was supposed to be an escape. Now I had to deal with not only Connor, but Mitch as well.

I didn't bother to wait for Garza and Cohen to finish their reminders on appropriate behavior and that we were representing Ulwich Preparatory Academy. I made my way to the elevators as fast as I could without actually running and pressed the call button. The doors on my left opened immediately, and I released a sigh of relief when I noted that the rest of our little group was only now making their way down the short hall. Still, I wasn't interested in sharing. I mashed the door close button with impunity until they finally started to slide shut. Not a moment too soon, either.

"Andy, hold up!" Mitch called as he skidded into view, clearly having missed the memo about not running in the lobby.

My heart lurched with a sudden panic that I might get stuck in the elevator with him. Then the doors finished sealing him from sight. I slumped against the wall and scrubbed at my face. How the hell had this happened? Dodging Mitch at school these last few weeks hadn't exactly been easy. It'd be damn near impossible here, especially given that we were sharing a room.

The elevator came to a smooth stop; the doors opening onto the artfully decorated seventh floor. I took a second to note which way my room was, then set off to the right. This definitely wasn't the first time I'd stayed at a luxury hotel, but even I could admit this place was nice. The deep blue carpet was so plush, it completely absorbed the sound of my footsteps. Unfortunately, that meant it also obscured the sound of Mitch running up behind me.

"What's the rush?" he asked, breathless, and I half wondered if he'd run up the stairs to catch me.

I could have given him a flat answer, but honestly, I wasn't in the mood. Instead, I left him panting for air while I opened the door. As much as I would have liked to explore the amenities in our room, I was more interested in getting away from Mitch as soon as possible.

"We're rooming together. That should be awesome. Not... whatever this is," he said as I stepped inside. "Andy!" he said louder at my turned back. "You can't just not talk to me," he pressed as he stopped the door from swinging shut in his face.

The urge to remain petulantly mute was beyond strong, but he wasn't wrong. Some amount of communication would have to happen. I walked to the far end of the room where the wall-to-wall window provided a truly stellar view of our country's capital and gestured to one of the queen beds. "You can have the one by the wall."

"Okay, sure." The bed made a loud poof as he dropped his duffel unceremoniously. "But, Andy, we really need to—"

"I'm going to unpack my toiletries and freshen up," I cut him off, already moving toward the bathroom, bag in hand. Regrettably, that put me in closer proximity to Mitch. He tried to grab my arm, and I danced out of reach. Barely. "Don't dawdle. We have exactly fifteen minutes to get our things organized and be back in the lobby for lunch and the 'fun outing'." Even saying it tasted bitter. No part of this trip would be fun now
.

I arrived in the lobby before the rest of our group and debated finding a place to hide while I waited. Mitch had still been getting situated when I scurried out of the room like my ass was on fire. But he wouldn't be long. I didn't know what he was so damn insistent we talk about, but I was fairly positive I didn't want to hear it. Once again, I had to face the fact that a good portion of my predicament was my fault. All I had to do was stay away. But he'd been sincere, and charming, and *hot*. It'd be nice to say that one of these days my hormones wouldn't get me into trouble, but that ship had already sailed. Me plus Mitch equaled zero self control.

I'd just decided that the decorative arrangement of flowers on a marble table was tall enough to obscure me when Garza entered the lobby.

"Gallagher, I'd like a word," he said in his no-nonsense tone. If he hadn't already written my recommendation for the Advanced Writing Program at the University of Chicago, I'd be worried. As it was, calm and unfazed weren't exactly me either.

I froze mid-step and turned on my heel to walk toward him instead. "Yes, professor?"

"Is there something we should discuss?" he asked, his thick, dark eyebrow arched high.

I glanced behind him to see the rest of our group spilling out of the elevators—including Mitch. I swallowed thickly and attempted to smile, though I was pretty sure it came out closer to a grimace. "Just getting adjusted to not being at school."

"Mmhmm," he mumbled, like he didn't believe a word of it. Which, to be honest, he shouldn't. "See that you refrain from skipping out on future directions until you've been dismissed. Just because the lot of you can legally fend for yourselves doesn't mean we're not still responsible for y ou."

"Understood. I'm sorry," I replied, abashed. Being in trouble was new for me, and I didn't like it one bit.

Garza's stern expression softened, and he lowered his voice, no doubt in response to the growing noise of approaching students. "I'm serious, Andy. If there's ever anything you need to talk about—scholastic or personal—I'm here for you. We may not be on campus, but I'm still your mentor."

I gave him a shaky, but more sincere, grin. "Thank you, professor. I'll keep that in mind."

He nodded, then turned around and seamlessly fell in step alongside Professor Cohen. "Do we have everyone?"

"We do now." Cohen glanced at me, then shared a look with his colleague that I wasn't sure I wanted to decipher. The rest of the group clustered around them as they led the way to the hotel restaurant. Cohen faced us as the host got our table ready, which involved pulling together a couple of smaller ones. "I know it's not very grand, but for today, I think we can make an exception." He smirked and Garza rolled his eyes.

"You're not going to let that go, are you?" Garza muttered.

Cohen leaned in and whispered back, "Not on your life."

Intrigued that the two professors might disagree over *anything*, I was going to ask for the story. But no sooner did the thought cross my mind than an arm landed on my shoulder. My tongue stuck to the roof of my mouth and my whole body went rigid. A second later, my brain finally made the connection that Mitch had somehow snuck up behind me and was now using me as an armrest.

I bit back a snarl and fought the impulse to shove him off. When the host returned to lead us to our table, I slipped out from underneath, then did everything short of pushing people to make sure I snagged a seat between Elliott and Gardener. I caught sight of Mitch's scowl before I turned to Elliott and struck up a conversation about what he was most excited to see while we were here. I couldn't get out of dealing with Mitch forever, but I could put it off as long as humanly possible.

Mitch

Andy was really starting to piss me off. First the sprint to the elevator, then the stunt at lunch, and now, we were in a kick ass retro arcade—an *arcade*—and the little shit was still dodging me. Clearly, this was an oversight neither Calvin nor I had considered. What good was trying to talk to him if he insisted on pretending I didn't exist? But I didn't excel at lacrosse for nothing. "Quitter" wasn't in my vocabulary and I wasn't about to add it today.

With soft steps that I normally reserved for sneaking up on my cat back home, I stepped up behind Andy. He was currently dominating Pac-Man, dodging the ghosts with the same efficiency he'd been dodging me all day.

"Maybe it's just me, but I don't remember you being that good at this game," I said playfully. Just like all the other times I'd managed to get close to him, he immediately turned into a statue. Within seconds, the yellow character got gobbled by a ghost and the familiar withering death cry filled the air. "Tough break," I said, in yet another attempt to thaw the damn glacier that seemed to have formed between us. If only I could gobble him up the way Blinky had Pac-Man. Now there was a thought. Andy definitely qualified as edible, especially in those tight ass pants… which were now walking off.

I sighed and opted to finish out his lives to give myself a chance to calm down before I did something really stupid like try to kidnap him. Pac-Man resumed his "waka-waka" as I guided him through the maze to get to the special pellets that let you eat the ghosts. Clearly, my approach of outright proximity wasn't working, but I was at a loss for what to do instead. The problem was, I didn't know what I was doing wrong. I got that he was upset—and rightfully so—but how was I supposed to apologize or make it up to him, or even better, *explain* when he wouldn't even look at me?

The game time ran out, and the scoreboard came up. Between the two of us, we'd managed a new high score. I entered Andy's name, then wandered off to find him again. My luck finally seemed to be changing when I spotted him walking by a dual player racing game that had just been vacated. I didn't bother to mask my steps this time as I rushed over to him, then yanked him into the seats.

"What the hell, Mitch?" he hissed as he landed awkwardly in the seat cradle.

"One game. Gimme one game and you can go back to ignoring me," I pleaded with the most earnest expression I could muster.

He mulled it over a moment before finally taking out the token card Cohen had given each of us. Finally, he gave me a clipped nod. "*One* game."

Joy washed over me and I didn't even bother to hide my ridiculous grin as I took out my card and swiped it as well. We picked our cars, ribbing the other's choice, then after a minor dispute over which track to do, we were watching the screen countdown.

I glanced at him and adjusted in my seat. "I'm totally going to kick your ass."

"Dream on," he said with a snort.

I probably shouldn't have glanced at him again. I definitely shouldn't have been appreciating how nice his thighs looked in those jeans or how similar the flush of excitement on his face was to when he was climaxing. The checkered flag dropped, and I twisted my attention back to where it should have been in time to watch Andy's car peel rubber.

"Damn it," I muttered. It took some aggressive passing and bumping of the other cars to catch up, but at last we were neck and neck.

"Not bad," he said, flashing me a smile. Then he twisted his wheel sharply and my car collided with his rear end. I was still regaining my bearings from the jolting and vibrating steering wheel, emulating the crash, when he leveled out and left me behind again.

"Oh, you are so gonna pay for that."

He laughed. "You have to catch me first."

"Keep talking smack. It's not over until we cross that finish line!" Except after his little stunt, there was no way I could regain the ground I'd lost.

He won the round easily, coasting across the finish line while a gold medallion with "#1" spun around on his screen. One game turned into best out of three, then best out of five. In the end, Andy came out ahead, but I couldn't be mad about it or even a little salty. It had been *fun*. For half an hour, we'd been ourselves. Before all the bullshit.

"Damn, when did you get so good at that?" I asked, bending to crack my back. Those seats were *not* comfortable. Still, no regrets.

The bright smile on Andy's face and shining in his eyes vanished as he abruptly shut down. All my hopes that I'd be able to convince him to keep playing together fell down into the sudden pit that opened up between us. Before I could push to see what had happened, the professors summoned everyone back to the front of the arcade.

"Yes, I know, everyone is having a good time," Garza said, sounding both put upon and entertained by the group's belly-aching. "Perhaps we'll have an opportunity to come back before we return to campus."

"But enough about games. Who wants pizza?!" Cohen shouted. Apparently, it didn't matter how old you got, you were always excited about pizza. Unsurprisingly, the exclamation was met with equal enthusiasm.

I shot Andy an excited look. I knew how much he loved pizza and hated how the academy refused to serve it. But he refused to meet my gaze, keeping his attention fixed on the professors. My smile instantly flipped to a frown. Why couldn't *anything* go my way? I gave myself a mental shake. I'd cracked his exterior once. I could do it again. Starting with sitting right next to his stubborn ass at dinner.

Chapter 11

Mitch

Darkness dogged my steps as I stalked after Andy toward our room. Dinner had been an unrivaled disaster that no amount of delicious pizza could remedy. Andy had gone from indifferent at the arcade to cold when I'd elbowed my way to sitting beside him at the checker patterned table at dinner, then outright rebellious when the professors had divided the group for different tours the next day.

"What the fuck is your problem?!" Andy yelled as he swung our hotel room door shut.

I barely caught it in time to prevent it from slamming into my face. "*My* problem? You didn't even fucking ask."

"I didn't know I had to. If you don't want to go to the Smithsonian, then don't," Andy snapped back as he violently plunked the bucket of ice he insisted we get on the dresser.

I clenched my jaw, a stupid attempt to prevent myself from shouting in return. "It's *not* that I don't want to go."

"Then what's the big fucking deal?" Andy asked, spinning back on me.

There was no tempering my growl. *He so doesn't fucking get it.* "The big fucking deal is that you didn't even bother to find out if I wanted to do something else."

"You're just upset that Brock and Connor are coming and it won't just be us," Andy said, waving his hands emphatically.

I blinked. He'd hit the nail right on the head. "He's going to be a prick the whole time," I said, trying to deflect.

"Then maybe you shouldn't have broken his nose!"

I bit off my knee-jerk response to tell Andy exactly *why* I'd broken Connor's stupid face. "Look, it's not just that. It's like you didn't even care to ask. Which might have been a hell of a lot easier if you weren't so hell bent on ignoring me."

"Why would I? We *always* do what you want!" Andy threw his hands up.

"Since when?" I fired back. Last I'd checked, pulling teeth was easier than getting Andy to do anything together.

"*Since when?*" he mocked. "Since always. *You* pick the hangout. *You* pick the prank. *You* pick the game. *You* pick the position."

My mind blanked. Sex? He was angry about how we'd had sex? Not *that* we'd had sex, but *how*?

A sneer twisted Andy's face. "Don't have anything to say to that, do you? It's never mattered what I wanted! It doesn't matter how I bend over to give you what you want, it's never enough. You always flip things around!"

"Are you serious right now? All of this, because I would rather look at your face than your back? What the fuck, Andy?" My outrage threatened to eat me from the inside out. I'd never heard anything more ridiculous in my life. I knew he was still mad after the episode in the storage shed, but I hadn't expected this at all.

He made a high-pitched sound at the back of his throat like I'd stepped on his tail. His eyes were green fire as he walked up and stabbed me in the chest with his finger. "I'll tell you what the fuck. I know exactly what you're doing."

"And what's that?" The argument had taken a hard left, and I was immediately wary of where it was headed. Wasn't this about me bottoming… or not, in this case?

"You're trying to make everything we do as different as possible. Heaven forbid anything we do even remotely resemble what happened four years ago," he said with all the conviction of someone who believes they've got it all figured out. In fairness, he was half right.

"For someone so smart, you miss a lot. You know that?"

"What's there to miss?" He pushed my chest with both hands and I stumbled back at the unexpected force. "You walk around like some kind of sports god and expect everyone to just fall in line. News flash. You're not *my* god. You're *supposed* to be my best friend. But you *never* ask what *I* want." He pushed again with more force. "And you Fucking. Dictate. Everything. Our whole friendship, our whole everything, has always been on your terms."

Oh, *fuck* that. Andy was the one calling the shots. His refusal to talk to me was why I'd weaseled my way into the DC trip to begin with. Before I could argue any of that, though, he advanced. He went to shove me again, but I was ready for him. I caught both of his wrists.

Contrary to being caught, he didn't back down. His eyes blazed with fury as he fought against the hold like some wild animal. "Fucking let me go. You motherfucking—"

I stopped the tide of expletives with a savage kiss that was sure to leave both of our lips bruised.

"Don't fucking touch me," he gasped as he squirmed furiously, his chest heaving. He wasn't fooling me. The flames in his eyes had an entirely different cast now.

I mashed my mouth down on his again, fueled by the anger and rage that had sprung up the moment he'd signed us up for the stupid excursion—half a second behind Connor. Andy's teeth dug into my lip. I didn't care. I bit him right back. "You fucking want to be bent over something? I'll fucking bend you over something." That was the only warning he got before I used my grip to spin him around. His hands smacked on the dresser as I pulled his hips backwards, nearly forcing him double.

"You son of a bitch! We're still doing whatever *you* want," he shouted over his shoulder, even as I yanked his shorts to the floor.

"No, we're not. We're doing what you want." I jerked his hips again, and he sprawled on the dresser, flinging his arms wide to catch himself a half-second too late. I slipped spit-coated fingers inside of him. He was so tight they instantly went numb. Then he let out a groan so low it could have been a growl. Whatever was left of my control went up in flames.

"You're an asshole," he snarled from where he was struggling to regain his bearings. Not exactly easy, considering I was pumping my fingers in and out of his perfect little hole. He flailed his hands as he fought to get them back under himself, knocking over a collection of fancy complimentary lotions.

I caught a bottle before it could roll onto the floor. A quick glance showed it was actually some kind of oil. Perfect. He finally lifted himself from the flat surface during my momentary distraction. I pushed him back down and removed my fingers long enough to dribble some of the oil down his crease. This time when I pushed my fingers in, there was no resistance, though he was still tight enough to make my head spin.

"Fuck. You," he growled, but there was no missing how he was driving onto my fingers with each thrust. I twisted them and he gasped. The way he squeezed cranked my desperate need to be close to him, to be inside of him.

I removed my fingers, distantly wishing that I had the patience to drag this out. No way in hell was that happening now, but he was going to have to fucking deal with it. Hard and fast was the only speed I had left. I shoved my shorts to the floor and added more of the oil to my already insanely hard dick, groaning at the feel. It had been weeks since we'd had sex. Weeks of him parading around oblivious and blaming me for everything. Rooming together was supposed to give us a chance to work through our issues, but all we'd done was argue since the second I'd set foot on that plane. That was clearly proving to be a mistake, and now I was out of control.

"Tell me to stop," I dared him. He responded with an incoherent snarl, but it sure as fuck wasn't "stop". I lined the swollen head of my cock up with his clenching hole. "Do it! Tell me to stop."

"No!"

I flattened my hand on his back, pressing his chest into the dresser so he wouldn't go anywhere. I didn't want to know what I would do if he tried to move. Mercifully, the most he did was squirm beneath the touch. Some tiny voice of reason raised a red flag.

This is insane. I can't treat him like this.

Another voice countered the logic. *Except he hasn't said stop, and he's not actually trying to go anywhere.*

An image of Connor's smug grin when Andy signed up for the outing filled my mind. Blind rage seared away any remnants of restraint.

That asshole is never going to fucking touch you again.

In one powerful stroke, I buried my entire length in Andy. His cry filled the room. I should have been concerned, or at the very least worried, about hurting him. But I wasn't. All reason was gone. His self-righteous anger had unleashed something in me, something that had been trying to get out for a long time. Without anything to hold me back, I drove mercilessly into him, punishing his body and mine.

"You like that?" I panted between thrusts. His channel tightened around me. "You do, don't you? You like being bent over and fucked so hard the only thing holding you up is my cock. You like being fucking railed."

He groaned and clawed at the dresser. He also angled his hips higher, as if seeking more.

I ripped off my shirt, which was just getting in the way. I shifted my angle and slid a fraction deeper. We both moaned at the same time. The sound of my pelvis slapping into his ass was joined by the dresser banging against the wall. The force of it sent more items tumbling off the dresser, including the damn ice. I rucked his shirt up his back so I could see my cock sliding in and out of him rapid fire. His ass was like the goddamn moon pulling my cock in like the fucking tide. I pushed the shirt higher so I could wrap a hand over his shoulder, forcing him back into me even as I pushed harder.

His nails scratched along the wood as he straightened his arms and continued to take the beating. The chaos inside me began to crystallize. I tightened my grip on his hip, digging my fingers in hard enough to bruise. It wasn't enough. I moved my other hand from his shoulder and wound it into his hair. Then I yanked his head back, bringing his face up to mine. His eyes were wild as they locked onto mine. "I need you to come," I grunted without relenting.

An undeniable fierceness flashed in his eyes. "Make me," he growled.

"You're going to fight me on everything, aren't you, you little brat?"

Andy glared at me and didn't even hesitate. "Yes."

I growled as the last of my restraint snapped. "You want it that way? So fucking be it." I flung his head down so hard he nearly went flat on the dresser. Then, with both hands on his hips, I drove hard and fast. With each punishing thrust, he let out a gasp. And. It. Still. Wasn't. Enough.

There's no fucking way I'm coming without him.

I gave up my hold, spit into my hand, and reached around to wrap my fingers around his perfect cock. Whatever else was happening here, he was fucking hard. I didn't even bother stroking him properly. Just picked a point and tightened my grip. Each thrust sent him sliding through my circled fingers. He gave a strangled cry at the added sensation and I pumped harder.

Fuck. I'm not going to make it. He's gonna make me come first. Then that'll be my fucking fault, too.

Furious, I yanked him back up by the hair with my free hand. Desperate for an outlet for all the emotions boiling over, I sank my teeth into his shoulder as I thrust into him hard enough to rock the dresser. His entire body tightened around me as he shouted his release. I managed one last thrust before I came deep inside of him.

My death grip slackened as all the anger that had fueled me was forcibly expelled from my body. I stayed exactly where I was, unable to do much more than stand, until I was soft enough to slip out. By then, my breathing was somewhere near regular, even if my thoughts were still in complete chaos.

What have I done?

I stumbled half a step back, still trying to wrangle them into some form of coherency. The movement broke the last remaining contact I had with Andy's body.

He spun around to face me and for a split second I was sure he'd hit me; part of me wanted him to. After what I'd just done, I deserved it. Rather than contacting with my face, though, his hand landed on my chest. "Mitch," he panted. "That was..."

"Andy I—"

"That was fucking incredible," he sighed.

I was so shocked that when his lips brushed mine, I didn't even respond. Then his other hand coasted up my chest. I looked down at him to see that all the fierceness was gone from his eyes. He quickly removed his shirt, the only scrap of clothing left between us, then resumed his kneading of my chest and shoulders. His fingers curled in my hair as he brought my mouth back down to his. The kiss was soft and exploratory, followed by several smaller ones. I wrapped my arm around his waist as I got lost in the sensuality of it.

What is going on? This is all backwards. You're supposed to make out and then *have crazy sex, not the other way around.*

Despite the contradiction, Andy continued to pull sweet kisses from my lips. I slid a hand up his back and wrapped it around his shoulder, pulling him closer. He made a small mewling noise and kissed me harder. Then he applied gentle pressure on my chest in the same spot he'd stabbed me before. He kept at it until the back of my legs hit the bed. Still confused as hell, I got on it. He immediately followed, curling into me even as he twined his body around mine and continued to shower me with tender kisses.

What the hell is going on? First, he's some kind of raging tiger that would tear me apart as soon as look at me. And now... What? He's like some kind of ginger house cat?

As if to emphasize the strange analogy, he made another of the odd mewling sounds and rubbed against me. “What are you thinking?” he whispered as his hands continued to touch every part of me.

“That I knew there was no way you could have hair that red and *not* have a temper,” I said, putting my doubts into the only words that seemed to make any sense.

He chuckled and reclaimed my mouth, sliding his tongue inside to tangle with mine. I wrapped my arms around him and fell into a deep kiss. He flinched when my hand touched his shoulder and moaned into my mouth. Then I remembered I’d bitten him—hard. Guilt stabbed through me at my total lack of control. “What can I say? You bring it out of me, Mitch. You bring a lot out of me,” he said low and husky.

I was astounded at the heat in his response and that he hadn’t commented on the bite. He brushed his thumb over my parted mouth.

“Tonight was perfect.” He teased my bottom lip, sucking on it before deepening the kiss once again.

Chapter 12

Mitch

The digital red numbers of the clock on the nightstand said it was five am. I groaned inwardly and rolled over to find that the bed was empty. My hand automatically brushed across the empty space even as I glanced over my shoulder at the other bed. It was vacant and undisturbed, but the sheets beside me still held a bit of warmth. I sat up and noticed that the bathroom door was partially open, allowing yellow light to pool in the short entryway. Curious, I slid out from under the comforter and went to investigate. I stopped short of going into the bathroom and glanced through the crack.

In front of the wall-sized mirror, Andy twisted around to inspect where I'd bitten him. My stomach clenched at seeing the angry red mark. Accompanying the circle impression was also an array of jagged lines running the length of his back.

I don't remember doing those.

He barely spared them a glance as he reached over his shoulder. He chewed on his lip while he gently traced the outline. His soft moan carried through the tiled room to where I stood shrouded in darkness. My guilt deepened.

He sucked in a breath as he fingered the bite. I was about to step inside when I realized he was getting hard. He gave another groan even as his hand quested down his abdomen to his rising cock. He never took his gaze or his touch away from the mark.

Oh my God. He's intentionally working himself up.

His fingers wrapped around his shaft at the same time he pressed into the marred flesh. His eyelids fluttered and he swayed. Suddenly, it all fell into place. The things I'd said to Andy earlier had been said in anger. I'd assumed his grunts were equally angry responses, but now I was starting to think they were sounds of agreement.

Holy shit. Andy really does like it rough.

My mind immediately tried to dismiss the idea. I mean *Andy*? Quiet, unflappable Andy, who spent more time with his nose in a book than seeing the world around him? It was impossible. And yet, the evidence was growing right in front of me.

"Looks like it hurts," I said, pushing the door further open and stepping into the light.

Andy's head whipped around, his face looking guilty as hell. "You're up."

"So are you." I pointedly did not look down at where he'd just released his cock, but that didn't stop his cheeks from coloring. I glanced in the mirror at his back, lined with red claw marks and the bite on his shoulder. "I shouldn't have bitten you like that. I'm so—"

"I like it," he cut me off.

Ironic to hear him say that after he chewed me out for giving him a hickey before Winter Break.

I stepped deeper into the room. "Can I see?"

He searched my face for a moment, then quietly turned around. I started at the small of his back and drifted my fingers up, lightly tracing the scratches. He shuddered at the touch. When I reached the bite, my caress got even lighter, barely even stirring the air above where I could distinctly see teeth imprinted on his sensitive, alabaster skin sprinkled with freckles. I placed a kiss dead center. He tried so hard, but there was no hiding his resulting moan.

"It might take a couple weeks, but it'll heal," he offered breathlessly.

I rubbed his arms and caught his gaze in the reflection. He seemed wary. I stared back into his green eyes. "Then I'll have to give you another one," I said levelly. His knees nearly buckled before I spun him around and pressed him into the counter, then captured his mouth. He didn't bother to hide his moan this time when I reached up and shamelessly pressed on the mark.

It had taken the better part of a decade, but I finally felt like I knew everything about Andy. I dug my fingers into his sides as I tried to pull his tongue deeper in my mouth. He ground against me, reminding me that touching the bite had only made him harder. I could help with that and this time I wouldn't be cheated.

I caught his gaze again, which was already hazed with lust. "If you pull your dick out of my mouth before I say so, then we're going to have a problem." I pointedly shifted my gaze to the reflection of his shoulder, then back at him.

A note of panic entered his eyes. He swallowed, but didn't argue. I kissed his lips once, then worked my way down his torso. Andy never let me kiss him like this, and I savored every second. When I finally got to his erection, he was already leaking precum. I placed a kiss on his pelvis and appreciated how beautiful it was that he was already crying for me.

Perfection like that deserves a fucking trophy.

I slowly took him, his mushroom sliding past my lips into the wet. His whole body relaxed as he rolled his hips forward, sinking deeper into the cavern of my mouth. His moan echoed off the tile, filling me with hunger.

Between the tutoring lesson last term, the first hand example from when he'd blown me, and now this new facet of Andy's desires, I swirled my tongue and hollowed my cheeks while I used my hand to stroke his base to bring him to the edge. I felt when he was about to come and dialed it back. A deep groan swallowed his strangled cry of frustration when I dug my nails into the soft globes of his ass. He gasped as I dragged them down the back of his legs. Once I was certain he wouldn't come anyway, I resumed the formula he'd so thoughtfully given me–lick, suck, stroke.

His sounds grew desperate and his legs unsteady as I brought him to the edge three more times. When I finally let him climax, he fisted his hand in my hair and I nearly gagged at the sheer force of his cum shooting down my throat. I pushed past the reflex and swallowed, incurring a whine from Andy that sounded like he was seconds away from collapse. He tasted every bit as perfectly as I'd imagined, though the hint of spice was probably my imagination.

I tenderly caressed the back of his thighs, which now sported their own set of red marks, and kissed my way back up his body. A thin sheen of sweat coated him that salted each taste of his quivering flesh. He didn't seem to care that there were still remnants of his seed in my mouth as he kissed me deep enough to touch my soul. But as much as he clung to me, he couldn't hide how he was shaking.

There's no way he's walking out of here.

I gave him a small kiss before scooping him up into a cradle. He wrapped his arms around my neck and sagged into my chest. The mewling returned as I carried him back to the bed and curled around him. My own neglected erection dug into his back and he ground against me. I kissed his shoulder, causing him to shudder.

"Later. You need rest," I whispered, brushing his hair back. His only response was to burrow deeper into me. I trailed my fingers lightly over his skin as his breathing found a deep, steady rhythm. For a while, I lay there simply watching him sleep.

This is my Andy. The tiger and the house cat.

A knock came at the door, persistent and loud, ruining the doze I'd fallen into. Andy twitched beneath my arm. I glanced at the clock, which now read seven. *Who the fuck could that be?* I pulled on some lounge pants and went to answer it before they could knock again. I still had a hope that Andy hadn't woken.

When I opened the door, it was to find Connor. The anger from yesterday surged forward with a vengeance. I barely got control of it in time to prevent it from showing on my face. I carefully closed the door a bit to obscure Andy naked on the bed, where he was hopefully still sound asleep. "What do you want?" I deadpanned.

Right, so that could have been a little friendlier.

Connor stopped trying to look past the door and met my gaze. "I came to talk to Andy. Where is he?"

I crossed my arms over my chest and leaned against the door frame. "Why?"

"I already told you. I need to talk to him."

I raised an eyebrow. Connor glared at me.

"About the museum today. Now where is he?" he asked again.

I glanced over my shoulder to see that my ginger kitten had yet to stir. *Good.* "He's still asleep."

"Andy doesn't sleep in."

"Poor cat is tuckered out," I said with a small smile, absently wiping the side of my mouth.

Connor narrowed his eyes. "Look, I just want to check on him. The whole fucking hotel heard you two yelling at each other last night."

Hadn't really considered that when I was fucking him hard enough to black out.

Connor took a step forward and his gaze fell on the ice bucket, which, along with an assortment of other things, was still on the floor. I saw the moment he leapt to conclusions. "What did you do to him? Is he really asleep? Or is he unconscious?" Connor made as if to force his way into the room.

I blocked him.

"He's sleeping. We'll be down in time for breakfast."

That gave Andy one more hour to recoup. I just prayed it would be enough. I was a little concerned he might not be able to walk. *He'll never forgive me if I make him miss the Smithsonian.*

Connor didn't look like he believed a single word of what I said. I didn't appreciate the insinuation. His face pinched as he pointed at me. "I swear to God, if you've hurt him…" I missed the rest of the threat as it suddenly dawned on me.

He has no idea about Andy's kink. He doesn't know anything about him. Not my *Andy, and certainly not the Andy I got to know last night.* That meant Andy had trusted *me* with that and no one else.

All of my hatred for Connor vanished. Well, almost all of it; he still had something that I would never have–four missed years.

"Look, tell Garza and Cohen that we'll be down—dressed, showered, and ready to explore—in an hour," I said, working *really* hard to keep my tone friendly.

Connor opened his mouth, no doubt to continue demanding to speak to Andy, and I closed the door in his face. I shook my head, a little impressed at his persistence, and made my way back to bed. Andy turned slightly to face me as I slipped in beside him.

"Who was that?"

"No one," I said, brushing his lips with a kiss.

He made a noncommittal noise and returned to his pillow, effectively cocooning himself in my arms. I buried my face in his auburn hair and inhaled his essence. Suddenly, he stiffened, and I feared I'd freaked him out.

"Did you call me a cat?"

I chuckled, sending hot air to caress his neck. Guess he hadn't been as asleep as I'd hoped. "Yes."

"Are you saying I'm a pussy?" The idea that Andy could ever be anything so crass was ludicrous.

I smiled and kissed the nape of his neck. "More like a Tom-cat."

"Hmm. I suppose I can live with that." I wisely failed to mention that he was definitely more of a kitten at the moment and brushed another kiss along his shoulder. The teeth marks caught my attention once more.

"You'll have to be careful with this," I said, blowing on it softly.

"Why?" he asked, almost turning. I danced my fingers over the bite, barely even touching it. He instantly let out a guttural groan that had me hard in a second.

Fuck. What am I going to do with him?

He ground his ass against my erection, making me groan as well.

I took a steadying breath and tried to think about anything else besides how good it would feel to have him wrapped around me again, squeezing, pulling me deeper with each thrust.

Not helping, Mitch.

"We don't really have time for that," I said aloud.

"I heard. And we still have to take a shower."

I kissed along his neck and whispered in his ear, "Then I guess *we* should take a shower."

Chapter 13

Andy

I sidestepped a tour group composed almost solely of exuberant seventh graders. Their enthusiastic chatter faded as I walked toward my destination. Mitch was still appreciating the impressive assortment of geodes they had on display, while I was much more interested in checking out the "Dawn of Man" exhibit. That we had separate interests had always been one of the best things about our friendship. We didn't *have* to do everything together. We chose to.

I leaned on the railing to admire the attention to detail in the side-by-side comparison of Neanderthal and Cro-Magnon. The movement caused my shirt to brush my sensitive shoulder, a subtle reminder of the previous evening. A smile spread across my face.

I always knew there was a beast inside of Mitch. He's too careful for there not to be.

Of course, the results of forcing it to the surface had been mind blowing.

I've never been so thoroughly fucked in my entire life. God, that was amazing. And then this morning… I practically hummed to myself as I thought about it.

Having Mitch walk in while I was getting off to that impressive bite had been less than ideal. I wasn't ashamed of my desires, just terrified of what he would think of them. I needn't have been so concerned. Mitch was one of the few people in this world that saw me as more than just a brain. He was intimately familiar with every part of me. My smile turned wicked as my thoughts strayed to the epic blowjob. Mitch was by no means a selfish lover, as he had proved repeatedly.

Of course, as incredible as the sex was, literally nothing compared to waking up wrapped in his arms. My smile faltered.

What am I going to do? This won't last—I know that. I'll be lucky if he stays interested through graduation.

One thing was for certain. I couldn't hide from my feelings for Mitch anymore. I was more in love with him than ever, and despite the imminent heartbreak, I was willing to enjoy this game for as long as he was willing to play.

"Looks like you've lost your bodyguard."

I looked away from the exhibit to see Connor walking towards me. While I didn't appreciate the insinuation that Mitch was my protector, there was no point in hashing that out now. "Mitch is around," I replied noncommittally.

I might have fibbed a little to Mitch this morning when I asked who had been at the door. Connor's whiny voice was difficult to mistake, though I hadn't really caught much of the conversation. I returned my attention to the display and hoped he would take the hint.

It really had been a mistake signing up half a second behind him. Honestly, I'd been aiming to sign us up first so we would be guaranteed spots. Apparently Connor had had the same idea and beat me to it. I was more than a little surprised considering Connor hated history and Mitch was right—he'd been a total prick lately.

That still doesn't explain Mitch's reaction. It's almost like he's jealous. But fuck me if I know why. It's not like he knows Connor and I used to be a thing. Or would care.

"You okay?" Connor asked, pulling up next to me.

I gave him a sidelong look. He was fishing for something. "Yeah. Why?"

"Sounded like things got pretty heated between you two last night."

You have no idea.

"We're good," I responded evenly, careful to keep my face neutral.

"You know you can always talk to me, Andy."

I snorted. Calvin *talked.* Mitch *talked.* Connor was only ever interested in getting laid. *Talking* was just a means to an end. "I'm good," I reiterated, then turned away from the exhibit I was nowhere near done with to move on to the next display.

"Don't be like that. We don't even share notes anymore since you and that jockstrap decided to be friends again."

I rolled my eyes. Like he was one to talk. "Not a lot to share," I said, still walking away.

"Andy."

I gasped as his hand landed on my shoulder and sent the bite mark roaring to life. My body's instant and traitorous reaction had me frozen.

Connor took full advantage of my paralysis, to step up behind me and cup my ass. "I know you still want me," he whispered in my ear, then promptly gave my ass a less than subtle squeeze.

The heat that had spread through me like wildfire turned violent in an instant. I spun around so fast, he never saw it coming. I couldn't very well break his nose in the middle of the museum, so I did the next best thing.

Connor's eyes bulged as my open hand made contact with his face. The angry red that immediately sprung to life matched the fire raging inside of me. Without another word or so much as a backward glance, I left the room. The group of seventh graders eyed me as I stormed past them into the geode room, then onto the aquatic exhibit where Mitch had apparently relocated.

I was still struggling with calming breaths by the time I pulled up next to him. He glanced at me out of the corner of his eye. I wanted more than anything to wrap my arms around his neck and bury my face in his shoulder; but that wasn't exactly an option. Not here, out in the open where everyone could see, where people would assume things about him, where my heart would be on full display for anyone who bothered to look. Instead, I focused on my breathing and stared straight ahead at the rather daunting display of a narwhal.

"Something happen?" Mitch asked.

I closed my eyes and took a deep breath, then let it out slowly. I loved that he didn't ask if I was okay, since I clearly wasn't, but I also couldn't tell him the truth. At the first mention of Connor, he was liable to walk back in there and break his nose again. It wasn't even about him trying to fight my battles for me, though that was definitely part of it.

He would get sent home for sure and probably expelled on top of it.

"Just stupid people being stupid," I said vaguely. It was as close as I dared get to the truth.

He leaned back to look through the entrance to the exhibit, where you could still see the tail end of seventh graders. I sent up a silent prayer that Connor wouldn't choose that exact moment to walk across the passage.

"Yeah, I know what you mean," he said, resuming his casual perusal of the horned creature. "Cats are so much easier to deal with."

I chuckled and shook my head, the tension from the encounter with Connor finally leaving me.

Only a cat person would ever say that.

"How is your cat, by the way?" I asked.

Mitch turned his head and gave me a strange look. "Pretty good, last time I checked," he said with a grin. The small smile spoke of mischief, but I couldn't think how that would apply to asking about his calico. He nodded toward the horned whale. "Incredible, don't you think? Doesn't seem possible or even likely. And yet, it's as real as you and me."

"I know what you mean. Even with science and all we've learned, some things still feel like magic."

He laughed to himself and looked down at his clasped hands. "Tell me about it." For some reason, I didn't think he was talking about the impossible mammal. Suddenly, he straightened back up and smiled at me. My heart stuttered.

It's gonna tear me apart when he leaves.

"Have you seen the Cretaceous exhibit?" he asked.

Despite my depressing thought, I grinned back. "Not yet."

Mitch

Everything was… perfect. Literally, the only thing that could make the day better was if I could blatantly walk around with my arm around Andy. I'd settle for holding his hand, but I didn't see that flying either. So I made do with just being near him and absorbing any accidental touches that came my way.

It finally felt like we were connecting again. Not just because of the sex or learning about Andy's kinks, but because we were laughing and sharing. He stayed with me through some of the exhibits I was most interested in until we finally circled back to the "Dawn of Man" exhibit, though I was surprised he hadn't already checked it out since he'd made no secret that it was the one he was most eager to see.

I held back as we entered the grand space with displays lining the room to appreciate Andy's wonder. And his ass. I was definitely also appreciating his ass. Jesus, where was he buying jeans? He spun around and glanced at me and I couldn't help but return his smile. I doubted Andy had any clue how truly beautiful he was.

"Come check this out," he said in an excited whisper that still carried.

I quickly crossed the room to join him at a display illustrating a typical hunting party as well as an example of housing. "What am I looking at?"

He jostled me. "Come on, you can't tell me that the way they're positioned doesn't look familiar." I peered closer, but still came up empty. He made an aggrieved sound when I shook my head and pointed to the hunters. "Tell me that doesn't look like a lacrosse play."

My eyebrow shot up in disbelief before I could stop it. "Since when do you know lacrosse? Pretty sure I've never seen you at a game." And I'd definitely looked. Every. Time.

His face pinked. "I've seen a few practices… with Calvin. Besides, I don't have to know all the ins and outs of sports ball to recognize the basics."

I snorted a laugh. "Sports ball, Andy? Really?"

"Shut up. But seriously, look. There's Benny out front with you and Brian close behind, flanked by John and Kyle." He leaned further and further over the railing separating us from the display in his enthusiasm until I was worried he'd flip over it.

I grabbed his hips to steady him. No way was I explaining to Garza how his star pupil had fallen into an exhibit. The rightness of holding him thrummed through my arms to resonate in my chest.

"Do you see it?" he asked over his shoulder, his green eyes as bright as ever.

I gently coaxed him off the railing and back onto the ground, but didn't let go right away. "You're half a team short, but, yeah, I think I see what you mean. There are a lot of similarities. And I guess instead of eating the ball or the other team, we simply score."

"Exactly!" he replied a little too loudly and glanced around. Luckily, none of the other visitors paid us any mind. We were still a hell of a lot quieter than the younger students running around. He cleared his throat and stepped to the side, forcing me to drop my hands from his hips. They tingled with the memory of him and my palms longed to feel him beneath them again. "Anyway, like I was saying, most sports harken back to typical hunting patterns. Even the premise is the same. It builds community and teamwork with a foundation of trust. Hell, they even 'provide' for the larger community," he added seriously, though the air-quotes were adorable.

I smiled at him, loving how he got whenever knowledge was involved. Andy could teach me whatever he wanted all day, every day, as long as he did it with that same excited gleam in his eyes. “Oh, yeah? And how does that ‘providing’ work in modern sports ball?”

He made a face at my obvious teasing, but it didn’t prevent him from elaborating. “Okay, so it’s a little different. They’re not exactly bringing home a mammoth carcass, but they do bring revenue to wherever they are playing. People come to games to watch and be entertained, some to even live vicariously. And while they’re there, they inject money into the local economy.”

“Providing,” I finished for him.

His chest puffed with obvious pride and his eyes shone such a bright green that it took every ounce of restraint I had not to kiss him. Andy was perfect in every way, and I never wanted him to change.

Chapter 14

Andy

"I think we're gonna need to get some more ice, though I still don't see why we need it," Mitch said, picking up the fallen ice bucket. I met his gaze and tried diligently not to grin like a fucking Cheshire cat. "At least the floor is dry now," he added, sparing the spotted carpet a speculative look.

I rolled my eyes, finally losing the battle with my stupid grin. "I'll get it," I offered. He passed me the empty container and returned to getting ready for bed. I stalled, enjoying the show until he vanished into the bathroom. I shook my head at my own antics and opened the door to go retrieve the ice. When I looked up, it was to see Connor poised to knock.

"Hey Andy."

"Connor," I said flatly, a little disappointed not to see a red welt on his face.

"Look, I just wanted to apologize about being a dick earlier. I was way out of line."

"Ya think?" I was dubious about finding him here in the first place, but I was officially intrigued. Connor and apologies didn't really go together. I took another step into the hall and half-closed the door behind me.

"Well, yeah." He gave a self-deprecating laugh and rubbed his arm. "Would you believe I thought this trip would give us a chance to—I don't know—be close again or something?"

I believed it. I glanced back toward the door as if I could see through it and the bathroom to Mitch on the other side, then looked back at him.

"Anyway, I'm obviously doing a terrible job of convincing you to give me another chance. Still, maybe—if I haven't royally screwed things up already—maybe we could study for finals together or something."

He's fucking hopeless.

I shook my head and sighed. "Connor, you're an alright guy, you really are." Hope flashed across his face. "But I'm just not interested in being study partners anymore."

His face immediately twisted at the blatant rejection. "You know, ever since you started being friends with Hudson again, you've been a real asshole."

"You're one to talk."

"Whatever, Andy. He can't give you what I can."

I glanced anxiously down the hall. "Would you lower your fucking voice?" I hissed.

"Yeah, wouldn't want anyone finding out your dirty little secret, now would we?"

"I swear to God, if you don't shut up..."

"Does your *bestie* know what you are? What you're willing to do in the dark?"

Anger burned my skin. It felt like I was on fire. "Leave him out of this. Your problem is with me and the fact that I won't be your standby anymore."

He licked his teeth, rage clearly stamped on his face. "He doesn't know you like I do. He can't—"

I was done. "Mitch knows *everything* about me and he's known *exactly* who I am for years," I cut him off.

"Is that why he up and dropped you five years ago?"

That's it. I'm breaking his face.

I had a spotless record. If I was lucky, the most that would happen to me would be getting shipped back home and detention for a week. If I was unlucky, I might get suspended for a few days as well. I could live with that. It wasn't like it could affect my application to the University of Chicago at this point, anyway.

"I'm right, aren't I? You told him what you are, and he fucking abandoned you."

I took a step toward him, fully prepared to claw his eyes out. At the same time, the door flung open behind me and a half-dressed Mitch launched into the hallway.

"Go inside, Andy," he ordered, taking the bucket from me.

"But..." I protested, more than a little alarmed at his abrupt appearance. How much had he heard?

"I've got this. Second-string here is going to give me a hand," Mitch said, practically daring Connor to contradict him.

Connor's sour face looked like getting ice was the furthest thing from his mind. I managed one step before Mitch grabbed my arm, pushed me back in the room, and closed the door.

I stood frozen in shock, listening as their footsteps got fainter.

What do I do? Do I race after them? Do I stay here? Do I get someone? I knew I should have paid closer attention to what rooms the chaperones were in.

I ran my hands through my hair and felt sick. I sat on the edge of the bed and put my head between my legs.

Oh God, he'll kill him.

For some reason, I couldn't understand, Connor was a trigger for Mitch. Probably had something to do with lacrosse. Calvin had mentioned something about them being rivals or something, hadn't he?

And now he's going to get himself kicked out of school because of it.

The hotel room swam before my eyes and I quickly ducked my head again.

Fifteen minutes later, the door opened and Mitch walked in, complete with an overflowing bucket of ice. The door thunked shut, and I leapt to my feet, getting a head rush for my trouble.

"What happened?" I asked, terrified of the answer.

"I got the ice," he responded, mischief sparkling in his eyes.

"That's not funny. What happened?" I repeated.

"We had a… chat. He won't be bothering you anymore," he said with a smug grin as he set the bucket down on the dresser.

"For fuck's sake. What did you do to Connor?" I had a very clear vision of Connor left a bloody mess in the room with the ice maker and vending machine. I could barely breathe as I asked, "Did you hurt him?"

Mitch's humor instantly dissolved into anger. "If you're so worried about him, Andy, then you can bunk with him tonight," he said hotly then stomped past me.

"What? No." My head was spinning. Why the fuck would I want to bunk with Connor?

Mitch ignored me and walked up to the still made bed. He punched the pillow hard enough to make me jump before taking a seat on the mattress, his back pressing the abused pillow into the headboard. His folded arms felt like ten foot high walls.

Shit.

"Mitch, please. I don't want to bunk with Connor, like ever." His fierce stance softened slightly. "But I need to know what you did to him. I need to know if you hurt him." There was no hiding my edge of panic, and his response was not helping matters.

Mitch's arms re-tightened and his glower intensified. "This is the thanks I get for sticking up for you?" he growled bitterly.

"I had it handled."

"Didn't sound that way to me."

"You were eavesdropping?" I asked, slightly sidetracked.

"Kind of hard not to when you're shouting at each other with the door open," he bit off.

Shiiit. He would have heard everything. How the fuck do I fix this?

I walked to the side of the bed and considered my options. He continued to glare at the far wall as if I wasn't right there. How did I get him to understand? I stared down at him where it looked like he was perfecting the art of brooding. I sighed inwardly. For starters, he'd have to look at me. "Mitch," I said.

Nothing.

"Mitch," I tried again with the same result.

Petulant child. You wanna play like that? Fine. We'll be children.

I leaned over and thumped him on the forehead.

"What the fuck, Andy?" he shouted as he turned on me. He was obviously angry, but at least he was looking at me.

Now that I had his attention, I intended to keep it. I swung a leg over his outstretched two and straddled him. "Let's try this again," I said, ignoring his surprised expression.

He narrowed his eyes at me and refused to uncross his arms.

I was careful to keep any wayward emotion from my voice as I continued. "Mitch, if you hurt Connor in any way—say, broke his nose again or beat him to a bloody pulp—then you'd have been shipped back early and probably expelled."

His lips parted slightly, and the barrier of his arms fell.

I raised an eyebrow. "Didn't think about that, did you?" I let that sink in a moment before adding, "I don't give a shit what happens to that jackass. I care about what happens to *you*, Mitch. And frankly, I'm not done enjoying my time with you." I punctuated the statement with a kiss.

Mitch licked his lips and stared back at me as he rested his hands on my waist. “I didn’t hurt him,” he finally said.

I could have cried with relief. Instead, I said, “Good,” and captured his mouth again. A gasp escaped me when his fingers slipped beneath my shirt and gripped the bare flesh. I glided my hands across his bare chest, exploring every inch of him as I tangled my tongue with his in an even deeper kiss.

He shifted his hands higher up and pulled me closer, his rigid cock now firmly pressed against me. I shifted to a more comfortable seat on his lap and arched into the touch to encourage his adventuring. I rolled my hips, brushing against his barely constrained erection, and smiled as I captured his groan.

“What are you thinking about?” he whispered when I ventured down to his clavicle.

I traced my tongue over the bony protrusion, then tasted his lips again. “All the different ways I want you to take me,” I said, grinding hard for emphasis. There was something rather liberating about telling him the truth. I ground down again, holding onto him for support. His fingers dug into my lower back, but he didn’t give into the kiss I was trying to tempt him with. Confused, I leaned back to look at him.

“Are you sure it’s not too soon?” His concern was so sincere I could have melted.

I gave up mapping his chest to cup his face, then kissed him thoroughly enough to elicit a moan. “Let me worry about that. We won’t be here much longer, and I want to enjoy every second I have with you.” I stared into him, meaning every word and saying so much more than I should have.

I’d meant to sweetly place my lips against his, but Mitch was having none of it. He dominated my mouth with a savage kiss that only stopped when he pulled my shirt over my head. His fingernails raked down my back and I arched into him, groaning. Before I knew it, we’d traded positions so that now I was the one leaning against the headboard. Lost in the heat of the moment, I barely registered the quick work he made of our pants, leaving nothing between us but heated skin.

I laughed as he pushed me higher up so that I was sandwiched between him and the headboard. “I thought we already cleared this up,” I teased, leaning back against the warm wood as he left to grab the oil he’d used the night before.

"Have a little faith, Andy. You'll get exactly what you want," he said as he crawled back between my legs, then kissed me hard enough to lift me off the bed. The bite flared to life as it pressed against the headboard and I groaned even as I had to hold on to his shoulders to support my increasingly suspended position. He tapped a slick finger at my entrance, and I instinctively shifted my legs to give him more room to work. I was on the verge of begging for more when he removed his fingers altogether. Then he slipped his arms beneath my legs.

My eyes widened when he hooked his forearms under my knees and I rose even higher. I met his gaze, surprised to find his hazel eyes filled with the same mischief I usually associated with pranks. He shifted, continuing to fold me nearly in half as he positioned himself better. There was no way to mask the shock clearly stamped on my face.

"Don't look so surprised. There's more than one way to skin a cat," he said, the words laced with heat. I barely even registered that he had made yet another cat reference before he added, "And this way, we both win."

I'm about to get the living daylights pounded out of me and he's talking compromises.

He started slow. Carefully sliding into me inch by torturous inch. By breath caught repeatedly despite my efforts to keep it steady and my body relaxed. Through it all, Mitch held my gaze, refusing to even blink as he took me. The drawn out taking was more than I could bear. It was intense and an entirely different kind of primal.

Desperate for an outlet, I tangled my hands in his hair as I explored his mouth with my tongue and adjusted to the feel of him rooted so deep. When I couldn't stand it any longer, I rolled my hips. His resulting groan said the delay was killing him as much as it was killing me.

The muscles in his arms tightened as he slid out and slowly back in. I moaned, and he repeated the steady move several more times. His mouth dropped to my neck as he stroked deep and hit my prostate.

My whole body shuddered, and I groaned. This wasn't compromise. This was torture. He'd barely even done anything, and I was already hanging on by a thumbnail.

He placed a searing kiss on my neck. The heat of it rippled through me and still that methodical stroking, slowly driving me insane. Suddenly he paused, mostly pulled out, and caught my eye. "Ready?"

"For what?" I asked, short of breath.

That mischief reentered his eyes. "To get exactly what you want."

"Sweet fucking hell, yes." The words scarcely left my lips, and he rammed into me so hard my head bounced off the headboard. He froze until I looked back at him. "Keep going," I ordered, then mashed my mouth against his.

He immediately resumed his hard thrusts, escalating his rhythm until the headboard was smacking against the wall in rapid time. I moaned and felt the sharp bite of his nails on my thigh.

"Yes," I panted as he continued to drive into me. "Don't. Stop." Every stroke hit that perfect spot, hard and exact. "Don't…" My head popped the headboard again, drowning out the rest. I was probably going to have a headache from how many times I'd hit the damn thing, but I couldn't care less. My climax built like a tidal wave ready to crash. My cock pulsed in time with my heart—or maybe it was his thrusts. It was hard to tell. They were both going so fast. "Stop. Don't. Stop," I moaned again. He hesitated, and my orgasm drifted out of reach. "Mitch," I whined at the denied release.

He didn't wait for more prompting, just resumed with a renewed fervor, biting lightly at my neck. It wasn't much, but it did the trick. My tidal wave rose back up fierce and ready to drown me in ecstasy. After a few more dominating thrusts and a particularly sharp bite, the wave broke, and I came hard, coating our abdomens. Not even half a second after, Mitch went off as well, shooting his release deep inside me. I moaned at the feel, positive that if I hadn't just come so fucking hard, I could have again just from that.

I clung to him with arms that were more like cooked noodles and didn't even want to consider what state of jelly my legs were in. Our heavy breathing filled the room now that the pounding of the headboard was no longer drowning it out. Mitch slowly lowered me back to the bed where I lay in a human puddle of contentment, then he got up and vanished into the bathroom.

I dug deep to shift my exhausted body to a cooler part of the bed. He returned a minute later with a damp towel. I cleaned up half-heartedly, unwilling and unable to do more.

"We're going to need a safe word if this is going to be a thing," Mitch said, joining me stretched out on top of the covers.

"Why is that?"

"Because 'Don't stop' can just as easily be 'Stop. Don't,'" he said, propping himself up on his elbow and looking down at me.

That explained the hesitation earlier. I nodded. "Fair point."

"But it has to be something that would never come up during."

"That should be easy. It's not like we're really talking," I quipped snarkily.

"You never know," he said, bending to kiss my chest.

I got lost in another kiss, hot and humid on my already flushed flesh and it took me a moment to pull my thoughts back together. "So, like what? Frogs?" I suggested with a chuckle.

"Frogs could work."

I gave him an incredulous look. "You can't be serious. I was kidding. That's completely ridiculous."

He shrugged and continued kissing along my torso. "It'd be really hard to mistake."

"Fine. Frogs it is. *For now*," I added, still unwilling to accept something so preposterous.

"Frogs," he said with a smile.

"For now," I repeated, rolling my eyes.

Suddenly, his teeth closed on my nipple. I gasped and arched off the bed as waves of pain woven with pleasure radiated through me. "God, I'm glad you figured that out," I said breathlessly when he switched to sucking on it.

"You could have just told me," he said, looking at me.

"Where's the fun in that?" I countered.

"You are such a brat." He laughed as he coasted his hand across my chest, which now that I thought about it, was a canvas of hickeys.

"Which is it Mitch? Brat? Or cat?"

"In my experience," he began, briefly pausing to acquire the comforter from the other bed. He threw it over us and curled around me before resuming. "Cats, by nature, are bratty. So there's no reason you can't be both."

"You are *such* a cat person," I sighed.

He slid his fingers through my hair and stole a languid kiss. "I most definitely am."

"Yeah… yeah." I yawned. After two nights of incredible pounding, I was fading fast. I twined my limbs through his and buried my face in his chest where the sound of his steady heartbeat encompassed me. His arms tightened around my exhausted body and I slipped blissfully into slumber.

Chapter 15

Mitch

I could really get used to waking up with Andy in my arms. Was there anything more perfect in the world? I burrowed my face into his hair, letting the silken strands caress me while his unique herbal scent filled my nose. Shame it couldn't last forever. Today was primed to be another full day of educational tours and sightseeing historical landmarks. But we still had a few minutes before the alarm went off and I planned to cherish every last one of them.

Andy mumbled against my chest and I fought the instinct to hold him tighter, to cling to this fleeting moment. Reluctantly, I left his nest of auburn hair and let my arm fall away as he lifted his head. He glanced around bleary-eyed until his gaze landed on me. The faintest smile touched the edges of his mouth, making my heart swell so much I was afraid it might actually burst. Could hearts do that?

"Morning, kitten," I said softly, brushing the hair back from his face and letting my thumb glide over his pronounced cheek.

His almost smile flipped into a scowl that was really more of a pout. "Mm, not a cat," he mumbled, and I had to hold back a laugh at how freaking adorable it was. For someone who never slept in, Andy really wasn't a morning person.

"Could have fooled me," I teased as I ran my hand down his arm to where he was essentially making biscuits on my chest.

He snorted and grumbled something I didn't quite catch. He also stilled his hands.

I finished my journey along his arm to take his hand. I thought about bringing it to my mouth to kiss his palm, but settled for stroking my thumb along the back. This moment felt too fragile to risk upsetting. “I don’t mind,” I whispered.

Andy blinked and looked back at me, his intense gaze searching my face. The quiet enveloped us once more as we continued to stare into each other. I couldn’t help but wonder—not for the first time—what would have happened if I’d been there when he’d woken up after that first night instead of running away like a coward so full of shame I could barely breathe. Would it have been like this? Soft and tender. Would he have come to his senses and been furious with me for what I’d done, for taking advantage of him? Those “what ifs” tortured me constantly, and it was past time I was honest with Andy. That’s what I was here for, after all. To make him hear me.

I gathered what I could of my tattered courage and braced myself for this beautiful morning to get ugly fast. “Andy—”

The alarm blared so loud that I jerked and nearly bit my tongue. Andy rolled away with a miserable groan. “I still don’t understand why we have to start the day at the crack ass of dawn,” he grumbled as he flipped the covers back and sat up, awarding me a stunning view of his creamy skin and smattering of freckles. I ignored the faint red lines still criss-crossing his back.

He stood and stretched his arms high over his head. No amount of telling myself to keep my gaze up could prevent me from appreciating the perfect curve of his ass. I fucking wanted to bite it. I shook my head, grateful he couldn’t see my open struggle with the horny monster I became whenever he was close… or naked. This wasn’t the time for lust, it was the time for talking.

“Come on, slowpoke. We should get ready. I’m not making do with another picked-over breakfast,” he said before walking that glorious ass into the bathroom.

I flopped onto my stomach in the spot he’d just vacated to soak up the last of his lingering warmth. Just like all the other times, I felt my opportunity slip through my fingers. Why did everything with Andy always have to feel so damn tenuous? What was the worst that could happen if I told him the truth?

Unfortunately, I already had a ready answer. He’d hate me. Forever. My betrayal would be so much deeper once he knew. I fisted my hands in the sheets that were definitely going cold while the sting of tears pricked my eyes. I really was a fucking coward. My father would be ashamed. I snorted to myself. Doubly so.

"Mitch, what part of 'get ready' sounds like 'go back to sleep'?"

I cracked an eye and waited for him to venture closer to the bed. When he was within reach, I lunged, yanking him back down onto the mattress. "This part!" I shouted triumphantly as I tickled his sides.

His howls of laughter chased away the gloom, infusing the morning with a brightness that was all his own. "Stahp!" he laughed, pushing me away, but not escaping. "That's not fair! You're not even ticklish." He wiggled and wormed in my grasp until he finally slipped free and landed with an "Oof" on the ground.

I quickly moved to check on him, but before I could check to see if he was hurt, he bolted upright.

"Victory!" he declared, his arms held high in triumph.

I laughed and smacked his ass, causing him to frown. "Looked like retreat to me."

He swatted at my hand when I reached for him again. "I'm not one of your teammates. Cut that out."

I scoffed and spun around so I could stand in front of him. He lifted his chin to meet my gaze, defiance shining brightly in his endlessly green eyes. "Something tells me you wouldn't mind so much if I had you bent over my knee when I did it." I cupped the telltale bulge in the briefs he'd apparently put on when he'd gone to the bathroom.

His face turned scarlet and I could literally feel the heat emanating off of it, but in true Andy fashion, he didn't back down. "We don't have time for this," he replied, his voice only cracking slightly.

"I know, I know. No sad, crumbly biscuits for you." I gave his swelling dick a light stroke through the thin material, enjoying the way his breath caught and his pupils dilated. "You're right, I'm starved. *Someone* made me work up an appetite. With workouts like that, I won't even need to hit the gym." I winked at him, then slipped past to take a leak and brush my teeth. Not that I'd be sacrificing so much as a millisecond of time with Andy for something as ridiculous as following Coach's orders to keep up the training regimen while I was in DC.

Andy

Mitch was going to be the death of me. How was I even fucking functional right now? Yeah, I'd always known he was a little on the cocky side, but literally nothing could have prepared me for that confident swagger. *Earned* swagger. The way he'd looked at me in the hotel room, his hazel eyes smoldering with promise while he literally held me in the palm of his hand...

I shuddered and gulped down several swallows of ice water. I'd have given my left nut for a coffee, but I needed to cool down more than I needed caffeine, and sadly, the hotel didn't have any ice coffee. I offered Professor Cohen a shaky smile as he sat beside at the round breakfast table and hoped like hell my face wasn't still a damn furnace.

"Anderson," he said pleasantly as he plucked a piece of bacon from his laden plate.

"Professor," I replied and did my best to mirror him.

His brow creased. "Are you feeling alright? You look a little flushed."

God damn it. "I'm fine," I said too quickly, my voice pitching high.

To my relief, he merely chuckled. "No need to be so worried. I trust you to tell me if you're genuinely unwell." He leaned closer with a conspiratorial smile. "Between you and me, we're pretty much the most responsible adults here."

"Uh, Professor Garza?"

Cohen's mouth twisted to the side. He angled his fork at where Garza was joining us with a veritable mountain of breakfast on his plate, while his full cup of coffee balanced precariously on top of his glass of orange juice. I ducked my head to hide my chuckle.

"What's so funny?" Garza asked as he plopped down, then rubbed his hands together excitedly, all but dancing with eager anticipation in his chair.

Cohen steepled his fingers and looked evenly at his colleague. "You know they're not going to take the buffet away for at least another couple of hours, right? You can make more than one trip."

Right on cue, Mitch sat on my other side with an equally heaping plate. "What?" he asked when Cohen and I shared a look.

I shook my head and schooled my laughter. "Nothing. You're a mess."

He made a noncommittal noise and finished getting situated. "Oh, they added these after you'd already gone through. Thought they'd make a good snack while we adventured today. I know how distracted you can get when exploring." He pulled out three small apples and as many oranges from his pockets and placed them on the table.

I huffed a laugh and picked up a shiny red apple. I really needed this man to stop doing things that made me love him. "Professors, is it okay if I run up to our room for a bag before we leave?"

"Absolutely," Garza said after swallowing a mouthful of the biggest omelet I'd ever seen. "That's quite proactive of you, Hudson. I'm glad to see Anderson has been rubbing off on you more than scholastically."

I nearly choked on my latest bite of waffle and pushed back from the table. "Come to think of it, I'll just go get it now. Don't want to forget." I kept my head down and scurried away from the table as fast as I could while their curious eyes followed my abrupt departure. I did *not* need to be thinking about rubbing off on Mitch, or heaven forbid, his casual suggestion to spank me, while eating breakfast with two of our professors, one of whom was my mentor.

I dumped out my satchel of books on the still as yet unused bed, quickly rubbed one out, and raced back down to breakfast. Hopefully, no one wondered why it had taken so long to grab a damn bag. There was just enough time to finish my breakfast, which unfortunately had gone cold, and scoop up the fruit before we had to leave for our bus tour of the city. It was no museum or Library of Congress—that was tomorrow—but I was looking forward to riding on top of the double-decker bus. I was not, however, looking forward to the cold.

Garza and Cohen handled the tickets at the station, then our small group made its way to our tour bus. To my surprise, both Garza and Cohen opted to stay below deck, as did a couple of other students, including Connor. Seriously, where was the fun in that? I was still pondering why any of my peers would voluntarily forgo the experience of riding up top when Mitch flagged me down.

"Andy, over here! I got us some seats." I glanced at where he was waving emphatically above the heads of the other passengers… at the back of the bus.

I schooled my frown. I was not a back-of-the-bus kind of person. I was very much a *front-of-the-bus* where you could actually hear the tour guide. Still, I offered apologetic smiles to our traveling companions and made my way to the back. I was all set to inform Mitch that we'd be moving when he turned a grin that could rival that sun on me.

"Took you long enough. Come on, we're pulling out soon." He patted the seat next to him. "I made sure to get us a spot by one of the heaters since *someone* never dresses warm enough despite always being cold. And even better, there's a speaker right there." He pointed to a discreet circle I'd missed as I walked by it. "Isn't this great?"

I couldn't help but smile as I scooted closer to Mitch and the heater. Yeah, actually. It was pretty great.

Chapter 16

Andy

Mitch's head popped through his polo, and I chuckled at how his hair stood out in all directions. "Yeah, yeah," he grumbled, leaning over to peer in the mirror over the dresser and attempted to flatten his hair. After a few failed tries, he let out a frustrated huff. "I swear there's something in the detergent they use on the bedding. I never have this much trouble with my hair anywhere else."

"You're hopeless." I moved the bucket of now melted ice closer to him and dipped my fingers into the cool slush. "Come here."

He turned to me with a pout and I had to bite the inside of my cheek to keep from laughing. "I can do my hair," he complained sullenly.

"Could have fooled me," I teased as I ran the water through his rebellious hair. He was right. He was perfectly capable of doing this himself. But I wasn't about to pass up the opportunity to touch him. Also didn't hurt the way he was looking at me with half-lidded eyes. It really was a shame guys didn't get their hair played with more often. It was nice. Finally, my excuse to touch him ran out, and I wiped my hands on my jeans to finish drying them. "There, at least it's not sticking straight up anymore."

He snorted. "Don't understand why it was in the first place."

I shook my head and laughed softly as I slipped into a light jacket. "It's the lack of humidity. The air is a lot dryer here and there's way more static." He gave me a goofy grin, and I paused mid-zip. "What?"

"Seriously, how are you so smart? It's one of the most amazing things about you."

I scoffed. "You say 'one of' like there's more."

He tugged my jacket collar closed and looked down at me. For a moment, everything else ceased to exist. There were only his hands and his soft hazel eyes. "There's plenty more than one." His playful smirk did nothing to temper the blush fiercely burning across my cheeks. He released my jacket and reached for his. "What are we doing today, again?"

I cleared my throat and braced myself. "I signed us up for the National Zoo excursion." I had just enough time to register his eyes widening with surprise before he grabbed my jacket and started shaking me.

"The zoo?! For real?" Abruptly he stopped shaking me and looked at me in concern. "What about the Library of Congress?"

I shrugged. "I'm always around books. Thought it'd be nice to mix things up. Doesn't hurt that it's going to be warmer today than it has been the last few days." I maybe also knew how much Mitch loved zoos. It was the thing he'd done with his dad when he'd been alive. And selfishly, I loved the way Mitch lit up at the news.

"As long as you're sure…" He gave me a dubious look.

"There's no going back now. Garza is waiting in the lobby for us to get our asses down there."

"Well, what are we waiting for?" He grabbed my hand and hauled us out of the room. I laughed as he dragged me in his wake. He was so excited, I was worried he might combust as we waited for the other two in our group. Thankfully, it didn't come to that and within an hour we were walking into the National Zoo.

Mitch was practically bouncing on his toes while Garza handed us our passes, and we meandered through security. I grabbed a map, though I wasn't sure if we'd actually use it, reassured Garza that we would stay out of trouble, then walked over to where Mitch was already impatiently waiting at the entrance to the Asia Trail.

"What took so long?" he asked when I finally joined him.

"Relax. There's still plenty of daylight and Garza confirmed that we're not under any kind of time crunch. Also grabbed this." I held up the folded map. Glee erupted on Mitch's face.

"Yass," he said, snagging it from me. He immediately opened it all the way and twisted it around, glancing up periodically to get his bearings.

I stepped close and looked at the marked trails he was peering intently at. "Where do you want to start?"

"Definitely want to see the Big Cats exhibit, but we'll have to wind our way there, since it's on the far side of the park."

I snickered, and he glanced at me.

"What?"

"You're such a cat person." I swiped the map from him and took off down the trail. Not that I got far before he caught up.

"What's wrong with liking cats?" I was pretty sure his scowly face was supposed to be intimidating, but it was really just cute as fuck.

I bumped him with my shoulder. "Nothing. You're just consistent is all." I glanced at the first exhibit on our path. "Now, are you going to tell me all about sloth bears, or do I have to do all the reading for myself?"

He took the map back from me, folded into a smaller square, and shoved it in his back pocket. "Prepare yourself to be edu-macated," he said, cracking his knuckles.

I laughed at his over the top declaration and kept laughing as we wound our way along the trail. We were playfully arguing over whether we should double back to a food spot we'd passed for lunch when he spotted the sign for the Great Cats exhibit.

"This is it!" He rushed ahead, and I ran after him. Adults we may have been, but sometimes it was nice to feel like a carefree kid again. No essays. No college applications. No exams. No responsibilities. Just two best friends having a great day.

"Where are you going?" I called when he didn't stop at the first group of cats.

He glanced over his shoulder, his joy positively radiating off of him. "I want to see the tigers first."

I laughed to myself and hurried to catch up. By the time I made it to the Amur tigers, he was already leaning on the railing with the happiest freaking smile. I stole a moment to appreciate how amazing he looked in his bluejeans and dark teal polo. I was in serious danger of traipsing off to fantasy land when he looked over his shoulder.

"Don't just stand there. Come here." He waved me over and stepped back from the railing to make room for me.

I frowned. "Where are they? I don't see anything." A quick peek at the information display said there should be two tigers, but as far as I could tell, the enclosure was empty.

"Right there." Mitch pointed toward a thick section of underbrush. As much as I squinted, though, I couldn't make out heads or tails or any other body parts.

"Still nothing."

He moved to stand behind me, then guided my focus. “Just wait. I think they’re coming out.” He pressed closer, his anticipation palpable.

I did as he said, though it wasn’t easy when all I could think about was how I was essentially cocooned against him. I was about to call it quits and move away for the sake of my sanity when a section of shadow detached from the trees and sauntered into the open. I released an involuntary gasp as the sunlight shone off the tiger’s fur in a blaze of orange.

“Remind you of anyone?” Mitch teased while the incredible animal vaulted into what amounted to a tree house.

“He’s beautiful,” I whispered in awe.

“Yeah, he is,” Mitch sighed as he rubbed my arms.

Before I could comment, another tiger emerged from the opposite side of the enclosure to prowl along the elevated edge. “There’s the other one!” I shouted, then clapped a hand over my mouth.

Mitch’s chuckle vibrated against my back as he ducked his head to hide his face in the crook of my neck. “You’re too cute.”

“Shut up,” I grumbled.

He raised his head and placed a firm kiss on the side of my temple. “I like seeing you excited like this. Reminds me of the summer you came to visit.”

Much as I would have liked to join him on memory lane, my brain was stuck on the kiss—in public—and that he’d called me cute. Realistically, I knew he didn’t mean that in a romantic "you’re attractive" sense, more like a "you’re so silly," but my stupid heart refused to be convinced.

He squeezed my biceps and stepped away, taking his warmth and all my misplaced fantasies with him. “Okay, *now* we can go see the lions.”

After the Great Cats, we continued along the winding path past the smaller cats and prairie dogs, then past the kid’s farm until we got lost in Amazonia.

“Look at the size of that thing,” Mitch said in awe, pressed up against the glass much like the eight-year-old a few feet away. He stepped back and shook his head. “Remind me to *never* go swimming anywhere where there are electric eels.”

I chuckled and chuffed him on the arm. “They don’t go after people.”

He glanced back at the leisurely swimming—extremely large—eel and shuddered. “I’m not taking my chances.” We continued to work our way through the darkened room, enjoying the other animals and, most importantly, the AC.

I stopped in front of a collection of small habitats spotted with neon colored frogs. At this point in life, I was pretty sure frogs would always hold a special place in my heart.

"Wow, those are really pretty," Mitch said, resting his head on my shoulder to see.

"You know, typically the prettier something is, the more dangerous it is."

"Can't argue with that," he replied with an undercurrent of something I couldn't place.

I turned my head to look at him, not realizing how close it would put out faces, or our lips. To my surprise, mischief glowed in his eyes. Or maybe that was the green-tinted lighting. Not that there was much of it in this shadowy corner. A corner where no one would see if I closed the meager distance to press my lips to his.

The same kid from earlier let out an ear-piercing shriek. "Piranhas!"

Mitch lifted his head and stepped back, leaving me to ache at the loss. "I think that's our cue to skedaddle."

I chuckled.

"What?" he asked.

"Just you and your old-timey words."

Mitch

I was pretty sure the last time I'd been to the zoo had been that same summer Andy had visited for a couple of weeks when we were thirteen. Before that had been with my dad. I'd always had a fascination with animals—especially big cats—and going to zoos had been our guy-time. Once in a while, mom would join, but it really wasn't her scene. That Andy had remembered and sacrificed going to the Library of Congress meant everything. And the best part? He was having as much fun as I was.

The trail curved, and we began making our way back toward the entrance, checking out all the little side paths, "inside the enclosure" viewings, as well as the animal houses. We'd forgotten about eating in all the excitement of the Great Cats, and were finally settling down for a *very* late lunch.

"I still don't see what you have against lizards," Andy said as he set his tray of over-priced chicken tenders on the table and took a seat. "Some of them were cool looking."

"Nope. No lizards for me. You want to make fun because I like cats? Well, cats *eat* lizards and good riddance." He laughed like I knew he would and another firefly joined the cloud already filling my chest. I never wanted today to end. We were happy. We were us. The same us from that summer. Inseparable and completely in sync.

He offered me a few fries, which I gladly exchanged for some of my onion rings. "You think we'll have time to check out the Elephant Outpost again before we leave?" he asked before chomping into the crispy batter.

"I thought you said we weren't on any timetable." I really wasn't ready for the day to end. Not when I finally felt like I had the perfect opening to tell Andy the truth about what happened that night five years ago. The truth about me.

"*We* may not be, but the zoo still has hours, Mitch." He threw a fry at me. It sailed over my shoulder to land on the walkway where it was promptly claimed by a squirrel with the skinniest tail I'd ever seen.

Someone nearby clearing their throat prompted us both to look over. "Now I know I don't see you gentlemen feeding the wildlife."

"No, Professor Garza. Unless you count Mitch as wildlife." Andy threw another french fry at me. Thankfully, this time I caught it.

Professor Garza huffed a laugh. "Would either of you mind if I joined you?"

"Not at all," Andy replied, already scooting his metal chair further away from me.

My heart sank as my golden opportunity evaporated before my very eyes. Garza was nice and all, but I wasn't really up for sharing Andy at the moment. I already counted it as a miracle that Connor hadn't been on this foray. Though after our chat, I suspected he'd be giving Andy a wide berth now that I'd made it clear that his constant pestering was upsetting him.

I tucked into my sad excuse for a burger while the two of them launched into a conversation about college and the advanced writing program Andy couldn't wait to join. From what I could gather, it sounded like Andy's attendance at the university was a done deal. I'd have to find another time to talk to him. Preferably with fewer interruptions.

"What about you, Hudson? Given any thoughts on which university you'd like to attend?" Garza asked, dragging me into the conversation.

I let out a humorless laugh. "I doubt any of them would want me."

"Hey," Andy said sharply, startling me and Garza. "Don't do that. You've worked hard to pull your grades up and you are *not* a bad student." He angled a fry at Garza. "Tell him."

Garza turned a sympathetic look on me before addressing Andy. "Your faith in your friend is admirable, Anderson. But it's no secret that Coach Santinelli isn't exactly the best mentor. I fear many of the athletes on the lacrosse team are in similar positions."

Splotches of red bloomed on Andy's face, making his freckles stand out in high relief and betraying how angry he was getting. "That's not... You can't... You're a professor! How can you say that?" he spluttered.

"Andy, it's okay," I tried to reassure him. "We always knew that me getting a scholarship outside of athletics was a long shot."

"No, it's *not* okay." He slammed his tray on the table, causing Garza and me to jump.

"It's really not a big deal," I tried again.

"Like hell it's not." He pointed an accusatory finger at Garza, who understandably recoiled in the face of Andy's fury. "You have no right to say anything even remotely detrimental about Mitch or his studies. What have *you* done to help him? What have you done to help any of the athletes you say are suffering under that godforsaken coach's tutelage? Mitch is a remarkable student, but you wouldn't know, none of you would. You know why? Because you couldn't be fucking bothered."

"Now, Anderson—" Garza attempted to interject, only to have Andy steamroll right over him.

"I'm not finished," Andy snarled. "You don't know anything about Mitch. You don't know what he's been through, how hard he's worked, the shit he has to put up with just to eke out a few hours to study. And until you do, you can keep your opinions about him to your damn self." Andy was positively shaking with rage now while Garza and I sat completely gobsmacked at his outburst. Andy really thought all that? About *me*?

Garza waited another second, then awkwardly cleared his throat. When Andy didn't try to stop him again, he spoke. "You're right. I understand very little of Hudson's circumstances. For that, I would like to extend my heartfelt sincere apologies. I spoke out of turn and did not express myself very well."

"You, uh, don't need to do that," I mumbled, though the fierce glare Andy kept trained on his mentor said otherwise.

"On the contrary. If you'd please permit me to clarify my tactless statement." He glanced at Andy, who narrowed his eyes at him. "I didn't mean to imply that you're unintelligent. Far from it. You may not have the same book smarts Andy does, but you're still bright."

I sank into my seat, feeling more awkward than ever. It was one thing for Andy to say he thought I was a decent enough student, but a professor? "You don't have to lie to make me feel better." I ducked my head in increasing shame. I was under no delusions when it came to my intelligence… or lack of.

"I'm so sorry, Mitch," Garza said again.

Andy held up a hand when I opened my mouth to protest. "No, I want to hear this and whatever you think, Mitch, this man owes you an apology and an explanation."

Garza shot Andy a surprised look, and I worked to hide my shock. I knew firsthand how fierce Andy could be. But I never thought in a million years he'd use that fierceness for my benefit, least of all with a professor he admired and respected. When was the last time *anyone* had stood up for me like this?

Garza sat a little straighter and pushed his half-eaten sandwich aside so he could lean on the table and meet my gaze. "I'm sorry this institution has failed you. Anderson is right. When given half a chance, you're an incredible student. Attentive, engaged. And before you argue again, you don't have to be Andy-smart to be an outstanding student or bright."

I glanced askance at Andy to see if this satisfied his criteria. I really hoped it did, because I wasn't sure how much more I could take before I couldn't pretend my face was burning from too much sun.

He took a deep breath and let it out slowly. "I'm going to toss this. Are you finished?" Andy asked, reaching for my tray.

"Yes?"

He added my tray to his and walked to the nearest trash receptacle. Even after his calming breath, I could all but see a ginger tail switching behind him with agitation.

"That was… unexpected," Garza said quietly as he picked his sandwich back up.

"He does have a bit of a temper on him."

Garza threw his head back and laughed.

Andy paused what he was doing to look back at us suspiciously.

“I, uh, better go. Since I’m done and all,” I said before Andy could stomp back over.

Garza nodded and finished chewing his latest bite. “For what it’s worth, I do believe you are a bright student and are fully capable of accomplishing whatever you set your mind to. As for Anderson…” He shook his head with a rueful smile. “You’re good for him, even if he doesn’t always see it. He needs you more than he realizes.”

I pushed back from the table beneath Andy’s watchful eye. “Thank you, sir.” Now if I could just find the courage to tell Andy how much *I* needed *him*.

Chapter 17

Andy

I would never be okay with Mitch thinking he was dumb. It actually hurt my heart to hear that he still did after all the work we'd done together to help him study and lift his grades. I thought we'd made genuine progress. But maybe I was wrong. Was I not encouraging him enough? My side, I could fix, but nothing could have prepared me for the overwhelming sense of betrayal when I heard Garza voice a similar sentiment. My *mentor*.

It was a good thing he'd sent his letter of recommendation for the Advanced Writing program last term, or might have very well torn it up and shoved it in his face. Even after Mitch had reassured me of what Garza had meant, it had taken most of our remaining time at the zoo for me to calm down.

Mitch's warm hand settled on the back of my neck, and he squeezed lightly. "You okay?" he asked, his voice lowered so it wouldn't carry to any of the other disembarking bus passengers.

"I'm… I'm…" I angled my head to look at him with suddenly water-filled eyes. "You don't really think you're dumb, do you?" I asked just as softly.

He stared at me for a long second while his thumb traced a delicate arch at the nape of my neck. "That's… that's not an easy question to answer." He must have seen the argument brewing on my face, because he gave my neck a slightly firmer squeeze. "I know I'm not… stupid." He glanced away, and my heart broke at the undercurrent in his voice. When he looked back at me, I didn't know who he was trying to convince with that wan smile. "I also know I'll never be smart like you." He ruffled my hair, and for probably the first time in *ever*, I didn't care.

"Mitch," I said with all the sincerity I could muster and still keep my voice low. "At the risk of sounding really full of myself, *most* people aren't smart like me. That's not a fair standard to hold yourself to."

He tucked his hand in his pocket and released a heavy sigh. "I know. I just wonder sometimes…" He shot me a furtive glance. "Forget it." He stepped toward the hotel and I grabbed his arm.

"No. Tell me. You wonder what?"

He gave a self-deprecating laugh and rubbed the back of his neck while he peered at me from beneath his absurdly long lashes. "We have so little in common. I wonder why you ever became my friend."

Indignation prickled on my scalp and wormed its way down to my toes. "I am your friend because you're awesome. You're kind and funny, and, yes, smart. It may not be the same smart as me, but that's the best part."

"Okay, okay. I get it. Simmer down, tiger." This time, his smile and laugh were genuine. I gave a sharp nod and let my hackles down. He glanced at the clock hanging in the lobby and his grin broadened. "We have a good bit of time before the group dinner. I think I have an idea to fill the time."

"Yeah?" I asked, perking up.

"It's been a pretty busy day. What do you say we wash off the dust from the zoo, then relax and read for a bit?"

I blinked, not sure I believed what my ears were telling me. "You… want to read?"

"Don't sound so surprised," he scoffed. "You already know I brought that space pirate book. Things are getting really intense and I want to know what happens."

I snorted. "You don't really need me for that."

"Maybe. But I didn't exactly pack a dictionary. Who else is going to tell me what some of the words mean?" He crossed his arms over his chest and smirked. "It's really a selfish suggestion, if you think about it."

I ducked my head to hide my laugh at how expertly he'd just handled me. "Sounds like a good plan to me." We turned as one and resumed crossing the lobby. If I didn't exactly meet Garza's eye as we passed, it was pure coincidence.

Mitch's great idea would have been a lot better if we'd "washed off the dust" together instead of taking turns. Though I was hard pressed to be genuinely disgruntled about my solo shower, given I'd walked out to the unexpectedly sexy sight of Mitch propped against the headboard reading intently… shirtless. The shirtless part was extra nice. While he was preoccupied, I shamelessly appreciated the light dusting of hair on his defined chest that trailed down his mouth-watering abs to disappear into the promised land. I wanted to lick him.

And with that intrusive thought, I finished rubbing my hair dry and subtly adjusted myself before joining him on the bed with my book. Equally shirtless, because why the hell not? Ten minutes later, I was completely absorbed in my book and my soul was at peace. I wasn't sure how much time had passed when Mitch let out a satisfied sigh and set his book down on the side table.

"That was really good," he mused softly.

I peeked up from my current page. "You finished?" I glanced down at my book, feeling torn. "Guess I can continue this later…"

He placed a hand on my shoulder. "No need to stop reading on my account. The quiet is nice. I'll nap or something."

"You sure you don't mind?"

"Why would I? Keep reading, Andy." The way he said my name had butterflies lazily flapping their wings in my chest.

I smiled and snuggled back into the pillows. "Okay."

Turns out "or something" won out over Mitch napping. The hand he'd originally placed on my shoulder journeyed down my side and continued its subtle exploration of every exposed inch of me within his reach. Eventually, he shifted closer and nuzzled the back of my neck before placing a gentle kiss on my shoulder. Each touch was light, almost absent-minded, and just shy of too distracting. Rather than ask what he was doing, I indulged in the unprecedented relaxation wrapped around me.

Mitch pressed his lips into my shoulder again while he ran his fingers feather-light along my arm. If there was a better feeling in the world than this, I hadn't found it. Everything about this moment was perfect. Surely this was what paradise looked like—my best friend and the man who'd stolen my heart, gently caressing me while I lay curled up with a good book.

A wave of goosebumps rose in the wake of his fingers and he smoothed them away with the flat of his warm palm. I let out a soft sigh, fully embracing the fantasy and losing my spot for the third time.

"Is this what it would be like?" His soft question tickled the back of my neck and popped my perfect bubble of bliss.

"What do you mean?"

He sat back, taking his warm caresses with him. "You know."

"You mean being gay?" I asked, praying like hell that wasn't what he meant at all.

"No. Well, kinda? I mean, I don't know about you, but I've never had a relationship with a woman that was, well, this easy."

"I've never been in a relationship with a woman," I snapped to hide the hurt threatening to well up and ruin our perfect day.

"Right, yeah. I'm just saying women are, I don't know, *complicated*."

"And you're saying I'm not complicated? Newsflash, Mitch, gay, straight, or whatever, *all* humans are complicated."

"I know that. But it's not the same. Ugh, this is coming out all wrong," he added, his voice muffled like he was rubbing his hands over his face.

I squeezed my eyes shut, grateful he couldn't see the hurt rippling across my face, and closed the paperback without marking the page. "Then maybe you should do a better job explaining what you're trying to ask."

"I'm sorry we can't all be as good at words as you are."

I swung my legs over the side of the bed, still facing away from him, and stood. "Just say what it is you mean."

"I'm trying. All I was asking was if you'd ever experienced anything like this before. That's all," he huffed, and he might as well have stabbed me with a knife.

"No, I haven't," I replied, my voice thicker than I would have liked. And I probably never would again. I doubted I'd ever find another man that owned me body and soul like Mitch did, who saw and accepted all of me.

"Oh." That single small sound lit something inside me.

I whirled on him. "What does that mean?"

"I just, I thought you… you know. I mean, you seem to know what you're doing."

The tiny ember burst into flame. "Are you seriously asking me if I've had sex with other men, right now?" Judging by the color draining out of his face, he was. "You are. Fuck, Mitch. Not that it's *any* of your fucking business, but yes. I've fucked other guys."

"No, that's not…" He scrambled off the bed and tried to approach me, but I shrugged him off and focused on getting out my clothes for dinner.

"What did you think? That after you fucked me in some secret room that I'd be broken forever? That your sexual 'prowess' would ruin me for other men? You've got some fucking nerve."

He looked like I'd slapped him, and it took him a moment to recover. "Jesus, Andy, that's not what I meant at all! Wait, are you comparing *me* to other men?"

No, because there was no comparison. Mitch would always win hands down. Even our completely inexperienced and awkward first time was better than any of the sex I'd ever had with Connor. But I wasn't about to tell Mitch that. "What right do you have to stand there and ask me that? Next, you're going to ask me how many."

"I mean, I'd be lying if I said I wasn't curious." At least he had the decency to look abashed at the confession.

"That's none of your goddamn business!" I'd known this would end eventually. Wasn't like we'd be in DC forever. But I'd really hoped we could hide in this fantasy where we were an actual couple instead of friends fooling around until the last possible second. I should have known better. I *did* know better. Mitch was straight—curious, but straight—and I was… convenient. Trustworthy. And now he was throwing it all in my face.

"That's why I didn't ask," he countered when he found his voice.

"Then what the fuck *are* you asking, Mitch? Because I'm completely lost here."

"I don't see why the hell you're acting so self-righteous. I just asked a question. Maybe not well, but that's all. I didn't do anything wrong."

I stared at him while my brain tried to process what he'd just had the audacity to say to me. "You didn't…" I released a derisive laugh that spread through my chest like acid, momentarily eclipsing all the other hurts vying to dominate me. "You know what? I'm not doing this with you. I'm just… not. It's been over four fucking years. I am *done* with letting that night hurt me."

His face crumpled, and I almost regretted saying it. Almost. "Andy, if you just let me talk to you, I can explain. I can explain everything."

I let out a stuttering breath. The other hurts wouldn't be quelled for much longer, especially not with him looking at me like that. Like I fucking *meant* something to him. More than an easy friendship and a convenient fuck. "Yeah? Well, I don't want to hear it."

"Tough shit, because I'm going to say it."

"No." I pushed past him again, this time to get to the bathroom.

"Andy."

I ignored the plea in his voice, even though it tore at my heart. My throat constricted, and a repressed sob nearly split me in half. I hastily made my way to the refuge of the bathroom so I could fall apart with at least the illusion of privacy. “I’m going to freshen up. I suggest you get dressed.”

How stupid do I have to be? This was never going to last. It was always going to come to this. No amount of my loving him would ever make this more than a temporary diversion for him.

“Andy, wait.” He lunged to catch me, but he was too late.

I slammed the door shut and locked it, then hastened to the sink. A twist of the faucet knob had the sound of water spray filling the room in an instant. My breath came in shallow bursts as I sank to the floor, my back pressed against the locked door, unable to stay away from Mitch even as my heart inevitably broke all over again. What was I thinking? How had I let myself fall so deep into the fantasy?

“Andy, please,” Mitch whispered through the pressed wood almost right next to me. The bitter sting of tears pricked at my eyes. I squeezed them shut, to no avail. “I’m sorry. I didn’t mean any of that the way it came out. You know I’m shit with words. But I’m trying. I’m really fucking trying. Please open the door, Andy. There’s so much… so much I want to say to you. Let me explain.”

It was likely me projecting my heartache that made it sound like he was hurting too. But that didn’t stop my resolve to keep the distance between us, to preserve some part of myself from crumbling like a bluff falling into the sea.

A mere heartbeat away from rising and flinging the door open, a sharp rap came on the main door to the hotel room. A beat of silence went by and it came again. Mitch’s sigh drifted through the door as he abandoned his entreaty to answer the insistent summons.

The swing bar slammed against the wall, and the lock clicked open. “Hey Professor, what’s up?”

“Forget about the group’s evening outing already, Hudson?” Professor Cohen’s familiar dry voice asked.

“Right, sorry. Must have lost track of time.” I flashed to what Mitch had been doing as he “lost track of time” and my heart ached all the more for what could never be.

“Where’s Gallagher?”

Mitch stumbled to answer. “He’s, uh… freshening up.”

Professor Cohen sniffed, likely unimpressed with the shallow explanation of my whereabouts. “He can join the others downstairs. As it is, we are running behind.”

"I can wait for him," Mitch countered.

"Gallagher is a fully capable young man. I'm sure he can manage to get himself downstairs in a timely fashion. That correct, Gallagher?" he asked louder to be heard through the bathroom door.

"Yes, professor," I called back, grateful my voice didn't break.

"After you, Hudson." Mitch didn't respond and in my mind's eye, I could clearly see him waffling about doing as he was told and stubbornly refusing to go without me. At last, there was a thin sigh of defeat and the door closed.

Loneliness wrapped around my shattered heart and strangled my repressed sob. I pushed myself up and staggered to the sink where I splashed frigidly chill water on my face several times. But no matter how cold the water was, it couldn't numb the ache taking me over.

Mitch

Every fiber of my being wanted to stay in that room until Andy came out. I'd wasted so much time, not just days or weeks, but *years*. And it was killing me. I needed Andy in my life more than I needed anything else, and it was about time he understood that. Except I was awkward and nervous and didn't know how to start. So, of course, I'd said the wrong thing, and he'd fled. Literally. Again.

Now I had to contend with Cohen giving me the stink eye, because we'd not only spaced on the time, but we'd both forgotten that we were going out for a special dinner to celebrate the last day of the trip. I quickly changed into appropriate clothes befitting the occasion, all while hoping Andy would emerge and Cohen would fuck off. But it seemed my rash of good luck had finally run out. Andy didn't come out of the bathroom, and Cohen stood like a sentinel just outside the partially closed door.

I cast a defeated look toward the bathroom as I walked past to join Cohen in the hall. "Don't forget your room key," I called to Andy, not sure what else I could really say with Cohen standing Right. Fucking. There. "I guess I'll, uh, see you downstairs."

A noncommittal noise came from beyond the door and I made peace with the fact that was likely all I'd get until I could sit him down and *make* him listen to what I had to say. Maybe I could find some rope and buy it on the sly while we were out.

"Move along, Hudson." Cohen placed a hand on my shoulder to steer me and called back before the door could fully close, "Don't dally, Gallagher. The entire group is waiting and our reservation is coming up."

"Yes, sir." Andy's muted reply sounded so hollow. I was gutted, since I was pretty sure that was my fault.

As I trudged after Cohen, I kept replaying what had happened. But no matter how many times I went over it, I was still lost. Why couldn't I get my words together? It wouldn't even take that many. The only thing holding me back was me. And fear. A lot of fucking fear. Andy would be upset—rightfully so—when the truth came out. What if he couldn't forgive me? What if I lost him for good this time?

"Jesus. Took you long enough," Connor complained when Cohen and I stepped off the elevator. His gaze slid past us and his cheek twitched. No doubt he wanted to ask where Andy was.

"Let's load up the taxi buses. Gallagher will be down imminently," Cohen declared. He and Garza exchanged a look, then herded everyone out the door.

We'd all just finished getting settled into the two taxis when Andy scurried out of the hotel and slipped into the last open seat. I hated that I wasn't next to him, but it couldn't be helped. At least we were in the same taxi, and he wasn't sitting next to Connor. Though judging by his body language, he wasn't exactly thrilled to be sitting next to Garza, either.

I spent the unexpectedly long drive trying to make out their whispered conversation, but it was impossible given my seat at the back. Eventually, we pulled up to a fancy restaurant that immediately had me disparaging my outfit. Not that I had anything fancier outside of my school uniform. Luckily, I wasn't the only one who looked like they felt a little underdressed.

We scooted inside and my eyes widened in awe at how freaking *nice* everything was. The host checked our reservation and led us across the restaurant to a private event room. I barely stopped my sigh of relief that the whole joint wasn't going to be watching and judging us. Not that anyone had bothered to give us more than a passing glance as we passed.

For once, I didn't have to push my way into sitting next to Andy. There were legit fucking place cards with our names on them, along with a sealed envelope on each plate. I stood beside Andy, not sure if we were supposed to sit right away and wondering if all the envelopes had the same thing or if it was different.

"If you would all please sit." Garza held out his arms to encompass the long table and remained standing while Professor Cohen sat beside him at the head. "I realize some of you are a little out of sorts at our unexpected venue. This is a surprise we like to plan for all our trips." He placed a hand on Cohen's shoulder, who smiled at us enthusiastically. "This excursion is not covered by your tuition or trip fees."

A collective murmur filled the table, and I flinched. How the fuck was I supposed to pay for this? I hadn't brought that kind of money. I didn't *have* that kind of money. Suddenly, warmth suffused my trousers over my thigh. I glanced down to find, of all things, Andy's hand on my thigh offering reassurance. I swallowed thickly and returned my attention to the professor.

"You can all stop panicking that you didn't save enough over the week. This treat is wholly on us and completely *off* the books, if you catch my meaning." He gave the table a meaningful look, and Cohen smirked. Instantly, the nervous murmurs turned excited.

"So sit back and enjoy. We'd love to hear what you enjoyed most about this trip and if there was anything you wished we'd done or spent more time on," Cohen added.

Garza gave his colleague's shoulder a squeeze, much like I'd done to Andy earlier. "Bon appétit." He sat with a smile and turned to respond to whatever the student next to him said.

I felt Andy's hand sliding off my leg and I quickly grabbed it, grateful for the extensive tablecloth hiding our hands from view. Andy's sharp intake of breath made my skin tingle, but I didn't let go. I leaned closer and dropped my voice so only he could hear. "I get that you're mad at me, but this is our last night and there's something I really want to talk to you about. Later, okay?" I squeezed his hand for emphasis, tracking the wariness on his face.

After a few fraught seconds, he flicked his bright green gaze to me and nodded. I let out a relieved breath and relinquished his hand. Tonight, after what promised to be an incredible meal, I was finally going to come clean with him. There was no telling how he would react—he could be fine, he could hate me forever—but the wait was over. That in itself had me feeling lighter than I had in years.

Chapter 18

Mitch

I kept a close eye on Andy throughout dinner. He smiled and laughed at all the right things, but something was off. At least I'd finally told him outright that I wanted to talk to him about something. Now I just had to not fuck it up. This was our last night, and I was officially out of chances to be honest with Andy about… well, everything.

I let out a long breath and instinctively reached for him under the table. Even having my hand on his leg settled me in ways I never could have imagined. Andy had been my rock since my father had passed. How could I not realize how adrift I'd been without him?

"You okay?" Andy whispered. I blinked to find him leaning in and looking at me with concern in his green eyes. He glanced down, drawing my attention to where my grounding touch had turned into more of a squeeze. He continued to search my face as he coasted his hand over mine.

"Yeah," I replied, my voice pitching embarrassingly high. I cleared my throat, and this time gave his thigh a more intentional squeeze before removing my hand. "I'm good. Got lost remembering all the places we visited."

He smiled, then we were pulled back into the conversation. I managed to keep my focus more present for the rest of the meal, but as we got closer to the hotel, my anxiety resurfaced. You'd think after having weeks, months, *years*, to figure out what to say, I'd be more prepared. Unsurprisingly, Andy was giving me curious looks as we split from the group and went up to our room.

The second the door shut behind us, I turned to him. "Andy–"

"We should pack first, don't you think? That way we don't have to worry about it later and can… can relax," he cut me off before I could build any kind of steam.

I rubbed the back of my neck and shrugged. "Um, yeah, I guess that makes sense."

"Glad you agree." He flashed me an overbright grin and turned into a whirlwind of copper hair. I shook my head and followed his lead. We hadn't exactly been messy, so in hardly any time we were back to where we'd started, with me being an awkward duck and him doing damn near everything possible not to meet my gaze.

"Hey, Andy?" I began, fighting back years' worth of nerves.

"Yeah?" he replied without looking up from whatever he was holding.

"There are some important things I want to talk to you about—to tell you—but first, I wanted to apologize." *Finally,* he looked up.

"For what?"

I scoffed. "For being a total jerk earlier. I shouldn't have said what I did, and I'm sorry. You have every right to your privacy. What you've done with your time and with who is none of my business. I lost any right to know about your personal life when I… when I…" I closed my eyes and swallowed hard while the familiar pain washed over me. This wouldn't be easy, but I owed him the truth. I owed it to both of us. His sudden sigh caught me off guard, and I met his gaze once more.

"While we're at it, I'm sorry, too."

My second scoff turned into a full on snort.

"No, hear me out. My getting defensive wasn't really helping. It's just, some people… some people look down on guys who bottom."

"That's really fucked up."

"No shit. But yeah. And I maybe was a little sensitive since I…" He paused and looked up at the ceiling. I held my breath while I waited for him to continue, but was completely unprepared when he admitted, "I've never bottomed for anyone but you." There was absolutely no mistaking his cringe, and I *prayed* my face wasn't doing something extra stupid.

"That's, um, unexpected." I could have smacked myself in the head. Just once, could words be my friend?

He shrugged, his gaze downcast once more, and I stepped toward him until I could tilt his chin up. The uncertainty in his eyes stabbed at my heart. I wanted to find every son-of-a-bitch on the planet who'd ever made him feel like bottoming was something to be ashamed of.

"Hey," I began softly, shifting my hold on his chin to cup his cheek, and absently ran my thumb along his defined cheekbone. "It's really messed up and hypocritical that there are people out there who think like that. I hope you know I would *never* think anything like that about you. Do you hear me? Never."

He continued to stare into me. Something shifted in his intense green eyes, filling them with determination and fierceness. My tiger, burning bright. "Fuck it," he said, then with absolutely zero warning, lunged forward to mash our mouths together.

His fiery kiss muffled my surprise while I reflexively wrapped my arms around him, dragging him tighter against me. "This isn't exactly talking," I mumbled against his determined lips when my brain came back online.

"Talk later," he replied, before searing my lips with another heated kiss.

"But," I tried again.

He pulled away with a gasp, his eyes still alight. "Later," he said more firmly. "I intend to enjoy every fucking second of our last night here." He held up the bottle he'd been holding, which turned out to be actual fucking lube. Not that I had any idea when he'd gotten it. He arched an eyebrow, a challenge written clearly across his face. "Still want to argue, or are you going to throw me on that bed and fuck me like you should have the second the door closed?"

I smirked. "Well, when you put it like that." He let out a squeak of surprise when I picked him up. His lithe body wrapped around me as he returned to dominating my mouth. Even with working out regularly, Andy wasn't exactly light, and I stumbled backward until we fell on the bed in a mess of limbs, with him landing on top of me. He stole my resulting laugh in a toe-curling kiss, turning it into a needy moan. "Fuck," I gasped as he relentlessly ground against my now achingly hard dick.

Mischief shone in his eyes as he leaned back and yanked his shirt over his head. "Come on, super star, show me what you've got."

Nothing got me so hot and bothered as Tiger Andy. And while I would happily die for kitten Andy, playful Andy would always be my favorite. I gripped his thighs to keep him in place and rolled my hips up so that my confined erection could glide along the swell of his ass.

"Yes," he gasped, dropping his head back while he kept both of his hands planted on my chest.

Something cool brushed my shoulder, and I shifted my head away from the gorgeous sight above me to see the bottle of lube rolling around. He must have released it when we fell. Fingers gripped my chin, forcing my gaze back to the beautiful man straddling me.

"Eyes up here. And clothes off. Now." I already knew Andy was a bit of a brat, but bossy Andy was… damn. Wow, bossy Andy was really fucking hot.

With a growl, I released my grip on his legs and struggled to get my shirt off without getting up or dislodging him. He helpfully tugged and pushed the fabric, clearly just as eager to be rid of it as I was. Once I was finally free, he leaned down to capture my mouth once more, his tongue sliding past my lips while his short nails bit into my pecs. Desperate for more of him, I curled my arms around him. He released a hiss that went straight to my throbbing dick as I dragged my nails down his back.

Abruptly, he broke the kiss and squirmed out of my grasp and down my body. My breath caught as his weight glided over my straining erection with nowhere near enough pressure. I pushed up to my elbows, ready to ask him where the fuck he thought he was going, but the words dried on my tongue when he gave me a heated look and reached for the button of my pants. In no time, he'd tugged them down my legs. When he pulled my briefs off and my cock bounced free, leaving a string of pre-cum on my lower stomach, I nearly choked at the unbridled hunger in his eyes.

I forgot how to breathe as he ran his tongue up my shaft, then licked the fresh bead of pre-cum off the tip. I honestly didn't know what was better—feeling his mouth on me or watching it. Then he took me down to the root in one go. I shouted obscenities and fisted my hands in his hair. Feeling it. Definitely feeling it. Goddamn, Andy's mouth was magic.

I struggled not to shoot off, no longer worried about how tightly I gripped his hair as he swallowed me down again and again. If anything, the harder I pulled, the deeper his moans got. He fisted my shaft while he teased the tip and rolled my increasingly tight balls with his other hand. He swirled his tongue around the head, then took me deep once more, hollowing his cheeks, and I nearly combusted. At my strangled sound, he pulled free, his lips puffy and red and tilted with a smug satisfaction that reflected in his eyes. He slipped off the bed and I shifted to follow.

"Who said you could move?" The unmistakable note of challenge in his voice stole my breath and froze me in place. He placed the tips of his fingers on my chest and pushed. A stiff wind could have blown me over, so it was no surprise that I fell back. "That's better."

I heard the distinct glide of a zipper and fabric rustling, then Andy was climbing back up my body. The moment he was within reach, I curled my hand around the back of his neck and brought his mouth down to mine in a punishing kiss. I roved my other hand along the smooth lines of his back until I reached the perfect curve of his ass. I squeezed the enticing globe, then smacked it as hard as my position would allow. The sound nearly eclipsed his sharp intake of breath, and there was no disguising the way his cock jumped against my abdomen in response.

We ground together a little longer, the friction of our cocks dragging against each other equal parts ecstasy and torture, while we ravaged each other's mouth and touched every inch of skin we could reach. Then Andy started flailing his hand around above me.

"Looking for something?" I asked, holding up the bottle of lube.

"Well? What are you waiting for?" He didn't wait for a response before dropping his mouth back down to merge with mine.

I pulled at his lips between fervent kisses and prayed he'd had the foresight to unseal the bottle earlier as I put my dexterity to work. Luckily, when I snapped it open, the liquid came out without resistance. Unluckily, it also got all over my hand.

He snickered. "I can do it." He reached for the bottle and I jerked it away.

"Like hell you will." Surprise blossomed on his face at my harsh insistence. "Scootch higher," I said, already reaching for his ass. He ducked his head, no doubt to hide the pink staining his face, but did as I said. "Much better," I crooned, grabbing his cheeks and pulling them apart to get to his tight pucker.

He buried his face in my shoulder with a whimper as I circled the ring of tight muscle with a slick finger. "Mitch, please," he whined, pushing back against my questing finger and testing every ounce of restraint I possessed.

I nipped at the side of his neck at the same time I slid the digit all the way in. He shuddered and rocked his hips against my lazily thrusting finger.

"More," he panted, briefly returning to tangle our tongues until I added another finger. He broke the kiss with a ragged moan and bore down harder. I twisted my fingers in search of that small swell inside him and knew the exact moment I found it. His whole body jerked, and he started riding my fingers in earnest, periodically returning to give me more panted kisses.

Eventually, he pushed my hand away and reached for the lube. He shimmied down once more until my cock slid along his crease. He continued rolling his hips, tormenting me with the sensation of being *so close*, while he reached behind himself to dribble more lube on my dick. He grabbed my base, lifting himself, and positioned it at his loosened hole. His gaze bore into me as he slowly sank down.

A herd of wild elephants, or fuck, a stampede of dinosaurs, could have torn through the room and I wouldn't have noticed. There was only the way Andy was looking at me and the hot vise of his channel taking me deeper inch by inch. Once I was fully seated, he let out a shuddering sigh. While he took his time to adjust, I roved my hands over every inch of him I could reach, starting with his trembling thighs and gliding up his torso. Then he moved.

He started slowly, bracing himself on my chest as he lifted his hips and brought them back down, as if testing his balance. Gradually, he picked up the pace until it was all I could do to hang on for dear life as he impaled himself on my dick, his head thrown back while he rode me with wild abandon. The slap of flesh filled the room, punctuated by deep moans. I was completely entranced by the flush darkening his porcelain skin, the way his cock bounced and left a string of glistening pre-cum in its wake, how each of his breaths expanded his chest, and how unbelievably tightly he was squeezing me.

I coasted my hands up his chest and tweaked his nipples, earning myself a sharp cry. He moved to grab his leaking dick, but I got there first. Between the mess of spilled lube and his precum, there was more than enough to provide the perfect glide. I stroked him in time with the rhythm he'd set, letting him fuck into my hand as much as he was fucking himself on my cock.

"Mitch." His voice broke, and so did my restraint.

I maneuvered my legs to get my feet under me and thrust up to meet him. His faltering cry was all the encouragement I needed to take over. I let him replace my hand stroking him to grab his hips and pound into him with everything I had. He dropped his chin to his chest, meeting my gaze with lust-filled eyes and pupils blown wide. I slammed into him, desperate for that one perfect look I'd become addicted to.

His strokes became erratic, and no sooner did he let his head fall back once more than he clamped down around me. With a wordless cry, he shot ribbon after ribbon of his release onto my chest and I'd never seen anything so perfect. Andy was absolutely beautiful when he came.

"Andy, I–" He squeezed around me again before I could finish the sentence that had lived in my heart for over seven years and my release slammed through me. My fingers dug into his hips hard enough to leave bruises as I pumped into him and rode out one of the most incredible orgasms of my life.

He collapsed on top of me while the aftershocks continued to play through us. I held him close, mindless of the cum that he was lying on or that was likely leaking out of him now that I'd softened. He took a stuttering breath that set my nerves on edge and clung to me tighter.

"Andy? Is everything okay?" I asked quietly.

He jolted as if he hadn't realized I'd heard him. "It's fine. I'm fine," he said, his voice sounding oddly tight.

Worry chased away the remnants of my bliss and I lightly stroked his back. He was shivering. "Are you sure?"

"Yeah." He straightened up, but didn't meet my eye. "I'm good. I'm just gonna... wash up." He peeled himself off of me, red splotches marking his pale body where we'd stuck together. When I shifted to get up as well, he paused, laying a hand on my leg. "Alone. If that's okay?"

I settled back. "Of course." Absolutely not. "Whatever you want." Fuck what he wanted.

"Thanks." The soft gratitude wasn't really helping matters, but I stayed put like he'd asked.

Andy

It took all of my self control to walk at a normal, casual pace to the bathroom. At least Mitch didn't insist on joining me. My relief was almost palpable as I shut the door and locked it. My hand shook as I turned on the shower as hot as I could stand. Within seconds, steam billowed through the small room. I stared fixated as I watched a bead of water roll down the damp walls.

It wasn't until I stepped beneath the scalding spray that I realized it wasn't just my hands shaking—it was my whole body. A sob tore through me, louder than the one that had slipped out while I was in Mitch's arms. I sunk to the floor, unable to hold myself up or together any longer.

Water pounded against my back while I sobbed into my hands. This week with Mitch had been all of my wildest dreams come true, and now the fantasy was over. In the morning, we'd return to the Academy, to reality. Mitch would go back to lacrosse like it didn't chip away at his soul. Gone were our days of studying together, of me sneaking looks at his soft hazel eyes, or enjoying the way his face lit up when he got a question right. He'd be at practice every second he wasn't in class. He'd give his all at games where I was neither wanted nor welcome. Just like when I'd first lost him, there was no room for me in that part of his life. I was delusional to ever think we could have something more–even if it was just our friendship back.

I scrubbed angrily at my face, though I wasn't even sure who I was mad at anymore. Mitch had hurt me—a lot—but at what point did I move on? The truth was, we'd both made poor decisions back then… and now. We never should have kissed again and we definitely shouldn't have hooked up. It didn't matter why he went with it. *I* knew better. But I'd been selfish. I wanted to know what it could be like if we were truly together. Now I did. My chest spasmed, and a fresh flood of tears burned down my cheeks. Apparently, my heart wasn't done ripping itself in two.

When my eyes were painfully dry despite the water still cascading around me, I pushed myself up and went through the motions of washing up. At least I'd be clean, even if I'd be stuck with this awful empty feeling for the rest of my life.

I turned off the water, dried off, and wrapped the towel around my waist. Then I took a deep breath and wiped the fog from the mirror. The man looking back at me might as well have been a stranger. There was no life in his red-rimmed eyes. The most color on his sallow face came from his swollen red nose. Even his freckles were muted.

Will I ever feel joy again?

The intrusive thought grew and grew until it strangled my already exhausted body. The stinging in my eyes returned, and I violently shook my head. I wouldn't fall apart again. Besides, I didn't have any tears left to mourn my broken heart or what could never be.

I padded to the door and carefully pushed it open. Relief flooded me as I caught the distinct sound of Mitch's deep breathing. Thank fuck he'd fallen asleep. Now he just needed to stay that way, so I didn't have to come up with some lie to explain why I looked like the shell of a person.

I left the bathroom light on, closing the door enough not to disturb him, but still provide enough light that I didn't trip over anything. A quick glance at the other bed showed that he'd stolen the clean comforter from it. With a resigned sigh, I moved toward the vacant bed, dirty sheets and all.

"Andy?" Mitch's sleepy mumble stopped me in my tracks. "Wha' took s' long? Come to bed." He absently pulled the covers back beside him.

I debated pretending I didn't hear him, but decided it wasn't worth it. Wasn't like I was going to be getting any sleep tonight anyway, might as well enjoy being near him a little longer. Without a word, I crawled beneath the covers. Before I had the chance to settle facing away from him, he wrapped an arm around my waist and tugged me closer.

My breath hitched, and he murmured again, but didn't wake. Thanks to the thin light from the bathroom, I had a perfect view of his beautiful face. It honestly hurt to look at him sometimes. Tempting fate, I wriggled an arm free and gently brushed the hair away from his forehead. In a few short months, we'd graduate from Ulwich Prep and go our separate ways. I'd go to the University of Chicago and he'd go... somewhere. Somewhere he'd forget all about the friend he'd played pranks with, who he'd whispered secrets to in the dark with... who he'd had sex with.

I lightly traced the perfect outline of his face. He'd go on to live his best life. Marry the perfect girl, have a cute little house with a white-picket fence and two-point-five kids. He'd cave and get them a dog, even though he was much more of a cat person. Everywhere he went, he'd make friends and be loved. He might laugh one day and tell stories about how he'd experimented back in his school days. But he'd never have sex with a man again. That part of him would always belong to me. And even if he forgot, I never would.

I barely even registered the slow glide of a tear on my cheek as I whispered my ultimate truth into the soft night. "I love you, Mitch."

Chapter 19

Mitch

The second the alarm sounded, I knew something was off. I slapped around until I silenced it and scrubbed at my face, but the strange feeling didn't subside. It was a lot like that lingering feeling you get after a particularly bad dream that clings to you even once you're awake. Except I hadn't had a single nightmare since coming to DC and I didn't remember dreaming.

Grumbling to myself, I rolled over. Whatever it was, it wasn't anything that cuddling with Andy couldn't fix. When I didn't immediately encounter a body next to mine, I groped around. All I found were cold sheets without so much as a hint of warmth. I bolted upright and blinked blearily to bring the dim room into focus.

At first glance, nothing seemed out of the ordinary. The curtains were still drawn. All the lights were off, including the bathroom. My suitcase was still zipped and waiting on the other bed. I did a double take. Andy's suitcase was gone.

My legs got tangled in the sheets as I hurried to get out of the bed and landed bodily on the carpet with a hard thump. I struggled back to my feet, looking for any sign that he might still be here. My search stopped when I reached the clock and the obnoxiously bright red numbers. How was it already 7:30? The alarm was supposed to go off at six. Had I hit snooze a bazillion times and not realized it?

I shook away the thought. No way Andy would have let that fly. Which meant… My heart sank into my stomach. Which meant Andy had intentionally changed the alarm. I'd have given my left nut to believe he'd done it out of consideration, but I knew him better than that. He'd done it so he could be gone before I woke and could pick our delayed conversation back up.

Growling to myself, I pulled on the clothes I'd left out, did a quick sweep to ensure nothing had been left behind, and sprinted for the elevator. As I suspected, everyone else was already downstairs. What was worse, they were nearly done with loading the taxi bus to the airport.

Professor Cohen raised a blond eyebrow as I rolled up, panting for breath. "I was wondering if you planned on returning with us."

I winced at his dry tone. "Sorry, professor. I slept through the alarm," I replied, doing my best to look past him into the vehicle. While I spotted Andy's telltale red hair, there was a definite lack of seating anywhere near him.

"If you would." The professor gestured for me to get a move on. "Much longer and we won't have time to get through security and to the terminal before boarding."

I begrudgingly took a seat in the front row beside Adams with my luggage awkwardly situated between my legs. Needless to say, once we got on the plane, Andy and I would be having words. Not only was this beyond uncool, but it was mortifying to be the one holding everything up.

Given how shitty my morning was going, I should have known it wasn't going to get better anytime soon. In fact, it got progressively worse. We barely made it to the gate in time before they closed the doors. My luggage ended up having to get checked due to how booked the flight was. Andy managed to dodge me during boarding. And if all that wasn't bad enough, somehow I ended up seated between two tourists, who both discovered at the same time that they'd grown up in the same small town in Nebraska and spent the entire flight talking over the top of me. Ask me anything about Cleveland, Nebraska. Go on. I fucking dare you.

After waiting what felt like an eternity for them to bring my luggage out, I raced after Andy, determined to be in the same cab. Relief flooded my chest when I caught sight of him still waiting on the curb. A couple of cars pulled up, and he moved toward them. I poured on the gas. When it didn't look like I'd make it before someone else got a seat beside him, I called out.

"Andy! Wait a sec!"

I swore the world slowed down as he turned. His copper lashes caught the light. The steady hum of voices faded into the background. He glanced in my direction. And looked right through me. All the air left my lungs in a rush and I stumbled to a stop. Without a word, or even so much as an acknowledgment, he stepped into the first vehicle. Then the door shut behind him.

I was still standing in a stupor when a heavy hand landed on my shoulder. I glanced to the side to find Professor Garza with an uncharacteristic look of sympathy on his face.

"Why don't you ride with us?" He gestured to the other car that had just enough room to accommodate two more.

I struggled to swallow past the lump in my throat and nodded. He took my luggage, and I slumped into the seat, my head still trapped in that moment. I now had a much greater appreciation for how Andy must have felt when I'd left all those years ago. He'd tried to tell me, but I hadn't gotten it, hadn't really heard him.

Pain lanced across my chest as I admitted the truth to myself for the first time. I hadn't just left. I'd ditched him. I'd forsaken my best friend in the entire world and it had broken him in ways I couldn't imagine. But now? I didn't have to imagine. Now I knew.

An hour later, the deep red brick of Ulwich Preparatory Academy came into view and I was shaking with the effort of keeping my meltdown to myself. All I wanted was to crawl into a hole so I could fall apart in private. But as we got closer to the school, it became abundantly clear by the crowd of people waiting that wasn't going to happen, nor was it likely to for a good long while.

"Is that the *entire* lacrosse team?" Adams asked behind me.

"Uh-huh," I responded in a monotone.

Garza glanced at me in the rearview mirror, an apology in his deep brown eyes. "I can insist we need to debrief before you can resume your normal schedule."

I was already shaking my head before he could finish. "It's okay." We both knew it wouldn't matter what he said. There wasn't a chance in hell the team was going to let me have even a second to myself. Not after the stunt I'd pulled.

The professor cleared his throat and swiveled to face me. "Would you like me to at least have your things sent to your room?" he asked in a lowered voice.

My eyes and nose stung at the unexpected offer. I ducked my head to hide the sudden well of tears. "That would be great. Thanks," I replied equally low, my voice scratchy.

I spent the precious few minutes it took to drive to the front of the academy to pull myself together. Whatever happened, I couldn't show weakness. I hadn't gone more than ten feet away from the vehicle when the team descended on me.

Brian walked up behind me and aggressively squeezed my shoulders. "I hope you enjoyed your little impromptu vacation. It's the last one you'll be getting until after the championship," he hissed into my ear.

I didn't bother trying to shrug him off or explain that it was for extra credit. A quick glance at the gathered group confirmed pretty much the whole team was accounted for. I caught Nate's eye, and he looked away, his face turning red. Guilt welled in my chest. Had they come after him when they realized I was gone?

"I'm still waiting for a response, Hudson. How are you feeling after your getaway?" Brian snarled.

I dug deep for a neutral tone, but was still surprised when words came out instead of a mindless scream. "Feel like I'm ready to win a championship."

There was nothing remotely friendly about his subsequent chuckle. "That's what I want to hear." He released his bruising grip, simultaneously pushing me forward.

"You need to get your shit or something?" John asked, looking back toward the cars.

I resisted the urge to look back as well, to seek out my beautiful ember of sanity. But it wasn't safe. They'd see. "No." Part of me wondered if Andy was watching this spectacle play out. I doubted it. He was probably already gone.

"Good, then we can head straight to the field," Brian declared, then led the pack toward the green. John and Kyle bracketed me like I'd ever be dumb enough to try to make a break for it.

To my surprise, Connor of all people caught my eye as the team led me away like a lamb for slaughter. The empathy on his face nearly broke me. Maybe now he finally got it. I'd gladly have given him my starting position if it meant freedom. But the only way I was ever getting off the team before the end of the season was in a body bag. I glanced up at the Tower with its missing window. Moments like this, I wish I'd been more resolute and taken that final step.

Andy

I was the shittiest of shitty people. Was I really so desperate to protect my already shattered heart that I was willing to do to Mitch exactly what he'd done to me five years ago? Apparently, I was, and I hated myself for it. Watching the lacrosse team all but tie him up and carry him off seconds after arriving on campus twisted my insides. They hadn't even let him grab his luggage. I was on the verge of volunteering to take it to his room myself when Connor grabbed Mitch's bag.

"What are you doing?" I asked once I was close enough to him.

He jumped as if he hadn't seen me and turned a wary look on me. "What's it look like?"

"I don't know, that's why I'm asking," I replied, a hair too aggressively.

He let out a heavy sigh I wasn't expecting. "Look, I know we haven't been on the best terms lately, but I'm not a complete asshole." He hiked a thumb toward where the lacrosse team was getting farther by the second. "That shit is fucked up. I'm starting to realize the game stopped being fun for Hudson a long time ago. I'd ask him why he doesn't just leave, except it's pretty obvious he's not there by choice. Not any more."

I blinked, not really sure what to say to his unprecedented display of introspection and empathy.

"Don't worry, I won't vandalize his things or his room."

"How do you know where his room is?" It wasn't completely unheard of, but I didn't expect Connor to know or give a shit.

He gave me a level look that spoke volumes. "The whole team knows."

A pit opened in my chest. The shitty feeling I'd been nursing before doubled. "Would it… would it be okay if I joined you?"

Connor's face scrunched in obvious confusion at the request. "Sure?"

We fell in step, walking in silence as we wound through the halls with our luggage in tow. When we'd gone a few minutes without anyone walking by, I plucked up my courage to ask the question that had been plaguing me for days.

"Connor, can I ask you what Mitch said to you that night?"

He shifted the strap of Mitch's duffel to a more comfortable position. "I guess. Though I'm surprised he didn't tell you himself."

"I asked him, but he was a little vague."

He chuckled dryly. "You do hate that."

"So, what did he say?" I pressed, trying hard not to hold my breath.

"Honestly? He told me the same thing that you've been telling me. That you're not interested in hanging out or studying together anymore and I should back off."

"Oh."

He glanced at me. "Why? What did you think he said?"

I gave a noncommittal shrug. "Mostly, I was worried he'd hurt you again."

He barked out a derisive laugh that echoed down the hallway. "Not gonna lie, was worried about that myself when he hauled me down to the ice room. Was amping up for a fight on the way. But when we got there, he just… talked. Said that if I was really your friend, then I'd respect your wishes and that insulting you was a really shitty thing to do."

We stopped a few feet shy of Mitch's door. "Did he hear any of what you said before he stepped in?" I asked anxiously.

"If he did, he didn't let on." We stood in awkward silence for a few moments, then he added, "For the record, I am really sorry. My behavior the last couple months has been… Well, it's been messed up. I think you were right about me being lonely. Maybe if I wasn't such an ass all the time, I'd actually have friends." His sardonic smile was a little too relatable.

I would probably live to regret this, but it needed to be said. "You know, we don't have to be hooking up to spend time together, to be friends."

Disbelief sparked in his blue eyes. "You actually *want* to be my friend?"

"Jeez, you make it sound like you're the epitome of unlikeable," I scoffed.

"Aren't I?"

I sighed and shook my head. "No, Connor, you're not. You've got a few rough edges and some stuff you need to work through, but you're not a bad guy. Most of the time," I added with a smirk.

"Okay, that's fair. So, um, I'm going to drop this off, then head down to the lockers to join practice."

"Really?" I asked, taken aback.

He shrugged. "If I have a prayer of playing in the championship—which we're totally going to—then I can't afford to miss any practices. It's about showing up as much as it's about putting in the work. Plus… Nevermind. Forget it."

"Plus, what?" I pushed.

He gave me a wan smile and stepped toward the door. “Someone’s got to watch Hudson’s back so one of those dicks doesn’t put a knife in it.”

I blanched, and his smile softened into a reassuring grin.

“Don’t worry. It took me way too many years, but I think I’m finally ready to be a team player and I’m choosing Team Hudson.” He twisted the knob, pushing the door open, and glanced back at me. “See you around, Andy. Maybe we can grab lunch sometime.”

“That’d be nice. Try not to start any more fights.”

He snickered. “No promises.”

Chapter 20

Mitch

Thank fuck no one expected me to smile or laugh as the team—aka my jailors—escorted me to the locker rooms, with our fearless team captain at the forefront. As we made our way to the practice green, Nate elbowed his way closer to me.

"So, uh, how you doing? Have a good time on the trip?" he asked, shoving his hands in his pockets.

I flashed to walking the streets of DC, marveling at the monuments, and waking up with Andy in my arms. "Parts of it were really great."

"That's cool. Shame the trip is so exclusive. I've always wanted to check out the capital." He scratched his chin. "Still not sure how Hendricks got on the roster." He glanced at me out of the corner of his eye and I picked up on the unspoken "or you."

"That makes two of us. I only got in thanks to an extra credit opportunity from Stein. Course, that means I have to write *another* damn essay." I rolled my eyes to lend an layer of believability. Not that I really needed to play up my irritation. I *wasn't* looking forward to that essay, especially now that it seemed I'd be writing it all on my own.

Nate sucked his teeth. "That bites."

Damn it. Now I was thinking about that bite mark on Andy's shoulder. Would he still be playing with it? Was he upset about the reminder of our time together? I shook my head to clear the thoughts and focused on the current conversation. "It is what it is. Not like I can't use all the help I can get."

"You know, we could always work on it together after practices. I wouldn't say no to some help with physics. That shit is kicking my ass."

I couldn't hold back an ironic laugh at the suggestion. Never in a million years did I think someone would ask *me* for help with schoolwork. "That's not a bad idea, Nate. Especially since we both know Coach is going to eat up all of our downtime, including taking over our free study period."

"Dude, you have no idea. Shit has been rough this last week." He winced, as if he hadn't meant to let that slip.

I lowered my voice and leaned a little closer as we continued down the hill to the lockers. "They didn't, you know, do anything to you, did they?"

"I caught some third degree, but it could have been worse." He shrugged, but the tightness in his shoulders gave him away. While he was probably telling the truth that it could have been worse, whatever they'd done had been plenty bad.

"I'm sorry I left you in a lurch like that. I've, uh, recently realized that I'm not so great at thinking things through. Let me make it up to you?" Not that I was sure *how* I would, but I could at least try.

He glanced at me, his surprise clear. "Um, sure. I wouldn't say no to some more free ice cream." He waggled his eyebrows, and I chuckled.

"Debbie still working there?"

"Not as much, but yeah."

I hated how jealous I was of his moony-eyed expression. Would I ever get to openly have that?

"Hudson. Hawthorne. Quit your gossiping and get your asses changed. We've got drills to run," Brian barked from the doorway of the locker room.

Nate and I shared a look, rolling our eyes behind his back, when Brian turned to go inside. We shuffled after him into the noise of the cement building echoing with over a dozen voices laughing and trying to talk over each other.

I walked to my locker, conscious of all the eyes following my every move. Jesus, these guys were relentless. Honestly, where did they expect me to go? I was *literally* surrounded. Between the sound of lockers opening and closing, it was almost impossible to catch the bang of the coach's door hitting the wall.

"What is this? A fucking tea party?" Coach Santinelli said in his overloud voice, cutting over the din. "Quit the chit chat. I have an announcement to make." He walked toward the center of the room so all eyes could be on him and placed his hands on his hips. It was then that I noticed someone had followed Coach out of his office. "With two games down, the season is in full force. We've had some good hustle and I know I can expect more great things from my team. I appreciate all of you who stayed in town and put in the extra hours of practice. It'll make all the difference this year."

Murmurs sprung up around me and a distinct itch settled between my shoulder blades.

Coach Santinelli held up his hands in a quieting gesture. "We've still got ten more games to win, then the playoffs. I've already started reaching out to scouts and had scouts reach out to me. Be sure to let me know if there are any schools in particular you'd like to see at games."

Scouts? When was the last time I'd thought about scouts? Never even occurred to me we could request *specific* scouts. It went without saying that Coach would make sure all the major collegiate teams would send representatives. But maybe all wasn't lost. If I could get scouted by a smaller program... say the University of Chicago, then maybe I still had a chance to mend things with Andy. A new school could make all the difference. The only hangup was that I couldn't ask Coach. He'd never support such a small program with no affiliation with the academy.

"Yes, yes, it's all very exciting. We have a top-notch team this year and I *know* we've got championship material on that field. So don't futz around in getting those requests in." He gave the room collectively a stern look, then clapped his hands. "In other news, we have a returning player to our ranks." He waved for the guy that had followed him out of his office to step forward. "This is Warren Singleton. Since the season has already started, he'll be part of the second string, but I have full confidence in his abilities. He's trained with me before and I know he's kept his skills sharp at the schools he's attended in the interim. Let's give him a warm welcome and be sure to show him the ropes. It's good to have you back at Ulwich, son." Coach slapped him on the back hard enough to hear as whoops filled the locker room.

The guy, Warren, stepped forward with an eager smile to high five several of the guys who rushed to greet him. I couldn't help but notice they were all legacies that had been attending Ulwich long before I'd arrived. I shook my head. The last thing we needed was another entitled prick on the team.

I caught Brian glaring at the spectacle as he leaned on the locker beside me and angled my head toward Warren. "So, who is this guy, anyway?" I asked.

"Some military brat, back so he can say he graduated from UPA. Apparently, he was some hot shot like eight years ago when he made the team.

But when his dad got an assignment overseas, his whole family moved. I don't even think he got to finish the season."

I frowned. "Eight years ago. Shouldn't he *already* have graduated?"

Brian's scowl deepened. "Word is that his schedule got all fucked up from transferring to so many schools, but I think he got held back."

I glanced at Warren. He definitely looked older than the rest of us. Whatever his excuse, he was definitely toeing the line. "Former player or not, I'm surprised you're okay with him being added to the team like this."

"Not like I got a say in the matter." He narrowed his gaze at me. "And neither do you. No more fucking around, understand? Your ass is at practice. All of them. I don't give a damn if it's at five in the morning or in the middle of your history class. You're there."

I swallowed a resigned sigh and finished putting away the clothes I'd worn on the airplane. "Heard."

"And, Mitch, I mean it. Don't test me on this. You may be Coach's golden boy, but you're not untouchable. This is our last season—our last chance to win the championship—and I won't let you fuck it up. So you'll be here and be present. You'll make weight and train harder than you ever have. After that last game, I don't give a fuck what you do with your time or your life, but until we get that trophy, your ass is mine."

I stared into Brian's dark brown eyes and fought back the panic threatening to seize me. This was nothing new. Nothing I hadn't expected. Even if I didn't desperately need an athletic scholarship to get into *any* university, I always knew this was how my last year would play out. I'd survive this, because I had to. And because I finally had a plan. I may not be able to talk Coach into getting a scout from the University of Chicago, but I had someone much better in mind.

Finally, Brian gave me a curt nod. "Be on the field in five. You've got a lot of time to make up for." He turned on his heel and walked away, already bellowing for others to get their asses in gear.

I let out a shaky breath as I watched him go. Personally, I didn't think five days was "a lot of time", but clearly I was in the minority. Connor passed Brian and a group of others as they exited the locker room. I was honestly a little surprised to see him, but then, it *was* a full practice. He'd never rebelled against them the way I had. Connor was what Coach called "hungry," though sometimes he was a little too hungry, too… *desperate*. He walked a few feet into the locker room, then came to a dead stop when he saw the new guy. I reflexively turned to see if Warren was doing anything unusual, but he was still changing and shooting the shit with his cluster of fanboys. When I turned back to Connor, he was looking right at me and had gone deathly pale.

He gave himself a good shake, but instead of moving to his locker, he made a beeline for mine. "I need to talk to you. *Now*," he said under his breath.

"We have practice. Brian'll skin my hide if I'm not out there ASAP."

"It's about Andy," he hissed, his expression more serious than I'd ever seen it.

Still not entirely sure what this was about, I nodded and shuffled along behind him toward the toilets. Connor kept glancing back like he was afraid someone might follow us, then turned on several faucets, before stepping close once more. "What's with all the cloak and dagger, Hendricks?" I asked.

"Lower your damn voice," he hissed, glancing back toward the sound of the others chatting animatedly. "That was Warren Singleton."

"Yeah, I know. Coach just told us he's back on the team. Well, second string anyway. Hella sus if you ask me. But why are you acting so weird about it? It's not like he'll actually get to play." I neglected to add, much like he wouldn't.

Connor ran his hands through his hair, his face the picture of anxiety. "Fuck. That's right. It was before you got here. Okay, so Warren is not a good guy. Scratch that, he's the worst of the worst."

"You sure? He might be a jerk, but the others seem to like him fine."

He leveled a glare at me. "That's because they're straight."

Feared curled in my gut. "What… What are you saying?"

He grabbed my arm and pulled me even deeper into the bathroom portion of the locker room. "He's done things. Really bad things. To Bridges."

"He hurt Calvin?" II couldn't imagine *anyone* who had the balls to mess with him. Well, aside from Benny, but apparently that was all for show, anyway.

"He did a hell of a lot more than hurt him."

I shook my head, not wanting to accept what he was clearly alluding to. "Like what?"

"Right before he left, he cornered Calvin in the showers… Alone. Maybe he did it because he knew he was leaving, or maybe he was confident no one would do anything about it. Whatever his reason, it didn't change the outcome."

“Wait, if there was no one else there, then how do you know he… he…”

“Raped him?” Connor said it so bluntly that I immediately wanted to throw up. “Because the fucker had the nerve to brag about it. Not outright. Just hints in closed circles, but enough to leave little doubt about how ‘he’d taught that fag a lesson about real men’.”

I swayed on my feet, and Connor reached out to steady me. “Why are you telling me this? What does it have to do with Andy?”

“Because Andy wasn’t *here* the last time Warren was. How long do you think it'll take that animal to sniff him out? He won’t care about your blanket ‘no-touch’ order. He’ll do what he wants because he can and he has the money and backing to get away with it. Andy is going to need every friend he’s got watching his back, and that includes us.”

I pulled at my hair, the panic I’d so effectively put off earlier rising in full force. “How the hell are we supposed to do *that*? We’re going to be practicing or playing virtually twenty-four-seven.”

He sagged against the painted concrete wall and ran his hands over his face. “I don’t know. But we have to try.”

“Hendricks! Hudson! Get your asses on the field!” Coach Santinelli hollered, peering around the edge of the lockers.

We both jumped, then shared a look before wordlessly joining the rest of the team outside. If I’d thought my day was bad before, it had just gotten infinitely worse.

Andy

I huddled closer to the window, the moon outside my only source of light. Had it really only been a week since we’d gotten back from DC? Since I’d walked away from Mitch? It felt like longer. Holding it together during the day as I went through the usual routine of classes and schoolwork took every ounce of focus I had. By the time the day was over, I didn’t have the energy to fight it anymore and the heartbreak was there, waiting to pounce.

Had I cried this much the first time? I didn’t think so. But then, I’d devoted the last five years to burying the hurt. But there was no burying this. Which was why I was in the haunted classroom. At night. Again. It was the only place I could be sure Mitch couldn’t find me and, damn, was he trying. The storage shack was a no-go since I’d taken him there. The secret room would never offer the refuge I needed. Sound carried in the Tower. And no way was I explaining to Lucien why I was such a fucking mess.

I took a shuddering breath, my ribs protesting after way too many hours spent crying. I couldn't keep doing this. Even if Chicago had already accepted my application and I'd been admitted to the Advanced Writing Program, nothing was guaranteed. My grades needed to stay up and for that, I needed sleep. No, not sleep. *Rest.* But every time I closed my eyes, I saw the hurt on Mitch's face. And if by some miracle I fell asleep, I always woke painfully aware of his absence. Who'd have thought I'd become accustomed to sleeping in his arms in such a short amount of time? Me. That's who. I should have known. I *did* know. And I'd done it anyway.

A noise infiltrated the darkness, piercing my bubble of misery. I jerked and pressed my back against the wall. Ghosts weren't real, and this room wasn't actually haunted. Despite the logic, my fear remained. Another sound drifted through the room and I fought to get control of my rising panic. Nothing was there. It wall in my head. Everyone else was fast asleep in their beds. Where I should have been.

The door to the haunted classroom burst open. I stifled a cry and ducked behind the nearest desk. Not that it offered significant cover from what might be coming. I held my breath and hoped that whoever or whatever it was would move on.

"There you are! Fuck. I've been looking for you everywhere."

I risked a peek over the desk to confirm what my ears were telling me. Yep. Calvin, the second to last person I wanted to see.

"Andy, please come out. I really need to talk to you about something. I'd have told you sooner, but it seems you've been avoiding damn near everyone since you got back. Including your mentor. He wants to speak to you, by the way. But more importantly, I've been worried."

"Sorry," I croaked as I pushed myself up. I winced at how raw my voice had become. There was a reason I hadn't been volunteering answers in class lately. I didn't bother trying to pat free the dust on my rumpled uniform. They all looked like this now. The beam of light from the flashlight Calvin was carrying swung my way, and he sucked in a breath.

"Jesus Fucking Christ, Andy. What happened?" he asked, stepping deeper into the room.

As much as I knew I shouldn't, I looked up to meet his worried gaze. There was no hiding my sallow features or my perpetually red-rimmed eyes.

"Did someone hurt you?" he asked softly, a strange tightness in his voice. He set the flashlight on the teacher's desk at the front of the room, so the light projected in my general direction without blinding me, and walked toward me. I genuinely thought I might be able to keep it all in. Then he placed a gentle hand on my arm and I shattered.

I collapsed onto his chest with heaving sobs that shredded me from the inside out. I clung to the soft cotton of his shirt like it was a life raft, but I was still drowning. Distantly, I was amazed there were any tears left. I'd thought they'd dried up days ago.

"Andy, please talk to me," he whispered while he rubbed my back. "What happened? You're scaring me."

"I'm such an idiot."

His hands faltered. "What?"

I looked up at him, clawing for the only thing that could get me through this—anger. "Why did I listen to you? *Carpe diem*. What a fucking joke." I shoved him away, catching a brief glimpse of his perplexed expression before I curled in on myself. "I *knew* better. Knew it was a mistake, but I did it anyway. I never should have renewed our friendship, shouldn't have kissed him, no matter how perfect it felt. And I *definitely* shouldn't have had sex with him. Shouldn't have gone there with him," I admitted, my voice cracking.

Calvin's mouth opened and closed while he clearly struggled to catch up with my outburst. "Are you fucking kidding me right now? This shit again?"

I winced at the rebuke, but refused to back down. "What do you care? This is what you wanted, right?"

"Fuck you, Andy," he hissed. "I thought you were hurt—really hurt. That maybe I was too late."

"Well, you are," I grumbled, wrapping my arms around myself like a shield. "I followed your stupid advice, and it only led to more trouble."

"I think you mean wallowing."

I snapped my head up to glare at him. "Excuse me?"

"That's right. Excuse *you*. What the fuck are you doing here, Andy? Because from where I'm standing, it looks like you're wallowing in self pity. Again. And frankly, I'm fucking over it. We have bigger problems right now than your inability to have an emotionally mature conversation with the guy you're obsessed with."

I pulled myself up to my full height, which was honestly laughable next to Calvin's six feet. "Where do you get off saying that to me?"

"Really? You wanna go there?" he scoffed. "Fine. I was hoping you'd be smart enough to figure it out on your own, but clearly the sense is going to have to be knocked into you. And when I'm done hammering it home, I'm coming for Mitch."

I gave a snort that was more snot than derision. "What could you possibly have to say about this?"

"Which one of us is in a healthy relationship? Hmm?" He quirked an eyebrow.

"I wouldn't call what you two have healthy," I said with a sneer to hide my jealousy.

"It's a damn cry better than this ridiculous cat-and-mouse game you and Mitch have been at for way too fucking long. At least we're honest with each other. Tell me, Andy, when's the last time you were honest with someone? *Including* yourself." He waited a moment, then continued when I didn't rise to the bait. "Face it. You've been lying to yourself and everyone else for ages. Sure, you can pretend that it's for safety or a desire for privacy. But the truth is you don't like yourself."

"Fuck you," I snarled. "What do you know?! You have your perfect life. No one dares to touch you. You're as loud and proud and in people's faces as you can possibly be. You've never had to hide. Never had to wonder what it would be like for someone to love you, accept you."

Rage flared in his eyes, and he opened his mouth. No doubt to tell me how horribly off base and out of line I was—which I already knew. To my surprise, though, the words didn't come. Instead, he took a deep breath and visibly regathered himself. "I'm not doing this. Not now and not ever again. I won't indulge your self-hatred and internalized homophobia anymore. And you can argue all you want, but at the end of the day, we both know I'm right. You decided a long time ago how everyone saw you, and no matter what I've done, you cling to it. So go ahead, blame me for all the things that have gone wrong with Mitch. We both know I'm not the one you're really mad at."

I looked away to hide my fizzling anger as his words tumbled through my head. He didn't deserve any of what I'd said, but was he right? Yes, part of me did blame him. And I didn't care how illogical it was. He was happy, and I was fucking miserable. But was that actually *my* fault? I shifted from side to side, increasingly uncomfortable as I looked back at all the times with Mitch that I'd intentionally sabotaged before he could get the chance.

"You can sulk all you like after I leave, but first I'm going to tell you what I've been trying to since you got back from DC. So pay attention," he said, piercing my darkening cloud of thoughts.

"What is it?"

He took a deep breath, like what he was about to say was life-alteringly monumental. "Warren Singleton is back."

"Who the fuck is that?" I asked, rubbing at my raw nose.

"He... He's a bad guy. Okay? A really bad guy. Stay away from him. And whatever you do, don't draw his attention."

I frowned at the anxiety threading through his voice. "Why?"

"You could say he hates queers. Homosexuals especially. He's a bully, Andy."

I huffed an ironic laugh. "Benny was all those things too and now you're fucking him."

Anger lit in his eyes again, and I instantly regretted what I'd said. "Warren is *nothing* like Benny. He's fucking evil incarnate. He will hurt you in ways you'll spend years trying to recover from."

"Pretty sure I'm already there," I mumbled.

"Damn it, Andy. I'm not messing around here. You can believe whatever you want, but trust me about this. Stay out of his way and *pray* he never realizes you exist."

I took a step back, startled at his vehemence. "O-okay. I'll do my best to avoid his attention."

He visibly relaxed, his shoulders drooping for a moment before he straightened again. "Right. Time to go. I'm walking you to your room. NO arguments. And these little late night pity parties? They're over. You understand me?" he asked with a fierce look.

"You're not the boss of me."

"I'm not trying to be. I'm trying to protect you. So no more sneaking out late at night to where no one can find you. If you have to go somewhere, take someone with you. Now grab your shit, we're leaving."

It rankled to be ordered about like a petulant child, but his demeanor was also freaking me out. Whoever this Warren guy was, he had to be bad if he could rattle Calvin. I slung my satchel across my body, sagging beneath the weight, and trudged toward Calvin. We walked in complete silence through the halls toward the East Dormitories. While I kept my head down, his head seemed to be on a swivel. Once we made it to my room, he reiterated his warning in hushed tones, then left still clearly on edge.

Chapter 21

Mitch

Practice was going to kill me. I was sure of it. After last week's game ended in an overtime victory, Coach was riding all of our asses. Sweat poured down my back, and I rested my stick across my knees as I panted for breath. Everything fucking hurt. My muscles were screaming for a break and I was on the verge of committing murder just for a drink of water.

"Run it again!" Coach Santinelli shouted. No one dared utter even a whisper of discontent. We'd learned the hard way the Sunday after the near-loss that so much as a groan would be severely punished with burpees and suicide sprints. Poor Nate had puked… twice. And I was fairly sure John had passed out from dehydration.

None of that stopped us from trudging back to our starting positions. I didn't know how we were expected to perform any better, given all of us were dredging the bottom of the barrel. But again, no point in arguing. If we were lucky, Coach would decide we could hit the lockers after this, or at least run a different play. If not… I shook my head. It wasn't worth thinking about.

I took my place on the field and waited for the ball to go live. Coach blew the whistle, and just like every other run, we all surged into action. The play was running perfectly and I could see the strain in my fellow players' faces to keep it that way so we could finally end this hellish practice. It looked like we might actually pull it off when the ball went wide and sailed past Brian.

Connor, quick as ever on his feet, got to it first, but was immediately crowded by Neil, Todd, Warren, and John. Sticks clacked together as they jockeyed for the ball while the rest of us spread out, ready to catch it from whoever won. John came up with the ball, sending it back to Brian.

No sooner did the group break apart, though, than Todd let out an ear-piercing scream and crumpled to the ground. Everyone froze, including Brian, who was already halfway to the goal. One look at how he was clutching his right leg and writhing in agony said it all.

"Cut the theatrics, Garwood!" Coach hollered from the sideline. "Get off your ass. We still have a play to run. Come on, walk it off!" He clapped his hands as if that was all the encouragement Todd would need to stop rocking on the ground.

"Coach! I heard a pop!" Neil shouted over his friend's screams.

Half of us dropped our sticks and rushed forward. Pops were never good and, unlike at a game, there wasn't an ambulance on standby to treat injuries.

"Move! Everyone back up!" Coach ordered as he jogged over. "Let me take a look. I swear to God, Garwood, if this is some ploy to get out of drills for shitty stick work..." The threat trailed off as he got closer and he grunted.

As one, we all took a step back, forming a ring around Todd, and shared anxious looks with each other. We watched on as Coach Santinelli got Todd to let go of his leg so he could get a good look. He gingerly touched Todd's rapidly swelling knee. Todd turned green, screamed again, then promptly fainted.

"Just what we fucking need." Coach glanced around, clearly not happy with whatever he was seeing. "Where the fuck is that damn trainer?! Useless piece of shit."

Everyone shuffled uncomfortably, but Aaron was the sad sap who spoke up. "Um, you fired him during the game last week, Coach. Remember?"

Storm clouds rolled across Coach Santinelli's face as he realized that *he* was the one responsible for dealing with this mess. After another moment in which his face turned a disturbing shade of purple, he swiveled around and barked, "Singleton! Run up to the school and see if that fucking nurse is still here! Daniels, go get the med kit. And bring me my phone while you're at it!"

Poor Brian looked like a deer in headlights. This was a fear for all of us. Not just getting injured, but being out for the season. Or worse, end our careers before they could even start.

"Don't just stand there. Double time!"

"The nurse, Coach?" Neil interjected even as Warren and Brian took off at dead sprints in opposite directions. "He needs a fuckton more than a bandaid and an ice pack."

"I already called 911. An ambulance should be here soon," Benny said, his cell phone still in his hand.

Coach leveled a glare at him. "Price, why do you have a cell phone on my field? As a prefect, you know damn well that they're forbidden on school premises."

Benny pocketed the device and walked closer to his fallen friend with a jug of water I hadn't noticed he was carrying. "With all due respect, sir, fuck you." He stopped beside an absolutely distraught Neil and patted him on the back while our coach looked like he was about to have a fit. "He's gonna be okay. The paramedics will be here soon," Benny reassured Neil.

Surprisingly, Coach S didn't fly off the handle again, though his face remained a blotchy red. He wrapped an ice pack in a towel before gently pressing it to the discolored part of Todd's knee. Then he glanced up at Benny, who was still trying to comfort his friend. "We'll address the phone issue later, but way to keep your head about you, Price." He looked around at our collectively stupefied faces.

Had Coach just apologized? Well, sort of.

"That's practice for today. Tomorrow, instead of running plays in the morning, we'll go over scout negotiation strategy. In the evening, we'll review game tapes for the upcoming game. Until then, ice what you need to ice, drink plenty of water, and rest up. Hopefully, by then, we'll have an update for Garwood." After a moment in which no one moved, he snapped, "What are you waiting for? Hit the showers! And I better not see a single piece of equipment left out! Is that understood?"

"Yes, Coach!" we all shouted in unison, then scrambled to get our asses in the locker room and out of his sight. I glanced back, surprised to find Benny and Neil staying behind with Benny wearing a thunderous expression that dared the coach to tell them off.

I studied the note for what felt like the thousandth time, then glanced around the dark, dusty room. I didn't know what was more unsettling: that someone had slipped it into my bag without me noticing, I didn't recognize the handwriting, or that they wanted to meet after hours in the haunted room. A shudder rippled through me as I stuffed it back into my pajama pocket and tried not to think about what heinous things might have happened here to give the room its nickname.

Logically, I knew there was no way this room was haunted. For one, ghosts weren't real. For two… Well, I didn't really have a two. But it didn't change the fact that this place was still creepy as fuck. There was a *reason* everyone avoided it. I was just about to call it what it was—a prank—and head back to bed when the door to the classroom flung open.

"Good. I see you got my note."

"Calvin? You're the one who left the note?" I asked once my heart climbed down from my ears.

"Who the fuck else would it be?" he countered as he made his way deeper into the haunted classroom. Thank fuck for the moonlight. I doubted I would have lasted as long in the pitch dark.

I shrugged. "Connor?" I definitely wouldn't recognize his handwriting. Though now that I thought about it, why would he give me a note instead of just talking to me at practice? *Aaand* now that I see the withering expression on Calvin's face, I wished I'd kept the suggestion to myself.

"Since when are you and Connor on speaking terms?"

I took a nervous step backward, not at all liking the shrewd expression on his face. "Um, it's a recent thing. We had… a chat in DC about how he was being a dick to Andy. Now, I guess we're good? Ish?"

"I'm so glad you brought up 'chats'." He glowered at me over his crossed arms, and I swallowed thickly.

"Oh?"

"Yeah. But before we get into that, I want to know what the fuck you did."

I glanced around the dreary room for a clue what he was talking about. "Um…"

He uncrossed his arms and smacked a nearby desk, causing me to jump. "What the fuck did you do, Mitch? Or better yet, what didn't you do? Because it damn sure wasn't talk. Andy may be a surly little shit who always thinks he's right, but if you'd talked to him like you were supposed to—laid everything out—then he wouldn't be currently throwing the world's biggest pity party." He pointed at me, anger positively shimmering off of him. "I warned you what would happen if you fucked up again. I'll ask you one last time. What. The. Fuck. Did you do to my friend?"

My brain stupidly got hung up on the part where Calvin called Andy "his friend". "He's my friend too," I fired back. Big mistake.

Calvin seemed to swell with fury before my very eyes. I was kinda glad there was still so much distance between us, because it looked like fire might actually pour out of his eyes. "You don't get to fucking say that to me. *I'm* the one who's picked up your mess every time you've fucked up. *I'm* the one who struggles to put him back together after you've broken him for the hundredth time. *I'm* the one who has been there every day, protecting him, keeping him safe, making sure all the negative attention stays on me," he continued, advancing on me until my back hit the wall.

"You want to know why no one at this school is a hundred percent sure if he's actually gay?" he challenged in a sinister tone that made my insides cold. "I'll give you a hint. It has nothing to do with that damn near useless 'no-touch' edict you declared five fucking years ago and have done shit all to back up. It was me. I kept the rumors from sprouting like weeds. Created an alternative narrative for people to fixate on, then get bored with and move on. Me." He stabbed a finger into my chest so hard I grunted.

"I… I…"

"Can your excuses. I'm done with you. I have exhausted my considerable talents trying to help you and I'm. Fucking. Done." He spun on his heel and started marching toward the exit.

I scrambled to say something before he left. "I tried to talk to him. I lost count how many times. He won't listen. He just kept sidelining me. I–"

Calvin held up a hand, and I snapped my mouth shut. "Fuck you. And fuck your excuses," he said over his shoulder without turning around. Then he huffed a bitter laugh. "You know, he actually blames me for some of this disaster. Guess it's a good thing he doesn't know I'm the one that got you on that plane and made sure you'd be in the same room."

"Is that why you wanted me to meet you here? So you could chew me out?"

"It's not the only reason, but it was the biggest." He resumed storming out, only to pause at the door and look to the side. "He's your problem now. Fix this. I'm not losing my only friend because of *his* fuck ups."

I had exactly half a second to wonder who the hell he was talking to when Benjamin Price IV filled the doorway. He cradled Calvin's head like he was the most precious thing in the world and planted a soft kiss to his temple. "I'll take care of it, babe. Try to get some rest." Calvin murmured something I couldn't catch in response, then was gone, leaving me alone with Benny.

Trepidation made my limbs buzz and had fear crawling up my throat as Benny shut the door behind Calvin.

"I'm not going to hit you, if that's what you're worried about. Though by all rights, I should," he growled, crossing the room to stand in a pool of moonlight. "Get your ass over here. I'm not shouting at you across the room."

I grudgingly did as he said, though I made sure to still keep a few feet between us, just in case. Most days I was confident in my ability to handle myself, but Benny was built bigger. I didn't have to be that smart to know he could kick my ass without even trying. "If you're not going to hit me, then what *are* you going to do?"

"Hopefully, I'm going to talk some sense into that thick skull of yours." He let out a heavy sigh and shook his head. "Fucking hell, Mitch. I get that being queer in this godforsaken place is damn near impossible, but how many opportunities do you need?"

I wet my lips and shuffled from foot to foot. "I don't know what you mean."

"Yeah, you fucking do. Listen, do you want things to work out with Andy? Don't give me some bullshit line. We're way past that. The truth. Do you or don't you?"

The part of me that I kept buried deep and coiled tight snapped. I flung out my arms, forgetting for a second that this was supposed to be a *secret* meeting. "Of course I fucking do! But you don't get it. I have fucked up so many things. Things I can never truly apologize for. I'd need a damn time machine."

"Well, you don't have one, so you're going to have to make do with trying to fix things in the present."

I shook my head. "Cornering him didn't make a difference. Even when I got him to agree to talk, he still found a way to weasel out of it. He *left*, Benny!" I cried in anguish. "He left, and he made sure I couldn't follow him."

Benny ran a hand over his head and let out a frustrated breath. "Maybe instead of focusing on *that* he left, try focusing on why he felt like he had to."

"What?" I whispered, the air gone from lungs as effectively as if Benny had socked me in the gut.

“You can start with why you did it to him five years ago. I suspect the reasons are nearly the same.”

Cold washed over me. “You… you know what happened?”

“Not the particulars, but enough. If you really want to fix things with him, you’re going to have to nut up and be in his face about it. Trust me, you don’t want to waste any more time than you already have.” He glanced back toward the door and added in a whisper, “It’s more precious than you know.” He shook himself and faced me again. “I don’t have all the answers or, fuck, even a half-assed suggestion. That’s on you to figure out.”

I nodded, though part of me was really disappointed he didn’t have some grand master plan for me to fix everything with Andy. Not that I’d done much with the last plan someone had given me on a silver platter.

“Before I leave, there’s another thing I wanted to talk to you about. You know about Warren?” he asked gruffly.

Dread lapped at my insides. “Yeah. Connor filled me in. We’ve been trying to keep an eye out for Andy, but it hasn’t been easy with Coach monopolizing every waking second that we’re not in class.”

“That’s good. It’s weird you two are getting along suddenly, but I’m glad you have each other's backs. You’re gonna need it." He gave me a shrewd look. "He know about you and Andy?"

"No. He doesn't know about me at all."

Benny rolled his eyes and mumbled, "Fucking drama queens." Then he huffed and squared his shoulders. "Problem for another fucking day. Anyway, this isn’t about what Warren did during his first stint at Ulwich, or even what he might do now.”

“Then what’s it about?”

“Todd’s injury. He tore his PCL. He’s out for the season.”

I frowned. “How do you know that? Will he ever be able to play again? Coach didn't even know. He had to call off practice again today to go to the hospital for an update about his accident.”

Benny just glowered at me. “The docs are optimistic about his recovery. With surgery and some serious PT, he should even get to play again in time for college. But you should know that it wasn’t an accident.”

“You don’t know that,” I argued. “That kind of shit happens all the time. It’s awful, but it’s true.”

“You’re not wrong about that, but I know because I saw it happen." Anger darkened Benny's face. "Right as everyone broke apart, Warren hooked Todd's knee with his stick. My guess is he wasn't satisfied riding the bench. He means to take Todd's position."

"Holy fuck!"

Benny nodded in agreement. "He's a bad dude. But thanks to his father's connections and more money than sense, he thinks he's untouchable. Someday, I'll show him he's not. Until then, we need to watch out for each other and the people we care about."

"Yeah. Absolutely."

He nodded again and turned to leave. "Don't waste any more time than you already have with Andy, either. If you want him, you need to fight for him," he said over his shoulder.

"Hey, Benny," I called after him.

"Yeah?"

"Thanks and, uh, let me know if there's anything I can do on the Warren front, 'kay?"

Rather than respond, he inclined his head and walked out, leaving me alone to mull over everything he and Calvin had said. They were right. I couldn't let my past fuckups hold me back any longer. There was never going to be a perfect time to tell Andy the truth. And waiting around for it was causing just as many problems as not being honest with him to begin with.

Chapter 22

Andy

I really hated when Calvin was right, which was far more often than he got credit for. But after sleeping on it—and, yes, agonizing over it—there was no denying I'd gone out of my way to make sure Mitch couldn't say or do anything to hurt me again. He'd told me repeatedly he wanted—no, *needed*—to talk to me about something important and rather than listen, I'd run away and stuck my head in the sand. I didn't have a clue what he needed to tell me so badly. I'd just been convinced I didn't want to hear it. That it would be bad.

There was a saying about "assuming" things that I never felt more keenly as I wandered the halls during study period and tried to figure out when I'd be able to talk to him. Hell, I'd almost gone to his game on Saturday on the slim chance that I'd get an opening. Thank God I wasn't that desperate. Not yet. But I was getting there.

I turned into the next hallway, giving the corner a wide berth, forgetting that I'd opted to leave my satchel in my room. If I had my books with me, I'd be far too tempted to squirrel up somewhere and read instead of figuring out how to talk to Mitch. While I was at it, I also needed to come up with a way to make up for my shitty attitude with Calvin. He'd been there for me at all of my lowest points, and how did I repay him? By fucking blaming him for my arguably self-inflicted problems.

I shook my head, ashamed of myself all over again. When had I become so ridiculously melodramatic? I didn't even recognize myself anymore. Small wonder Calvin wanted to shake me. Slap me too, if I was being honest. If I was *really* being honest, I deserved it.

"Andy!"

I looked up at the shout and immediately frowned. Great, now I was seeing *and* hearing things. My preoccupation with Mitch had officially gone too far. Except he was still jogging toward me.

"I'm glad I caught you," he said, barely out of breath after sprinting the length of the long hallway. He glanced around, but there was no one else to be seen. "You weren't headed anywhere important, were you?" His gaze flicked down to my side, where my satchel was noticeably absent.

"Uh… no, I wasn't. But aren't you supposed to be at practice? I thought all the team's 'free time' had been commandeered." Not that study period should count as free time, but here we were.

He smiled broadly. "Oh, I'm definitely supposed to be there. Told Coach that my ankle was feeling twingy and he ordered me to go back to my room and ice it immediately. After Todd's injury, he's not taking any chances with the rest of us."

I grabbed his arm and started dragging him toward the wing that held his room. "Then what the fuck are you doing running down the halls? Come on. I can grab you some ice once we get your leg elevated."

"Andy. *Andy.*" He laughed as he tugged back, forcing me to stop my determined march. "I lied. It was an excuse to get out of practice. Coach has been more relentless than usual and I think all of us would benefit from some more down time. I skipped to come find you."

"Oh." My heart did the same flutter it always did. Except this time, I didn't push it away. I embraced it. Maybe it could give me the strength to say all the things I needed to. To be honest with Mitch and, most importantly, myself.

"Someone still owes me that talk he agreed to in DC." He raised an eyebrow and I cringed.

I let out a big breath. "Yeah, about that…"

"If you're about to find some other way to wiggle out of it—"

"No! No, I promise I'm not. I want to apologize. What I did… skipping out on you like that. It was petty and uncalled for."

He shrugged and offered me a soft smile. "Petty, maybe. I don't know about uncalled for. I kinda had it coming."

I chuckled, because I honestly had zero clue what to say next. "Maybe we should go somewhere that's not the hall?" I suggested.

"I don't see any prying ears, or eyes, for that matter. Do you?"

"No?"

"Then here is great. Besides, it'll look a lot more conspicuous if you take off." He paused, giving me just long enough to wonder why he thought I'd run and then realize that it was exactly what I'd done every other time he'd tried to talk to me. "Or if you decide to hit me. Though, in all fairness, if you decide you need your pound of flesh afterward, I wouldn't hold it against you."

I couldn't resist looking around again in search of any witnesses. I hadn't really planned on confessing my feelings out in the open, but if this was the only chance I was going to get, I wasn't about to waste it. "If you're sure..."

"I'm very sure." He stepped closer, angling us toward the wall, and I reflexively stepped backward. He took a deep breath, a lot like the one I'd taken earlier. "I don't know why the hell this is so damn hard to say. Well, I do. But you're my best friend. You did it. And I can do it too."

"Mitch, what are you talking about?" I asked, getting turned around by his sudden bout of rambling.

"I love you," he said in a rush.

I diligently ignored the heat rushing to my face, as well as the absolute riot of butterflies that threatened to explode out of my chest. Calm, cool, collected. We were friends again. Real friends. And friends could tell each other they loved one another. "Uh, I love you too, Mitch," I replied so awkwardly you'd think I'd never told another person "I love you" before. But this was different. This was Mitch. And he was *awake*.

He shook his head, his eyebrows coming together in an unexpected scowl. "I don't think you're hearing me. I love *you*, Andy."

"I heard you," I replied defensively. "What are you implying? That I'm one of those friends that can't say I love you?"

He arched an eyebrow. "That's not what I'm talking about, and you know it."

"I know what you *think* you mean. But I also know you, so that can't be it." God, I hated this. Why did I have to be the responsible one and point out the obvious? "Things got... confusing in DC. I, *we*, did things that we probably shouldn't have." I made an exasperated sound. "Look, is this really a conversation we should be having right here?" I checked the hall behind him, but we were still alone.

He made a rude noise at the back of his throat. "I love you, Andy, I really do. But sometimes your stubborn determination to misunderstand everything I say makes me want to throw you over my knee and spank your ass raw."

I probably looked like a fish with my eyes open impossibly wide and my mouth hanging open, and there wasn't a damn thing I could do about it. All words and coherent thought had fled at the image Mitch painted, because that should *not* have turned me on. As my brain slowly came back online, I finally got my mouth to close, though it didn't stop my face from burning.

"Please stop looking at me like that. And don't even try to pretend you don't think that sounded every bit as hot as I did." He reached down to adjust himself and my brain threatened to blue screen again.

"Wh-What is happening right now?"

His face softened, and I melted into his soft hazel eyes. He cupped my face with both hands while he studied me. I swallowed thickly as the fear I'd lived with constantly since coming out to him waged war with the spark of hope that refused to die. For maybe the first time since that fateful night five years ago, the hope was winning. "Oh, Andy," he sighed, his breath ghosting over my face. "I do love you as a friend, and I always will. But I also love you so much more than that." He traced the outline of my lips with his thumb and I was suddenly consumed with a need to know what caused people to spontaneously combust.

"Mitch?" I asked shakily, barely above a whisper.

He lifted his gaze from my mouth. "I'm in love with you, Andy, and I have been for a very long time."

"So you're… bi?" I finally pushed out with a Herculean effort.

He chuckled and shook his head, but didn't release my face.

I frowned, not sure what the hell was so damn funny about this. "So, still straight."

"Jesus, Andy. I'm gay. Really fucking gay."

Now I was shaking my head. Maybe my brain had broken more than I thought. "But you're not."

"Excuse me?"

I tried to pull away, but he'd done a damn good job cornering me and using his larger frame to block me in. Not to mention he was Still. Holding. My. Face. Finally, I gave up and latched onto the biggest argument I could think of. "But the girls. You've slept with girls. A lot of them."

He glowered at me, and I wilted against the wall. "Because no gay man in the history of ever has slept with a woman. And for the record, I *didn't* have sex with most of them." He shuddered. Actually fucking shuddered.

"But... but..." I stammered. Mitch wasn't gay. He *couldn't* be.

"Oh yeah, there's definitely some serious spanking happening in your future," he said with a glare that went straight to my dick and had me flushing from head to toe. "I'm gay, Andy, and I've been head over heels in love with you since the day you ran into me."

"Ran into..." I wracked my brain for when he could be referring to, but only one moment stuck out. "The day we met?"

He brushed his knuckle along my cheek and his gaze turned dreamy. "I'd never seen anyone so beautiful. Then you casually declared we'd be best friends, and I'd have gone along with anything you wanted if it meant getting to be near you."

Despite my brain doing its damndest to start glitching again, I violently seized onto reason. "That was seven years ago!" My voice rang through the hall and I clapped a hand over my mouth at the same time we both glanced around. "Are you fucking serious?!" I hissed angrily. "Why didn't you say anything? Sooner," I added with narrowed eyes when I sensed his likely reply that he was telling me now.

"Back then, I didn't say anything because I was scared. Being gay was what had gotten me kicked out of my previous school. I wasn't as cautious as I should have been."

"You never told me that."

"Why would I? It was pretty clear, in the beginning at least, that you didn't feel the same way. I didn't care, though. It was enough just to be around you. And I *know* I should have said something the night you came out, but... But no matter how hard I tried to get the words out, they wouldn't come. So, I kissed you."

That didn't make sense. I would have remembered Mitch kissing me. After all, I'd been pretty damn in love with him myself at the time. "Except I kissed you." Only I wasn't so sure of that now. I remembered thinking at the time that I'd lost my damn mind. One minute we'd been laughing, the next I was having the first best kiss in history of first kisses. Then he'd pulled away. "You freaked."

He crowded against me, sandwiching me between the wall and the warmth of his firm body. "Oh, Kitten. I didn't freak, not the way you think I did. It was the same mistake I'd made before—kissing before thinking. Just because you were gay didn't mean you were suddenly into me the way I'd always wanted." His hands slid from my face and I'd have given anything to get them back.

My eyes stung, and I blinked rapidly to dispel the oncoming tears. I was *done* crying. "But I was. I am. Mitch, I love you. I never stopped loving you, though damn if I didn't try."

He searched my face as if he couldn't believe what I was saying anymore than I believed what he'd said. "You really mean that? But what about..." He trailed off, but we both knew where he was going—the night that ruined everything, or morning, in my case.

Before he could finish, I surged forward, mashing my mouth against his and wrapping my arms around his neck. He made a muffled sound of surprise and, for a second, I thought he might insist on finishing his awful thought first. Instead, he wound his arms around my waist and crushed me against him, kissing me back hard enough to bruise. I lost all sense of self as I accepted that somehow my wildest dream had come true.

"Fuck, Andy. I don't know how I've lived without you. I put on a brave face, but every day was torture," he rasped, then returned to kissing me like he wanted to brand it on my soul. Fine by me.

I barely repressed a moan as his tongue slipped past my lips to deepen the kiss. He gripped my ass, leveraging his position to grind me against him and pushing me closer to a finish line I hadn't known was there. When he nipped at my sensitive bottom lip, I was positive I was gonna come just from fucking wish fulfillment.

A discreet cough pierced our bubble. We pulled apart and simultaneously turned to face the source of the interruption. My mentor, Professor Garza, and Professor Cohen stood shoulder to shoulder as they stared at us a mere five feet away from where we were currently making out like touch-starved animals. Mitch went noticeably pale while my face burst into flames.

"Professors," Mitch said, his voice strained. Professor Cohen's eyebrows climbed up his forehead into his impeccably styled golden hair, while Garza looked like he was fighting back laughter.

"Perhaps the hallway is not the most appropriate place for such... displays," Professor Cohen said with more decorum than could be found in an eighteenth century sitting room.

To my astonishment, Garza took Cohen's hand and placed a tender kiss on the back of it. "Don't be cruel, Samuel," he said, rubbing his thumb along the lighter skin of Cohen's hand. The hand he was holding. And kissing. What *the fuck* was going on?

Cohen huffed and rolled his eyes. “I’m being practical, not cruel. The hallways of Ulwich are not safe for such declarations, and study period will be over soon. You know I’m right, Ari.”

Professor Garza cleared his throat and softly touched Cohen’s arm. “As you usually are.”

A pleased smile curled Cohen’s mouth, then he turned back to us. “I don’t mean to be callous. We’re both very happy you have finally found each other, but Ulwich is still… Ulwich,” he finished with a heavy sigh. “I’d recommend continuing your… conversation,” Garza’s lips twitched at Cohen’s delicate word choice, but he didn’t interrupt, “someplace more private.”

“Yes, sir. Sirs,” I squeaked.

Garza’s repressed grin burst free, and he nodded before turning to look at Cohen. A silent conversation passed between them, that I couldn’t help but envy, then as one they turned forward and resumed their trek down the hall. “I’ll see you at our next mentor meeting, Anderson,” Garza said over his shoulder. "We have some important things to discuss."

I nodded, though he couldn’t see me, having used up my capacity for speech. Mitch and I remained frozen in place as we watched them continue down the hall until it turned and they disappeared from view. As one, we erupted into laughter. We eventually sobered and rested our foreheads against each other’s.

“He’s right,” I sighed, flexing my arms around Mitch’s neck in an effort to convince myself to let go.

Mitch squeezed my waist in response. “There’s still a lot we need to talk about.”

“I know. Think you could slip away tonight? We could meet up at the storage shed.”

“No,” he replied forcefully.

I lurched my head back to look at him. “No, you can’t get away?”

He shook his head. “I can sneak out just fine, but not the shed. Let’s meet in the secret room. Fitting, don’t you think? Midnight?”

“I suppose…” Though it didn’t explain the vehemence with which he’d shot down the storage shed. I’d be digging into that later, for sure. “I’ll see you at midnight.” We finally released each other and went our separate ways, though this time I felt like I was floating.

Chapter 23

Mitch

I paced the secret room for what had to be the hundredth time. Would Andy show? My confession earlier had gone… remarkably well. Way better than I ever dared to hope. But there were a lot of hours between then and now. Hours that Andy could have spent realizing he *didn't* actually feel the same, that he was too angry to forgive me. To be fair, I hadn't actually expected his forgiveness, or an apology, or for him to say he loved me back.

The same smile I'd been fighting since we parted ways in the hall twitched on my lips. This time I set it free. There was no one around to ask why I was suddenly in such a good mood, or want to know what was "funny", or to berate me for not keeping focused. Andy loved me, and nothing was *ever* going to pierce that fog. Except he wasn't here. Then again, I was early. Really early. Like two hours too early. Okay, three. I blew out a breath with the hope that it would also expel my nerves. Nope. At this rate, I'd go insane before he arrived. Assuming he showed.

"Fuck this. I need to do something," I muttered, shaking my arms out and jumping in place. When that still didn't do the trick, I moved toward the hidden door. Maybe I could filch us some pudding or another treat to kill time. Then I wouldn't be standing around like the impatient fuck I was, slowly driving myself insane.

I was still a few feet away from the exit when the outside painting that made up the door shifted to the side. I froze as I waited to see who it was. The lighting in the secret room was crappy on the best of days and so far all I could make out was a walking oversized lumpy… something. My mysterious guest made a noise like they were struggling before finally clearing the entrance and letting the founding headmaster portrait swing shut behind them.

"Out of my fucking mind. Who does this? Me, that's who. Because I'm an over-achieving dum–"

"Andy?" I asked the grumbling creature, sending up a silent prayer that our secret spot hadn't been compromised like the shed.

The lumpy figure froze, then a familiar red haired head poked around what I could now see was a haphazard stack of pillows and blankets. "Mitch?"

I gave him a small wave.

He shook his head like he was clearing cobwebs. "Sorry, I just need to confirm something real quick. Because if I just lied to myself about what I think happened earlier today, I need to get professional help."

"If you did, then we must be living in the same fantasy," I replied with a smirk.

"Holy fuck, I didn't imagine it. You... you're..."

"Gay," I filled in, fighting back a laugh.

He swallowed hard. "And you... you..."

"Am desperately in love with you?"

He nodded. "Yeah. That."

"You didn't imagine it," I said with a broad smile that I couldn't have tempered if I'd wanted to.

"Oh, thank fuck!" He dropped his collection. Then, before I could do more than register blankets hitting the floor, he'd leapt over the pile and into my arms.

Only quick reflexes honed by years of learning to catch anything thrown at me prevented me from dropping Andy or from falling over. He wrapped his arms around my neck and slammed his mouth down on mine while I struggled to get a better grip on him. I shifted his legs slightly higher, and he tightened them around my waist, helping to secure his precarious position.

"I didn't imagine it," he repeated breathlessly when he finally came up for air.

"Did you really think you had?" I teased.

He hiked his shoulder in a shrug and dropped his gaze to where my collar had been pulled askew to reveal skin. "Wouldn't be the first time."

Well, that was a fucking gut punch. I cleared my throat and shifted my grip, suddenly very conscious of how I was holding his ass.

His head flew up, a mild panic stamped plain as day across his face. "I didn't… That's not…"

"Yeah, it is," I said softly. "And it's okay. That's why we're here, right? To finally say all the things."

He nodded, but didn't look convinced.

"Hey," I said, using my hold to bounce him. He reluctantly met my gaze again. "Since we're putting everything out there, I've fantasized about this moment more than I care to admit."

"Seriously?"

"Seriously." I shuffled to look past him. "Can I ask what the deal is with the blankets now?"

He chuckled and buried his face into the crook of my neck, squeezing me tightly with his whole body. I held him just as fiercely until he relaxed his grip and stood on his own once more. "Figured it was better than sitting on the cold floor and I wasn't sure how long we'd be here."

"That's smart. And you're two hours early because?"

His cheeks turned a bright pink that he tried to hide by moving to pick up the spilled blankets.

I grabbed the pillow closest to me and waited for him to meet my gaze. When he did, I couldn't help but smile again. "I was here three."

He fought to keep a smile from surfacing, but it spread across his face anyway, though the pink in his cheeks remained, making his freckles stand out in high relief. "Seeing as how we both have zero chill, help me spread these out?"

I grinned harder and helped him lay down the blankets. Once the ground was appropriately padded, I went to sit.

"Wait," Andy said, and I awkwardly stopped mid-descent.

"What's up?" I asked, trying to hide my sudden spike of anxiety.

He gave me a playful smile, then stepped close. "One more before we get into the deep stuff." He rose to his toes and pressed his lips against mine in a tender kiss. He made a happy humming sound as he slanted his mouth to deepen it.

Fireflies had nothing on this. I felt like someone had dropped a carton of Mentos into a vat of diet soda. I cradled his face as I kissed him back and relished the fizzle of happiness.

When he lowered himself back to the ground, he was still smiling. "Sorry, I know we need to talk, and I promise neither one of us is leaving this room until we're all talked out. But I just…" He shrugged again, then seemed to realize I hadn't said anything. His brow furrowed in mild confusion. "Why are you looking at me like that? Do I have something on my face? Oh, God! Is my breath terrible?" He slapped a hand over his mouth. "I *knew* I should have brushed again before coming here.

"Your breath is fine, Andy."

"Then what?" he asked, dropping his hand.

"That's the first time you've ever smiled when kissing me."

Surprise rippled across his features, making his jaw slack and his eyes widen. "That's not true. Can't be."

"Believe me, it is. I'd have noticed if you'd done it before. Lord knows I've dreamed about it long enough." I took a deep breath and let it out slowly. "On that note, we should probably settle in. I have a feeling this is going to be a long night." He didn't argue—for once—and followed my lead in getting comfy on the floor.

"So, um, where do you want to start?" he asked as he played with the edge of a blanket.

I huffed a laugh. "Honestly? I have no fucking clue. I feel like I've practiced what to say so many times over the years, and now…" I held up my hands in a show of defeat.

"I know what you mean." He placed his hand on my knee and gave it a reassuring squeeze. "How about you tell me when you realized you were gay?"

Where I expected there to be an edge to the suggestion, there was only patience and understanding. Things I didn't feel like I deserved at all, but was grateful for nonetheless. "Suppose that's as good a place as any. Before I came to Ulwich Prep, I was at St. Benedict's Catholic School." He grimaced, and I nodded. There weren't many places that could compete with UPA for awfulness, but a rigid private Catholic school was definitely up there. "I'd gotten to the age where everyone kept asking me what girls I thought were pretty and who I would go out with if I could. But the more people asked, the more I realized the answer was none of them. I could recognize they were pretty just fine, but I didn't *care* about them the way the other boys did."

Andy smiled knowingly as he grabbed a pillow and hugged it to his chest. "Who woke you up?"

My smile was bittersweet. "His name was Robert McCaffery. I'm still not sure where I went wrong." I shook my head as I thought back. "He had light brown hair and stormy eyes that were more gray than blue. He also didn't seem all that interested in girls. Maybe I was seeing what I wanted to see, or maybe it was because I was always sneaking glances at him, but it felt like he was looking at me too."

"I can relate."

"Noticed that, did you?" I asked him with a cheeky grin.

He shrugged. "I assumed it was wishful thinking. *A lot* of wishful thinking." I reached over to squeeze his thigh and he gave me a wan smile. "I didn't mean to interrupt. What happened then?"

"One day out of the blue, he asked if I wanted to hang out. I don't even remember what game we ended up playing, just that it was going really well. We were clicking, you know?" He nodded and I let out a heavy breath. "Anyway, after a few weeks of things going well, we ended up… close. Kissing him felt like the thing to do. At first, I was so excited to actually be kissing someone that I didn't realize that he'd locked up. Then he shoved me away, called me some really ugly names, and hightailed away from me as fast as his legs would take him."

"Wow. That sucks." Andy gripped my hand, which apparently had never left his thigh.

"No shit. The next day, he and a group of other boys beat the shit out of me. A few days of that went by, then I got called to the headmaster's office. To my surprise, my uncle was sitting there instead of my mom. Not that I'd told either of them why I was getting the crap beat out of me every day."

"Your Uncle Terry?"

"The one and only. He took one look at me and lost his shit. Apparently, the headmaster was planning to expel me for fighting." Andy snorted, and we shared a look. "Since he and my dad both went to Ulwich, he was able to get me in as a legacy. He's also been footing the bill."

"Did he… Does he know you're gay?"

I couldn't help but smile. "Yep. Turns out he'd had his suspicions for a while. When he pulled me aside after telling me what was going to happen, I freaked out. I'll never forget it. He said, 'Mitch, my boy, relax. As for how I knew, takes one to know one.' Then he winked. I'm having a crisis of identity, full on panicking that I'm about to get kicked out of my house as well as my school, and the motherfucker goes and winks." I laughed and shook my head.

"That's something, at least."

"Yeah. He also warned me that I'd have to be even more careful here. That Ulwich wasn't friendly to queers. But he figured if he could survive, then so could I, and I'd get to roam the same halls as my father. That last part didn't turn out as awesome as I thought."

Andy scooted closer, causing the blankets beneath him to bunch. "What do you mean?"

"Let's just say being part of the lacrosse team came with a lot of really messed up expectations. It's hard to imagine my father doing those things. Or worse, enjoying it. Plus, Coach fucking hated him. So I didn't exactly get to hear any fun stories from their time at school together." I clasped my hands together and stared down at my interwoven fingers as something occurred to me. "I think their rivalry might have actually been a lot like the one between me and Connor. On the field," I added when I looked up and saw Andy's stricken expression.

"So, um, Connor. I'm guessing you've, uh, figured out..." he trailed off, dropping his gaze to the lumps of fabric between us.

"Oh yeah. That day at the library is actually when I put it together."

"Fuck." He rubbed his hands over his face, then paused and stared intently at me. "That's why you broke his nose!"

"Hey! In my defense, he goaded me." My shoulders sagged. "Not my proudest moment."

Andy cleared his throat and went back to fraying the edge of the blanket. "Does he know about... You know, us?"

"I don't think so. Pretty sure he thinks I busted his face for implying I *might* be doing more than studying with you."

His face turned a dark shade of pink. "'Studying' was our code word for hooking up."

I barked out a laugh that turned into several more. "No wonder he was so pissed when I said all we were doing was studying."

Andy chucked a pillow at my face, which I caught. "Shut up. We were already over by the time I found you in the Tower at the start of fall term. He just—"

"Didn't get the message?" I ventured.

"I thought it was mutual, but apparently not. He was so convinced we could be good together if we gave it half a chance. Which, okay, we had our moments, but we weren't good *for* each other, if that makes sense. He still has a lot of shit to work through and I..." He darted a cautious glance at me. "I was still trying and failing to get past you."

"I know the feeling. I know I said earlier that I didn't actually have sex with most of the girls everyone thinks I did. It was really only two. The first one…" I paused and shuddered. "I don't want to talk about that. The other was actually Trixie, and it was *awful*. Like the only way I made it through was by picturing you."

His expression of concern morphed into disgust. "Ew, I don't want to know that," he said, smacking me with the other pillow he'd brought. This time, he was smart enough not to let it go.

"I thought we were being open and honest," I said with a laugh as I fended him off.

He huffed and stopped attacking. "Fine. Since we're over-sharing, Connor's the only other guy I've had sex with, and I never bottomed."

I blinked in shock. Sure, Andy had topped me, but I couldn't imagine him doing it *all* the time. Oh God, what if he wasn't as much of a bottom as I'd thought he was?

"Ugh, this is why I didn't want to bring it up."

"What? I didn't say anything, and *you* brought it up."

"Damn it. I did, didn't I?" He sighed. "It shouldn't matter whether I bottomed or topped. I know that. But…" He looked at me, his green eyes as earnest as I'd ever seen them. "I thought you might want to know."

"Um, thanks. Just to be clear, though, you *are* a bottom?"

His laugh rang out, filling the room with a brightness that threatened to overtake the dim lighting. "I could be persuaded to top, but as Calvin so eloquently told me once, I have 'bratty bottom energy leaking out my ears'."

I chuckled. "You're definitely a brat," I said, and he stuck his tongue out in response. "And Calvin is fucking terrifying when he's mad."

"No shit. Wait, did he talk to you, too?"

"Oh yeah. *And* Benny." Andy let out a low whistle, and I shrugged. "Eh, it wasn't so bad. I expected him to smack me around a bit, but he basically told me to get my head out of my ass and stop wasting time."

Andy's chuckle rang of disbelief. "Full disclosure, Calvin could have totally beat your ass if he'd wanted to, and he'd have won. Dude is secretly ripped. It's scary, to be frank."

"No shit," I said, struggling to reconcile the image he was painting. He shook his head with a smile. "Huh, go figure. Guess I should be glad he decided he was done helping me and sent in the cavalry. Did you ever tell him about what happened between us?"

His shoulders caved inward, but as much as I wanted to take back anything that might hurt him, we'd danced around this long enough, so I kept quiet. “I told him some. He kind of guessed at the outset that something had gone down. But I think part of why I never told him more was because I didn’t really understand it myself.” He squeezed the pillow he was holding tighter as he looked at me with misty eyes. “Mitch, what *happened* that night?”

It had taken long enough—five years too long—but we were finally here and it still hurt so fucking much. “I–” My voice broke, and I had to pause to collect myself before pushing on, to admit the darkness that had dogged my steps every day since. I took a fortifying breath that was more shaky than helpful. “I was convinced that I’d taken advantage of you. That I’d wanted you so badly that if at any point you’d told me to stop, I wouldn’t have heard it. Between my growth spurt and training for my first lacrosse season, I could easily overpower you. Would I have even noticed if you’d pushed back?” I looked at him with equally watery eyes. “You were so scared when I brought you to the secret room and everything escalated so quickly. What if you’d only gone through with it because… because…”

“You thought I had sex with you for self preservation,” he finished when the words wouldn’t come.

I squeezed my eyes shut, causing a tear to spill over, and nodded. “And after, when you admitted you’d never done any of that before… It all came crashing in. I was disgusted with myself. How could I do that to not only the guy I was hopelessly in love with, but to my best friend? What kind of monster did that make me?” I released a stuttering breath as the grief and shame twisted together in an ugly rope that wound around my chest, squeezing tighter and tighter until it felt like I’d never breathe again. Before I knew what was happening, Andy launched himself across the little distance separating us and tackled me with a fierce hug.

“Fuck, Mitch. That’s what you really thought? And you’ve been carrying that weight around all this time?” He squeezed me tighter, and it was all I could do to cling to him.

“So you don’t think I’m a monster?” I hiccuped into his shoulder.

“Of course not! I was mad and hurt that you left. I thought you were rejecting me. But I never once thought you were a monster, and I never will.” He buried his face against my neck and was quiet for a few moments before whispering, “Why were you in the Tower?" He leaned back to look at me. "The day I found you. What were you doing there?"

There was no point in denying it, so I didn’t bother. “I was going to jump. But I was too much of a coward.”

His face crumpled. Then he disentangled one of his arms and gently brushed the tears from my cheeks. “You know, most people would say that jumping would have been the cowardly thing. Which, by my logic, makes you one of the bravest men I know.”

“I’m not brave, Andy. A brave man would have set aside his fear and fought for you instead of running and telling himself it was for the best.”

“I could have fought harder for you, too.”

I grabbed his hand and placed a kiss on his palm. “Not exactly like I gave you anything worth fighting for.”

He shook his head. “That’s not true. You were my best friend. And I was in love with you. I *am* in love with you.” His sincerity, the way his green eyes caught the light, his adamant denial that I was a monster, his pure Andy-ness undid me. I pulled him back down on top of me, appreciating the way his weight settled me, and held him close.

At some point, we must have fallen asleep. Next thing I knew, I was rolling over with an ache in my back that rivaled the time John had bowled me over during a practice match. I reflexively tightened my arm and realized Andy was lying on top of it. I tried to wriggle it out from under him without disturbing him. Successful at last, I snuck to the entrance and peered into the hall. As I feared, we’d slept through the night. Apparently, finally telling the truth takes it out of a guy.

“Mmm,” Andy mumbled sleepily as I walked back to him. “What time is it?”

“Not sure,” I said, doing my best not to laugh at how fucking cute he looked with his red hair pointing in every direction. “Still pretty early, judging by the light outside, but I saw a few people walking around.”

“Fuck,” he grumbled as he sat up and attempted to stretch his back. “The blankets did *not* help. Why the fuck couldn’t we meet in the shed again?”

I looked at him as he blinked blearily. “Because it’s not safe anymore. I saw Singleton and some of his followers coming out of there the other day.”

He huffed and stood up, stretching again. “You know, I caught a glimpse of this Warren guy and honestly, I don’t see what the big deal is. He’s no more of a douche than anyone else on the lacrosse team.” He spared me a glance. “No offense.”

“None taken. But I’m confused. Calvin didn’t tell you?”

"He told me to stay away from him." He gave me a scrutinizing look. "But that's not what you're talking about."

I shook my head. I couldn't fathom why Calvin wouldn't have told Andy why he should avoid Warren Singleton at all costs, but he needed to know, and it looked like I was going to have to be the one to tell him.

Chapter 24

Andy

I peered anxiously past the last stack of books into the oasis of privacy Calvin and I frequented. Given how many times I'd checked it over the last few days, only to find it empty, I was a little surprised to finally see Calvin. Originally, when I couldn't seem to track him down, I assumed it was because he was still irate from our last conversation. The one where I'd had the audacity to blame him for my problems with Mitch. Considering most of my "problems" ended up being of my *own* making, I owed him more than an apology.

Except I hadn't been able to find him. On the rare occasion I'd caught a glimpse of him in the halls, he'd vanished by the time I'd gotten there. Now that I finally had my opportunity, my nerves were a tangled mess. While I'd presumed he was still upset after our argument–which, to be fair, he could be—now I was more concerned about why he was really avoiding me. Now that I knew the truth about what had happened to him before I'd ever even stepped foot on Ulwich grounds.

Mitch hadn't exactly come right out and said that Calvin was the one Warren had sexually assaulted, but it didn't take a genius to put the pieces together. And I *was* a genius… and at a complete loss for what to say to him. Did I let him know I'd figured it out? That I'd read between the lines of his warning? Or did I pretend to still be ignorant? Before I could come to a decision, the choice was taken out of my hands.

"You can stop lurking. I can see you," Calvin said dispassionately.

I let out an awkward huff of laughter and stepped from behind the shelf that was apparently doing an appalling job of obscuring me from view. "Hey, it's, uh, been a while."

He flicked his gaze up from his small sketchbook and raised an eyebrow. "I meant what I said before. I'm done coddling you. If you're looking for sympathy for your self-imposed relationship drama, you can turn right back around."

"That's fair." I stepped cautiously into the alcove and dared to lower my satchel to the ground. "Sorry doesn't really cover my behavior or how I treated you, but I am. Sorry, that is. You were right."

A familiar smirk curled his lips, and he leaned over his sketchbook. "About?"

"Everything," I grumbled. With a put-upon sigh, I plopped down onto the carpet next to him. "Normally I'd say there's no need to be so damn smug about it, but I think, in this case, it's totally earned."

"Damn right it is." He snapped his sketchbook shut and set it aside. "Only took you five fucking years to listen to me. Five years in which you *could* have been fucking, I might add."

"Ugh, why do you have to be so crass?" I shoved his shoulder, but if anything, his grin widened.

"It's part of my charm."

I rolled my eyes. "Keep telling yourself that. And for the record, I *was* having sex."

He snorted, but didn't dispute it. "So, I take it you two dumbasses finally talked?"

"Is the name calling really necessary?" I asked, to which he merely raised his eyebrows. "Fine. Yes, we did."

"And… How was it?"

I shifted. "Parts of it were uncomfortable and we still have a lot to cover, but we're getting it all out there. We've already met up a couple of times in the secret room to continue clearing the air."

Calvin ran a hand over his face and made an aggrieved sound. "*Please* tell me you're meeting up in the middle of the day and not sneaking out at night."

"Only on the nights Benny is doing rounds," I replied defensively. "I'm not an idiot."

"Except you are. What the hell about "no sneaking out at night' says 'sneak out to hook up with your long-lost beau?'"

I scowled at him. "Are you really berating me right now for doing something that you practically wrote the book on?"

"This is different. If you get caught out of bed by the wrong person, you won't be written up or given detention or whatever worse thing your nerd brain can think up. It's dangerous, Andy." His intense sincerity had my nerves jangling again, but I refused to be cowed. Mitch and I had fought too damn hard to get here, and we'd be fools not to spend every possible second together.

"Mitch will keep me safe."

His resulting scoff put my hackles up. "Yeah? Is he escorting you from bed to the secret room and back again like some Victorian gentleman?"

"Don't be ridiculous."

"Or maybe he's watching from a distance, not getting too close, but keeping you in sight?" he continued, undeterred.

"How should I know?"

"Because if you're going to be that fucking reckless, then you damn well better know how your 'protector' is keeping you safe. And while we're at it, who's keeping *him* safe?"

My stomach swooped unpleasantly.

"Judging by your dumbstruck expression, that didn't even occur to you," he sneered.

"Okay, fine, you're right, it didn't. But that doesn't mean we're not being careful. Give us *some* credit. Or at least me. Forget for a fact that I used to sneak around this place all the damn time and never once got caught. *You're* the one who taught me even better ways to go unnoticed."

He sighed heavily, betraying how weary he really was, and rested his arms on his knees. "I know. And I know you're not being stupid about it, but these aren't normal times. I worry about you."

"I worry about you too." I placed a hand on his shoulder. He huffed, but didn't shrug me off. "So, you know, how *are* you doing? Portfolio going well? Still hot and heavy with your paramour?" I teased.

He snickered. "I'm not showing you any of my scandalous sketches." He paused and turned his head to give me a wicked look. "Unless you ask really nicely."

I mimed gagging, though part of it might have been real. "Hard pass."

"Oh, 'hard' is definitely involved," he teased mercilessly.

"Ew, no. I don't need to know that."

"Me thinks thou doth protest too much. It's okay to be curious." He wiggled his eyebrows suggestively as he reached for his sketchbook. "I've got some right here… As a matter of fact, I think there are a few you'd appreciate. Artistically, of course."

"Fuck you," I said with a laugh as I slammed my hand down on his, pushing the threatened sketchbook to the ground. No way was I ever about to admit that I was actually tempted to look.

He chuckled and raised his free hand in surrender. When I was moderately sure he wouldn't open the sketchbook anyway, I released his other. "Don't worry, I won't accost your delicate sensibilities."

I snorted. I seriously doubted "delicate" people came so hard they nearly passed out when their partner bit them hard enough to leave a mark, but he didn't need to know that. "Anyway," I emphasized, "how are you? Really?"

A crease formed between his eyebrows as he straightened up. "I already told you, I'm good."

"That's not what I meant."

"Then what do you mean?" he fired back with a decided edge.

"Come on. I'm not the only one who should be on alert where a certain student is concerned."

Calvin stiffened, his face going unnaturally pale.

"I mean, I assume Benny is watching out for you, but…"

"But what?" he asked, his voice tight.

"Why didn't you tell me? You warned me to stay away, but you could have told me why he was so dangerous. What he did… back then," I said as gently as I could.

In the blink of an eye, the color returned to his face in abundance and his tight lips morphed into a snarl. "Who told you?"

"Did you think you couldn't trust me? Were you worried what I might say?"

"Who. Fucking. Told. You?" His growl made the hairs on the back of my neck stand up.

"M-Mitch," I stammered and immediately cringed at basically throwing him under the bus. In my defense, Calvin was really hard to lie to convincingly, especially when he already had you backed into a corner.

He shut down so fast I got whiplash, though I could still feel the anger radiating off of him. He reached for his sketchbook and shoved it into his bag, ignoring how he bent the pages.

"He told me what Warren had done. How bad he really is." I scrambled to my feet as he stood and continued to put away the art supplies he'd laid out. There weren't many. "Calvin, talk to me."

"You know, I don't think it's smart for us to be seen together. Two fags hanging out draws too much attention."

I recoiled at the slur he'd never once in all our years of friendship aimed at me. "Wouldn't it draw more attention if we suddenly *stopped* spending time together?" I argued, though it was clear the battle was already lost. Calvin finished slinging his bag across his body and walked out of our refuge without looking back. I fell back against a shelf in shock as I struggled to wrap my head around how badly I'd just fucked up.

Mitch

"I hope everyone enjoyed their little break," Coach Santinelli barked.

The team shared anxious looks with each other. Practice today had been fucking brutal. Coach was clearly determined to make up for the few days we'd "taken things easy". Apparently, not even a starting player being majorly injured would stop him from putting the rest of us through the ringer.

"Now that it's clear Todd will be out for the rest of the season, we'll need a new starting defender to fill his position. Singleton, I know you're only recently back with us, but you have a firm grasp of the plays. What do you say? Think you can handle it?"

Warren's shit-eating grin while his groupies slapped him on the back made my stomach curdle. "I know so," he replied with more arrogance than I thought the field could hold.

I glanced at Brian out of the corner of my eye. Judging by the rage burning in his eyes, he had *not* been consulted despite being the team captain. "Hey, Coach," I said before my brain could catch up with my mouth.

"Yes, Hudson?" Coach replied, his smile tilting into a frown.

"That's not right."

"Excuse me?" He stepped toward me menacingly, but I couldn't back down. Not now that I'd gone and opened my big, stupid mouth.

Everyone was watching me, waiting to see if I had the balls to stand up to Coach's unilateral decision. I caught sight of Warren smirking as he talked to one of the guys that had taken to following him around and decided right there that I'd rather have my PCL torn like Todd than let that asshole play on *my* team.

"I said, that's not right. There are plenty of guys here who've put in a ton of work for *years* and are still riding the bench. They should get to play. Not someone who's literally never played a full match with any of us."

Behind Coach, Warren's face twisted into a savage snarl. Oblivious, Coach crossed his arms and glowered at me. "Is that so?"

"Yeah, Coach, it is," Brian said, stepping up beside me.

"Yeah," a couple others echoed from the back of the huddle.

"And did you have someone in mind?" Coach asked with an insincere smile that made my skin crawl.

Brian glanced at me for an answer since apparently this was my shit show. I don't think he, or anyone else, including myself, expected the name that popped out of my mouth.

"Hendricks," I said without an ounce of hesitation.

Coach barely repressed a laugh. "You want *Hendricks* to take Todd's spot? As a D-man?"

"He can do it. He's practiced every position on the team. And he's *been* here. He knows how all of us play, how to read the field and anticipate."

Coach gestured for Connor to move to the front. "Hendricks, get your ass up here." Once Connor was standing beside me, chest puffed out defiantly and an edge of wariness in his eyes, Coach returned his focus to me. "He doesn't exactly have the physique we look for in a Defender," he said as if Connor wasn't standing two fucking feet in front of him.

"Maybe not, but what he lacks in bulk, he more than makes up for in speed and determination. Plus, he's got some of the fanciest fucking footwork I've ever seen."

Coach studied me, then Connor and Brian, followed by the rest of the team, now shifting uncomfortably. Never in a million years did I think I'd actually be *advocating* for Connor, but I wouldn't take it back. He deserved that spot and over my dead body was I going to stand there and let Coach just hand it to Singleton. Finally, Coach's mouth pinched into a thin line. "You have one game, Hendricks. You do well and I'll let you stay on as a D-man." I could practically feel Connor swelling with excitement beside me. "But if you fuck it up, you won't even get to ride the pine. Understood?"

All the air went out of Connor at the threat of being kicked off the team altogether. We may have our issues, and I had no clue if he was banking on an athletic scholarship, but even I thought that was cruel. To his credit, Connor kept his shoulders square and his voice firm. "I won't let the team down, Coach. That Championship trophy is coming home with us this year."

Rather than slapping him on the back for saying exactly what he'd wanted to hear, Coach let out a gruff, "We'll see," then ordered us all to hit the showers with a not so friendly reminder not to be late to morning practice.

Connor gave me a small nod of appreciation before peeling off to get cleaned and changed. It wasn't until the last of us were filing out of the locker room to trudge back to the school that Brian appeared once again at my shoulder.

"That was a bold move, Hudson," he said quietly as he fell in step.

"Do you disagree?"

"That Singleton has no business starting? Not at all. Fucker shouldn't have even been allowed on the team this far into the season. Hendricks, on the other hand." He glanced at me, the setting sun bathing his brown face in bronze. "You really think he can do it?"

I fought the urge to clench my fist at hearing his obvious doubt. "Yeah, I do. The better question is, why don't you?" Before he could respond, I surged ahead into a lopping run that my sore legs didn't appreciate at all. I was nearly to the cafeteria—and sweating again—when an iron door I'd never really noticed suddenly opened up and someone yanked me inside.

"What the fuck?" I snapped as I threw my hands out to defend against whoever had grabbed me while I blinked rapidly to adjust to the gloom. At the sound of a lock clanging into place, my heart leapt into my throat. "What's going on? Who's there?!"

"Calm down. It's me."

It took a second and a few more blinks before the voice registered. "Calvin?" I asked, squinting as if that would somehow make the shadowy room brighter.

"The one and only."

"Is that a light in here or something?"

On cue, I heard the click of a switch and soft yellow light similar to that in the secret room illuminated the area. The first thing I noticed was the giant fucking cross on the far wall, followed by the rows of pews, a short table with candles on it, and finally, Calvin's stormy expression.

I took a nervous step back, and the cold iron of the door leached through my shirt. "Uh, hey. What's up?"

"We need to have words." His clipped tone only made me more nervous.

"Is this about Andy? Because I talked to him. We got everything out there. I swear. Is this a church? How long has this been here?" I rambled.

"Forget the chapel!" he shouted, and I winced. "Who told you?"

"Told me what?" I asked shakily. Angry Calvin really was terrifying and now I had Andy's little insight that he could totally kick my ass running through my head.

"You know damn well what. You weren't even here when it happened. I want to know who the fuck told you about what went down with Warren and where the fuck you get off telling Andy."

I blanched.

"Well! Who was it?!"

"Connor," I blurted. "He pulled me aside the day we got back from DC and filled me in. Told me we needed to keep an eye out for Andy."

"And you just took it upon yourself to make sure Andy knew all the sordid details."

My spine finally decided to make a reappearance, and I stopped cowering against the door. "Look, it wasn't like that. This isn't about you. I have every right to tell my *boyfriend* that there's a predator on campus that targets people like him, like us." Calvin opened his mouth, probably to lay into me some more, but I cut him off. "And for the record, I only told him the bare minimum. He needed to know what Singleton is capable of. He didn't know why we both were so adamant that he stay away from him. But I *never* mentioned your name. If he figured it out, that's not on me."

"Fuck," Calvin groaned, slumping against the wall. "Does everyone fucking know?"

"I don't think so. I don't even know how Connor knew, but I'm glad he told me. Why didn't you tell Andy the truth when you warned him?" I asked tentatively.

Calvin's sigh might as well have been dredged from the bottom of his soul. "Because he's my only friend. He's looked up to me, *depended* on me. I couldn't bear the thought of him suddenly pitying me, seeing me as broken."

"For what it's worth, I'm sorry. I didn't mean to jeopardize your friendship. I just wanted to keep him safe," I said softly.

"I know. These last couple weeks have been... Well, they've been a lot."

I shifted to rest against the wall beside him. "Tell me about it. I just went toe-to-toe with Coach to get him to give Connor Todd's spot on the team instead of Warren."

"No shit?" He huffed a laugh and shook his head. "Bet he took that with the grace of a pineapple being shoved up his ass."

"Sounds about right."

He straightened and ran his fingers through his curls, drawing attention to the dark circles under his eyes. I wanted to ask if he was sleeping, but it wasn't my place and I'd already done enough damage. "Sorry about..." He waved a dismissive hand.

"Don't worry about it," I said, though he'd thoroughly scared the shit out of me.

"Oh, I'm not. Seemed like the thing to say." He moved toward the door and I stepped out of his way as he produced an impressive iron key. He slid it into the lock, then looked at me. "And, Mitch, you two need to stop sneaking out at night. I mean it."

I nodded, though it was clear by the look in his eyes he didn't buy it. Probably for the best, since I had zero intention of stopping. Andy was safe with me. I'd never let anyone harm a single red hair on his head. Finally, Calvin pushed the door open, then waited for me to exit the chapel before locking it back. He gave me another searching look before walking away.

Chapter 25

Andy

"Oh God. Mitch," I gasped as he rammed back home. I was barely even aware of the wall at my back or his bruising grip on my thighs, I was so focused on where he was absolutely wrecking my hole. The sound of our flesh slapping together was almost too much. It filled the room, punctuated with ball-tightening pants and moans. I clawed at Mitch's shoulders, torn between the desire to get away from the punishing thrusts and desperation for more. Thank God the secret room was virtually soundproof.

"You gonna come for me?" he asked as he shifted his grip, angling my hips just enough so his next drive pegged my prostate.

"Fuck!" I yelled as the overwhelming pleasure threatened to make me do just that. When I gathered enough coherency and was sure I'd staved off the pending orgasm, I met his lust-blown hazel eyes. "Make me."

"Such a brat," he said with a smirk. If anyone else had the gall to call me that, I'd have ripped them a new one, but when Mitch said it, I felt special, cherished. And most definitely like a brat. Abruptly, he gripped my hair and yanked my head back, then mashed his mouth against mine in a bruising kiss. When he pulled away, he was panting for air, and there was a fierceness in his gaze. "Whose are you?" he growled.

I whimpered, and my traitorous hole clenched at the blatant possessiveness.

"Say it," he demanded, jerking on my hair and forcing me to look at him while he continued slamming his length into me again and again. "Whose are you?"

"Yours," I gasped, lacking the willpower to deny him anything.

"Say it again." He emphasized the order with another punishing thrust.

"I'm yours. Always."

"Damn right you are." He slashed his mouth over mine in a messy kiss, then lowered his head to my chest. The sharp prick of his teeth against my flushed skin rocketed me toward my denied orgasm. Then he bit down hard right over my heart.

I threw my head back with a shout as I clenched around his cock and unloaded on his abs. He continued to plow into me as my release threatened to turn me into a jellyfish. With a fierce cry of his own that he muffled against my chest, he buried himself in my ass one last time. We moaned in tandem as the aftershocks of my orgasm milked him dry.

Once our breathing had steadied somewhat, he gingerly lowered me to stand on my own. Which became immediately apparent wasn't happening. I slumped against him while my legs did a fair imitation of a jello fresh out of the mold. Lime, of course. How we got to the blankets we'd accumulated was a blur, but Mitch's mouth back on mine was crystal clear in that soft dream-like way.

The kisses stayed relatively tame. But one press of lips turned into another and another. I didn't ever want to stop kissing him. It still didn't feel real that he felt the same way. Eventually, the need for oxygen won out. I rolled onto my back with a groan, equal parts exhausted and sated. Was there such a thing as enough Mitch?

The soft brush of lips on my shoulder startled me out of my reverie and I blinked up at the man in question. "How you doing, kitten?"

I hummed contentedly, because words were hard, and shuffled closer to him. "Love you," I mumbled against his chest as he wrapped his arm around me and pulled me closer.

"Love you too."

We lay wrapped in each other until the discomfort of drying cum forced us to move. We cleaned up as best we could, given what we had on hand, and pulled our pajama pants back on. I vetoed replacing our shirts. I wasn't finished with skin-to-skin contact yet.

"Fuck," Mitch groaned as he settled back on the makeshift mattress of layered blankets. "We keep going like this, and I'm gonna have to start wearing a shirt at practice."

"Why's that?" I asked, scooting in close again.

He laughed. "Because everyone's gonna want to know when the hell I had time to put in extra ab workouts."

I echoed his humor and ran a hand over the defined ridges of his stomach. "You won't hear me complaining."

"Oh, I see. You only want me for my hot, dumb jock body," he teased.

"First off, you *are* hot. Insanely fucking hot. I won't deny that I'm a total sucker for the hot jock. But not dumb. Never dumb."

Mitch's resulting smile, despite my serious tone, had butterflies swirling in my stomach. "I know. My wicked smart boyfriend does an amazing job of reminding me."

Heat blazed on my face and I tried desperately to hide the ill-timed blush, as well as my ridiculously happy grin.

"What? Too much?"

I pushed through my embarrassment to meet his hazel eyes and shook my head. "No. It's not. I just wasn't expecting it."

He searched my face for a moment. "Is it a label thing? Or do you not want to be my boyfriend?"

"Oh my God, Mitch. What part of this asinine grin says I *don't* want to be your boyfriend?"

He smirked, and I realized I'd been played. "Well, when you put it like that." He pulled me down for a kiss. We were still laughing when he pulled away.

"Oh fuck," I said, as something finally clicked. I pushed up to look down at him and couldn't realize how daft I'd been.

"What is it?"

"This is what you meant. In DC. When you asked if this is what it would be like. You weren't talking about being gay at all. You were talking about being together. With me." I smacked my forehead. "I'm such an idiot."

"No, you're not," he said as he gently pulled my hand away from my face to cradle over his heart. "You're the smartest person I know."

"Can I at least call myself a stubborn fool?"

His smile widened. "I'll let you have that one."

I tried to smack him in the chest, but didn't manage much, considering he held one hand captive and the other was holding me up. I gave it up as a lost cause and flopped on his chest with a harrumph. The quiet of the room wrapped around us like a blanket, making me feel snuggly and warm. That, combined with Mitch's hand slowly rubbing up and down my back, was the perfect recipe for drifting off. Which we definitely could not do.

I shook myself to throw off the impending fog of sleep and maneuvered to prop my chin on his chest. He ran his fingers through my hair and I couldn't repress another happy hum. For some reason, that made him smile. "Tell me about the game last week. Did Connor really hold his own?"

"You know, you could always *come* to a game," he suggested playfully. I snorted, but he didn't take it too seriously. "As for the game, it actually went really well. I think it went a hell of a lot better than anyone expected. Connor blended right in like he'd been playing on the team as a D-man for years instead of a week. He even managed a few goal assists."

"That's great!"

"Yeah, turns out having him fight tooth and nail *with* you is way better than against you."

I rolled my eyes. "Go figure. So you think Coach Santinelli will let him continue?"

"Seems like a sure thing to me. But we'll find out for sure after we watch the game tape in a couple days."

"It's kind of weird, you and Connor getting along. And you're sure he doesn't know about us?" I wasn't sure why it mattered, but I knew it did. I was really happy for Connor finally getting his chance to play, to be an integral part of the team. But realistically, I also knew he'd be furious if he ever learned that Mitch had been his rival in more ways than one… and that he'd never stood a chance.

"I don't know if I'd go so far as to say we're friends or anything, but not trying to kill each other is a welcome change. And as far as I know, he's still in the dark about me. All he knows is that we were best friends a long time ago and now we are again."

"That's something, I guess." I pushed back up to a sitting position and stretched, appreciating the tenderness of my ass. That would be a nice reminder during the day.

Mitch's hand trailed down my back as he sighed. "Is it really time to go already?"

I twisted around to look at him. "Yeah. We don't want to linger too long." I watched as he sat up and reached for his shirt, Calvin's concern about who was looking out for Mitch playing through my mind. "Mitch?"

"Yeah?" His head popped through the top of his shirt and he looked at me askance.

"You're careful when you come here, right? And when you go back to your room?"

"Of course. Besides, if I got caught out, the only way you would know is if I didn't show. And I'm never *not* going to show." He leaned forward to cradle my cheek. "Never again."

I smiled and closed the distance to place a lingering kiss on his lips. "Okay. Just wanted to make sure."

"What brought this on?" he asked, his face still showing concern.

I sighed. "Something Calvin said."

Mitch studied me for a moment, then asked, "He still not talking to you?"

"Nope," I replied, popping the P and betraying my frustration. "And he's doing a damn good job of dodging me, too. No sooner do I catch a glimpse of him in the hall than he disappears. I didn't mean to upset him." I darted a glance at Mitch. "Or get you in trouble. It's not like you outright told me he was the one Warren had hurt. I just wanted to show him support. Be there for him like all the times he's been there for me."

He wrapped his arms around me, and I rested my head on his shoulder. "He'll come around. You'll see."

It was really hard not to walk around like I was floating on cloud nine. Already a few of my classmates had asked what had me in such a good mood. I was starting to think that I must look like a surly shit most of the time for the distinction to be so noteworthy. But it wasn't like I could tell them that I was madly in love with my boyfriend—boyfriend!—who also happened to be my best friend and we were having the most incredible sex, and talking, and cuddling. Honestly, the only thing that could have made our evenings any better was if we didn't have to separate. And a bed. A bed would be heaven. So I told them the next best thing.

Not only had I been accepted to the University of Chicago, but I'd also been admitted into their prestigious Advanced Writing program. And all on a full scholarship that included housing. That was more than enough for most of them to start congratulating me and letting my ultra happy demeanor slide. To be fair, general admittance hadn't been much of a concern for me, but the full ride was definitely a surprise.

Considering all that, it felt a little weird to continue meeting with my mentor. Then again, Garza was also one of the few people I could be open with about why I was so damn happy. Besides, with added lacrosse practice commandeering Mitch's study period, it wasn't like I could spend more time with him. Might as well make the most of it.

"I know it may seem premature to be reviewing schedules now, especially since some of the classes might not exist by the time you're set to take them—"

"But it never hurts to be prepared," I filled in, picking up the thread of conversation easily, despite being distracted—again—with thoughts of Mitch.

"Exactly," Garza said. He stood and walked around his desk, bringing him closer to where I sat in the front row. "So, how are *other* things going?" he asked with a knowing grin.

I didn't even have the wherewithal to be embarrassed about the smile that nearly split my face in two. "*Things* are going great. I never knew I could be this happy. Especially not here."

Garza chuckled and nodded. "I know what you mean."

"If it's not too presumptuous, can I ask how you do it? I know that we're not exactly operating at the same level, but I can't imagine that makes it any easier."

"No, it does *not*." He released a long-suffering sigh.

"Then why stay? Surely there are more," I darted a glance at the closed door, "progressive places to teach."

"You'd be surprised. At the end of the day, it really boils down to this is where Sammi wanted to be." He shrugged. "I could explain why a dozen different ways—the prestige, the benefits, the accommodations—but honestly, it has as much to do with the past as the future."

I frowned. "I'm not following."

"I'm sure it comes as no surprise that when I got hired on at Ulwich, I was considered an outsider," he said with a smirk as he casually gestured at his tawny skin. That it did not. If the student body was whiter than Wonder Bread, the faculty might as well be bleached flour. "Samuel, much like yourself and many of the other young men here, is a legacy. His great grandfather was one of the founding members. He's determined to steer the academy into the future, to make things better for everyone. When he asked me to stay and fight with him, I couldn't bear to say no."

"Wow. I had no idea." I stopped myself from adding that I'd never witnessed anything remotely anti-establishment since I'd been here.

"Well, it's been more of a struggle than I think either of us anticipated. Our efforts have been subtle, to say the least. I'm still convinced that eventually something so bad that it can't be ignored will happen and that will be our opening to crack this place wide open. What that could be, though, makes me even more anxious than our stilted efforts at change."

It was on the tip of my tongue to ask if he knew about Warren Singleton's sordid past at Ulwich, but the bell signaling the end of study period cut me off before I could start.

"I guess that's time." Garza swiveled around to resume his position behind his desk in preparation for his next class. He paused before sitting and looked at me, his expression serious. "You *are* being careful?"

He could have been talking about safe sex or any number of things, but I had a feeling that wasn't it. "Yes, sir. We're being smart."

"I would expect nothing less," he said with a nod. "I'll see you at next week's meeting, and I expect that writing prompt to have at least a couple of pages."

"Yes, professor," I said over my shoulder as I opened the class door. Life really couldn't get any better. Then I stepped into the hall and *into* another student.

The student slowly turned around and looked down at me with unforgiving storm blue eyes, his light brown hair falling across his forehead. The apology on the tip of my tongue died a merciless death. My heart lurched into my throat and I stopped breathing altogether as it sunk in that I'd just done the number one thing I shouldn't have. I'd attracted Warren Singleton's attention.

His lips curled into a smile that was as far from friendly as a Great White shark was from a Golden Retriever. "You must be the Anderson Gallgher I've heard *so* much about." His predatory gaze flicked to my bright auburn hair, leaving little doubt how easy I was to single out. "At long last we meet. I confess, I've been curious about the mysterious person under Hudson's protection. His 'no-touch' edict is so... sweet, now that I've met you."

"I don't know what you're talking about," I said, doing my level best not to sound nervous and failing miserably. "I'm sorry for running into you. I should have paid better attention to where I was going."

Something dark entered his eyes and cold trickled down my spine. "You should be. Clearly, this place has gone to shit while I've been gone. The name *Ulwich* used to mean something. Now they'll let anyone in. And here I thought I took care of that the last time I was here. No worries though, there's still time to take out the trash." He bared his teeth in what

I assumed was supposed to imitate a smile as he slowly looked me over from head to toe.

My entire body vibrated with the desperate need to bolt. To drop my overweight satchel and run as fast as my legs could carry me. I couldn't think straight. A single word blared in my head like a siren, screaming at me to seek shelter: *DANGER*. But I couldn't make my feet move, couldn't force any more words out, couldn't even swallow. Fear had me completely paralyzed.

Warren slowly dragged his gaze back up my body until he met my wide-eyed gaze once more. "Run along, Anderson. I'll be seeing you around." His following smile held a dark promise that finally got my limbs moving.

I stumbled backward, nearly falling on my ass and dumping my books on the floor. By some miracle, I kept my footing. I didn't even care that his laughter chased me down the hallway while I scrambled away as fast as I could manage. I clung with a white-knuckle grip to the only thought that kept me from dissolving into a hyperventilating panic right there in the hall—I had to find Mitch.

Chapter 26

Mitch

Andy came careening around a corner, panic clear in his over-bright eyes and flushed face. Before I could ask what was wrong, he grabbed me by my jacket lapels and whispered, "Secret room. Now."

If I wasn't worried before, I definitely was now. Andy didn't skip class. I was also suddenly very glad that Coach had held me back from the others to gruffly "commend" me on my suggestion to have Connor take Todd's place. It meant that I didn't have to make excuses to teammates or figure out how to ditch them. However, they would notice if I didn't make it to class.

I hastened my steps to reach my math class, where I immediately begged forgiveness for being tardy and for needing to duck to the nurse's office, as I wasn't feeling well. The professor grumbled something about "it better all be worth it for that damn trophy," and sent me off with a half-hearted wave. I didn't waste any time doubling back to the secret room.

I barely had a chance to adjust to the dim lighting when Andy grabbed the front of my jacket once more. When I looked into his eyes, I realized he wasn't just panicked; he was fucking terrified.

"Mitch, I fucked up. We have to stop meeting at night. It's not safe. How could I have been so stupid? Of course, Calvin was right. I should have been more careful, paid better attention. Warren knows who I am. I ran into him outside of Garza's. He said something about your protection and a 'no touch' order. What was he talking about?" His words spilled over each other so fast it was almost impossible to keep up. Then the "no-touch order" registered and all the blood drained from my face.

"Fuck!" I shouted. This was bad. This was worse than bad. I'd pissed off Warren by pushing for Connor to fill the D-man position and, thanks to that stupid order I'd issued five years ago, I'd all but painted a target on Andy's back.

"Mitch!" he shouted to get my attention. "Are you listening to me? What was he talking about? What order?"

I wrapped my hands around his wrists to ground myself. "It was a long time ago. I was trying to keep you safe. It was the only way I could think to protect you."

He shook his head, seemingly unaware that he was simultaneously tightening his fingers on my jacket. "What? When was this?"

"After we... broke up," I said awkwardly, because, honestly, what else could I call it? "Some guys on the team were chasing you down the hall. You fell down after running into me."

"I remember," he said so softly I almost didn't hear.

"You have to understand. I wanted so much to go with you. But they were still coming, and I *knew* what they would do if they caught you. So I stayed. One thing led to another, and I ended up low-key threatening anyone who touched you. I played it off, saying you'd had my back once, and I was returning the favor."

He shoved me away, anger now battling fear for dominance on his face. "What the fuck were you thinking?!"

"I wasn't. Please believe me, I didn't mean for it to become a thing, but I also couldn't bring myself to take it back. I couldn't be close to you any more, but I could still protect you from a distance."

"Jesus, Mitch! I know you meant well, but how could you be so shortsighted?"

I puffed up defensively. "It didn't seem shortsighted at the time. I was desperate to keep you safe. And for the record, it *worked*. For four years, no one has laid so much as a finger on you. Yeah, they still talked shit, but no one was willing to find out what would happen if they crossed the line. *You're welcome*."

"And I appreciate what you tried to do. But I never said I needed your help. I can take care of myself," he pushed back.

"I know you can."

"Then how could you not see that issuing an order like that could make things so much worse? I love you, I do, but *fuck*, Mitch." He grabbed his hair. "We're getting off track. We can't undo the past. All we can do is deal with the consequences in the here and now. And right now, we've got a pretty fucking big one to deal with."

"Warren."

"Warren," he repeated. "The way he looked at me, Mitch." He shuddered. "I've never felt so unclean in my life. I wanted to bathe in acid. Still do," he added, looking off to the side.

I didn't think twice about wrapping my arms around him. "We'll figure this out, kitten. I promise."

He buried his face against my chest and took a stuttering breath. "How?"

"For starters, you're right. It's not safe to sneak out at night anymore. No matter how much I want to see you or hold you, I won't put you at risk like that."

He lifted his head and blinked at me with wet lashes. "What about you? How are you any safer?"

I forced a smile that probably looked as fake as it felt. "Because I'm Coach's shiny star. Warren may hate me, but he'd have to be a special kind of stupid to go after me like he did Todd."

Andy tightened his arms so much that my ribs cracked. Not that I for a second considered asking him to ease up. "What about Connor? He's the one who got the spot, after all."

I shook my head. "Same deal. It would be suspicious as fuck if Connor got hurt during a practice like Todd. Plus, I don't think the rest of the team would stand for it."

"Okay. That's good. So no more meeting up. What else?"

"Let's start with what he said to you."

He stuttered through what Warren had said to him in the hall. All of it was upsetting, but none more so than the last thing he'd said—*I'll be seeing you around*. When he finished, we stood in silence, holding each other, while the ominous promise seemed to fill the room.

"I'm scared," he whispered eventually.

"Me too," I admitted. "We'll get through this. I won't let him hurt you."

Andy sniffled and pulled away. "We should get to class. Neither of us showing will raise suspicions."

"Even though we're in different classes?" I asked.

"Especially because we're in different classes. Better to be safe."

"Okay." I cupped his face and placed a soft kiss on his still trembling lips, then rested my forehead against his. "Be careful."

He looked at me with shiny green eyes that still held a shadow of fear. "I will."

Folding chairs squeaked as two dozen of my teammates grew increasingly restless. This was our third time watching the most recent game tape, and it wasn't any easier than the first. The game had been brutal. Norwood Academy had put up a hell of a fight and we'd barely eked out the W. It wouldn't surprise me if we ended up facing them again in the championship. And they'd be out for blood. Not that they hadn't been during this game.

Everyone winced as the clack of helmets ricocheted through the locker room. On the screen, the Norwood player walked away while Connor hit the ground like a sack of potatoes. The image of Singleton's smirk swam before me, though it hadn't been captured on the tape. Pity. Though, judging by the furtive looks everyone kept sneaking at Warren, I doubted I was the only one who believed he'd paid the other team to take out Connor.

I returned my attention to the flurry of activity on the screen. After a few minutes of trainers attending to Connor's fallen form, he miraculously got up and walked. Even through the grainy footage, you could make out the stubborn set of his mouth and the determined square of his shoulders. It was going to take a lot more than a cheap foul to keep him down.

"Right. I think that's enough for today." Coach paused the video on Connor mid-stride. "I've been holding off officially naming Hendricks as Garwood's replacement, but after last week's game, I'd say he's more than proved his worth. You've got some real mettle in you, Hendricks." He slapped Connor on the shoulder.

While the rest of the team echoed their praise on how Connor had rallied for the last game, I stole a glance at Singleton. I'd never really understood the phrase "so mad you could spit nails", but one glance at the unfettered rage blanketing Warren's face remedied that. Beside me, Brian leaned forward, resting his dark brown forearms on his knees.

"Serves that fucker right," he said under his breath.

I looked over at him. "Just hope it doesn't blow back on anyone else."

He snorted. "The team'll be fine. Everyone has their eyes peeled for any more underhanded shit."

I darted a glance at the legacies that had taken to hanging around Warren. "You sure about that 'everyone', Captain?"

"They're not dumb enough to step out. Singleton may think he has them in his pocket, but this is still *my* team."

I angled closer to him and dropped my voice. "Don't get me wrong, I don't want him here any more than you do. He's scum through and through. There were a dozen other ways he could have taken out Garwood, and he went with one that could have taken him out of the game for good. He did him dirty, and from what I can tell, he doesn't have a speck of remorse. If he's willing to do that out on the field where everyone can see, what'll he do when no one is looking?"

"Then I guess we'll have to make sure we've always got eyes on him." Brian's intense gaze took on a familiar glint, and I was relieved that for once it wasn't aimed at me.

Coach made a single loud clap, cutting through the murmurs and dropping the room into expectant silence. "We've got an all-star lineup this season. We've already had one shake up and I'm not looking to have another. Thanks to Headmaster Torsney, we finally have a half competent trainer on staff and Hendricks has proven he can run more than his mouth." He stabbed the screen with his middle finger, right where Connor was frozen mid walk-it-off. "Our opponents are clearly coming with everything they've got. Make sure you're covering each other on the field and off. We're a team and a team has each other's backs. Is that understood?"

There were several head nods and some muffled agreement.

"I said, is that understood?!" he repeated.

"Yes, Coach!" we all shouted in unison.

"Good, now get your asses fed and in bed. I want all of you rested and ready to hit the field in full gear tomorrow for morning *and* midday practice."

No one dared groan out loud, but you could fucking *feel* the misery in the room. There was something truly unholy about having a full-dress practice in the middle of the day. It was bad enough before when we barely had a chance to wipe down before returning to class. Now, we wouldn't even have that. There was no use in complaining, though. Best to just roll with it. There were only three more regular season games, followed by six playoff rounds and, heaven help us, the championship, then it was less than a month to graduation. Which reminded me, I needed to follow up with my Uncle Terri about that scout. But first, I needed to touch base with Connor and Benny.

Chapter 27

Mitch

There was only one word for our current state—gross. I felt like I'd been wrung through one of those old-fashioned laundry presses, only I was still soaked with sweat. Double gross. It was a true testament to everyone's level of exhaustion that no one so much as groaned while we peeled off our disgusting gear and tugged back on our school uniforms. Hell, as it was, I was trying not to even breathe through my nose, we were so fucking ripe. Not that breathing through my mouth was doing me any favors. I could *taste* the stench. I half expected every professor with a lacrosse player in their class to insist we either sit at the back or in the hall.

I'd just finished forcing my sticky arms through the sleeves of my button down when Coach Santinelli stormed into the locker room with fire blazing in his eyes. "Daniels!"

Brian jerked out of the daze he'd been in, straightened, and turned to face Coach. "Yes, sir?"

"Where the hell is Singleton?"

Brian and I shared a look, as did most everyone else in the room. I'd assumed he'd been riding the pine since he no longer had a shot of playing and I'd been too busy busting my ass to pay him any mind. Brian cleared his throat. "Uh, maybe he's in the showers?"

It was a poor guess, seeing as how we'd have heard the water running in that case. The bigger question was: when was the last time *anyone* had seen him? My stomach sank as I realized *I* didn't even know the last time or place that I'd noticed him.

"Nice try. He's been MIA all practice. Unless someone saw him and didn't tell his ass that being benched doesn't excuse him from being present?" Coach stared down the legacies that normally clung to Warren like velcro.

With each one that offered a clueless expression and shook their head, my stomach dropped further and further while my heart climbed into my throat. This wasn't happening. Did *no one* know where he was?

"The first one that sees him, you tell him I want him in my office ASAP, and I don't give a damn what class he does or doesn't have." The entire team remained frozen in place as Coach stomped over to his office and slammed the door behind himself.

The crash of blinds was still ringing through the room as I looked across the locker room and met first Benny's and then Connor's worried faces. As one, we dropped everything and bolted out of the lockers. Not even screaming hamstrings could slow me down as I poured every drop of energy I had left running to the main building.

"Any idea where they might be?" Connor panted as he ran beside me, for once not out-stripping me.

"Andy has his mentor meeting today, but the bell's going to ring any minute. He could be anywhere," I replied haltingly. "Benny?" I nearly stumbled when I caught the dire expression on his face.

"I know where Cal is. You two find Gallagher."

Just like when we coordinated on the field, the three of us wordlessly split apart the second we stepped inside. Each sprinting down a different hallway. Every corner I turned, I prayed I'd see Andy's bright red hair. But the halls were empty. Most everyone would still be in study period. The second the bell rang, though, my search would get infinitely harder.

I forced my aching limbs to go faster and crashed against the wall as I careened down the next hallway. My heart nearly stopped when the sun shone copper off Andy's head further down. "Andy!" I shouted.

He stopped mid-stride and turned a confused expression on me. "Mitch? What are you—"

The rest of whatever he was going to say lurched out of his mouth as I grabbed his arm and hauled him to the small bathroom nearby. I didn't slow until I'd shut us inside the farthest stall from the door.

"Thank fuck you're okay," I said between gulps of air, then I mashed my mouth against his. Much as I wanted to kiss him deeper, I was still out of breath. I released his lips and began doing a full pat down to confirm what my eyes were telling me—Andy was okay. He was safe.

“Mitch, what is going on?”

“Nothing, kitten. Everything’s fine.” I captured his mouth once more. Oxygen be damned.

“We can’t do this here,” he hissed. “And why are you so sweaty?”

“I know. I know. I ran straight here from practice,” I gasped, still crowding him against the stall wall and peppering his lips with kisses as much as my lungs would allow.

“Why?”

I finally stopped trying to pull him inside me long enough to meet his understandably freaked out gaze. “No one’s seen Warren. He wasn’t at practice.”

Andy’s eyes widened, filled with horror. “Maybe he had a meeting with a professor or had to go to the nurse?” he hazarded, though his heart wasn’t in it.

“Maybe. But I doubt it. Either way, the second we realized no one knew where he was, we weren’t taking any chances. I don’t know what I would do if something happened to you.” I let out a breath that carried all my fears and worries for Andy, along with my immense relief at finding him unharmed.

“Mitch,” he said, his voice uncharacteristically thick. “Wait. We?”

I huffed a laugh. “Yeah, me, Connor, and Benny tore out of the locker rooms like we were on fire. Should probably find Hendricks and let him know you’re okay.” I studied Andy’s surprised gaze. “I can’t say I won’t always be jealous of the time that you two had together or that he won’t regularly piss me off just for breathing, but he really cares about you.”

“He should be more worried about himself.”

“Maybe,” I replied absently, turning his head this way and that, then pushing up his sleeves to check for bruises from someone grabbing him.

He jerked back his arm after I’d only managed one. “What are you doing?”

“I need to be sure.”

“Sure of what?” he huffed, his irritation obvious.

I glanced up to catch his green eyes. “That you’re okay.”

“I already told you, I’m fine.”

"I know. I know. But I needed to see it for myself. Fuck, Andy, I was so scared. I don’t know if I’ve ever been more scared in my life." Without preamble, I mashed my mouth against his. I didn’t want to know what I would do if something ever happened to him. What I’d be capable of.

In the blink of an eye, my reassuring brush of lips morphed into a tongue-tangling, clothes-pulling make out. If we were quiet, we might even be able to sneak in a quickie before we had to show up for class. Though I wasn't sure if Andy was capable of being quiet.

The debate was snatched out of my hands when Andy suddenly pulled away. I began to ask what was up, but didn't make it past the first "W" when he clamped a hand over my mouth. Then I heard it—the bathroom door closing and at least two new voices. We shared a panicked look. This was exactly why this was a bad idea.

I sent up a silent prayer that they wouldn't need the stall and that they'd be gone quickly. Meanwhile, Andy nudged me backward and used me to balance as he climbed to stand on the toilet. It took me longer than it should have to realize what he was doing and why. Whether someone needed the stall or not, two pairs of feet sharing it was still damning.

Andy

I love him, I reminded myself for the twentieth time as I crouched on a fucking toilet behind Mitch. But seriously, what had he been thinking? What had *I* been thinking? Once I realized why he was so freaked, I should have immediately gotten us out of here. But *no*, I had to be seduced by his concern, and soft touches, and intense kisses. Really, I was just as much to blame for the absurd predicament we found ourselves in.

I was debating whether I could get away with sliding under the divider into the next stall and escape that way when the bathroom door slammed against the wall.

"Holy fuck!" an unfamiliar voice shouted.

"Jesus, Frank, you scared the shit out of me," one of the guys who'd already been here said. The other chuckled at his ironic turn of phrase.

"What's got your panties in a twist?" yet another voice asked. Three? There were three of them?! Well, four now. I glowered at Mitch, who at least had the decency to look abashed.

"Benny Price is carrying Calvin Bridges naked down the hall," Frank spat out. "They're covered in blood!"

There was a collective gasp, mingled with cries of "Fuck!" and "Holy shit!", which thankfully hid mine and Mitch's equally involuntary reaction to this news. Terror strangled my heart. I immediately began tugging on

Mitch to get him to trade places with me. The other boys' voices blended with the dull roar filling my ears. I needed to get out of here. Now.

Mitch only had one foot on the seat when my impatience got the better of me. I threw caution to the wind and burst out of the stall, startling the—yep, four—guys into silence.

"Where?" I demanded. When Frank didn't immediately respond, I advanced on him, fully prepared to shake the answer out of him if I had to.

He glanced at the others with wide eyes and took a nervous step back as I bore down on him.

"Where?" I repeated more forcefully.

"The infirmary," Frank said, the words bursting out of him.

I glanced in the mirror across from the stall I'd just vacated. Mercifully, the door had swung partially shut, but I could still catch a glimpse of Mitch's worried gaze. He gave me a nod, and I didn't hesitate to tear out of there, much like I imagined Mitch had done earlier when he'd come to find me.

Guilt writhed and twisted in my gut as I made my way as fast as I could toward the infirmary. Unfortunately, the bell had rung at some point and the hall was now filled with the excited chatter of students. I caught snippets of conversation that confirmed what Frank had shared in the bathroom. Only, it was so much worse.

I learned that Calvin was actually wrapped in a towel and not actually naked-naked. He also wasn't in a fireman's carry or anything similar, but in a bridal carry. The closer I got to the infirmary, the more detailed the descriptions of his state got. Calvin looked like he'd been through hell. Was his eye swollen? His cheek was definitely busted. Was he even conscious?

Benny's knuckles were bleeding. They'd left a trail of blood in their wake. Price was… crying? Had he done it? He wouldn't say. Was any of the blood on him his or was it all Bridge's?

Finally, the sign for the nurse's office came into view. The hall blurred, and I swayed in place as I braced myself for the worst. Once I was mostly sure I wouldn't simply pass out, I pushed open the door.

Angry shouting washed over me, and it took a second to place the owner. Benny snarled something I couldn't quite make out as I slunk closer to the half-glass wall separating the medical exam room from the waiting area. My gaze was drawn to where Benny was apparently laying into the nurse and Professor Nolan, then it slid to the prone figure lying on the table.

I covered my mouth with both hands, though it did little to stifle my horrified gasp. The only thing remotely recognizable about Calvin was his hair. But even his curls were matted with blood, destroying their usual rebellious bounce. His face was a distortion of swollen, broken skin, and darkening bruises. The towel Benny had carried him in was indeed soaked with blood, most of which had absolutely come from Calvin. Abruptly, Benny moved around the table, providing an unobstructed view of the rest of my friend. Then I saw the blood running down the inside of his legs.

Black curled around my vision as I swayed once again and stumbled backward. I fell heavily into a chair, though I doubt I would have noticed if I'd landed on the floor. Tears rolled unhindered down my face. This was my fault. I should have tried harder to get Calvin to talk to me, should have insisted we stick together.

The door to the infirmary and Headmaster Torsney stalked in. "Where is he?" he snapped.

I pointed shakily at the room across from me that looked straight out of a horror movie.

He turned and rapped on the glass. When everyone inside—minus Calvin—turned to look, he pointed aggressively at Benny and gestured for him to come out.

Benny whispered something to Calvin and lightly stroked a part of his arm *not* covered in gore. Then he spared a glare at the other two in the room and walked over to rip the door open. "If you're here to—"

"What the hell do you think you were doing?!" Torsney cut him off. "Destruction of school property, accosting another student. You're lucky the ambulance got here in time. You nearly killed Singleton."

"You gave that asshole my ambulance?! That's Calvin's fucking ambulance!" Benny gestured emphatically to where Calvin still hadn't moved.

Torsney drew himself up to his full height. Not that it could compete with Benny's. "You will mind your tone with me, Mr. Price. Another ambulance can be called. Mr. Bridges... injuries don't seem nearly as severe. He can wait. Mr. Singleton could not."

In all the years I'd known him, all the verbal sparring, all the low blows, I'd *never* seen Benny so blindly furious. His grip on the door turned white knuckle. "With absolutely no respect, *sir*, fuck you. I hope that fucking asshole dies." He spat on Torsney's pristinely polished shoes, then slammed the door shut in his face. The headmaster was mid-apoplectic fit when

Benny pulled out possibly the only cell phone on campus and dialed emergency services for the second time.

Chapter 28

Andy

Fuck small towns and fuck this school. Hylestead didn't have its own hospital, so the original ambulance had come from the county hospital over thirty minutes away. Like the community it served, the facility was relatively small. They also *conveniently* didn't have another ambulance available anytime soon. Which was why Benny was on the other side of the glass, pacing and clearly yelling as he tried to secure a private EMT to come get Calvin while I sat in the room with my beaten and broken friend.

I'd tried to clean the blood off of him, but no matter how gentle I was, he still winced in pain, though he'd yet to regain consciousness. Finally, I lost my nerve. There was too much blood, too many cuts, and I didn't know if anything might be broken. So I sat beside him and apologized for not being a better friend, for not being there, all while carefully avoiding looking at his blood stained legs. Not that I could see them anymore, thanks to the sheet someone had placed over him. But I was positive the image was burned into my brain. All of it was.

The door clicked open, and I glanced up as Benny entered the room and quietly shut the door behind him. It was just the two of us in here with Calvin now. Not long after he'd had his altercation with Torsney, he'd declared the others completely fucking useless and kicked them out as well. Mitch had attempted to stop by, but I'd shaken my head for him to go before Benny could see him.

"Any news?" I asked, painfully aware of Calvin's labored breathing even in his sleep. At least, I hoped it was only sleep.

Benny pocketed his illegal cell phone and ran a hand through his hair, his knuckles still raw. "I finally got someone to commit to being here as soon as possible."

"How long is that?"

"Another twenty minutes at the earliest."

"Fuck," I hissed. It had already been an hour.

"Yeah, and it took the promise of a hefty 'donation' to even get that. If I didn't know better, I'd think that the Academy heads told all emergency services not to respond."

We shared a look. We both knew better, and we both knew that was absolutely a possibility.

"How is he?" Benny asked as he sat in a chair on the other side of the table.

"Same as far as I can tell. I tried to… I couldn't…"

"I know." He shook his head and delicately twined his fingers with Calvin's. "Nolan actually had the audacity to suggest that Cal brought this on himself. That he'd *asked* for it."

I drew in a sharp breath. "What the fuck?"

"Yep. Because every queer wants to be sexually assaulted. Obviously." His cynicism curdled my stomach, but I didn't dispute it. Calvin was living proof of the depths homophobic assholes would sink. Oh God, please let him live.

The door opened again, and we looked up to find not just Professor Garza but Professor Cohen as well. "Both of you get up. You're going to help us get him out of here," Garza declared.

"Ari, are you sure this is the best option?" Professor Cohen asked quietly as he shut the door behind them. He glanced at Calvin and went noticeably green. "Is it safe?"

Professor Garza cupped Cohen's face and planted a firm, albeit chaste, kiss to his lips. "Samuel, I know you're scared. I know you don't want to make waves. And I know you believe that slow change is lasting change. But we're a little past that."

Professor Cohen swallowed thickly, but didn't look away from Garza's entreating gaze. "I know. We should have done more."

Garza nodded and placed a softer kiss this time. "We should have," he echoed, then turned to a surprised me and a stupefied Benny. I was technically in the "know" and *I* was taken off guard. I couldn't imagine what was going through Benny's head.

Professor Cohen squared his shoulders and stepped away from his lover's touch. "Mr. Price, what's the ETA on that ambulance?"

"At least another twenty," he replied hollowly.

"Mierda!" Garza hissed. "We're not waiting on that nonsense. We're taking him. Now."

"What do you need us to do?" I asked, eager for direction.

I stared down at my obnoxiously nutritious lunch. I needed to eat, but my appetite had been lacking since Calvin had been injured. The metal of the fork dug into my hand as I tightened my grip and squeezed my eyes shut. Not injured. *Attacked*. Sexually assaulted, regardless of if Calvin pressed charges. I wouldn't—*couldn't*—sugar coat it. Not like the rest of the school was hell bent on doing.

From the professors to the students, no one would talk about it. Not the truth, anyway. And Headmaster Torsney was spearheading the campaign to sweep what had happened under the rug. The few people I'd tried to illuminate hadn't been interested in the truth—that Warren was the villain, *not* the victim. They didn't want to know the real reason Benjamin Price IV had beaten him within an inch of his life, taking out a porcelain sink in the process. It was too ugly, too *real*.

I'd never felt so helpless. There had to be something I could do. Anything was better than this *nothing*. To my surprise, someone slid onto the bench across from me. I looked up, hoping to see Mitch, though I knew the lacrosse team had completely monopolized him since the incident. Which made who I did see that much more of a surprise.

"Benny?" I squeaked, barely keeping myself from shouting. "What are you doing here? Why aren't you at the hospital? Oh my God, did something happen?" Worst-case scenarios played through my mind, making me lightheaded with fear.

"Take a breath, Gallagher. Cal is fine."

I deflated so fast it was a wonder I didn't slide off the bench into a pool of relieved goo. Unable to help myself from years of caution, I glanced around to see who might be taking an interest in my unexpected companion. Short answer: no one. Real answer: everyone. If the students around us tried any harder *not* to look, they'd be openly staring.

"Why are you here?" I whispered.

He leaned on the table, and I realized how weary he looked. Not just tired—likely from his long nights of bedside vigil—but a bone deep exhaustion. The circles under his eyes had circles. "Cal gets released tomorrow."

"That's great!" I shout-whispered. When Benny looked more harrowed than excited, I frowned. "Isn't it?"

"Yes… and no. It's a total clusterfuck. I've spent the last five days doing everything in my power to make sure he gets the help he needs, but I feel like I'm fighting *him* as much as I'm fighting everyone else."

"What do you mean?"

He scrubbed his hands over his face as if to wake himself up. Not that it did any good. "Someone—I'm guessing the headmaster—tried to prevent the doctors from running a rape kit."

A gasp slipped out before I could stop it.

"Oh, it gets better. Cal tried to stop them, too. Luckily, I got him to agree before it was too late. As if that's not bad enough, they're trying to have him expelled."

"What the fuck?" I hissed, my ears burning with the onrush of anger. "If *anyone* was going to be expelled, it should be Warren and, honestly, you."

He leveled a dark look at me. A subtle reminder that no way in hell would his father, Benjamin Wallace Price III, ever allow that to happen. "In the meantime, they're attempting to force him to sign a gag order."

"He wouldn't say anything anyway," I inserted.

"I know, but you know him. *Because* they want him to, he won't. Not that I'd let him without a fight. The Academy heads are implying that his being able to return is contingent upon signing the order." I snorted, but didn't interject again. "As it is, I'm having a hell of a time convincing them that Warren is a danger and *he* should be expelled."

"It shouldn't be that hard. I mean, the police report alone should more than guarantee that he can't come back. Hell, he'd be tried as an adult. He'd go away for years," I added with a touch of malicious glee.

"He would."

"Judging by your face, I'm gonna go out on a limb and say that's not happening."

Benny sighed so heavily, *I* felt it. Defeated wasn't a word one associated with Benjamin Price, but that's exactly what he looked—defeated. "Calvin won't press charges. And he all but outright lied to the officers that took his statement."

"Surely his mom won't stand for that," I said, grasping at straws.

"She doesn't know. About any of it. He's legally an adult. The hospital is not obligated to contact his legal guardian." I couldn't tell if Benny was repeating what he'd heard verbatim or if he was just that acquainted with the law. Given his family's reputation in court, it could go either way. "As for the school," he continued, "whether they're required to or not is irrelevant, because we both know they'll find a way around it. Can't risk anything tarnishing their hallowed halls." His sneer made the hair on the back of my neck stand up.

I pushed my tray away and dropped my head in my hands. This place was the worst. No amount of supposed prestige could ever be worth letting such blatant violence go unaddressed. "I don't even know what to say."

"Say you'll help me."

"Yes, of course," I said, straightening. "Um, what am I helping you with?"

He leaned closer and dropped his voice so low that I had to lean forward as well to hear. "It'll be risky and it might not even work. But I have to do something. There's no way I can let Singleton come back to Ulwich."

"Fuck. They'd really let him come back?"

He nodded. "Wouldn't be long after Calvin, assuming I can prevent them from expelling him in the first place."

"If there's even a chance, I'm in."

"I was really hoping you'd say that." His smile was tight and a little frightening.

"What did you have in mind?" I asked, increasingly worried that I might have gotten myself in over my head.

His eyes glinted with pure, stomach-turning malice. "We're going to blackmail the school."

Chapter 29

Mitch

"He's not there. So you can stop looking," Connor said as we jogged into position for the next play.

I grunted. Of course he wasn't. It had never been all that smart for Andy to watch our practices before. But he'd had Calvin then. Also, the only reason Connor could possibly know that Andy wasn't sitting at the top of the hill was because he'd been searching for him, too.

"How's he doing, by the way?" he asked without looking at me.

Wasn't that the million dollar question? Ever since Benny had approached him with the scheme to blackmail the school with a scathing tell-all article, Andy had withdrawn, not just from me, but from *everything*. Putting together the article consumed him night and day and it showed. Honestly, I was really worried about him, but between grueling practices, keeping up with grades, and the team constantly around me, there wasn't much I could do.

"This isn't tea time! Get your asses in position!" Coach shouted from the sideline.

Connor lingered another moment, and I took the chance to quickly respond to his earlier question. "He's as well as he can be." He nodded in what I assumed was understanding, then hot-footed it to his starting position. I followed his lead and put my head down, pushing all my worries about Andy, Calvin, Benny, and fuck, *even me*, to the back of my mind.

Oliver and Brian faced off at midfield, their hands and knees to the ground, ready to jockey for the ball. Coach blew the whistle, and the ball went live. Within seconds, Brian gained control of it and sent it sailing in my direction. The weight of it hit my net, then I raced down the field. As long as that ball was in play, my head was in the game. I couldn't afford for my concentration to be anywhere else.

Back in the locker rooms, exhaustion warred with the knowledge that we'd had a damn good practice this afternoon. Normally, laughter and teasing, broad smiles and general excitement would fill the room. Not today. Not now. The oppressive atmosphere kept what smiles there were small and furtive. Without the game to keep us focused, everyone was just going through the motions.

Stripping off gear. Hanging it up. Letting the hot spray of the shower rinse away the grime and sweat of yet another demanding practice. Drying off. Putting fresh clothes on. Several of us were already slipping our shoes on when Brian exited Coach's office and leapt onto a bench in the center of the room.

"That was a great practice, everyone. Saw some good teamwork and the plays are looking tight. Evansville Christian won't know what hit 'em!" he shouted, though the response was nowhere near as enthusiastic as it normally would have been.

"Which is why," Coach Santinelli began, as he stepped out of his office, "we're all headed to town for some much deserved R and R." Many of my teammates shared disbelieving looks. "Did I mention there'd be pizza as well?" he added with a smirk. "We set out in fifteen."

The shift in the locker room was equivalent to the power coming back on after an intense storm. An unexpected lightness filled the room at the chance to forget all the drama, the game coming up, finals getting closer, and the championship. Infectious chatter banished the heavy quiet as guys picked up the pace to get cleaned and changed. Even I got caught up in the excitement and added some hustle to my movements. But as I made my way to the door, my gaze fell on Benny and shame dragged the smile off my face.

What right did I have to be happy? To be relieved? Andy was safe, but his closest friend had endured one of the worst things imaginable. Would I look any different from Benny if it had been the love of *my life* fighting not just for his life, but to get help at all? As if picking up on my gruesome thoughts, Benny glanced in my direction. He turned to answer whatever it was Neil asked him with a shaking head. Thoroughly humbled, I trudged outside with the others.

The animated conversations kept up as we fell into a haphazard column and began the twenty-minute trek to town. Somehow, the promise of pizza and games at the end eliminated everyone's fatigue. Unsurprisingly, my roommate, Nate, ended up walking beside me. He'd become pretty used to my moodiness the last few days and thankfully, didn't encourage me to talk as we walked.

Off to our left, I was more than surprised to find both Todd and Neil walking along. Well, rolling in Todd's case thanks to one of those knee-scooter-things. It was odd to see the pair of them without Benny, though I could understand why Benny would choose to sit out the "festivities."

Nate considered them a moment, then asked, "Hey, is it true that Price moved Bridges into his room?"

Neil stiffened, and Todd turned a furious glare on my roommate. "What's it to ya?" Todd snarled.

"Nothing. I was just asking." Nate threw his hands up in a defensive gesture.

"Is it?" I asked, drawing their attention. No one ever said I had good sense.

Neil and Todd shared a look, but it was Neil who answered this time. "Yeah. It's true. Bridges needs a lot of help and..." he trailed off, clearly not sure how much he could say and I realized that they both knew Benny and Cal were an item. Whether Benny had actually told them or they'd figured it out on their own, the important part was that they were ready to defend them both. Who knew they were actually Benny's *friends* and not just his lackeys?

"You got a problem with that?" Todd snapped at both of us, still on the offensive.

"Nope," Nate said quickly, his ears turning bright pink.

"Good for him," I said with a short nod.

Todd and Neil blinked at me, then looked at each other again. "Good practice today, Hudson. You too, Hawthorne," Todd said gruffly, then they moved away.

"Well, that was weird," Nate said under his breath. "What do you think that was about?"

I caught a glimpse of Connor out of the corner of my eye on our right and knew he'd heard the exchange as well. "I think it means this school is about to get the shakeup of the century."

"Damn right!" Kyle crowed, coming up behind us and hooking his arms over my and Nate's shoulders. "Evansville's not gonna know which end of the stick to catch the ball with when we're through with them! Isn't that right, John?"

"You know it!" John shouted and several others picked up the cheer.

Pizza and arcade games were great and all for lifting the spirits of downtrodden teenagers, but some of us had bigger things at stake. Once I had an opening to slip away without anyone immediately trying to track me down, I pocketed some change and made a break for the east side of town.

I sagged against the cool glass pane of an antique telephone box that had somehow survived not only the decades, but the town's numerous renovation projects. Andy teased me mercilessly about my affinity for all things vintage, but there was something about the phone booth that set me at ease. Maybe it was the clear definition of it, or how it felt like I stood on an island looking out at the world, witnessing, but not participating. It also offered a clear view of the back street and the building beside me, both of which were currently devoid of life.

I double checked to make sure the glass-paned door with its chipped red paint was completely closed, before picking up the receiver and sliding change into the slot. This wasn't a conversation I wanted overheard, thus my calling on the outskirts of town in a derelict phone booth with a clear line of sight in every direction. Calling in the relative safety of my dorm room or even the secret room would have been preferable, but I'd have needed a cell phone for that. Yet another way, the school kept us in line and under control.

The line picked up, and happiness pulsed through my chest at the warm voice on the other side. "Hello, Mitchum. It's been awhile. How are you?"

"Hey, Uncle Terri. I'm..." I debated lying to him like I lied to everyone else, like I lied to myself, and immediately dismissed it. Uncle Terri was one of the few people I could be completely honest with. "I'm tired." My shoulders slumped with the admission. "So very tired, Uncle."

"I understand," he responded, voice gentle. "You're almost done."

My chest tightened at the reassurance. Was I? Two months didn't seem like a lot in the grand scheme of things, but it felt like an eternity, and then what? Would I ever truly be out? It didn't feel like it. Especially after what had happened to Calvin. Was anywhere truly safe?

"Tell me what has you at odds," he prompted when I was quiet for too long.

I kicked at a bottle cap someone had left behind. It vaulted onto its side and rolled in an arc until it met with a rude end at the base of the booth. "It's all the pretending. It's exhausting. I don't know how much longer I can go on like this," I confessed, the weight on my chest growing heavier with each word. He let out a commiserate sigh.

"I know. Just a little longer, Mitch, then you'll be free to live your life the way you want." I shook my head, though he couldn't see it. While I appreciated the effort, the platitude still felt empty.

"I feel trapped." The words seemed to tear their way out of me, coming out raw and bleeding. I swallowed, but it did little to ease the feeling of razor blades in my throat. I couldn't even openly comfort my boyfriend, and it was killing me.

"I'm familiar with the feeling." His voice dropped again, empathy and a unique understanding of my situation coloring the sentiment. "I promise, it gets better. Maybe not easier, but better." My hand tightened around the phone until my fingers ached.

"Do you think... do you think my dad would have been proud of me?" I whispered. I hated asking Terri about my dad, not because he was unwilling, but because it hurt so damn much.

"Yes, without a doubt. You've grown into quite the remarkable young man, Mitch. Don't ever doubt that."

"But what about—"

"He knew, Mitch," my uncle interjected before I could finish asking the question that plagued me nearly nonstop every day. "He always knew, and he loved you all the more." My nose burned and my eyes stung with unshed tears. I wanted to believe him more than anything, but I was just so scared.

I sniffed hard and worked to pull myself together. "I'm sorry, I didn't even ask. How are you two settling in up there?"

"Canada is fucking cold and don't believe what anyone else tells you." He laughed, and a smile tugged at my mouth. "We're settling in okay. Boxes are still everywhere, but we're slowly chipping away. The community has been every bit as welcoming as we'd hoped."

"That's good. You two deserve to be happy."

"So do you, Mitch. The offer still stands, the apartment and the tuition."

"The apartment is already too much and you've already paid for one school. I can't let you pay for another. Not to mention, you two need every extra penny to establish your new home."

"I appreciate the concern, but we can manage. I don't want you to feel like you have to do this. You've worked so hard not to have to take an athletic scholarship. A scout is serious business. If they come, they'll expect an answer."

"And they'll have one."

"Mitch—"

"Look, we both know even with improved grades, I'll never get into that school without a scholarship. Will you call or not?" I asked and held my breath for his response. So much hinged on if the scout would even show up and even more if they'd make an offer.

"Yes, I'll reach out to my contact and have them secure footage of your games," he grumbled.

"I know you don't like it, but—"

"No, I can't very well tell you to follow your heart and then take issue with how you choose to do it."

I let out a relieved breath. "Thanks, Uncle Terri."

"Yeah, yeah. Tell me what else is going on. Have you talked to Andy about any of this?"

"Some," I deflected. Andy knew about the grades and about me not wanting to take an athletic scholarship, but not much else. Definitely not my plan to secure a scout from the University of Chicago.

"Only some? I thought you two were reconnecting."

"We were. We *have*. Things were even really good there for a while."

"I'm sensing a but."

"I've been busy with practice and he's had his own preoccupations. Some... things have happened since I asked you to look into the scout for me." I cringed at my inability to come right out and say what had happened.

"Like what? More bullying issues?"

I rolled my shoulders and dug deep for the courage Andy believed I had. "This is so much worse than bullying, Uncle."

"What do you mean?" he asked with a hard edge. "Did someone hurt you? Hurt Andy?"

"No! No, we're both okay. But, uh, Andy's friend wasn't so lucky." My breath hitched as the fear that had propelled me to find Andy that afternoon washed over me.

"Take a deep breath. I'm glad to hear you and Andy are okay. Maybe if you tell me what happened to his friend, I can help." Uncle Terry's steady voice soothed my nerves enough to venture the dark truth.

"So a guy transferred to Ulwich like last month. Apparently, he went here a long time ago. Before Andy or I started. He seemed like a real jerk, but that wasn't any different from any of the others."

"Okay," my uncle said. "What changed?"

There was an awful pinch in my chest, and my vision blurred. "I pissed him off. He hurt Todd real bad one day at practice and Coach just wanted to give this new guy his spot, but I didn't think he should have it. So I spoke up and Brian had my back. He didn't want this guy on the team anymore than I did. But this guy, Warren—I don't think I told you his name yet—he's bad news."

"Mitch, breathe," Uncle Terri said firmly.

I tried, but my chest just got tighter and the words spilled over each other. "He threatened Andy. Then, a couple of weeks ago, he wasn't at practice. And I didn't even notice! I raced to find Andy. But what if I was already too late? Fuck, Uncle, I've never been so scared in my life."

"I thought you said Andy was okay?"

"He was. Warren didn't go after him. He went after Andy's friend Calvin."

"Calvin... I know that name. Isn't that the kid you said was living out and proud?" Uncle Terri asked.

"He was." My voice cracked, and I closed my eyes.

"Mitch. What. Happened?"

"Warren raped him." Even though I could barely push the words out, it sounded like I'd shouted them. I hiccuped and rubbed the heel of my palm under my eyes to wipe the sudden stream of tears. "He beat the shit out of him and then he raped him. And all I can think is 'what if that had been Andy?'. What kind of selfish asshole does that make me? Andy's friend was assaulted—*raped*," I rasped, my voice painfully tight, "and it's all my fault. But all I care about is that it *wasn't* Andy." I curled in on myself, shame and guilt making my stomach cramp.

"Jesus, Mitch, why didn't you call me sooner?" he asked, just shy of shouting. I winced, but before I could respond, his voice became faint, like he was talking to someone else on his end. Probably his partner, Paul.

When he came back, his tone was softer, though still firm. “First off, this is *not* your fault.”

“But—”

“No. You may have pissed him off, but he’s responsible for his own actions. No one else. So you can drop that shit right now.”

I shook my head, though he couldn’t see me. “You don’t understand, Uncle. As worried as I was for Andy, I should have *known* Calvin was just as much a target. Maybe more so.”

His heavy sigh carried through the line. “Why would you say that?”

“Because it wasn’t the first time,” I said in a whisper.

“The first time he’s sexually assaulted someone or the first time he’d gone after a fellow student?”

“The first time he’s raped Calvin. He did it before, way back when,” I replied brokenly, pressing my fist against the glass.

“And the Academy let him come back?!”

“I don’t think they knew. Someone—a friend who was here then—told me.”

Uncle Terri cleared his throat, though his voice still sounded strained when he said, “I’m going to need the last name of this boy.”

“Singleton. Warren Singleton.”

“Thank you, Mitch. I know this is hard and scary, but you can’t blame yourself. It’s an awful thing to happen to anyone. But it is Not. Your. Fault. The reality is that people like this Warren exist everywhere. They enjoy hurting people.”

I sniffed. "I feel so stupid. I figured since he’d already hurt Calvin, he’d be looking for someone new to terrorize."

“I understand why you would think that. Unfortunately, some of these types of people get off on re-victimizing people they’ve harmed in the past. Have you talked to Andy about any of this? I can’t imagine he’s handling the powerlessness that comes with these situations any better than you are.”

I let out a derisive laugh. “That’s one way to put it. Andy hates being out of control, and he’s not really talking to me. It doesn’t help that Calvin refuses to see him.”

“You think he blames you,” he said, accurately summing up my latest insecurities with Andy.

“Shouldn’t he?”

"Whether he should or shouldn't is beside the point. You are not to blame for Warren's actions. What Andy needs right now is a friend, even if he can't admit it."

"But he won't talk to me," I argued.

"Then just be there. He'll talk when he's ready. I suspect Andy might be struggling with some similar guilt."

I released a heavy sigh and sagged against the side panel. "Fuck. You're right. No wonder he doesn't want to talk to me. And Calvin keeping him at a distance probably makes him think Calvin blames *him*. I really am the worst friend and I'm already an extra shitty boyfriend."

"Don't be so hard on yourself. You're both young. Communication comes with time and a willingness to listen. But you actually have to *be* there. You hear me, son?"

"Yeah. Loud and clear." My gaze caught on three familiar figures as they separated from a wall less than a block away and made a beeline toward me. "Shit. I gotta go. Thanks again, Uncle. Give Paulie my love." I scrubbed at my face as discreetly as I could to hide the evidence of my sudden crying jag.

"Will do. Take care, Mitch. Love you."

"Love you too," I croaked, then plunked the phone in the cradle as Brian slid open the door.

"There you are. You're a stealthy son of a bitch. One minute you were playing a motocross game, the next you were gone."

I cleared my throat and pushed past.

Brian eyed the nearly antique phone booth. "What are you doing in this piece of shit, anyway?"

"Overdue to call my mom back." Lie. "She gets mushy." Lie. "I'm ready now." Extra lie. "You guys hit up the corner store yet?" I asked, continuing my way to where they'd emerged.

Brian raked a skeptical gaze over me and fell in step with the others trailing behind. "Nah. We were waiting for you. And you didn't answer the question. If you were just calling your mom, why'd you come all the way out here? There are less sketchy phones in town."

Tension tightened my shoulders at the prodding. I willed them to relax and answered as calmly as I could. "Like I said, she gets a bit mushy, and she expects mush right back. Like I need you fuckers hearing that." I smiled, though it hurt. Almost done.

"Aw, does Mitchy miss his mommy?" John cooed to a chorus of heckling laughter.

"Fuck you." I forced a laugh that turned my stomach. Despite the painful twist in my gut and the unnerving feeling of being caged by sharks, I kept the false cheer plastered on my face.

Just a little longer.

Chapter 30

Andy

I caught sight of Calvin in the hall with his now ever-present shadow, Benny, and made my way toward them. The hallway was quickly emptying as my peers ventured off to wherever they planned to spend the study period. With the end of term practically around the corner, hopefully some of them actually intended to study.

Benny caught my eye as he maneuvered Calvin's books on top of his and gave me a subtle nod. I took a bracing breath and quickened my pace. My nerves ricocheted with anxiety as I got closer. Thankfully, no one called out to me and Calvin was too absorbed in what appeared to be a whispered argument with Benny to turn around.

"I can handle it," Calvin hissed as I got near enough to overhear. "You have to stop coddling me. I'm not a child."

"No, you're recovering and the doctors said to take things easy," Benny pushed back.

Calvin snorted. "I hardly think they meant carrying my own books."

"Actually, I recall them specifically saying that you weren't to carry any weight at all," Benny countered without missing a beat. "Your shoulder will take a while to heal. Over-exerting yourself won't make the process go any faster."

Calvin grumbled something I couldn't catch.

"I know you're frustrated, baby. But if you won't do it for yourself, then do it for me. Please," Benny implored softly, his voice full of tenderness. Clearly, that was Calvin's kryptonite because his shoulders instantly sagged.

If Benny hadn't arranged for this impromptu run-in, I'd have scampered away from intruding on their intimate exchange. But nerves or no nerves, I wanted to be there for my friend, even though he'd done everything short of issuing a restraining order to keep me at a distance.

Benny glanced up and smiled, then said as if he hadn't already seen me, "Hey, Gallagher." At hearing the greeting, Calvin instantly stiffened.

"Hi, Benny. Calvin," replied by rote and glanced at my friend.

"Andy," he said flatly, pointedly looking away from me. My heart sank. If he wouldn't even glance in my general direction, how was I supposed to get him to talk to me?

Benny hesitated a beat, then forced a smile. "I'm glad you're here. You can help us out. Take these." He dropped Calvin's books into my arms and I nearly fell over at the sudden weight. "I have to get to that stupid midday practice. Cal was wanting to head to the library, but it's in the opposite direction of the field and I'm already running late."

"Sure, I can do that. I was actually headed there myself," I replied, following the script Benny had put together for this little "run-in". Not that it would have mattered where Calvin was going, because I'd have been conveniently going there as well.

"Perfect!" he said with way too much cheer while Calvin glared at him. "Okay then, I'll be on my way. Just be sure to take it slow. He's supposed to taking things easy, and he gets winded pretty quickly. Oh, and make sure he drinks water and doesn't pick up anything too heavy or reach high, or—" With each new instruction, Calvin's glower intensified and his face got darker.

"Uh, Benny?" I interjected.

He abruptly cut off and looked at me. "Yeah?"

"I think we can handle it. Can't we?" I looked to Calvin for confirmation, afraid that he'd insist on sending me away, like he had all the other times I'd tried to talk to him after he got back from the hospital.

"Yes," he snarled.

Benny released an awkward laugh and absently reached for Calvin's good arm. "Of course. Sorry. I'll just..."

"Go?" Calvin filled in with an arched brow and a look that could have drawn blood, effectively halting Benny's hand in its tracks.

Benny's face turned bright pink. "Guess I'll see you later," he said, then turned on his heel and made a beeline for the exit.

I shifted Calvin's books to a more comfortable position. "To the library, right?" I asked cautiously.

Calvin huffed and started walking way faster than I suspected was Benny-approved. As if to drive home all of Benny's cautions, Calvin did get winded fairly quickly and within a couple minutes, he'd reduced the speed of his determined walk by half. I wisely did not comment on it.

After walking another minute in silence, I tread into what I hoped would be neutral waters. "So, Benny's being pretty protective. That's kind of sweet."

Calvin made a strangled choking sound. "Sweet? It's fucking mortifying! I'm a grown-ass man. I can take care of myself! And this. God. Damn. Thing. Is a nuisance!" He struggled with his sling until he finally disentangled himself from it and threw it down the hall, back the way we'd come. Then he sagged against the wall, his shoulders caving inward as he dropped his head forward in such a show of defeat that I had to catch myself from gasping.

I stood in silence, not sure what to do. Did I comfort him? Did I say something? Did I run back for his sling? I felt completely powerless to help my friend, and I *hated* it. Calvin was always so strong for me. Why couldn't I be that for him?

Then it hit me. Calvin was strong. Only maybe he really wasn't. What if he'd only pretended to be for me? And now his fragile core was exposed for everyone to see. To hurt. Abruptly, I realized the soft sound tickling my ears was muffled crying. And it was coming from Calvin.

"I'm going to grab your sling before some first-year trips over it." I scurried the few yards to retrieve the discarded sling. Part of me feared that Calvin would take the opportunity to make a break for it, but he was still there when I returned.

"Thanks," he whispered, his voice barely more than a croak.

"Did you want to put it back on?"

He sighed and straightened. "I should." He leaned to the side enough for me to get it over his head, then I carefully positioned his arm in the cradle. He winced, but didn't protest at the manhandling. "Do you think…"

"Yeah?" I asked, a touch too eagerly.

He cleared his throat. "I have a hair band in my blazer pocket. Do you think you could pull my hair back?" He lifted his gaze long enough for me to catch a glimpse of his red-rimmed eyes and the mottled bruising still marring his light brown face.

I wasn't sure if I'd ever touched Calvin's hair before, but I wasn't about to let that stop me. I'd helped my older sister plenty of times. This couldn't be that much different. "Sure thing. But you'll, uh, need to sit do wn."

He glanced sharply at me with his brows pinched together.

"I'm short, remember? Unless you were planning to just squat here in the hallway so I can reach."

He huffed what could have been a laugh. "Come on. I know a place." He shifted his injured shoulder to what I hoped was a more comfortable position, despite the pain that flashed across his face. Then started walking down an adjacent hall that did *not* end at the library. We hadn't gone too far when he slowed and looked around before producing an old iron key from his trouser pocket. It was only when he reached out to put it in a lock that I realized we'd stopped in front of an iron-banded door.

In all the time I'd been at Ulwich, I'd never seen it open. I'd just assumed it was sealed shut. Maybe even bricked over on the other side. It didn't have any bearing on anything I did, so I got used to ignoring its existence altogether. "Oh," I said, when the lock silently slid free. Leave it to Calvin to have his own secret room.

"After you," he said, taking a step back.

I nodded and pushed open what turned out to be a very heavy door. Though like the lock, the hinges were also silent. I held it for Calvin, who ghosted inside, then immediately slumped into a seat. No, not a seat, a pew. This was a small chapel. "Cool place," I said as I closed the door behind us. Luckily, light shone through the stained glass windows at the far end, so the room wasn't overly dark.

"It's quiet," he murmured.

I set his books down, along with my satchel, and moved to his side. "Okay, where's this hair band?"

"In my left pocket."

Ah. That explained part of why he hadn't pulled it out himself. It was on the same side as his sling. But it also *didn't* explain it? "Um, not to be insensitive, but why'd you put it in your left pocket?"

He spared me an irritated look. "I always keep a hair band in my left pocket. Not that I ever use them. Thing's probably been in there since the Mesozoic era." Despite the exaggerated statement being reminiscent of his usual deadpan humor, there was nothing remotely funny about the cynical way he said it.

"Right. Of course," I said, my face heating. I fished out the band, doing my best not to jostle his arm too much, then moved behind the pew. "Do you want it high or low?" I asked as I gently combed his curls back with my fingers. And *holy shit,* were they soft.

"High. Otherwise, it'll get tangled in the sling."

"Got it." I adjusted my combing to position the band higher up his head. With more care than I'd ever shown my older sister's tender head, I tied his hair back firmly, but not too tight. "There. How's that?"

"It's fine."

I took a deep breath and walked back around the pew so I could sit beside him. "Glad I could help."

He shifted his head enough to look at me out of the corner of his eye. "Don't tell Benny, okay?"

"Tell him what? About this room? Sweet setup, by the way."

He shook his head. "About pulling my hair back. Benny already knows about the room. He's the one who gave me the key."

"Oh. Um, why don't you want him to know about the hair-thing?"

He released a long-suffering sigh. "Because it's just one more thing he'll fret about. He fusses over me enough as it is. And I know how much he loves my hair. I don't... I don't want to take that away from him, too." The agony in his voice was like a spear through the middle of my chest, punching out all my oxygen.

I quickly pulled myself back together. It was clear the last thing Calvin wanted was anything that even remotely resembled pity. "He won't hear anything about it from me. Did you want me to do anything else?" He shook his head, and we lapsed back into silence.

After a while, he inhaled deeply and leaned back to rest his head on the back of the pew. "I feel like half a person. I hate how everyone looks at me. The pity in their eyes. Hate that they *know* what he did to me."

I bit my lip to stop myself from offering what would probably sound like empty condolences and platitudes. Or worse, telling him about the project Benny had enlisted me for on his behalf.

"The worst part is that he probably wouldn't have beaten me if I hadn't fought back. But I couldn't *not*. I worked so hard to never be the victim again." His breath hitched, and my eyes burned. "It still wasn't enough." A sob that would have broken the strongest of people ripped out of his chest. "It wasn't enough. I'm a victim. A helpless, disgusting victim. And that's all I'll ever be." His chest rose and fell with his stuttered breaths between soul-wrenching sobs.

I swallowed thickly and sniffled, not sure when I'd started crying too. "Calvin, this doesn't define you."

He rolled his head to look at me. His normally piercing brown eyes held a wealth of suffering that rivaled any tragedy I'd ever read. "Doesn't it? I'm weak. I can't even defend myself. How can I defend others? This isn't supposed to happen to men. And I let it happen. *Twice.* "

Understanding bloomed. This was why he'd been avoiding me. For five years, he'd gone out of his way to protect me and who knew how many others from the ugliness of this world. And now he thought he couldn't; that he never could. "Don't say that. You're still the strongest person I know and you always will be. You didn't *let* anything happen."

He snorted and shifted his focus back to the ceiling.

"I mean it. Just because something unimaginably awful happened to you, that doesn't make you weak."

"Andy, don't."

"No! I'm not going to sit here and let you blame yourself for something that was in no way your fault. If our roles were reversed, you'd never let me get away with that shit."

"You finished?"

I let out an angry huff and slammed my back against the pew. "If anyone is to blame, it's this wretched school. This place is a fucking cesspool. Neither one of us should ever have had to fear for our fucking *safety* while we were here. Someone should burn this place to the ground."

"Easy there, my budding arsonist."

"I didn't say *I* would do it," I grumbled.

"Uh-huh. You really don't think I know about the firework incident?" He glanced at me with a raised eyebrow.

I ducked my head. "Technically, that was Mitch."

"Or the convenient Bunsen Burner explosion?"

I opened my mouth to protest and promptly closed it. "Okay, that was me."

"That's what I thought." He shifted in his seat, wincing as he did so, and I couldn't help but imagine all the bruises I couldn't see. "Look, I'm sorry about avoiding you. I—"

"You have nothing to be sorry for. At all. Was I hurt? Yeah. But only because I wanted to be there for you. I get that you hate asking for help—for needing it. But that doesn't make you weak." A smile tugged at my lips. "You taught me that."

"I suppose I did. Damn. I must be awesome or something," he replied with a hint of his usual cavalier attitude. Relief flooded me to see that part of my friend was still in there, albeit beneath a world of hurt, but still alive.

"Or something," I quipped.

He shoved me with his good arm. "Brat."

"Hey!" I laughed. "Only Mitch gets to call me that."

Both of his eyebrows shot up and a devilish grin spread across his face. "Is that so? Do tell."

I rolled my eyes. Though I wouldn't normally, I spilled all the dirty details. By the time we heard the bell signaling the end of study period and parted ways, I finally had hope that we'd be okay. But more importantly, that he would.

Chapter 31

Andy

"Damn, Andy. This is a lot of work," Benny said aloud as he read over the blackmail article that had been my *life* for the last week. He'd stalled the school from expelling Calvin, but it wouldn't last. This was our ace in the hole to make sure it stuck and that Warren Singleton never stepped foot on Ulwich grounds again.

"Yeah. I didn't want to leave anything out." Or to chance. I wrung my hands as I continued to walk the secret room. Shockingly, Benny hadn't known about it.

He released a low whistle. "You certainly didn't shy away from name dropping."

I halted my pacing to look at him, my anxiety spiking all over again. "Wasn't I supposed to? Is it too much? I can always dial it back. Redact a few. Fuck knows Calvin will murder me if he ever finds out about this."

"Relax." He gripped my shoulder with a firm hand. "This is *exactly* what I wanted. More than I was hoping for, to be honest. I'd like to see the heads of the school try to discount *this*. Not only do you establish a precedent of the Academy covering up scandals, you also cited verifiable resources."

I released a stuttering breath as I attempted to force the tension from my body and gave him a shaky smile. "So you think it'll work?"

He continued to scan the pages of precise type, then nodded. "I know it. And once they meet our demands, we can banish this to the bottom of a drawer and we can all move on."

There was nothing forced about my relieved exhale this time. "Thank God, you think so too. I don't want to imagine how all of this could blow up if we actually had to publish the damn thing."

He carefully folded the paper and stuck it in the inside pocket of his school blazer. "No shit. We'd be better off burning the school to the ground before we let these names go public."

"Calvin told you about that, huh?" I laughed and shook my head.

"Like he wouldn't," Benny replied with a smirk.

"Thanks again for orchestrating that little run-in. It was nice to talk to Calvin again, even if it was only for a little while."

He scoffed. "I'm the one who should be thanking you. Cal seems so much more… I don't know. Settled since that afternoon. And it was nice to not get bitched out for missing practice… Again."

"What's this about missing practice?" Mitch asked as he stepped into the secret room, the painting that was the door swinging shut behind him. "We're mid-playoffs. You better not be missing *any* practices." He walked across the room to stand beside me, casually throwing an arm around my shoulders. "So, what do you think?" he asked Benny.

"I think they're not gonna know what hit 'em. Anyway, I better get going. I need to check on Cal, then work on getting all the people who need this kick in the ass," he patted his blazer over where he'd squirreled the article, "in one room away from prying eyes."

"What do you mean? I thought you were going to send it to the local paper?" Mitch asked. I glanced at him to find him frowning.

"That's the threat. If everything goes according to plan, it won't come to that," Benny explained, though it didn't appear to put Mitch at ease.

I grabbed his hand, which was hanging over my shoulder, and squeezed lightly. "Hey, there are a lot of names in there. Not just the faculty at fault over the years, but student names. Culprits *and* victims." I thought about how Calvin still refused to give the police anything to go on about what happened to him and wouldn't press charges, solely because he didn't want to be associated with what had happened. "This article would not only drag up some awful memories for a lot of them, but expose their darkest moments to the world."

"Okay, but couldn't you just leave out the victims' names?" he pressed.

I shook my head. "Even if I omitted victims' names, there are enough details that someone not even trying very hard could put two and two together. The only way it could even sort of be released to the public would be if *all* student names were stripped from the article. Which would kinda defeat the point."

"I suppose," he grumbled. "I still don't like it. Doesn't feel like enough."

"No, it doesn't," Benny agreed. "These people should have to answer for what they've done and what they've covered up, but we're not in a position to make that happen. Blackmail is dangerous enough as it is. Andy is taking a massive risk helping me with this. If we were to get caught, we could be charged with a felony and face multiple years in prison. Luckily, the people being called out in the article have a vested interest in making sure it stays quiet. Otherwise, they'd have to admit a lot more than that the article exists."

Mitch huffed beside me, but didn't continue to push. I absently rubbed his back in an attempt to soothe him. While he leaned into me more, his muscles remained taut, as did the hard edge of his jaw.

"Thanks again for doing this, Andy. I can't imagine reading about all the awfulness that has happened here was pleasant. But I really believe this will tip the scales. I'll see you two around." Benny nodded at us, then turned on his heel and slipped back out into the hall.

"It's not right," Mitch grumbled again once Benny had gone.

"None of this is right," I replied, finally letting myself feel the exhaustion from prioritizing research over sleep, showers, and even sex.

"Hey, how are you doing? You've been going pretty hard this last week." He gently turned me to face him and I could have easily melted into the concern in his eyes.

"I'll be okay. Just need to recharge," I replied, resting my head on his broad chest.

"Aren't you the one who's supposed to be getting on to me about burning the candle at both ends?"

I huffed a tired laugh. "I didn't want to let Calvin down."

"And you won't. Even if the blackmail doesn't work, you haven't let him down." He gently pushed me back enough so that he could hook a finger under my chin and tilt my head up. "You're amazing, and that article is a fucking masterpiece. It's almost a shame no one will ever know you wrote it."

Against odds a smile curled my lips. "You're sweet. Biased, but sweet."

"You forgot 'and right', but I'll let it slide. This time." He gave me an over-the-top serious expression and a laugh burst out of me. His face softened, and he gently trailed the back of his hand along my cheek. "I love you, Anderson Gallagher."

My original tiny smile grew into a ridiculous grin as he leaned down to press a kiss to my lips. “I love you too, Mitchum Hudson,” I breathed into him.

“This’ll work,” he reassured me.

“I hope so.”

Mitch

“What do you mean they’re not going to publish it?!” Connor asked—well, more like *shouted*.

“I’m not any happier about it than you are,” I snapped back as I shoved the last of my gear into my duffle bag. The away game had gone great, and we were officially that much closer to the championship. Only a couple more games, and that assumed our closest contenders didn’t bomb. But it was hard to enjoy the victory given everything else going on.

Connor crossed his arms and scowled out the hotel window. Thankfully, Brian was more interested in celebrating than hanging out in the room and packing. To be fair, I was a little surprised that Connor wasn’t down in the hotel restaurant with the rest of them, considering he’d yet again been instrumental in the win.

“There. All packed up and ready for the early morning bus ride,” I declared, mentally crossing my fingers that he’d take the hint and leave so I could pass out.

He spun around, but sadly didn’t look any more ready to leave than he had twenty minutes ago. "We have to do something. They can’t get away with this. Don’t get me wrong, I’m super glad it worked and Benny got that scumbag out for good. But this still sucks." He smacked his hand on the desk. "It’s not enough. Someone needs to pay. There *has* to be more we can do."

“And what would that be?” I sat beside my duffle on one of the queen beds with an exasperated huff. This conversation had been going in circles for way too long.

He threw up his hands. “I don’t know. We need to *tell* someone. Someone with more authority than either of us.” He snapped his fingers. “I know. You can get the article from Andy and *we* can publish it.”

I rubbed my forehead with the tips of my fingers. “It’s more complicated than that.”

"How so?"

"Something about names and anonymity and protecting former students. Andy could explain it better."

He bared his teeth in a snarl. "Some of them don't deserve to be protected."

"Besides, I'm like ninety percent sure Benjamin Price, through either money or family connections, has people at the *Hylestead Press* who wouldn't dare run the article against his wishes." I wasn't entirely sure how true that was, but I wouldn't put it past Benny given how protective he'd been of Calvin.

"Then we'll have to go over his head. We'll go national. That would really show those assholes. Ruin their 'pristine' reputation." His lip curled with obvious distaste.

I fought not to roll my eyes. It wasn't that I didn't understand where he was coming from—I was right there with him—but he was asking for a miracle. "Oh yeah, and how do you propose we do that? Got some secret ultra-high up connections in the media I don't know about?" If anyone had something like that, it'd be Benny and I didn't see him budging any time soon about *not* publishing the article.

Connor let out a defeated sigh and plopped down on the other side of my duffle bag. "No. Don't suppose you know anyone with connections in the national news?" He huffed a laugh. "Something like the *Washington Post* or the *New York Times*?"

I was on the verge of laughing with him at the ridiculous idea that either of us might have those kinds of connections when it hit me. I reached over and grabbed his bicep. He glanced at me and I met his curious gaze. "I think I might."

His eyes widened, and his jaw dropped, but he quickly recovered. "What? Who?"

I lurched upright and nearly tripped over my feet in my effort to get to the room's phone. "I have to call my uncle first. I could be wrong." Or about two decades too late.

"You have an uncle?" Connor asked as he joined me by the corded phone.

"Would you focus? Help me figure out how to dial out on one of these damn things."

He snickered. "It's not that hard, Hudson. You just press nine first."

"And what about for an international call?" I fired back.

"Well shit. How should I know?"

We both leaned over the device and read over the instructions stuck to the desk. After a couple false starts, we finally got the number order correct, and the line started ringing. I gave him a thumbs up. It wasn't until my uncle's sleepy voice came on the line that realized he and Paul were probably already asleep.

"Hello? This is Terri Hudson. I swear if this is another telemarketer—"

"Hey, Uncle Terri. It's Mitch."

"Mitchum. Is everything alright? I wasn't expecting to hear from you again so soon. Did something happen?" he asked in rapid fire, noticeably more alert.

"Everything is fine. Look, I'm really sorry about calling so late."

"Is it about the scout? I was able to pull a few strings. The usual know a guy who knows a guy," he cut in before I could get out the reason for the call.

I couldn't help but perk up at the news. He'd actually pulled it off. A scout from the University of Chicago was going to come see me play. "Really?"

"Really. Though there's a catch. They'll only come out if you're in the Championship game. From what I gather, they've already finished their recruiting for the next year and don't have much of a budget for it anyway."

"Don't worry. We'll be in the finals."

Connor frowned at me in confusion, unable to hear what my uncle was saying on the other end. I quickly got back to our purpose.

"As awesome as that is, that's also not why I'm calling."

"Oh," he said, and I got the distinct sound of sheets ruffling in the background. "Then what's up?"

I shared a look with Connor and went for broke. "I was hoping you could pull some more strings. Well, that Paulie could pull some strings. Is he still good friends with the people he used to work with at the *Washington Post*?"

"Why?"

"Remember that article I told you about? The one Andy was working on? Well, it worked. The only thing is, turns out they were never planning to publish it."

I heard a whispered, "Paul, wake up." Followed by a louder, "Okay, we're both here."

"Hey, Paulie. Sorry to wake you, but I didn't think this could wait," I said.

"Hey yourself, Mitch. And you know I'm always here for you," Paul replied groggily. "If this is about the Warren kid, we've done a lot of digging, but we've hit a wall. Seems General Singleton has a lot more pull than we expected."

I grinned at Connor. "I may have a way around that. You think you could get the *Post* to publish a 'tell-all' article?"

"Now you have my attention. I presume this would be the article Anderson wrote?" It warmed my heart how both my uncle and Paul had accepted Andy into my life so easily.

"Yep. I think I can get it to you by the end of the week."

"Think you could make it Wednesday? I'll want to review it—no offense to Andy—before sending it over. You can send it to Terri's email."

I bit the inside of my cheek as I debated how I was going to get the article in the first place. Surely I could convince Andy. "Yeah, I think I can pull that off."

"Excellent! I'll reach out to my friend in the editor's office to give her a heads up."

"You're the best Paulie. Sorry again for waking you."

"No need to apologize," he said at the same time my uncle said, "Anything we can do to help."

"Oh! One more thing. Do you think it would be weird if all the student names were stripped from the article?"

There was a beat of silence and I could imagine the two of them sharing a look along with that freaky silent communication thing they had going on. "I can understand why that would be desirable," Paul said at last.

"Very prudent of you, Mitchum. I'll keep an eye on my email. We'll talk again soon. Love you," Uncle Terri said, the last bit echoed by his partner.

"Love you too. And thanks." I hung up and released a long breath. "I can't believe that worked." I glanced at Connor.

"Those fuckers are going down," he said, sporting a disturbingly evil grin.

Chapter 32

Mitch

I let out a relieved breath when I spied Andy sitting at a table in the library. To be fair, it was also the first place I checked. I slid into the seat across from him without bothering to remove my satchel.

His gaze flicked up from the textbook he was absorbed in and a subtle smile stretched his lips. "I hear congratulations are in order."

It took me a second to realize what he was talking about. "Oh, yeah, the game. We did really well. Only a couple more to go."

"That's fantastic!" he shout-whispered. "But what did you think I was talking about?"

I wasn't ready to tell him about the scout my uncle had arranged from the University of Chicago, at least not until I'd actually spoken with the guy. "Is there somewhere a little more secluded we could talk?"

"How secluded are we talking?" he asked, raising an eyebrow skeptically.

"I'm not planning to maul you, if that's what you're asking."

He ducked his head and chuckled. "Well, *that's* disappointing. Not quite what I meant, but I suppose it's answer enough. Yeah, I know a place."

I waited impatiently for him to finish packing his things, using the time to go over what I wanted to say. Connor and I had brainstormed a number of arguments on the way back from the game. But I was secretly hoping it wouldn't take *that* much convincing to get Andy to agree to publishing the article. I just had to pick the right angle.

"Okay, follow me. Though, uh, maybe not too close?" he added, subtly looking around to see if anyone had taken an interest in our conversation.

I nodded and let him get a few steps ahead before trailing after him. I couldn't wait to be somewhere no one would speculate about us standing too close as we walked or spending too much time together or, heaven forbid, laughing together. Even more, I longed for us to be able to hold hands as we walked, to be unapologetically together.

We wound through the stacks, getting deeper and deeper into the library. I was a little embarrassed to realize that I'd never even been to this part of the massive room. Finally, Andy turned down a narrow passage that ended in a kind of sub-room, walled off by extra massive book stacks. One thing was for sure: this space was definitely secluded.

"Will this work?" Andy asked, turning to me.

"It's perfect. How did you know this was here?" I glanced up at the only wall not covered in books. Somehow we'd wound up beneath one of the big-ass stained glass windows.

He smiled softly as he un-shouldered his bag and let it slump to the floor. "This is where Calvin and I normally hang out."

"Huh. So the talk went well, I take it?"

He nodded. "Thanks to Benny."

"I'm glad. Speaking of Benny…" I began tentatively. A frown creased Andy's brow. "And the article you wrote. I still think we should publish it."

He let out an exasperated sigh. "We've talked about this. It's too risky. Not just for *all* the people I referenced, but for me, too. I didn't even sign the copy I gave Benny."

"And I hear you, I really do. But this is about more than us. More than you and me. More than Benny and Calvin. More than our whole grade level. We're in a position to make a difference. We *owe* it to those same people you reference in the article and for any that might come after."

Andy stared up at me, his green eyes dark with thought. He chewed his bottom lip, then admitted, "You have a point. And I have to confess, I've been thinking a lot about this since I gave Benny the finished article." I diligently schooled my face and did *not* crow at the impending victory. This wasn't about winning. This was about doing what was right.

"I know there's a chance things could blow back and I get that it's dangerous. You can still remove or change any names you feel need to be protected. You could even use a *nom de* something like Agatha Christie did."

"Plume?"

"That's it."

He arched a copper eyebrow. "Someone's getting fancy."

"Hey, I can do research, too." I stuck out my tongue, and we shared a laugh. "But in all seriousness. Think about it. What happened to Calvin—both times—might not have happened at all if someone had said something sooner. Both options are bad. Which bad are we willing to live with?"

"Whoa. Okay." He let out a heavy breath. "Damn. I knew it was bothering me, but I hadn't looked at it like that. The biggest reason I've been thinking about it is because Benny couldn't convince Calvin to file a police report. The worst thing that was going to happen was that Warren wouldn't be able to come back and would be denied any association with the academy. It doesn't… doesn't…" He shook his head.

"It doesn't feel like enough."

He raised his gaze. "No, it doesn't. I've been warring between that and betraying Calvin."

"You're not betraying him, Andy. If anything, you're supporting him *and* the future men of Ulwich."

He stubbornly shook his head again. "He won't see it that way. But… you're right. I can't sit by. Other people need to know what's been happening here. And we won't get a better opening than now."

"Funny you should mention that," I said with a mischievous grin.

"What's that look for?"

My smile grew. "You're going to want to pick a really professional sounding fake name."

We missed my initial goal to get the article to Paulie by Wednesday, but I couldn't complain. Andy was on board, and I was more than willing to give him the time he needed to make any necessary edits. I was even a fan of his very official-sounding nom de plume, E. R. Daring, though for a hot second it looked like he might use his actual name when he found out the article was being published in the *Washington Post*.

Despite all the ways we thought this could shake out, neither of us considered the biggest blow up of all—several national broadcasts picked up the story. We'd wanted action and ooh boy did we get it, and then some.

Scandal rocks East Coast as a prestigious school is found to be complicit in cover-up.

Abuse rampant at renowned educational institution.

Governor demands investigation at New England school.

Charges imminent at Ulwich Preparatory Academy.

So far, the "investigation" had largely focused on senior faculty, but it was only a matter of time before students started being questioned. I didn't know what kind of outcome I'd expected sending the article to a national source, but I was pretty sure it wasn't this. The academy resembled more of a kicked ant hill these days than a school one week away from the end of term. Even the fact that we'd made it into the championship couldn't distract from the chaos.

"This is insane," Andy said as he stepped up beside me where myself and several others were watching men in suits tear apart the headmaster's office. We shared a grim look.

"No kidding," Connor echoed, appearing out of nowhere.

"You think they'll find anything?" Andy asked, though I wasn't sure who he was asking.

Connor shrugged. "Guess it depends on what they're looking for and who their source is."

I resisted the urge to shoot him a look. All three of us knew who the fucking "source" was. Was he *trying* to out us? Before I could say anything, I caught sight of Calvin further down the hall. "Uh, guys. Is something up with Bridges?" I asked.

No sooner did I say something, and the others turned to look, than Calvin's frantic gaze fell on us. He practically sprinted the distance separating us. Clearly, he was moving around much better these days. Even the dark bruises had faded into barely there yellows beneath his light brown complexion.

He skidded to a stop in front of us and I realized he was clutching what appeared to be a worn journal. "Have any of you seen Benny?" he asked, not even pausing for breath.

The three of us shared a collective look, but Andy was the one to speak up. "No, we haven't. Is something wrong?" he asked quietly.

Calvin's face contorted with pain. "I can't find him *anywhere*. He tried to give me his class ring the other day, and I told him no. At first, I thought he was just mad at me. But then he didn't come back to the room that night or the next. I was getting some things from my old dorm room earlier today and I found this on the bed." His fingers dug into the worn binding, his knuckles turning white.

"What is it?" Andy asked.

"It's Benny's collection of stories... about *me*," Calvin replied in anguish.

"Come on, we should get out of here," Andy said, reaching for the increasingly distraught Calvin.

"Where *is* he, Andy? You have to help me find him. He has to be somewhere." It was a true testament to how upset he was that he didn't comment or even seem to notice Headmaster Torsney being escorted out of his office by a pair of the men in suits.

Abruptly, Connor cleared his throat—not that Calvin noticed—and nudged me. "We should probably get going, too. Not like Coach is likely to let a little thing like a school-wide investigation hinder practice. Not with the championship coming up."

"Uh, yeah." I nodded and leaned forward to whisper in Andy's ear. "You got this?"

He looked at Calvin, who was now muttering to himself, "He has to be here somewhere," while hugging the journal tightly to his chest and scanning the hallway. "We'll manage." He gave Connor and me a pointed look. "Try to stay out of trouble."

I attempted a smile, but it felt more like a grimace. In my defense, Connor didn't seem to be faring any better on the believability front. We set off together and, for once, I was actually glad that we had another grueling practice ahead of us.

Outside, away from curious ears, Connor glanced at me. "Did we fuck up?"

"I was just about to ask you the same thing."

Andy

Calvin was a wreck. I knew there would be consequences—fall out—for publishing the article, but I never imagined this would be one. The school was overrun with Department of Justice investigators. The professors were jumpy. And Benny was nowhere to be found. At all. As if that wasn't bad enough, while Calvin had been scouring the school looking for him, someone had come along and packed up Benny's dorm room. The only sign he'd been there at all was a single nail still stuck in the wall. He was just… gone.

If I had to guess, even though all student names had either been redacted or changed for privacy, Benny's father had still put it together. Either that, or one of the guilty faculty members had ratted him out. Whatever the case, there wasn't a doubt in my mind that Benny wouldn't be coming back. Not for the championship. Not for graduation. And not for Calvin. That journal that Calvin was clinging to like a lifeline was as good as a goodbye.

"How did they find out?" Calvin whispered as he rocked back and forth on Benny's old bed.

"I don't know." As much as I hated lying to him, the rot at Ulwich was long overdue to be exposed and rooted out. I felt horrible that yet again Calvin had been the one to pay such a heavy price, but I also stood by my decision. The abuse had to stop.

"He's gone, isn't he?" Calvin whispered, staring blankly across the room.

I moved to sit beside him and rubbed his back. "I think so."

"It was his fucking father," he snarled. "I know it. That bastard has never let his son have anything!" The sudden burst of energy faded, and he crumpled in on himself. "I should have taken the ring. Who cares that anyone who took one look at it would know whose it was? Everyone already knew I was staying in his room." He buried his head in his arms.

At a loss for what to do, I kept rubbing his back and making soothing noises. Then the door opened. I jumped to my feet so fast I nearly fell over. "It's not what it looks like," I blurted before I registered who was standing in the doorway. I blinked as both Todd and Neil stepped inside.

"He's not here," Calvin mumbled.

"Uh, we know," Todd said.

Neil awkwardly rubbed his arm, then shoved his hands in his pockets. "He asked us to put the journal in your room."

Calvin's head shot up. "You talked to him? Where is he?"

"His dickhead dad pulled him out," Neil said.

Todd pulled out a folded piece of paper and added, "We didn't exactly talk to him. He sent one of these. Well, two actually. One's for you. It was hidden inside the one addressed to us."

Calvin launched off the bed to tear the letter from Todd's outstretched hand. He opened it so fast that I feared for the integrity of the paper. Then he narrowed his eyes at the two. "Did you read it?"

"Not on purpose," Neil chimed in when it looked like Todd had swallowed his tongue. "Like he said, it was hidden inside. But we didn't read anything we didn't already know."

Calvin and I stared at them in mutual surprise. "You—both of you—knew Benny and I were together?" Calvin asked, a touch of wonder in his voice.

Todd was back to the awkward shuffling, his face getting redder by the second. "We may have overheard some… things a few months back."

"And you didn't say anything?" Calvin didn't seem to believe it any more than I did.

They shrugged in unison. "Why would we?" Neil asked.

"Why?" Calvin echoed, incredulous. "Why *wouldn't* you?"

"Because he's our friend," Todd said at the same time Neil said, "You made him happy."

I stepped forward as Calvin dropped back onto the mattress and tried to wrap his head around this mind-blowing revelation.

"Why are you here now?" he asked.

Todd took a deep breath to answer, but Neil beat him to it. "We figure it's what Benny would have wanted. He's not here to look out for you, so we will."

Wow. The surprises just kept on coming. Neil glanced at me and I realized I accidentally said that out loud.

"I get it. We don't have the best history when it comes to you guys." Neil ducked his head as if to hide his shame.

"We're not proud of it," Todd chimed in. "But we can do better. You mattered to Benny, so you matter to us."

"I don't need your protection.," Calvin mumbled glumly. "I can take care of myself."

"Without a doubt," Todd said, without missing a beat. "But if it's all the same to you, we'll hang around, anyway."

Neil swiveled the desk chair around and plopped into it. "And, you know, if you ever want to talk about Benny…"

"We'd like that," Todd finished.

I shook my head, but it didn't make any of what was happening right now more believable. Calvin didn't respond, but he also didn't send them away. Not sure what else to do, retreat seemed to be the best option. "I'll catch up with you later. If you need anything, you'll let me know?" I waited for Calvin to meet my gaze.

"Yeah, I'll let you know," he said, while his new bodyguards gave me reassuring nods.

I returned the nod, feeling like an ass, and left them to their collective grief. Just when I thought things couldn't get any worse for Calvin, he lost Benny. If the school wasn't currently being turned upside down, I'd think there was no justice in the world.

Chapter 33

Mitch

This was it. I was meeting with a scout. An honest to God lacrosse scout from the University of Chicago. Something I didn't even think I wanted when my senior year had started. And now I was a tangled bundle of nerves, anxiously pacing the small conference room at the Hylestead Inn.

I peered out the window at the cobbled street below. It was impressive how well the town had resisted most modernization, but its proximity to an Academy oozing money had something to do with it. It was nice. Now if only my tie would stop trying to strangle me. I tugged at the knot for the hundredth time, then smoothed my jacket, straightened my cuffs, and made sure my shirt was still tucked in. My gaze caught on my loafers. Fuck, I should have polished them. Why hadn't I polished them?

"Mr. Hudson, I'm pleased to see you here. I hope I haven't kept you waiting long."

I spun around at the voice and did my best to swallow my nerves. "Not at all. Thank you for meeting with me." To my surprise—and relief—the scout wasn't some stuffy old guy like Professor Nolan with a sharp suit and withering gaze. He had light brown hair, looked to be in his mid-thirties, and was wearing a sweater vest, of all things. And even though his eyes were decidedly blue, he kind of reminded me of Andy. Probably had something to do with the nerd-vibe coming off of him.

He smiled and held out a hand. "I'm Edgar Quinn. And I believe that was my line."

Heat warmed my face. "Sorry about that, Mr. Quinn. Guess I'm a little nervous. I've never spoken with a scout before." I mentally kicked myself as I accepted his hand. Now he was going to think that no one wanted me. And if no one else wanted me, then why should Chicago?

"Please, call me Edgar. And there's nothing to be nervous about." He gestured for me to take a seat at one of the tables in the room. He set his things down, then sat across from me. "I have to admit, after watching some of your game tapes and seeing you at practice yesterday, I'm surprised that more scouts haven't sought you out."

"You were at practice? I didn't see you." Panic bubbled up my throat. Had I made an ass of myself? Had I given it my all? Had I already screwed my chances?

Edgar tapped the side of his nose and gave me a wry smirk. "That's the general idea. The last thing we want is for your performance to be affected because you know someone is watching. Whether that be simple mistakes due to nerves or over-taxing yourself and causing an injury."

I sank against the back of my chair and immediately sat straighter. "Yeah, I guess that makes sense."

"So tell me, Mr. Hudson. Why *haven't* more scouts shown an interest in you? You're obviously a very talented player. And your coach strikes me as… enthusiastic."

I bit back a snicker. That was one way to describe Coach Santenelli. "Honestly, my grades haven't always been that great."

He nodded, reaching inside his bag to pull out a blue binder. He flipped through to what I assumed was my transcript. "True. But I know of many athletic programs that are more than willing to help their athletes maintain their scholarships. I also see that your grades have experienced an impressive uptick this past year." I tried to decipher his expression, but it remained neutral.

"There's also probably the fact that I didn't show any interest in getting a scout. Until recently, I'd been hoping to avoid taking an athletic scholarship," I admitted. It might kill my shot, but I'd talked with my uncle about this and we both agreed that transparent honesty was the best move.

"Interesting." He rested his elbows on the table and steepled his fingers as he leaned forward, a spark of curiosity in his eyes. "May I ask what changed?"

I shifted in my seat and took a deep breath. This was my moment of truth. I wouldn't live in the closet anymore. I owed it to myself, and I owed it to Andy. "My boyfriend is going to the University of Chicago and an athletic scholarship is the only way I can do that."

Edgar's eyes widened slightly, but otherwise he didn't react to the bomb I'd just dropped. My heart felt like it was going a mile a minute and I fought to keep my breathing even.

"Will that be a problem? My being gay and out?" I asked when he didn't say anything.

He searched my face for a moment, then leaned back in his seat. "I take it that it *has* been a problem here?"

"You could say that. Though I'm not out at Ulwich." It was on the tip of my tongue to add that it wasn't safe.

Empathy shone in his eyes. "I read the article. I can only imagine how difficult it must have been."

"My boyfriend is actually the one who wrote it." I caught myself rubbing the back of my neck and snatched my hand down. "Yeah."

His eyebrows rose up his pale face. "Impressive. UChicago is fortunate to have such a talented writer joining our ranks."

"He got into the Advanced Writing Program. He's insanely smart. It's actually thanks to him that my grades have been so much better this year." I realized how that sounded and threw out my hands in a stopping motion. "Not that he did any of my work for me. Just tutored. Believe me, he made me earn every single grade."

He chuckled. "Relax, Mr. Hudson. I've already seen how well you play and work with your team. This conversation is to get to know you better and make sure we're a good fit. As far as your sexuality is concerned, it's a nonissue. It's not relevant to your grades or your athletic performance."

"It's amazing to hear you say that—it really is—but that doesn't mean the team or the coach will see it that way. Fuck knows Coach Santinelli would shit a brick if he knew he had queer players." I scrunched my eyes shut and grimaced. Wow, when I wanted to fail, I really went all out.

Edgar released a loud laugh, and I nervously cracked an eye. "I can certainly understand your reservations, but I'm confident they wouldn't find issue with it either. Unlike many programs I've visited, UChicago's lacrosse program prides itself on being a family. In fact, a fair number of the team-building exercises and events involve players' partners to further foster that feeling."

"Wow. I had no idea." I couldn't even imagine what that would be like.

He shrugged. "It's a different structure and not one meant for everyone. Winning is nice and while it brings significant revenue to the school, we value having outstanding players that are also outstanding people. In the interest of honesty, that's largely the reason we rarely scout from Ulwich Prep. Your coach's reputation precedes him."

"Someone should tell him it's not a good thing," I mumbled.

"For many universities, it is probably helpful."

"Just not for UChicago," I filled in.

"Precisely." He returned his attention to the folder, flipping through a few more pages before stopping again. "Have you given any thought to your major?"

"I'm guessing 'whichever one will take me' isn't the right answer," I said sheepishly. Edgar gave me an indulgent smile, but didn't comment. "I considered going into business, since that seems to be the athlete go-to, but it's not really for me. I'd rather do something more focused on people. I read that the university's social science programs are incredible. While I'm a little intimidated about the analytic writing aspect, I'm also excited to challenge myself."

"And your boyfriend is in the Advanced Writing Program," he added with a smile that I returned.

"He might be willing to tutor me again if it came to that. *And* if it didn't interfere with his own course work."

"At some point, I hope I get to meet this boyfriend of yours. He sounds quite impressive." He cleared his throat and his face took on a more serious expression. "Let's get down to brass tacks."

I took a deep breath and willed my anxiety to chill the fuck out. "Okay. Lay it on me."

"At first impression, I believe you would make an excellent addition to the Chicago Maroons. You have the right attitude, you certainly have the skill, and you've shown a dedication to your education."

"I'm sensing a but," I said when he paused.

"Perhaps not the one you're expecting. Funds—scholarships—for recruits are incredibly limited and we are already very late in the season. You'd be a last-minute addition and would be bypassing tryouts."

"So… it's a no." I tried not to let my disappointment show on my face, but was pretty sure it was a lost cause. Now I was really glad I hadn't mentioned this as a possibility to Andy.

"No. It means that I can only extend this offer under exceptional circumstances."

I instantly perked up, damn near drooling with renewed hope. "Like what?"

"Like, you would have to not only win the championship at the end of the week, but be integral to the victory."

That took the wind out of my sails. "So, like scoring the winning goal?"

"That would be one way. Ultimately, I will be the one who determines how integral a role you played should Ulwich secure the win. Though, again, after seeing you play, I find it difficult to envision a scenario in which you don't."

"Wait. *Wait.* Are you saying what I think you're saying?" My heart was pounding again, though this time in excitement.

Edgar pushed his chair back and stood, extending his hand. "Contingent on a championship victory, I would like to extend a full athletic scholarship for you to attend the University of Chicago starting this fall. Well, summer, really."

"Oh my God, yes!" I surged out of my seat and eagerly shook his hand.

He smiled as he released my grip and began gathering his things. "I'll report back to the recruitment office and work on getting a contract drawn up. I should have it ready for you to sign prior to the game. Did you have any other questions before we part ways?"

"Actually, yeah. I assume you'll put the bit about having to cinch the championship into the contract."

"I will," he answered with a nod.

"Could you also include a clause that prevents me from being harassed or terminated from the team for being gay?" I never thought I'd actually be grateful for Coach Santinelli's contract negotiation strategy lessons, but it was nice being able to hold my own with confidence.

"Harassment or hazing of any kind is strictly prohibited at UChicago, but given where you've been the last seven years, I can understand your concern and need for caution. I'll be sure to add the distinction to the contract. In the meantime, here's my card with my cell number should you have any more questions or concerns." He artfully pulled a crisp card from his chest pocket and passed it to me. It might as well have been the Holy Grail for how carefully I accepted it.

I swallowed thickly, suddenly overcome with emotion. It wasn't exactly a done deal, but it was more promise than I'd dared to hope for. "Thank you, Edgar. For everything." I held out my hand, surprised at how steady it was.

"It was a genuine pleasure." He wrapped his fingers around my hand once more. "I look forward to seeing you win on Saturday." He winked, then released my hand and picked up his bag.

I stayed behind a few extra minutes to wrap my head around what had just happened. I was going to be a Maroon. Andy and I wouldn't have to go to separate colleges. We could stay together, not just as friends, but as a *couple*. I wasn't under any delusion that it would be easy, but it was *possible*. Now I just had to be the MVP of the championship. Piece of cake.

Chapter 34

Mitch

Patience had never been my strong suit, and it wasn't now either. I was bursting at the seams with the need to tell Andy about the meeting with Edgar. Except it wasn't a *done* deal. But it was so close I could taste it. In less than a day, my fate would be decided. Was it worth telling Andy now, or would it be smarter to wait? I absently rounded a corner into another hallway, worrying my thumbnail as I continued to turn the dilemma over in my mind.

"Hey, you. Since when do you bite your nails?" Andy asked.

At his voice, my head shot up and a grin split my face at seeing him walking toward me. "Hey. What are you doing wandering the halls? I figured you'd be in the library studying for final exams."

He arched a copper brow. "You mean where *you* should be?"

"Busted." I laughed, but it trailed off awkwardly.

He finished closing the distance between us and lowered his voice. "Is everything alright? If you're worried about finals, you know I'm happy to help."

I actually didn't, but hearing him say so set loose a tizzy of fireflies in my chest. "It's not that." He gave me a knowing look, and I caved. "Okay, it's not *just* that."

"Talk to me. What's up?" He gently steered us toward the side of the hallway, and I obligingly went along.

"So, what would you say if I told you I had access to an apartment in Chicago?"

He tilted his head to the side, clearly trying to figure out what to make of my cryptic question. "Um, I'd say that's great. But what does it have to do with anything?"

"Would you be interested in living with me?"

"Like after college? I mean, I've always wanted to live in Chicago. But I'm still lost here, Mitch." He shifted the strap of his overweight bag and glanced down the hall.

"Right, yeah. I should probably start at the beginning."

He gave me a small smile that shone in his eyes. "It might help."

"I spoke with a scout today." His eyes widened and his mouth opened. I quickly pushed on before he could interject. "From the University of Chicago."

He spun around and landed heavily against the wall with an exhale. "Fuck, Mitch. Way to bury the lead. But isn't it a little too late for all of that?"

"Sort of. But!" I quickly threw out my hands to stop whatever argument he already had ready. "My athletic skills are impressive and, thanks to you, my grades are halfway decent. They could be willing to make a special exception."

"You're shitting me. *You* could be going to *the* University of Chicago. With me." He shook his head like he couldn't really believe it. To be fair, I'd been working toward this for months and I wasn't sure *I* did. Finally, he stopped shaking his head and squinted at me. "Have you even applied? Far as I know, the acceptance window is closed. So, this would be for next year."

I smirked. "This would kind of skirt around that. Athletic scholarships are fun that way."

He leaned forward to brace his hands on his knees and took several deep breaths. "Holy fuck, this is actually happening."

"Well… almost."

His head jerked up. "What?"

"I still have to do one more thing before the offer is official."

"Right. Finals. Of course."

I blinked. Whoops, forgot about those in all the excitement. "Well, two things."

He narrowed his eyes at me. "Would it kill you to spit it all out at once, or are you *trying* to kill me?"

"Sorry. Besides finals, I just have to pull off the teeny tiny task of winning the championship. And maybe being the MVP." I grimaced as I waited for his reaction, but he kept staring blankly at me.

"Minimum Viable Product?"

I stared at him, at a complete loss for where the fuck that had come from. "Uh, no. It means *most valuable player*. Basically, I need to be a big reason we win."

He nodded, his gaze sliding away from me. "Yeah. Okay. No big deal. You just have to single-handedly win a championship that Ulwich Academy hasn't even managed to get to in the whole time we've been here. No problem there." He huffed a disbelieving laugh.

"No one said anything about it being single-handed," I countered. "Just a major contributor."

"This is *insane*," he muttered under his breath, then added louder, "you didn't even *want* an athletic scholarship."

"I know, but the reasons for that won't be at UChicago." My abbreviation of the university caused his lips to twitch with a smile. "Just for a second, let's put all that aside. Would you still want to be with me? Live with me?"

"I'm pretty sure my scholarship dictates at least one year in a dormitory."

"Andy," I deadpanned.

"Of course, I'd still want to be with you!" he hissed. "Wait, is that the only reason you'd be going to UChicago?"

I seriously debated lying, but dismissed it. Lying had already cost us too much. "If there are other reasons—reasons that make me really happy—does it matter that you're the first?"

He opened his mouth and closed it a couple of times without saying anything. Eventually, he gave me a searching look. "Are there really other reasons?"

"There are. Their social sciences program sounds amazing and honestly, the way Edgar—the scout—described their lacrosse team sounds like everything I ever wanted when I first tried out here. But I'd be lying if I said that you weren't the reason I got Uncle Terri to send the scout in the first place."

He stared at me for another long moment, his eyes getting liquid. "I really wish I could kiss you right now."

I darted a quick glance down each end of the hallway. When I was sure it was clear, I stepped forward, caging Andy against the wall, and pressed my lips to his in a firm kiss that didn't come anywhere near capturing how I felt in this moment. "I love you, Anderson Gallagher."

"I love you too," he sighed, peering up at me with his vibrant green eyes. "Guess this means I'm going to the game tomorrow."

Fuck fireflies. I turned into the goddamn Human Torch. Andy had literally *never* been to a game before. And I would know, because I always looked for him. "Really?"

He hiked a shoulder and smiled. "How could I not? My boyfriend's going to win a championship so he can be with me."

Andy

I waited for Mitch's dorm room door to open with a level of patience that should have afforded me sainthood status. Some time after midnight, Mitch's roommate, Nathaniel, slipped quietly into the dark corridor. I clung to the shadows as I trailed after him to ensure he really was leaving the school and not just out for a bathroom visit. Given that he was in casual clothes instead of pajamas, it seemed like a safe bet, but I wasn't taking any chances. Then I took my time doubling back to where I'd started.

Outside Mitch's door, my doubts resurfaced. The team's superstition—or was it a ritual?—of getting laid the night before a big game for good luck was admittedly ridiculous. Then there was the fact that Mitch really needed his rest if he was going to be at peak performance for the championship game. And if I was being really paranoid, there was no telling when Nate would return from his outing.

What if he doesn't want me here? I forced the insecurity back into the dark where it belonged. Mitch had made it abundantly clear he wanted me any way he could have me. He'd asked me to live with him, for fuck's sake. My heart gave another little thrill at the prospect. And when all was said and done, *I* wanted this. Not just for Mitch because "ritual", but for me, too.

I bypassed knocking and slowly opened the door. To my surprise, Mitch was pacing the room, illuminated by a lamp partially covered by a shirt. He was also chewing on his thumbnail again. I smiled to myself. Coming tonight had been the right decision.

"Hey, handsome," I said quietly.

His head shot up. "Andy. What are you doing here?" He altered the course of his latest circuit to walk over. He peered past me into the still thankfully empty hall, then carefully shut the door.

"Don't worry, I made sure Nate was long gone before letting myself in," I said with a grin.

He shifted to face me, raising a hand to cup the side of my face. I couldn't help but lean into the caress. Fuck, I loved when he did that. "It's late. Why aren't you asleep?"

"I could ask you the same thing," I teased, earning a crooked smile.

"Wasn't for lack of trying. I think I'm too excited, and nervous, about tomorrow." He glanced over at the digital clock on his desk, winced and dropped his hand. "Fuck. Today, now." He took a few steps back, so he wasn't crowding me against the door. "But you haven't answered my question. What brings you here at this time of night?"

I desperately wanted to play it cool, but didn't have much faith in my ability to keep a straight face, especially when a smirk tugged at my lips. "Should think it's obvious."

He frowned.

Biting back laughter, I leisurely closed the distance between us. "I'm here for the same reason your roommate snuck out."

He blinked. "That stupid good-luck ritual?" I arched an eyebrow as if to say "what else" and he gave me a smile sweeter and softer than the best ice cream. "Andy, you don't need to do that."

I nodded and drifted around his room. "So, you don't believe it brings good luck?"

"Honestly? Not really. I think it has more to do with that the guys on the team believe it does, so..." He shrugged.

I trailed a finger along his spotless desk and for the first time wondered if the reason he didn't have little knickknacks and photos was because he wasn't out. Did he have a photo of me somewhere? I glanced around as if the answer to my question would leap out or at least have the decency to glow like a hint in a video game. No luck.

"Anyway, yeah, haven't really ever been a fan of the whole get laid before a big game nonsense," he said when I kept silently exploring his room.

"That's a shame."

"Why?"

I glanced over my shoulder at him. "Because it's something I've always wanted to do." I let that sink in a moment before turning around completely to face him. God damn, he was edible. The way his dark gray pajama pants hung low on his waist was a sin. I wanted to lick my way up that delicious V and trail my tongue over the ridges of his abs before burying my face in his defined pecs. Finally, I lifted my gaze to his shocked face.

"Wait. So, you never… Not even with…"

I slowly shook my head and let my grin spread. "You're the only one I've ever been interested in doing this with. Plus," I gave a nonchalant shrug, "as *skilled* as you are, I figure an extra bit of luck couldn't hurt. But if you're not interested, then I guess I'll have to find another way to take advantage of the prep I did before coming." Okay, so I wasn't very chill *or* subtle.

He made a strangled sound, which I hoped was a good thing. Not easy to tell in the half-light. "You're serious. You really want to do this? Tonight?"

I was done pretending to be coy. I stalked over to him and looked up into his doubtful face. "You tell me, Mitch. Are you going to fuck me, or what?"

As if it was the last push he needed, he surged forward to capture my mouth. My dick jumped to attention from the half-hard state I'd been battling since I'd decided to do this. His tongue pushed past my lips and I moaned into him while he held my face exactly where he wanted it. Abruptly, he pulled back.

"What's wrong?" I asked, not appreciating the shift.

"Just a sec." He walked over to his dresser and dug around before coming up with—a sock? Then he went to the door, cracked it open, and hung it on the knob facing the hall. I bit my lip to stifle a chuckle as he dusted his hands. "There, at least now, if Nate strikes out and heads back early, he won't just barge in."

"Clever. Now where were we?"

His grin shone in his eyes as he reached for my shirt.

I firmly put my hand on his to stall him. "How about I get that?"

His bottom lip jutted out in a pout so cute I wanted to tackle him to the ground. "Why?"

"I love you, babe, but you suck at getting my shirts off." To illustrate my point, I pulled off the cotton tee in one fluid motion.

He snorted, then grabbed my hips and spun me around. "Perhaps, but I'm positive I've never had any issues getting you out of your pants," he whispered huskily in my ear. I gave an involuntary shudder and did what I could to smother a whimper. He slipped his hands inside my plaid pajama pants and slid them down, all while somehow managing to caress the full length of my legs.

"Damn, Mitch," I panted as my already aching cock sprang free.

He nipped lightly at my neck while he massaged the back of my thighs, slowly working his way higher. I had to stifle another moan as he dug his fingers into my cheeks, then spread them enough to run a finger along my crease. "You sly imp. You really did get started without me," he commented as he teased the slick rim of my hole.

"I didn't know how much time we'd have," I replied breathily as I wriggled my ass against his feather light touch in an attempt to get him to go deeper.

Without any warning, he removed his exploratory fingers. I had exactly half a second to be upset about it when the flat of his palm came down sharply on my ass. The sound exploded in the room as he growled, "Don't do it again."

I didn't think about how the sound carried. I couldn't. The sharp sting had turned into a full body wave of pleasure that made my dick pulse and a pearl of precum dribble out.

"Fuuuck," he groaned as he slipped first one and then a second finger inside, creating the most exquisite burn. "One of these days, I'm going to enjoy taking my time spanking your sweet ass until it's the perfect shade of red."

"Mitch," I whined, barely even recognizing my voice.

"Get on the bed."

He didn't have to tell me twice. I scrambled onto the mattress, which was mercifully less squeaky than mine. Before he could join me, I swiveled around on my hands and knees to face him. I swiftly liberated his erection and swallowed him down.

"Oh God, Andy," he choked out as he twined his fingers tightly in my hair.

I hummed appreciatively at the tugging sensation, then ran my tongue up his length while I cupped his balls with my hand. I teased his slit before sucking lightly on the cap. He tasted divine. If only there was some way to have him in my mouth and in my ass at the same time. Damn, I was a greedy brat.

"If you don't stop, you're going to have to wait for me to recover before I can plow you into the mattress," Mitch said above me, loosening his grip on my hair enough to stroke it.

I immediately relented with a pop. Yep. Greedy *and* impatient.

He smirked. "That's what I thought. We can play more with that gifted tongue of yours another time. Right now, I want to be buried so deep in your ass that it's all you can think about tomorrow."

I had to bite the inside of my cheek to prevent myself from groaning loudly like the slut I apparently was. Who said jocks weren't poets? Fuck tomorrow, it was all I could think about *now*. "How do you want me?" I asked once I was sure I had myself mostly under control.

He hooked a finger under my chin and used it to encourage me up onto my knees where he could look me in the eye. It was a good thing he wrapped his other arm around my waist to press me against his bare chest, because the look of absolute love and adoration on his face threatened to make my legs give out. "Oh, kitten, you already know the answer to that." He slanted his mouth over mine in a sweet kiss that became deeper and needier with every second that passed.

I took full advantage of Mitch's steadying hold to let my hands rove over every sculpted inch of him. Our tongues tangled in a sensuous glide of give and take, stoking the heat already burning in my lower belly. I grabbed a double handful of his firm ass and squeezed, pulling him close enough that his cock left a smear of precum on my abdomen.

He nipped at my lip, then pulled back enough to gaze at me with hooded eyes. "Hands and knees, facing the top of the bed." He stole another quick kiss, then released me.

I repositioned the way he wanted me, my dick swelling painfully in anticipation. Out of the corner of my eye, I saw him grab what I presumed to be lube from a drawer and finish kicking off his pants. Then the bed dipped with his weight as he climbed up to join me.

"Jesus, you're beautiful," he whispered reverently as he coasted his hands over my sides. *Beautiful* wasn't really a word I normally associated with myself—handsome, maybe—but the way Mitch said it sounded more like the way one would talk about mountains or oceans or vast plains of wildflowers. The kind of beauty that boggled the mind and stole your breath away.

I was on the verge of demanding he fuck me before I died of blue balls, when his fingers made a return, this time with significantly more lube. I gasped as the slight burn dissolved into toe-curling pleasure. Then he lazily thrust his fingers in and out, opening me more and brushing my prostate with each pass. I flailed for his pillow and dragged it close just in time to moan loudly into it.

As if it was some kind of secret cue, he removed his fingers yet again, leaving me clenching air and aching for more. Then the blunt head of his cock pressed against my hole. I released a satisfied sigh as he pushed slowly in, relaxing my body and taking every inch he had to give. By the time his pelvis met my ass, I wasn't sure which of us was shaking more. He pulled almost all the way out and snapped his hips forward. I knew two things for certain right then: I was *never* going to be good at quiet sex and I would be absolutely devastated if Mitch didn't come with me to Chicago.

He set a punishing pace that lit up every sensitive nerve ending and wrecked me in the best way. He reached forward to grip my shoulder, forcing me back against him and helping him to drive deeper. My channel fluttered around his hot length as I free-fell toward release. Not ready for the ecstasy to end, I gripped the base of my cock hard enough to stem my imminent orgasm.

Mitch moved his hand from my shoulder so that his fingers delicately covered my throat. At the hint of pressure, I let him guide me back up to my knees so that my back was flush against his chest. I got lightheaded as he dug the fingers of his other hand into my hip and sucked bruises out on the side of my neck. I loved that he was marking me, claiming me as his. I wanted him to mark me more.

"Jerk yourself for me," he panted while he continued to drive mercilessly in and out of me.

I shook my head, unable to form words.

He mouthed the shell of my ear, nibbling the lobe, and there was absolutely nothing dignified about the small whine I emitted. "I want to feel you come."

"No. Not yet," I pleaded.

"Yes. I want that hot ass to tighten around me, to squeeze me until I can't take it anymore."

Oh God. I wasn't going to make it. Already my hand was shuttling up and down my cock with a mind of its own. I wanted to tell him how much I loved him. How happy I was that he was back in my life. How perfect we were together. And how I wanted this moment to last forever. But I didn't manage any of that. "Mitch," I sighed, giving myself over to him completely.

"I'm right here, kitten. I'll always be right here." He pressed a firm kiss onto my shoulder, then before I knew what was happening, his teeth sank into the tender flesh.

Pain coiled with mind-blowing pleasure and I came all over my hand. I clenched around his length and rode a wave of release that didn't seem to have an end in sight. He plunged into me three more times, pegging my prostate with each thrust, then muffled the groan of his orgasm against the bite he'd just given me. His cock pulsed as he filled me and mine gave another half-hearted spurt.

I slumped against him, completely spent, letting him support most of my weight. He curled his arms around me and I'd never felt more safe or cherished in my life. He nuzzled into my neck and I hummed happily back at him. I wanted to say something, but words were hard and this was perfection. Or it would have been if he hadn't started to pull out. I grumbled incoherently, hating the empty feeling left in his wake.

"I know, kitten. Someday," he murmured and placed a gentle kiss on my cheek. I hummed again at the beautiful promise. *Someday* we wouldn't have to part. Hopefully, someday soon. He slid off the bed, leaving me to sway in place as I tried not to collapse and get even more cum on his pillow.

Faster than I expected, he returned with a damp towel. I'd have asked where he'd gotten it, but that required the power of speech. He peppered me with light kisses as he wiped down my softened cock and cum-covered hand. Then he flipped over his pillow and had me lie down so he could wipe down the rest of me. Like the greedy bottom he'd made me, I couldn't help but push back as he ran the cloth over my now super-sensitive rim.

When he was done, he tossed the towel into a hamper and crawled in beside me on the narrow mattress. "Come here," he whispered, holding his arms open for me.

I shimmied closer until my head was resting on his chest and our legs were intertwined. The soft lamplight peeking out from beneath the shirt attempting to obscure it wrapped around us. I closed my eyes and listened to the steady thud of his heart as we came down from our high. It was probably pure romanticism that made me believe even our heartbeats were in sync.

"I wish you could stay," he said after a while.

"Me too. But you know I can't. Besides, you need to rest for the big game."

He held me tighter. "I know, but we *both* know I'd sleep better if you were here."

I angled my head to look up at him. "I love you."

His responding smile made my heart flutter. "I love you too," he said softly, caressing my cheek with his knuckle. He awkwardly leaned down, and I stretched my neck to meet him halfway in a lingering kiss. When we parted, he let out a heavy sigh. “I really wish you could stay.”

I smiled at him as I maneuvered off the bed. “Me too.” With a groan he got up and pulled on his pants, then passed me my shirt, which I’d apparently thrown onto Nate’s bed. Whoops. “I think that’s everything I came with,” I said once I was finished dressing.

Mitch followed me to the door, where he stole another kiss. “You’ll really be there tomorrow?”

“I wouldn’t miss it for anything.”

He beamed at me, like I’d just told him he’d won the lottery, or a free trip to space. My poor heart was going to need some serious attention with all of this fluttering going on. “You know, if I *do* get to go to UChicago, I’ll expect you to come cheer me on at all my games.”

“What? That wasn’t part of the agreement. I take it back,” I said in the most alarmed way I could manage, then promptly ruined it by grinning. “Of course, I’ll be there. Rain, shine, home, or away. And what’s this ‘if’ business? Maybe it’s the sex-high talking, but I’m positive we racked up enough good luck energy for a couple of games.”

He chuckled. “That’s not exactly how it works, but you won’t hear me arguing. I’ll see you later,” he finished, punctuating the statement with a kiss. “Sleep well, kitten.”

I absolutely did *not* croon at the odd endearment he’d settled on. “You too. Good night.” He cracked the door to peer out and ensure the way was clear, then opened it for me. I stepped into the much darker corridor, smiling back at him, before making my way back to my room.

Chapter 35

Andy

"Please come with me," I begged Calvin for the dozenth time. I'd use puppy eyes if I thought they'd work. That's how desperate I was. The library table he'd commandeered was by one of the large windows that offered an incredible view of the academy grounds and the perfect day outside. So perfect, in fact, that we were the only ones inside. Everyone else was either enjoying the sunshine or had made their way to the fleet of buses waiting to whisk us off to the stadium. The championship was set to start at two, which didn't leave me much time to convince Calvin to join me.

He obstinately ignored me, keeping his focus on the landscape he was currently sketching, the scritch of his pencil the only sound in the otherwise empty library. After Benny left, it was all he'd sketched. I knew he'd gotten more comfortable with portraits and even self portraits, which he abhorred on principle, but that was all gone now. It didn't take a genius to recognize he was depressed. Maybe a lot more than depressed, but I didn't know what went deeper than that—not that I'd ever be dumb enough to point it out. All the more reason to get him out of the school and into the sunshine.

I invaded his space, leaning over the table to disrupt his light. As expected, he looked sullenly up at me. "If you don't go, who's going to explain to me what the hell is going on? You *know* I don't know shit about lacrosse."

"Don't be so dramatic," he grumbled, shifting his sketchpad slightly to catch the few rays of light my small body couldn't obscure. "You're smart and you've seen their practices. You'll figure it out."

"That's not the same," I huffed. "Watching a bunch of sweaty guys run around half naked doesn't equate to understanding the rules of the game."

"Can't you get someone else to fill you in?"

I walked around the table and sat in the chair beside him. "Most of the people I would ask are *on* the team and the others won't get why I'm suddenly so invested in a game I didn't give two shits about a week ago."

"Still can't believe Hudson found a way to get into UChicago," Calvin mumbled with a distinct edge of bitterness.

"It's not a guarantee," I replied gently.

He snorted. "Still closer than I got."

"Oh yeah, because having to go to Yale is the absolute *worst*." I scowled at him, hoping he could hear how ridiculous he sounded. Plenty of students would kill to go to Yale and it had been his *backup*.

He finally set his pencil down and leaned back. Try as he might, though, he couldn't mask the sadness that eclipsed his face. "Believe me, I get how ungrateful I sound. But… what if Benny is at UChicago?" he finished in a whisper, turning his brown eyes on me.

"Still haven't heard from him?"

He shook his head. "Not that I'm surprised. His dad could give dictators lessons on how to be a controlling asshole."

"I'm guessing Neil and Todd haven't heard anything either."

"Nothing past that first letter." He ran his hands over his face. "I'm just so, so…"

Lost, was the first word that came to my mind, quickly followed by bereft.

"Angry," he finally said, surprising me. "I'm so fucking angry. At everything. I'm angry at Warren. Angry at myself. Angry at Benny for putting himself in the middle of it. Angry about that godforsaken fucking article."

A pit opened in my stomach as I came face to face with the consequences of my actions. My friend was hurting, and it was partly my fault. I'd planned to never tell Calvin about my hand in things, but now I realized I couldn't keep that truth from him. Not just because it was steadily eating away at my conscience, but because he *deserved* to know.

"Why are you looking at me like that?" Calvin snapped.

"So, this probably won't help my chances of convincing you to come to the championship with me—like, at all—but I need to tell you something." He stared impassively at me. I took a deep breath and let it out slowly. "I wrote the article."

"I know."

My jaw dropped. "I... what? How? Did Benny tell you before he..."

"Really, Andy? We've been friends for five years. You don't think I'd recognize your handiwork?" He rolled his eyes. "You're very voicey."

"I don't know if that's meant to be a good thing or a bad thing."

He shrugged. "It's a thing. Even with all the stats and professional language you used, I'd know your style anywhere."

"Um, thanks? You should know that I never meant to make things worse for you. I had no idea that it would blow back on Benny. I'm really sorry." I tentatively touched his arm. Physical affection had never really been a hallmark of our friendship, but it was the only way I could think to show support.

Calvin let out a heavy sigh. "I know you meant well, that you were only trying to help. And honestly, if his dad wasn't such a dick, I don't think it would have been a problem. But it wasn't all on you. Benny—" His voice cracked, and he had to pause to collect himself. "Benny leveraged his status as a Price to make a lot of things happen. Things he did for me. Part of me can't help but think we were doomed from the start."

"I don't believe that," I said, tightening my hand on his arm. "You two are amazing together."

"Maybe, but don't be naïve. Benny comes from a world of expectation. While I live my life giving other people's expectations the middle finger." I chuckled as he gave the empty library two aggressive middle fingers. "Like I said, doomed." He slumped back in his seat, his moment of energy snuffed as soon as it began, and I could sense that I was losing him again.

"You can't stop fucking with people's expectations now. What better way to show that nothing cows Calvin Bridges than to go to that game? Be loud. Cheer with me. Show those people exactly what they can do with their preconceived notions," I said with gusto.

His eyes glinted, and I nearly crowed with imminent victory. I really should have started with this track rather than asking nicely. A challenged Calvin was a *motivated* Calvin.

"I mean, it would be kinda weird if the most consistent spectator didn't show at the biggest game of the last decade. You know we're playing Norwood Academy, right?" I personally didn't know why that was a big deal, but judging by the snarl that twisted Calvin's darker features, it definitely was.

"Those fuckers are overdue to be knocked down a few pegs. Cheating bastards. Did you know they tried to take out a key Midfielder at last year's championship? And they tried to do the same thing to Connor earlier in the season." He scowled into the distance, momentarily wrapped up in his grievances with a rival team. I *didn't* know that, but it seemed prudent to keep that to myself.

"All the more reason to go. Who else is going to shout at the ref for bullshit calls?" I mentally crossed my fingers that I was using the jargon correctly, and that was an actual thing in lacrosse.

Calvin raised a dark brown eyebrow and side-eyed me, not fooled by my sudden ability to talk sports ball. "Been doing your research?"

"Maybe. But it's no substitute for someone who really understands what the hell is going on. Please come with me. We can root for Mitch and Connor together. Not to mention Neil and Todd."

"Todd isn't playing. Torn PCL. He'll heal, but he's been out a good chunk of the season."

"Maybe. But I hear he's been taking his new role as water boy *very* seriously." I gave Calvin an intense look until he broke and laughed out loud.

"Oh my God, I fucking hate you. Fine, I'll go to the stupid game." He shoveled his art supplies off the table into his satchel. "But *only* so you don't accidentally end up cheering for the wrong team. I'd never be able to show my face again."

A victorious grin split my face. I quickly reached into my satchel—which felt weird without a shit ton of books weighing it down—and pulled out a wad of fabric. "Will you still hate me if I give you this to wear to the game?" I opened the material with a flourish that I hoped would make Calvin proud, then held my breath as I waited for his reaction.

"How… how did you get this?" he whispered in awe as he cautiously touched the shirt.

"Mitch stole it from the locker rooms. Don't worry, I washed it." Calvin slowly took the material from me and I dove back into my bag. "He gave me one, too. Though apparently it's the 'away' jersey?"

Calvin's gaze flicked over to take in the white jersey with HUDSON spelled out in navy block letters across the back. "Yeah, they wear different colors to distinguish the home team."

I frowned and studied the two jerseys. "But aren't both schools technically 'away'?"

He made an aggrieved sound and clutched Benny's home jersey to his chest. "God help me. This is going to be rough."

Mitch

If my nerves didn't kill me, I didn't know what would. I wanted to fly and throw up all at the same time. Add to that the overwhelming pressure that this was the first championship game Ulwich Prep had been part of in fifty years, and, yeah, I was a mess.

"Alright, men, huddle up!" Coach Santinelli's voice cut through the babble of excited voices ricocheting around the strange locker room. It felt weird and a little intimidating to be in such a large stadium—a college stadium—but if all went well, I'd be doing it for every game going forward. And it didn't hurt that neither team had homefield advantage.

The team clumped around where Coach was standing in the middle of the room with Brian beside him. As I looked around, I realized I wasn't the only one feeling the nerves. This was a big game for all of us, though I doubted the others were banking on a win to go to college. I met Todd and Neil's gaze on the opposite side of the cluster and we nodded at each other. I was glad Coach had let Todd come. Even though he couldn't play, he was still part of the team and deserved to be here.

At a subtle tap on my elbow, I turned to the side to find Connor. "You ready for this?" he asked, keeping his eyes trained on Coach.

"As much as I can be. You?"

"Fuck yeah, I am. I've been busting my ass for years to get here," he replied with his usual intensity.

I shoulder-checked him. "I'm glad you are. You're a damn good player."

He glanced at me, a confused smile on his face. "Yeah?"

"Hell, yeah."

"Alright, alright. Cut the chit-chat. Hey! I said zip it!" Coach shouted and silence dropped like a stone. "That's better. Now, I don't need to tell all of you what a big day this is, not just for the Academy, but for each one of you. Every face I see before me has shed blood, sweat, and tears for this team. You've given your all at each practice and game. I'm so proud of the athletes you have become. And even though we've had to cross some major hurdles," he inclined his head at Todd, "this really is a team of champions. It's hard to believe that for many of you, this will be our last game as that team."

The room went quiet again as we all waited for what he would say next. So far, this pep talk bore no resemblance to the aggressive speeches we'd gotten at all of our previous games that sounded a lot more like "win or die trying". The silence continued to stretch until we started sharing concerned looks. Was that it?

Coach clapped his hands, and I was relieved to see I wasn't the only one who jumped. "Alright, enough with the sappy shit. You all have practiced hard, studied the plays, and gotten us this far. Now let's go out there and kick Norwood's ass!"

I raised my fist in the air and whooped and hollered along with everyone. The energy was palpable and I let it fill me up to bursting. For all the bad days I'd had, this feeling never got old. Each of us was a live wire ready to explode and together, we were gonna make one hell of a bang.

Still shouting, we ran out of the locker room, where a stadium full of cheering hit us like a wall. I slowed down to a jog, scanning the home side for familiar faces. In next to no time at all, I spotted a shock of auburn hair toward the front of the bleachers. A smile threatened to rip my face in two as I took in both Andy and Calvin, standing and shouting and waving the arms in the air. I might have been a little biased, but Andy looked damn good in my jersey, even if it *was* two sizes too big for him. And was he wearing face paint?

A laugh of pure joy burst out of me, then my gaze landed on Edgar Quinn standing a few rows over from them. The scout shifted his gaze from where I'd been looking and gave me a thumbs up. It seemed ridiculous to be happy about basically a random stranger's approval of my boyfriend, but he was also one of four people who knew. So, ridiculous or not, it mattered a lot to me.

I gave myself a good shake as we went through our warm up. It felt like in no time at all we were doing the coin toss and taking our positions on the field. Brian gave each of the players on the field a "let's get this" expression, then turned to face Norwood's Attackman at the line. The referee placed the ball between them, held up his hands as he backed up a few steps, then blew the whistle stuck between his lips. The clack of sticks jockeying for the ball filled the air, along with shouts of encouragement from the stands. As one, we surged forward. It was game time.

Chapter 36

Mitch

I'd never sweat so much in my fucking life. I was sure of it. Every muscle burned and exhaustion crept closer with each ragged breath I took. Part of it probably had to do with how stupidly hot it was. Regular season ended in April, so we didn't really have to contend with summery weather. A larger part of it likely had to do with the fact that we'd given a hundred and fifty percent *and* we were in double-overtime.

I gratefully accepted the water bottle Todd passed me. My attempt at a smile of thanks was more of a grimace, but he got the idea. I squirted a stream of water in my mouth, gulping it down, before dousing my face. Given just how amazing the cool water felt on my skin, I was pretty sure I was getting a sunburn on top of everything else.

The ref's whistle cut through our collective ragged breathing, and we all tossed our bottles to the ground before scurrying back to the field. Brian waved for us to circle up so he could give us the next play.

"I know we're feeling it, guys. Norwood has put up one hell of a fight," he said, to which several of my teammates growled. "Yeah, they've had some dirty plays, but that's only because they know we have them beat!" I joined the enthusiastic shout of agreement. "This is *our* championship! Now let's go out there and win it!" There was another round of shouting as the huddle broke a part.

Much as I wanted to glance up at the stands, to seek out Andy, I didn't want to risk losing focus. One more play and it would all be over. If we scored, we walked away champions. If we didn't... I wasn't sure any of us had anymore left to give.

I jogged over to my position by the goal, keeping an eye on the Defensemen there. I couldn't remember which one had cross-checked me earlier, but I wasn't taking chances. These assholes spent as much time in the penalty box as they did on the field. The whistle blew, capturing my attention, and I danced forward. I'd gotten right up the edge of my zone prepared for a pass, when a Norwood Midfielder stole the ball from John. He snarled and turned to go after him while I was left behind, cursing.

Adrenaline kept me light on my feet and ready to spring into action, but my heart lurched into my throat as the ball got closer to our goal. My pulse pounded in my ears and I held my breath as the player broke through our defenses and bore down on our Goal Keeper. Then, out of nowhere, Connor checked the guy so hard that he went down and the ball went sailing. Connor swiped it out of the air and flung it to Brian in one fluid motion.

I was already running full-tilt for the Norwood goal before I even registered that I was moving. A quick glance behind me showed Brian coming in hot. One of the Norwood defenders moved to block him and I twisted just in time to catch Brian's pass. I took exactly one microsecond to register that I had an opening and sent the ball hurtling toward the goal. I skidded to a halt inches from the crease as the ball flew past the Goal Keeper and caught the net.

I was still processing that I'd just scored the winning goal when the whole damn team slammed into my back. Suddenly I realized the roaring wasn't just in my head, it was the stadium losing its ever loving mind. I struggled to keep my footing as my teammates continued to converge on me, shouting, waving sticks in the air, and slapping my back.

For the first time since we'd walked out on the field, I let myself look over at the stands. It took me a beat to realize Andy had moved from his original seat to stand at the edge of the bleachers. He was leaning over the horizontal railing with his hands cupped around his mouth and cheering for all he was worth. Without a second thought, I dropped my stick, pushed past my celebrating teammates, and sprinted for the stands.

In a single bound, I landed on the railing opposite Andy. His face paint had smeared in all the heat, and his face was pink from too much sun. But my number was still clear on his cheek, and I'd never seen anything more beautiful.

"Holy shit!" he shouted, though it was still hard to hear him over the rest of the crowd, even though I was literally standing in front of him. "You did it! Mitch, you won!"

There were a million and one things I could say in that moment—that I wanted to say—but in the end, none of them came close to capturing how I felt. So, I hooked my leg on the middle bar of the railing, grabbed Andy's face with both hands, and kissed him for all I was worth.

It wasn't until a sharp wolf whistle pierced the air that it dawned on me what I'd just done. I pulled away, letting my hands drop back to the hot metal rail. I caught a glimpse of the source—of course it was Calvin—and released a self conscious cough. "I did it. I actually did it."

"Fuck yeah, you did!" He fisted a hand in my sweaty jersey and yanked me forward to sear me with another kiss. "If that doesn't earn you MVP, I don't know what will!" He lightly pushed my chest. "Now go get your trophy!"

I glanced over my shoulder to see the rest of my team still going absolutely bananas as they made their way to center field. I leaned forward to steal another swift kiss, then hopped down and raced to join them. From there, it was a blur of shaking hands, back-slapping, posing for pictures, water being thrown on everyone, and general chaos.

By the time we meandered our way back to the locker room, any doubts I had about what I was about to do had evaporated. I let out a piercing whistle once I was sure most of the team was inside. A bunch of sweaty, excited faces turned to me. "Guys, that was awesome!" A few enthusiastic shouts rang out in agreement. "I couldn't think of a better time to finally tell all of you something I've wanted to for years. I'm gay."

There was a beat of silence in which anxiety crawled up my spine like some kind of evil spider, then Brian said, "No fucking shit."

I did a double take as he crossed his dark brown arms and glowered at me. "What?"

"Dude, the whole fucking stadium saw you macking on Gallagher," Kyle chimed in.

"Oh. Right," I said, deflating.

Brian walked forward and clapped a hand on my shoulder. "Good for you. Don't get me wrong, I'm still pissed as hell about the months of bullshit you put us through, but yeah. Good for you." He gave my shoulder a firm squeeze, then walked past me to hit the showers. To my amazement, most of the rest of the team did much the same thing. By the time Nate walked up to me, I was actually a little light-headed, and I didn't think it was from too much sun. Unlike everyone else, though, he grabbed my arm and yanked me off to the side.

"What's up, man? I know it was kinda out of nowhere and I'm sorry I didn't tell you sooner, especially with you being my roommate and all," I said sheepishly.

"Forget all that. *Andy* was in our room last night?!"

"Uh... yeah?"

Nate went bright red and white as a sheet in equal turns. "So *he's* the one that made all those noises?" Nate sounded like he was on the verge of a fit or a seizure or something.

Then what he said clicked. I frowned at him. "Wait, were you *listening*?" He made a sound that I was positive was never intended to come out of a human and staggered away without answering. I was debating going after him when Connor stalked up to me and shoved me against the wall.

"I should have fucking known," he snarled.

"Excuse me?" I asked, reflexively bowing up.

"You... you..." He flailed his hands around as he struggled to get his words together, then stabbed a finger into my chest. "It was always you. You're the one who broke his heart, the reason he was never interested in more. It was fucking *you*! And to think I believed we were finally becoming friends."

"We were. We *are*," I argued.

"Some fucking friend you are," he spat.

I glanced past him to where Nate was now full-on freaking the fuck out at the other end of the locker room. "Look, I'm really sorry you feel that way. I didn't set out to hurt you."

He curled his lip, but I didn't have time for his righteous anger right now. I was really worried about Nate. As if sensing my look, Nate glanced up and went pale all over again.

"You can be pissed later. Right now, I need to ask a favor."

He let out an indignant shriek that could have broken glass if there'd been any around. "A favor?! You've got some fucking nerve, you traitor."

Yeah, I wasn't going anywhere near that. "It's not for me. It's for him." I grabbed his shoulders and spun him around so he could see Nate, who now looked on the verge of passing out. "Can you talk to him? He's not handling me coming out very well."

Connor shook me off. "Talk to him, your damn self. I don't owe you shit."

"No, you don't. But I don't think me talking to him will help. It might actually make it worse."

He narrowed his eyes at me. "Why?"

"I think he... heard some things and doesn't know what to make of it now that he knows the truth," I admitted, my face heating.

He glanced at Nate again, then back me and rolled his eyes. "Fine, but I'm not doing it for you."

I held my hands up in surrender. "Understood. Thanks anyway. And you played a hell of a game today."

"You too," he admitted grudgingly, before stomping off toward Nate.

I lingered long enough to watch him grab Nate's arm and Nate's surprised horror as Connor dragged him into the outside hall. Then I raced to take the quickest shower known to man, packed up my gear, and bolted out of the locker room.

"Hey you," Andy said the second I stepped outside. His hair shone like fire in the sunlight and his pink face had way more freckles than it did yesterday. Even a sweaty, sunburned mess, he was the most beautiful person I'd ever seen.

I dropped the bag holding all my gear, raced over to him, and wrapped him in a hug before spinning him around. Laughter poured out of him and didn't even stop when I set him down to kiss him. "I came out to the team," I said, out of breath.

He giggled. "Pretty sure the whole school and all the alumni know, too."

"Shit. Sorry. I wasn't thinking. I—"

He covered my mouth with his hand and smiled. "I don't care. I'm just so fucking happy." He removed his hand and wrapped his arms around my neck, then pressed a kiss to my lips. Someone nearby cleared their throat, and we separated with nervous laughter.

"I hope I'm not interrupting," Edgar said as he stepped closer.

"Not at all!" I said, throwing an arm around Andy's shoulders and pulling him close. "Andy, this is Edgar Quinn, the scout I told you about."

"Hello," Andy said, extending a hand.

Edgar shook it and smiled. "It's a pleasure to meet you, Andy. Your writing skills are quite impressive." It was hard to tell under the sunburn, but I was pretty sure Andy was blushing. Edgar turned back to me. "Again, please forgive my intrusion of your well-earned celebration. I just wanted to be the first to congratulate you and welcome you to the University of Chicago."

I accepted his hand, but could barely focus enough to let go of it after we shook, thanks to all the buzzing in my head. “Thank you.”

He nodded. “I’ll leave you to it. See you around, Mr. Hudson.”

He’d barely gone a few feet away when Andy grabbed my shirt and violently shook me. “Holy shit, you’re going to Chicago!”

I grabbed his hands, so full of happiness and excitement for the future, it was a wonder I didn’t combust. “*We’re* going to Chicago.”

Epilogue

Five months later

Andy

I raced down the dormitory hallway, dodging students, and trying like hell not to fall over.

"What's the rush, Andy?" one of Mitch's teammates asked as I barreled past.

"Got a letter!" I shouted over my shoulder, holding it up high.

The guy laughed, no doubt at how excited I was over something so simple. "Hudson should be in his room."

"Thanks!" I dodged another one of his teammates, who smiled at me. By now, everyone on the UChicago Men's Lacrosse team knew who I was and about my relationship with Mitch. None of them had batted an eye as far as I knew. In a word, it was liberating.

I finally caught sight of Mitch's room. Thankfully, the door was propped open. Not an uncommon occurrence around here. I skidded inside, barely slowing down enough not to miss the opening.

"Hey, Andy. What's the rush?" Mitch asked from where he was currently sitting on his bed.

I didn't even think twice about climbing into his lap. "Got a letter from Garza," I said, holding up the envelope.

"Who's Garza?" Mitch's roommate asked. "And who even sends written letters anymore?"

"Oops. Sorry, Devon. Didn't see you there," I said, shifting to a more comfortable position without actually getting off of Mitch. Devon was used to it by now.

He chuckled. "Don't worry about it. I'm sneaky, like a ninja."

I barked out a laugh, both at his preposterous rendition of a sneaking ninja and at the idea that the six-foot-four D-man could be anything sneakier than a foghorn.

"Garza was one of our professors at Ulwich Prep and Andy's mentor," Mitch said in answer to Devon's question as he wrapped his arms around me. I happily snuggled deeper into his embrace.

"Oh cool. I think? What's the old prof got to say?" Devon asked, plopping onto his mattress on the opposite side of the small room.

Mitch chuckled. "It's cool. Garza was one of the good ones and he was this imp's mentor," he said, ruffling my hair. I batted him away, but the damage was already done.

"Ugh," I groaned, "you're the *worst*."

"Eh, you love me. Now, what does he have to say?" Mitch asked, propping his head on my shoulder to peer at the letter.

I unfolded it and quickly scanned the page for the highlights. "Oh! Professor Cohen has been named the new headmaster!"

"No shit! That's awesome!" Mitch exclaimed, then turned to his roommate to elaborate. "Cohen and Garza were in a secret relationship the whole time we were there. We didn't even know until our last term."

I squealed in delight, recapturing their attention. "Not so secret anymore, it seems."

"Damn, things really are changing over there," Mitch said, squeezing me tightly. "Any other news?"

"Nothing as big. Things are going well. Apparently, they tore down that old storage shed after they realized students were getting high there."

"And other things," he whispered in my ear before nipping at it.

I squirmed in his grasp, but didn't get anywhere. "They want to know how we're doing here." I twisted to look at Mitch. "Wanna write back with me?"

"Of course," he replied with a grin before placing a kiss on my neck.

"Hey, what about me? I don't get invited to write to these super cool professors?" Devon teased.

Mitch threw his head back in a laugh. "Sure. Why the hell not? What do you say?" he asked me.

"Totally. It'll be fun." I beamed at Mitch, more in love than I knew a person could be, and falling more so every day. We were finally together and absolutely nothing was ever going to keep us apart again.

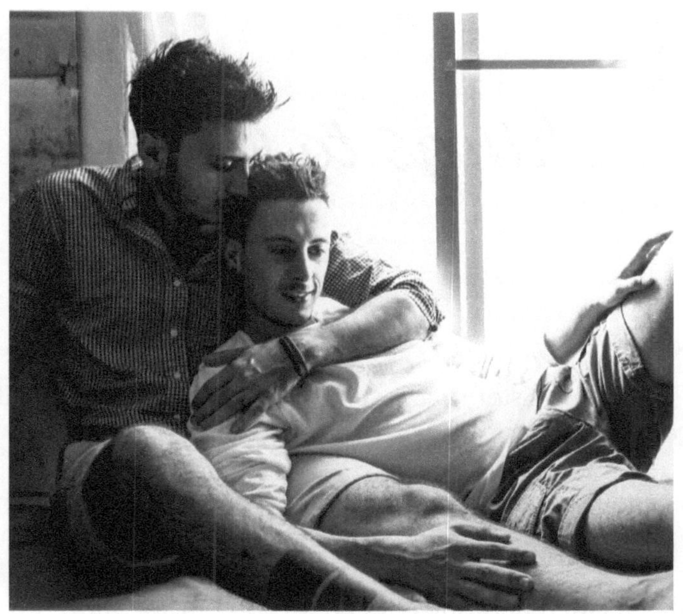

Things to Come

Benny and Calvin's story will resume in *The Promise,* which will be part of the *Men of Ulwich* series.

Curious about Nate and Connor's conversation? Be sure to check out *Men of Ulwich: The Question*.

Need more Mitch and Andy? Keep an eye out for short stories that highlight their college years together!

About the Author

Sam Bolanos (she/they) is a genderqueer author and founder of Chaotic Neutral Press LLC. They believe in love, equality, and the Oxford comma. When not playing with her three dogs, who you can follow on Instagram @austendogs, or spending time with her incredible husband, she's probably agonizing over edits or escaping into her latest fantasy.

Welcome to the adventure!

NEWSLETTER: SUBSCRIBE
WEBSITE: BOOKSBYSBOLANOS.COM
FACEBOOK: @BOOKSBYSBOLANOS
READER GROUP: SAM'S SUNBEAMS
INSTAGRAM: @SBOLANOSBOOKS

www.ingramcontent.com/pod-product-compliance
Lightning Source LLC
Chambersburg PA
CBHW020303030826
48979CB00027B/2009/J

* 9 7 8 1 9 5 6 1 2 8 5 3 6 *